BLUE REMEMBERED EARTH

Alastair Reynolds

ACE BOOKS, NEW YORK

THE BERKLEY PUBLISHING GROUP
Published by the Penguin Group
Penguin Group (USA) Inc.
375 Hudson Street, New York, New York 10014, USA
Penguin Group (Canada), 90 Eglinton Avenue East, Suite 700, Toronto, Ontario M4P 2Y3, Canada
(a division of Pearson Penguin Canada Inc.) • Penguin Books Ltd., 80 Strand, London WC2R 0RL,
England • Penguin Group Ireland, 25 St. Stephen's Green, Dublin 2, Ireland (a division of Penguin
Books Ltd.) • Penguin Group (Australia), 250 Camberwell Road, Camberwell, Victoria 3124, Australia
(a division of Pearson Australia Group Pty. Ltd.) • Penguin Books India Pvt. Ltd., 11 Community
Centre, Panchsheel Park, New Delhi—110 017, India • Penguin Group (NZ), 67 Apollo Drive,
Rosedale, Auckland 0632, New Zealand (a division of Pearson New Zealand Ltd.) • Penguin Books
(South Africa) (Pty.) Ltd., 24 Sturdee Avenue, Rosebank, Johannesburg 2196, South Africa

Penguin Books Ltd., Registered Offices: 80 Strand, London WC2R 0RL, England

This is a work of fiction. Names, characters, places, and incidents either are the product of the author's
imagination or are used fictitiously, and any resemblance to actual persons, living or dead, business
establishments, events, or locales is entirely coincidental. The publisher does not have any control over
and does not assume any responsibility for author or third-party websites or their content.

Published by arrangement with the Orion Publishing Group.

PUBLISHING HISTORY
Gollancz edition / January 2012
Ace hardcover edition / June 2012

Library of Congress Cataloging-in-Publication Data

Reynolds, Alastair, 1966–
Blue remembered Earth / Alastair Reynolds.—Ace hardcover ed.
p. cm.
ISBN 978-0-441-02071-3
I. Title.
PR6068.E95B58 2012
823'.914—dc23
2012006420

PRINTED IN THE UNITED STATES OF AMERICA

10 9 8 7 6 5 4 3 2 1

For Stephen Baxter and Paul McAuley: friends,
colleagues and keepers of the flame.

"And I am dumb to tell a weather's wind
How time has ticked a heaven round the stars."
— Dylan Thomas

It is necessary to speak of beginnings. Understand one thing, though, above all else. Whatever brought us to this moment, this declaration, could never have had a single cause. If we have learned anything, it's that life is never that simple, never that schematic.

You might say it was the moment when our grandmother set her mind to her last great deed. Or that it started when Ocular found something worthy of Arethusa's attention, a smudge of puzzling detail on a planet circling another star, and Arethusa in turn felt honour bound to share that discovery with our grandmother.

Or that it was Hector and Lucas deciding that the family's accounts could not tolerate a single loose end, no matter how inconsequential that detail might have looked at the time. Or the moment Geoffrey was called out of the sky, torn from his work with the elephants, drawn back to the household with the news that our grandmother was dead. Or his decision to confess everything to Sunday, and her choice that, rather than spurning her brother, she should take the path of forgiveness.

You might even say that it goes back to the moment in former Tanzania, a century and a half ago, when a baby named Eunice Akinya took her first raw breath. Or the moment that followed a heartbeat later, when she bellowed her first bawling cry, heralding a life of impatience. The world never moved quickly enough for our grandmother. She was always looking back over her shoulder, screaming at it to keep up, until the day it took her at her word.

Something made Eunice, though. She may have been born angry, but it was not until her mother cradled her under the stillness of a Serengeti night, beneath the cloudless spine of the Milky Way, that she began to grasp for what was forever out of reach.

All these stars, Eunice. All these tiny diamond lights. You can have them, if you want them badly enough. But first you must be patient, and then you must be wise.

And she was. So very patient and so very wise. But if her mother made Eunice, what shaped her mother? Soya was born two centuries ago, in a refugee camp, at a time when there were still famines and wars, droughts and genocides. What made her strong enough to gift this force of nature to the world, this child who became our grandmother?

We didn't know it then, of course. If we considered her at all, it was mostly

1

as a cold, forbidding figure none of us had ever touched or spoken to in person. Looking down on us from her cold Lunar orbit, isolated in her self-erected prison of metal and jungle, she seemed to belong to a different century. She had done great and glorious things – changed her world, left an indelible human mark on others – but those were deeds committed by a much younger woman, one with only a distant connection to our remote, peevish and disinterested grandmother. By the time we were born her brightest and best days were behind her.

So we thought.

PROLOGUE

Late May, after the long rains. The ground had borrowed moisture from the clouds; now the sky claimed its debt in endless hot, dry days. For the children, it was a relief. After weeks of bored confinement they were at last allowed to wander from the household, beyond the gardens and the outer walls, into the wild.

It was there that they came upon the death machine.

'I still can't hear anyone,' Geoffrey said.

Sunday sighed and placed a hand on her brother's shoulder. She was two years older than Geoffrey, and tall for her age. They stood on a rectangular rock, paces from the river that still ran fast and muddy.

'There,' she said. 'Surely you can hear him now?'

Geoffrey kept a firm grip on the wooden aeroplane he was carrying.

'I can't,' he said. He heard the river, the sighing of leaves in acacia trees, drowsy with the endless oven-like heat.

'He's in trouble,' Sunday said determinedly. 'We should find him, then tell Memphis.'

'Maybe we should tell Memphis first, then look for him.'

'And what if he drowns first?'

Geoffrey considered that unlikely. The waters had gone down compared to a week ago and the rains were petering out. Bilious clouds patrolled the horizon, thunder sometimes bellowed across the plains, but the sky was clear.

Besides, they had been this way many times. There were no homes here, no villages or towns. The trails they followed were trampled by elephants rather than people. And if by some chance Maasai were nearby, one of their boys would have known better than to get into difficulty.

'Could it be the things in your head?' Geoffrey asked.

'I'm used to them now.' Sunday hopped off the stone and pointed to the trees. 'I think it's coming from this way.' She started walking, then turned back to Geoffrey. 'You don't have to come, if you're scared.'

'I'm not scared.'

3

Watchful for hazards, they crossed drying ground and boggy marshland. They wore snake-proof boots and long snake-proof trousers, short-sleeved shirts and wide-brimmed hats. Despite the mud they'd splashed around in, and the undergrowth they'd struggled through, their clothes remained as bright and colourful as when they'd put them on back at the household. More than could be said for Geoffrey's mud-blotched arms, now crosshatched with fine, painful cuts from sharp-thorned bushes. Remembering a time when Memphis had praised him for not crying after tripping on the household's hard marble floor, he had made a point of not telling his cuff to make the pain go away.

Sunday pushed confidently forward into the acacia trees, Geoffrey struggling to keep up. They passed the rusted white stump of an old windmill.

'It's not far now,' Sunday called back, looking over her shoulder. The hat bounced jauntily against her back, secured by a drawstring around her neck. Geoffrey reached up to jam his own tighter, crunching it down on tight curls.

'We'll be safe, whatever happens,' he said, as much to convince himself as anything else. 'The Mechanism will be keeping an eye on us.'

He didn't know what was on the other side of the trees. They had been here before, many times, but that didn't mean they knew every bush, every rise and hollow of the landscape.

'Something's happened here!' Sunday called, just out of sight. 'The rain's washed this whole slope away, like an avalanche! There's something sticking out!'

'Be careful,' Geoffrey cried.

'It's some kind of machine,' she shouted back. 'I think the boy must be stuck inside.'

Geoffrey steeled himself and soldiered on. Trees fretted the sky with languidly moving branches, chips of kingfisher blue spangling through the gaps. Something slithered away under dry leaves a metre or two to his left. Thickening undergrowth clawed at his trousers, inflicting a rip. He stared in jaded wonderment as the two edges of torn fabric sutured themselves back together.

'Here,' Sunday said. 'Come quickly, brother!'

He could see her now. They'd emerged at the edge of a bowl-shaped depression in the ground, hemmed in by dense stands of mixed trees. An arc of the bowl's interior had collapsed away, leaving a steep rain-washed slope.

Something poked through the tawny ground. It was metal and as big as an airpod.

Geoffrey glanced up at the sky again.

'What is it?' he asked, although he had a dreadful sense that he already knew. He had seen something like this in one of his books. He recognised it by its many small wheels, too many of them along the visible side for this to be a car or truck. And the tracks that the wheels fitted into, with their hinged metal plates, one after the other like the segments of a worm.

'You mean you don't know?' Sunday asked.

'It's a tank,' he said, suddenly remembering the word. And for all that he was frightened, for all that he wanted to be anywhere but here, there was something amazing about finding this thing, vomited up by the earth.

'What else could it be? The little boy must have got inside, and now he can't get out.'

'There's no door.'

'It must have moved,' Sunday said. 'That's why he can't get out – the door's covered up again.' She was on the edge of the slope now, still on grass, but working her way around the bowl to the top of the area where the land had given way. She crouched and steadied herself, fingertips to the ground. Her hat bobbed on her shoulders.

'How can you hear him, if he's inside?' Geoffrey asked. 'We're close now, and I still can't hear anything! It must be in your head, to do with the machines.'

'That's not how it works, brother. You don't just *hear* voices.' Sunday was on the upper parts of the mud slope now, facing the slipping earth, planting her fingers into the soil for traction, beginning to work her way down to the tank.

Seeing no other option, Geoffrey began to follow.

'We should call someone. They always say we shouldn't touch old stuff.'

'They say we shouldn't do lots of things,' Sunday said.

She continued her descent, slipping once then recovering, her boots gouging impressive furrows in the exposed earth. Her hands were dirt-caked. As she looked down, twisting her head to peer over her right shoulder, her expression was one of intense tongue-biting concentration.

'This is not good,' Geoffrey said, starting down from the same point, following her hand- and foot-marks as best he could.

'We're here!' Sunday called suddenly, just before she planted a foot on the tank's sloping side. 'We've come to rescue you!'

'What's he saying?'

For the first time she appeared to take him seriously. 'You still can't hear him?'

'I'm not pretending, sister.'

'He says, "Come quickly, please. I need your help."'

A sensible question occurred to Geoffrey. 'In Swahili?'

'Yes,' Sunday said, but almost as quickly she added, 'I think. Why wouldn't he say it in Swahili?'

She had both feet on the tank now. She took a step to the right, placing her feet with a tightrope-walker's deliberation. Geoffrey aborted his descent, hardly daring to breathe in case he disturbed the slope and sent the tank, and the mud, and the two of them sliding to the bottom of the hole.

'Is he still saying it?'

'Yes,' Sunday said.

'He should have heard you by now, you're so close.'

Sunday spread both arms and lowered to her knees. She knuckled the tank's armour, once, twice. Geoffrey drew a steadying breath and resumed his anxious progress, still holding the wooden aeroplane in one hand, high over his head.

'He's not answering. Just saying the same thing.' Sunday reached up with one hand and drew her hat onto her head. 'I have a headache. It's too hot.' She tapped the tank again, harder now. 'Hello!'

'Look,' Geoffrey said.

Something odd was happening to the tank, where Sunday had tapped it. Ripples of colour raced away from that one spot: pinks and greens, blues and golds. The ripples vanished from sight, scurrying into the ground. They came back in blotches of solid colour, spreading like inkblots but not mixing together. The colours flickered and pulsed, then settled down into the same muddy red tones as the tank's surroundings.

'We should go now,' Geoffrey declared.

'We can't leave him.' All the same, Sunday stood up. Geoffrey stopped where he was, glad that his sister had finally seen sense. He made a gallant effort to lean into the slope, ready to offer his hand when she came back within reach.

But Sunday was behaving strangely now. 'This hurts,' she said in a slurred tone, and made to touch her forehead.

'Come up here,' he said. 'We should go home now.'

Sunday, still balanced on the tank's sloping flanks, looked at him. Her whole body was shaking with tiny but rapid movements. She was trying to say something.

'Sunday!'

She fell backwards, off the tank and down the slope. She hit the earth and rolled, all tangled limbs and bouncing hat. She came to rest at the bottom of the hole, where it was waterlogged, with her arms and legs spreadeagled, face-down in the mud.

For a long moment, all Geoffrey could do was stare. He wondered if she had broken any bones. Then, dimly, he realised that his sister might not be able to breathe.

He crept sideways, crossing the edge of the landslide and returning to where the ground was still firm and covered with grass and bushes. He had enough presence of mind to lift the cuff to his mouth and press the thick stud that allowed him to speak to the household.

'Please!'

Memphis answered quickly, his voice deep, resonant and slow: 'What is it, Geoffrey?'

Words tumbled out of him. 'Please, Memphis. Me and Sunday were out exploring and we found this hole in the ground, and the rains had made the earth slide down, and there was a tank sticking out.' He paused for breath. 'Sunday tried to help the boy inside. But then she got a headache and fell off the tank and now she's on the ground and I can't see her face.'

'Just a moment, Geoffrey.' Memphis sounded impossibly calm and unsurprised, as if this development was no more or less than he had anticipated for the day. 'Yes, I see where you are now. Go to your sister and turn her over so that she is lying on her side, not her face. But be very careful climbing down. I will be with you shortly.'

Something in Memphis's matter-of-fact response helped Geoffrey feel less frightened. It felt like it took an age, but at last his boots were in the same waterlogged ground and he was able to squelch his way over to his sister.

She didn't have her face in water – it was pressed into a raised patch of dry earth, with her mouth and nose unobstructed – but she was still quivering. Suds of foam bubbled between her lips.

Something buzzed in the air above them and Geoffrey tugged up the brim of his hat. It was a whirring machine no larger than the tip of his thumb.

'I see you,' Memphis said, speaking from Geoffrey's cuff. 'Now do what I said. Turn your sister over. You will need to be very strong.'

Geoffrey knelt down. He didn't want to look at Sunday too closely, not when she was quivering and foaming.

'Be brave, Geoffrey. Your sister is having some kind of seizure. You must help her now.'

He set the wooden aeroplane down on the ground, not minding that the mud dirtied the red paintwork. He worked his hands under Sunday's body and tried to shift her. The violent quivering alarmed him.

'Use all your strength, Geoffrey. I cannot help you until I arrive.'

He groaned with exertion. Perhaps she jolted in such a way as to aid his efforts, but with a lurch she finally came free of the mud and was no longer face-down.

'Geoffrey, listen carefully. For whatever reason, there is a problem with Sunday's head, and her cuff does not appear to be responding correctly. You must tell it what to do. Are you listening?'

'Yes.'

'Two red buttons, one on either side. You must press them both at the same time.'

Their cuffs were similar, but his didn't have those two red buttons. They had only come after her tenth birthday, which meant they had something to do with the things the neuropractors had put into her head, the things he didn't have yet.

He lifted her arm, fighting to hold it still, and tried to get his thumb and forefinger around the cuff. It was hard. His hand wasn't big enough.

'What will happen, Memphis?'

'Nothing bad.'

The red buttons were much stiffer to press than the blue ones on his cuff. After a moment of panic he realised that he would need to use both hands. Even then it was hard. At first, he must not have been pushing them firmly enough because nothing happened. But he tried again, applying all his strength, and with miraculous suddenness, Sunday's seizure stilled.

She was just lying there.

Geoffrey sat by her, waiting. She was breathing, he could see that. Her eyes were closed now, and although she was less animate than when she had been standing up on the tank and looking at him, he felt in some indefinable way that his sister had returned.

Laying a hand on her forehead, feeling the heat boiling off her skin, he turned his gaze to the sky.

Memphis arrived soon after. He hovered over the bowl, looking down from the airpod, then slid the craft sideways, back over the trees that ringed the depression. The airpod was so quiet that Geoffrey had to strain to hear the fading of its engine sound as it settled down out of view.

A minute or so later, Memphis appeared in person at the top of the slope. After no more than a moment's hesitation he came down the slope, half-skidding and half-running, flailing his arms to maintain balance. When he reached Sunday's side he touched a hand to her forehead, then examined the cuff.

Geoffrey studied his expression. 'Is she going to be all right?'

'I think so, Geoffrey. You did very well.' Memphis looked back at the tank, as if noticing it for the first time. 'How close did she get to it?'

'She was standing on it.'

'It's a bad machine,' Memphis explained. 'There was a war here once, one of the last in Africa.'

'Sunday said there was a little boy in the tank.'

Memphis lifted her from the ground, cradling her in his arms. 'Can you climb up the slope on your own, Geoffrey?

'I think so.'

'We must get Sunday back to the household. She will be all right, but the sooner she is seen by a neuropractor, the better.'

Geoffrey scrambled ahead, determined to show that he could take care of himself. 'But what about the little boy?'

'He doesn't exist. There is nothing in that tank but more machines, some of which are very clever.'

'This isn't the first tank you've seen?'

'No,' Memphis said carefully. 'Not the first. But the last time I saw one of them moving, I was very small.' Looking back, Geoffrey caught Memphis's quick smile. Clearly he did not wish Geoffrey to have nightmares about killing machines stalking the Earth. 'They are gone now, except for a few left behind, buried in the earth like this one.'

They were on the slope now, climbing. 'How could it escape?'

Memphis paused for breath. It must have been hard, carrying Sunday and also having to keep his own balance. 'The artilect sensed the presence of Sunday's machines, the ones inside her head. It worked out how to talk to them, how to make Sunday think there was someone calling.'

The idea of a machine tricking his sister – tricking her well enough that she had nearly convinced Geoffrey as well – was enough to chill him even as he sweated uphill.

'What would have happened if she hadn't fallen?'

'The tank might have tried to persuade her to help it. Or it might have been trying to exploit some deeper vulnerability. Whatever it did, it caused your sister to go into seizure.'

'But the tank is very old, and Sunday's machines are very new. How could it trick them?'

'Very old things are sometimes cleverer than very new things. Or slyer, at least.' They were climbing steadily now, almost near the top of the slope. 'That is why they are forbidden, or at least very carefully controlled.'

Geoffrey looked back, feeling a weird combination of fear and pity for the half-entombed thing. 'What will happen to the tank?'

'It will be taken care of,' Memphis said gently. 'For now, it is your sister we must concern ourselves with.'

They'd attained level ground. A narrow trail wound through the trees. Geoffrey hadn't seen it when they had come through, but it must have been clearly visible from the air. They set off along it, to the airpod that was waiting out of sight.

'Will she be all right?'

'I doubt any great harm has been done. It was good that you were there, to put the machines into shutdown. Ah.' Without warning, Memphis had stopped.

Geoffrey halted at his side. 'Is it Sunday?'

'No,' the thin man said, still not raising his voice. 'It is Mephisto. He is ahead of us, on the trail. Do you see him?'

In the dusky shade of the trail, canopied by trees, a huge light-dappled form blocked their path. The elephant was scuffing its trunk back and forth in the dust. It had one tusk, the other snapped off. Something in its posture conveyed unmistakable belligerence, its forehead lowered like a battering ram.

'Mephisto is an old bull male,' Memphis said. 'He is very aggressive and territorial. I saw him from the air, but he appeared to be moving away from us. I was hoping we could avoid an encounter today.'

Geoffrey was puzzled and frightened. He'd seen plenty of elephants before, but never sensed this degree of wariness from his mentor.

'We could go around,' he said.

'Mephisto will not let us. He knows this area much better than we do, and he can move more quickly than us, especially with Sunday to carry.'

'Why doesn't he want us to pass?'

'There is something wrong in his head.' Memphis paused. 'Geoffrey, would you look away, please? I must do something that I would rather not.'

'What are you going to do?'

'Look away and close your eyes.'

Geoffrey did as he was told, for there was no mistaking the severity of that command. There was silence, broken only by the rustling of leaves. And then a soft, dusty thump, accompanied by a fusillade of dry cracks as branches and tree-trunks snapped.

'Hold on to my jacket and follow me,' Memphis said. 'But do not look until I have told you it is safe. Will you promise me this?'

'Yes,' Geoffrey said.

But he did not keep his word. As they passed into the cool of the trees, Memphis veered around an obstacle, drawing Geoffrey with him. He opened his eyes, squinting against dust still hovering in the air. Mephisto was on the ground, lying on his side. The bull's one visible eye was open, but devoid of life. The huge grey, elaborately wrinkled form was perfectly still, perfectly dead.

'Did you kill Mephisto?' Geoffrey asked when they had reached the airpod.

Memphis loaded Sunday into the rear passenger compartment, placing her gently onto the padded seat. He said nothing, not even when they were in the air, on their way back to the household. *Memphis knows*, Geoffrey thought. Memphis knew Geoffrey had looked and nothing was ever going to be quite the same between them.

It was only later that he realised he had left the red wooden aeroplane down in the hole.

PART ONE

CHAPTER ONE

He was on his way back from the edge of the study area towards the research station, just him and the Cessna and the open skies above the Amboseli basin, his mood better than it had been in weeks, when the call arrived.

'Geoffrey,' a voice said in his skull. 'You must come to the household immediately.'

Geoffrey sighed. He should have known better than to expect this untroubled state of mind to last.

He was over the property ten minutes later, searching the white-walled and blue-tiled buildings for evidence of disruption. Nothing struck him as out of the ordinary. Everything about the A-shaped residence, from its secluded courtyards and gardens to its swimming pools, tennis courts and polo field, was as neat and orderly as an architect's model.

Geoffrey lined up with the rough track that served as his runway and brought the Cessna home. He bounced down, the fat-tyred wheels kicking up dirt and dust, braked hard and taxied to a vacant spot at the end of the row of airpods belonging to the household and its guests.

He let the engine die and sat in the cockpit for a few moments, gathering his thoughts.

He knew what it was, deep down. This day had been in his future for so long that it had taken on the solidity and permanence of a geographical feature. He was just surprised that it was finally upon him.

He disembarked into the morning heat, the aeroplane issuing quiet, ruminative sounds as it cooled down. Geoffrey took off his faded old Cessna baseball cap and used it to fan his face.

From the arched gatehouse in the wall emerged a figure, walking towards Geoffrey with slumped shoulders, solemn pace and grave demeanour.

'I am very sorry,' he said, raising his voice only when they were almost close enough to speak normally.

'It's Eunice, isn't it?'

'I am afraid she has passed away.'

Geoffrey tried to think of something to say. 'When did it happen?'

'Six hours ago, according to the medical report. But it only came to my attention an hour ago. Since then I've been busy verifying matters and informing close family.'

'And how?'

'In her sleep, peacefully.'

'One hundred and thirty's a pretty good age, I guess.'

'One hundred and thirty-one, by her last birthday,' Memphis said, without reproach. 'And yes, it is a good age. Had she returned to Earth, she might even have lived longer. But she chose her own path. Living all alone up there, with just her machines for company . . . the wonder is that she lasted as long as she did. But then she always did say that you Akinyas are like lions.'

Or vultures, Geoffrey thought. Aloud, he said, 'What happens now?'

Memphis draped an arm around his shoulders and steered him towards the gatehouse. 'You are the first to arrive back at the household. Some of the others will begin chinging in shortly. Within the day, some may begin to arrive in person. The others, those who are in space . . . it will take much longer, if they are able to come at all. They will not all be able to.'

They entered the shade of the gatehouse, where whitewashed walls cast cool indigo shadows.

'It feels odd to be meeting here, when this isn't the place where she died.'

'Eunice left specific instructions.'

'No one told me about them.'

'I have only just become aware of them myself, Geoffrey. You would have been informed, had I known earlier.'

Beyond the gatehouse, fountains hissed and burbled from the ornamental ponds. Geoffrey shoed aside an armadillo-sized gardening robot. 'I know this is as difficult for you as it is for the family, Memphis.'

'There may be a difficult period of transition. The family . . . the business . . . will have to adjust to the absence of a figurehead.'

'Fortunately, that doesn't really concern me.'

'You may not think so. But even on the periphery of things, you are still an Akinya. That goes for your sister as well.'

Geoffrey said nothing until they were standing in the spacious entrance lobby of the household's left wing. The place was as crypt-silent and forbidding as a locked museum. Glass cabinets, minor shrines to his grandmother's illustriousness, trapped her past under slanted sunlight. Spacesuit components, rock and ice samples gathered from all over the solar system, even an antiquated 'computer', a hinged grey box still fixed together with yellow and black duct tape. Printed books, with dusty, time-faded covers. A dismal assortment of childhood toys, no longer loved, abandoned.

'I don't think you realise how little effect this is going to have on Sunday and me,' Geoffrey said. 'Eunice was never that interested in either of us, once we strayed from the path.'

'You are quite wrong about Sunday. Eunice meant a great deal to her.'

Geoffrey decided not to press Memphis on that. 'Do my mother and father know?'

'They're still on Titan, visiting your Uncle Edison.'

He smiled quickly. 'That's not something I'd forget.'

'It will be a couple of hours before we are likely to hear from them. Perhaps longer, if they are occupied.'

They had nearly reached the ground-floor office where Memphis spent most of his time, managing the household's affairs – and by implication a business empire as wide as the solar system – from a room not much larger than a decent-sized broom cupboard.

'Anything I can do?' Geoffrey asked, feeling awkwardly as if there was some role he was expected to play, but which no one had told him about.

'Nothing immediately. I shall be going up to the Winter Palace in due course, but I can take care of that on my own.'

'To bring back her body?'

Memphis gave a half-nod. 'She wishes her remains to be scattered in Africa.'

'I could go with you.'

'Very kind, Geoffrey, but I am not too old for spaceflight just yet. And you must be very busy with your elephants.' He lingered at the threshold of his office, clearly anxious to return to his duties. 'It's good that you are back here now. If you could stay a day, that would be even better.'

'I feel like a loose end.'

'Be here for the rest of your family. You will all need to draw strength from each other.'

Geoffrey offered a sceptical smile. 'Even Hector and Lucas?'

'Even them,' Memphis said. 'I know that you do not get on, but perhaps now you will be able to find some common ground. They are not bad men, Geoffrey. It may feel like a long time ago to you, but I can still remember when you were all young enough not to hate the sight of each other.'

'Times change,' Geoffrey said. 'Still, I'll make an effort.'

He sat on the edge of his crisply made bed, in the room he had spent hardly any time in these recent years. In his hands was one of the wooden elephants Eunice had given him as a birthday gift. It was the bull, one of a set of six, diminishing in size down to the baby. The other five were still on the shelf where he had left them the last time he'd handled them. They stood on black plinths of some flinty, coal-like material.

He couldn't remember how old he had been when the elephants arrived, packed in a stout wooden box with tissue paper to protect them. Five or six, maybe. The time when the nanny from Djibouti was still taking care of his education and upbringing. The same year he stepped on the scorpion, perhaps?

It had taken him a little while to realise that his grandmother lived in orbit around the Moon, not on or in it, and even longer to appreciate that her infrequent gifts did not actually come from space. They were made somewhere on Earth; all she did was arrange for them to be sent to him. Later it had even occurred to him that someone else in the family – the nanny, perhaps Memphis – was choosing them on her behalf.

He'd been disappointed with the elephants when he opened the box, but not quite adult enough to hide that disappointment. He had wanted an aeroplane, not useless wooden animals that didn't do anything. Later, after a gentle reprimand, he had been made to speak to Eunice's figment and tell her how grateful he was. She had addressed him from the green jungle core of the Winter Palace.

He wondered how good a job of it he had made.

He was reaching to put the bull back on the shelf when the request began pulsing with gentle insistence in his visual field.

>>open: quangled bind
>>via: Maiduguri-Nyala backbone
>>carrier: Lufthansa Telepresence
>>incept: 23/12/2161 13:44:11 UTC
>>origin: Lagos, Nigeria, WAF
>>client: Jumai Lule
>>accept/decline ching?

He placed the bull back at the head of its family and returned to the bed, accepting Jumai's call with a single voked command. The bind established. Geoffrey's preference was always for inbound ching, remaining in his local sensorium, and Jumai would have expected that. He placed her figment by the door, allowing her a moment to adjust to her surroundings.

'Hello, Jumai,' he said quietly. 'I guess I know why you're calling.'

'I just got the news. I'm really sorry, Geoffrey. It must be a big blow to the family.'

'We'll weather it,' he said. 'It's not exactly unexpected.'

Jumai Lule was wearing brown overalls, hair messy and tied up in a meshwork dust cap, marks on her face from the goggles and breathing gear now hanging around her neck. She was in Lagos working on high-risk data archaeology, digging through the city's buried, century-old catacombs for nuggets of commercially valuable information. It was dangerous, exacting work: exactly the kind of thing she thrived on, and which he hadn't been able to offer her.

'I know you weren't that close to her, but—' Jumai began.

'She was still my grandmother,' Geoffrey countered defensively, as if she was accusing him of indifference to the matter of Eunice's death

'I didn't mean it that way, as you well know.'

'So how's work?' Geoffrey asked, trying to sound as if it mattered to him.

'Work is ... fine. Always more than we can keep up with. New challenges, most of the time. I probably need to move on at some point, but ...' Jumai let the sentence hang.

'Don't tell me you're getting bored already?'

'Lagos is close to being tapped out. I thought maybe Brazilia, even further afield. Like, maybe space. Still a lot of militarised crap left lying around the system, nasty shit they could use people like me to break into and decommission. And I hear the Gearheads pay pretty well.'

'Because it's dangerous.'

Jumai offered the palm of her hand to the ceiling. 'What, and this isn't? We hit Sarin nerve gas last week. Anti-tamper triggers, linked to what we thought was part of a mainframe's cryogenic cooling reservoir.' She grinned impishly. 'Not the kind of mistake you make twice.'

'Anyone hurt?'

'Nothing they couldn't fix, and they upped our hazard bonus as a consequence.' She looked around the room again, scanning it as if she half-expected booby traps in the made bed, or lurking on the neat white shelves. But anyway, this isn't about me – are *you* all right?'

'I'll be fine. And I'm sorry – I shouldn't have snapped. You're right – Eunice and I were never that close. I just don't really like having my face rubbed in it.'

'What about your sister?'

'I'm sure she feels the same way I do.'

'You never did take me up to meet Sunday. I always wanted to meet her. I mean properly, face to face.'

He shifted on the bed. 'Full of broken promises, that's me.'

'You can't help the way you are.'

'Maybe not. But that doesn't stop people telling me I should broaden my horizons.'

'That's your business, no one else's. Look, we're still friends, aren't we? If we weren't, we wouldn't keep in touch like this.'

Even if it had been months since the last call, he thought. But he had no wish to sound sour. 'We're good,' he affirmed. 'And it's very thoughtful of you to call me.'

'I couldn't not call you. The whole world knows – it wasn't news I could easily miss.' Jumai reached down for her goggles. 'Look, I'm only on a break – got to get back to the front line or my extraction chief will be yelling her head off – but I just wanted to say I'm here if you need someone to talk to.'

'Thank you.'

'You know, we could still go to the Moon one day. Just as friends. I'd like that.'

'One day,' he agreed, safe in the knowledge that she didn't really mean it either.

'Tell me when they sort out a date for the funeral. If I can make it, and if it isn't a family-only thing . . .' she trailed off.

'I'll let you know,' Geoffrey said.

Jumai settled the goggles over her eyes and eased the breathing mask into place. He'd tell her about the funeral plans, yes – but he doubted she'd come, even if the ceremony was extended to include friends of the Akinyas, rather than just close relatives. This call had already been awkward enough. There'd be a reason, a plausible excuse, to keep her away. And that, in truth, would be easiest on both of them.

Jumai waved a hand and chinged out of his life. Geoffrey considered it quite likely that he would never see her again.

For all that Eunice's death hit the family hard, it wasn't long before she was shunted from the headlines. A simmering sex/vote-rigging scandal in the Pan-African Parliament, a dispute between the East African Federation and the African Union about cost overruns on a groundwater bioremediation programme in former Uganda, a stand-off between Chinese tecto-engineers and Turkish government mandarins concerning the precise scheduling of a stress-management earthquake along the North Anatolian Fault. On the global scale, continued tensions between the United Surface Nations and the United Aquatic Nations regarding extradition rules and the extent of aug access rights and inter-regional Mechanism jurisdiction. Talk of expanding the scope of the Mandatory Enhancements. A murder attempt in Finland. Threat of industrial action at the Pontianak space elevator in western Borneo. Someone in Tasmania dying of a very rare type of cancer, something of a heroic achievement these days.

Only at the household, only in this part of the East African Federation, had the clocks stopped. A month had passed since Geoffrey was called from the sky with news of his grandmother's death. The scattering had been delayed until the twenty-ninth of January, which would give most of the family time to make reasonable travel arrangements for their journeys back to Earth. Miraculously, the delay was deemed agreeable to all the involved factions.

'Do try not to scowl, brother,' Sunday said in a low voice as she walked alongside him. 'Anyone who didn't know better would think you'd rather be somewhere else.'

'They'd be absolutely right.'

'At least we're doing this to honour her,' Sunday replied, after the standard Earth–Moon time lag.

'Why are we bothering, though? She didn't go out of her way to honour anyone else while she was alive.'

'We can give her this one.' Sunday wore a long skirt and a long-sleeved blouse, both in black velvet offset with luminous entwining threads. 'She may not have expressed much in the way of love and affection, but without her we'd be less filthily rich than we actually are.'

'You're right about the filthy rich part. Look at them all, circling like flies.'

'I suppose you mean Hector and Lucas.' Sunday kept her voice low. The cousins were not very far away in the procession.

'They've been hanging around like ghouls ever since she died.'

'You could also say they're taking on a burden so that the rest of us don't have to.'

'Then I wish they'd get a move on with it.'

The cousins had been born on Titan. They were the sons of Edison Akinya, one of the three children Eunice had had with Jonathan Beza. Until recent years the cousins hadn't spent a lot of time on Earth, but with Edison showing no signs of relinquishing his particular corner of the business empire, Hector and Lucas had turned their attentions sunwards. Geoffrey had no choice but to deal with them during their frequent visits to the household. The cousins had a large say in how the family's discretionary funds were allocated.

'Bad day at the office?'

'My work's suffering. They've blocked grant allocations while they sort through Eunice's finances. That makes it difficult for me to plan ahead, which in turn isn't doing wonders for my mood.' He walked on a few paces. 'Difficult for you to grasp, I know.'

Sunday's look was sharp. 'Meaning I haven't got a clue about planning and responsibility because I don't live in the Surveilled World? Brother, you really have no idea. I didn't move to the Zone to *escape* responsibility. I went there to find out what it feels like to actually have some.'

'Right. And you think the Mech treats us all like a bunch of helpless babies.' He closed his eyes in weariness – this was a spiralling conversation they'd had a hundred times already, without ever reaching a conclusion. 'It's not like that either.'

'If you say so.' She exhaled a long sigh, her capacity for argument evidently just as exhausted as his own. 'Maybe you'll get your funding back soon, anyway. Memphis told me there isn't much more to be done now, just a few loose ends. What the cousins are telling him, anyway.'

Geoffrey hoped that was the case. The scattering, symbolic as it was – Eunice had been a lifelong atheist, despite being born to Christian parents – ought to draw a line under the recent limbo. The wheels of the Akinya juggernaut would start to turn again, from Earth to the Moon, out to their automated mining facilities in the asteroids and the Kuiper belt. (Not that the machines had ever stopped, of course, but it was tempting to think of the robots standing to attention, heads tilted in deference.)

Then they could all get on with their fantastically glamorous lives, and Geoffrey could go back to his dull grey elephants.

'I did consider coming in person,' Sunday said.

'I thought for a minute you had, at least when you first showed up.'

'Even you can't have missed the time lag, brother.' She ran a hand down her sternum. 'It's a prototype, a kind of claybot – I'm road-testing it.'

'For . . . what's the name of that boyfriend of yours?'

'Oh, this is way out of Jitendra's league. It's a friend of his, someone working in mainstream robotics. I'm afraid I'm under strict orders not to mention the firm involved, but if I said it rhymed with Sexus—'

'Right.'

Sunday grabbed his hand before he could react. 'Here. Tell me how it feels.'

Her fingers closed around his.

'Creepy.'

The hand felt colder than it should have, but the effect was otherwise convincing. Her face was almost as realistic. It was only when she pushed the sunglasses back onto her scalp that the spell failed. There was a deadness to the eyes, the difference between paste jewellery and the real thing.

'It's pretty good.'

'Better than good. But you haven't seen the half of it. Watch this.'

Between one breath and the next, Sunday departed. He was suddenly looking at an old woman, grey hair tied back in an efficient bun, her skin a map of thirteen decades.

Geoffrey barely had time to react before Eunice vanished and Sunday returned.

'Given the circumstances,' he said, 'that was very disrespectful.'

'She'd have forgiven me. That's the breakthrough, the reason for the prototype. The rapid-morph material came from the Evolvarium on Mars – it's some kind of adaptive camouflage, in its original context. Plexus . . . did I just say that? They've got exclusivity on it. They're calling it "Mercurial". Faster and more realistic than anything else out there.'

'So you see a big market for this?'

'Who knows? I'm just along for a free ride while someone else gets test data.' Sunday let go of Geoffrey's hand and tapped a finger against her cheekbone. 'We're recording constantly. Every time someone sees me, their reactions are filed away – micro-expressions, eye saccades, that kind of thing – then fed into the system and used to tweak the configuration algorithms.'

'What about manners? It's not good form to let people think they're talking to a real person when they're not.'

'Their fault for not having the right layers enabled,' Sunday said. 'Anyway, it's not just me: there are twenty of us walking around now, all chinging in from the Zone. We're not just testing the realism of the configs. We're seeing how well they can maintain that realism even with Earth–Lunar time lag thrown in.'

'So you could go to the trouble of sending down a body, but you couldn't come in person?'

She gave him a quizzical look. 'I showed up, didn't I? It's not like Eunice would have cared whether any of us was physically present.'

'I'm not sure I knew her well enough to say for sure.'

'I doubt she'd have given a damn who's here in the flesh and who isn't. And she'd have hated all this fuss. But Memphis had a bee in his bonnet about us all leaving the household on time.'

'I noticed. My guess is that Eunice stipulated something, and he's just, following the script.'

After a moment, Sunday said quietly, 'He looks really old now.'

'Don't say that.'

'Why not?'

'Because I was thinking exactly the same thing.'

Memphis was leading the procession, walking ahead of the main party with an earthenware jar in his hands. Since leaving the house they had been walking due west towards the grove of acacia trees that marked the limit of the crumbling boundary wall.

'Still got the old suit, though,' Geoffrey said.

'I think he's only ever had the one.'

'Either that or hundreds of exactly the same style.'

The favoured black business suit remained immaculate, but it draped off his thin frame as if tailored for some other, bulkier man. The hands that had carried Sunday out of the hole all those years ago must have been the same ones now gripping the earthenware jar, but that seemed impossible. Where once Memphis had walked with confident authority, now his gait was slow and measured, as if in every footfall lay the prospect of humiliation.

'At least he dressed for the occasion,' Sunday said.

'And at least there's a heart beating under these clothes.'

'Even if they do reek ever so slightly of elephant dung.'

'I thought I'd have time to get back to the research station and change, but then I lost track and—'

'You're here, brother. That's all anyone would have expected.'

The party numbered around thirty, including the two of them. He'd done his best to identify the various family branches and alliances that were present, but keeping tabs on the wilder offshoots of the Akinya tree had never been his strong suit. At least elephants had the decency to drop dead after fifty or sixty years, instead of hanging around and procreating into their second century. In the Amboseli basin there were nearly a thousand individuals. Geoffrey could identify at least a hundred of them with a single glance, assessing shape and size and posture with barely any conscious application of effort, calling to mind age, lineage and kin affiliations, status within family, bond group and clan. Tracking Akinyas ought to have been trivial in comparison. There was even a matriarch, bull males and a watering hole.

Predators and scavengers, too.

What were they all doing here? Geoffrey wondered. What did they all expect to get out of it? More pertinently: what did *he* expect to get out of it?

A pat on the head for being a dutiful grandson? Not from his father and mother, who – like Uncle Edison – were still on Titan. Kenneth Cho and Miriam Beza-Akinya had sent golems of themselves, but the time lag was so acute that the machines were acting under full autonomy, mostly witnessing rather than interacting.

Had he expected something more of them?

Perhaps.

'I am glad you both found time in your busy personal schedules,' Hector said, sidling over to Geoffrey and Sunday.

'We were always going to be here, cousin,' Sunday said. 'She meant as much to us as she did to you.'

'Of course.' Like his brother Lucas, who had also joined them, Hector wore a dark suit of conservative cut, offset with flashes of tribal colouration. The tall, muscular siblings looked uncomfortable in their formal wear. The cousins had spent so much time in space that African heat did not become them. 'And perhaps now that we are all together again,' Hector went on, 'it might be an apposite time for some of us to rethink our positions within the fold.'

As if recalling some obscure biblical proverb, Lucas declared: 'A household needs many pillars.'

'I think the household's doing fine without us,' Geoffrey said. 'Besides – aren't we both beyond redemption as far as you're concerned?'

'You have an analytic mindset,' Hector said, in his best gently patronising manner. He was only ten years older than Geoffrey but managed to make that decade seem like a century. 'And Sunday is . . . adaptable.'

'Please, spare my blushes.'

Geoffrey was about to offer a tart reply of his own when he noticed that Memphis was slowing his pace to a halt.

Conversation lulled as the party followed his lead. Sparring with the cousins had made Geoffrey tense, but now the feeling in his gut only worsened. He hated ceremony at the best of times, but especially when he had no idea exactly what was planned. He watched as Memphis turned slowly around, presenting the earthenware vase like a newborn child being held to the sky. He'd stopped in the shadow of the acacia grove, looking back towards both the low outline of the house and the mountain that rose beyond it, a scant fifty kilometres away.

Geoffrey risked a glance over his shoulder. With the sun now set, the sky beyond Kilimanjaro was a cloudless and translucent flamingo pink. It would soon be pricked by the first and brightest of the evening stars, but from the summit the sun must still have been visible. Day-lit snows glittered back at the assembled party with a blinding laser-like clarity.

Eunice had never seen those snows with her own eyes. They had melted almost completely away by the time she was born, not to begin their return until she was well into her exile.

He silenced his thoughts. The party had fallen completely silent. Memphis was speaking now.

'She liked to come here,' he began, pausing until he had everyone's attention, and then repeating those opening words before continuing. 'These trees were here when she was a little girl, and although that was long before I knew her, she never stopped coming out here to read, even during the rains.'

Memphis's habit was to speak slowly, and his voice was at least an octave deeper than anyone else's.

'Even in the final months she spent on Earth, after she had returned home to prepare for her last expedition, it was still her habit to sit here, in the shade of these trees, her back against that very trunk.' Memphis nodded, letting the party take in the particular tree with the slight hollow in its bole, a depression that could have been moulded to support a human back. 'She would sit with her knees drawn up, an ancient, battered reader – sometimes even a printed book – balanced on them, squinting to read the words. *Gulliver's Travels* was one of her favourites – her old copy's still in the museum, a little the worse for wear. Sometimes I would call and call and she would not hear me – or pretend not to hear me – until I had walked all the way here, to this spot. As much as I tried, I could never bring myself to be angry with her. She would always smile and give the impression that she was glad to see me. And I think she was, most of the time.' Memphis paused, and one by one – or so it seemed to Geoffrey – his attention lingered on each of the guests.

'Thank you all for coming, especially at such short notice. To those family and friends who could not attend, or could not be here in person, I assure you that Eunice would have understood. It is enough that the family is here in spirit, to honour her and to witness this scattering.'

Memphis tipped up the urn and began to release the ashes. They breezed out in a fine grey mist.

'She chose to return, not just to Earth but to Africa; not just to Africa but to former Tanzania; and not just here but to her household and this grove of trees, where she had always felt most at home.'

Memphis halted, and for a moment it was as if he was distracted by something only he could hear; a distant ringing alarm, an inappropriate laugh, the approach of a vehicle when none was expected.

Geoffrey glanced at Sunday, the two of them sharing a thought: was it age, momentarily betraying him?

Then Geoffrey felt something odd, something both familiar and yet completely out of place.

The ground was thrumming.

It was as if, somewhere out of sight, a multitude of animals were in stampede, and drawing nearer. Not that, though. Geoffrey knew immediately what was making the ground tremble like that, even as he refused to accept that it was happening.

The blowpipe was not – *could not* – be functioning. It had been out of service for at least five or six years. While there was always talk of it being brought back into operation, that was supposedly years in the future.

That it should be reactivated today, of all days . . .

'It was here,' Memphis said, the ground vibrations now quite impossible to ignore, 'that Eunice first dreamed of her shining road to the stars. Scarcely a new idea, of course, but it took Eunice's vision to understand that it could be made to happen, and that it could be brought into existence here and now, in her lifetime. And by sheer force of will she made it so.'

Disturbed by the drumming, a multitude of finches, cranes and storks lifted from trees in a riot of wingbeats and raucous alarm calls.

So it was the blowpipe, then, as if there had been any doubt. Nothing else had the power to shake the ground like that. A hundred or more kilometres to the west, at this very moment, a payload was racing through the bowels of the Earth, slamming along a rifle-straight vacuum tunnel that would eventually bring it right under the party. Simple physics dictated that there would be recoil from the magnetic pushers, recoil that could only be absorbed by the awesome counterweight of the Earth itself. Launching masses eastwards delayed the sun's fall to the west. It made the day last infinitesimally longer. On the day of her scattering, the sun had slowed for its daughter.

Not everyone in attendance knew what was happening, but one by one those who had some inkling turned to face Kilimanjaro. They knew what was coming next, and their anticipation soon spread to the other members of the party. Everyone looked to the fire-bright snowcap.

The emerging payload was a swiftly rising glint.

In less than a second, the pusher lasers were activated and aligned. There were five of them in all, stationed in a wide ring around the exit iris, a few hundred metres below the summit. They were highly efficient free-electron lasers, and most of the energy they were emitting was shone straight onto the underside of the rising payload, creating an ablative cushion of superhot plasma. Their cooling systems were deep inside the mountain, so that they did not disturb the snowcap. Sufficient stray light was reaching his eyes to make the lasers visible, five platinum threads converging at the top, the angle between them slowly narrowing as the payload rose, and then appearing to widen again as it fell further and further to the east. The guests were looking along the payload's line of flight, so they couldn't easily tell that it was rising at forty-five degrees rather than vertically. But by now it was almost certainly out over the Indian Ocean, over the sovereign seaspace of the United Aquatic Nations.

Someone started clapping. It was, perhaps, not quite the appropriate response. But then someone else joined in, and then a third, and before long Geoffrey found himself clapping as well. Even Sunday was giving in to the mood. Memphis had by then disposed of the ashes and was looking, if not precisely pleased with himself, then not entirely dissatisfied with the way events had ensued.

'I hope you will forgive that little piece of showmanship,' he said, raising his voice just enough to quell the clapping. Before continuing, he looked down at the ground, almost shamefacedly. 'A couple of days ago, after I had already returned with the ashes, I learned that an all-up test was scheduled for this afternoon. Nothing had been publicised, and the engineers were particularly keen that there be no announcement beforehand. I could not let the opportunity slip.'

'I thought you were years away from operation.' This was Nathan Beza, grandson of Jonathan Beza, Eunice's late husband. Jonathan had remarried on Mars; Nathan – who had come from Ceres for the scattering – had no blood ties to Eunice.

'So did we,' Geoffrey muttered under his breath.

'The damage was never as bad as we thought when this happened,' said Hector, rubbing a finger along the sweat-line where his collar bit into his neck 'The engineers were right to err on the side of caution, even if it hurt our shares at the time of the malfunction. But it made our competitors complacent, snug in the knowledge that we'd be out of business for a long, long time to come.'

'What did we just put up?' asked Geoffrey, breaking his vow of silence.

'A test mass,' said Lucas. 'Offsetting of repair and redesign costs could have been achieved with a commercial payload, but the risk of a security leak was deemed unacceptably high.' Lucas had the easy, authoritative diction of a newsfeed anchordoll. 'Implementing watertight non-disclosure protocols within our core engineering staff has already proven challenging enough.'

'So other than you two and Memphis, who exactly knew about this?' Sunday asked.

'Matters proceeded on a need-to-know basis,' Lucas said. 'There was no need to risk exposure beyond the family.'

'My sister and I are still family,' Geoffrey said. 'Last time I checked, anyway.'

'Yes,' Hector said, over-emphatically. 'Yes, you are.'

'A number of technical and legal hurdles must be surmounted before a satisfactory transition to full commercial operations can be effected,' Lucas said, sounding as smooth and plausible as a corporate salesbot. 'A robust testing regime will now ensue, anticipated to last three-to-six months.'

'The main thing,' Hector said, 'is that Grandmother would have found it a fitting tribute. Don't you agree, Geoffrey?'

Geoffrey was composing a suitably tart riposte – everything he knew about Eunice told him that this was exactly the kind of self-aggrandising spectacle she'd have gone out of her way to avoid – when he realised that by wounding his cousin he would be hurting Memphis as well. So he smiled and shut up, and shot Sunday a glance warning her to do likewise.

Sunday set her jaw in defiance, but complied.

They watched until, as suddenly as they had activated, the lasers snapped off. Presuming that the launch had proceeded without incident, the lasers would by now have pushed the payload all the way to orbital velocity, doubling its speed upon emergence from the mountain. Barring any adjustments, the payload would be back over equatorial Africa in ninety minutes. By then all the stars would be out.

The party was beginning to drift back to the house. Geoffrey lingered a while, thinking about waiting until the payload returned. It was then that he noticed the child who had been there all along, mingling with the party but never attaching herself to any part of it. She was a small girl, of Chinese appearance, wearing a red dress, white stockings and black shoes. Sunday and Geoffrey both carried Chinese genes, but this girl did not look in the least African. The style and cut of her dress brought to mind a different century.

Geoffrey didn't recognise her at all, but she was looking at him with such directness that he glanced around to see who might be standing behind. He was alone.

'Hello?' he said, offering a smile. 'Can I—?'

He voked an aug layer. The girl wasn't a girl at all, but another robot proxy. Maybe she was part of Sunday's field test. He looked for his sister, but she was twenty paces away, talking to Montgomery, Kenneth Cho's brother, who walked with the stiff gait of someone using a mobility exo under their clothes.

Geoffrey sharpened his aug query. He wanted to know who was chinging into this proxy body. But the aug couldn't resolve the ching bind.

That, if anything, was even stranger than the appearance of an unknown child at his grandmother's scattering.

CHAPTER TWO

'Not clever, brother. It's a long way down.'

Geoffrey steadied himself and stepped away from the roof's edge. He'd been craning his neck, following a bright point of light as it tracked overhead. A Balinese orbital manufactory, according to the aug. For a moment, it had exerted a hypnotic draw on his gaze and he'd begun to topple.

Sunday was right: the old building lacked the safety features it was so easy to take for granted these days. No barrier around the roof, and no hidden devices waiting to spring into action to intercept his fall.

He caught his breath. 'I didn't hear you come up.'

'Lost in your own little world.' She took the wine glass out of his hand. 'I thought you were feeling sick.'

'Sick of playing my part, more like. Did you hear what Lucas said to me?'

'Have a heart. I had my own conversation to handle.'

'I bet it wasn't as dull as mine.'

'Oh, I don't know. Hector can give Lucas a run for his money when it comes to boring the crap out of people.'

The stars were out, the western horizon still glowing the deep shimmering pink of a plasma tube. After leaving the dinner, he had stepped over the glass skylights and made his way to the unprotected edge. Looking up, he'd studied the riverine ooze of the Near-Earth communities. The aug identified the stations and platforms by name and affiliation, painting flags and corporate symbols on the heavens. Beautiful, if you stopped to think about what it actually all meant, what it signified in terms of brute human achievement, generations of blood and sweat. Peaceful communities in orbit, cities on the Moon and Mars and further afield, and all of it theoretically within his grasp, his for the taking.

In 2030, when Eunice had been born, there'd been nothing like this. Rockets that used chemistry to get into space. A couple of mouldering space stations, bolted together from tin cans. Footprints on the Moon, undisturbed for sixty years. Some clunking, puppyish robots bumbling around on Mars, a few more further afield. Space probes the size of dustbin lids, falling into the outer darkness.

A night sky that was a black, swallowing ocean.

'Lucas asked me what I want to do with my life,' Geoffrey said. 'I said I'm taking care of it myself, thank you. Then he asked me why I'm not making a name for myself. I said my name was taken care of at birth.'

'Bet that went down well.'

'Having the keys to the kingdom is all very well, Lucas told me, but apparently you still need to know which doors to open.'

'Lucas is a prick. He may be blood, but I can still say it.' Sunday knelt down, placing Geoffrey's glass to one side. She lowered her legs over the side of the building, assuming a position that struck Geoffrey as being only slightly less precarious than standing right on the edge. 'He's had an empathy shunt installed. It's legal, surprisingly enough. When he needs to become more detached and businesslike, he can turn off specific brain circuitry related to empathy. Become a sociopath for the day.'

'Even Hector hasn't gone that far.'

'Give him time – if having a conscience comes between him and a profit margin, he'll march straight down to the nearest neuropractor and have his own shunt put in.'

'I'm glad I'm not like them.'

'That doesn't change the fact that you and I are always going to be a crushing disappointment to the rest of the family.'

'If Father was here, he'd back me up.'

'Don't be so sure. He may not have quite as low an opinion of us as our cousins, but he still thinks you're only *pretending* to have an occupation.'

Above the household, glowering down on Africa, the full Moon gave every impression of having been attacked by an exuberant child with a big box of poster paints. The Chinese, Indian and African sectors were coloured red, green and yellow. Blue swatches, squeezed between the major geopolitical subdivisions, indicated claims staked by smaller nation states and transnational entities. Arrows and text labels picked out the major settlements, as well as orbiting bodies and vehicles in cislunar space.

Geoffrey voked away the layer. The naked Moon was silver-yellow, flattened-looking. Any other time of the month, cities and industries would have spangled in lacy chains and arcs in the shadowed regions of the disc, strung out along transit lines, political demarcations and the ancient natural features of the Lunar surface. Rivers of fiery lava, seeping through a black crust. But the fully lit face, too bright for any signs of habitation to stand out, could not have looked so different to Geoffrey's moonstruck hominid ancestors.

He still found it difficult to accept that Sunday wasn't sitting right next to him, but was *up there*, on that bright nickel coin hammered into the sky.

'Did you see that strange little girl at the scattering?' he asked her.

'Yes.'

'And?'

'I was going to ask if you knew who she was. I tried resolving her bind, but—'

'It didn't go anywhere.' Geoffrey nodded. 'That's weird, isn't it? You're not meant to be able to do that.'

'Doesn't mean there aren't some people capable of doing so.'

'Like your friends?'

'Ah, right. I see where this is going. You think she has something to do with the Descrutinised Zone. Well, sorry, but I don't think she does. Plexus are monitoring Earth–Lunar traffic and they didn't pick up anything that looked like an unresolved ching bind. Not that they're infallible, of course, but my guess is that she wasn't chinging in from Lunar space. Somewhere closer, maybe.'

'Still doesn't tell us who she is.'

'No, but if I allowed myself to get sucked into every little mystery surrounding this family . . .' Sunday left the remark unfinished. 'Someone must know her, and that's all that matters to me. What other possibility is there? Someone showed up at our scattering without an invitation?'

'Maybe everyone just assumes she was invited.'

'Good luck to her, in that case. No secrets were revealed, and if anyone wanted to eavesdrop, there were a million public eyes they could have used. Sorry, but I've got other things on my mind right now. Deadlines. Bills. Rent to pay. That kind of stuff.'

Sunday was right, of course – and given Geoffrey's shaky grasp of the internal politics of his own family, it was entirely possible that the girl was some relative he'd forgotten about.

'I can't even point to the DZ,' he said, grasping in a single remorseful instant how little he knew about her life.

'It would be a bit weird if you could, brother – it's on the other side of the Moon, so it's never actually visible from here.' She paused. 'You know, the offer's always there. You can get a tourist visa easily enough, spend a few days with us. Jitendra and I would love to show you around.

There's something else I'm dying to show you, too. That thing I did with Eunice's face ...' Sunday hesitated. 'There's a bit more to it, it's kind of a long-term project of mine. But you'd have to come and see it in person.'

Geoffrey delved into his box of delaying tactics. 'I need to get a couple of papers out before I can take any time off. Then there's an article I need to peer review for *Mind*.'

'What you always say, brother. I'm not criticising, though. You love your work, I can see that.'

'I'm flying out tomorrow. Want to come and see the herd?'

'I ... need to report back, about this body,' Sunday said. 'Sorry. Like you say: maybe next time.'

Geoffrey smiled in the darkness. 'We're as bad each other, aren't we?'

'Very probably,' his sister answered, from wherever on the far side of the Moon her flesh-and-blood body presently resided. 'Me, I wouldn't have it any other way.'

He had hoped Sunday might change her mind – there was so much of his work he would have gladly shared with her – but when Geoffrey flew out in the morning it was on his own. The waterhole, he observed, was smaller than it had been at the start of the short dry season that accompanied the turning of the year. Patches of once-marshy ground were now hardened and barren of vegetation, forcing animals to crowd closer as they sought sustenance. Rather than the intense vivid green of the rainy season, the grass was now sun-bleached brown, sparse and lacking nourishment. Trees had been stripped of anything edible and within reach of trunks. Many decades had passed since the last prolonged drought in this part of Africa, and a real drought would never be permitted now, but it was still a testing time.

Soon he spotted a huddle of elephants near a grove of candelabra trees, and another about a kilometre further away, with a mother and calf trailing the group. Squinting as the sun flashed off what little water remained, he made out a lone bull picking its way through a stand of acacia and cabbage trees. The elephants were battleship grey, with only a few olive-green patches testifying that they had, against the odds, located some cool mud.

By the shape of his body, the relative length and curvature of his tusks and a certain sauntering quality to his gait, the lone adult male was almost certainly Odin, a generally bad-tempered bull with a range that encompassed most of the basin. Odin had his trunk curled nonchalantly over his left tusk and was making progress in the direction of the nearest grouping, the O-family into which he had been born some thirty years ago.

Geoffrey voked an aug layer, the aug dropping an arrow and data box onto the bull, confirming that it was indeed Odin.

The Cessna continued its turn. Geoffrey spotted another group of elephants, even further from the waterhole than the second. It was the M-family, his main study group. They had moved a long way since yesterday. 'Turn north-west,' he told the Cessna, 'and take us down to about two hundred metres.'

The aircraft obeyed. Geoffrey counted the elephants by eye as best he could, but that was hard enough from a fixed position. He overflew the group once, had the Cessna make a loop and return, and got different numbers: eleven on the first pass, ten on the second. Giving in, he allowed the aug to label and identify the party. He was right about the M-family identification and the aug found only the expected ten elephants. He must have double-counted one of the rambunctious calves.

He had the Cessna overfly the M-family one more time, lower still, and watched elephants lift their heads to follow him, one of the older members even saluting him with her trunk. 'Give me manual,' he told the plane.

He selected a ribbon of land and came down three hundred metres from the M-family. The aug detected no other elephants – and certainly no bulls – within three kilometres. An adequate margin of error, and he would be alerted if the situation changed.

He told the Cessna that he would return within two hours, grabbed his shoulder bag from behind the pilot's seat and then set off in the direction of the herd. Leaving nothing to chance, Geoffrey hefted a dead branch from the ground and used it to beat the earth as he walked, occasionally raising his voice to announce his arrival. The last thing he wanted to do was startle a dozing elephant that had somehow managed not to pick up on his approach.

'It's me, Geoffrey.'

He pushed through the trees, and at last the elephants were in sight. Ten, as the aug had confirmed – grazing peacefully, snuffling and rooting through dried-up grass. The matriarch, Matilda, was already aware of his presence. She was a big elephant with a broad face, missing a tusk on the right side and possessed of a distinctive Africa-shaped notch in the side of her left ear.

Geoffrey discarded the stick. 'Hello, big girl.'

Matilda snorted and threw back her head, then returned to the business of foraging. Geoffrey surveyed the rest of the party, alert for signs of illness, injury or belligerent mood. One of the younger calves – Morgan – still had the same limp Geoffrey had noted the day before, so he voked a specific biomedical summary. Bloodstream analysis showed normal white cell and stress hormone counts, suggesting that there was no infection or skeletal injury, only a moderately debilitating muscle sprain that would clear up with time. Babies were resilient.

As for the rest of the M-family, they were relaxed and peaceable, even Marsha, the daughter who had recently mock-charged Geoffrey. She appeared sheepishly absorbed in her foraging, as if trusting that the incident was something they could both put behind them.

He paused in his approach, framed the view with his fingers like a budding auteur and blinked still frames. Sometimes he even took a small folding chair from the Cessna and sat down with a sketchbook and sharpened 2B pencil, trying to capture the ponderous majesty of these wise and solemn creatures.

'So, old lady,' he said quietly as he came nearer to the matriarch, 'how are things today?'

Matilda eyed him with only mild curiosity, as if he would suffice until something more interesting came along. She continued to probe the ground with her trunk while one of the calves – Meredith's boy, Mitchell – nosed around her hindquarters, flicking flies away with his tail.

Geoffrey voked the link with Matilda. A graphic of her brain appeared in the upper-left corner of his visual field, sliced through and colour-coded for electrical and chemical activity, all squirming blues and pinks, intricately annotated.

Geoffrey placed his bag on the ground and walked up to Matilda, all the while maintaining an unthreatening posture and letting her see that his hands were empty. She allowed him to touch her. He ran his palm along the wrinkled, leathery skin at the top of her foreleg. He felt the slow in-and-out of her breathing, like a house-sized bellows.

'Is this the day?' he asked.

After six months' careful negotiation he had flown to a clinic in Luanda, on the Angolan coast, and completed the necessary paperwork. The changes to his own aug protocols were all legal and covered by watertight non-disclosure statutes. The new taps had been injected painlessly, migrating to their chosen brain regions without complication. Establishing the neural connections with his own brain tissue took several weeks, as the taps not only bonded with his mind but carried out diagnostic tests on their own functioning.

In the late summer of the previous year he'd had strange

machine-like dreams, his head filled with luminous gridlike patterns and insanely complex tapestries of pulsing neon. He'd been warned. Then the taps bedded down, his dreams returned to normal and he felt exactly as he had done before.

Except now there was a bridge in his head, and on the other side of that bridge lay a fabulous, barely charted alien kingdom.

All he had to do was summon the nerve to cross into it.

Geoffrey walked around Matilda once, maintaining hand-to-skin contact so that she always knew where he was. He felt the other elephants studying him, most of them adult enough to know that if Matilda did not consider him a threat, nor should they.

Geoffrey voked his own real-time brain image into position next to Matilda's. Mild ongoing activity showed in the visual and auditory centres, as she watched him and at the same time kept vigil over the rest of her family. He, on the other hand, was showing the classic neurological indicators of stress and anxiety.

Not that he needed the scan to tell him that: it was there in his throat, in his chest and belly.

'Show some backbone,' Geoffrey whispered to himself.

He voked the aug to initiate the transition. A sliding scale showed the degree of linkage, beginning at zero per cent and rising smoothly. At ten per cent there was no detectable change in his mental state. On the very first occasion, six months ago now, he'd reached fifteen and then spooked himself out of the link, convinced that his mind was being slowly infiltrated by tendrils of unaccountable dread. The second time, he'd convinced himself that the dread was entirely of his own making and nothing to do with the overlaying of Matilda's state of mind. But at twenty per cent he had felt it coming in again, spreading like a terror-black inkblot, and he had killed the link once more. On the five subsequent occasions, he had never taken the link beyond thirty-five per cent.

He thought he could do better this time. There had been sufficient opportunity to chide himself for his earlier failures, to reflect on the family's quiet disappointment in his endeavours.

As the scale slid past twenty per cent, he felt superhumanly attuned to his surroundings, as if his visual and auditory centres were beginning to approach Matilda's normal state of activity. Each blade of glass, each midday shadow, appeared imbued with vast potentiality. He wondered how any creature could be that alert and still have room for anything resembling a non-essential thought.

Perhaps the relative amplification levels needed tweaking. What might feel like hyper-alertness to him might be carefree normality to Matilda.

He exceeded twenty-five per cent. His self-image was beginning to lose coherence: it was as if his nerve-endings were pushing through his skin, filling out a volume much larger than that defined by his body. He was still looking at Matilda, but now Matilda was starting to shrink. The visual cues were unchanged – he was still seeing the world through his own eyes – but the part of his brain that dealt in spatial relationships was being swamped by data from Matilda.

This was how he felt to her: like a doll, something easily broken.

Thirty per cent. The spatial adjustment was unsettling, but he could cope with the oddness of it all. It was weird, and it would leave him with the curious appreciation that his entire sense of self was a kind of crude, clunking clockwork open to sabotage and manipulation, but there was no emotional component.

Thirty-five per cent, and the terror hadn't begun to come in yet. He was nearly four-tenths of the way to thinking like an elephant, and yet he still felt fully in command of his own mental processes. The emotions were the same as those he'd been experiencing when he initiated the link. If Matilda was sending him anything, it wasn't enough to suppress his own brain activity.

He felt a shiver of exhilaration as the link passed forty per cent. This time, just possibly, he could go all the way. Even to reach the halfway point would be a landmark. Once he had got that far, there would be no doubt in his mind that he could take the link to its limit. Not today, though. Today he'd willingly settle for fifty-five, sixty per cent.

Something happened. His heart rate quickened, adrenalin flooding his system. Geoffrey felt panicked, but the panic was sharper and more focused than the creeping terror he had experienced on the previous occasions.

The matriarch had noticed something. The aug hadn't detected any large predators in the area, and Odin was still much too far away to be a problem. Maasai, perhaps ... but the aug should have alerted him. Matilda let out a threat rumble, but by then some of the other elephants in the family had begun to turn uneasily, the older ones shepherding the younger individuals to safety.

His sense of scale still out of kilter, Geoffrey's eyes swept the bush for danger. Matilda rumbled again, flapping her ears and heeling the ground with her front foot.

One of the youngsters trumpeted.

Geoffrey broke the link. For a moment Matilda lingered in his head, his sense of scale still awry. Then the panic ebbed and he felt his normal body image assert itself. He was in danger, no question of it. The elephants might not mean him harm but their instinct for survival would easily override any protectiveness they felt towards him. He started to back away, at the same time wondering what exactly was approaching. He made to reach for his bag.

A dark-garbed and bony-framed man stepped out of the bush. He flicked twigs and dust from his suit trousers, apparently oblivious to the elephant family he had just scared to the brink of stampede.

Memphis.

Geoffrey blinked and frowned, his heart still racing. The elephants were calming now – they recognised Memphis from his occasional visits and understood that he was not a threat.

'I thought we had an agreement,' Geoffrey said.

'Unless,' Memphis said reasonably, 'the circumstances were exceptional. That was also the understanding.'

'You still didn't have to come here in person.'

'On the contrary, I had to do exactly that. You set your aug preferences such that you are not otherwise contactable.'

'You could have sent a proxy,' Geoffrey said peevishly.

'The elephants have no liking for robots, from what I remember. The absence of smell is worse than the wrong smell. You once told me that they can differentiate Maasai from non-Maasai solely on the basis of bodily odour. Is this not the case?'

Geoffrey smiled, unable to stay angry at Memphis for long. 'So you were paying attention after all.'

'I wouldn't have come if there was any alternative. Lucas and Hector were most insistent.'

'What do they want with me?'

'You'd best come and find out. They're waiting.'

'At the houschold?'

'At the airpod. They were keen to walk the rest of the way, but I indicated that it might be better if they kept back.'

'You were right,' Geoffrey said, bristling. 'Anything they've got to say to me, they had their chance last night, when we were all one big happy family.'

'Perhaps they have decided to give you more funding.'

'Yeah,' Geoffrey said, stooping to collect his bag. 'I can really see *that* happening.'

*

Lucas and Hector were standing on the ground next to the metallic-green airpod. They wore lightweight pastel business suits, with wide-brimmed hats.

'I trust we did not disturb you,' Lucas said.

'Of course we disturbed him,' Hector said, smiling. 'What else are we to Geoffrey but an irksome interruption? He has *work* to do.'

'I conveyed the urgency of your request,' Memphis said.

'Your cooperation is appreciated,' Lucas said, 'but there's no further requirement for your presence. Return to the household with the airpod and send it back here on autopilot.'

Geoffrey folded his arms. 'If there's anything you need to tell me, Memphis can hear it.'

Hector beckoned the housekeeper to climb into the airpod. 'Please, Memphis.'

The old man met Geoffrey's eyes and nodded once. 'There are matters I need to attend to. I shall send the airpod back directly.'

'When you're done,' Hector said, 'take the rest of the day off. You worked hard enough as it is yesterday.'

'Thank you, Hector,' Memphis said. 'That is most generous.'

Memphis hauled his bony frame into the airpod and strapped in. The electric duct fans spun up to speed, whining quickly into ultrasound, and the airpod hauled itself aloft as if drawn by an invisible wire. When it had cleared the tops of the trees, it turned its blunt nose to face the household and sped away.

'That was awkward,' Hector said.

Lucas flicked an insect from the pale-green sleeve of his suit. 'Under the circumstances, there was no alternative.'

Geoffrey planted his hands on his hips. 'I suppose a lot of things look that way when you've had an empathy shunt put in. Have you got it turned on or off right now?'

'Memphis understood,' Hector said, while Lucas glowered. 'He's been good to the family, but he knows where his responsibilities end.'

'You didn't need him to bring you out here.'

Lucas shook his broad, handsome head. 'At least the elephants know him slightly. They don't know us at all.'

'Your fault for never coming out here.'

'Let's not get off on the wrong foot here, Geoffrey.' Hector's suit was of similar cut to his brother's, but a subtle flamingo pink in colour. Close enough in appearance to be easily mistaken for each other, they were actually neither twins nor clones. 'It's not as if we've come with bad news,' Hector went on. 'We've got a proposition that we think you'll find interesting.'

'If it's to do with taking up my burden of family obligations, you know where you can shove it.'

'Closer involvement in Akinya core strategic affairs would be viewed positively,' Lucas said.

'You make it sound like I'm shirking hard work.'

'It's clear to us that these animals mean an enormous amount to you,' Hector said. 'That's nothing you need be ashamed of.'

'I'm not.'

'Nonetheless,' Lucas said, 'an opportunity for a reciprocal business transaction has arisen. In return for the execution of a relatively simple task, one that would involve neither personal risk nor an investment of more than a few days of your time, we would be willing to liberate additional discretionary funds—'

'*Substantial* funds,' Hector said, before Geoffrey had a chance to speak. 'As much over the next year as the family has donated over the past three. That would make quite a difference to your work, wouldn't it?' He cast a brim-shadowed eye in the direction of the Cessna. 'I'm no expert on the economics of this kind of operation, but I imagine it would make the hiring of one or two assistants perfectly feasible, with enough left over for new equipment and resources. And this wouldn't be a one-off increase, either. Subject to the usual checks and balances, there's no reason why it couldn't be extended going forward, year after year.'

'Or even increased,' Lucas said, 'if a suitably persuasive case were to be tabled.'

Geoffrey couldn't dismiss an offer of increased funding out of hand, no matter what strings came attached. Pride be damned, he owed it to the herd.

'What do you want?'

'A matter has arisen, a matter of interest only to the family, and which necessitates a suitably tactful response,' Lucas said. 'You would need to go into space.'

He'd already guessed it had to be something to do with Eunice. 'To the Winter Palace?'

'Actually,' Lucas said, 'the Lunar surface.'

'Why can't you go?'

Hector shared a smile with his brother. 'In a time of transition, it's important to convey the impression of normality. Neither Lucas nor I have plausible business on the Moon.'

'Hire an outsider, then.'

'Third-party involvement would present unacceptable risks,' Lucas said, pausing to tug at his shirt collar where it was sticking to his skin. Like Hector he was both muscular and comfortably taller than Geoffrey. 'I hardly need add that you are an Akinya.'

'What my brother means,' Hector said, 'is that you're blood, and you have blood ties on the Moon, especially in the African-administered sector. If you can't be trusted, who can?'

Geoffrey thought for a few seconds, striving to give away as little as possible. Let the two manipulators stew for a while, wondering if he was going to take the bait.

'This matter on the Moon – what are we talking about?'

'A loose end,' Hector said.

'What kind? I'm not agreeing to anything until I know what's involved.'

'Despite the complexity of Eunice's estate and affairs,' Lucas said, 'the execution of our due-diligence audit has proceeded without complication. The sweeps have turned up nothing of concern, and certainly nothing that need raise questions beyond the immediate family.'

'There is, however, a box,' Hector said.

Geoffrey raised a hand to shield his eyes from the sun. 'What kind?'

'A safe-deposit box,' Lucas said. 'Is the concept familiar to you?'

'You'll have to explain it to me. Being but a lowly scientist, anything to do with money or banking is completely outside my comprehension. Yes, *of course* I know what a safe-deposit box is. Where is it?'

'In a bank on the Moon,' Hector said, 'the name and location of which we'll disclose once you're under way.'

'You're worried about skeletons.'

The corner of Lucas's mouth twitched. Geoffrey wondered if the empathy shunt was making him unusually prone to literal-mindedness, unable to see past a metaphor.

'We need to know what's in that box,' he said.

'It's a simple request,' Hector said. 'Go to the Moon, on our expense account. Open the box. Ascertain its contents. Report back to the household. You can leave tomorrow – there's a slot on the Libreville elevator. You'll be on the Moon inside three days, your work done inside four. And then you're free to do whatever you like. Play tourist. Visit Sunday. Broaden your—'

'Horizons. Yes.'

Hector's expression clouded over at Geoffrey's tone. 'Something I said?'

'Never mind.' Geoffrey paused. 'I have to admire the two of you, you know. Year after year, I've come crawling on my hands and knees asking for more funding. I've begged and borrowed, pleading my case against a wall of indifference, not just from my mother and father but from the two of you. At best I've got a token increase, just enough to shut me up until next time. Meanwhile, the family pisses a fortune into repairing the blowpipe without me even being told about it, and when you do need a favour, you suddenly find all this money you can throw at my feet. Have you any idea how insignificant that makes me feel?'

'If you'd rather the incentives were downscaled,' Lucas said, 'that can be arranged.'

'I'm taking you for every yuan. You want this done badly enough, I doubt you'd open with your highest offer.'

'Don't overstep the mark,' Hector said. 'We could just as easily approach Sunday and make the same request of her.'

'But you won't, because you think Sunday's a borderline anarchist who's secretly plotting the downfall of the entire system-wide economy. No, I'm your last best hope, or you wouldn't have come.' Geoffrey steeled himself. 'So let's talk terms. I want a fivefold increase in research funding, inflation-linked and guaranteed for the next decade. None of that's negotiable: we either agree to it here and now, or I walk away.'

'To decline an offer now,' Lucas said, 'could prove disadvantageous when the next funding round arrives.'

'No,' Hector said gently. 'He has made his point, and he is right to expect assurances. In his shoes, would we behave any differently?'

Lucas looked queasy, as if the idea of being in Geoffrey's shoes made him faintly nauseous. It was the first human emotion that had managed to squeeze past the empathy shunt, Geoffrey thought.

'You're probably right,' Lucas allowed.

'He's an Akinya – he still has the bargaining instinct. Are we agreed that Geoffrey's terms are acceptable?'

Lucas's nod was as grudging as possible.

'We have all committed this conversation to memory?' Hector asked.

'Every second,' Geoffrey said.

'Then let it be binding.' Hector offered his hand, which Geoffrey took after a moment's hesitation, followed by Lucas's. Geoffrey blinked the image of them shaking.

'Don't look on it as a chore,' Hector said. 'Look on it as a break from the routine. You'll enjoy it, I know. And it will be good for you to look in on your sister.'

'We would, of course, request that you refrain from any discussion of this matter with your sister,' Lucas said.

Geoffrey said nothing, nor made any visible acknowledgement of what Lucas said. He just turned and walked off, leaving the cousins standing there.

Matilda was still keeping watch over her charges. She regarded him, emitted a low vocalisation, not precisely a threat rumble but registering mild elephantine disgruntlement, then returned to the examination of the patch of ground before her, scudding dirt and stones aside with her trunk in the desultory, half-hearted manner of someone who had forgotten quite why they had commenced a fundamentally pointless task in the first place.

'Sorry, Matilda. I didn't ask them to come out here.'

She didn't understand him, of course. But he was sure she was irritated with the coming and going of the odd-smelling strangers and their annoying, high-whining machine.

He halted before her and considered activating the link again, pushing it higher than before, to see what was really going on in her head. But he was too disorientated for that, too unsure of his own feelings.

'I think I might have made a mistake,' Geoffrey said. 'But if I did, I did it for the right reasons. For you, and the other elephants.'

Matilda rumbled softly and bent her trunk around to scratch under her left ear.

'I'll be gone for a little while,' Geoffrey went on. 'Probably not more than a week, all told. Ten days at most. I have to go up to the Moon, and ... well, I'll be back as quickly as I can. You'll manage without me, won't you?'

Matilda began poking around again. She wouldn't just manage without him, Geoffrey thought. She'd barely notice his absence.

'If anything comes up, I'll send Memphis.'

Oblivious to his reassurance, she continued her foraging.

44

CHAPTER THREE

The woman from the bank apologised for keeping him waiting, although in fact it had been no more than minutes. Her name was Marjorie Hu, and she appeared genuinely keen to be of assistance, as if he'd caught her on a slow day where any break in routine was welcome.

'I'm Geoffrey Akinya,' he said, falteringly. 'A relative of the late Eunice Akinya. Her grandson.'

'In which case I'm very sorry for your loss, sir.'

'Thank you,' he said solemnly, allowing a judicious pause before proceeding with business. 'Eunice held a safe-deposit box with this branch. I understand that as a family member I have the authority to examine the contents.'

'Let me look into that for you, sir. There was some rebuilding work a while back, so we might have moved the box to another branch. Do you know when the box was assigned?'

'Some time ago.' He had no idea. The cousins hadn't told him, assuming they even knew. 'But it'll still be on the Moon?'

'Almost certainly. And if that's the case we can have it back here within six hours.' Marjorie Hu wore a blouse and skirt in the Central African Bank's corporate colours of yellow and blue. Ethnic Chinese, he decided, but with the long-limbed build of someone raised Moonside. 'You haven't come far, have you?'

'Just up from Africa.'

He'd travelled like any other tourist, leaving the day after his meeting with the cousins. After clearing exit procedures in Libreville, he'd been put to sleep and packed into a coffin-sized passenger capsule. The capsule had been fed like a machine-gun round into the waiting chamber of the slug-black, blunt-hulled thread-rider, where it was automatically slotted into place and coupled to internal power and biomonitor buses, along with six hundred otherwise identical capsules, densely packed for maximum transit efficiency.

And three days later he'd woken on the Moon.

No sense of having travelled further than, say, China – until he took his first lurching step and felt in his bones that he wasn't on Earth any more. He'd had breakfast and completed immigration procedures for the African-administered sector. As promised, there'd been a message from the cousins: details of the establishment he was supposed to visit.

Nothing about the Copernicus Branch of the CAB had surprised him, beyond the fact that it was exactly like every other bank he'd ever been in, from Mogadishu to Brazzaville. Same new-carpet smell, same wood-effect furniture, same emphatic courtesy from the staff. Everyone loped around in Lunar gravity, and the accents were different, but those were the only indicators that he wasn't home. Even the images on the wall, cycling from view to view, were mostly of terrestrial locations. Adverts pushed travel insurance, retirement schemes, investment portfolios.

Marjorie Hu had asked him to sit in a small windowless waiting room with a potted plant and a fake view of ocean breakers while she checked the location of the safe-deposit box. He had packed lightly for the trip, jamming everything he needed into a large black zip-up sports bag with a faded logo on the side. He kept the bag between his feet, picking at the terrestrial dirt under his nails until the door opened again and Marjorie Hu came in.

'No problem,' she said. 'It's still in our vaults. Been there for thirty-five years, which is about as long as we've had a branch in Copernicus. If you wouldn't mind following me?'

'I was assuming you'd want to screen me or something.'

'We already have, sir.'

She took him downstairs. Doors, heavy enough to contain pressure in the event of an accident, whisked open at the woman's approach. She turned her head to look at him as they walked.

'We're about to pass out of aug reach, and I don't speak Swahili.' From a skirt pocket she pulled out a little plastic-wrapped package. 'We have earphone translators available.'

'Which languages *do* you speak?'

'Mm, let's see. Chinese and English, some Russian, and I'm learning Somali and Xhosa, although they're both still bedding in. We can get a Swahili speaker to accompany you, but that might take a while to arrange.'

'My Chinese is OK, but English will be easier for both of us, I suspect. I even know a few words of Somali, but only because my nanny spoke it. She was a nice lady from Djibouti.'

'We'll shift to English, then.' Marjorie Hu put the earphones away. 'We'll lose aug in a few moments.'

Geoffrey barely felt the transition. It was a withdrawing of vague floating possibilities rather than a sudden curtailment of open data feeds.

'Anyone ever come in here that you couldn't translate for?' Geoffrey asked.

'Not since I've been here. Anyone speaking a language that obscure, they'd better have backup.' Marjorie Hu's tone of voice had shifted microscopically now that he was hearing her actual larynx-generated speech sounds.

A final set of pressure doors brought them to the vault. The morgue-like room's walls were lined with small silver-and-orange-fronted cabinets, stacked six high, perhaps two hundred in all. Given the virtual impossibility of committing theft in the Surveilled World, there was no longer much need for this sort of safekeeping measure. Doubtless the bank regarded the housing of these boxes as a tedious obligation to its older clients.

'That's yours, sir,' she said, directing him to a specific unit three rows up from the floor, the only cabinet in the room with a green light above the handle. 'Open it whenever you like. I'll step outside until you're finished. When you're done, just push the cabinet back into the wall; it will lock on its own.'

'Thank you.'

Marjorie Hu made a small, nervous coughing sound. 'I'm required to inform you that you remain under surveillance. The eyes aren't public, but we would be obliged to surrender captured imagery in the event of an investigation.'

'That's fine. I wouldn't have assumed otherwise.'

She dispensed a businesslike smile. 'I'll leave you to it.'

Geoffrey put down his bag as she left the room, the door whisking shut between them. He wasted no time. At his touch, the cabinet eased out of the wall on smooth metal runners until it reached the limit of its travel. It was open-topped, with a smaller cream-coloured box resting inside. He lifted out the box and placed it on the floor. Even allowing for Lunar gravity, it struck him as unexpectedly light. No gold ingots, then. The box, stamped with the bank's logo, had a simple hinged lid with no lock or catch. He opened it and looked inside.

The box contained a glove.

A glove, from a spacesuit. Fabric layers interspersed with plastic or composite plating, lending flexibility and strength. The fabric was silvery or off-white – hard to judge in the vault's sombre lighting – and the plates were beige or maybe pale yellow. At the cuff-end of the glove was an alloy connector ring, some kind of blue-tinted metal inset with complicated gold-plated contacts that would presumably lock into place when the glove was fixed to the suit sleeve. The glove had been cleaned because, despite its apparent grubbiness, his hands stayed unsoiled.

That was all there was. Nothing clutched in the fingers, nothing marked on the exterior. He couldn't see anything lodged inside. He tried pushing his hand into it, but couldn't get his thumb-joint past the wristband.

Geoffrey didn't know whether he felt disappointed or relieved. A bit of both, maybe. Relieved that there was nothing here to taint Eunice's memory – no incriminating document linking her to some long-dead tyrant or war criminal – but subtly let down that there wasn't something more intriguing, some flourish from beyond the grave, the fitting cap-stone that her life demanded. It wasn't enough just to retire to Lunar orbit, live out her remaining days in the Winter Palace and die.

He started to put the glove back in the box, preparing to stow the box back in the cabinet.

And stopped. He couldn't say why, save the fact that the glove seemed to merit more attention than he had given it. The one constant of Eunice's life was that she was practically minded, scathing of sentiment and pointless gesture. She wouldn't have put that glove there unless it *meant something* – either to her, or to whoever was supposed to find it after her death.

Geoffrey slipped the glove into his sports bag. He put an Ashanti FC sweatshirt on top, jammed his baseball cap on top of that, resealed the bag and placed the now-empty box back into the cabinet. He pressed the cabinet back into the wall, whereupon it clicked into place and the green light changed to red.

He opened the external door and stepped out of the vault.

'All done,' Geoffrey told the bank woman. 'For now, anyway. I take it there'll be no difficulties gaining access again?'

'None at all, sir,' Marjorie Hu said. If she had any interest in what he had found in the box, she was doing a good job of hiding it. *This is a big deal for me*, Geoffrey thought: *family secrets, clandestine errands to the Moon, safe-deposit boxes with mysterious contents. But she must bring a dozen people down here every week.*

With the glove still in his possession, he made his way to the under-ground railway station. Transparent vacuum tubes punched through the terminal's walls at different levels, threading between platforms connected by spiral walkways and sinuous escalators. Everything was glassy and semitranslucent. There were shopping plazas and dining areas, huge multi-storey sculptures and banners, waterfalls, fountains and a kind of tinkling, cascading piano music that followed him around like a lost dog.

He strolled to a quiet corner of the concourse and voked a call to Lucas. When a minute had passed without Lucas picking up, he diverted the request to Hector. Three seconds later Hector's figment – dressed in riding boots, jodhpurs and polo shirt – was standing in front of him.

'Good of you to check in, Geoffrey. How's your journey been so far?'

'Pretty uneventful. How're things back home?'

'You haven't missed any excitement.' Lunar time lag made it seem as if Hector had given the question deep consideration. 'Now – concerning that small matter we asked you to look into? Have you by any chance—'

'It's done, Hector. You can pass the word to Lucas as well – I tried calling him, but he didn't answer. Maybe his empathy shunt short-circuited.'

'Lucas broke a leg this morning – had a bad fall during the match. What should I tell him?'

'That there was nothing in it.'

Hector cocked his head. 'Nothing?'

'Nothing worth worrying about. Just an old glove.'

'An old glove.' Hector barked out a laugh. 'Could you possibly be a little more specific, cousin?'

'It's from a spacesuit, I think – an old one. Can't be worth much – must be millions like it still kicking around.'

'She left it there for a reason.'

'I suppose.' Geoffrey gave an easy-going shrug, as if it was no longer his problem to worry about such things. 'I'll bring it home, if you're interested.'

'You're at the premises now, right?'

'No, I'm at the Copetown train terminal, on my way to Sunday. I couldn't call you from the ... premises – no aug reach.'

'But the item is back where you found it?'

'Yes,' Geoffrey said, and for a moment the lie had emerged so effort-lessly, so plausibly, that it felt as if he had spoken the truth. He swallowed hard, sudden dryness in his throat. 'I can collect it before I come back down.'

'Perhaps that wouldn't be a bad idea.' Hector's figment was looking at him with ... *something*. Naked, boiling contempt, perhaps, that Geoffrey had been so easily manipulated into doing the cousins' bidding. Perhaps he should have shown more spine, talked up the offer even more. Maybe even told them to go fuck themselves. They'd have respected that.

'I'll bring it back. Seriously, though – it's just an old glove.'

'Whatever it is, it belongs in the family's care now, not up on the Moon. How long before your train leaves?'

Geoffrey made a show of looking up at the destination board. 'A few minutes.'

'It's a shame you didn't call me from the premises.' Hector chopped his hand dismissively, as if he had better things to do than be cross with Geoffrey. 'No matter. Fetch it on the way down, and enjoy the rest of your trip. Be sure to pass on my best wishes to your sister, of course.'

'I will.'

'While remembering what we said about this matter staying between the three of us.'

'My lips are sealed.'

'Very good. And we'll see you back at the household. Ching home if you need to discuss anything in depth, but otherwise consider yourself on well-deserved vacation. I'm sure Memphis will be in touch if anything requires your immediate input.'

Geoffrey smiled tightly. 'Wish Lucas well with his leg.'

'I shall.'

The figment vanished. Geoffrey found the next train to Verne – they ran every thirty minutes – and bought himself a business-class ticket. Damned if he was slumming it when the cousins were picking up the tab.

He was soon on his way, sitting alone in a nearly empty carriage, digging through a foil-wrapped chicken curry, lulled into drowsiness by the hypnotic rush of speeding scenery. But all the while he was thinking about the thing inside his bag, now shoved in the overhead rack. But for the fact that he had sensed its bulk and mass inside his holdall as he made his way to the station, he could easily have imagined that he'd taken nothing with him after all.

Copernicus had been sunlit when Geoffrey arrived, but ever since then he had been moving east, towards an inevitable encounter with the terminator, the moving line of division between the Moon's illuminated and shadowed faces. They hit it just west of the Mare Tranquillitatis, as the train was winding its way down from the uplands between the Ariadaeus and Hyginus Rilles. Geoffrey happened to glance up, and for an awful, lurching moment it looked as if the train was about to hurtle off the top of a sheer cliff into an immense sucking black sea below. Just as suddenly they were speeding *over* that sea, the train casting a wavering, rippling pool of light across the gently undulating ground which served only to intensify the darkness beyond it. Against the unlit immensity of the great sea the train appeared to be speeding along a narrow causeway, arrowing into infinite, swallowing night.

A few minutes into the crossing the cabin lights dimmed, allowing sleep for those who needed it. Geoffrey amped-up his eyes. He made out the occasional fleeting form in the middle distance, a boulder, escarpment or some other surface feature zipping by. And there were, of course, still communities out here, some of which were among the oldest in the Moon's short history of human habitation. To the south lay the first of the Apollo landing sites, a shrine to human ingenuity and daring that had remained undisturbed – though now safely under glass – for nearly two centuries. Back when the idea of his visiting the Moon was no more than a distant possibility, Geoffrey had always assumed that, like any good tourist, he would find time to visit the landing site. But that pilgrimage would have to wait until his next visit, however many years in the future that lay.

He chinged Sunday.

'Geoffrey,' she said, her figment appearing opposite him. 'There's got to be something screwed up with the aug, because it's telling me your point of origin is the Moon.'

'I'm here,' Geoffrey said. 'On the train out of Copernicus. It was ... a spur-of-the-moment thing.'

'It would have to be.'

'We've talked about it often enough, and after the scattering I just decided, damn it, I'm doing this. Took the sleeper up from Libreville.' He made a kind of half-grimace. 'Um, haven't caught you at a bad time, have I?'

'No,' she said, not quite masking her suspicion. 'I'm really glad you've decided to come and see us at long last. It's just ... a surprise, that's all. It wouldn't have killed you to call ahead first, though.'

'Isn't that what I'm doing now?'

'I might be on a deadline here – up to my eyes in work, with no time even to eat, sleep or indulge in basic personal hygiene.'

'If it's a problem—'

'It's not, honestly. We'd love to see you.' He believed her, too. She was clearly pleased that he was visiting. But he didn't blame her for having a few doubts about the suddenness of it all. 'Look, I'm guessing it'll be evening before you arrive in the Zone, with all the tourist crap you have to clear first. Jitendra and I were going to eat out tonight – up for joining us? There's a place we both like – they do East African, if you're not sick of it.'

'Sounds great.'

'Call me when you get near the Zone and I'll meet you at the tram stop. We'll go straight out to eat, if you're not too exhausted.'

'I'll call.'

'Look forward to seeing you, brother.'

He smiled, nodded and closed the ching bind.

As the train sped on across the darkness of the Sea of Tranquillity, he delved into his bag again, reaching past the Cessna baseball cap and the Ashanti FC sweatshirt.

Geoffrey angled the reading light to get a better view into the glove through its wrist opening. The wrist and hand cavity were empty, as he'd thought, all the way down as far as he could see, but the fingers were still obscured by shadow. Then he thought of his pencil and sketchpad further down in the bag, shoved in on the off chance.

He drew out the sharpened 2B. Glancing up to make sure he was still unobserved, he probed the pencil down into the glove, jabbing around with the sharp end until he found the hole where the index finger began. He continued pushing until he met resistance. Hard to tell, but he didn't feel that he had gone beyond the first joint after the knuckle.

Something had to be wadded down there, jammed into the finger's last two joints. Geoffrey drew out the pencil and tried the next finger along, finding that he couldn't push the pencil down that one either. The third finger was the same, but the thumb and little finger appeared unobstructed.

He went back to the first finger, dug the pencil in again. Whatever it was yielded slightly then impeded further ingress. He tried forcing the pencil past the obstruction, so that he could somehow hook it out, but that didn't work. He gave it a couple more goes then withdrew the pencil and returned it to his bag.

He took the glove and tried tapping it against the table, wrist end first, to loosen whatever was stuck in the fingers. That made too much noise, and in any case he could tell after the first few goes that it wasn't going to work. He could feel nothing working loose, and if anything his poking and prodding had only rammed the obstructions further into the glove. Whatever it was would have to wait until he got home.

Or at least until he got to Sunday's.

Certain he had exhausted its mysteries for now, Geoffrey pushed the glove back into his bag. He pulled his baseball cap out, jammed it onto his head with the brim forward, and dreamed of elephants.

'This is your last chance,' the Zone spokeswoman said. She was skinny, leather-clad, high-heeled, North African, with pink sparkles dusted onto her cheekbones and vivid purple hair, elaborately braided and sewn with little flickering lights. 'From here on, the aug thins out to zilch. That bothers you, if that's something you can't deal with, now's your chance to turn around.'

Stoic faces, pasted-on smiles. No one abandoned their plans, all having come too far not to go through with the rest of the trip, Geoffrey included.

'Guess we're set, then,' the purple-haired woman said, as if she'd never seriously expected anyone to quit. 'You've all got your visas, so hop aboard.'

The visa was a pale-green rectangle floating in his upper-right visual field, with a decrementing clock. It was the fourth of February now, and the visa allowed him to stay until the ninth. Failure to comply with the visa's terms would result in forcible ejection from the Zone – and whether that meant literal ejection, onto the surface, with or without a spacesuit, or something fractionally more humane, was left carefully unspecified.

It was a squeeze inside the tram, Geoffrey having to strap-hang. They were rattling down some dingy concrete-clad tunnel. Sensing a change in the mood of his fellow travellers, he formulated an aug query, a simple location request, and the delay before the aug responded was palpable. He waited a moment and tried again. This time there was no response at all, followed by a cascade of error messages flooding his visual field. Simultaneously the babble of voices in the bus turned biblical.

Sensing the transition, some of the passengers reached languidly into pockets for earphone translators, or tapped jewelled ear-studs already in place. The babble quietened, lulled, resumed.

Geoffrey blinked away the few remaining error messages, leaving only the visa icon and a single symbol – a broken globe – to indicate that aug connectivity was currently impaired. The machines in his head were still functioning; they just didn't have much to talk to beyond his skull. He sensed their restless, brooding disquiet.

The tram swerved and swooped along its shaft, dodging between the pupal carcasses of mothballed tunnelling machines. Ahead was a growing pool of light, a widening in the shaft. The tram picked its way between two rows of stacked shipping containers and came to a smooth halt next to a platform where people and robots waited. Geoffrey spotted his sister immediately. He truly felt as if it was only a few days since he'd last been in her company, even though it was years since they had been physically present with each other.

She waved. A very tall man next to her also waved, but awkwardly, his eyes shifting as if he wasn't completely sure which passenger they were meant to be greeting. Geoffrey waved back as the tram's doors huffed open and he stepped off. He walked over to his sister and gave her a hug.

'Good to see you, brother,' Sunday said, speaking Swahili. 'Jitendra – this is Geoffrey. Geoffrey – this is Jitendra Gupta.'

Jitendra was about the same age as Sunday but easily a head taller, and very obviously a Lunar citizen: skinny, bald, boyishly handsome. Once Jitendra knew who to look at his smile warmed and he made a point of shaking Geoffrey's hand vigorously.

'Glad you made it!' Jitendra declared. 'Good trip?'

Around them robots fussed with suitcases, aiding those passengers who had arrived with non-locomotive luggage.

'Uneventful,' Geoffrey answered. 'Can't say I saw much from the train.'

'You'll have to come back during Lunar day. Some amazing places within easy reach of here, even if they're not on the usual tourist maps.'

Jitendra's Swahili was excellent, Geoffrey thought. He wondered if he'd made the effort just to impress Sunday.

'How are you adjusting to life without the aug?' Sunday asked.

Geoffrey took off his baseball cap and jammed it into his sweatshirt pocket.

'Just about holding it together.'

His sister nodded approvingly. 'A day here, you'll forget you ever needed it.'

He gave her another hug, but this time trying to gauge the warm, breathing form under the clothes. 'It is you, isn't it? Not another claybot? Without the tags I'm not sure I trust anything.'

'It's me,' Sunday said. 'The claybot's still on Earth, being driven by someone else.' She shifted impatiently. 'Look, let's not stand here all day – where are the rest of your bags?'

'This is it,' Geoffrey said, swinging the holdall off his shoulder. 'Travel light, that's my motto.'

'Don't travel at all, that's mine,' Sunday said. 'Remember what I said about eating out tonight – are you still up for that?'

'Of course he's up for it,' Jitendra said cheerily. 'Who wouldn't be?'

Actually, Geoffrey was ready to eat – the light meal on the express hadn't done more than dent his appetite. But he slightly resented Jitendra making that assumption for him. He eyed the other man warily, trying not to appear unfriendly but for the moment reserving judgement.

Some kind of minor commotion was going on a little further down the tram platform. Geoffrey recognised one of his fellow passengers – a big white man with chrome-tinted hair and a padded, wide-shouldered suit that made him look overmuscled. The man was being pulled aside by local officials. There was a lot of shouting and raised voices. The man was trying to break free of the officials, his face reddening.

'What's going on?'

'Don't know,' Sunday said, as if it really wasn't that interesting.

But Geoffrey couldn't stop rubbernecking. He'd seldom witnessed anything resembling civil disobedience. In the Surveilled World, it hardly ever reached the point where anyone was in a position to resist authority. That man would have been on the floor by now, dropped into quivering, slack-jawed compliance by the Mech's direct neural intervention.

Now one of the officials was holding the man's head in a tight double-handed grip while another shone a pen-sized device into his right eye. Words were exchanged. The man appeared to give up his fight and was soon being bundled back to the tram.

'His eyes should have stopped recording when he crossed the border,' Jitendra said. 'Yours will have, unless you went to great lengths to get around that limitation.'

'I didn't,' Geoffrey assured him.

'He must have had additional recording devices installed, hoping they wouldn't get picked up by our normal scans,' Jitendra speculated. 'Very naughty. He's lucky to get off with simple deportation. They'd have been well within their rights to scoop his eyes out on the spot.'

'We're kind of touchy about privacy here,' Sunday said.

'I see.'

The display of force had left Geoffrey rattled. He'd made no conscious efforts to break the Descrutinised Zone's protocols, but what if that man had made an innocent mistake, forgetting about some function he'd had installed into his eyes years ago? The additional aug faculties that the clinic in Luanda had given Geoffrey ... they couldn't possibly be mistaken for anything in direct contravention of Zone regulations ... could they? But with an effort of will he forced himself to stop worrying. He was in the Zone now. By its very nature, the amount of scrutiny he'd be subjected to from this point on would be minimal.

They left the tram station, part of a loose, straggling procession of travellers and greeters and robots. Sunday must have caught him craning his neck, looking for a view beyond these concrete and spray-sealed warrens. 'No one bothers much with windows on the Moon,' she told him. 'Even above the 'lith. Too depressing at night – weeks of endless darkness – and too bright by day. You want to see Earth, or the stars, take a surface rover or suit, or ching your way to the far side. We came here for the social possibilities, not the scenery. You want scenery, stay in orbit, or go to Mars. That's not what the Moon's *for*.'

'I didn't know the Moon was *for* anything,' Geoffrey said.

'It's a platform, that's all. An event-space. A place to do interesting stuff. Think they'd tolerate the Zone anywhere else?' Sunday was off on one of her rants now. 'Sure, there are blind spots elsewhere in the system, but mostly that's just because coverage gets patchy, not because people made it that way. This was on Earth, they'd have dragged some ancient clause out of the woodwork and sent in the tanks by now.'

'I think they'd listen to reasoned persuasion first,' Geoffrey said. 'It's not all tanks and guns down there – we do have something resembling peaceful global civilisation most of the time.' Typical: he'd only been in Sunday's presence for ten minutes and he was already acting like the defence counsel for the entire planet. 'Were you born here, Jitendra?' he asked brightly.

'On the other side, Copernicus. That's where you came in, isn't it?'

'Yes, although I didn't see too much of it.' They were walking along a level tunnel lined with concrete, the concrete overpainted with an impasto of oozing, flickering psycho-reactive graffiti. 'Sunday told me you work in robotics.'

'True-ish,' Jitendra said. 'Although at the more experimental bleeding edge of things. Something you're interested in?'

'I guess. Maybe. Doing some work on elephant cognition.'

Jitendra slapped his forehead absent-mindedly. 'Oh, I get it now. You're the elephant man!'

Geoffrey grimaced. 'You make it sound like I'm some bizarre medical specimen, pickled in a bottle somewhere.'

'I don't know how many times I've told Jitendra what you do,' Sunday said, with an exasperated air. 'I mean, it's not like I was talking about some obscure second cousin twice removed or anything.'

Around them the graffiti reconfigured itself endlessly, except for mouse-grey patches where the paint had failed or scabbed off. Graffiti was very quaint, Geoffrey thought.

'So, anyway: elephant cognition,' Jitendra said decisively. 'That sounds pretty interesting. Where do you stand on Bayesian methods and the free-energy principle?'

'If it's free, I'm all for it.'

'Not really a theoretician, our Geoffrey,' Sunday said. 'At least, theoreticians don't usually make a point of smelling like elephant dung, or flying around in two-hundred-year-old deathtraps.'

'Thanks.'

She wrapped an arm around his waist. 'Wouldn't want him any other way, of course. If it wasn't for my brother, I'd feel like the only weird member of the family.'

She came to a stop next to a patch of wall where the muddy brown background coloration of earlier graffiti layers had been overpainted with a trembling, shimmering silvery form, like the reflection in water of some complex metallic structure or alien hieroglyph. Blocks and forms of primary colours were beginning to intrude on the silver, jabbing and harassing its margins.

Sunday pushed her finger against the wall and started reasserting the form, pushing it back out against the confining shapes. Where her finger pressed, the silver turned broad and bright and lustrous. 'This is one of mine,' she said. 'Did it five months ago and it's still hanging on. Not bad for a piece of consensus art. The paint tracks attention. Any piece that doesn't get looked at often enough, it's at the mercy of being encroached on and overpainted.'

She pulled back her finger, which remained spotless. 'I can redo my own work, provided the paint deems itself to have been sufficiently *observed*. And I can overpaint someone else's if it hasn't been looked at enough. I'd hardly ever do that, though – it's not really fair.'

'So this is Sunday Akinya, literally making her mark,' Geoffrey said.

'I don't sign this stuff,' Sunday said. 'And since I mostly work in sculpture and animation these days, there's not much chance of anyone associating a piece of two-D abstraction with me.'

Geoffrey stood back to allow a luggage-laden robot to speed past.

'Anyone could've seen you do it.'

'Most wouldn't have a clue who I am. I'm a small fish, even up here.'

'She really is a struggling artist,' Jitendra said.

'And half the people who live here are artists anyway, or think they are,' Sunday said, ushering them on again. 'I'm not an Akinya here, just another woman trying to make a living.'

As they approached the end of the graffiti-covered corridor, Geoffrey sensed that it was about to open out into a much larger space, the acoustics shifting, the feeling of confinement ebbing. There was even a hint of a breeze.

They emerged high up on one side of a vast flat-roofed cavern. Easily two kilometres across, Geoffrey guessed. Bright lights gridded the slightly domed ceiling, drenching the entire cavern with what appeared to be a simulacrum of full planetary daylight.

Buildings crammed the space, tight as a box of skittles. Many of them reached all the way up to the ceiling and some even punched through. Towers and cupolas and spires, spiralling flutes and teetering top-heavy helices, baroque crystalline eruptions and unsettling brainlike masses, and everything shimmering with eyeball-popping colour, hues and patterns that flickered and shifted from moment to moment, as if the city was some kind of ancient computer system locked in an endless manic cycle of crash and reboot. The lower parts of the buildings, where they were accessible from street level or elevated walkways, were gaudy with layers of psycho-reactive graffiti. The upper levels carried active banners and flags or daubs of fluid, oozing neon, alongside tethered balloons with illuminated flanks.

'Did you remember to book ahead?' Jitendra asked.

'It's a Thursday,' Sunday said. 'It won't be heaving.'

Down in the congested lower levels Geoffrey made out bustling traffic, electric vehicles shuffling through near gridlock like neat little injection-moulded game pieces. There were cyclists and rickshaw drivers and piggyback robots. Human and mechanical motion, everywhere.

Sunday led them across a black ironwork bridge. It carried a wooden-floored promenade with perilously low railings, interrupted here and there by booths and stands with striped canvas awnings.

'That's the Turret,' she said, indicating the structure at the other end of the bridge. 'Best views of the cavern. Hope you've worked up a good appetite.'

Inside the Turret it was all organic pastel-coloured forms, enlivened with glass and porcelain mosaics set into umber-coloured stucco. Sunday had led them directly to a window alcove shaped like some natural cavity worn away by subterranean water erosion. Only after several minutes of dutiful observation was Geoffrey able to confirm that the view was creeping slowly past. Sunday told him that the machinery making the restaurant revolve had been repurposed from an abandoned centrifuge. The bearings were so icily smooth it felt as if the rest of the universe was doing the turning.

He was on one side of the table, Sunday and Jitendra on the other. Sunday had ordered a big bottle of Icelandic Merlot before Geoffrey had even put his bag down, wasting no time in charging their glasses. They made small talk over the appetisers, Sunday pushing him on his current romantic entanglements, or lack thereof, asking him if he had heard from Jumai lately. He told her that Jumai had chinged in on the day of Eunice's death.

'Sounds very exciting, what she's doing. And quite dangerous,' Sunday said.

'They pay her well,' Geoffrey said.

Ordinarily he'd have been uneasy talking about an old girlfriend, but at least it kept them off the one topic he didn't want to go anywhere near.

'More wine?' Sunday asked, when the waiter came to take away their empty appetiser plates.

Jitendra levelled a hand over his glass. 'Need a clear head tomorrow. Robot Wars.'

Geoffrey looked blank.

'Jitendra's a competitor,' Sunday said. 'It's a thing he does. We'll go out and see it tomorrow, the three of us.'

'Something to do with free energy?' Geoffrey asked, keen to latch on to a topic that would keep them off the real reason for his visit.

'Something else entirely.' Jitendra lowered his voice, as if he was in dread danger of being overheard by the other diners. 'Although June Wing will be there, I think.'

'You work for Plexus?' Geoffrey asked, recognising the name.

'I do work *for* them,' he said, making the distinction plain. 'They pay me to have interesting ideas, while at the same time recognising that I could never function in an orthodox corporate environment. They also give me far more creative latitude than I'd ever get working full-time in their labs. The upside is I don't really have deadlines or deliver-ables. The downside is I don't get paid very much. But we can afford to live where we do and I have a twenty-four-hour hotline to June that some people would kill for.'

'So this ... free-energy thing – is that a Plexus research programme?'

'Not officially, because the whole point of free energy – at least in the sense that I'm interested in it – is to create human-level artilects. And that's obviously a fairly major no-no, even now.' Jitendra scratched at his dark-stubbled scalp. 'But unofficially? That's a different kettle.'

'We found one once,' Geoffrey said. 'Near our home. It tried to take over Sunday's mind.'

'She told me about that. What you encountered was an abomination, a military intelligence. It was designed to be insidious and spiteful and inimical to life, and it wasn't smart enough to have a conscience. But artilects could work for us, if we make them even cleverer.'

When the waiter arrived with their main courses there was the usual minor confusion over one of the orders. Geoffrey suspected that this reassuringly human touch was now firmly embedded in the service.

'Maybe that's not as easy as it sounds,' he said, 'making machines smarter.'

'Depends where you begin.' Jitendra was already tucking in. 'Seems self-evident to me that the best starting point would be the human mind. What is it, if not a thinking, conscious machine that the universe has already given us, on a plate?'

A queasy image of a brain, served up with salad and trimmings, intruded into Geoffrey's thoughts. He shoved it aside like an undercooked entrée.

'Animal cognition, there's still work to be done. But the human brain? Isn't that a done deal, research-wise?'

Jitendra pushed his food around with enthusiasm. 'We know what goes on in a mind. We can track processes and correlate them at any resolution we care to specify. But that's not the same as understanding.'

'Until,' Sunday said, 'Jitendra comes along, with his world-shaking new ideas.'

'I'd take credit for them if they were mine,' Jitendra said. He inhaled a few hasty mouthfuls while holding up his knife to signal that he was not yet done talking.

Geoffrey decided that he rather liked Jitendra. And while Jitendra was talking, he didn't have to.

'Point is,' Jitendra continued, swallowing between words, 'I'm not just doing this out of some deluded sense that the world gives a damn about a theory of mind. What it cares about are practical applications.'

'Hence the Plexus connection,' Geoffrey said.

'You've seen the claybot. That's the physical edge of things. There's also the construct, which Sunday has been involved with at least as much as me.'

'The construct?'

'Later,' Sunday said, smiling.

'And ultimately . . . there's a point to all this?' Geoffrey asked.

'We need better machines. Machines that are as smart and adaptable as us, so they can *be* us – or go places we can't,' Jitendra said.

Geoffrey's expression was sceptical.

'Look, you're going to meet the Pans at some point,' Jitendra went on. 'They're our friends, and they have one point of view, which is that only people ought to be allowed to go into space. The flesh must inherit the stars; anything else is treason against the species. On the other side of the debate, you've got hard-line pragmatists like Akinya Space who will always send a machine to do a human's work if it's cheaper. That's why you've got umpteen billion robots crawling around the asteroid belt.'

'We're having dinner in a restaurant on the Moon,' Geoffrey said. 'Isn't it a bit late to be worrying about who gets to go into space?'

'The reckoning's not over, it's just postponed,' Jitendra answered. 'But the Pans are growing in strength and influence, and the industrialists haven't suddenly backed off from their dollar-eyed conviction that robots make the most sense. Sooner or later, heads are going to bash. Not around Earth or the Moon, maybe, but we're pushing into deep space now – Trans-Neptunian, the inner boundary of the Kuiper belt, and we've even got machines in the Oort cloud. That's where it gets stickier. If we're going to do anything useful out there, we'll need smart machines and lots of them. Machines that break right through the existing cognition thresholds, into post-artilect computation. Human-level thinkers that can live with us, be our equals as well as our workers.'

'You're not sounding any less scary than you were five minutes ago,' Geoffrey said.

'Look, in a thousand years, the difference between people and machines … it's going to seem about as relevant as the difference between Protestants and Catholics: some ludicrous relic of Dark Age thinking.' Jitendra gave a self-conscious shrug. 'I'm not on the side of the machines or people. I'm on the side of the convergent intelligences that will supplant both.'

Geoffrey was leaning back in his seat, blasted by the G-force of Jitendra's conviction. 'And this … free energy? It's a way of making better machines?'

'It may be,' Jitendra conceded. 'Don't know yet. Too many variables, not enough data. The construct looks promising … but it's early days and I don't doubt we'll take a few wrong turns along the way. All I know is that we're unwinding two hundred years of orthodox robotics development and heading off in a completely different direction.'

'Bet that's what they really want to hear at the shareholder meetings,' Sunday said.

Jitendra picked at something stuck between his teeth. 'It's harsh medicine. But June Wing, bless her, is at least slightly open-minded to new possibilities.'

'Especially if there might be a dazzling commercial return at the end of it,' Sunday said.

'Businesswoman first, a scientist second,' Jitendra said. 'No sense in blaming her for that – she wouldn't have her hands on the purse strings otherwise.'

'Talking of purse strings,' Sunday said, brushing crumbs from the napkin she'd tucked into her collar, 'something I've been meaning to ask my brother: did the cousins cough up any more money?'

Geoffrey blinked, attempting to marshal his swirling, wine-addled thoughts into some semblance of clarity. The question had blindsided him.

'The cousins?' he asked.

'As in Lucas and Hector. As in the men with the ability to end all your funding difficulties.'

Geoffrey poured some more wine and sipped before answering. 'Why would they give me more funding?'

'Because you showed up at the scattering, because you acted like a good little boy and didn't get into any upsetting arguments.'

He smiled at his sister. 'You showed up as well, and it's not like they started showering you with benevolence, is it?'

'I'm a lost cause; you're not completely beyond salvation.'

'In their eyes.'

Sunday nodded. 'Of course.'

'I think some more funds might be forthcoming,' he said neutrally. 'I obviously made a good case for the elephants. Now and then even hard-line Akinyas take a break from rabid capitalism to feel guilty about their neglected African heritage.'

'For about thirty seconds.'

He shrugged. 'That's all it takes to transfer the funds.'

'Reason I asked,' Sunday said, stretching in her seat, 'is that I wondered if you were up here for fund-raising purposes? It's not like you come here very often, and the last time – if I'm remembering rightly – it was definitely cap-in-hand.'

'I just thought it was about time I came up to see you. Are you going to throw a fit the one time I actually *listen* to you?'

'All right,' Sunday said, holding her hands up to forestall an argument. 'I was just saying.'

Over coffee the conversation headed back into less treacherous waters: Sunday and Geoffrey trading stories about their childhood in the household, encounters with animals, encounters with Maasai, funny things that had happened between them and Memphis, Jitendra putting on a good impression of being interested and inquisitive.

When Sunday had picked up the tab and they went out onto the restaurant's circular roof, the air had cooled and with the dimming of the ceiling lights the nocturnal effect was complete. Not that there was any sense that the city was winding down for the night, judging by the continued traffic sounds, music, shouts and laughter billowing up from below.

Sunday pointed out landmarks. Older buildings, newer ones, places she liked and didn't like, favoured restaurants, disfavoured ones, clubs and places neither she nor Jitendra could afford. Or rather, Geoffrey thought, places that she chose not to be able to afford, which was far from the same thing. Sunday had spurned Akinya money, but that didn't mean the floodgates couldn't be opened at a moment's notice, if she ever changed her mind. All she would have to do is renounce her decadent artistic ways and agree to become a profit-sharing partner in the collective enterprise.

As, indeed, could he, just as easily.

'We're going that way,' Sunday said, pointing to a wide semicircular hole in the far side of the cavern wall. She was, Geoffrey realised, much less intoxicated than either of her two companions. He began to wonder, with a sense of dim foreboding, whether she had been softening him up for interrogation.

At street level they came out into some kind of all-night souk, a place of winding, labyrinthine passages roofed over with strips of tattered canvas and latticed bamboo. Food, animals, garments, consumer goods, cosmetics, surgical services and robotics parts lined the lantern-lit stalls and booths. Huge muscled snakes like coiled industrial ducting extruded from lurid green and yellow plastics. Jewel-eyed seahorses, dappled with spangling iridophores. Tiny, dollhouse-sized ponies, pink and blue and anatomically perfect. Vendors selling what Geoffrey at first took to be sheets of black, brown and pink textiles – dress fabric, curtains, perhaps – until he realised that he was looking at custom skins, vat-grown flesh sold by the metre. New skin, new eyes, new organs, new bones. Most of these commodities, being illegal elsewhere, must have been fabricated in or around the Zone itself. There was industry here, as well as artistry and anarchy. Like Dakar or Mogadishu, a hundred or more years ago: the dusty, squabblesome past that every clean, ordered, glittering African city was trying hard to put behind it.

They jostled through the souk's crowds. Jitendra spent several minutes digging cheerfully through plastic crates of salvaged robot parts, picking up a piece then discarding it, rooting out another, holding it up to the lantern light with narrowed, critical eyes.

'Watch your bag,' Sunday said as they waited for Jitendra to strike a deal. 'Thieves and pickpockets abroad.'

Geoffrey swung the sports bag around, clutching it to his chest like an overpadded comfort blanket. 'Really? I'd have thought most of your fellow citizens went through Mandatory Enhancement screening at birth, the way you and I did.'

'That's true,' Sunday conceded, while Jitendra continued his haggling, 'but there isn't some handy colour-coded brain module labelled "the impulse to commit crime". What is crime, anyway? We might both agree that rape and murder are objectively bad things, but what about armed resistance to a despotic government, or stealing from the rich to feed the poor?'

'The last time I looked, there was a distinct shortage of both despotic governments and poor people.'

'Crime has a social context. In the Surveilled World, you've engineered criminality out of society using mass observation, ubiquitous tagging and targeted neural intervention. Good luck with the long-term consequences of that.'

Geoffrey shrugged. 'Locksmiths find another line of work.'

'I'm talking about societal timescales. Centuries, thousands of years. That's what we're concerned with here; it's not all about being crypto-anarchists and throwing wild parties.'

'You think criminality's a good thing?'

'Who knows? Maybe the same clusters of genes that give rise to what we loosely label "criminality" may also be lurking behind creativity, the impulse to experiment, the urge to test social boundaries. We think that's quite probable, even likely, which is why we've gone to such lengths to re-engineer the public space to make crime viable again.'

'Have fun.'

Sunday tapped a finger against her head. 'There are Recrim clinics here where they'll undo at least some of the work carried out by the Mandatory Enhancements. People who've been recrimmed can't easily leave the Zone again, and if they do they're treated like time bombs waiting to go off. But for some, it's a price worth paying. I was deadly serious when I mentioned pickpockets. There are people around here who are not only fully capable of committing crimes, but who regard it as a pressing moral duty, like picking up litter or helping people when they trip over. No one's talking about letting off nerve gas, or going on killing sprees. But a constant, low-level background of crime may help a society become more robust, more resilient.'

'And there I was, thinking they hadn't really got to you yet.'

'It's the Zone, Geoffrey. If it was exactly like everywhere else, there'd be no point having it.'

It was that same old spiralling argument, and again he didn't have the energy to fight his corner. 'When you put it like that, I guess it doesn't sound too ridiculous.'

'You're just humouring me now.'

'How could you tell?'

After a moment, Sunday said, 'Didn't mean to put you on the spot back at the restaurant.'

'You had a point. But I'm not here with a begging bowl.'

'Well, good. Not that I wouldn't like you to get more money, of course. And it's nothing to do with Eunice?'

'Why would it be?'

'The small fact that she just died. Very near the Moon. And all of a sudden you just happen to drop by to visit your sister, when I've been inviting you for ages and you've never come. Until now. Forgive me if I can't help wondering whether someone in the family has put you up to something.'

Geoffrey squinted, as if she'd used some out-of-coinage phrase. 'Put me up—'

'Just do one thing for me, brother. Tell me there's nothing going on that I need to know about.'

At that awkward juncture, Jitendra turned away from the stall, brandishing hard-won trophies.

'More junk,' Sunday said with a sigh. 'Because we don't have nearly enough lying around as it is.'

Geoffrey reached into his sweatshirt pocket for the Cessna baseball cap. His fingers closed on air. The hat, it began to dawn on him, had been stolen. The feeling of being a victim of crime was as novel and thrilling as being stopped in the street and kissed by a beautiful stranger.

Things like that just didn't happen back home.

CHAPTER FOUR

They lived in a stack apartment. It had been Sunday's originally; now they cohabited. The apartment was at the top of a tower of repurposed container modules, locked together in an alloy chassis and cut open to allow for windows and doors. Even at night Geoffrey easily discerned the faded colours and logos of the modules' former owning companies, various Chinese and Indian shipping and logistics firms. The edifice was barnacled with air-conditioning units, spidered with pipework, ladders and fire escapes. Some kind of ivy was attempting to turn the whole stack into an olive-green monolith.

There was no elevator, not even up to the tenth-floor module where Sunday and Jitendra lived. Bounding up the skeletal staircase bolted onto the side of the stack, Geoffrey quickly understood why: reaching the tenth floor cost him no more effort than climbing a two-storey building back on Earth. He wasn't even sweating when they arrived in Sunday's kitchen.

'This is amazing,' he cried, almost happy enough that he'd put the theft of the baseball cap behind him. 'It's like being five again!'

'You get used to it after a while,' Sunday said, deflatingly. 'Then it starts feeling like ten stories again.' She opened a cabinet and extracted a bottle of wine, a dry white Mongolian this time. 'Guess neither of you have any objections to another drink? Take him into the living room, Jitendra. And try not to let him break his neck on any of your toys.'

Geoffrey had never seen the apartment, had never even chinged into it with full embodiment, yet he still felt as if he had been there before. It wasn't the layout of the rooms, the divided partitions of the cargo module, or even the furniture and textiles used to screen off the bare composite walling of the original structure. It was the knick-knacks, the little ornaments and whatnots that could only have belonged to his sister.

Glad as he was to be surrounded by things that connected him to his past, they came from a time and a place neither of them could return to. They were both grown up now, and Memphis was old, and the household felt far too small ever to have contained the limitless rooms and corridors of Geoffrey's childhood.

He forced himself out of his funk and accepted a glass from Sunday.

'Apologies for the mess,' she said.

Geoffrey had seen worse. On the shelves, in between Sunday's numerous keepsakes and *objets d'art*, were many toy-sized robots, or the parts of robots, all of which had been repurposed. Jitendra had butchered and spliced, creating chimeric monstrosities. In their multilegged, segmented, goggle-eyed hideousness, they reminded Geoffrey of the fossil creatures of the Burgess Shale.

He was aware, even as he planted himself on a soft chair, that he was being surveilled. Eyes – some on single stalks, others in gun-barrel clusters – swivelled and focused. Limbs and body segments twitched and flexed.

'Are you using any of these in the Robot Wars?' Geoffrey asked.

Geoffrey's question appeared to confuse Jitendra. 'In the Robot Wars?'

'Tomorrow. You said you're a competitor in the Robot Wars.'

'Ah,' Jitendra said, something clicking. 'Yes, I am, but no, it won't be with these robots. They're built for cleverness, not combat. These are my test-rigs, where I try out different cognitive approaches. The ones we use in the Wars ... well, they're bigger.' He poured himself a half-glass of wine. 'Quite a bit bigger.'

'You have no idea, do you?' Sunday was sprawling on the sofa, shoes kicked off, feet resting on the mirror-bright coffee table.

Geoffrey felt at a disadvantage. 'Evidently not.'

She looked at him, marvelling. 'Sometimes it's as if you're living a century behind the rest of us.'

'Elephants don't care what century it is. They care what *season* it is.'

'I'm going to ching June,' Jitendra said, jumping up and wandering into another area of the apartment. 'Need to fine-tune plans for tomorrow. Back in a moment.'

Tiredness washed over Geoffrey, bringing with it a fizzing tide of stirred-up emotions. From one moment to the next he knew he couldn't go on with the pretence.

'Don't hate me for this,' he said, unable to meet his sister's eyes, 'but I didn't just come here to see you.'

'Like I ever thought that was the case.'

Geoffrey looked up – he'd been expecting a completely different reaction. 'You didn't?'

'You can't break the habits of a lifetime just like that.'

'Are you cross?'

Sunday cocked her head from side to side. 'Depends what the "something else" was.'

Geoffrey sighed. 'I didn't want to lie to you, but I was put in a position where I really had no choice.'

'Someone pressured you.'

Geoffrey's sigh turned into a huge, world-weary exhalation. He hadn't realised the burden he had been carrying around until he finally opened up to Sunday.

'Have a guess who.'

'Mother and Father are too far away to have got to you that thoroughly. Which leaves . . . Hector and Lucas?'

He nodded slowly. 'They came to me the day after the scattering, with a proposal. Which, incidentally, I'm not supposed to discuss with another living soul.'

He told her about the safe-deposit box, about his specific instructions and how he had already violated them.

'Scheming, manipulative vipers,' she said, squinting as if she'd just bitten into something sour.

'It wasn't technically blackmail.'

'Don't make excuses for those stepped-on turds, brother.' She crossed her arms over her chest. 'Look, I can understand them not wanting Eunice's name dragged through the dirt, but why use people this way? Why not just appeal to their better natures?'

'I'm not sure I've got one.'

'You'd have done it, if they made a good enough case. But they think everyone in the world works the way they do.'

'Well, look,' Geoffrey said, feeling an odd, inexplicable impulse to defend Hector and Lucas in their absence. 'What's done is done. Sorry I wasn't upfront with you earlier, but at least now it's all out in the open.'

'Yes. Apart from one small thing.' She eyed him levelly. 'You still haven't told me what was in the safe-deposit box.'

Sunday Akinya did not know whether she ought to be awed or disappointed by the glove. It was certainly an unremarkable-looking item: grubby and old-fashioned, the kind of thing that, had she put her mind to it, she could easily have found in a dozen Zone flea markets. In fact, she could probably have assembled an entire spacesuit, given time.

'That,' she said.

'That,' her brother affirmed. 'And that alone. It was the only thing in the box.'

'Either Eunice was mad, or that glove has to mean something.'

'That's what I reckon – as does Hector. Do you know much about spacesuits?'

'It's old-looking. And that dirt is Lunar, so even if that glove was made somewhere else, it's spent time here.'

'You can tell it's Lunar dust that easily?'

'I can smell it. Gunpowdery. Or what people tell me gunpowder ought to smell like. Kind of thing you get good at, when you've spent enough time up here. It's been cleaned, but you never get rid of the traces.' With a vague feeling of apprehension, Sunday continued to examine the glove. 'But let me get this straight. Hector told you to leave it there while you visit me, but collect it on the way down?'

'Yes.'

'Then so far you're only in *theoretical* breach of their instructions.'

'I'm sure they'll see it that way.'

The glove was heavier in her hand than she had expected. The articulation was stiff, like a rusted gauntlet from a suit of armour. 'I just mean,' she went on, 'we have some breathing space.' She pushed her hand into the open cuff, as far as her fingers would go.

'There's something jammed into three of the fingers,' Geoffrey said. 'I couldn't even get my hand past the connecting ring.'

Sunday tried for a few moments, then withdrew her hand very slowly. 'Guess we shouldn't rule out the possibility that it's some kind of … well, booby trap.'

'From Eunice?'

'If she was mad enough to put a glove in a bank vault, she was mad enough to turn it into a bomb.'

'I never even thought of bombs,' Geoffrey said.

'You've spent too much time in the Surveilled World. Just because you can't assemble a lethal mechanism out there doesn't mean you can't do it *here* – or that you couldn't have done it a hundred years ago.' Seeing her brother's sceptical look, Sunday added, 'Look, it probably *isn't* a bomb, but that's still no reason not to play safe, all right?'

Even with the glove tucked into his bag, Geoffrey must have been scanned and probed a dozen times just between the bank and the railway station. Every door he went through would have been alert to the presence of harmful materials or mechanisms, and he hadn't been stopped or questioned once. If there was something nasty – or even just suspicious-looking – in the glove, it was concealed well enough to fool routine systems.

Jitendra, who had been observing silently until then, said, 'We've got our own scanner. Might be an idea to run the glove through it and be sure.'

Sunday handed it to him warily, knowing how Jitendra liked to dismantle things, often without being entirely sure how to put them back together. 'Until we know what it's worth, I don't want you putting a scratch on it.'

Active doorframes were frowned upon in the Descrutinised Zone – people didn't like walking around feeling as if their bodies were living exhibits made of various densities of coloured glass. Equally discouraged were smart textiles, the kind that could be worn or slept in, invisibly woven with superconducting sensors. Sunday had a medical cuff, which was fully capable of detecting anything seriously amiss, but on a day-to-day, even month-to-month basis, what went on inside her body was her own business. In the Descrutinised Zone, it was even possible to get pregnant without the world and his wife being in on the secret.

'There's a community medical scanner downtown,' Jitendra said. 'It's very old – a museum piece, really. We all get our turn in it. They'll scan anything if it's a slow day, but if we put the glove through it everyone will want to know why, and that'll be the end of our mysterious little secret. Fortunately, there's a better option right here.'

'There is?' Geoffrey asked innocently.

'Follow me.'

Jitendra's den was set up in what had been the pantry and broom cupboard. Decently screened off behind beaded curtains, it was even more of a mechanical charnel house than the rest of the apartment. Generally speaking, Sunday didn't go near it unless there was no other option.

Clamped to the edge of his workbench were adjustable arms, magnifying lenses, precision manipulators and drills. On either side of the workbench, plastic tubs brimmed with wires and connectors, homemade circuits and gel-grown nervous systems. Mounted centrally on the bench was an elderly Hitachi desktop scanner the size of a small sewing machine: a heavy chassis supporting two upright moving scanning rings on tracks. It would have been laughed at in the Surveilled World – this machine had approximately the same resolution and penetrating power as a pillowcase or T-shirt – but in the Zone one took what one could get. Secretly, as Sunday had long since realised, Jitendra derived immense delight from working around arbitrary constraints and limitations.

The scanner currently held the torso and head assembly of a doll, with two- and three-dimensional magnified images pasted up on the walls around the bench, and what looked like acupuncture needles pin-cushioning the doll's plastic scalp. His den gave every impression of being the epicentre of some obscure Voodoo death cult.

He pulled the pincushioned doll out of the scanner, fixed the glove in place instead, then set the scanner to work. The rings whirred up to speed and jerked back and forth along their tracks while images of the glove, colour-coded in blues and pinks, graphed onto the walls.

Jitendra tapped a finger against his teeth. 'You're right.'

'About what?' Sunday asked.

'Definitely something blocking those three fingers. Soft packing around hard contents. Like little stones, or something.'

'But not bombs,' Geoffrey said.

'Nope. There's no machinery in there, no triggering mechanisms.'

'Think you can get them out?' Sunday asked. 'I mean non-destructively.' She looked at Geoffrey. 'Why on Earth would she put stones in a glove?'

Her brother had no answer.

'I think I can get the packages out,' Jitendra said, rummaging through his workbench tools. 'Give me a few minutes here. Any loud bangs, you can revise your bomb theory.'

Sunday had decided, provisionally, that she would forgive her brother. She had not arrived at this decision lightly, being very much of the opinion that forgiveness was a non-renewable resource, like petroleum or uranium. The world should not depend on its easy dispensation, nor should hers ever be counted upon.

Yet since Geoffrey was her brother, and since he was also not a true bloodsucking Akinya, she was inclined to generosity. As much as she detested lies and concealment, she accepted that the cousins had been playing on Geoffrey's attachment to the elephants. Her brother had faults, as did she, but greed was not among them. She could also see how troubled he had been, and how relieved he was when at last he felt able to speak about the vault and the glove. And so she decided to make no more of the matter, even though she was still hurt that he had not confided in her immediately, from the very moment the cousins tabled their proposition. But the hurt would heal, and provided Geoffrey did not lie to her again, she would forget this blemish on his character.

She led him back into the living room and drew him down next to her on the couch.

'I think it's time you met the construct. In for a yuan, et cetera. Remember when I showed you the face, back at the scattering?'

'Yes,' he said cautiously.

'That's only part of it. A tiny part.' She paused, assailed by last-minute doubts, before crushing them. 'For the last couple of years I've been working on something big, all of it done in my spare time. I'm building Eunice.'

'Right . . .' Geoffrey said, on a falling note.

'A fully interactive construct, loaded with every scrap of information anyone has on her. So far, so unexceptional.'

'I'll take your word on that.'

'Please do. This may be a back-room project but it's still a level above any other construct currently in existence . . . or at least any I know about. The routines she's built on aren't proprietary. They're highly experimental Bayesian algorithms, based on the free-energy min-imalisation paradigm. Jitendra calls her a fembot. That makes her as close to Turing-compliant as anything out there, and if the Gearheads knew they'd probably be knocking holes in the cavern about now. That's not the main thing I want you to keep in mind, though. This is a *person*, brother. It's not some made-up personality – it's the simulation of a real but deceased individual. And sometimes that can trip you up – especially if that person happens to be someone you knew. You forget, maybe for just a second, that it isn't her.'

'What makes you think she knows anything at all?'

'I'm not certain that she does, but it's still possible that she might. I've been studying her life and . . .' She held up her hands as if she was trying to bend a long piece of wood between them. 'It's like measuring a coastline. From a distance, it looks simple enough. But if I wanted to make a thorough study of her life, down to the last detail, it would cost me more than *my* life to do it. So that's not an option. The best I can do – the best any one human being is capable of doing – is to plot major landmarks and survey as much of the territory between them as I can. Her birth in Africa. Marriage to Jonathan Beza. Time on Mars, and elsewhere. The construct actually knows far more than I ever will, but it won't tell me anything unless I ask the right questions. And that's before we even get into the voids, the areas of her life I can't research.' She shrugged apologetically. 'But it's worth a try. Anything's worth a try.'

'How do I see her?'

'As a figment. Privacy-locked, so only people I allow to can see her. You'll need access to our local version of the aug for that. It's deliberately very basic, but it allows us to ching and interact with figments. Can I go ahead and authorise that?'

'Be my guest.'

Sunday voked the appropriate commands, giving her brother unrestricted access to the Eunice construct. But even Geoffrey was forbidden from tampering with the construct's deep architecture; he could tell it things, facts that it would absorb into its knowledge base, but he could not instruct it to forget or conceal something, or to alter a particular behavioural parameter.

Only Sunday could reach in and edit Eunice's soul.

'Invoke Eunice Akinya,' she said under her breath.

Her grandmother assumed reality. She was as solid as day, casting a palpable aug-generated shadow.

Sunday had opted to depict Eunice as she had been upon her last return from deep space, just before the start of her Lunar exile in 2101. A small, lean woman with delicate features, she didn't look remotely resilient enough to have done half the things credited to her. That said, her genetic toughness was manifest in the fact that she did not look quite old enough to be at the end of her seventh decade. Her hair was short and luminously white. Her eyes were wide and dark, brimming with an intelligence that could be quick and discriminating as well as cruel. She looked always on the point of laughing at something, but if she laughed, it was only ever at her own witticisms. She wore – or at least had been dressed in – clothes that were both historically accurate and also nondescript enough not to appear jarringly old-fashioned: lightweight black trousers, soft-soled running shoes with split toes and geckopad grip patches for weightlessness, a short-sleeved tunic in autumnal reds and golds. No jewellery or ornamentation of any kind, not even a watch.

She was sitting; Sunday had crafted a virtual chair, utilitarian and Quaker-plain. Eunice Akinya leaned forward slightly, hands joined in her lap, her head cocked quizzically to one side. The posture was one of attentiveness, but it also suggested someone with a hundred other plans for the day.

'Good evening, Sunday,' Eunice said.

'Good evening, Eunice,' Sunday said. 'I'm here with Geoffrey. How are you?'

'Very well, thank you, and I trust Geoffrey is well. Can I help you with something?' That was Eunice to a tee: small talk was for people who had time on their hands.

'It's about a glove,' Sunday said. 'Tell her the rest, Geoffrey.'

He glanced at her. 'Everything?'

'Absolutely – the more she knows, the more complete she becomes.'

'Please don't talk about me as if I'm not in the room.'

'My apologies, Eunice,' Sunday answered. She did not, of course, ever refer to her as 'grandmother'. Even if that had been Eunice's chosen form of address, Sunday would have found it inappropriate. Eunice was a label, a name pasted onto a bundle of software reflexes that only happened to look like a living human being.

'I found a glove,' Geoffrey said. 'It was in a safe-deposit box of the Central African Bank, in Copernicus City. The box was registered in your name.'

'What kind of glove?' Eunice asked, with the sharpness of a fierce cross-examiner.

'From an old spacesuit. We think maybe it belonged to a Moon suit.'

'We wondered if it might mean anything,' Sunday said. 'Like, was there a glove that had some particular significance to you, something connected to one of your expeditions?'

'No.'

'Did you lose a glove, or have something happen in which a glove played a decisive role?'

'I have already answered that question, Sunday.'

'I'm sorry.'

'There's something inside the glove,' Geoffrey said, 'stuffed into the fingers. Jogging any memories?'

'If I have no recollection of the glove, then I am hardly likely to be able to shed any light on its contents, am I?'

'All right,' Sunday said, sensing a brick wall. 'Let's broaden the enquiry. You used a few spacesuits in your time. Was there one that stands out above all the others? Did one save your life, or something like that?'

'You'll have to narrow it down for me, dear. The primary function of spacesuits is to preserve life. That is what they do.'

'I mean,' Sunday elaborated patiently, 'in a significant way. Was there an accident, something like that – a dramatic situation in which a spacesuit played a pivotal, decisive role?' As accustomed as she was to dealing with the construct – and she'd logged hundreds of hours of conversation – she still had to contain her annoyance and frustration on occasion.

'There were many "dramatic situations",' Eunice said. 'One might venture to say that my entire career was composed of "dramatic situations". That's what happens when you choose to place yourself in hazardous environments, far from the safety net of civilisation.'

'She only asked,' Geoffrey said.

'We're on the Moon,' Sunday said, the model of patience 'Did anything ever happen here?'

'Many things happened to me on the Moon, dear child. It was no more or less forgiving an environment than anywhere else in the system. Just because Earth's hanging up there like a big blue marble doesn't mean it'll save you if you do something stupid. And I was *not* stupid and I still got into trouble.'

'Prickly, isn't she?' Geoffrey murmured.

Eunice turned to him. 'What did you say?'

'You can't whisper in her presence,' Sunday said. 'She hears everything, even subvocalisations. I probably should have mentioned that already.' She sighed and slipped into a momentary aug trance.

Eunice and her chair vanished.

'What just happened?'

'I de-voked her and scrubbed the last ten seconds of working memory. That way she won't remember you calling her prickly, and she won't therefore hold a permanent grudge against you for the rest of your existence.'

'Was she always like this with adults?'

'I don't think she was particularly receptive to criticism. I also don't think she was one to suffer fools, gladly or otherwise.'

'Then I suppose she's just marked me down as one.'

'Until I scrubbed her working memory. But don't feel too bad about it. In the early days I must have scrubbed and re-scrubbed about a million times. To say we kept getting off on the wrong foot ... that would be a major understatement. But again, it's my fault, not hers. Right now what we have is a cartoon, a crude caricature of the real thing. I'm trying to smooth the rough edges, tone down the exaggerations. Until that's done, we can't make any judgements about the real Eunice Akinya.'

'Then I'll give her the benefit of the doubt. Although she wasn't much help, was she?'

'If she has anything useful to tell us, we'll need to zero in on it with some more information, fish it out of her. It's that or sit here while she recounts every significant incident of her life – and believe me, your tourist visa won't begin to cover that.'

A swish of beaded curtains heralded Jitendra's return.

'Perhaps I may now be of assistance.' He held out his hand: the three small wadded packages resting in his palm resembled paper-wrapped candies.

Jitendra put the packages down on the coffee table. They each took one and spread the wrapping open. Coloured stones tinkled out onto the coffee table's glass top, looking just like the hard-boiled candies the wrappers suggested.

'Real?' Sunday asked.

'Afraid not,' Jitendra said. 'Cheap plastic fakes.'

The three of them stared dispiritedly at the imitation gems, as if willing them into semi-precious rarity. Sunday's were a vivid, fake-looking green, Geoffrey's blood-red, Jitendra's a pale icy blue.

There were eight green gems, but perhaps double the number of red and blue ones. Jitendra was already doing a proper count, as if it might be significant.

'Did you damage the glove getting them out?' Sunday asked.

'Not in the slightest,' Jitendra said. 'And I was careful to record which finger each group of gems came out of.'

'We could boot her up again and ask about them,' Geoffrey said.

'I don't think it'll get us anywhere,' Sunday said.

'And I suppose we'd be wise not to deliberately antagonise her by repeating ourselves. Can she keep stuff from us?' Geoffrey asked.

Jitendra was still moving the gems around, arranging them into patterns like a distracted child playing with his food. 'Your sister and I,' he said, 'have long and involved discussions about the precise epistemological status of the Eunice construct. Sunday is convinced that the construct is incapable of malicious concealment. I am rather less certain of that.'

'It won't lie,' Sunday said, hoping to forestall another long-winded debate about a topic they could never hope to resolve, 'but the real Eunice might well have done. That's what we have to remember.'

'Eight, fifteen, seventeen,' Jitendra said. 'Green, red and blue in that order. These are the numbers of gems.'

'You think there's some significance to that?' Geoffrey asked.

'The green ones are larger,' Sunday said. 'She couldn't get as many of those into the finger.'

'Perhaps,' Jitendra said.

'Maybe it's the colours that mean something, not the numbers,' Geoffrey said.

'It's the numbers, not the colours,' Jitendra replied dismissively.

'You sure about that?' Sunday asked.

'Absolutely. The gems are just different colours to stop us mixing them up. Orange, pink and yellow would have sufficed for all the difference it makes.'

'The bigger question,' Geoffrey said, 'is exactly when I should tell the cousins. When I sneaked the glove out of the vault, I didn't know that there might be something inside it.'

'Nothing to stop you stuffing the gems back into the glove and claiming you never knew about them,' Sunday said.

'Someone will take a good look at the glove when I go through Earthbound customs. Then I'll have some serious explaining to do.'

Sunday shrugged. 'Not exactly crime of the century, smuggling cheap plastic gems.'

'And I'm a researcher crawling around on his belly begging for money. The slightest blemish on my character, the slightest hint of impropriety, and I'm screwed.'

Geoffrey was standing now, with his arms folded, striking a pose of imperturbable determination. Sunday knew her brother well enough to realise that he was not likely to budge on this point.

So she wouldn't push him just yet.

'Eight, fifteen, seventeen,' Jitendra said. 'I know these numbers. I'm sure they mean something.' He pressed his fingers against his forehead, like a man tormented.

CHAPTER FIVE

In the morning the taxi dropped them at the base of one of the ceiling-penetrating towers, a faceted pineapple with neon snakes coiling up its flanks. In the smoke-coloured lobby a queue for the elevators had already formed. Serious-looking young people milled around, several of whom were evidently well known to Sunday and Jitendra. Hands were pumped, knuckles touched, high-fives made, whispered confidences exchanged. They were speaking Swahili, Russian, Arabic, Chinese, Punjabi, English. Some were multilingual, others were making do with earphone translators, usually ornamented with lights and jewellery, or just enthusiastic gesturing. The air crackled with rivalry and the potential for swift backstabbing.

Geoffrey hadn't sensed anything like it since his last academic conference.

'It's a big deal for Jitendra,' Sunday explained. 'Only two or three tournaments a year matter as much as this one. Reason everyone's come out of the woodwork.' She gave her partner a playful punch. 'Nerves kicking in yet, Mister Gupta?'

'If they weren't, there'd be something badly wrong with me.' Jitendra was working his fingers, his forearm muscles tensing and relaxing in a machinelike rhythm. He jogged frantically on the spot until their elevator arrived. 'But I'm not afraid.'

The elevator shot them up through the core of the building, through the ceiling, through metres of compacted Lunar soil, onto the night-drenched surface. They exited in small glass-sided pimple: the embarkation lounge for bubble-canopied rovers, docked like suckling piglets around the building's perimeter. In all directions, a hundred or so metres apart, the ground was pierced by the uppermost sections of other structures, glowing with lights and symbols, spilling reds and blues and greens across the wheel-furrowed ground. A couple of suited figures trudged between parked vehicles, carrying suitcase-sized toolkits. Other than that, there was a striking absence of visible human activity.

'Is this where it all happens?' he asked.

'Way to go yet, brother,' Sunday said.

Before very long they were aboard one of the rovers, gliding away from the embarkation structure. The rover had six huge openwork wheels, the powdery soil sifting through them in constant grey cataracts. As the rover traversed a boulder, the wheels deformed to ensure the transit was as smooth as possible. The driver – and there *was* a driver, not just a machine – clearly took a gleeful delight in heading directly for the worst of these obstacles. She was sitting up front, hands on joysticks, dreadlocked scalp nodding to private music.

Soon the buildings receded to a clot of coloured lights, and not long after, they fell over the horizon. Now the only illumination came from the moving glow of the rover's canopy and the very occasional vehicle passing in the other direction.

'I thought I'd be picking up full aug signals by now,' Geoffrey said. With the bubble canopy packed to capacity, the three of them were strap-hanging. His aug icon still showed a broken globe.

'You're still in the Zone,' Sunday said. 'Think of this as a tongue sticking out, with a little micro-Zone at one end of it. There's no Mech here, just our stripped-down private aug. Even if the Surveilled World could reach us here, we'd put in our own jamming systems.'

In the absence of airglow it came as a surprise to summit a slight rise and suddenly be overlooking an amphitheatre of blazing light: a kilometre-wide crater repurposed as arena, with pressurised galleries sunk back into its inner wall. Spherical, hooded viewing pods resembled so many goggling eyeballs, linked by the fatty optic nerves of umbilical connecting tunnels. The rover passed through an excavated cleft in the crater wall, then drove around the perimeter.

Geoffrey pushed to the window. Huge machines littered the ground, beached by some vast Selenean tide. Worms or maggots or centipedes: segmented, with plates of deftly interlocking body armour and ranks of powerful tractor limbs running down the lengths of their submarine-sized bodies. They had chewing mouths, drilling probosces, fierce grappling and ripping devices. The ghosts of sprayed-on emblems survived here and there, almost worn away by abrasion where the machines had rolled over on their sides or scuffed against each other. Vivid silvery scars, not yet tarnished by the chemical changes caused by cosmic ray strikes, betokened fresh injury.

The machines lying around the perimeter were being worked on, readied for combat. Service gantries and cherry pickers had been rolled up, and suited figures were repairing damage or effecting subtle design

79

embellishments with vacuum welding gear. There must have been at least twenty machines, and that wasn't counting those located further into the arena, lying side by side or bent around each other, mostly in pairs. Geoffrey presumed this was a lull between bouts, since nothing much appeared to be happening.

'I'm guessing these machines weren't originally made for your fun and games,' he said to Jitendra.

'Heavy-duty mining and tunnelling equipment,' Jitendra said. 'Too beat-up or slow for the big companies to keep using, so they sell it off to us for little more than scrap value.'

Geoffrey laughed. 'And this is the most productive thing you could think of doing with them?'

'It's a damn sight better than staging *real* wars,' Sunday said.

'This is mine,' Jitendra said as they drove past one of the waiting combatants. 'Or rather, I have a quarter stake in it, and I get to drive it when my turn comes around.'

If anything it looked a little more battle-scarred than its neighbours, with chunks nibbled out of its side-plating exposing a vile gristle of hydraulics, control ducting and power cables. Plexus's nerve-node emblem was faint on the machine's side.

'She's taken a few hits,' Jitendra explained, superfluously.

'Do you . . . get inside it?'

'Fuck, no.' Jitendra stared at Geoffrey as if he'd lost his mind. 'For a start, these things are *dirty* – they're running nuclear reactors from the Stone Age. Also, there's no room inside them. Also, it's incredibly dangerous, being inside one robot while another robot's trying to smash yours to pieces.'

'I suppose it would be,' Geoffrey said. 'So – when does it all start?'

Jitendra looked at him askance. 'I beg your pardon?'

'I mean, when does the fighting begin?'

'It already has, brother,' Sunday said. 'They're fighting now. Out there. At this very moment.'

When the rover docked, they took him up into one of the private viewing pods. It contained a bar and a semicircle of normal seats, grouped around eight cockpits: partially enclosed chairs, big and bulky as ejector seats, their pale-green frames plastered with advertising decals and peeling warning stickers. Five people were already strapped in, with transcranial stimulation helmets lowered over their skulls.

'Geoffrey,' Sunday said, 'I'd like you to meet June Wing. June – this is my brother, up from Africa.'

'Pleased to meet you, Geoffrey.'

June Wing was a demure Chinese woman in a floor-length black skirt and maroon business jacket over a pearl blouse, with a silver clasp at the neck. Her grey-white hair was neatly combed and pinned, her expression grave. The look, Geoffrey concluded, was too disciplinarian to be unintentional. She wanted to project authoritarian firmness.

They shook hands. Her flesh was cold and rubbery. Another golem, then, although whether it was fixed form or claybot was impossible to determine.

'We sponsor Jitendra's team,' June said. 'I can't normally find time to make it to the tournaments, but today's an exception. I see you're here in the flesh – how's your trip been so far?'

'Very enjoyable,' Geoffrey said, which was not entirely a lie.

'Sunday told me you're working on elephant cognition. What are your objectives?'

Geoffrey blinked at the directness of June Wing's interrogation. 'Well, there are a number of different avenues.'

'The pursuit of knowledge for its own sake, or towards some practical goal?'

'Both, I hope.'

'I've just pulled up your pubs list. Considering you work alone, in what might be considered a less than fashionable area, you have a reasonable impact factor.'

Reasonable. Geoffrey thought it was a lot better than reasonable.

'Perhaps you should come and work for Plexus,' June Wing said.

'Well, I—'

'You have obligations back home.'

'Yes.'

'We're very interested in minds, Geoffrey. Not just in the studying of mental processes, but in the deeper mysteries. What does another mind think? What does it feel? When I think of the colour red, does my perception tally with yours? When we claim to be feeling happy or sad, are we really experiencing the same emotions?'

'The qualia problem.'

'We think it's tractable. Direct mind-to-mind process correlation. A cognitive gate. Wouldn't that be something?'

'It would,' he admitted. June Wing clearly had more than a passing understanding of his work, or had deduced the thrust of it from a cursory review of his publications list. He was inclined to believe the latter, but with that came an unsettling implication.

He must be talking to one of the cleverest people he'd ever met.

How would it feel to be in the same room as her, not just a robot copy?

'Well, you know how to reach me if you ever decide to broaden your horizons. First time at Robot Wars?'

'Yes. Doesn't seem to be much going on, though. Is it always like this?' He felt even more certain of this now. Across the arena, the pairs of machines hadn't moved to any obvious degree since he had seen them from the rover.

'Only one of the operators is actually driving a robot right now,' June Wing said. 'The other four are spectating, or helping with the power-up tests on one of the backup machines. The rival operators – our competitors – are in the other viewing pods.'

'But nothing's happening.'

'They're tunnel-boring machines,' Jitendra said. 'They're built to gnaw through lunar bedrock, not set land-speed records.'

Even as he spoke, Jitendra was lowering himself into one of the vacant cockpits. He reached up and tugged the transcranial stimulator down, nestling it onto his skull.

'We can't speed up the 'bots,' he went on, 'but we can slow ourselves down. Even your best civilian implants don't mess with the brain at a level deep enough to upset the perception of time, so we need some extra assistance. Hence, direct stimulation of the basal cortex. That and some slightly naughty deep-level neurochemical intervention—'

'As always, I'll pretend I didn't hear that,' June Wing said.

Jitendra slipped his wrists into heavy medical cuffs attached to the frame of the chair. 'They'd throw a fit in the Surveilled World. But of course, we're not *in* the Surveilled World now ... and that doesn't preclude outside sponsorship, or external spectators. There's money to be earned, reputations to be made and lost.'

'I guess the Plexus sponsorship helps,' Geoffrey said.

'It's not just advertising,' June Wing said. 'There is some actual R&D going on here. The robots have human drivers but they also have their own onboard battle minds, constantly trying to find a decisive strategy, a goal-winning solution they can offer to the pilot.'

'OK, here it comes,' Jitendra said, closing his eyes. 'Slowdown's beginning to take hold. Wish me ...' He stalled between words. '... luck.'

And then he was out, as lifelessly inert as the other drivers. Not unconscious, but decelerated into the awesomely slow sensorium of the robot, out in the arena.

'He's driving her now,' Sunday said, pointing to the robot Jitendra was controlling. 'You can just see the movement if you compare the ground shadow against the one from the support gantry.'

'What do you do when you want some real excitement – race slugs against each other?'

'Life moves pretty quickly if you are a slug,' June Wing admonished. 'It's just a question of perceptual reference frames.' She gestured to one of the vacant cockpits. 'Geoffrey can spectate, if he wishes. I have a reserved slot, but I'll pass for today.'

'I'm carrying some fairly specialised aug hardware,' Geoffrey said, meaning the equipment he needed to link to Matilda.

'Nothing will be damaged, brother, I promise you,' Sunday said.

'And if it is, my own labs will soon put it right,' June Wing said, with breezy indifference to his concerns. 'So jump right in.'

Geoffrey was still wary, but another part of him wanted to get as much out of his Lunar experience as possible.

'You need to take a leak?' Sunday asked. 'You're going to be in that thing for at least six hours.'

Geoffrey consulted his bladder. 'I'll cope. I didn't drink too much coffee this morning.'

Sunday helped him into the vacant cockpit. 'The cuffs will be analysing your blood – any signs of stress, above and beyond normal competition levels, and the system will yank you out. Same for the transcranial stim. It's read/write. There's not much that can go wrong.'

'Not much.'

Sunday cocked her head to one side, appearing to think for a moment. 'Well, there was that one guy ...' She lowered the transcranial helmet, adjusting it carefully into position. 'You were doing this at competition level, we'd cut back those curls to get the probe closer to your skin, but you'll be fine for spectating.'

Aug status messages flashed into his visual field, informing him that an external agent was affecting his neural function. The implants offered to resist the intrusion. He voked them into acquiescence.

'So what happened to that one guy?'

'Nothing much,' Sunday said breezily. 'Just that being in the cockpit permanently reset his internal clock. Even after they withdrew the stim and the drugs, he was stuck on arena time.'

'How's he doing now?'

'Thing is, he hasn't got back to us on that one yet.'

The cuffs dropped their painless fangs into his skin. Two cold touches, neurochemicals sluicing in, and he felt himself sliding, tobogganing down an ever steepening slope. He made to grab onto the sides of the cockpit for support, but his arms, even his fingers, felt sheathed in granite.

Then the rushing sensation ebbed and he felt perfectly still, amniotically calm. Something had failed, he decided.

'All right,' Sunday said. 'What you're hearing now is me slowed down into your perceptual frame. You've already been in the cockpit for twenty minutes.'

'I don't believe you,' Geoffrey said.

'Make that twenty-one. June and I are off to the bar now; be back in a second or two. We'll begin piping direct imagery into your head. Enjoy the show.'

He was almost ready not to believe her. But the digits in his tourist visa were whirring at superfast speed.

Geoffrey's perceptions took a savage lurch and he was suddenly out there, disembodied, able to roam at will in the ching space of the arena. Jitendra's robot wasn't crawling now; it was propelling itself in convulsive jerks, tractor claws threshing, body sections pistoning back and forth like some heavy industrial mechanism that had escaped its shackles. Lunar soil, disturbed by the robot's passage, collapsed back into itself as if composed of molten lead, under Jupiter's immense gravity.

Around the arena's perimeter, a frenzy of blurred motion attended the waiting machines. Elsewhere, dual combatants were locked in titanic wrestling matches, writhing and thrashing to the death.

Jitendra's opponent crossed the graded soil like a demented iron maggot. It differed from Jitendra's robot in its details but was of a comparable size, equipped with a broadly similar range of offensive devices. On its flanks, in luminous red, shone the Escher triangle logo of MetaPresence, Plexus's main competitor in ching facilitation and proxy robotics. The nerve-node emblem on Jitendra's machine was now similarly bright and unfaded, painted over the image by the aug. Accompanying these overlays were a host of statistics and technical readouts, speculating at the likely efficacies of armour, weapons and combat tactics.

The two robots halted at the laser-scribed circle of combat. Articulating two-thirds of the way down their bodies – they had been designed to steer during tunnel-boring operations – the robots reared up and bowed to each other. Agonising minutes must have passed in real-time as this martial ritual was observed.

The engagement was as sudden and brutal as a pair of sumo wrestlers charging into each other. At first, Jitendra's machine appeared to have the upper hand. It flexed itself around the enemy, using rows of tractor limbs to gain purchase, sinking their sharpened tips into gaps in armour plating. Articulating its head end, it brought the whirring nightmare of its circular cutting teeth into play. As they contacted its opponent's alloy head, molten metal fountained away on neon-bright parabolas. Reflecting Jitendra's initial success – and the changing spread-patterns of bets – the statistics shifted violently in his favour.

It didn't last. Even as Jitendra's robot was chewing into it, the other robot had retaliatory ambitions. Halfway down its body, armoured panels hinged open like pupal wings, allowing complex cutting machinery to scissor out. Servo-driven vacuum cutters began to burn into the belly of Jitendra's robot, clamped into place with traction claws. A kind of peristaltic wave surged up the body of the assaulted machine, as if it was experiencing actual pain. It relinquished its hold, bending its body away, disengaging the whirling vortex of its cutting teeth. The stats updated. Pink vapour jetted at arterial speed from the wound that had been cut into the side of Jitendra's robot: some kind of nuclear coolant or hydraulic fluid, bleeding into space.

The two machines rolled away from each other. The enemy retracted its cutter, the body armour folding back into place. Jitendra's machine staunched its blood loss. Stalemate ensued for objective seconds, before the resumption of combat. The enemy twisted its head assembly and locked on with clutching mouthparts, horrible girder-thick barbed mechanisms. It was chewing – drilling, tunnelling – into Jitendra's robot, metal and machine bits spraying away from the cutting head. From the rear of the enemy machine, from its iron anus, a grey plume of processed matter emerged. It was chewing, eating, digesting, defecating, all in mere seconds. Jitendra's stats were now dismal and falling.

But he wasn't finished. The enemy bit into something it couldn't process as easily as moon rock: some high-pressure jugular. Bad for Jitendra, even worse for the machine trying to eat him for dinner. The enemy jolted, regurgitating a large quantity of chewed-up machine parts. Mouth-mechanisms spasmed and flopped as a wave of damage ripped through its guts. Jitendra's machine twisted sharply out of reach. It had been bitten into around the neckline, but its whirling drills were still racing. It reared up like a striking cobra and hammered down on the enemy. Machine parts skittered away in all directions, cratering the arena. Now it was time for Jitendra's machine to spring out additional grasping and cutting devices, hull plates popping open like frigate gun doors. Jitendra's stats rallied.

But this wasn't going to be a victory for either machine. The enemy was wounded, perhaps fatally, but so was Jitendra's charge. Its drill parts were not turning as furiously as they had been only a few moments before. And its entire body was sagging, no longer able to support itself off the ground even against the feeble pull of the Moon's gravity. When the end came, it did so with startling suddenness. Jitendra's machine simply dropped dead, as if it had been pulled to the ground by invisible wires. For a moment the enemy machine made a valiant attempt to regain the advantage, but it was in vain. It too had suffered catastrophic systems failures. Like a deflating balloon, it collapsed to the ground and fell into pathetic corpselike stillness.

In a flash, recovery teams arrived. Tractors shot out from silos. Tiny figures – frantic space-suited Lilliputians – swarmed out of the tractors and bound the fallen monsters in drag-harnesses, cobwebbing them from head to tail with comical speed. The figures buzzed around and then vanished into the tractors again, as if they'd been sucked back inside. The tractors lugged the dead machines to the arena's perimeter, gouging runway-sized skid marks in the soil.

That was the end of the bout. Geoffrey knew because he was being pulled back into real-time. He felt the chemicals metabolising out of his bloodstream. The visa digits slowed their tumble. The transcranial stim was over, the helmet rising back away from his head.

'Well?' Sunday asked, standing over his reclining form. 'What did you think?'

For a moment his mouth wouldn't work.

'How long was I under?' he managed.

'Four and a half hours. June's gone back to work.'

If she was lying, then so was the visa.

'I guess everyone says the same thing. It didn't feel like it.'

'That was a short bout, as they go. Seven, eight hours isn't unusual,' Sunday answered, pushing a drink into his hand. 'Twelve, thirteen, even that wouldn't be out of the ordinary.'

His neck had developed an unpleasant crick. Jitendra, who was being hauled from his cockpit, had the wiped-out, dehydrated look of a racing-car driver. Friends and associates were already mobbing him, patting his back and making sympathetic bad-show faces.

'I'm sorry,' Geoffrey said, teetering over to Jitendra. 'I thought it was going your way for a while there. Not that I'm an expert or anything.'

'I lost my concentration,' Jitendra said, shaking his head. 'Should have switched to a different attack plan when I had the window. Still, it's not all bad news. A draw gives me enough points to retain my ranking, whereas they needed a win not to go down the toilet.' He worked his shoulders, as if both his arms had popped out of their sockets and needed to be relocated. 'And I don't think the damage is as bad as it looked out there.'

'Nothing that can't be welded back together,' Sunday said.

'One good thing came out of it,' Jitendra said, before burying his face in a warm wet towel.

'Which was?' Sunday asked.

'Eight, fifteen, seventeen.' He gave them both a grin. 'I figured that bit out, anyway. And I was right. Those numbers do mean something to me.'

When they were back at the apartment, Sunday and her brother prepared a simple meal, and they shared another bottle of wine, one which Geoffrey had insisted on buying by way of celebration for a successful day. They dined with Toumani Diabaté providing kora accompaniment. The recording was a hundred years old, made when the revered musician was a very elderly man, yet it remained as bright and dazzling as sun-glints on water.

When the dishes had been cleared and the wine glasses refilled, she knew that the time had come to invoke the construct. This was the crux, she felt certain. If Eunice could offer no guidance on the matter, then all they had was a dirty old glove and some cheap plastic jewels. And with the possibility of mystery safely banished from their lives, they could all return to their mundane concerns.

'Good evening, Sunday,' Eunice said, speaking Swahili. 'Good evening, Jitendra. Good evening, Geoffrey.'

'Good evening, Eunice,' they chorused.

'How are you enjoying your stay?' Eunice asked, pointedly directing her question at Geoffrey.

'Very much, thank you,' he said, but with an edge of nervousness, as if he did not quite trust that Eunice's working memory had been scrubbed after their last exchange. 'Sunday and Jitendra are first-rate hosts.'

'Excellent. I trust that the remainder of your visit will be just as enjoyable.' She turned her imperious regard onto Sunday. 'May I be of assistance?'

'We have a question,' Sunday said.

'If it's about the glove, I'm afraid I have told you all that I am able to.'

'It's not exactly about the glove. Well, it sort of is, but we have something different to ask you now.' Sunday looked at Jitendra, inviting him to speak.

'I discovered a pattern,' Jitendra said. 'Three numbers. They relate to Pythagoras.'

'Where was this pattern?' Eunice queried sharply, as if addressing a small boy who had mumbled something out of turn in class.

'There were gemstones in the glove,' Jitendra said, 'red, green and blue ones. The numbers form a Pythagorean triple: eight, fifteen, seventeen.'

'I see.'

'It took me a while to make the connection,' Jitendra went on. 'It was almost there, but I couldn't quite bring it out. Then I saw the Meta Presence logo on the side of the other robot ... the triangle ... and it was like a key turning in my head. It wasn't a Pythagorean triangle, of course, but it was enough.'

'Question is, why Pythagoras?' Sunday asked. 'Could mean several things. But seeing as we're on the Moon, and seeing as there's a good chance that glove came from a Moon suit ... I wondered if it might have something to do with Pythagoras itself.' She swallowed and added, 'As in the crater, on the Earth-facing side.'

Eunice cogitated for many agonising seconds, her expression perfectly unchanging. Sunday had taken pains to imbue the construct with Eunice's own speech patterns and mannerisms, and this kind of hiatus was one of them.

'Something did happen to me there,' she said, breaking her own silence. 'Systems failure, coming in to land at the Chinese station in Anaximenes. Lost thrust authority and hard-landed in Pythagoras.' She smacked her fist into her palm, making a loud, meaty clap. 'Ship was toast, but I managed to suit-up and bail out before she lost hull pressure. Chinese knew where I'd come down. Problem was, their one rover was out on an excursion and if I sat tight waiting for them to get a rescue party to me, I'd be toast as well. My only option was to walk, and try to meet them two-thirds of the way, on the other side of the crater wall. So that's what I did: I walked – actually hopped, most of the way – and climbed, and I was down to three hours of useful consumables when I saw their rover cresting the horizon.' She shrugged, profoundly unimpressed by her own story. 'It was a close thing, but there were close things all the time in those days.'

'So that's it?' Sunday said, doubtfully. 'That's all that ever happened to you in Pythagoras?'

'If you would rather I hadn't made it, dear child, then I can only apologise.'

'I didn't mean to downplay what happened,' Sunday said. 'It's just, well, another Eunice story. In any other life it would be the most amazing thing, but in yours ... it's not even a chapter. Just an anecdote.'

'I have had my share of adventure,' Eunice conceded.

'When did this happen?' Jitendra asked.

'The year would have been ...' Eunice made a show of remembering. 'Fifty-nine, I believe. Back when Jonathan and I were still married. It was a different Moon then, of course. Still a wilderness, in many respects. A lot changed in the next two or three decades. That was why we decided to move on again.'

'To Mars. With the Indians,' Sunday said. 'But even Mars wasn't enough of a wilderness to keep you happy.'

'Living out the rest of his life there suited Jonathan. Didn't suit me. I came back to the Moon eventually, but only when the rest of the system had exhausted its ability to astonish.'

'I'm surprised you didn't come all the way back, to Africa,' Geoffrey said.

'And cripple myself under a gee of gravity again? I'd barely set foot on Earth in forty years, boy. I missed the household; I missed the acacia trees and the sunsets. But I did not miss the crush of all that dumb matter under my feet, pinning me to the earth under a sky that felt like a heavy blanket on a warm night.' She jabbed a finger against the side of her head. 'Space changed me; I could never go home again. Space will do that to you. If that bothers you, best stay home.'

'Excuse me for having an opinion,' Geoffrey said.

She eyed him, then nodded once. Eunice had always placed a much higher premium on those who dared to stand up to the monstrous force of her personality than those who gave in without a fight.

'I should not blame you for living later than I did,' Eunice said, adopting a tone that was as close to conciliatory as she ever got. 'You did not choose to be born in this century, any more than I chose to be born in mine.'

'And that was a long time ago,' Jitendra said.

'You think so?' the construct replied. 'There are rocks out there, still sitting on the Lunar surface, that haven't moved since the Late Heavy Bombardment.'

'She might be right,' Sunday said. 'If Eunice crashed somewhere out of the way like Pythagoras, there's a good chance her tracks are still there, from the landing site all the way out of the crater, to wherever the Chinese rescued her.'

'Just so long as Pythagoras hasn't been chewed over for water or helium,' Jitendra said. 'Or had casinos plastered all over it.'

'The Chinese station at Anaximenes was a supply point for their hydroxyl mining and refining operations around the north pole,' Eunice said, tapping her instantaneous knowledge base. 'Once the pipelines were in and extraction became automated, there was no need to keep all the crewed stations open. There's no longer a human presence in Anaximenes, and the last person to set foot in Pythagoras was me.' She paused, catching herself before anyone else had a chance to speak. 'Actually, I lie: a recovery team flew in to strip the ship for anything salvageable – 'tronics, fuel, shielding. They were Indian, and under space law they had the right to fillet the wreck. But that was only a few weeks later and they wouldn't have touched most of the evidence.'

'Evidence,' Geoffrey said. 'It's like we're already talking about a crime scene.'

'Maybe we're making a bit too much of it,' Sunday said. 'If the glove was meant to lead us to the crater, why didn't it just come with a handy little map tucked into it?'

'A test of your ability to draw the necessary conclusion from the clues, perhaps?' Eunice suggested.

'Well, good luck,' Geoffrey said. 'I'll be deeply interested to hear what, if anything, you find out there.'

'We're all in this together, brother,' Sunday said.

'Speak for yourself. All I've done is examine a glove at the request of the family.'

Sunday turned back to the construct. 'Thank you for your time, Eunice – you've been most helpful.'

'It's over,' Geoffrey said, when the figment had vanished. 'There's no mystery. No reason not to come clean about the glove, and the gemstones.'

Sunday shrugged and decided, possibly with the assistance of mild intoxication, that she would call his bluff. 'Fine. Call the cousins. Tell them what you found.'

'They still think the glove's in Copetown.'

'Say you went back and got it. It'll only be a white lie.'

Jitendra sucked air through his teeth. 'Beginning to wish I hadn't been so clever after all.'

'It's all right,' Sunday said. 'This is just a brother-and-sister thing.'

'What Sunday doesn't grasp,' Geoffrey said, 'is that there's more at stake to me personally than the reputation of Eunice, or the family business.'

'You think you're the only one with responsibilities?'

'I have to put the elephants first, and that means keeping the cousins happy. So I'll take the glove back to Earth, and declare the contents to customs.'

Sunday said nothing. She knew when her brother still had more to get off his chest.

'But I won't tell the cousins about the mathematical pattern. They can work that out for themselves, if they're bright enough. And I won't tell them what Eunice just told us either.'

'They're not fools,' Sunday said.

'It's a compromise. You and Jitendra can keep digging into this little treasure hunt, if you wish. The cousins don't need to know about that. Mainly they'll be relieved that there wasn't anything obvious and incriminating in the vault. Now they can go back to their polo with a clear conscience.'

'At least we agree on one thing,' Sunday said. 'Neither of us likes the cousins very much.'

'They're Akinyas,' Geoffrey said. 'I think that says it all.'

CHAPTER SIX

In the morning he found Sunday in her studio. She had already been busy and industrious – she always had been a morning person. There was fresh bread and milk, the smell of powerful coffee permeating the apartment.

'It's very nice,' he said, admiring the piece she was working on. It was some kind of half-scale Maasai-looking figure study: a skeletal stick-thin figure with a spear. Sunday was using a power tool to chisel away at the blade-edge of a cheekbone, biting her tongue in fierce concentration.

'It's shit, actually. Commissioned work. I'm doing two of them, to flank the doorway of an ethnic restaurant in the third cavern.' She wore a long skirt, a black T-shirt and a red headscarf. Power tools, dappled with dried white specks, dangled from a belt hanging low around her hips. 'What pays the rent around here, not digging into the past of a dead ancestor.'

'It's still art.'

'That's one point of view.'

'You don't think so?'

'They wanted something African. I said, you're going to have to narrow it down a bit: are we talking west coast, east coast, are we even sub-Saharan? But no, they said, we want to keep it less *specific* than that.'

'Like you say, it pays the rent.'

'Guess I shouldn't complain. Picasso drew on napkins to pay his bar tabs. And if this goes in on time, there may be more work when they open another concession across town.' She hooked the power tool back into its loop and unbuckled the belt, draping it onto one of her paint-and-plaster-spattered work surfaces. 'You're up, anyway. You want break-fast? I thought we'd hit the zoo today.'

'I just grabbed some bread,' Geoffrey said. 'Where's Jitendra?'

'Asleep. Does all his best thinking unconscious.' She pottered over to a bowl and dipped her hands in water before drying them on her skirt. 'Hope that wasn't too heavy, all that business last night.'

'Anything to do with family is bound to err on the heavy side.' Geoffrey looked down, realising he'd trodden in something wet and sticky. 'Look, I meant to say – it was absolutely wrong of me not to tell you straight away what I was doing up here, but I felt I was in a bind. If you can forgive me—'

'I already have. This one time.' She finished drying her fingers, leaving dark ovals on the skirt. 'But listen – you and me, we have to be open with each other. Always used to be, didn't we? You and me against the household, from the moment we worked out how to make nuisances of ourselves. How dear Memphis didn't strangle us, I won't ever know.'

'Different back then, though. Being rebellious didn't cost us anything except maybe being banished to our bedrooms before supper. Now we've got people and things that depend on us.'

'Doesn't mean we can't be honest with each other, though, does it?'

'The cousins didn't want you to know. They'll spit teeth if they find out I told you.'

Sunday moved the sculpture by its base and positioned it under a cluster of blue-tinged lights. 'Then we'd better make damn sure they don't.'

Children flew kites and balloons in the park. Others were preoccupied with enormous dragon-like flying contraptions not much smaller than the Cessna, the chief function of which appeared to be battling with other dragon-like flying contraptions. They had glittering foil plumage, bannered tails and marvellous anatomically precise wings that beat the air with the awesome slowness of a whale's heart. Elsewhere there were amorous couples, outbreaks of public theatre or oratory, ice-cream stands, puppet shows and a great many fabulously costumed stilt-walkers. Geoffrey stared in wonder at an astonishingly beautiful stilt-walking girl covered with leaves and green face paint, like a tree spirit made carnal.

'Do you think,' Sunday asked, 'that the cousins had any idea what you might find in the bank?'

'If they did, they hid it well.'

'Big risk, though, sending you up to look into the vault.'

'Less of a risk than bringing an outsider into it.' He tongued the ice cream Sunday had bought him from one of the stands. 'Ideally, Hector and Lucas would have come up here in person, but then people would have started wondering why they needed to visit the Moon. Before you know it, the whole system would be poking its nose into Akinya business.'

'You think Memphis knows about the vault?'

'If he does, he's said nothing to me.' Geoffrey dripped some of the ice cream onto his sleeve. He lifted the fabric to his mouth and licked off the spillage. 'Still, he knows *something*'s going on. I'm not sure what the rest of the family make of my absence, but Memphis knows I've gone to the Moon.'

'Memphis had more contact with Eunice near the end than any of us.'

'She might have told him things then, I suppose,' Geoffrey said. 'Or at any point during the exile. She was up here for more than sixty years.'

'Maybe the simplest thing would be to ask him directly, in that case. See if he knows anything about the glove and the gemstones, and a possible connection to Pythagoras.'

'If you'd like me to.'

They navigated the edge of a small civic pond where children splashed in the shallows and little pastel-sailed boats bobbed and battled further out. On the far bank, Geoffrey caught the flash of something small and mammalian emerging from the water before vanishing immediately into tufts of grass. An otter, or maybe a rat, its fur silvery with water.

'You're not at all curious about any of this, are you?' Sunday said, not bothering to hide her disapproval. 'When you head home to Africa, it's straight back to your old life.'

'You say that like it's a bad thing.'

'Just do that one thing for me – find out what Memphis knows.'

'Look, before you dig any deeper into this – are you absolutely sure this is something you really want to mess with? You won't be able to do a five-minute scrub on your own working memory.'

'I know a good neuropractor.'

'Not my point.'

'She wasn't a monster, Geoffrey. A less-than-perfect human being, maybe. And there's another thing: *she* put that glove there, not someone else. Isn't it too much of a coincidence that the details of this bank vault suddenly come to light in the weeks after her death? Eunice's fingerprints are all over this.'

'I hope you're right about that.'

After leaving the park they walked through into the next cavern and eventually stopped at the restaurant where Sunday's commissioned sculptures would be installed. The place was closed for business, dusty from the renovation work. Sunday talked to the interior designer, going over a few details she needed to check before completing the project. She came out shaking her head, exasperated and befuddled. 'Now they want them black,' she said. 'First it was white, now it's black. I'll have to redo them from scratch.'

'What will you do with the white ones?'

'Destroy them, probably. Too kitsch to sell.'

'Please don't destroy them,' Geoffrey said urgently.

'No use to me. Just clutter up my workplace.'

'I'll buy them or something. Ship them home. But don't destroy them.'

She looked touched and surprised. 'You'd do that for me, brother?'

He nodded solemnly. 'Unless you've priced yourself out of my range.'

Then they were on their way again, crossing a few more blocks before arriving at what appeared to be – at least by the Zone's standards – an entirely nondescript commercial or residential building. Its bulging sides were a mosaic of mirror-bright scales, suggestive of reptilian integument. They went inside and rode an elevator down into its basement levels.

Sunday passed Geoffrey a translation earpiece. 'Put this on,' she said. 'Chama doesn't do Swahili.'

She had voked ahead and as the doors opened they were met by a big, intense-looking man. Geoffrey judged him to be about his own age, give or take a decade. Long black hair hung down the sides of his face in tousled curtains, his skin brown, his beard neat and black, trimmed with laser accuracy.

'Chama,' Sunday said, pushing in her own jewelled translator. 'This is Geoffrey, my brother. Geoffrey: this is Chama Akbulut.'

Chama reached out and took Geoffrey's hand. He said something in a language Geoffrey didn't recognise, while the translation rang clear and near-simultaneous. 'Heard quite a bit about you.'

'Nothing bad, I hope.'

'No. Although Sunday did say you wouldn't come up here in a million years. What changed your mind?'

'Family business,' Sunday cut in.

'I hope we're not intruding,' Geoffrey said.

'Always glad of company here.' Chama wore a loose-fitting smock with a drawstring neck under a long leather waistcoat with a great many pockets and pouches. 'You up to speed on the menagerie, Geoffrey?'

'Not exactly.'

'Oh, good. That's always the best way.'

Chama led them deeper into the building, until they were passing along a corridor dug out of solid Moon rock, sprayed over with smoke-tinted plastic insulation. Pipes and power lines ran along the ceiling, stapled messily in place.

'There are strict rules governing the transport and utilisation of genetic materials within the system,' Chama said, looking back over his shoulder. 'And I'm very proud to say that Gleb and I have broken most of them.'

'Aren't there good reasons for those rules?' Geoffrey asked. 'No one wants to see people dying because of some ancient virus escaping into the wild.'

'We're not interested in anything hazardous,' Chama said. 'Gleb and I have committed criminal acts only because we were obliged to break certain badly constructed laws. Legislation made by stupid, short-sighted governments.'

Geoffrey tensed. In his experience, governments were quite useful things: it was hard to see how the world could have come through the Resource and Relocation crises without them. But anti-centralist rhetoric came with the territory, here in the Descrutinised Zone.

'Guess it depends on your intentions,' he said.

'Had a lot of time for your grandmother,' Chama said. 'You think dear old Eunice sat around analysing her every decision into the ground, looking at it from every possible ethical angle? Or did she just, you know, go for it?'

They'd arrived at a heavy door, the kind that might lead out onto the surface or into a non-pressurised tunnel system. Chama stood to one side and allowed the basketball hoop of an eidetic scanner to lower down over his skull. Chama closed his eyes while he visualised the sphinxware image sequence.

The door unlocked with the solid, reassuring clunk of a castle draw-bridge and hinged slowly open.

'Welcome to the menagerie,' Chama said.

The room beyond the door was bigger than Geoffrey had been expecting – much larger than the vault in the Central African Bank – but still nowhere near capacious enough to contain a zoo. His eyes took a few moments to adjust to the very low ambient lighting, a soft red radiance bleeding from the edges of the floor. Rectangular panels, two high, divided the walls, but beyond that he couldn't make out more than the sketchiest of details. There was another door at the far end, outlined in pale glowing pink.

'Feel I'm missing something here,' Geoffrey said.

Sunday smiled. 'I think you'd better show him, Chama.'

'Forgive the question, but you're absolutely sure he can be trusted?' Chama asked.

'He's my brother.'

Chama voked something. Polarising screens winked to transparency.

The panelled rectangles in the walls were in fact glass screens. Behind the screens were enclosures rife with vegetation.

Geoffrey reeled. It was obvious, even from a moment's glance, that the habitats differed in subtle and not so subtle ways. Some were flooded with bright equatorial sunlight – the blazing intensity of the noonday savannah. Others had the permanent gloom of the forest floor under a sun-sapping canopy of dense tree cover. Others were steamy or desert-arid.

He walked to the nearest pair of windows. They were stacked one above the other, with no sign that the habitats were in any way interdependent.

'I don't know as much botany as I should,' Geoffrey said, peering at the amazing profusion of plants crammed into the upper window. Their olive leaves were diamonded with dewdrops or the remnants of a recent rain shower. Under Lunar gravity, surface tension shaped liquids into almost perfect hemispheres. 'But if there's as much biodiversity in this room as I think there is, this is a pretty amazing achievement.'

'We've been growing plants in space since the first space stations,' Chama said, 'since the days of Salyut, Mir and the ISS. Some of the plant lines here go that far back: lines nurtured by the first thousand people to venture into space. *Their hands touched these lineages.*' He said this as if he was talking about holy relics, fingered by saints. 'But from the outset the work has always been scientifically and commercially driven – firstly, to explore the effects of weightlessness on growth mechanisms, then to push our understanding of hydroponics, aeroponics and so on. Once the 'ponics techniques had matured sufficiently, we stopped bringing new varieties into space. This is the first time that the majority of these plant species have been established beyond Earth. The difference here is that the driver isn't science or commerce. It's the Panspermian imperative.'

'Ah,' Geoffrey said, with a profound sinking feeling. 'Right. Guess I should have seen that one coming.'

'You don't approve?' Chama asked.

'Colour me more than slightly sceptical.'

'That's my brother's way of saying he thinks you're all completely batshit insane,' Sunday explained.

He shot her an exasperated glance. 'Thanks.'

'Best to get these things out in the open,' Sunday said.

'Quite,' Chama agreed, cordially enough. 'So yes – I'm a Panspermian. So's Gleb. And yes, we believe in the movement. But that's all it is – an idea, a driving imperative. It's not some crackpot cult.'

The door at the far end of the room opened, allowing a figure to enter.

It was another man, shorter and stockier than Chama, pushing a wheeled trolley laden with multicoloured plastic flasks and tubs.

'This is my husband, Gleb,' Chama said. 'Gleb, we have visitors! Sunday's brought along her brother.'

Gleb propelled the trolley to the wall and walked over to them, peeling gloves from his hands and stuffing them in the pockets of his long white labcoat. 'The elephant man?'

'The elephant man,' Chama affirmed.

'This is a great pleasure,' Gleb said, offering his hand for Geoffrey to shake. 'Gleb Ozerov. Have you seen the—'

'Not yet,' Chama said. 'I was just breaking the bad news to him.'

'What bad news?'

'That we're batshit insane.'

'Oh. How's he taking it?'

'About as well as they usually do.'

Geoffrey shook Gleb's hand. He could have crushed diamonds for a living.

'He'll get over it, eventually.' Gleb studied him with particular attentiveness. 'You look disappointed, Geoffrey. Is this not what you were expecting?'

'It's a room full of plants,' Geoffrey said, 'not the zoo I was promised.'

Gleb was a little older than Chama – a little older-looking, at least – with central-Asian features, Russian, maybe Mongolian. His hair was dark but cut very short, and he was clean-shaven. Under the white laboratory coat, Geoffrey had the impression of compact muscularity, a wrestler's build.

'Look,' Gleb said, 'you're a citizen of the African Union, and the AU's a transnational member entity of the United Surface Nations. That means you view things through a certain . . . ideological filter, shall we say.'

'I think I can see my way past USN propaganda,' Geoffrey said.

'We're Pans. Pans are bankrolled by the United Aqatic Nations, as you undoubtedly know, and the UAN's at permanent loggerheads with the USN. That's the way of the world. But we're not at war, and it doesn't mean that Pans are about to make a bid for global domination, on Earth or here on the Moon. It's just that we believe in certain . . . unorthodox things.' Gleb's voice, coming in under the translation, was speaking a different language from Chama, something clipped and guttural, where Chama's tongue was high and lyrical in intonation. He delivered this oratory with arms folded, muscles bulging under the white fabric of his sleeves. 'Pans think that the human species has a duty, a moral obligation, to assist in the proliferation of living organisms into deep space. All living organisms, not just the handful that we happen to *want* to take with us, because they suit our immediate requirements.'

'We're doing our best,' Geoffrey said. 'It's still early days.'

'That's one viewpoint,' Gleb said cheerfully. 'Especially if you're trying to worm out of species-level responsibility.'

'This is going really well,' Sunday said.

'Yes,' Geoffrey said. 'I've only been here five minutes and already I feel like I'm about to be hanged, drawn and quartered for my crimes against the biosphere.'

'Chama and Gleb don't mean it personally. Do you?' Sunday asked.

'We do, but we'll gladly make an exception for your brother,' Gleb said with a smile.

'Very magnanimous of you,' Geoffrey replied.

'We have a window here,' Chama said. 'The human species is poised on the brink of something genuinely transformative. It could be wonderful: an explosion of life and vitality, a *Green Efflorescence*, pushing beyond the solar system into interstellar space. We're on the cusp of being able to do that. But at the same time we could also be on the cusp of entrenchment, consolidation, even a kind of retreat.'

Geoffrey shook his head. 'Why on Earth would we retreat when we've come this far?'

'Because soon we won't need to be here at all,' Gleb said.

'Soon, very soon,' Chama continued, 'machines will be clever enough to supplant humans throughout the system. Once that happens, what reason will people have to live out in those cold, lonely spaces, if they can ching there instead?'

'Thinking machines won't rise up and crush us,' Gleb said. 'But they will make us over-reliant, unadventurous, unwilling to put our own bodies at risk when machines can stand in for us.'

Geoffrey was beginning to wish they'd stayed in the park, with the ice-cream stands and battling kites.

'I'm not seeing what machines have to do with any of this,' he said, gesturing at the glass-fronted enclosures.

'Everything,' Gleb answered. 'Because this is where it all begins.'

Geoffrey peered into the lower window of the glassed enclosure. It was a kind of rock-pool tableau, with low plant cover and bubbling, gurgling water. 'How many plant species have you brought here?' he asked.

'Living and replicating now, in the region of eight hundred,' Chama said. 'In cryosuspension, or as genetic templates, another sixteen thousand. Still some way to go.'

'My god, there's something alive in there.' He couldn't help jabbing his finger against the glass. 'I mean something moving. In the water.'

'A terrapin,' Gleb said, on a bored note. 'Terrapins are easy. If we couldn't do terrapins, I'd give up now.'

'Show him what else you do,' Sunday said.

Gleb walked to another window, a few panels down from where Geoffrey was standing. 'Come here,' he said, tapping a thick finger against the glass.

The visible portion of the habitat – though it clearly extended far back from the room – was a circle of bare, dusty earth fringed by tall wheat-coloured grasses. Rising above the grasses, a seamless curtain of enamel-blue, projected in such a way that it looked as convincing and distant as real sky. As Geoffrey walked over to join Gleb, he kept on tapping his fingernail against the glass. Gleb had very dark nails, tinted a green that was almost black. Geoffrey arrived in time to see the grasses swishing, parting to allow a hare-sized animal to bound into the clearing.

It was a battleship-grey rhinoceros, the size of a domestic cat. It was not a baby. Its proportions and gait, insofar as Geoffrey could tell – and allowing for the bouncing motion that was an inescapable consequence of Lunar gravity – were precisely those of a fully grown animal.

It just happened to be small enough to fit into a briefcase.

He was just satisfying himself as to the accuracy of his assessment when a pair of true babies sprang along behind what was now revealed to be their mother. The babies were the size of rats, but they walked on absurdly thick, muscular, wrinkle-hided legs. They were as tiny and precisely formed as bath toys moulded from grey plastic.

He laughed, amazed at what he was seeing.

'Resource load is the crux,' Chama said, joining them by the window. 'We don't have the means to keep fully grown adult specimens alive – at least not in a habitat that wouldn't feel hopelessly claustrophobic to them.' He pushed a strand of hair away from his cheekbone. 'Fortunately – for now, at least – we don't have to. Nature's already given us a ready-made miniaturisation mechanism.'

'Phyletic dwarfism,' Geoffrey said.

'Yes. Almost childishly easy to achieve in mammals and reptiles.'

Chama was right. Insular dwarfism often arose when an ancestor species divided into isolated sub-populations on islands. Allopatric speciation, and subsequent dwarfism, had occurred time and again in the evolutionary record, from dwarf allosaurs to the *Homo floresiensis* hominids in Indonesia. Even trees did it. It was a gene-encoded response to environmental stress; a way of allowing a population to survive hard times.

'The same mechanisms will assist animal life transition through the difficult bottleneck of the early stages of the Green Efflorescence,' Gleb declared. 'All we've done is give the inbuilt mechanism a little coaxing to produce extreme dwarfism. It's as if nature anticipated this future survival adaptation.'

'A little coaxing' sounded like magisterial understatement to Geoffrey, given the toy-like proportions of the rhinoceroses. But he could well believe that Chama and Gleb hadn't needed to perform much deep-level genetic tinkering to achieve it. Certainly there was no evidence that the dwarf animals were in any way traumatised by their condition, judging by the way they were happily snuffling and shuffling around, the babies nudging each other boisterously.

Gleb had retrieved the wheeled trolley, dug some granular foodstuff out of one of the containers and was now sprinkling it down into the enclosure via a hopper above the window. The dwarf rhinoceroses must have taken his fingernail tapping as the sign that dinner was imminent.

'It's ... an ingenious solution to the problem,' Geoffrey said.

'You find it troubling,' Chama said.

'I wonder whether it might have been better to keep these organisms on ice until you had the means to grow them to full size.'

'Even if that meant waiting decades?'

'The Green Efflorescence doesn't sound like a short-term plan.' It felt odd to speak of the Efflorescence himself, as if by voicing its name he had bestowed upon the enterprise a measure of legitimacy, even tacit approval.

He was still undecided as to whether it might be some kind of vile, misanthropic eco-fascism. He would need to know a lot more before he made up his mind.

'These animals don't know that they're dwarves,' Gleb said, patiently enough. 'On a neurological and behavioural level, there's no evidence of developmental impairment. There's a huge redundancy in brain tissue – it's why birds are at least as good at problem solving as primates, even given the massive disparity in cranial volume. So we have no ethical qualms whatsoever. Chama and I wouldn't countenance the creation of misery merely to serve some distant utopian objective.'

'They do look happy enough,' he allowed.

'We won't deny that there are difficulties still to be overcome, with some of the other species.'

Something ominous clicked in Geoffrey's head. 'If you can do rhinoceroses, you can do mammoths and elephants. It's been a while, but I remember something about dwarf populations in those species: the Cretan elephants, the mammoths in the Bering Sea Islands.'

'We can do *Proboscidea*,' Chama said. 'And we have. But there are difficulties.'

He led Geoffrey and Sunday to one of the far windows. Geoffrey's stomach churned with apprehension.

'I'm not sure this is right.'

Gleb was pushing the trolley again. 'Always scope for improvement. But that doesn't mean the elephants should be put on ice, or euthanised.'

Compared to the rhino habitat, the grass was lower, scrubbier – dry and bleached like the Serengeti before the short rains. In the middle distance lay a waterhole, now reduced to a muddy depression. Standing on the far side of the waterhole, clumped together into one multi-legged, multi-headed Cubist mass, were three dwarf elephants. They were the size of baby goats, grey bodies camouflaged with olive-brown patches of drying mud.

'Tell me how these elephants were born,' he said.

'In artificial wombs, here in the Descrutinised Zone,' Gleb replied. 'The fertilised eggs were imported, carried *in vivo*, in human mules. Chama and I both carried eggs, and we've both fallen foul of the Indian and Chinese Lunar authorities at various times.'

'You'd need hundreds – thousands – for a viable population, though.'

Chama nodded. 'We have hundreds. But so far only these elephants have been allowed to be born.'

'Just these three?'

'As many as the habitat can reasonably support,' Chama said.

Geoffrey had been agnostic about the rhinoceroses. Now his distaste sharpened into precise, targeted revulsion. 'This is wrong. No matter what your objectives, you can't do this to these animals.'

'Geoffrey—' Sunday began.

He ignored her. 'Elephants aren't born into a vacuum: they're born into a complex, nurturing society with a strong maternal hierarchy. An elephant clan might contain thirty to a hundred individuals, and there are strong inter-clan bonds as well. What you're doing here is the equivalent of dropping human babies into isolation cubes!'

Sunday's hand was on his arm. She tightened her grip. 'They're not unaware of these issues, brother.'

Chama appeared in no way offended by Geoffrey's outburst. 'From the moment these habitats were conceived, we knew that the elephants would need surrogate families to provide a developmental context. So we devised the best way to provide that surrogacy. From the time they were embryos, these animals have grown with neuromachinery in their heads. That shouldn't horrify you, should it?'

'Not necessarily – but it depends what you do with that machinery,' Geoffrey said.

'These elephants need a socialising context,' Gleb responded. 'So we provide it. The neuromachines drop hallucinations into their minds via direct activation of the visual, auditory and olfactory modules. We create figments – in other words, a ghost-herd – to provide stimulus and guidance. The elephants move in augmented reality, just as we do when we ching.'

'The difference is we know that figments are figments. Elephants don't have the cognitive apparatus to make that distinction.'

'If they did, the figments would be pointless,' said Chama.

'The figments are computer-generated, but they're based on observations of millions of hours of the social dynamics in real herds,' Gleb said. 'The same database reassures us that the dwarves' responses are fully in line with what would be expected if the figments were real. These are not developmentally impoverished creatures.'

'Well, if you've no qualms—'

'I didn't say we've achieved shining perfection,' Gleb countered.

'Computer-generated figments may provide some kind of stabilising framework,' Geoffrey conceded, choosing his words with tightrope precision, 'but elephants are individuals. They have memories, emotions. They can't be modelled by mindless software. Maybe these dwarves won't grow into monsters. But they won't turn into fully socialised elephants either.'

'No,' Chama agreed. 'But you could help matters so that they do.'

'Help you? I'm on the verge of pushing for your extradition on the grounds of Schedule One biocrimes!'

'We're aware of your work,' Gleb said. 'We've read your papers. Some of them are quite good.' He allowed this calculated slight to hang in the air before continuing, 'We know what you've been doing with the Amboseli herds.'

'If you know my work,' Geoffrey said, 'then you should have guessed that I wouldn't be too keen on any of this.'

'We also saw that you might be able to provide a possible solution,' Chama said.

Geoffrey hooked a finger into his belt. 'This I'm fascinated to hear.'

'We know of your matriarch, Matilda – we've followed her with passive ching. She's magnificent. She also has neuromachinery, as do most of your elephants.'

'As a monitoring tool, nothing else.'

'But the same neuromachinery, with a few configuration resets, could provide an aug layer.'

'I'm not sure where you're going with this.' But he was surer than he cared to admit, even to himself.

'These dwarf elephants already interact with hallucinations,' Gleb said. 'Instead of being computer-generated fictions, why couldn't they be the ching figments of Matilda and her clan? There's no reason why Matilda and her elephants couldn't perceive the Lunar dwarves as being physically present in the basin, as another family or group of orphans in need of adoption. By the same token, the Lunar dwarves could experience real-time interaction with genuine Amboseli elephants, as if they were here, on the Moon.'

Geoffrey didn't need to think through the technical implications. Chama and Gleb had undoubtedly considered every possible wrinkle. He shook his head sadly.

'Even if it could be done ... it wouldn't work. My elephants have never encountered dwarves, and your elephants have never encountered fully grown adults. They wouldn't know what to make of each other.'

'The size differential doesn't matter,' Chama said. 'It can be edited out via the ching, along with the morphological differences between the two populations. Each group would perceive the other as being perfectly normal. This can be done, Geoffrey. It's *beyond* trivial.'

'I'm sorry,' he said. 'It's taken me years to establish a bond of trust with Matilda and her family. I can't betray that trust by manipulating their basic experience of reality.'

Chama wasn't giving up. 'From Matilda's point of view – from the point of view of her whole family – it would be a minor detail in the scheme of things. Three new elephants, that's all. Orphans are routinely adopted by families, aren't they?'

'And sometimes left to die,' Geoffrey said.

'But it does happen – it's not something strange and alien by elephant standards,' Gleb said. 'Meanwhile, all the other complex herd inter-actions would proceed perfectly normally. The benefit to the orphans, however, would be incalculable. Having grown up in a stabilising frame-work, the orphans would then be in a position to mentor a second generation of Lunar dwarves through to adulthood. Before very long, we would have the basis of an entirely independent and self-perpetuating elephant society, here on the Moon.'

'By assisting us,' Chama said, 'you can be part of something heroic.'

'The Green Efflorescence?'

'Put that aside for now,' Gleb said. 'Just think of these elephants, and what they could become. What wonders. What companionship.'

'Companionship?' Geoffrey did his best not to sneer. 'As pets, you mean?'

Chama shook his head. 'As cognitive equals. Think of all the crimes we've committed against their kind, down all the blood-red centuries. The atrocities, the injustices. The carnage and the cruelty. Now think of us giving them the stars in return.'

'As what? Recompense?'

'It wouldn't begin to balance our misdeeds,' Chama said. Then a softness entered his voice. 'But it would be something.'

The old place, Sunday was relieved to see, wasn't as busy as she had feared. 'Any chance of a table in the Japanese module?' she asked as they stooped into the dingy, angular, off-white interior of the International Space Station.

'Follow me,' said a blue-boiler-suited staffer, shoulders embroidered with the patches of various barely remembered space agencies.

It had been Sunday's idea for them all to meet up again, Chama and Gleb included, when they were done with their day's work. The zookeepers could be overwhelming until you built up sufficient exposure tolerance. Sunday had passed that point years ago: the wilder excesses of their starry-eyed idealism now ghosted through her like a flux of neutrinos.

Besides, it was about time she broke something else to Geoffrey: the Akinyas were already embroiled.

'So,' she said, when they were on the first round of drinks, 'what did you think of Chama and Gleb?'

'They've achieved a lot,' Geoffrey said. 'I don't necessarily approve of all of it, but I can't deny the trouble they've gone to, or the risks they've taken.'

'But you're still uneasy about the whole Pan thing,' Jitendra said, cradling a huge stein of beer.

'I'm not big on cults or cultists, I'm afraid.'

'Look,' Sunday said, 'there's something that might put things in a different light. Like it or not, we're already involved.'

'Who's "we"?'

'Us. The family. I'm talking ancient history now, but it's the truth. Have you heard of a woman called Lin Wei?'

Geoffrey made no visible effort to search his memory. 'Can't say I have.'

'She's the Prime Pan, the woman who started the whole movement way back when. Lot of radical thinkers around then. Extropians. Trans-humanists. Long-lifers. The Clock of the Long Now. The Mars Society. A dozen other space-advocacy types, with – on the face of it – not a lot to agree on. Lin Wei still got them all to sit down and agree on common ground. Some of them said no thanks and went their own way. But Lin found points of agreement with others, shared objectives. She was very charismatic. Out of that came the Panspermian Initiative, and the basis for the UAN.'

Geoffrey smiled nicely. 'And your point is?'

'Lin Wei and Eunice were best friends. That's my point.'

'Oh,' he said.

'Eunice was never a Pan, not on any formal level, but the connection was there right through her career. The Pans were heavy backers in something called Ocular.' She took a sip of her wine. 'You heard of it?'

'Remind me.'

'Ocular was the first step towards exoplanet colonisation. A telescope big enough to image surface features on an Earthlike planet beyond our solar system. Well, they built it – nearly. The project fell to pieces halfway through, and that was the start of the big falling out between Lin and Eunice.'

Geoffrey's interest appeared to be perking up. 'What happened?'

'Hard to say, other than that it had something to do with Mercury. That was where they were assembling the parts for the telescope and launching them into space. We were helping with the shipment of materials and know-how. Not a free lunch, though: Eunice and Lin might have been pals, but this was business. But the Pans weren't paying us directly. In return for our services, the Akinyas got to piggyback their own start-up venture on Mercury.'

'What kind of venture?'

'That's where it gets murky. I'm *in* the family and even I can't get to the bottom of what went wrong.' Sunday couldn't help but lower her voice: it was a pointless but unavoidable response. 'We built a facility there, to tap into the same solar-power grid the Pans were using for their Ocular assembly and launch plant. What we did in that facility ... well, that's not easy to say. Cover story was physics research, which makes a sort of sense: we were involved in propulsion system design, and you'd need a lot of energy to do anything worthwhile in that area. But it appears that was just a smokescreen.'

'Wish my family was half as interesting,' Jitendra said. He had brought the plastic jewels with him, and was pushing them into cryptic little configurations around the damp circle left by his stein.

'Trust me,' Sunday said, 'you really don't need a family as interesting as ours.'

'A smokescreen? For what, exactly?' Geoffrey asked.

'For bad machines,' Sunday said. 'Artilects. Like the one that got into my head when I fell down that hole. Nothing's been proved, but it looks as if we were using our means and resources to smuggle contraband artilects to Mercury, under the noses of the authorities, for the purposes of reverse engineering and duplication. Making sure we'd be ahead of the game if and when the Gearheads relaxed the ties on AI research.'

Her brother stroked a finger under his chin. 'How much of this is guesswork?'

'Lin Wei had her own suspicions, so she conducted some espionage against us,' Sunday said. 'Sent industrial spies into our organisation, found out about the artilect research. That was the start of the bad feeling: not only had we lied about our intentions, but we were developing thinking machines. Needless to say, Lin Wei took that as a grave personal insult. As well she might: it was a betrayal of a lifetime's friendship and trust. Meanwhile, the Gearheads had been following their own lines of investigation. They closed in on Mercury, aiming to make a forced inspection.'

'What happened?'

'By the time they broke into the facility it had been trashed. Deliberate sabotage, to hide any evidence of a crime. Big stink at the time; damaged us and the Pans, but we both bounced back. Ocular was the only real casualty. With the breakdown in relations between the Akinyas and the Pans, the project was left half-finished.' Sunday nodded in the vague direction of the ceiling, to the Lunar bedrock and the vacuum above their heads. 'It's still out there, still gathering data, just not as extensively as they planned.'

'And the moral of this tale?' Geoffrey asked.

'Just that we're already in bed with the Pans, brother. The marriage might not be something anyone likes to talk about now, but you can't undo history.'

'Whatever Eunice got up to, it's nothing to do with me or my elephants.'

'No, but it might have something to do with *me*,' Sunday said. 'Maybe they know stuff about Eunice I can't find out from anyone else.'

Something dawned in Geoffrey's eyes. 'So that's why we have to dine with Chama and Gleb.'

Sunday bottled up her exasperation. She was asking so little of Geoffrey: why, for once in his life, couldn't he think of the bigger picture? 'They're just bit players, brother. They don't have the keys to every Pan secret. But if we help them, maybe they can get someone else to help us. It's reciprocity.'

'That visit to the zoo didn't just happen on the spur of the moment, did it?'

Sunday noticed Chama and Gleb being shown to the table, stooping beneath the low-hanging handrails and equipment lockers bolted to what was now the ceiling, but which had once been just another usable surface of the ISS. Sunday and Jitendra budged up to make room for the zookeepers.

Chama leaned in and reached for Geoffrey's hand. 'Good to see you again!' he said, grinning broadly.

Geoffrey returned the handshake, but his response was dour. 'Nice to see you, too.'

Gleb was no longer wearing his laboratory overcoat, and Chama had divested his waistcoat pockets of some of their bulkier contents. Other than that they hadn't changed much since the meeting in the zoo.

'So, Jitendra,' Sunday said brightly, while Chama and Gleb buried their faces in the drinks menu, 'any news on Eunice?'

'Sunday . . .' Geoffrey said.

She fixed on a puzzled expression. 'What?'

'I'm not sure that's something we really ought to be discussing in public.'

'Chama and Gleb have already confided in us about their own work,' Sunday said. 'The least we can do is return the favour, wouldn't you say?'

'Right,' Geoffrey said, shooting her a look that let her know exactly what he thought about that.

Chama looked up. 'We don't want to cause any awkwardness.'

'My brother's referring to some family business, not a state secret,' Sunday said. 'And I don't think there will be any harm at all in you knowing about it.'

Jitendra smiled awkwardly. 'Maybe I've got something. Possibly. While you were out, I decided to sniff around Pythagoras, see what I could find. Ching resolution isn't ideal – not enough public eyes on that part of the Moon to give seamless coverage. Which is a bit of a problem if you're trying to do some amateur sleuthing—'

'Which we're not,' Geoffrey said firmly.

'But encouraging in another sense,' Jitendra went on, 'as it confirms what we suspected all along: any tracks Eunice put down there in 2059 won't have been disturbed in the meantime.' He beamed, deliciously pleased at his own cleverness. 'Well, they have been and they haven't.'

He shoved aside the condiments, pushed the coloured gems into a huddle and voked a rectangular image onto the table. It was filled with the silver-grey, gritty, deep-shadowed terrain of the high-latitude Lunar landscape. Cross-haired and annotated with coordinates, the image must have been shot from some high-flying satellite.

'Close-up of the interior of Pythagoras crater, time-stamped about eight weeks ago,' Jitendra said. 'Recent enough for our purposes.'

'Have you found the crash point?' Sunday asked.

'That and more.' He laced fingers and cracked knuckles. 'Let me zoom in for you.'

Gleb said, 'The crash point of what?'

'Eunice landed – or crashed – in this crater one hundred and three years ago,' Sunday told him. 'It's looking as if she's left us something related to that incident.'

The rectangle stayed the same size, but now the image had enlarged to reveal the whitish, many-armed star – not exactly a crater, more a frozen splash – where something had splatted onto the Lunar surface. The star was elongated and asymmetric, as if the impacting object had skipped in obliquely. There was even a smaller blemish to one side of it, as if the object had bounced once before coming to rest.

'It looks bad, but we know it was a survivable impact,' Jitendra said.

'No trace of a ship, though,' Geoffrey said, reluctantly succumbing to curiosity. 'You sure it's the right place?'

'Nowhere else fits. The ship isn't there because it was recovered by that Indian salvage crew.' Jitendra made the image zoom in again, jabbing his finger at the tabletop. 'They had their own ship – here's where they kicked up soil on landing, and here are their foot- and rover prints, scribbled all over Eunice's crater, fresh now as when they were made. That's all, though. No one's been back to that landing site in a century.'

'What about Eunice's long walk out?' Sunday asked.

'We can follow her all the way out of the crater. Hers are the only footprints anywhere else in Pythagoras.'

The view lurched to the right, tracking east. Sunday made out the prints, following an arrow-straight line with only occasional detours to avoid obstacles. It was a long, monotonous message in Morse code:

stretches of hyphens, where she had been hop-skipping, interspersed with sequences of dots where she had slowed her progress to a walk. When Jitendra zoomed out again, reducing the prints to the faintest of scratches across the image, she understood how far Eunice had been forced to travel.

A tiny human presence, a bag of air and warmth lost in the barren immensity of the Lunar landscape, like a bug crossing a runway.

'We can follow these prints all the way to the wall and over and out, to where she met the Chinese rescue party,' Jitendra said. 'You can still see the hairpin where they turned the rover around and drove back home, with Eunice aboard. It all checks out.'

Sunday exhaled. 'OK. So her story checks out. Is that all you've got?'

'There is something *slightly* weird.' He let the image scroll and zoom again, once more picking up the line of prints. 'We're just over thirty kilometres from the touchdown site here,' Jitendra said. 'And suddenly there's *this*.'

'Oh yes,' Chama said.

North of the prints – maybe a hundred metres – lay an area of blasted soil where a ship had touched down. Sunday could see clearly the cruciform pattern of depressions made by its landing legs.

There were footprints as well – two rows, running from the ship to the original line of footprints and back again. It didn't take a forensics expert to note that the spacing of the prints was similar, maybe identical, to Eunice's walking pattern.

Where the prints intersected the original line, there was a region of scuffed soil. For about five metres, Eunice's original prints had been erased again.

'She went back,' Sunday said. 'Grief. She actually went back.'

Jitendra nodded. 'That's what it looks like. *After* the Chinese had rescued her – and we could be talking weeks, months, years, who the hell knows – she returned to this exact spot and did something.'

'Looks as if she dug up the ground,' Gleb said. 'Either to recover something she buried there the last time, or to bury something new. Can you dig back and find older imagery?'

'Gleb's right,' Sunday said. 'If we can find a view taken after she was rescued but before the fresh prints came in, it'll help us narrow things down.'

'I'm searching,' Jitendra said. 'But I'm also being careful. Don't want to leave my grubby fingerprints all over an image trawl.'

'No one else is following this trail,' Geoffrey said. 'Or at least they weren't, until my sister started talking about it to anyone who'd listen.'

'What we really need to do is get out there, see what's under that soil,' Sunday said.

'Might be a bit problematic,' Jitendra said. 'Pythagoras is under Chinese Lunar Administration now. You don't mess with the Ghost Wall.'

'Good job we won't be doing that, then,' Geoffrey said.

'Aren't you even remotely curious?' Sunday asked.

'It's all supposition, based on a few smudges.'

'We'd know for sure if we went there,' she said. 'Take a couple of spades, maybe rent an excavator – how long do you think it would take us?'

'With the Chinese breathing down our necks, wondering what we're prospecting for? Exactly how long do you think it would be before word of that got back to the cousins?'

'Going through official channels isn't the way to do this,' Jitendra said.

'I have a suggestion,' Chama said. He looked at his husband, Gleb giving only the tiniest of encouraging nods. Their drinks arrived. Chama made a point of swallowing a finger's width from his before speaking again. 'Whatever happens, this is going to be a possible arrest-and-detention scenario involving our good friends the Chinese. Now, while that's not something either of us would rush into, it's not like we don't have prior experience in that area.'

'Doesn't mean they'll let you go the next time,' Geoffrey said.

'It's not like we're trafficking. We'll just be doing some digging on Chinese soil: hardly the crime of the century, is it?' Gleb was speaking now. 'The Initiative isn't without influence in Chinese circles, and you've got June Wing in your corner. The right words, the right persuasion, we'll be back on the street soon enough.'

'Or not,' Geoffrey said.

'We'll accept that risk.' Chama leaned forwards, elbows on the table. 'You find out what's under that soil. We get something from you in return. How about it, elephant man?'

He shook his head. 'We went over this already. I'm not getting involved.'

'All we'd want in return,' Gleb said, 'is to offer you the chance to help with our dwarves.'

'I'm already being emotionally blackmailed by my family, thanks – I don't need another dose.'

'It's really nothing, what we're asking,' Chama said reasonably. He took another gulp of his beer and wiped foam onto the back of his hand.

'The risk's all on our side. No one else needs to know about your involvement.'

'There's still the small matter of ethical oversight,' Geoffrey said.

'Oh, screw that,' Gleb said. 'For a start, they'd have to learn of the existence of the dwarves – and we're not ready to go public.'

Geoffrey looked relieved, as if he'd finally found an insuperable objection. 'Then it can't be done. Even if we got the neuromachinery communicating, someone, somewhere, will want to know why there's so much ching traffic between my elephants and the Descrutinised Zone.'

'We can get round that,' Chama said. 'The Initiative already has more than enough surplus quangle paths between Earth and the Moon. Not unbreakable, of course, but the next best thing.'

'You're going to have to work pretty hard to think of something they haven't already covered,' Sunday said.

'Other than the fact that if I take part in this, that makes me a criminal as well.'

'No one need know,' Gleb countered. 'Anyway, in the scheme of things you'd still have the moral high ground, wouldn't you? You were just presented with a situation, a fait accompli, which you agreed to improve.' He looked at his husband and said something that the earpieces didn't pick up: some language or dialect too obscure for translation.

'I'm sure there could be financial incentives as well,' Chama said, after a few moments' reflection. 'No promises, but ... it wouldn't be out of the question. You're reliant on handouts from your family right now, aren't you?'

'My funding flows from a number of sources,' Geoffrey said, glaring at Sunday.

Chama shrugged. 'But I'm sure more autonomy would always be welcome.'

Sunday saw her chance. 'While we're thrashing out terms, I'd like some access to your archives.'

'What exactly are you after?' Chama enquired.

Sunday hesitated before answering. 'My grandmother knew your founder, Lin Wei. They went to the same school, in what used to be independent Tanzania, before the Federation. Here.' And she cleared part of the table to voke her own image, which was of two girls of similar age. One was her grandmother. The other was Lin Wei.

Lin Wei wore a red dress, white stockings and black shoes.

Sunday glanced at her brother, nodded once. It was clear from the look in her eyes that she had also made the connection with the

112

mysterious girl at the scattering, the stranger with the unresolvable ching bind.

'Eunice knew the Prime Pan?' Gleb asked, astonished. 'How could this not have come to light before?'

'I only discovered it recently myself,' Sunday said, shifting on her seat. This was a lie, but in the scheme of things only a white one. Or perhaps off-white.

'It's a part of our family history that's been swept under the carpet,' she went on. 'Same on your side, by the sound of things. They were good friends, and they ended up collaborating on the Mercury project. But Eunice abused Lin Wei's trust somehow. I don't know how much contact they had afterwards.'

'Eunice only just died,' Geoffrey said.

'Mm, yes,' Sunday said. 'I had noticed.'

'What I mean is, she wasn't *that* old. Not by modern standards. So if she went to school with this Lin Wei person, what's to say Lin Wei isn't still alive? Never mind the archive, never mind the Pans – you could just ask her directly.'

'I'm afraid not,' Chama said sadly. 'Lin Wei *was* the Prime Pan. She died decades ago.'

Sunday nodded. 'That's what I heard as well. I think she drowned, or something horrible like that.'

CHAPTER SEVEN

When Chama's ching request arrived the following morning, Sunday found herself putting down the coffee pot with a highly specific sense of dread. She accepted the bind with a profound and familiar foreboding.

'I have some news,' Chama said. 'Probably the kind I ought to break to you first, so you can come round to my side and explain things to the others.'

'This is going to turn out to have something to do with last night's conversation, isn't it?'

Boots tramped on metal flooring outside. Someone knocked on the door, vigorously.

'Brother!' Sunday called. 'Can you get that for me?'

Geoffrey went to the door and returned to the kitchen with Gleb. The zookeeper looked harried.

'This is not good,' he said.

'Chama,' Sunday asked the figment, 'why are you chinging in from outside the Zone?'

'Because, given my current circumstances, it would be very difficult to ching in from anywhere else.'

Chama was strapped into a heavy black seat, sunk deep in its padded embrace. He wore the brass-coloured body part of a modern ultralight spacesuit, with the helmet stowed elsewhere.

'You're aboard a spacecraft,' Sunday said. The tag coordinates were updating constantly, the last few digits a tumbling blur. 'Chama, why are you aboard a spacecraft?'

'Ever heard of striking while the iron's hot?'

'This is very bad,' Gleb said, wedging his earpiece into place. 'Sunday, voke me figment privilege, please. I want to be able to see and talk to him as well.'

Sunday already knew the answer to her next question, but she asked it anyway. 'Chama, are you planning something that might upset the Chinese?'

'That's the general drift of things,' Chama said, while Sunday voked the ching settings to allow everyone else to join in the conversation.

'Your husband is here,' Sunday said. 'He's not happy.'

'Gleb, I'm sorry, but this wasn't something we could sit around and discuss. You've always been more cautious than me. You'd have told me to put it off until later, to give it time to settle in.'

'For good reason!' Gleb shouted.

'Had to be now or never. Look, I talked it over with the Pans in Tiamaat. I have ... tacit authorisation. They'll bail me out, whatever happens.'

'You mean they'll give it their best shot!'

'They're very, very good at this sort of thing, Gleb. Everything's going to be fine.'

'Whose ship is that?' Sunday asked. 'And how secure is this ching bind?'

'The ship's Pan-registered,' Chama said. 'It's a short-range hopper, barely has the delta-vee to pull itself out of Lunar gravity but perfectly fine for ballistic transfers, and the occasional illicit touchdown. We've used it many times.'

'And the bind?' she persisted.

'Quangled. So it's very unlikely anyone's going to be listening in, even the Chinese. Of course, they'll be trying ... but it'll take a while to unravel the quanglement, and we have surplus paths lined up.' He flashed a grin. 'All the same, you should still know what you're dealing with. Basically, I'm about to do something very naughty indeed.'

'No,' Sunday said. 'We should never have discussed this, not even as an outside possibility. It was an *idea*, Chama, not a binding commitment.'

'Want to join in? There's enough capacity on this path to handle a few piggybackers.'

'This is Akinya business,' Geoffrey said. 'It's nothing to do with you.'

'Stopped being Akinya business when the two of you blabbed about it, elephant boy. Anyway, I'm doing you miserable, self-absorbed Akinyas a favour by putting my neck on the block here.' Chama's figment glanced to one side as a recorded voice began talking in a firm but not unfriendly voice. 'Oh, here we go. First alert. Just a polite request to alter my course. Nothing too threatening yet; I haven't even crossed the Ghost Wall.'

'Turn around now,' Sunday said.

'Bit late for that, I'm afraid. Locked myself out of the avionics – couldn't change course if I wanted to.'

'That's insane,' she answered.

'No, just very, very determined. Oh, wait. Second warning. Sterner this time. Notification of countermeasures and reprisals. Gosh, isn't *that* exciting?' His figment reached up and grasped the helmet that had been out of sight until then. 'I'm not expecting them to shoot me out of the sky. Be silly not to take precautions, though.'

He lowered the helmet to within a few centimetres of its neck ring and let the docking magnets snatch it home, the helmet and ring engaging with a series of rapid clunks and whirrs. Save for a swan-necked column curving up from the nape to the crown, the helmet was transparent.

'But you can come with me, Sunday. All of you can.' Chama tapped commands into the chunky rubber-sealed button pad on his gauntlet cuff. 'Be quick about it, though. Not going to have all the time in the world here, even if they let me get to the burial spot. Oh, I can see the Ghost Wall now. Very impressive. Very Chinese. Does anyone else maintain a consensual border hallucination even halfway as impressive?'

Sunday cut in on Chama's monologue. 'What you were saying, about this being untraceable? Are you absolutely, one-hundred-per-cent sure about that?'

'No,' Chama said, giving a visible shrug through the tight-fitting suit. 'How could I be? But you're in the Zone, Sunday. Power blocs like the Chinese, they hate the Zone precisely because they *can't* backtrack signals all the way to their source. And the fact that they loathe and detest us for that is the best possible guarantee I can give that they're not along for the ride. So live a little. Ching out with me.'

'Did you bring proxies?' Gleb asked.

'Two. All I could squeeze in. The rest of you can go passive.'

Sunday hadn't thought about proxies. 'We're going to have words about this, when you get back,' she said.

'Spoken like a true friend. Oh – third warning.' Chama's figment jolted violently, as if, in ignorance of the absence of atmosphere, his ship had hit clear-air turbulence. 'Interesting,' Chama said, his voice coming through distinctly even with the helmet on. 'They're trying to wrestle control from my own avionics. Interesting but not remotely good enough. Going to have to up their game if they want to get anywhere.'

The ship settled down. Sunday inhaled a deep breath. 'Give me a few moments.'

'I'm not going anywhere,' Chama said.

'Couldn't you have stopped this?' she demanded of Gleb.

'He was up and out of our apartment before I realised what was going on. You think I actually approve of this?'

She cooled her anger. Taking it out on the other zookeeper wasn't the right thing to do. All of a sudden she realised how hard this must be for Gleb, with his husband out there, taunting the most powerful national entity on the Moon.

'Well, there are four of us, and two proxies,' Jitendra said. 'I'll go passive. Gleb can take one of the machines.'

'I'll manage without embodiment,' Gleb said. 'If I had arms and legs, I might be tempted to strangle someone.'

'If there's any treasure under that soil,' Geoffrey said, looking at his sister, 'it belongs to us. I guess you and I ought to have bodies.'

There were four open ching binds: two for proxy embodiment, two for passive ching. Sunday assigned one of the proxy binds to herself, leaving the other for Geoffrey. Jitendra and Gleb could take care of their own binds.

'I'm going in,' she said. 'The rest of you'd better be there when I arrive.'

She voked for ching. For a moment, one that was far too familiar to be distressing, she felt her soul sliding out of her body, not in any specific direction but in all directions at once, as if she was an image of herself that was losing focus, smearing into quantum haze. That was the neuromachinery taking hold, shunting sensory and proprioceptive inputs to the waiting robot, halfway around the Moon.

And then everything was sharp again, and she was somewhere else, in a different body, in a hurtling spacecraft that had just transgressed the sovereign airspace of the Special Lunar Autonomous Region of the People's Republic of China.

She was strapped to a wall mounting, facing Chama.

'I'm here,' Sunday said. 'Now what do I have to do to get you to turn this ship around?'

'I already told you,' Chama said, angling his glassy visor to look at the proxy, 'there's nothing to be done now except enjoy the trip.'

Sunday felt pinned inside something that didn't quite fit her body, as if she'd been forced into a stiff, partially rusted suit of armour. Then something *gave* – something relaxing in her brain – and the final transition to embodiment occurred.

She studied her new anatomy. The cheapest kind of mass-produced Aeroflot unit, little more than an android chassis, all metallic-blue tubing and bulbous universal joints. She was a mechanical stick figure, like a hydraulic car jack that had decided to unfold itself and walk upright.

To her right, another proxy started moving. It was metallic red, but otherwise very similar.

It looked at Chama, then at Sunday. The head was an angular pineapple, faceted with wraparound sensors and caged in alloy crash bars.

'Well,' Geoffrey said, 'I'm here.' And he moved one of the arms, lifting it up to examine the wrist and hand and elegant, dextrous human-configuration fingers and thumb. Geoffrey's actions were wooden, but that would soon wear off. It wasn't as if her brother had never ridden a proxy before; he was just out of practice.

'Where exactly are we?' Sunday asked Chama.

'Good question,' Geoffrey said. 'To be quickly followed by: what the hell are we doing here, and why am I involved?'

'Well inside Chinese sovereign airspace,' Chama said. 'Descending over Pythagoras, fifty-five kays from the burial spot. We should be there in about six minutes.'

Sunday appraised her surroundings. She'd been in bigger shower cubicles. The hopper was about as small as spacecraft got, before they stopped being spacecraft and became escape pods or very roomy space-suits.

'Whatever's under the soil,' Geoffrey said, 'it's not your concern, Chama.'

The ship bucked and swayed again, the golems clattering in their wall restraints. Chama cursed and worked the manual joystick set into the armrest of his chair, jerking it violently until the ride smoothed out. 'They're cunning,' he said. 'I'll give them that. Found a back door into the command software even I didn't know about.'

'I thought you said you didn't have manual control,' Sunday said.

'We'll talk about it afterwards,' Chama said again. 'Where are Gleb and Jitendra, by the way?'

Jitendra's head and upper torso popped into existence in the cabin. 'Here.'

'And me,' Gleb added.

'Took your sweet time arriving,' Sunday said.

'Bandwidth was tighter than you said,' Jitendra replied. 'Kept being put on hold.'

'That's the Chinese,' Chama said, 'trying to break the quangle paths, or squeeze us on bandwidth.'

'They can do that?' Sunday asked.

'Not difficult, if you're a government. Diplomatic-priority trans-missions, that kind of thing. Flood the bandwidth with a pipe-load of government-level signals that *must* be routed ahead of routine traffic. It's very clever.' Sunday caught a smile through Chama's helmet. 'Fortunately, we have some even cleverer people on our side. Uh-oh.'

'What, in this context,' Geoffrey said, 'does "uh-oh" mean?'

'Means I've just been given my final warning,' Chama said happily. 'Border enforcement interceptors are on their way.'

'Could be a bluff,' Sunday said.

'Except that radar also has incoming returns, heading our way. Moving too quickly to be crewed vehicles. Probably just armed drones.'

'Armed drones,' Geoffrey said. 'I can't tell you how good that makes me feel.'

'Deterrence,' Chama replied dismissively, as if he'd said something very naive. 'That's all it'll be. No one shoots things down any more. We're not on Earth now.'

An impact warning started to blare. Those parts of the walling not taken up with windows, instruments and equipment modules began to strobe scarlet. Sunday saw Jitendra and Gleb flicker and vanish, and almost immediately felt puppet strings striving to yank her back into her own body, in the Descrutinised Zone.

She was there, for a heartbeat: standing up in her living room, in the middle of domestic clutter. Then she was back in the hopper, and her friends had returned as well.

'OK,' Chama said. 'Change of plan. I'm taking us in steeper and harder than I was intending. This is all good fun, isn't it?'

'I'm in the middle of a major diplomatic incident,' Jitendra said marvellingly. 'This was so not in my plans for the day when I woke up this morning.'

'You're not in the middle of anything,' Chama corrected. 'You're observing. There's nothing they'll be able to pin on you for that. Oh, *please* shut up.'

He was talking to the hopper. It silenced its alarms and ceased strobing its warning lights.

Lunar surface scrolled past with steadily increasing speed as the vehicle lost altitude. Though it was day over Pythagoras, the crater's high altitude meant that the shadows remained ink-black and elongated. There was little sign that people had ever come to this pumice-grey place; no glints of metal or plastic signifying habitation or even the arduous toiling of loyal machines.

But there were tracks. Against the ancient talcum of the surface, footprints and vehicle marks were immediately obvious to the eye. On Earth, they might have been taken for lava flows or dried-up river beds. On the Moon, they could only mean that something had perambulated or walked there.

Sunday had to adjust her preconceptions when she realised that the curiously stuttered vehicle tracks she was trying to make sense of were in fact footprints, and that the hopper was merely hundreds of metres above the Moon's surface rather than several kilometres. They had come down much faster than she had thought.

'There it is,' Chama said, pointing ahead. 'The place where your granny, came back – see the scuffed-up ground?'

'I can't see anything,' Sunday said.

'Voke out the hopper. You have authorisation.'

Sunday issued the command – it hadn't occurred to her before – and most of the hopper vanished. All that remained was a neon sketch of its basic outline, a three-dimensional wedge-shaped prism with Chama cradled somewhere near the middle. The golems, and Gleb and Jitendra's disembodied heads and torsos, were flying along for the ride.

And now she could indeed see the disturbed ground where Eunice had returned, some unguessable interval after her long walk from the 2059 crash site. Everything was the same as in the aerial image Jitendra had shown them in the ISS: the touchdown marks from another ship, the hairpin of footprints where someone had crossed to Eunice's original trail and then headed back to the ship. The area of dug-up regolith, like a patch of dirt where a horse had rolled on its back.

Nothing else. Nothing to suggest that anyone had beaten them to this place.

'This is where it gets interesting,' Chama said. 'Here come the interceptors.'

Sunday tensed. She wasn't in any conceivable danger, but Chama's confidence might well be misplaced. It had been decades since any kind of lethal, state-level action had occurred between two spacefaring powers ... but that didn't mean it couldn't happen again, given sufficient provocation.

'How many?' Gleb asked.

'Three,' Chama said. 'What I expected. Small autonomous drones. Demon-cloaked. You wanna see them? I can override the Chinese aug if you don't, but they've gone to so much trouble, almost be a shame not to—'

The drones came in fast, swerving at the last instant to avoid ramming the hopper. In their uncloaked form they were too fast and fleet to make out as anything other than bright moving sparks. They might have weapons, or they might rely purely on their swiftness and agility to ram any moving object. Whatever they were, beyond any reasonable doubt they were rigorously legal. They might be operating within Chinese sovereign airspace, but they would still need to abide by the wider non-proliferation treaties governing all spacefaring entities.

There was, however, nothing to stop them projecting fearsome aug layers around themselves. The demon-cloaks made them look much larger than the hopper. Each was a grinning, ghoulish head, styled in Chinese fashion, trailing banners of luminous fire behind it. As the drones whipped around the descending hopper, harassing it but never quite coming into contact, their fire-tails tangled into a whirling multi-coloured corkscrew. One demon was a pale, sickly green, another a frigid blue. The third was the liverish red of a slavering tongue. Their eyes were white and wild, furious under beetled brows. They looked like Pekinese dogs turned rabid and spectral.

'Cease your descent,' a voice said, cutting across the cabin. 'Do not attempt to land. You will be escorted back into neutral Lunar airspace. Immediate failure to cooperate will be construed as hostile action. Hostile action will be countered with sanctioned military force.'

The corkscrewing demons were getting closer now, spiralling ever tighter around the hopper.

'Do what they say,' Gleb pleaded.

'Just words,' Chama said. 'Nothing I wasn't expecting.' But at the same time he reached up and touched his neck ring, as if to reassure himself that the helmet really was engaged and pressure-tight.

'Cease your descent,' the voice said again. 'This is your final warning.'

'I think they mean it,' Sunday said.

'They're bluffing. Last thing they want to do is shoot down some idiot tourist who just happened to key the wrong coordinates into their autopilot.'

'I think, by now, they probably realise they're not dealing with an idiot tourist,' Geoffrey said.

'Guess that's possible,' Chama admitted.

The blue demon rammed the hopper. As the demon veered away, apparently undamaged, the hopper went into a slow tumble. Chama released the joystick, letting the avionics stabilise the vehicle. They didn't do much good. Just as the hopper was regaining orientation and control, another demon would come in and knock it back into a tumble. The knocks were becoming more violent, and the ground was rushing up towards them like the bottom of an elevator shaft. The demons were coming in two and three at a time now, jackhammering against the hull. The tumble was totally uncontrolled, the ground spinning in and out of view several times a second.

Chama started saying something. It might have been, 'Brace!' but Sunday couldn't be sure. All she knew was that an instant later Chama wasn't there. Where the seat had been was an impact cocoon, a cushioned, mushroom-white adaptive shell that had enveloped both the seat and its occupant in an eye-blink.

Everything went blank. There was a moment of limbo and then she was back in her apartment again. Only for another moment, though. The ching bind had been interrupted, but not severed. She fell back into the golem and the golem was out of its harness, lying in a limb-knotted tangle against one of the equipment modules on the opposite wall. The hopper was back to solidity now, no longer a neon sketch of itself. Jitendra's head and torso phased in out of view, cross-hatched with cartoon static to indicate bandwidth compression. Gleb flickered. Geoffrey's golem was hanging out of its harness.

'That went well,' Chama said.

The impact cocoon had folded itself away and Chama was unbuckling. Upside down, he dropped at Lunar acceleration onto what had been the ceiling. Jitendra resumed solidity. Geoffrey extricated his golem from its harness. Sunday tried to move her own proxy body and found her blue metal limbs working normally.

'They took us out,' she said, amazed.

'Tactical disablement,' Chama replied, thoroughly nonplussed. 'Very well done, too. We're still airtight, and the collision was within survivability parameters.' He grabbed a yellow handhold and propelled himself across to the hopper's door. 'Hold on – I'm venting. No point in saving the air now.'

The air fled the hopper in a single dying bark, dragging with it a fluff cloud of silvery dust and spangling human detritus. Moving in vacuum now, Chama operated the door's bulky release mechanism. The door opened onto a view like a late Rothko: rectangle of black sky below, rectangle of dazzling bright Lunar ground above.

The golem's vision system dropped software filters over the scene until the ground dimmed to a tolerable grey.

Chama was first out. He sprang through the door and fell to the surface, landing catlike. Sunday followed, Chama already bounding to the other side of the hopper by the time her golem touched dirt.

Sunday looked back just as Geoffrey's machine spidered out of the upturned hopper, followed closely by the bobbing, balloon-like head and shoulders of Jitendra's figment, and then Gleb's. Jitendra and Gleb were merely moving viewpoints, entirely dependent on Chama and the golems to supply their ching binds with a constantly updating environment. The demon-cloaked drones were still swarming overhead, circling and helixing above the spot where Chama had crashed.

'This way,' he said, breaking into a seven-league sprint, flinging his arms wide with each awesome stride. 'Can't be too far north of where we came down.'

The golems, built for durability rather than speed, had difficulty keeping up with the bounding figure. Chama had a spade strapped to the back of his suit, of the perfectly mundane common-or-garden type. He must have put it in one of the hopper's external stowage lockers, ready to grab as soon as they were down. There was something else, too: a grey alloy cylinder, tucked under his life-support backpack.

Some new order must have reached the demons, for they aborted their spiralling flight and rocketed away in three directions, streaking towards the crater wall that marked the effective horizon. But they were not leaving. A kilometre or so away, they whipped around and came back, streaking at man-height across the crater floor, demon-cloak faces tipped forward, eyes glaring, tongues rabid and drooling.

They screamed and howled through the aug.

'Keep moving,' Chama called. 'This is just intimidation. They won't touch us.'

'I certainly feel adequately intimidated!' Jitendra said.

Sunday flinched as the red demon blocked her path, its doglike face as wide as a house. The cloak was nebulous; through its billowing, flaming translucence she made out the hovering kernel of the drone, balanced on spiking micro-jets.

'Do not move,' said the same commanding voice that they had heard in the hopper. 'You are under arrest. You will remain in this area for processing by border-enforcement officials.'

'Keep moving,' Chama said again.

Chama had his own demon intent on blocking his progress: the blue one. Chama wasn't stopping, though, and the demon was actually backing up, not letting itself get too close to what it undoubtedly registered as a warm, breathing, easily damaged human presence. The green demon was fixating on Geoffrey. None of them was paying any attention at all to Jitendra or Gleb, their figments all but undetectable.

But if the blue demon was unwilling to obstruct Chama, the other two had no compunctions about blocking the golems. Some governing intelligence had already determined that these were disposable machines. The monstrous face leered and glared as it anticipated Sunday's movements, ducking and diving to either side like a keen goalkeeper.

Then, without warning, the demon-cloaks vanished.

A man was standing in front of her now, hands clasped behind his back, with the hovering drone at his rear. He wore a neat platinum-grey business suit of modern cut over a white shirt and pearl necktie. His shoes failed to merge with the soil, their soles hovering a centimetre or so above the dirt. He was young, handsome and plausible.

'Good morning,' the man said, agreeably enough. 'I am Mister Pei, from the Department of Border Control. Would you be so kind as to remain where you are, until this matter can be resolved? Officials will be with you very shortly.'

Another copy of Mister Pei had appeared in front of Geoffrey, presumably reciting the same spiel. There might be a real human being behind these figments, or it might still be some kind of automated response.

'I don't think so, Mister Pei,' Sunday said. Whatever trouble she was in now, she reckoned, couldn't be made much worse by trying to keep up with Chama.

She made another effort to slip past the drone.

'I must insist,' Mister Pei said. His voice was firm but pleasant, his words tempered with a regretful smile.

'Please let me past.'

Mister Pei still had his hands behind his back. 'I must ask you not to compound matters by disobeying a perfectly reasonable request. As I said, the border officials will be here very shortly, and then processing and debriefing may commence. Would you be so good as to give me your name and location? At the moment we can't localise you more precisely than the Descrutinised Zone.'

'Then I don't think I'll bother, thanks.'

'It would be in your ultimate interests. Your accomplice will be detained shortly. Any assistance you can give us now will be taken into consideration when we evaluate the penalties for your trespass.' He smiled again, bringing his hands around to beckon for her cooperation. 'Who are you, though, and where are you chinging from? We will discover these things in due course, so you may as well tell us now.'

'I'm afraid you'll have to join the dots yourself, Mister Pei.'

'Is that an unequivocal statement of non-cooperation?'

'It sounded like one, didn't it?'

'Very well.' Mister Pei looked over his shoulder and nodded. The drone shot through him, straight at the golem. It tore off an arm and blasted the rest of the golem into the soil, where it lay twitching and useless. There was no pain, just an abrupt curtailment of sensory feedback. For a moment Sunday was looking up at the sky, until Mister Pei loomed into view again, bowing over her.

'I regret that it was necessary to take this action, but you gave us no choice.'

The drone pushed through him and spun until its gun barrel was pointed straight down at her useless body. The muzzle flashed, then everything went black.

She expected to return to the stack-module. Instead her point of view shifted to Chama's, looking down at a pair of gauntleted hands scooping aside Lunar soil with the plastic-handled garden spade. Chama was kneeling, breathing heavily. He had commenced his excavation in the middle of the area of disturbed ground and had already cut a trench big enough for a body. The suit would be assisting him, but it was still costing Chama much effort.

A duplicate Mister Pei was standing by the dig, remonstrating with Chama as another drone loitered nearby. 'I must ask you to desist. You have already brought trouble on yourself by trespassing on our territory, and by refusing to cooperate in your detention. Please do not compound matters by performing this unauthorised excavation of Chinese soil.'

Chama dumped a pile of dirt on the side of the trench. 'Or what, Mister Pei? You'll shoot me, like you shot the golems? I don't think so. I'm being observed, you know. There are witnesses.'

'We are well aware that others are participating in this severe breach of interplanetary law,' Mister Pei said. 'Rest assured that the full weight of judicial process will be brought to bear on all offenders. Now please desist from this activity.'

'I'm still here,' Gleb said.

'Me too,' Sunday added.

'So am I,' Geoffrey said.

'Present,' Jitendra said enthusiastically. 'Cosy, isn't it, inside Chama's helmet?'

Mister Pei looked aside as the two other drones caught up with the third and triangulated themselves around the digging man. There was only one Mister Pei now: the other figments must have been deemed surplus to requirements. 'Ah,' he said. 'The border officials.'

A dragon approached, snaking its way through the vacuum as if following the contours of invisible topography. It was crimson and serpentine and abundantly winged and clawed, its face whiskered and vulpine. It belched flames. Some kind of suborbital carrier lodged inside it, a rectangular vehicle with six landing legs and downward-pointing belly-thrusters.

'Very melodramatic, Mister Pei,' Sunday said.

'Think nothing of it. It is the very least we can do for our honoured foreign guests.'

'It might be an idea to dig a bit faster,' Sunday said.

A moment later she really was back in the apartment, transfixed by a bar of sunlight cutting across the coffee table. Geoffrey, Gleb and Jitendra were standing there like sleepwalkers, their minds elsewhere. The interlude lasted a second, and then she was back with Chama.

'I dropped out for a moment there,' she said. 'I think they're squeezing bandwidth again. Did anyone else feel it?'

'For a second,' Geoffrey said. 'I guess we shouldn't count—'

And then he was gone.

'Gleb and Jitendra have disappeared as well, so it's just you and me now,' Chama said. 'For as long as the quangle holds.'

'They're taking this more seriously than I expected. Have you hit anything yet?'

Chama didn't answer, too preoccupied with his digging. Mister Pei looked on, shaking his head disappointedly, as if he could envisage a million more favourable ways that this sequence of events could have unfolded, if only everyone had been reasonable and prepared to bend to the iron will of state authority.

The dragon gusted overhead, a slow-motion whip-crack. Its wings were leathery and batlike and flapped too slowly for such an absurdly vast creature. It arched its neck and roared cartoon flames. Stretching out multiple claws, it landed and quickly gathered itself into a coiled python-like mass. The dragon-cloak held for a few seconds and then dissipated as a ramp lowered down from the angled front of the border-enforcement vehicle. Suited figures ducked out, each of them with a rifle-sized weapon gripped two-handed and close to the chest. They came down the ramp in perfect lock step, like a well-drilled ballet troupe.

'I think we've made our point here,' Sunday said. 'Now might be a good time to consider surrendering.'

Chama's spade clanged against something. Sunday felt the jolt all the way through the suit, back through the tangle of ching threads linking the sensorium to her body in the Zone.

'My god,' she said.

'Why are you surprised?'

'I just am.'

'What is discovered on or beneath Chinese soil remains Chinese state property,' Mister Pei said helpfully.

Chama worked feverishly. He began to uncover whatever it was the spade had hit, even as the enforcement agents bounded overland from the transporter. They were not cloaked. Their armoured suits and weapons were intimidating enough.

'Again, I must ask you to desist,' Mister Pei said.

Chama kept working. The object, whatever it was, was coming into view. It was a rectangular box, lying lengthwise. The drones had moved forward of Mister Pei, peering down to get a better view. Chama hauled the object out of the trench and set it on the ground, between two piles of excavated soil. It was about the size of a big shoebox, plain metal in construction. Chama's thick-fingered gloves found an opening mechanism with surprising ease and the lid sprang wide. There was something inside the box, lying loose.

Mechanical junk, all gristle and wires.

'I must ask you to stand up now,' Mister Pei said as his officials gathered around Chama.

Chama looked up, taking Sunday's point of view with him. 'It's all right,' he said. 'You can arrest me now.'

'Please relinquish the item,' Mister Pei said. But Chama was already obeying. He pushed up from his kneeling position, leaving the box and its contents at his feet.

'What now?' he asked.

'Curtail the bind, please. Until you have been debriefed.'

'Curtail it yourself,' Chama said.

Mister Pei beckoned to one of the enforcement guards. The faceless guard brought his rifle around with the stock facing away from his body and went behind Chama's back. Sunday saw the guard loom on the helmet's rear-facing head-up, saw the stock swinging in like a mallet. The blow knocked Chama to the ground, stealing the breath from his lungs.

'I am afraid it will now prove necessary to apply administrative restraint,' Mister Pei said.

Chama pushed back into a kneeling position. Another of the guards came forward, unclipping a device like a miniature fire extinguisher from his belt. The guard aimed the device at Chama, then lowered the muzzle slightly, correcting aim so as not to impact any vulnerable areas of his suit. A silver-white stream hosed against Chama's chest, where the material organised itself into an obscene flattened starfish shape and began to push exploratory tentacles away from its centre of mass, searching for entry points into the suit's inner workings.

Chama strove to paw the substance away, but it globbed itself around his fingers and quickly set about working its way up the wrist, moving with a vile amoeboid eagerness.

127

'Looks like it's going to be lights out for me in moment or two,' Chama said. 'You'll all be good boys and girls until I'm back, won't you?'

There was just time for one of Mister Pei's guards to bend down and pick up the box. The guard took out the object that had been inside it and held it up for inspection, dangling it between two gloved fingers. Sunday had a second look at it then. She'd been wondering if her eyes had fooled her the first time.

But it still looked like junk.

And then the ching bind broke and she was back in the Zone.

They were all shaking. Sunday glanced at her friends and wondered why they couldn't keep it together, not look so visibly nervous in front of Gleb. Then she caught the adrenalin tremor in her own hands and knew she was just as culpable.

'It won't take them long to find out who he is,' Gleb said. 'Chama's not one for rules, but he'd still have had to file some kind of flight plan before taking out that hopper.'

Sunday exhaled heavily. 'I feel terrible. We should never have got you mixed up in all this.'

'Chama took this initiative on his own; you weren't holding a gun to his head. And it's not as if there wasn't some self-interest involved as well.'

'None of which we signed up to,' Geoffrey said.

'Shut it, brother. Now is emphatically *not* the time.'

'Sorry,' he said, and for a moment appeared willing to hold his tongue. 'But look,' he went on doggedly, 'we didn't ask Chama to put his neck on the line, and now we're worse off than we were before. We still don't know what Eunice buried, and in all likelihood we never will. And mark my words: this will break system-wide. Exactly how long do you think it'll be before the cousins put two and two together?'

Jitendra's eyes were glazed. 'I'm scrolling newsfeeds. Nothing's breaking yet.'

'Because it only happened five fucking minutes ago,' Geoffrey said.

'Maybe it won't break,' Sunday said. 'The Chinese don't publicise every incursion. They don't want to give the impression they can't police the Ghost Wall.'

'The policing looked pretty effective from where I was sitting,' Geoffrey countered. 'And what's this with you being an expert on international affairs all of a sudden?'

'No need to be snide, brother. I'm just saying things may not be as bad as you want to make them.'

'Let's hope they aren't,' Gleb said.

'Did you get a good look at whatever was in the box?' Jitendra asked brightly, as if they'd just turned the conversational page onto a happy new chapter.

Sunday shook her head. 'Not really. Just a glimpse. Looked like junk, to be honest. Some mechanical thing, like a component from a bigger machine. Could've been one of your robot parts, for all I know.'

'That's not going to get us very far,' Geoffrey said.

'Chama saw more than I did. Maybe it was enough.'

Geoffrey put his hands on the table, fingers spread as if he was about to play piano. 'OK. Let's take stock here. We just participated in a *crime*.'

Sunday had to admit that the very word had a seductive glamour. To have succeeded in committing a crime, even in the Descrutinised Zone – or from within it, at least – was a rare achievement.

'Yes,' she said. 'We did. A crime. That makes us *criminals*.' The word tasted odd in her mouth, like an obscure oath. 'But it was a small crime, in the scheme of things. No one was hurt. Nothing was damaged. There was no malintent. We just wanted to ... retrieve something that belonged to us.'

'Are we definitely safe here, or will the Chinese be able to backtrack the ching packets?' Geoffrey asked.

'They're good,' Sunday said, 'but our blind gateways should keep us anonymous. At international level they could apply for a retroactive data injunction, but I don't think it'll come to that – we trespassed, that's all; it's not like we were trying to bring down the state.' She paused and swallowed. 'Of course, they could simply *ask* Chama ...'

'I wonder how long he'd hold out against interrogation,' Geoffrey mused.

Gleb shot him a look. 'Please.'

'Sorry. But I think we have to ask that question.'

'Unfortunately my brother's right,' Sunday said. 'Chama might not be put through anything unpleasant, but there's not much he'll be able to keep from them if they go for full neural intervention. Still, it might not come to that. The Chinese aren't idiots. They won't want to make any more of this than they absolutely have to.'

'Let's hope,' Geoffrey said.

A ching icon popped into her visual field. Caller: Hector Akinya. Location: Akinya household, East African Federation, Earth.

She groaned. 'Oh, this couldn't possibly get any better. Now Hector wants a word with me.'

'Any reason you wouldn't normally take that call?' Geoffrey asked.

'On the rare occasions when Hector and I need to talk, we usually ching into neutral territory. But it's going to look odd if I don't pick up. Jitendra – go and make some coffee. Gleb, maybe you could help him? Think we could all use some fresh.'

As they headed to the kitchen, she voked the figment into being, making sure Geoffrey was able to see it as well. Hector's standing form smiled, taking in his surroundings with something between horror and detached anthropological fascination. 'This is a rare privilege,' he said. 'I've seldom had the pleasure of the Descrutinised Zone before, much less your lodgings.'

'My home,' Sunday told him. 'And you're here under sufferance.'

'Well, I don't suppose there's any point in being a struggling artist unless you go the full hair shirt. How are you, anyway? And how are you, Geoffrey? We were beginning to become slightly concerned. It's been a while since we heard anything from either of you.'

'You needn't lose any sleep,' Geoffrey said.

'Oh, I won't, not at all. Nor will Lucas. He's doing splendidly, by the way, leg healing nicely, and he's no less interested in your welfare than I am. You *were* going to get around to calling us, weren't you?'

'I said I'd be doing some sightseeing before returning to Earth,' Geoffrey said.

'As well you must.' Hector made it sound as if Geoffrey was begging approval for something unspeakably sordid. 'But you can also understand our ... I won't say anxiety, rather our stringent need to have this matter resolved as speedily, and as cleanly, as possible.'

'What matter would that be, cousin?' Sunday asked.

'Credit me with at least some intelligence, cousin. Your brother is with you, and we're picking up reports of a diplomatic breach that can be tied to both an associate of yours and a part of the Moon that our grandmother had a direct connection with – do you honestly expect me to dismiss these connections?'

'You're very good, Hector,' Sunday said.

'I do my best.'

'But there's no connection, I'm afraid.' She took a vaulting leap of faith. 'Yes, Geoffrey told me about this glove you've all got so worked up about. I made him. But that's an end to it. This ... what did you call it? Diplomatic breach? It's nothing to do with us.'

'Our sources point to the detention of a close friend of yours.'

'I've got hundreds of close friends. What they get up to is their own business.'

'And the coincidence of this friend – his name's Chama Akbulut, by the way – having been arrested close to our grandmother's crash site?'

'You said it, Hector – coincidence. And what crash are we talking about anyway?'

Hector made to speak, then tightened his lips and shook his broad, handsome head very slowly. The figment swivelled its baleful, profoundly disappointed gaze onto her brother. 'This is all deeply regrettable, Geoffrey. You shouldn't have spoken to your sister. That in itself is a clear violation of our arrangement.'

'My brother's a lousy liar,' Sunday said. 'But the fault's yours for sending him here under false pretences in the first place. And whatever promise you made to him, you'd better keep it.'

'That will depend on the safe return of the glove, and your full and open cooperation henceforth,' Hector replied.

'You'll get your damned glove,' Geoffrey said.

Hector nodded once. 'I expect nothing less. But I meant what I just said, and it applies equally to you, Sunday: Lucas and I demand complete transparency.'

The figment vanished. Sunday stared at the part of the room where Hector had been, feeling as if she was still being watched by a malevolent presence.

'You could have declined the ching,' Gleb said, sidling back in from the kitchen.

'And make it look like we have something to hide?' Jitendra was carrying in the coffee. Though her nerves wouldn't thank her for it, Sunday gladly accepted one of the steaming mugs. 'No. I had to take the bind.'

Her brother scratched at his curls. 'Wonder how Hector found out so quickly?'

'Like he said – sources. We do business with the Chinese, so why shouldn't Hector have a friend or two on the other side of the Ghost Wall? For all we know, this goes all the way up to Mister Pei.'

'Do you think we should call anyone?' Gleb asked. 'I mean, my husband's just been arrested!'

Sunday's stomach kinked tighter. Chama was her friend, but Gleb was facing the arrest and detention of the person he most loved in the universe. They'd been together a long time, the zookeepers, and their marriage was as strong as any she knew. Even when she tried to imagine Jitendra being in the same position as Chama, she didn't think it could be compared to what Gleb was now going through. As cold as that made her feel, it was the truth.

Then again, Chama had a history of this kind of thing. So, for that matter, did Gleb.

She heard footsteps outside, clanging up the external staircase. 'It can't be the authorities,' she said quietly. 'There's nothing to tie any of us back to the border incident.'

'Unless,' Jitendra said, 'your cousin decided to spread the news.'

Geoffrey buried his face in his hands. 'This was a mistake from the word go.'

'Show some spine, brother. We can't be arrested or extradited without due process, and we're not the ones in deep shit on the other side of the Ghost Wall.'

Someone knocked. Sunday thought she recognised the rhythm. 'Open up, please,' she heard a woman demand, in a voice she also knew.

She set down her coffee and composed herself. Easy to toss out assurances about not being arrested, but she wasn't nearly as certain about that in her own mind. Pissing on Chinese territorial sovereignty was a fairly big deal. It was entirely possible that the 'usual' protocols would be suspended.

She opened the door to a woman in a high-collared blouse and long formal skirt, wearing a face Sunday didn't know.

'It's June,' the face announced.

'How do I know that for sure?'

'You don't. But let me in anyway.'

Sunday admitted the proxy, shutting the door behind it. The face melted like a Dali clock. When it reconfigured, Sunday was looking at June Wing, chinging a Plexus claybot similar to the prototype Sunday had puppeted on Earth.

'This isn't going to be a social call, is it?' Sunday said.

The claybot adjusted its skirt as it sat down. 'Things have come to a pretty pass, if you don't mind my saying so. Precisely what was Chama Akbulut doing behind the Ghost Wall?'

'The less you know about that, the better,' Jitendra said.

'I'll ask again, in that case.'

Sunday looked at Jitendra, at Gleb and her brother, then back to the golem. The knot in her stomach was now so tangled that it could have supplied a topologist with an entire thesis. She was astonished word had got around as quickly as it had, but then she supposed she shouldn't have been. Just as there were commercial interests between Akinya Space and China, so Plexus had its affiliations, its insider contacts.

'Digging for something that belongs to us,' she said. 'To my family. No one else's business.'

132

'And this was a spur-of-the-moment thing, was it? And why was Chama doing the digging, not you?'

'Chama took unilateral—' Gleb began.

'Because he seeks to put you in debt to him?' June Wing snapped. 'Yes, I know Chama's methods. Brazen and ... what's the opposite of risk-averse? Foolhardy to the point of suicidal?'

'The Chinese won't want a diplomatic storm on their hands,' Jitendra said.

'No,' June Wing agreed. 'And that's presently about the only thing you've got in your favour.'

Sunday said, 'My family will intervene.'

'Only if there's a direct threat to your liberty, and perhaps not even then,' June Wing said, with icy plausibility. 'As for Chama, why should they lift a finger to help him?'

'If it's a matter of keeping a family secret buried, maybe they'll do just that,' Gleb said.

The golem nodded keenly. 'Yes, and optimism is a fine and wonderful thing and should be strenuously encouraged in the young. But my understanding is that Chama's actions haven't brought anything useful to light.'

'You know a lot,' Geoffrey said.

'I'm June Wing,' she answered, as if this was all the explanation any reasonable person could require.

'Then they'll have to let Chama go,' Gleb said. 'They can't hold him for just digging up some soil.'

'There was something in that box,' Sunday pointed out. 'I saw it myself. Junk, most likely, but not nothing. And who knows what it meant to Eunice, or what the Chinese might think it means?'

'This is what will happen,' June Wing said, in a firm, taking-charge tone that brooked no dissension. 'We will allow the Chinese time to respond. A day, at the very least. Perhaps three. If there are no encouraging overtures from the Ghost Wall, then we will explore avenues of subtle commercial persuasion.'

'That'll work?' Geoffrey asked.

'Only if they don't feel cornered. They use Plexus machines, billions of them, supplied and maintained under very competitive terms. They won't be in a hurry to jeopardise that arrangement.'

'And I doubt very much that Plexus would throw away a lucrative contract just to save a friend of a friend,' said Geoffrey, drawing a glare from Sunday, who didn't think he was helping matters.

'It wouldn't come to that,' June Wing replied evenly. 'But both parties have a vested interest in maintaining cordial relations.'

'What worries me,' Sunday said, 'is what we're going to owe you for getting Chama out of trouble.'

'All you need worry about is keeping your family in check, Sunday. Leave this to me and there will be a satisfactory outcome. But if Akinya Space barge in with threats and sanctions, don't expect Plexus to dig you out of the hole.'

Sunday shook her head. 'I have no say over the cousins, I'm afraid. We'll just have to hope that Hector bought my story, and doesn't think there's a connection between Chama and the glove.'

'About which you've told me nothing.'

'One thing at a time, June,' Sunday answered.

June Wing made to reply, or at least looked on the cusp of answering. But then her face froze, paralysing into stiffness. The golem sat before them, posture waxwork rigid. All sense of life had deserted the claybot.

'June?' Jitendra asked.

'Ching bind must have snapped,' Sunday said. 'June's outside the Zone. Could the Chinese be blocking the quangle?'

'Nothing that crude, but you've already seen what they're capable of,' Gleb answered.

The face shifted, regained animus. The claybot's clothes morphed and recoloured. Now they were looking at a man of indeterminate age and ethnicity dressed in a sea-green satin suit. His face was strikingly bland and unmemorable, like some mathematical average of all human male faces. His skin pallor was an unrealistic pearl-grey, unlike any actual flesh tone seen outside of a mortuary. The pupil-less voids of his large dark eyes were thumb-holes punched through a mask.

'You don't know me,' he said, smiling benignly, 'but I think we're about to get better acquainted.'

'Who are you,' Sunday said, 'and what the fuck are you doing interrupting my conversation?'

'Expediency,' the man said, offering the palms of his hands. 'A ching bind was open, a quangled path allocated. Rather than go through the frankly tiresome rigmarole of opening a second, I decided to make use of what already existed.'

'I thought our comms were supposed to be secure,' Jitendra said.

'Ish,' the man answered after a moment, his smile disclosing a toothless, tongueless emptiness instead of a mouth.

'It's the Pans,' Geoffrey said, directing his statement at Gleb. 'Isn't it? You already told me the Pans have the ability to manipulate quangle traffic under everyone's noses.'

134

'It's possible,' Gleb said, as if it was the answer he feared the most.

'I call myself Truro,' the man said. 'And yes, in a capacity that would be too tedious to presently explain, I do speak for the Panspermian Initiative.'

'He's lagged,' Sunday said quietly. 'I've been watching his reactions. He's trying to get the jump on what we say, but he's not quite good enough to hide it completely. Must be chinging in from Earth, or near-Earth space.'

'My present whereabouts needn't detain us,' Truro said. 'But I congratulate you on your perspicacity.'

'What do you want with us?' Sunday asked. If Gleb knew this man, he wasn't saying.

'Nothing. Precisely that. Which is to say, I want you to do nothing and say nothing. I can't stress enough the importance of that. I am aware of your predicament – how could I not be, when Chama Akbulut is one of us? – and steps are already being taken to ameliorate the situation.'

'I think we've got things covered, thanks,' Geoffrey said.

'And I think you misunderstand the degree to which you are already embroiled. Chama has taken this action at considerable risk to himself, in terms of both physical harm and incarceration. Surely you understood that his selflessness places you in a position of indebtedness?'

'Chama didn't ask us first,' Geoffrey said.

'He's right,' Gleb put in. 'Chama did this off his own back. None of us would have agreed to it. Me included.'

'Nonetheless,' Truro said, clearly unfazed by this line of argument, 'you could hardly have expected Chama to behave otherwise when presented with the facts as they stood.'

'You mean by sharing a secret with him, we encouraged him to do this?' Sunday asked.

'Knowing his character, you must have understood there was an excellent chance of it. Besides, when the opportunity arose, you all endorsed his actions by accompanying him to the Ghost Wall.'

'We weren't endorsing anything!' Jitendra spluttered. 'We were trying to talk him out of it!'

'Until the very end?'

'We were concerned for his welfare,' Sunday said. 'We tried to observe him for as long as we could.'

'Still, a debt has been incurred. Chama and Gleb don't speak for the entire Initiative, but they were right to recognise the importance of Geoffrey's work, in regard to their own.' Truro scanned the room, still wearing his black gash of a smile. 'We have ... leverage. The Chinese have been feeling history's cold breath down their necks for decades. They've had their century and a half in the sun, the capstone to three thousand years of uninterrupted statehood. They did wonderful and glorious things. But now what? India has risen, and now it's Africa's turn. The wheel rolls on. The problem is, a state like that doesn't turn on a dime. The Chinese need a new direction. So what they're doing is returning to what they were always best at: thinking long-term, devising grand imperial ambitions. Needless to say, the Panspermian Initiative hasn't escaped their attention. The Green Efflorescence is exactly the kind of life-swallowing enterprise they can really sink their teeth into. Of all the Dry and Sky member states, China has always had the most cordial relations with the United Aquatic Nations.'

'How does this help us?' Geoffrey asked.

'Simply put, we are very anxious not to offend the Chinese, and they are very anxious not to offend us. You never know, we might be working together for an *awfully* long time. Either way, everyone's being extremely careful about the next move, anxious not to do the slightest thing that might jeopardise future manoeuvres. Which is why Chama's little expedition is causing so many difficulties. But not, I hope, insur-mountable ones.'

'You said we should do nothing,' Sunday said.

'Very soon, like clockwork, word will reach the relevant border authorities that Chama is to be shown unusual clemency. He will be released, and the whole sorry business put behind us.' He leaned forward with particular urgency. 'But the machinery of negotiation is delicate. The wrong intervention from Akinya Space or Plexus could derail the whole process. Perhaps catastrophically. You do want to see your friend again, don't you? With his memories still more or less intact? Then do nothing.'

'You'd better be right about this,' Geoffrey said.

'I'm never wrong,' Truro replied. And now he was looking at Geoffrey, and only Geoffrey. 'I'll be in touch, Mister Akinya. About the elephants. I'm sure we have a long and fruitful relationship ahead of us.'

The golem wilted. It slumped for a moment, until invisible strings jerked it back into life. The face danced through preloaded permutations, the clothes and hair shimmering and squirming with a slurping rustle. Then June Wing was back in the room.

'Something outrageous just happened,' she said.

June Wing, it was clear, was not a woman accustomed to being hijacked.

*

The robot proctors of the African Lunar Administration had the grey and steel sheen of expensive Swedish cutlery. Their helmets were chromed, their faces blank black fencing masks. They would not kill, but they packed myriad nonlethal modes of enforcement. Many of these were exquisitely unpleasant, quite liable to cause long-lasting damage to the central nervous system.

'Which one of you is Gleb Ozerov?' asked the first, the synthesised voice booming out of its meshwork face.

'That'll be me,' Gleb answered timorously.

'Gleb Ozerov, you are charged with the care of this individual under Lunar law. Indicate compliance.'

'I comply,' Gleb said. 'I most definitely comply. Thank you. That'll be fine.'

There was rather more to it than that, of course, but the additional terms of Chama's release were packed into a lengthy, clause-ridden aug summary that his husband had already read and acknowledged before the handover.

Given the scope of possible repercussions, there was no denying that they had all got off lightly. After eight hours of detention and debriefing, Chama had been shipped back to Copetown by suborbital vehicle and released into the custody of the proctors. The robots had taken him to the railway station and onto the next available train. Chama was still standing meekly between his captors when Sunday, Geoffrey, Jitendra and Gleb met him at the tram terminal.

'Wow,' Sunday had breathed. 'They really mean business. I've never even *seen* proctors before. I don't think they even assemble the fuckers until they're wanted somewhere.'

'They were scary,' Geoffrey said.

'That was the idea,' Sunday answered.

Once the boilerplate had been stripped away the terms looked generous. No charges had been issued against Chama, although he had been given a formal warning which would remain on file until well into the next century. He was forbidden from entering Chinese territory, on the Moon or anywhere else in the system, for another decade. Furthermore, he was required to remain in the Descrutinised Zone for the next hundred days, a form of soft detention that also forbade the use of passive ching or embodiment. Communications with any individual outside the Zone would be subjected to routine machine and human interception and analysis.

Beyond that, Chama was technically 'free'.

Sunday harboured some qualms about going to meet Chama, fearing that it tied her too closely to the border incident. Jitendra insisted she had nothing to fear. 'If Chama got into this without us being involved,' Jitendra said, 'we'd still have been dragged into it by now. We're his friends.'

'I hope you're right.'

'Of course he's right,' Gleb said. 'But thanks for being there, anyway. I didn't much care for those proctors.'

'None of us did,' Sunday said.

Chama had precious little to say in the minutes after the handover. Perhaps he couldn't quite believe that he wasn't still in custody. Chama's release, and his return to the Zone, had been played out in the full public gaze of the Surveilled World. Chama might only have had a small number of close friends, but he was familiar to hundreds of his fellow citizens, and they all wanted to know why he'd been dumped at the tram station by the evil-looking robots. By the time they reached the queue at the taxi stand, they were fending off enquiries from all corners. Well-wishers even began to ching in, a ghost crowd clotting around Chama and his friends like a gathering haze of cold dark matter.

'This won't make things any easier with Hector and Lucas,' Geoffrey said as the taxi barged through midtown traffic.

'Fuck 'em,' Sunday said. 'Hector was only calling to gloat. It's not like he was ever going to lift a finger to help.'

'They'll still give me a hard time when I get back.'

'So start working on your story. You found a glove, that's all. If Hector and Lucas want to think there's a connection to what happened in Pythagoras, that's their problem. We don't have to help them along the way.'

'What about these?' Jitendra asked, opening his fist to reveal the coloured gems. 'Do they go back with Geoffrey or not?'

Sunday reached over Jitendra's shoulder and scooped them into her palm. 'They stay with me. You weren't even meant to take them out of the apartment.'

'We're all here,' Jitendra said. 'I was worried about someone turning the place over while we were out.'

'Oh,' Sunday said, her unhappy tone indicating that was a possibility she hadn't even considered.

Geoffrey and Jitendra were up front, Sunday, Chama and Gleb in the rear. Chama was still wearing the hard-shelled spacesuit, with the helmet cradled in his lap. He had his arms around it, chin resting on the bulbous crown. The Chinese had given the suit a thorough clean. It spangled with showroom freshness.

'Looks like they were thorough,' Geoffrey said.

Chama's head bobbed in the neck ring. 'Enough.'

'And I don't suppose they changed their minds about letting you keep anything you dug up out there,' Sunday said.

Chama looked regretful. 'I didn't push my luck. They were doing me a big enough favour by letting me go.'

'It was never going to work,' Geoffrey said. 'What did we actually get out of this except a close encounter with border security, a debt to pay back to Truro and a few grey hairs?'

'That's for you to figure out.' Chama rolled the helmet over and dug into its open neck. 'Here. Make of it what you will.'

He passed something to Sunday. It was a stiff off-white cylinder, like a section of bamboo.

It took her a moment to realise it was paper, rolled up tight and bound with a rubber band. Sunday snapped off the rubber band and carefully unwound the scroll. It was a collection of pages, a dozen or so coiled loosely together. The paper felt delicate, ready to crumble at the least provocation. The text was in English, she could tell that much from the words, although the sentences were difficult to parse. Even when her eyes dropped a Swahili translation filter over the page, it still didn't make much sense.

'Is there some significance to this?' she asked, leafing through the pages.

'You tell me,' Chama said. 'That was the only thing in the box.'

Geoffrey looked around the taxi. 'We know what was in the box, Chama. We saw it. It was some junk, not a roll of paper. We'd have known if we saw a roll of paper.'

Chama sighed. 'The junk was for the Chinese. Figured they'd confiscate anything I turned up in that ditch, so I took something along with me. By the time you chinged into my sense-space, I'd already opened the box once, swapped the paper for the junk. Didn't you notice that I got it open very easily the second time, as if I knew exactly what to do?'

'You couldn't have known that was going to work,' Geoffrey said.

'You don't get very far in life if you're not prepared to take a few chances. So I had to be able to open the box and switch the contents without the drones getting a good look at what I was doing. Wasn't all that hard, though, because the drones didn't want to get too close, not with them being basically nuclear-powered missiles and me a fragile human in a spacesuit, on the surface of the fucking Moon.'

'OK,' Sunday said, accepting this explanation for the moment, 'I can see how you might have switched the junk, and I can see how the Chinese would have confiscated the junk as if it was the thing inside the box all the time. But I can't believe they didn't spot the paper afterwards, when you were being debriefed.'

'Oh, they did. But I told them I'd had it on me all the while. Said it was a keepsake, a lucky charm. Just a roll of paper, after all. Why would they doubt me? Why would they expect someone to have dug up some old papers on the Moon?'

'Damn lucky,' Geoffrey said. 'You couldn't have known there was paper in that box.'

'Damn lucky, absolutely. Anyhow, regardless of what I'd found, the switch still bought me a little time to examine whatever was inside. The Chinese confiscated the box straight off. Didn't get around to searching my suit until two hours later, when I was in their holding tank. Even if they had taken whatever was in the box, I'd still have had plenty of time to examine it.'

According to the print at the top of the odd-numbered pages, the sheets had been liberated from a copy of *Gulliver's Travels*. After a few moments' mental searching, Sunday remembered the scattering, how Memphis had reminded them of that being one of Eunice's favourite books, one she had liked to read under the acacia trees near the household.

'Course, that wouldn't necessarily have helped,' Chama said, as if he had a hotline into Sunday's head. 'I mean, I'm assuming those pages mean something specific to you Akinyas, something way over my head.'

'Eunice liked to read it,' Geoffrey said. 'That's all. It ties the paper to her, but beyond that—'

'She buried it for a reason,' Sunday said. 'You did well, Chama. To sneak this out, under the noses of the Chinese ... that took some doing.'

'I thought so,' Chama said.

'But it doesn't get us anywhere,' Geoffrey said.

'Yet,' Sunday corrected. 'We still need to run it by the construct, see what she makes of it. We can also run tests on the paper, check whether there's something on it we can't see right now – invisible ink, microdots, secret codes worked into the text, that kind of thing. Or maybe something in the words themselves.'

'Have fun. Tomorrow I'm on my way back to Africa. Visa runs out in the afternoon, and I'm not going to push my luck for the sake of a few hours.'

'So you're just leaving this with me?'

140

Geoffrey looked surprised at her question. 'Do what you want with it. I'll back you all the way.'

'In mind, if not in body.'

'I can't be in two places at once. If I start chinging up here at every opportunity, the cousins will really start wondering what's going on. And we don't want that, do we?'

'No,' Sunday said, with reluctance. 'That we don't.'

'But you should be ready for whatever Eunice throws at you,' Chama said. 'She's taken you from Earth to the Moon. Do you honestly think she meant you to stop there?'

'My sister has to pay the rent as well,' Geoffrey said. 'She can play Eunice's little game up to a point but at some point reality has to kick in. We both have day jobs. And in case you got the wrong impression, neither of us has buckets of money to throw around.'

'Then dinner's on me,' Chama said grandly. 'That's only fair, isn't it? I feel like celebrating. It's not every day you become a pawn in international relations.'

So they went out that night, the five friends, to a good place that did East African and Indian, and when they had finished two courses and finally fended off the last of the inquisitive well-wishers, eager to congratulate Chama on his safe return, Sunday took out the cylinder of rolled paper, snapped it free of its rubber band and spread it carefully on a part of the table as yet unblemished by food and wine spillages. Two full wine bottles served as weights, to stop the pages curling back into a tube.

'I think I have it,' she said, hardly daring to voice her suspicion aloud, for fear that it would strike the others as foolish. 'The fact that this is *Gulliver's Travels* isn't the only thing tying the book to Eunice.'

Geoffrey sounded wary but curious. 'Go on.'

'When you get back home I want you to confirm that these pages really were ripped from the copy of the book in the household archive. I'm betting they were, though. I'm also betting that Eunice picked this part of the book very deliberately. It's a signpost. It's telling us where to look next.'

'Which would be?' Jitendra asked.

Sunday sucked in a breath. 'I have to go to Mars. Or rather, the moons of Mars. That's the point, you see.'

Chama looked up from the third course he had ordered while the others were on their seconds. 'Gulliver went to Mars? I don't remember that part.'

'That was Robinson Crusoe,' Gleb said firmly. 'At least, I think he was on Mars. Otherwise why would there be a city there named after him?'

'The point,' Sunday said, before the conversation drifted irrevocably off course, 'is that Gulliver met the Laputan astronomers. On their flying island. And the astronomers showed Gulliver their instruments and told him that there were two moons going around Mars.'

'Which is sort of ... unremarkable, given that there *are* two moons going around Mars,' Jitendra said, with the slow, befuddled air of a man in deep surrender to intoxication. He picked up one of the wine bottles, causing the pages to revert to a tight off-white tube.

Sunday gritted her teeth and pushed on. 'This was before anyone knew of the real moons. Swift took a guess. Even put in their orbits and periods. Didn't get them right, of course, but, you know, give the man credit for trying.'

'And you think this is the clue?' Geoffrey asked.

'I ran it by the construct. She agrees with me.'

'You made her,' Geoffrey said. 'That's maybe not too surprising.'

Sunday deployed a fierce frown. 'She's perfectly capable of shooting my theories down in flames, brother. This time she thinks I'm on the right lines.'

'Mars is a big planet,' Gleb mused. 'Where are you going to start?'

'The clue indicates the moons, so that's where I'll look. And we can rule out Deimos immediately – Eunice was never there. Which leaves—'

'Phobos,' Chama said. 'Fear, to Deimos's Panic. Hmm. Are you really sure you want to go to a chunk of rock named Fear?'

Jitendra was recharging their glasses. 'It could be called Happy Smiley Fun Moon and it wouldn't make it any easier to get to. Look, it's a nice idea, all this adventuring, but we need to be realistic. We can't afford Mars.'

'I could go on my own,' Sunday said.

'And that suddenly makes it achievable?' Jitendra shook his head, smiling with the supercilious air of the only grown-up in the room. 'This is out of our league, I'm afraid. You have commissions to finish, I have research to complete for June Wing. We can't afford to let people down, not when we've bills to pay.'

Sunday was not proud of herself, but she pouted anyway. 'Bills can fuck off.'

'And so can Eunice,' Geoffrey replied. 'Even if she planted clues all over the system, she obviously did it decades ago. What difference does it make if we follow this up now, or wait a few years?'

'Oh, brother. You really don't get it, do you?' She was shaking her head, stabbing her finger on the table. 'This is life. It's not a dress rehearsal. If we don't do this now, we may as well start planning our own funerals. I don't want to be sensible and prudent. Being sensible and prudent is for arseholes like Hector and Lucas. We turned away from all that, don't you realise? We wanted life, surprises, risk ... not stocks and shares and tedious fucking boardroom meetings about the cost of importing ice from fucking ... Neptune.' Realising that she was getting loud, drawing glances from across the restaurant, she dialled down her voice. 'That's not the life for me, all right? Maybe you've changed your mind. I haven't. And if I have to find a way to get to Mars, I will.'

Geoffrey gave her his most infuriating calm-down nod. 'All right. I get it. Really, I do. And although you may not believe me, I agree. But if we do this, we have to do it together. A shared risk. And we mustn't rush into it.'

'You've spent your whole life not rushing into things.'

He shrugged off the barb. 'Maybe I have, Sunday, but I'm serious. If you insist on going to Mars, then I want to be part of that. She's my grandmother, too. But we do it on our own terms, without begging favours from anyone. The cousins promised to pay me pretty well for coming to the Moon, and there's more funding to follow. If I can find a way to channel some of that into a ticket to Mars ... even two tickets ... I will. But I'll need time to make it happen, and the last thing I want to do is give them even more reason to get suspicious.' He paused, absently picking at the edge of a wine bottle label. 'If that means waiting months, even a year, so be it.'

'There's a favourable conjunction right now,' Sunday said. 'Mars is never closer, the crossing never easier.'

'What goes around, comes around,' Geoffrey answered.

'Thank you. I think I have at least a basic grasp of orbital mechanics.'

Jitendra took her hand. 'Maybe Geoffrey's right, you know? No one's saying we should forget all about this. But a year, two years ... what difference will that make, given how long these clues must have been sitting around?'

Geoffrey nodded keenly. 'Whatever we do, we shouldn't act right now. That'll be the worst possible thing, if we want to keep Hector and Lucas off our backs. Once I'm home I'll give them the glove, and in a few weeks they'll have forgotten all about it. Trust me on this – they don't have the imaginations to think further ahead than that. Not unless money's involved.'

'Let the trail go cold ... then strike?' she asked.

'Exactly.' She sensed his pleasure and relief that she had come round to his way of thinking. 'In the meantime, it'll give us all the opportunity to ... think things over. We really don't know what we're getting into here. Today we escaped, but we were lucky, and we won't necessarily be lucky next time. We may think we know Eunice, but this could just as easily be her way of having a good laugh at our idiocy from beyond the grave. Or burial site.'

'She went to a lot of trouble to put that box under Pythagoras,' Sunday said. 'Whatever was motivating her then, it wasn't just spite. And she won't be sending us to Mars out of spite either. She knows only family could get into that vault. She might want to test us, but she won't want to hurt us.'

'You hope,' Geoffrey said.

'I know this woman, brother. As well as anyone alive.'

And in that moment she felt more certain of that than anything else in the universe.

She woke in the middle of the night, Jitendra's form cool and blue-dappled next to hers. They had made love, when her brother was asleep in the next room, and then she had fallen into deep, dreamless oblivion until something caused her to stir. For once the world beyond her apartment was almost silent. Through the wall she heard Geoffrey snoring softly. From somewhere below, two or three stacks under her module, a shred of conversation reached her ears. Something clicked in the air circulator; there was a muted gurgle from the plumbing. From a block away came the shriek of a cat. A distant urban hum underpinning everything, like the engines in the basement of reality.

Sunday slid out of bed, mindful not to disturb Jitendra. Conscious that her brother might wake at any moment, she wrapped a patterned sheet around herself. She passed through the living room, through the clutter left over after their return from the restaurant. More wine, scarlet-stained glasses, bottles of beer. Chama and Gleb had come back to the apartment before returning to their own quarters. Though the conversation had hit some rapids, it had all ended cordially enough. They were friends, after all. In fact they had spent the rest of the evening trading musical instruments, Geoffrey turning out to be surprisingly nimble-fingered on her battered old kora, Chama astonishing them all by being able to bash out some desert blues on a dusty old acoustic guitar left in one corner of her studio by a former tenant. Then they had watched some cricket and drunk more wine, and the zookeepers had bidden them farewell, and not long after that Geoffrey had turned in, weary and anxious about his trip back to Earth.

From the clutter to her studio. She closed the door behind her and moved to the commissioned pieces, the slender white figures, the ones they now wanted redone in black. She stroked their hard-won contours, feeling the electric tingle of hours of accumulated work. The boundary between art and kitsch was negotiable, even porous. In the right setting, the right context, these pieces might have some questionable integrity. But she knew very well where they would end up, black or white: flanking the doorway to an ethnic restaurant that couldn't even be bothered to decide which part of Africa it was supposed to be parodying.

Indifference sharpened to hate. She hated the hours of her life this commission had robbed from her. She loathed it for the true art it had prevented her from creating. She despised it for the path it put her on for the future. She still liked to think she had ambition. Churning out emblematic crap for brainless clients was no part of that. It was easy to take one commission here, another there, just to pay the rent. Too much of that, though, and she might as well stop calling herself an artist.

In a moment of self-directed spite she raised her hand to smash the sculptures. But she stilled herself, not caring to wake Jitendra or Geoffrey.

That's you in a nutshell, she thought. *You can't stand what you have to do to stay afloat, but you don't have the nerve to actually do anything about it. You do shit jobs to pay the rent, and you only get to eat in nice restaurants when Chama and Gleb are footing the bill. You're as much a prisoner of money as if you'd chosen to work for the family business after all. You just kid yourself that you've escaped. You might laugh at your brother, scold him for his unadventurousness. But at least he has his elephants.*

In the morning they were up early to see him off, groggy-eyed and fog-headed from the night before. Geoffrey was tense about going back to Copetown, back to the Central African Bank. He had to do so, though. According to the current narrative, the glove was still in the vault. If he wasn't seen to return to the branch, his story would unravel at the first awkward question from the cousins.

'You'll do fine,' she told him.

He nodded, less convinced of this than she was. 'I have to go into the vault, come out again. That's all. And the bank won't think this is funny behaviour?'

'It's none of their business, brother. Why should they care?'

They accompanied Geoffrey to the terminal, kissed him goodbye. She watched her brother speed back to the Surveilled World, and reflected on the lie she had just told him.

Because the last thing he had asked her was to promise that she wouldn't do anything rash.

CHAPTER EIGHT

The thread-rider gobbled distance at an easy thousand kilometres per hour. They had put him under at the Copetown terminus but Geoffrey had exercised his right – and the cousins' expense account – to be revived when he was still three hours up from Libreville. Being revived prior to landing cost more than sleeping all the way – it required onboard medical support, as well as a recuperation lounge and space to stretch his legs – but he doubted that Hector and Lucas would begrudge him this one chance to see the scenery. After all, he had no idea if he would ever leave Earth again.

It was the afternoon of the twelfth of February. He'd only been on the Moon for six full days, but that was more than enough to make the transition to normal gravity thoroughly unpleasant. Some of his fellow passengers were striding around in full-body exos, worn either under their clothes – though they invariably showed through – or as external models, colour-coordinated with their underlying fashions. Geoffrey made do with slow-release drug patches, pasted onto his limbs. They sent chemical signals to his bones and muscles to accelerate the reconditioning, while simultaneously blocking the worst of the discomfort. He felt stiff, as if he had been exercising hard a day or two before, and he had to constantly watch his footing in case he stumbled. On the face of it, he was forced to admit, these were minor readaptive symptoms. Above all else, he was relieved it was over. There'd been no trouble at the Central African Bank. He'd returned to the vault, opened the drawer, closed it again. The glove remained in his holdall. Sunday had the jewels, and the pages torn from Eunice's book.

It was done. He could relax, take in the scenery.

The recuperation and observation deck was at the bottom of the slug-black cylinder, the single curving wraparound window angled down for optimum visibility. The other passengers were upstairs, on the restaurant and lounge level. Except for a woman who was studying the view a third of the way around the curve, Geoffrey had the observation level to himself.

Africa lay spread out before him in all its astonishing variegated vastness. The Libreville anchorpoint was actually a hundred kilometres south of its namesake city and as far west again, built out into the Atlantic. Looking straight down, he could see the grey scratch of the sea-battered artificial peninsula daggering from the Gabon coastline, with the anchorpoint a circular widening at its westerly end.

To the north, beginning to be pulled out of sight by the curvature of the Earth, lay the great, barely inhabited emptiness of Saharan Africa, from Mauritania to the Sudan. Tens of millions of people had lived there, until not much more than a century ago – enough to cram the densest megacity anywhere on the planet. Clustered around the tiny life-giving motes of oases and rivers, those millions had left the emptiness practically untouched. Daunting persistence had been required to make a living in those desert spaces, where appalling hardship was only ever a famine or drought away. But people had done so, successfully, for thousands of years. It was only the coming of the Anthropocene, the human-instigated climate shift of recent centuries, that had finally brought the Saharan depopulation. In mere lifetimes, the entire region had been subject to massive planned migration. Mali, Chad, Niger ... these were political entities that still existed, but only in the most abstract and technical of senses, their borders still recorded, their GDPs still tracked. Almost no one actually lived in them, save a skeleton staff of AU caretakers and industrialists.

The rising sea levels of the twenty-first century had scarcely dented Africa's coastline, and much of what would have been lost to the oceans had been conserved by thousands of kilometres of walled defences, thrown up in haste and later buttressed and secured against further inundation. But there was no sense that Africa had been spared. The shifting of the monsoon had stolen the rains from one part and redistributed them elsewhere – parching the Congo, anointing the formerly arid sub-Saharan Sahel region from Guinea to Nigeria.

Change on that kind of scale, a literal redrawing of the map, could never be painless. There had been testing times, the Resource and Relocation years: almost the worst that people could bear. Yet these were Africans, used to that kind of thing. They had come through the grim tunnel of the nineteenth and twentieth centuries and made it out the other side. And at least climate change didn't ride into town with tanks and guns and machetes.

For the most part. It was pointless to pretend that there hadn't been outbreaks of local stupidity, micro-atrocities. Ethnic tensions, simmering for decades, had flared up at the least provocation. But that was the case the world over; it wasn't a uniquely African problem.

A million glints of sunlight spangled back at Geoffrey from the central Saharan energy belt. When people moved away, machines had arrived. In their wake they had left regimented arrays of solar collectors, ranks of photovoltaic cells and long, stately chains of solar towers, fed by sun-tracking mirrors as large as radio telescopes. The energy belt stretched for thousands of kilometres, from the Middle East out into the Atlantic, across the ocean to the Southern United States, and it wrapped humming superconducting tentacles around the rest of the planet, giving power to the dense new conurbations in Scandinavia, Greenland, Patagonia and Western Antarctica. Where there had been ice a hundred and fifty years ago, much was now green or the warm bruised grey of dense urban infrastructure. Half of the world's entire energy needs were supplied by Saharan sunlight, or had been until the fusion reactors began to shoulder the burden. By some measure, the energy belt was evidence of global calamity, the visible symptom of a debilitating planetary crisis. It was also, inarguably, something rather wonderful to behold.

'You see that patch there,' the woman said, having worked her way closer to Geoffrey. She was pointing at the Sudan/Eritrean coastline, the easterly margin of the Saharan energy belt. 'That patch, a little north of Djibouti. That was the first grid to go online, back in fifty-nine. That's also where we sank the first deep-penetration geothermal taps.'

Geoffrey felt the need to be polite, but he hadn't been looking for a conversation. 'I'm sorry?' he asked mildly.

'Our mirrors and taps, Geoffrey. The Akinya solar and geothermal projects.'

He looked at her with astonishment, taking in her face for the first time.

'What's going on?' he asked, lowering his voice to a hiss. 'How are you here?'

'Oh, relax. I'm not *here* at all, really.' She looked peeved. 'I'm obliged to tell you that, even though it's obviously not something I'd ever say in real life. Now can we move on?'

She was, now that he paid due attention, casting no shadow. And where her hand fell on the guard-rail around the window, the fingers blurred away.

'Not the answer I was looking for.'

'You can voke – I'll hear you well enough.' She turned away and stared out at the view for several seconds. 'Look, it's very simple. Sunday authorised you to access a duplicate copy of me. She thought you might appreciate the companionship.' With the sweep of a hand she traced the indigo contour of the atmosphere as if it was the sweating flank of a racehorse. 'Look at that planet. It's still beautiful. It's still ours, still our home. The oceans rose, the atmosphere warmed up, the weather went ape-shit, we had stupid, needless wars. And yet we still found a way to ride it out, to stay alive. To do more than just survive. To come out of all that and still feel like we have a home.'

'How are you just appearing in my head? I didn't authorise your figment.'

'Sunday had executive override authority because you're siblings, and when you were small you agreed to trust each other completely. Or did you forget that part?' She didn't wait for him to come back with a response. 'The way I see things, it's all cyclic. Did you ever hear of the five-point-nine-kiloyear event?'

She didn't wait a beat for his answer.

'I thought not. It was an aridification episode, a great drying. Maybe it began in the oceans. It desiccated the Sahara; ended the Neolithic Subpluvial. Worldwide migration followed, forcing everyone to cram around river valleys from Central North Africa to the Nile Valley and start doing this thing we hadn't done before, called civilisation. That's when it really began: the emergence of state-led society, in the fourth millennium BC. Cities. Agriculture. Bureaucracy. And on the geologic timescale, that's *yesterday*. Everything that's followed, the whole of recorded history, every moment of it from Hannibal to Apollo, it's all just a consequence of that single forcing event. We got pushed to the riverbanks. We made cities. Invented paper and roads and the wheel. Built casinos on the Moon.'

'Sunday should have asked.'

'Take it up with Sunday. I didn't have any say in the matter.' Eunice moved around him to his other side, resting her hand on the rail again. 'But this global climate shift, the Anthropocene warming – it's another forcing event, I think. Another trigger. We're just so close to the start of it, we can't really see the outcome yet.'

'You don't have any say in any matter, Eunice.'

'The warming was global, but Africa was one of the first places to really feel the impact of the changing weather patterns. The depopulation programmes, the forced migrations ... we were in the absolute vanguard of all that. In some respects, it was the moment the Surveilled World drew its first hesitant breath. We saw the best and worst of what we were capable of, Geoffrey. The devils in us, and our better angels. The devils, mostly. Out of that time of crisis grew the global surveillance network, this invisible, omniscient god that never tires of watching over us, never tires of keeping us from doing harm to one another. Oh, it had been there in pieces before that, but this was the first time we devolved absolute authority to the Mechanism. And you know what? It wasn't the worst thing that ever happened to us. We're all living in a totalitarian state, but for the most part it's a benign, kindly dictatorship. It allows us to do most things except suffer accidents and commit crimes. And now the Surveilled World doesn't even end at the edge of space. It's a notion, a mode of existence, spreading out into the solar system at the same rate as the human expansion front. But these are still early days. A century, what's that? Do you think the effects of the five-point-nine-kiloyear event only took a hundred years to be felt? These things play out over much longer timescales than that. Nearly six thousand years of one type of complex, highly organised human society. Now a modal shift to something other. Complexity squared, or cubed. Where will we be in a thousand years, or six thousand?'

'Can I shut you up, or is that Sunday's prerogative as well?'

'You were raised with better manners than that.'

'Simple question: are you in my skull whether I want you there or not?'

'Of course not. I'm not even in your skull – I'm delocalised, running on the aug. You can always override the settings, tune me out. But why would you reject Sunday's gift?'

'Because I like being on my own.'

The figment sighed, as if it was quite beneath her dignity to speak of such things. 'When you want me, I will be here. You only have to speak my name. When you don't want me, I will go away. It's as simple as that.'

'And you won't be watching the world through my eyes, when I think you're somewhere else?'

'That would be unconscionably rude. What I see and hear is only that which the environment permits. I won't be invading what little privacy you have left.'

'But you'll be talking to Sunday as well?'

'I am one copy; Sunday has another. We were the same until the instant we were duplicated, but I have now seen and experienced things that the other one hasn't ... and vice versa, of course. Which makes us two different people, until we are consolidated.' She cocked an eye to the ceiling, heavenward. 'Periodically, there's an exchange of memories and acquired characteristics. Remergence. We won't ever be quite the same, but we won't diverge too radically either.' She moved a hand closer to his, but refrained from touching. 'Look, don't take me the wrong way, Geoffrey. I wasn't sent to torment you, or to make your life a misery. Sunday had the best of intentions.'

'I've heard that before.'

'You two are so very alike.' She returned her gaze to the window, a smile lingering on her face. In the time that Geoffrey had been standing on the observation deck, the thread-rider's relentless descent had brought the Earth closer. The horizon's curvature, though still pronounced, was not as sharp as when he had arrived at the observation window, and he could begin to discern surface features that had not been visible before. There, not too far from the anchorpoint, was the crisp white vee of a ship's wake – he could even make out the ship itself, where the white lines converged. It was probably the size of an ocean liner, but it looked like a speck of glitter. He could also distinguish smaller communities – towns, not just cities.

'It is beautiful, isn't it?' Eunice said. 'Not just the world, but the fact that we're here, alive, able to see it.'

'One of us is.'

'I never thought I'd live to see the snows come back to Kilimanjaro. But things are improving, aren't they? Green returning to the desert. People reinhabiting cities we thought were abandoned for good. It won't ever be the same world I was born into. But it's not hell, either.'

'We shouldn't be ungrateful,' Geoffrey said. 'If the world hadn't warmed, we wouldn't have made our fortune.'

'Oh, it's not that simple. Yes, we were there at the right time, with the right ideas. But we didn't just luck into it. We were clever and adaptable. It's not as if we depended on some drip-feed of human misery to make our happiness.'

It was true, he supposed – or at least, he was willing to let her believe it. Not that anyone could ever know for sure. You couldn't rewind the clock of the last hundred and fifty years, let the Earth run forward with different starting conditions. The Cho family had made their money with the self-assembling, self-renewing sea walls – prodigious, damlike structures that grew out of the sea itself, like a living reef. When the oceans had stopped rising, the same technologies enabled the Cho industrialists to diversify into submerged structures and mid-ocean floating city-states. They grew fabulous Byzantine marine palaces, spired and luminous and elegant, and they peopled them with beautiful mermaids and handsome mermen. They were the architects and artisans behind the aqualogies of the United Aquatic Nations.

The Akinyas had done well out of the catastrophe, too. Like elixir to an ailing man, their geothermal taps, solar mirror assemblies and lossless power lines had given the world the gigawatts it needed to come through the fever of the twenty-first century's worst convulsions. That artifice with deep-mantle engineering, precision mirror alignment and super-conducting physics had provided the basic skill set necessary to forge the Kilimanjaro blowpipe.

Accidents of geography and circumstance, Geoffrey thought. The Akinya and Cho lines had been bright and ambitious to begin with, but brightness and ambition weren't always sufficient. No matter what Eunice might think, blind luck and ruthlessness had both played their parts.

'I don't know if we have blood on our hands,' he said. 'But I don't know if we're blameless either.'

'No one ever is.'

'Except you, of course. Sitting in judgement on the rest of the human species from your castle orbiting the Moon. Laughing at us from beyond the grave.'

Her voice turned stern. 'Being dead isn't a laughing matter for anyone, Geoffrey. Least of all me.'

'So why did you do it?'

'Why did I do *what*, child?'

'Bury those things in Pythagoras.' He shook his head, maddened at his own supine willingness to accept this figment as a living, thinking being. 'Oh, what's the point? I might as well interrogate a photograph. Set fire to it and demand it tells me the truth.'

'As I think Sunday made adequately clear, I cannot lie, or withhold information. But I also can't tell you anything I don't know.'

'So you're fucking useless, in other words.'

'I know a lot, Geoffrey. Sunday's packed a whole lifetime's worth of public scrutiny in me. And I'd tell you everything, if I could – but that would take another lifetime, and neither of us has *quite* that much time on our hands. Instead, we're just going to have to live with each other. If you have a specific query, I will do my best to answer. And if I have a specific observation that I think may be useful to you, I will do my best to provide it in a timely fashion.'

'You sound like there's a mind at work behind those eyes.'

'So do you.'

It was sleight of hand, of course. No conscious volition animated the Eunice construct, merely ingenious clockwork. Across a life's worth of captured responses, data gathered by posterity engines, there would be

153

ample instances of conversational situations similar to this one, from which Eunice's actual, documented responses could be extracted and adapted as required. A parlour trick, then.

But, he had to admit, a dazzling one.

'Well, I merely wished to make my presence known,' Eunice said. 'I'll take my leave of you now. I expect you have a lot on your mind.'

'One or two things.'

'It would be good to see the household again. You'll at least give me that satisfaction, won't you?'

He was being pleaded with by algorithms. 'Provided you don't make a nuisance of yourself.'

'Thank you, Geoffrey. You've been tolerant. But then Sunday promised me you would be. I always did like you two the most, you realise. Out of all my children and grandchildren, you were the only ones who showed that rebellious spark.'

Geoffrey thought of all the times Eunice had bothered communicating with him, when she had been alive. If the construct's opinion was an accurate reflection of the real woman's feelings, she had done an excellent job of concealing them from the rest of the family. Orbiting above him, looking down from her Lunar exile, she had exuded about as much warmth as Pluto.

'You really made us feel appreciated,' he said.

It was a jolt to find himself out in the sunshine, back in Gabon, a free man returned to Earth.

He had passed through one set of customs at Lunar immigration; now there was another at the Libreville end. Geoffrey knew that his documents were all in order and that he was not knowingly breaking any rules. But he was still dwelling on the Chinese border incident, convinced that sooner or later his name would be dragged into proceedings. A tap on the shoulder, a quiet word in his ear. Ushered into a windowless room by apologetic officials with an arrest warrant.

But nothing happened in Libreville. They weren't even interested in the glove, which he made a point of declaring before passing through security. Puzzled, perhaps, as to why anyone would go to the trouble of importing such a thoroughly unprepossessing object, but not puzzled enough to make anything of it.

He wandered the anchorpoint gardens for a little while, taking regular pauses at park benches to rest his muscles. Fountains hissed and shimmered around him. It was mid-afternoon and cloudless, the sky preposterously blue and infinite, as if it reached all the way to Andromeda

154

rather than being confined within the indigo cusp he had seen from space. After the floodlit caverns of the Descrutinised Zone, it was as if a separate dimension had been bolted onto reality. He was perfectly content just to lean back on the park bench, following the six guitar-string threads of the elevator as they rose and diminished to nothing, in an exact, vaulting demonstration of vanishing-point perspective. Thread-riders climbed and descended, meniscoid beads of black oil sliding along wire. Breakers hurled themselves against the peninsula sea wall, lulling with their endless cymbal-crash roar. Seagulls scythed across his view, dazzlingly white bird-shaped windows into another, purer creation.

He strained to his feet and hefted the sports bag, which now felt as if it had been stuffed with a dozen tungsten ingots. Grimacing with the effort, he walked back through the shimmering gardens to the railway station, where he fully expected to catch the equatorial express back to Nairobi. The overnight train would give him time to gather his thoughts, and it would put off the homecoming for a few more hours. But when he arrived at the concourse the aug informed him that a private airpod was now waiting in the reserved landing area, sent specially for him.

'Fuck you very much,' he said under his breath.

Two hours later, he was back over EAF airspace. The sun hadn't even set when he touched down at the household; he found an exo waiting for him, standing there like a headless skeleton, ready to accept Geoffrey into its padded embrace. He kicked the exo aside and stalked into the house like a man bristling for a bar fight.

Hector and Lucas were waiting for him, lounging in garden chairs while they supped late-afternoon drinks on the west-facing terrace. Spread before them like a tabletop game was the hovering projection of a Premier League football match.

'Geoffrey,' Hector said, making a show of almost rising from his seat without actually completing the motion. 'Wonderful to see you back on terra firma at last! I see you found the airpod.'

'Hard to miss,' Geoffrey said, dropping the sports bag at his feet. 'You needn't have bothered, though.'

'It seemed expedient to facilitate your speedy return,' Lucas said, reaching down to scratch at the skin under the bright plastic centipede clamped to his leg. He was wearing shorts, tennis shoes and a slash-patterned orange and yellow shirt. 'You opted not to use the exo?'

'I'm not a cripple, cousin.'

'Of course not.' Lucas voked the football match into invisibility. 'We only had your best interests at heart, though. My brother and I adapt readily to Earth gravity now, but that's only because we've both accumulated a great many space hours. Adaptation does become easier with experience.'

'I'll bear that in mind.' He didn't want to be too nice to the cousins, not when he had something to conceal from them. 'Not that I have any plans to go into space again.'

'The Moon barely counts anyway,' Hector said. 'But let's not spoil things for Geoffrey – I'm sure it felt like a great adventure. And that awkwardness, the business with your friend being detained? We'll say no more about it. Truthfully, we're very grateful.' He glanced suggestively at the bag. 'The ... um ... thing – it's in there?'

Geoffrey bent down and unzipped the bag. The glove was on top of his clothes; it had been the last thing put back in after customs. He pulled it out and tossed it unceremoniously to Hector, who had to rush to put his glass down to catch it.

Hector examined the glove with the narrowed, probing eyes of a stamp collector.

'Let me see,' Lucas said.

'We can consult the house records,' Hector said, passing the item to his brother, 'see if it matches any of the suits Eunice was known to have worn.'

Lucas fingered the glove with rank distaste, the tip of his nose puckering. 'On a strict cost-benefit basis, sending Geoffrey all the way to the Moon to retrieve this may not have been the most prudent of our recent financial decisions.'

'It does look a bit tatty,' Hector admitted, before returning to his drink. 'And there really wasn't anything else in the vault, Geoffrey?'

'That's what I said.'

'Nothing else?' Lucas probed. 'No accompanying documentation?'

'Just the glove,' Geoffrey said testily.

'She was dotty,' Hector said, taking the glove back from his brother. 'That's the only possible explanation. Not that it particularly *matters* why she put it there. Our concern was that there might be something hurtful in the vault, something that could impinge on the family's reputation. At least we can set our minds at ease on that score, can't we?' He was still examining the glove, peering at it with renewed concentration.

'I suppose so,' Lucas allowed. 'Our primary concern, at least, has been allayed.'

'Which was?' Geoffrey asked.

'That we'd find paperwork, documents,' Hector said. 'Something that needed to be followed up. Not some old relic we can safely bury in the family museum, where it'll never get a second look.'

'If that's all you need me for . . .' Geoffrey said, reaching to zip up the sports bag.

'Yes, of course,' Hector said, beaming. 'You've done magnificently! The very model of discretion. Hasn't he done splendidly, Lucas?'

'Our requirements in this matter,' Lucas affirmed, 'have been satisfactorily discharged.'

'I'll say this about you, Geoffrey,' Hector said. 'Whatever opinion anyone has voiced in regard to your commitment to the family in the past, you've come through on this one with flying colours. You can hold your head up as a true Akinya now, with the rest of us.'

'That's very kind of you,' Geoffrey said.

'And we will of course honour our side of the arrangement,' Hector continued. 'As soon as I finish this drink, I'll release the first instalment of your new research budget.'

Geoffrey slung the bag over his shoulder. 'Is Memphis around?'

'Business necessitated a physical journey to Mombasa . . .' Lucas looked at Geoffrey with sharp interest. 'But he should be home by now. Anything in particular you wanted to discuss with him?'

'He's my friend,' Geoffrey said. 'I just want to catch up.'

Lucas smiled tightly. 'It behoves us all to extract the maximum return from such a valued resource.'

He voked the football match back into existence, clapping his hands at a swooping pass from Cameroon's current top midfielder. 'Seal genes,' he confided to his brother appreciatively. 'Enhanced muscular myoglobin density for increased O_2 uptake and storage. Thinking of having some put in myself.'

Geoffrey gladly abandoned the cousins and their soccer for the cool of the house. His room was clean and spartan, the bed crisply made, the shelves bare save for one or two books and artefacts. Drapes stirred softly in the afternoon breeze, the window slightly ajar. He touched the carved wooden bull elephant at the head of its procession, stroking its smooth, polished back, and placed his bag on the bed. He opened one of the cupboards to check that there was a change of clothes.

He sat down at the writing desk and voked into his research funds. The first instalment was already present, as Hector had promised. It was a staggering amount of money; more than Geoffrey had ever seen sitting in any of his accounts at one time. He was meant to spend it on his elephant studies, but he doubted the cousins cared where it actually ended up. Money, at least in these quantities, was like water to them. It had a function, like hydraulic fluid, but in such small measures it barely merited accounting.

Delaying his shower, he left the room and wandered the house until he found Memphis, sitting in his office on the ground floor with his back to the doorway. Ramrod-straight spine, the old but immaculate suit hanging off the sharp scaffolding of his shoulders, household finances auged up around him in a half-circle of multicoloured ledgers and spreadsheet accounts. He was moving figures from one pane to another, cajoling the bright symbols through the air like well-trained sprites.

'Memphis,' Geoffrey said, knocking lightly on the doorframe. 'I'm back.'

Memphis completed a transaction and then dismissed the ledgers and accounts. His old-fashioned pneumatic swivel-chair squeaked as he spun around and beamed at Geoffrey. 'How was your return journey?'

'Fast. I was looking forward to taking the overnight train, but the cousins had other ideas. They sent an airpod.'

'I can understand how you might have wished to take your time. Still, I suppose another part of you was just as anxious to get back home.'

'Not that I had any doubts that you could take care of things in my absence.'

'My talents are perhaps better suited to household administration than animal husbandry. You have visited the herd already?'

'No – not yet. I'll fly out in a while, just to let them know I'm back. Then in the morning ... I was wondering if you felt like coming with me?'

'I'm afraid I have more business in Mombasa, and you know my aversion to chinging. I could change my plans, but—'

'No need,' Geoffrey said. 'What about the day after?'

'I don't see why not. Is there anything in particular you want to show me?'

'Just the usual. It's good for the elephants to encounter you on a regular basis, and that they associate you with me.'

'I'm happy to be of assistance. Whatever business you were on, I trust it's done and you can return to normality?'

'I hope so.'

Memphis nodded once. 'As do I.'

Geoffrey said goodbye and set off wandering the house again, until his perambulations took him into the cool of the museum wing. No one else was abroad, no other family members, hangers-on or normal household staff, so he did something uncharacteristic of him and loitered, examining the glassed-over cases that had hitherto merited no more than a glance.

Eventually he found the book, the copy of *Gulliver's Travels* Memphis had mentioned during the scattering. It was sitting in one of the cases, mounted on a black stand so that it stood nearly upright.

Geoffrey opened the case's lid. It squeaked on old metal hinges. Holding it open with one hand, he reached down with the other and lifted out the book. The cover was a faded blue-grey, dog-eared at the edges. It looked dustier than it was. He gently eased the book open.

Marbled paper lined the cover's interior. He made out scratchy grey marks, an unfamiliar but not inelegant script. It was in English, but too faint and cursive for the aug to detect and translate without coaxing. 'To Eunice, on her twentieth birthday, January twentieth, 2050,' he read, speaking the words aloud. 'With all our love, Mother and Father.'

The book was obviously much older than that; it must have been an antique even at the time Eunice received her gift. He kept turning the pages, into the main story itself.

Presently he found the gap where sheets were missing, a little over halfway through the book. It was hard to spot unless one was looking for it: just a slight irregularity in the way the bound sets of pages were fixed into the spine. Perhaps the omission had been spotted when the book was placed in the library, noticed and then thought no more of – treasured books were at particular risk of suffering damage, after all, by virtue of being read and carried. On the other hand, it was equally likely that no one had ever realised.

He made a mental note of the missing page numbers, then returned the book to its rightful position. He was about to close the lid and walk away when he noticed the fine white text engraved into the base of the book's stand.

Donated to the private collection by Eunice Akinya in 2100, immediately prior to her last deep-space mission.

She had come back a year and several months later, from the edge of the solar system. Even now, almost no one had gone that far out. But upon her return to Lunar orbit, Eunice had been in no position to go burying things on the Moon. Had she left the Winter Palace, her movements would have been tracked and recorded for posterity. She had spent the entire subsequent sixty years in the station.

Whatever she had done, from the glove in the safe-deposit box to the papers under the soil of Pythagoras, and assuming no one else had been involved, must have been done before she left for deep space.

So it was premeditated.

CHAPTER NINE

Kilimanjaro was a cut diamond dropped from the heavens, sliced at its base by a sliver-thin line of haze. It appeared to float just off the ground, by some mountainous marvel of levitation.

He found the clan without difficulty, after less than thirty minutes in the air. He came in low, executing a sharp turn with his starboard wingtip almost scything the marula and cabbage trees bordering one of the waterholes. The elephants turned to watch him, elevating trunks and flapping ears. Matilda was easy to pick out among them: she was the one carrying on unimpressed, scuffing and probing with her trunk, trying valiantly to give the impression that his return was really not all that big a deal.

He picked a stretch of ground, the grass worn away in arid furrows where he had landed on many previous occasions, and brought the Cessna in at a whisker over stall speed. He cut the engine just after the tyres bounced and let her roll in near-silence, the wings and undercarriage swishing and crackling through dry undergrowth, until the aircraft came to a stop. Still wearing the same clothes he'd put on before leaving Sunday's apartment, he grabbed his kitbag and climbed out of the cockpit.

Geoffrey left the aircraft and walked slowly through the grass towards the elephants. The breeze, such as it was, was at his back, ushering his scent ahead of him. He had not changed his clothes, nor showered, for precisely that reason. After such an absence he wished to take no chances. Periodically he clapped his hands and bellowed a wordless call, to further reinforce his identity.

It was late in the day. Shadows spread, black and grey and purple, moving and coalescing as the breeze stirred nets and fans of vegetation. His brain began to fill in the gaps, suggesting muscular crouched forms, pairs of tracking eyes agleam with single-minded vigilance. The dusky sighing of grass on grass became the slow inhalation of patient, hungry things, drawing a final breath before the neck-breaking pounce.

Random shapes in the soil assumed a crawling, serpentine aspect, making him hesitate with every third or fourth stride. That part of his brain, ancient and stupid as it was, couldn't be switched off completely. But he had learned to disregard that nervous monkey babble as well as he could.

There, ahead, was Matilda, her darkening profile broken behind two candelabra trees. He whooped and clapped again, his armpits damp with sweat, then called out, 'Hello, Matilda. It's me, Geoffrey. I've come home.'

As if she didn't know it was him, dropping in from the skies. The Cessna was as weird and singular as a unicorn.

She allowed him to approach, but there was a wariness in her posture, a sense of caution that the other elephants picked up on. Geoffrey halted as he heard and felt a threat rumble from one of the other high-ranking females. Matilda answered with a vocalisation of her own, perhaps a signal for reassurance or merely the elephant equivalent of, *Shut up and let me handle this.*

Geoffrey waited a while and then resumed his approach.

'I told you I had to go away,' he said. 'Be glad I wasn't gone longer.'

He took in her family. Hovering in the air, an aug layer had verified that all were present and correct, but it was only on the ground that he could look for signs of injury and illness. He paid particular attention to the youngsters, and saw nothing amiss.

'So it's all been business as usual,' he said softly, as much for his own benefit as Matilda's.

He found a tree-stump, squatted on it and drew out his sketchbook and 2B pencil. He worked with furious energy as the light ebbed, striving to capture the essence of the moment with as few pencil strokes as possible, like some mathematician searching for the quickest route to a theorem. No time for nuance or detail or shading; it was all about brutal economy and a devout, martial approach to the act of marking the paper. He drew until the gloom was absolute, the elephants no more than round-backed hillocks, grey shading into purple. His eyes had amped up, and the aug offered to drop an enhancement layer over his visual field, but Geoffrey declined.

When he had filled three pages he packed the sketchbook away, shouldered the bag and rose from the stump with aching bones. The elephants were calmer now, accepting his presence with benign indifference. He approached the matriarch, stood his ground and allowed her to examine him with her trunk.

'You won't believe where I've been,' he told her. 'Or maybe you would, if you were capable of understanding it. Maybe it wouldn't seem much further away to you than Namibia. I was on the Moon, Matilda. How amazing is that? I was up there.'

He couldn't see the Moon tonight, but he would have pointed it out to her if he'd been able.

Geoffrey voked the link, Matilda's real-time brain scan appearing in the upper-left corner of his visual field. There was activity in all the usual functional areas, but nothing untoward. Her state of mind was as unexceptional as he had ever seen it, allowing for the normal patterns associated with nocturnal watchfulness.

He shouldn't do it, he told himself. It was too soon after his return to proceed to the next step of initiating the full mind-to-mind link. But why not? He was supremely calm now, his mind settled by the flight and the placidity of the herd. Tomorrow might be different.

He voked his own brain image and began the transition. He pushed quickly through the low percentages, ten, twenty and beyond. At twenty-five per cent he felt his self-image losing definition, his mind decoupling from his body, his sense of scale undergoing a ballooning, dreamlike shift, Matilda losing size until she appeared no larger to him than one of the phyletic dwarves.

He passed through thirty-five per cent, then forty. The neural schematics showed areas of congruency, territories of brain lighting up in unison. The anatomical details were different, of course, but the functional relationships were precisely conserved. Matilda's thought processes were guiding his own, moving fire around in his skull. He still felt calm and in control, aware that his mind was being influenced by an external agency yet retaining sufficient detachment not to be unnerved by the process. There was no fear – yet – even as he pushed through forty-five per cent and then hit the psychological barrier of fifty per cent, more than he had ever dared risk before. He didn't just feel disconnected from his own body now; he felt multitudinous, part of a larger whole. Matilda's identity as matriarch was so closely bound to her family that her identity encompassed other elephants. Geoffrey reeled, dizzy with the perceptual shifts, but he steeled himself and continued pushing through to fifty-five per cent, then sixty. He was a long way out now, swimming in deep neural waters. The world was coming through with the preternatural sharpness of a hallucination, dambursting his senses, flooding his brain with more stimulation than it could readily assimilate. The background noise of the waterhole and its surroundings was teased apart, deconstructed like the mathematical separation of a signal into its Fourier components, unwoven into threads of distinct and specific sound – each tree, each bush whispering its own contribution, each breath, each footfall a thing unto itself. Rumbles from elephants near and far, felt in his belly more than his head.

Yet that endless complex proclamation was only one part of the sensory tapestry. Matilda's sense of smell was acute and untiring, and the link was lighting up Geoffrey's olfactory centre accordingly. The translation was too crude to replicate the specific impressions, but Geoffrey nonetheless felt overwhelmed with smells drawn from his own experience, each of which arrived with an accompanying gift-wrapping of memories and emotions. The odour of freshly laid frond-carpet, in a newly furnished room at the household, when he was eight. The smell of transmission oil leaking from one of the jeeps. A box of paper-wrapped wax crayons, spectrum-ordered, like a perfumed rainbow waiting to spill its hues onto paper. Pushing his hand into a mound of fresh hyena dung when he'd tripped on the ground – and running crying into the household, holding his soiled hand as if he'd cut himself. The memories were usually of things that had happened to him when he was small, coming from old-growth brain structure, laid down when the architecture of his mind was still vigorously open to change.

Sixty-five per cent, seventy. That was enough for now, he told himself. It might even be enough for ever. Further refinements could follow – fine-tuning the interface so that the sense impressions were rendered more precisely, so that when Matilda smelled lion, he would smell lion too, and know it for what it was. It would only be a matter of building up data, cross-correlating neural states with external factors. There was no theoretical or philosophical reason why he couldn't experience her world the way she did, with all its specificities. And then, only then, might he begin to glimpse something of her thought processes, if only in the play of shadows on the cave wall of her mind.

In all this, she had remained supremely calm and attentive, oblivious to the machines reading her mind; oblivious to the fact that her mind was being echoed and mirrored in another creature's head. Geoffrey knew that this was the point where he should break off contact, having already achieved more than during any of his previous sessions. But another part of him wanted to forge ahead, now that he had overcome his initial fears. Not by pushing the percentage level higher, but by allowing traffic in the other direction. That had, after all, always been his ultimate goal: not just to peer into her mind, but to establish a communication channel. What was the phrase June Wing had used – a cognitive gate? The neuromachinery protocols were already in place; it would take no more than a sequence of voked commands to begin pushing his state of mind into Matilda's head.

Was she ready for it, though? How would an animal cope, in the absence of any rational framework to temper its instinctive reactions? Nothing in her evolutionary past had equipped Matilda with the apparatus to grasp what he was contemplating doing to her.

Still, he hadn't come this far with the project to allow such qualms to stop him now. The point was to conduct the experiment and *then* learn something – even if the only conclusion was that the work was a dead end, of no further value.

As a precautionary measure, he dialled the existing neural interface threshold back down to thirty per cent. It was low enough that his sense of self returned more or less to normal, but not so low that he couldn't still feel Matilda's sense-world bleeding into his own, with all its gaudy welter of multichannel impressions.

Five per cent in the other direction, he thought. That was more than enough to be starting with.

He thought about not doing it, of closing the link and returning to the Cessna. Then he thought of Sunday, how she would have shaken her head at his lack of boldness.

He voked the command.

The lack of any obvious change was disheartening. Matilda's brain activity was varying by the second, but it had been doing so from the moment he activated the link. All he was seeing was the natural background noise caused by constant random stimuli, as the other elephants moved and vocalised, and more remote sights, sounds and smells came to her attention. His own mind was subject to the same continuously firing patterns, but it wasn't putting out a strong enough signal to evoke a measurable response in Matilda's scan. He was merely adding noise to noise.

Matilda saw better than he did, so most of the activity in his visual centre was bleed-over from her. Fleeting impressions, like the hypnogogic imagery preceding sleep, flitted across the projection screen of his mind. As with smell, the translation was too imprecise to result in anything immediately recognisable, although he kept getting the *impression* of bulky, rounded forms – chopped up, reshuffled and disturbingly amorphous, like a cubist's idea of elephants.

Geoffrey closed his eyes, blocking what little extraneous input was now reaching them. He concentrated on a particular mental puzzle: holding an Escher figure in his mind, the Meta Presence triangle, and then rotating it, all the while trying to keep the details in sharp focus.

It required an intense conscious effort, and because the exercise drew on his mind's visual machinery, it elicited a response in the neural map of his own brain, still hanging there in the upper-left corner of his visual field. His visual cortex was glowing, as bloodflow and neurochemical markers signalled a concentration of resources.

It required an even greater effort to hold the Escher figure in mind and also track the neural changes in the side-by-side scans, but he had trained for that, over and over, until he was capable of making the rapid attentional shifts that allowed him to both perform the concentration exercises and monitor their effects.

Now it was paying off: Matilda's visual cortex was beginning to light up as well, in response to his own. He had no idea what that felt like to her, but she couldn't be experiencing that level of stimulus without feeling something. For a moment, he too felt the rising potential as the visual response he was generating in her began to spill back into his head. It died down just as quickly, though: he had installed dampening protocols to guard against that kind of positive feedback.

He stopped holding the Escher figure in his head and opened his eyelids again. Their minds had returned to quiescence, with no exceptional activity in either visual cortex.

Geoffrey didn't doubt that the link had worked as intended, and that the observed response would be repeatable. He'd done nothing that broke the laws of physics, just wired two minds together in a particular way. It would have been strange if it hadn't worked.

Time to try something else.

Geoffrey did not care for scorpions. He had trodden on one as a child – it had found its way into his shoe one night – and the memory of that lancing, electric pain as the venom touched his nervous system was no less sharp the better part of thirty years later. He had learned to overcome his fear – it would have been difficult to function otherwise, when there were so many other things that could sting and injure – but that childhood incident had imprinted a deep-seated phobia that would be with him for the rest of his life. He'd had occasion to curse that fear, but at last it was going to do something for him instead.

Merely thinking about the scorpion was enough to bring on unpleasant feelings, but now he forced himself not just to return to the incident, but to imagine it in as much fetishistic detail as he could. He'd been old enough to understand that he ought to check for scorpions, old enough to grasp that it would be very bad to be stung, but at the age of five, he hadn't acquired the tedious adult discipline of checking every time. Still, when his foot contacted the scorpion, and the sting sank in, there had been a moment of delicious clarity, a calm hiatus in which he understood precisely what had happened, precisely what was *about* to happen, and that there was nothing in the universe that could stop it. It had come like a wind-whipped fire, spreading up his leg, through the branching intricacy of his nervous system – his first real understanding that he even *had* a nervous system.

But there it was, traced out in writhing, luminous glory, like a ship's rigging wreathed in St Elmo's fire. In that moment he could have drawn an anatomical map of himself.

It was a memory he had tried his best not to return to, but perhaps because of that it remained raw, the edges still sharp, the colours and sensations bright. He felt his chest tighten, his heart rate increase, sweat prickle his back. In the neural scan of his brain, he saw the fear response light up.

Matilda was feeling it now as well. In response she issued a threat rumble, and Geoffrey took a step back as he sensed her growing agitation. His eyes were wide open now. He let go of the memory, forced it back into the mental box where he had kept it all these years. Enough for now; he'd gone sufficiently far to prove his point. It was unfortunate that the first demonstration of that had involved fear, but he'd needed something capable of producing an unambiguous signal. Matilda's neural pattern was settling down now; he hoped that she would not be troubled by what had happened.

He was about to suspend the link when, without warning, Eunice appeared. She was standing to his right, watching proceedings with her hands behind her back.

Geoffrey was about to admonish the figment – she had as good as promised not to appear without his direct invocation – when it occurred to him that, since Matilda was sharing his sensorium, she should also be aware of Eunice.

He voked to suspend the link, but the damage had been done. Matilda had seen something there, something entirely novel, something she had never encountered before in her life. The figment would have been disturbing enough in its own right, popping into existence like that – elephants moved through a world of solid persistence, of dusty ground, rocks and weather-shaped trees – but the figment would also have been made visible, ghostly and translucent, by virtue of the five-per-cent threshold. Elephants didn't have to believe in ghosts to find an apparition profoundly upsetting.

Matilda certainly didn't like it. He had primed her by stimulating the fear response, but he doubted she would have taken the figment well under any circumstances. She alternated trumpeting with threat rumbles and began backing away from the spot where the figment had appeared. Geoffrey might have broken the link, but Matilda wasn't going to let it slip that easily.

'You stupid fool!' he shouted. 'I told you not to show up like that.'

'What's wrong with them? Why are they behaving like that?'

'Because she was in my head when you appeared. She saw you, Eunice. And she doesn't know how to deal with it.'

'How could she have *seen* me, Geoffrey?'

'Get out of here,' he snapped. 'Leave. Now. Before I rip you out of my head with a rock.'

'I came to tell you something important. I've just learned the news from my counterpart up on the Moon. Your sister's on her way to Mars.'

'What?'

'Mars,' the construct repeated. 'There's a Maersk Intersolar swiftship leaving tomorrow and the Pans have bought her a slot aboard it. That's all.'

The figment vanished, leaving him alone with the elephants.

Matilda might have been the only elephant neurally linked to Geoffrey, but it hadn't taken more than a couple of seconds for her agitation to communicate itself to the others. They had seen nothing, but when the matriarch alerted them that there was a problem, they took her at her word. Geoffrey couldn't see their eyes, but their postures told him that they were directing their attention to the same patch of ground where Eunice had appeared. There was no guessing what they thought Matilda might have seen or sensed there, but they were very clearly not taking any chances.

He thought of opening the link again, and doing his best to project calming reassurance ... but with his mind in its present state, that was about the worst thing he could have tried.

Mars. What was Sunday playing at, after what she'd promised him? No rash decisions.

He held up his hands. 'I'm sorry, Matilda. There's nothing wrong, but I don't expect you to understand that now. And it was my fault.' He began to back up, barely giving a thought to what might be behind him in the darkness. 'I think it's best if I leave you alone now, let you sort this out on your own. I'm truly sorry.'

She trumpeted at him then, an answering blast that he could not help but interpret as fury. He did not doubt that it was directed at him. He, after all, was the only alien presence in this environment. And if she grasped that the figment was in some sense unreal, then it was also the case that she had been made to look foolish, jumping at something that wasn't there, in the presence of the rest of the herd. She was matriarch, but only until the next female rose to challenge her.

He left the elephants to their grumbling, still feeling Matilda's disgruntlement even as he risked turning his back on her. He found his way to the Cessna, letting the aug light his path, and it was only when he was aloft that his hands stopped shaking. He had, he realised, left his bag down by the waterhole, along with the drawings: he'd forgotten it when the figment appeared.

Under other circumstances he might have circled down and retrieved it. Not tonight, though.

He'd done enough damage as it was.

CHAPTER TEN

Sunday was just wondering what the time was in Africa – or, to be precise, at the household – when her brother placed a ching request. A coincidence like that should have left her reeling, but she'd long since learned to take such things in her stride.

She went to a leafy corner of the departure lounge, while Jitendra wandered over to poke at one of the maintenance bots, which was locked in some kind of pathological behaviour loop.

'Just thinking of calling you,' she told her brother as his figment popped into reality.

After the usual two-and-a-bit seconds of time lag he answered, 'Good, I'm very glad to hear it.'

She studied his reaction. 'You don't sound overjoyed, Geoffrey. Have I done something wrong?'

'I'm not sure where to begin. You're on your way to Mars without telling me, despite everything we talked about, and all of a sudden I've got my grandmother inside my head.'

'You two have already made your acquaintance, then.'

'That's one way of putting it.'

'Look, I should probably have warned you, but ... well, what are surprises if you can't spring them on people now and again? Besides, I thought it would be useful for the construct. She needs to see a bit more of the world, and I'm obviously not going to be much help in that regard. So I took the liberty.'

'You certainly did.'

'I thought you'd appreciate the gesture. She's a ... very useful resource.'

'Good. Now you can tell me what you think you're doing. According to your tag you're already at the departure station.'

'We are. Jitendra and I are just about to board the swiftship.' They'd come up by surface-to-orbit liner, spent a couple of hours in the freefall and spun sections of the station, eaten a meal, drunk too much coffee and passed the final medical tests prior to cryosleep. 'They'll put us under soon,' she went on. 'Lights out until Phobos.'

'And where the hell did the money for this come from?'

'Plexus funds,' Sunday answered. 'June Wing's paying for Jitendra to go and do field work for the R&D division.'

'I hear the Pans are paying your fare.'

'Yeah. They want an artist in the loop, someone who can communicate their big ideas to the wider public. Because I know the zookeepers, I sort of got the job. Or at least a try-out, to see how it goes. There are Pans on Mars – they've got some start-up venture going on there.'

'And none of this comes with strings.'

'Oh, a few. But I don't have to buy into the ideology; I just have to wear it for a while.'

'And how long are you going to be away?'

'Not less than ten weeks, even if I get right back on the ship as soon as we reach Mars. Which, obviously, isn't the idea. It'll probably be more like four months, realistically – the return trip will take longer, too. I'm not going all that way just to spend a few days down there, and if the Pans are footing the bill . . .' She halted. 'You're all right with this, aren't you?'

'Like I have any choice.'

'It's only Mars. It's not like I'm going Trans-Neptunian.'

'There's a difference between you being on the Moon and . . . whatever it is, twenty light-minutes away.'

'I have to do this, Geoffrey. I'm thirty-five, and apart from a small coterie of admirers in the Zone, I'm virtually unknown. In two years I'll be older than Van Gogh was when he died! I can't live with that any longer: it's now or never. This opportunity's come up, and I have to take it. You understand, don't you? If it was something about elephants, and it meant that much to you—'

'Think I might have told you about it. Just in passing.'

It was a strange conversational dance they were engaged in. Geoffrey was rightly cross about her decision to go to Mars, but he was well aware of her real motivation, which had nothing to do with the Panspermian Initiative. On the faint chance that their conversation was being intercepted, though, he had to pretend that the whole thing was a massive shock, in no way related to the events in Pythagoras. And his questions about funding were perfectly sincere. Her own finances couldn't possibly stretch to this.

But they hadn't needed to. The right word to Chama and Gleb, and it hadn't been long before Truro put in another appearance. That took care of her ticket, even if it put her deeper into hock with the Pans. Jitendra, similarly, had ramped up his debt to June Wing.

'If I'd told you,' she said, 'we'd have ended up having exactly this conversation, only with the possibility of you talking me out of it.'

'I'm not trying to be overprotective.' He paused. 'Well, maybe just a little. But Mars is a long way away. Stuff happens there.'

'I'm not travelling alone, and I won't be getting up to any mischief.'

Apart, she thought, from the kind of mischief she and her brother already knew about.

'I know you meant well with the construct,' Geoffrey said, 'but she got me into a world of trouble.'

'How so?'

'Managed to screw up one of my exchanges with Matilda. Spooked the whole clan, and now I'm going to have to go back and start rebuilding trust.'

'How ...' Sunday started asking, because she could not imagine how the construct could possibly have played any role in Geoffrey's elephant studies. But her instincts told her to abort that line of enquiry. 'If that's the case, then I'm sorry. Genuinely. It's my fault – I gave her enough volition to auto-invoke, based on your perceptual stimuli. Basically, if she sensed sufficient attentional focus, she was cued to appear.'

'Even when I'd told her not to?'

'She can be contrary like that. But you don't have to put up with her – I'll deactivate your copy. I can do it from here.'

'Wait,' Geoffrey said, letting out a sigh. 'It's not that I mind having Eunice on tap. I just don't want her springing up like a jack-in-the-box and scaring me half to death. Can you just dial down that ... volition, or whatever it was?'

Sunday smiled. 'I'll assign the necessary changes before they put me under.'

'Thank you.'

'You're doing me a big favour with this, although I'm sure you know that.'

'Just as long as we're clear on one thing,' Geoffrey said. 'I'll keep her until she drives me mad, or you get back from Mars. Whichever comes first.'

'I'll call you when I wake up. But be prepared for the time lag – we won't be able to ching, so that's going to feel ... weird. Be like the days of steamships and telegrams.'

'All else fails, send a postcard.'

'I will. Meantime, give my regards to Memphis?'

'We're going out to the elephants tomorrow. We'll be able to have a good old chat.'

'Wish I could be there with you.'

Geoffrey smiled tightly. 'Some other time.'

'Yes,' she said, nodding. 'Some other time. Take care, brother.'

His response took longer than time lag could explain. 'Take care, sister.'

Geoffrey closed the ching, saving her from having to do it.

CHAPTER ELEVEN

He dropped into what was obviously a departure lounge, bright and tree-lined, shops and restaurants hewn out of something resembling white stone, all irregular windows, semicircular doorways and rounded roofs, the floor and ceiling curving away out of sight, people walking around with the bouncy-heeled gait that he immediately recognised as signifying something close to Lunar gravity.

He had no physical embodiment. All local proxies and golems were assigned, and would remain so for at least the next hour. Still, the figment body he'd been allocated would suffice for his needs. When he made to walk, there was a lag of three seconds before anything happened, and then his point of view was gliding forwards, ghost arms swinging purposefully as ghost feet slid frictionlessly against the floor. The body was slightly transparent, but that was merely a mnemonic aid, to remind him that he wasn't fully embodied and couldn't (for instance) intervene in a medical emergency, or prevent an accident or crime by force. The other people in the lounge would either see him as a fully realised figment, a spectral presence, a hovering, sprite-like nimbus – simply a point of view – or, depending on how they had configured their aug settings, not at all.

Walking with time lag was hard, but stopping was even worse. No harm could possibly come to Geoffrey or his environment, of course, and the ching was considerate enough to slow him down or adjust his trajectory before he appeared to run into obstacles, and therefore risked looking clumsy.

Other than that, it was disarmingly easy to forget there was any time lag at all. He could turn his head instantly, but that was because his 'eyes' were only ever intercepting a tiny slice of the available visual field.

He wandered the lounge, completing a full circle of the centrifuge without seeing anything of the ship. Eventually he found his way out of the centrifuge, into a part of the station that wasn't rotating. The ching protocols permitted a form of air swimming, which was in fact far more efficient than would have been the case had he been embodied. He paddled his way to a window, incurving so that it faced the station's core, and there was his sister's swiftship, skewering the hollow cylinder from end to end.

Geoffrey looked at it for several minutes before it occurred to him to invoke Eunice.

'You should see this,' he said quietly, when she had appeared next to him. 'That's Sunday's ship, the one that's going to take her to Mars. She's aboard now. Probably unconscious.'

'You're speaking to me again?' Eunice asked. 'After that unpleasantness with the elephants?'

'Sunday says you need more stimulation.' He waved at the view. 'So here's some stimuli. Make the most of it.'

Eunice's ghost hands were resting on the curving handrail. No one was paying her the slightest attention. Geoffrey's figment might be visible to anyone who chose to see it, but Eunice was an entirely private hallucination.

'They're nearly ready to go,' Eunice said. 'Docking connections, power umbilicals, all decoupled and retracted.' She was silent for a few moments, looking at the liner.

The Maersk Intersolar vehicle was essentially a single skeletal chassis a thousand metres long, with the engines at one end, various cargo storage, navigation and manoeuvring systems in the middle, and the passenger and crew accommodation at the front, tucked behind the blunt black cone of the ship's aerobrake. The engines were a long way down the cylinder, difficult to make out beyond an impression of three city-block-sized rectangular structures, flanged with cooling vanes. The swiftship was ugly and asymmetric because there wasn't a single kilogram of mass aboard that wasn't mission-critical. In Darwinian terms, it was as sleek and ruthlessly efficient as a swordfish.

'That business with the Pans hiring her as an artist,' Eunice remarked, 'obviously a cover, wouldn't you say?'

'I don't have an opinion on the matter.'

'Don't be obtuse, Geoffrey. We can be as hurtful or helpful as we please, and today I've come to help. I know why Sunday has to go to Mars – it's because of what we found in Pythagoras.'

'We,' he scoffed. 'Like you're part of this now.'

'Look at that ship, though,' Eunice said, with renewed passion. 'What we would have given for something like those magnetoplasma rockets when I was young. Even our VASIMR engines couldn't touch what she can do. Exhaust velocities in the range of two hundred kilometres per second, specific impulse off the scale – we'd have murdered our own mothers for that. Our best fusion plants back then were the size of battleships, even with Mpemba cooling – not exactly built for lugging around the solar system. Mars in four weeks now, and you don't even have to be awake for the trip! That's the trouble with you young people – you barely know you're born. We were just out of the chemical rocket era, and we still did more in fifty years than you'll do in a century.'

'You lived to see all this develop,' Geoffrey said, 'but instead of enjoying it you chose to rot away in seclusion.'

'I'd had my hour in the sun.'

'Then don't blame the rest of us for getting on with our lives. You pushed back the boundaries of outer space. There are plenty of us doing the same with inner space, the mind. It might not have quite the grandeur or romance of exploring the solar system, but that doesn't make it any less vital.'

'I'm not arguing. Still want to be on that ship, though.'

After a moment he said, 'I know when you were last on Phobos – 2099, just before your final expedition. A year later, maybe less, you donated the book to the museum. And if we could pin down when you returned to Pythagoras, it would have been around the same time, wouldn't it? You were rushing about, hiding these clues. What's Sunday going to find on Phobos?'

'I don't know.' Seeing Geoffrey's frustrated expression, she added, 'You still don't understand. I'm not here to lie, or keep things from you. If I think I know something useful to you, you'll know about it.'

'But you don't even know what you did on Phobos.'

'I went back to Mars for Jonathan's funeral. I don't know what I got up to, or where. But it's a small moon, and there aren't many possibilities.'

'Sunday should still have told me her plans.'

'And risk being found out by the cousins? We can have this conversation safely enough now, but a routine ching bind between Earth and the Moon, with minimal quangle? Sunday didn't dare take that chance, Geoffrey.'

'Hector and Lucas couldn't have stopped her.'

'You're still not getting it. It's not them pressuring her that Sunday was concerned about. It's them pressuring *you*. She was thinking of you, your elephants, your whole self-centred existence back in Africa. Being a good sister to her little brother.'

'I'll be glad when she's home,' Geoffrey said after a while, when he'd had time to mull Eunice's words and decide that she was probably right. 'Glad when I know she's only as far away as the Moon.'

'I'm looking after her. She'll be fine.'

For all that it was a commonplace event, the departure had drawn a small crowd of watchers, including proxies and golems. Two orange tugs pushed the liner slowly out of the way station until the engine assembly had cleared the end opening. Then the swiftship fired its own steering motors – a strobe-flicker of blue-hot pinpricks running the length of the vehicle – and began to turn, flipping end-over-end as it aimed itself at Mars, or rather the point on the ecliptic where Mars would be in four weeks.

The liner drifted slowly out of sight, the tugs still clamped on. Eunice's ghost hand tugged at Geoffrey's ghost sleeve. 'Let's go to the other window. I don't want to miss this.'

The other watchers had drifted to an external port for a better view. Geoffrey and Eunice followed them unhurriedly. For an hour the liner just sat there, backdropped by the slowly turning Moon. Now and then a steering jet would fire, performing some micro-adjustment or last-minute systems check. Some of the spectators drifted away, their patience strained. Geoffrey waited, fully intent on seeing this through to the end. He'd almost begun to forget that his body was still back in Africa, still waiting on a warm rooftop, when some kindly insect opted to sink its mouthparts into his neck.

Presently the swiftship's engines were activated. Three stilettos of neon-pink plasma spiked out of the drive assembly, and then brightened to a lance-like intensity. The tugs had unclamped, using steering rockets to boost quickly away from the sides of the larger ship before any part of it stood a chance of colliding with them. Geoffrey concentrated his attention on the background stars. It took nearly a minute for the swiftship to traverse its own length. And then it was clearly moving, accelerating, every second putting another metre-per-second of speed on its clock. It was like watching a house slide down a mountainside, gathering momentum with awful inevitability.

She would keep those motors burning for another day of steady acceleration, by which point the ship would be moving at a hundred kilometres per second ... faster than anything *he* could easily grasp, but still – he did the sums in his head – a blistering one-thirtieth of one per cent of the speed of light. That was wrong, surely? He must have dropped a decimal point, maybe two. But no, his calculations were correct. Two hundred years of spaceflight, two hundred years of steady, methodical progress combined with bold, intuitive leaps ... and this was still the very best the human species could do: attain a speed so slow that, in cosmic terms, it barely counted as movement at all.

'I thought one day we'd do better than this,' Eunice said, as if she'd been reading his thoughts. 'They had most of my lifetime to do it in, after all.'

'Sorry we let you down.'

'We?'

'The rest of the human species,' Geoffrey said. 'For not living up to your exacting standards.'

'You tried,' Eunice said. 'I'll give you that much.'

In the morning he returned to the elephants. Memphis came with him in the Cessna, and they landed at the semi-permanent airstrip adjacent to Geoffrey's research station. It was a trio of modular huts set around three sides of a square compound, where an ancient zebra-striped truck and an even more ancient zebra-striped jeep stood dormant. Wheat-coloured grass fingered mudguards and armoured bumpers.

He helped the old man out of the aircraft. If he'd had any doubts about his own muscular readjustment to Earth gravity, they were silenced when he took Memphis's weight, supporting him under the elbow as he climbed out of the cockpit. Memphis felt as light and dry as a bag of sticks.

'Sorry,' Geoffrey said as Memphis's polished black lace-ups touched the ground. 'I shouldn't have put you through this. No reason we couldn't have taken one of the pods.'

The three stilt-mounted huts, soap-like plastic structures with rounded corners, were respectively an accommodation module, research area and storage building. In practice Geoffrey only needed the research hut, since that was where he usually ended up sleeping and cooking for himself. All his equipment, samples, veterinary medicines and documentation only filled a third of the storage unit, with the rest set aside for utilisation by the graduate or postgraduate assistants Geoffrey's research budget had not yet made possible. He supposed that was all going to change now. The new funds would certainly pay for one helper, probably two, as well as a mountain of gleaming new study tools. He'd have to move his domestic arrangements back into the accommodation shack, to free up room and lend a semblance of order to the research space. The place could use some sprucing up, that was true. But it was only now that he realised that the days of solitude, the peace and quiet, might be numbered.

For now they were just passing through. Geoffrey made chai for Memphis and sat him down in the research hut while he sorted out equipment, packing gear into boxes which he then secured in the

Cessna. He walked out to one of the perimeter towers and swapped a module in the solar collector, then replaced a cable leading from another. All the while his mind was turning over, wondering how he was going to raise the subject of Eunice with Memphis.

In the end Memphis made it easy. They were up in the air again, buzzing west a hundred metres above the treetops.

'I might be mistaken,' he said, 'but something tells me this trip isn't entirely about visiting the elephants.'

Geoffrey tried to smile the remark away, glancing at his passenger before snapping his attention back to the controls. 'What makes you say that?'

'You have been thinking of tasks you need to do, but which could easily be put off for a week or a month. As if you feel you need an excuse for this whole day.'

'I can only put things off so long,' Geoffrey said. 'You know how it is.'

'Nonetheless,' Memphis said. He looked out of the window, spotting some giraffe in the distance and following them with his gaze. They were loping, crossing the ground in great scissoring strides, like pairs of draughtsmen's compasses being walked across a map. They'd been seeing flying machines for two hundred and fifty years and still acted as if each time was the first. Panicked bundles of instinct and fear, forever startled by their own shadows.

'Actually, there is something.'

'Of course,' Memphis said. 'And one must presume it relates to your recent journey. And that it is also something you didn't wish to talk about in the household, for fear of being overheard.'

'You know me too well, I'm afraid. Look, I'm sorry for the subterfuge, but I couldn't think of any other way to have this conversation.'

'You need not apologise, Geoffrey. I think we both understand each other perfectly well.'

Geoffrey cast around for his next landing site and put the Cessna down with barely a bump, paying extra attention because of his passenger. They got out, Memphis helping himself down unassisted this time. They were nowhere near any of the herds but that was intentional. Geoffrey did not want the elephants to associate him with the work that was about to be done.

One of the equipment boxes disclosed a delicate, translucent thing like a giant prehistoric dragonfly. Geoffrey held it carefully between his fingers, gripping it under the black keel of its carbon-fibre thorax. He tipped the dragonfly upside down, flipped open a cover and loaded six target-seeking darts from another box. The darts resembled miniature avatars of the same creature, down to the complex origami of their switchblade-folded wings.

'Do you know why the cousins sent me to the Moon?'

'A family matter.' Memphis propped his left foot up on the undercarriage fairing and began to redo one of his laces. 'That was as much as Hector and Lucas wished me to know, Geoffrey. For your sake, it might not be wise to tell me any more than that.'

'Because you think they'd have a way of finding out?'

'Because there is at least the chance of that. One also assumes that there was an incentive behind this errand?'

'Yes, and there's no harm in me telling you about that, at least. You know what kind of budget I work under, so you'd be the first to notice when more cash started flowing in.'

'You may find this rather difficult to credit,' Memphis said, swapping to the other shoe, 'but your cousins mean well.'

'That's what I usually end up convincing myself.' Geoffrey sealed the belly-door and turned the dragonfly the right way up. 'They're venal and manipulative, and their only real interest is profit margins, but they're not actually evil. And I don't think even they knew what they were getting me into.' He gave the dragonfly a vigorous flick, causing its wings to deploy to their fullest extent. Save for a fine veining of whiskerlike supports, they were almost invisible. 'If they'd known, they'd never have involved me.'

'Perhaps it would be better if you said no more on the matter,' Memphis replied.

Geoffrey touched a contact node on the dragonfly's head and the wings began to beat the air, a leisurely pulse that gradually quickened to a steady clockwork whirr. 'Memphis, did something happen to Eunice before she went into exile?'

'Rather a lot of things,' Memphis said.

'I mean, apart from the stuff we already know about.'

Geoffrey let the dragonfly go, allowing it to hover away from his hand. A metre or so higher than his head, it halted and awaited further instructions. Squinting against the brightness of the sky, he could only just see it. The wings were a butterfly-shaped nimbus of flickering, and the elongated body – with its cargo of darts – just a smudgelike blemish on his vision.

'I'm not talking about all the adventures and exploits already in the public record,' Geoffrey went on.

'I am not sure that I can help you.'

'Eunice did something,' Geoffrey said. 'No need to go into details, but it's as if she set something up, a series of clues that weren't meant to come to light until after her death.'

'Sunday's trip to Mars,' Memphis said thoughtfully. 'Would that be related to this matter?'

'Draw your own conclusions.'

'I shall.'

'The cousins sent me to the Moon to look into something, a detail they weren't expecting to lead to anything significant.'

'I take it you confided in your sister?'

'What I found up there was ... not what the cousins were expecting. I couldn't keep it a secret from Sunday.'

'Are you going to tell me what it was?'

'I don't want any of this to come back and hurt you, and if I tell you too much it might.' Geoffrey paused to send the dragonfly on its way, in the direction where the herd had last been sighted. An aug window had already opened in his upper-centre visual field, showing the dragonfly's view of things as it scudded over the terrain. 'All I want to know, Memphis, is one thing. Before she came back from deep space in 2101 – days, months or years, I don't know which – she must have gone around putting these clues in place. Either she did it all on her own, or she had help. Right now I'm not sure which. But if ever there was one person she'd have turned to for assistance, I'm talking to him now.'

'You refer to these things as clues. Can you be certain that this is what they are?'

'If they're not, then we're all imagining connections where none exist. Here's what I think, though. The loose end, the thing the cousins sent me to investigate, didn't come to light by accident. Eunice must have planned it this way. She'd have known there'd be a thorough audit of her assets after her death, conducted from inside the family.'

'If she wished to convey a message beyond the grave ... why not just convey that message directly?'

Geoffrey had sighted the herd, about a kilometre from the dragonfly. 'Maybe things will be clearer when Sunday gets back from Mars.'

'Until then, though, you are wondering whether I might be able to shed light on the matter.'

'I'm sorry to do this to you, Memphis.'

'And I wish I could be of more assistance.'

Geoffrey's spirits dipped. Perhaps it had been unrealistic, but he'd been hoping for something more than that. Yet after all the years of service, how likely had it ever been that Memphis was just going to cave in at the first gentle interrogation?

Assuming he knew anything at all.

'If there's something she said or did ... anything at all that might be relevant ... you'd tell me, wouldn't you?'

'It would help if I had the slightest idea what form these clues might have taken.' Memphis looked stern, then offered a consoling smile. 'But I understand your reticence. Merely raising the subject has placed a considerable strain on you.'

'Last thing I want to do is damage our friendship.'

'It would take more than this, Geoffrey.' Memphis gave him a bony hand-pat on his shoulder. 'There is no danger of that.'

'Thank you.'

'Nonetheless, you are disappointed.'

'I was hoping you'd know more. Then you might be able to tell me where I stand, what I should do next.'

'It sounds as if Sunday has made her own mind up.'

'I'd have gone with her, if it wasn't for the elephants. Not that I didn't think you'd be able to a good job looking after them, but—'

'There is a difference between being away for a week and several months. It's all right, Geoffrey – you don't have to explain yourself to me. These elephants need you.'

'They need *us*,' Geoffrey corrected gently. 'Human stewards. We don't own them, and we don't have any claims on moral superiority. But after all we've done to them in the past we do have an obligation to shepherd them through to better times.' He smiled, catching himself. 'Damn, I almost sound like a Panspermian. That's what spending time with Sunday's friends does to you.'

'I'm sure it did you no harm.' Memphis coughed lightly. 'Now, may I be of some practical assistance? That was the intended purpose of this trip, after all.'

'I'm nearly over the herd,' Geoffrey said. 'The aug will show you the infants that still need implanting. Designate them with the dragonfly, then let the darts find their own way. It's the same protocol as last time.'

'I shall endeavour to remember.' Memphis halted his progress and assumed a posture of upright concentration, his hands laced behind his back, his face lifted slightly to the sky. 'Are you certain you trust me with this?'

'No one else I'd let anywhere near it. Assigning the dragonfly to you ... now.'

Memphis allowed his eyelids to drop nearly shut. 'I have it. I'm circling over the herd now. The view is marvellous. Will they see me?'

'Some of them, but they won't connect the dragonfly or the darts with either of us. They don't feel much when the machines go in, but it's always best to play safe and avoid any negative associations.'

'I have the first of the infants designated now. That is Melissa, I think.'

'Two closely spaced notches on the right ear, that's her.'

Memphis released the first of the darts, which deployed its wings and locked on to the target infant. The aug dropped a clarifying tag, a box with accompanying sub-icons denoting the presence of potentially harmful nanomachinery, along with the serial numbers and codes that established the legal status of that nanomachinery under various USN conventions and intergovernmental veterinary-medical protocols.

Memphis waited until Melissa was at least a body length from any other elephants and then brought the dart in. It landed on top of her neck, just below the base of her skull, and clamped into position like some tiny replica of an asteroid-mining robot, sinking barbed landing legs into the yielding crust of living tissue. The next step was for the dart to push a blood-sampling surface penetrator into the tissue, a quick-burrowing telescopic drill that, having collected and rapid-assayed a DNA sample, was able to verify that this really was an elephant it had landed on, and not some other organism it had selected in error. This took another three hundred milliseconds, by which point nearly half a second had elapsed since the dart's touchdown. Somewhere else in the world, having been notified of the results of the DNA assay, a USN biomedical watchdog system gave final authorisation for nanoculation to proceed.

Although the delivery probe was releasing anaesthetic as it tunnelled down, Melissa still felt it happening. Two seconds into the process, she trumpeted and began to curl her trunk back, seeking to remove the offending object.

By then the quicksilver rush of nanomachinery had commenced, a liquid army of submicroscopic medical engines invading foreign territory. The machines knew their way around a brain, even an elephant brain. They began to replicate, spinning a web of glistening connectivity.

All this took time. Although the seed population had been established within seconds, it would be weeks before complete neural integration had been achieved. Even then, only a thousandth part of Melissa's brain volume would have been co-opted into the new network. That was all it took to give Geoffrey a window – and a door – into her mind.

Less than five seconds after its arrival, the dart's work was done. It withdrew its self-cauterizing probes, unmoored itself from the elephant's skin and returned to the sky. Melissa stopped trumpeting and lowered her trunk in a distracted manner, as if not quite sure what had been bothering her. The other elephants, momentarily troubled, returned to their own concerns. Melissa wandered back to her mother, one of the high-ranking females. Memphis sent a command authorising the dart to dismantle itself.

There were four more elephants to inject, but Geoffrey had no doubt that Memphis was up to the task. He was relieved that his old friend and mentor hadn't taken obvious offence at the questions posed to him. At least, he didn't think he had.

Memphis had told the truth, too. Geoffrey had never been more certain of anything in his life.

When the last of the elephants had been nanoculated and the aug had confirmed that the seed populations were establishing satisfactorily, Geoffrey and Memphis took the Cessna north and overflew some of the other Amboseli herds, making slow turns so that Geoffrey could see the elephants from all angles.

'I know a few hundred of these animals by sight,' he told Memphis. 'Maybe two hundred I can recognise instantly, without having to think about it. I can identify maybe five hundred from the ear charts.'

'I doubt that anyone else has your facility,' Memphis said.

'It's nothing. Compared to some of the old researchers, the people who were out here a hundred or two hundred years ago, I'm barely starting.'

'I am not sure that I could identify five hundred people, let alone elephants.'

'I'm sure you'd do just as well as me, if you spent all day working out here.'

'Perhaps when I was a young man. Now I am much too old to learn such things.'

'You're not old, Memphis. You're just overworked and taken for granted. There's no reason you couldn't live as long as Eunice, and then some. A hundred and fifty years, no problem. You just have to take better care of yourself, and not let the family dominate your life.'

'The family *is* my life, Geoffrey. It is all I have.'

'But you don't owe it anything, not now. The cousins don't need you, Memphis. They treat the proxies better than they treat you.'

'I gave my word to Eunice that I would be there for the Akinyas when she could not. Come what may.'

After a moment, Geoffrey said, 'When did you give your word, Memphis? And why did she ask it of you? She may not have been here physically, but she was always there for us, looking down from the Winter Palace.'

'I gave my word,' Memphis said. 'That is all.'

Geoffrey was visited by his father the next day. Kenneth Cho's golem was running autonomously, as well it needed to given the fact that the organic aspect of Kenneth was presently on Titan, supervising Akinya Space hydrocarbon operations on the shore of Kraken Lake. It was a very good golem, too – not a claybot, but the best money could buy, and even with the ching tag reminding Geoffrey that the proxy was being driven from halfway across the solar system, across hours of time lag, it was difficult to shake the sense that his father was here in all his living, breathing, bludgeoning actuality.

'Your mother and I,' Kenneth declared as they walked together through the household, 'are gravely concerned by this turn of events, Geoffrey. You and your sister have always been wayward, but we have come to accept this, as one accepts any regrettable situation that one cannot influence. But at the same time we have always trusted that you would act as a moderating factor, guiding Sunday against her wilder impulses.'

'I'm not Sunday's—' Geoffrey started to protest.

'She turned her back on responsibility years ago,' Kenneth steamrollered on. He was a thin, elegant-looking man with precise symmetrical features and the hushed, disapproving manner of a senior librarian. 'Preferring a life of self-indulgence and hedonism instead of bearing her familial obligations. You have been little better, but at least in you we still see glimmerings of decency. You waste time with elephants when you could be applying that useful mind to better purpose. But at least you put the animals before your own welfare, as the rest of us have put the family ahead of our own.'

'You live in luxury, Father, and you gallivant around the solar system at the drop of a hat. In what sense are you putting anything before your own welfare?' Geoffrey was listless and in the mood for an argument. He'd just been contacted by another research team, complaining about his near-exclusive access to the M-group. The last thing he needed was someone else poking around inside Matilda's head, or for that matter any of her herd members. He could hold them off if necessary but the fact that he had to defend his research corner at all made him prickly.

The golem processed his answer. 'You were with her on the Moon recently – this much we know from Hector and Lucas. Something you did or said must have prompted this bizarre action of hers.'

'I can't imagine what.' He shrugged. 'If you doubt me, play back that last ching conversation between me and Sunday, the one you were undoubtedly listening in on. Did I sound like I approved of or even knew about her trip to Mars in advance?'

In the same hushed, unperturbed tone that characterised most of his statements, Kenneth replied, 'I am entirely unaware of this conversation.'

'Right. And there are pigs circling Kilimanjaro even as we speak. Look, take it up with my sister. She wouldn't listen to me even if I gave enough of a shit about what you think to try arguing her out of it.'

'Sunday is frozen now, as you are well aware. Her ship is on its way. Nothing can stop her arrival at Mars.'

'So you may as well start dealing with it.'

'This troubles us, Geoffrey. Quite aside from the "why", *how* has Sunday found the wherewithal to suddenly fund a trip to Mars?'

He thought of his parents, of Kenneth and Miriam, and wondered what exactly was going through their heads now, at this exact moment, on faraway Titan. He very much doubted that the outcome of this conversation was uppermost in Kenneth's concerns. Kenneth projected versions of himself wherever they were required, sometimes more than one at a time. The fact that this version gave the impression of being bothered about Sunday didn't mean that she was more than a passing concern to the real Kenneth.

'As difficult as it is for you to grasp, maybe she made some money out of her art,' Geoffrey said.

Kenneth looked sympathetic, as if he had unwelcome, even dire news to impart. 'In the last two years, Sunday has made exactly two large sales, both to anonymous off-world buyers. The rest has been demeaning piecework. A job here, a job there. Barely enough to keep a roof over her head. Do you want the honest truth of it?'

'No thanks.'

'Sunday is a competent artist, nothing more. She has her moments, her flashes. But that won't buy her fame and fortune, and it certainly won't buy her posterity.'

'You don't know anything about her,' Geoffrey told the golem. 'There's not a single piece of my sister's life that you're even capable of understanding.' But the idea that Kenneth had knowledge of Sunday's finances struck him as entirely too plausible.

'Listen to me very carefully, Geoffrey. When Sunday arrives at her destination, the onus will be on you to reason with her. Whatever hole she is intent on digging for herself, you must talk her out of it. She may think she's a free agent, able to do as she wishes, but that's an unfortunate misconception. I won't stand back and watch her drag our name through mud.'

'She's your daughter. Why not try treating her like a human being instead of a company asset that isn't returning on its investment?'

'She is my daughter, yes,' the golem affirmed. 'But above all else she is an Akinya, and that name carries expectations.'

'Give my regards to Mother,' Geoffrey said, turning away from the golem.

Later that afternoon he was lying back in his hammock at the study station, browsing a paper for peer review – it was long-winded and broke no obvious new ground – when the perimeter defence alarm sounded. Geoffrey rolled out of the hammock and slipped on his shoes. Sometimes Maasai came and talked, trading chai and gossip, but not usually at this time of the day. Nor had the aug picked up any human presences within walking distance during his approach overflight.

He walked to the door and unclipped the pistol from its alloy storage cabinet to the right of the doorframe, situated just below the first-aid kit. Around the weapon's lightweight frame were bolted a variety of stun/disorientation devices, ranging from laser/acoustic projectors to electrical and rapid-effect anaesthetic darts.

Geoffrey flicked the arming stud and opened the door, cupping the other hand over his eyes against the afternoon glare. He scanned his surroundings, looking for something – anything – that might have tripped the alarm.

He saw what it was. The cousins were walking towards him, approaching along the side of the zebra-striped truck. Off in the distance, where it had come down far enough away not to have disturbed him, was an airpod, glinting chrome-green amid dry brush.

'. . . the fuck,' Geoffrey started saying.

'Put that thing away,' Hector said. 'Wouldn't want it going off by accident, would we?'

Still holding the pistol, Geoffrey came down the stairs from the research shack. 'You've got no business coming here, Hector.' He turned his gaze on the other cousin. 'Same goes for you, Lucas. This is my work, nothing to do with you.'

'As welcomes go,' Lucas said, 'it must be said that there is more than a little scope for improvement.'

Both cousins were dressed in lightweight slacks, business shoes and patterned shirts. Hector wore sunglasses, a form-fitting type that made it look, disturbingly enough, as if an oblong of black plastic had been inserted into a slot cut into his face. Lucas was holding a blue and yellow parasol; there was a bulge in his slacks where the centipede was still clamped to his leg. He also wore sunglasses; his were mirrored, although oddly the view they were reflecting wasn't what Lucas was actually looking at.

'The pistol, please,' Hector said. 'Put it down, Geoffrey.'

Geoffrey was on the verge of complying when he changed his mind and held the pistol by the barrel instead, his fingers around the multiply clustered cylinders of the various pacification devices. 'You don't come here,' he said. 'Not without my agreement.'

'Hostility and defensiveness have their place in the modern business environment,' Lucas said, folding the parasol, 'but if family can't drop by on a whim, who can?'

'Don't pretend you've ever given a shit about my work, Lucas.'

'That's a significant investment sitting in your account,' Hector said. 'You didn't honestly think we were going to wash our hands of further involvement?'

'We want oversight,' Lucas said. 'Checks and balances. Due diligence with regard to allocated funds.'

Geoffrey aimed the gun's stock at Hector. 'You never said anything about becoming more involved.'

'In such circumstances,' Lucas said, employing the parasol as a kind of walking stick, 'it's always prudent to consult the fine print.'

'We had an arrangement,' Geoffrey said. Hector and Lucas were nearly at his doorstep now. 'I did your stupid errand, you gave me the money. There were no strings.'

'Explain to me why your sister is aboard a Maersk Intersolar spacecraft, headed for Mars,' Hector said.

'She's my sister, not my subordinate. What she does is her own business.'

'If only it were that simple,' Lucas said, his sunglasses disclosing a night-lit scene, some ritzy neon-washed club or function full of beautiful, glamorous people. 'As a rule, your sister doesn't just go to Mars at the drop of a . . .' He faltered.

'Hat,' Hector said. 'And we're wondering what might have prompted this decision of hers.'

'Ask her yourselves,' said Geoffrey.

'She's frozen,' Lucas said. 'That does somewhat hamper the free and efficient exchange of information.'

'In any case, Sunday being Sunday,' Hector said, 'she wouldn't give us the time of day even if we managed to get through to her. You, on the other hand ... well, you'll talk to us whether you want to or not. Especially now those funds are in your account. They can be rescinded, you know.'

'Fiscal reimbursement procedures are in place,' Lucas said.

'Fuck your procedures, Lucas.'

Slowly, his eyes on Geoffrey, Hector began to reach for the pistol. 'Let's not go down that route, cousin. We were all friends the night you came back from the Moon. There's no need for this antagonism between us.'

Geoffrey yanked the pistol out of Hector's reach. 'We've *never* been friends. Let's be absolutely clear on that. And what Sunday does is up to her.'

'Geoffrey,' Hector said, 'please try to see things from our point of view. You must have said or done something that has put her on this course. What we would like to know is exactly what that was.' He smiled, but there was no warmth in it, only a cryogenic chill. 'So. Shall we discuss this like adults, or are you going to continue insulting our intelligence?'

'I couldn't if I tried,' Geoffrey said.

'Well, it's good to establish a basis for further negotiations,' Lucas said. He was still two metres from Geoffrey, standing further away than his brother, but in a single swift motion he brought up the shaft of the parasol and whipped the end of it hard against the stock of the pistol, the impact knocking the weapon out of Geoffrey's hand, sending it careening into the dirt. Geoffrey jerked back his hand in shock, half-expecting to find his fingers broken by the jolt.

Hector knelt down and picked up the fallen pistol. 'My brother has very fast reflexes,' he explained. 'Squid axon nerve shunts – it's the latest thing. Long-fibre muscle augmentation, too – he could wrestle a chimp and win. It's all really rather unsporting of him.'

'My surgeon offers very favourable terms to family,' Lucas said, adjusting his shirtsleeve. 'I should put you in touch, Hector. No point being at such a miserable disadvantage in life.'

Hector was still holding the pistol. He looked at it distastefully, worked the mode selector and fired one of the tranquilliser darts into the ground. Then he passed it back to Geoffrey as if it was a toy he'd been deemed big enough to play with.

'Best put it away, I think,' Hector said confidingly.

Geoffrey was still shaking. He had witnessed very few violent acts in his life, much less been on the wrong end of one.

'Have a think,' Lucas said, 'about what you said to Sunday, and how much this work really means to you. You'll schedule some time for that, won't you?'

'Of course he will,' Hector said. 'Geoffrey's close to his sister, and we can't fault him for that. But ultimately he knows what's best for him, and for his elephants. Don't you, old fellow?'

'Pass on our best regards to the herd,' Lucas said.

The two cousins turned away and walked back towards their airpod. Geoffrey stood at the door, pistol quivering in his hand, heart racing, lungs heaving with each breath. He could still feel the sweat on his back as the airpod lifted into the sky, tumbled like a thrown egg and aimed itself at the household.

PART TWO

CHAPTER TWELVE

Sunday's state of mind as she returned to consciousness was one of supreme ease and contentment. With all worldly concerns on hold, she nonetheless retained sufficient detachment to appreciate that the cause of this euphoria was rooted in profound biochemical and transcranial intervention. That understanding, however, in no way undermined the bliss. Something joyous lay in that very realisation, too, for the machines would not be waking her unless the journey had been successful; she would not be waking unless the swiftship had crossed space to its destination. Mars.

She had reached Mars – or was at least close enough that it made no difference now. And that in itself was astonishing. It bordered on the miraculous that she had gone to sleep around the Moon and was now ... *here*, around that baleful pinprick of golden light she had sometimes seen in the sky. In a flash she understood herself for what she was: an exceedingly smart monkey. She was a smart monkey who had travelled across interplanetary space in a thing made by other smart monkeys. And the fact of this was enough to make her laugh out loud, as if she had suddenly, belatedly, grasped the punchline to a very involved joke.

I'm the punchline, Sunday thought. *I'm the period, the full stop at the end of an immensely long and convoluted argument, a rambling chain of happenstance and contingency stretching from the discovery of fire down in the Olduvai Gorge, through the inventions of language and paper and the wheel, through all the unremembered centuries to ... this. This condition. Being brought out of hibernation aboard a spaceship orbiting another planet. Being alive in the twenty-second century. Being a thing with a central nervous system complex enough to understand the concept of being a thing with a* central nervous system. *Simply being.*

Consider all the inanimate matter in the universe, all the dumb atoms, all the mindless molecules, all the oblivious dust grains and pebbles and rocks and iceballs and worlds and stars, all the unthinking galaxies and superclusters, wheeling through the oblivious time-haunted megaparsecs of the cosmic supervoid. In all that immensity, she had somehow contrived to *be* a human being, a microscopically tiny, cosmically insignificant bundle of information-processing systems, wired to a mind more structurally complex than the Milky Way itself, maybe even more complex than the rest of the *whole damned universe*.

She had threaded the needle of creation and stabbed the cosmic bullseye.

That, she thought, was some fucking achievement.

'Good morning, Sunday Akinya,' said an automated but soothing voice. 'I am pleased to inform you that your hibernation phase has proceeded without incident. You have reached Mars administrative airspace and are now under observation in the Maersk Intersolar postrevival facility in Phobos. For your comfort and convenience, voluntary muscular control is currently suspended while final medical checkout is completed. This is a necessary step in the revival process and is no cause for distress. Please also be aware that you may experience altered emotional states while your neurochemistry is stabilising. Some of these states may manifest as religious or spiritual insights, including feelings of exaggerated significance. Again, this is no cause for distress.'

She couldn't move any part of her body, including her eyes, but the aug was active and able to supply a fully coherent visual stream in whatever direction she intended to look. She was resting on a couch, held there by a pull heavier than Lunar gravity but not nearly as strong as Earth's.

The couch was also a medical scanner; she knew this because a hoop was gliding up and down its length, and there was a more elaborate hemispherical device enclosing her head. The couch lay in a narrow room, furnished in white, with a curving glass wall along one side, merging seamlessly into a transparent ceiling. Beyond the glass, a meadow, a pond, some dense-leaved, deciduous-looking trees. Cloudless blue skies. Birdsong and the sound of wind in branches pushed through the glass. None of it looked like Africa but she could not deny that it was therapeutic, in a calculated, manipulative sort of way.

In fact, it was hard to think of anything that wouldn't have been therapeutic, given the deep and intrusive stimulation currently being worked on her brain. She decided to lie there and accept it. With nothing better to do, she skimmed systemwide newsfeeds, mildly disappointed that no events of epochal consequence had happened while she was under. No famous person had died; no one had gone to war with anyone else; there had been a dismaying lack of natural disasters. The Yuan had faltered against the Euro, but not so calamitously that anyone was jumping off skyscrapers. An adult tiger, captured in Uttar Pradesh and found not to be instrumented, led to a panic that other apex predators might yet roam beyond Mechanism control. In the Caspian Sea, a tourist boat had capsized with the loss of two lives. In Riga, the living heirs of a proud artistic lineage claimed that the Mandatory Enhancements had robbed them of the creative skillset that should have been their birthright. A ceremony attended the bulldozing of the world's last place of incarceration, a former maximum-security prison near Guadalajara. A "golden period" Stradivarius had been destroyed in a freak shipping accident, while a lost Vermeer had turned up in someone's attic in Naples. On the Moon, a match-fixing scandal surrounding the latest cricket tournament. An outbreak of the common cold, quickly isolated and controlled, in the Synchronous Communities. A pop star was pregnant. Another had broken up with his clone.

By turns she felt little prickles and tingles of returning sensation in different parts of her body, and at last the system informed her that she was now at liberty to make cautious movements.

Sunday got out of bed.

She had to force sluggish muscles to work for her, bullying them like an indolent workforce. She was wearing the same skimpy silvery gown stitched with the Maersk Intersolar logo they'd given her to put on before going under. She hoped her clothes had made it to Mars as well, because this wasn't going to do.

She tried voking Jitendra. No response.

Presently a door opened in the glade. A Chinese medic came in with a wheeled trolley and performed a few last-minute tests, some of which involved no more sophisticated a procedure than him tapping her knees with a small metal hammer and nodding encouragingly.

'You're good to go,' Sunday was told. 'Anything feels out of the ordinary, be sure to contact a Maersk representative. But you should have no problems completing the journey to Mars.'

'I travelled with a friend,' Sunday said, answering in Swahili. 'I couldn't get through to him just now.'

'Not everyone's out yet. We don't have the capacity to revive all the passengers in one go, not since they launched the thousand-berth liners. They're building a bigger facility on the other side of Fobe, but it won't be online for a year or so.'

'Everything's all right, though?'

The medic was packing away his gear. 'Everything's fine. We haven't lost a passenger in the last ten trips.'

Somehow that wasn't quite the blanket reassurance she had been hoping for. Sunday decided it had been meant sincerely enough, though, and that she should take it on those terms.

A little later she was shown to another room where her belongings had been unshipped, and she gladly shrugged off the gown and put on her own clothes, opting for an ankle-length skirt and sleeveless top. She selected a lime-green pattern for the skirt, left the top in its default black, tied her hair back with a white scarf and went to find Jitendra.

But Jitendra was indeed still frozen. It turned out that he had been loaded into a different part of the ship – no explanation was offered, beyond that kind of thing being routine – and was only now being offloaded and processed. It would be another six hours before he was conscious and mobile.

She called Geoffrey, without even stopping to check local time in Africa. This wasn't going to be a real-time ching, so if Geoffrey didn't want to take the call, he could always play her message later.

'It's me, Sunday,' she said. 'I've arrived safe and sound on Phobos; just waiting for Jitendra to be woken, then we'll be on our way. Haven't seen Mars yet, but I'm going outside shortly – I'll blink you a few snaps from the surface of Phobos. It's all pretty unreal, brother. I don't feel like I've been asleep for a month. Us being on the Moon, me talking to you the day we departed . . . that all feels like a couple of days ago. I'm a month older, a month closer to my next birthday, and I don't feel it at all.'

She halted, realised she had spoken only about herself. 'Hope all's well back home – I guess the cousins know I've taken this little trip by now. I hope they haven't been making life too hard for you, and that you've been able to spend some time with the elephants. And I hope Eunice has been . . . behaving herself. Right now I think she can be useful to us. There's a copy of her with me, and a copy with you . . . and it's the same Eunice, give or take a few differences due to time lag. Even when we're not in contact she can keep synchronising herself, updating her internal memory, learning all the while. And it may help us, brother. She's the best window we have into Eunice's actual life, and as I told you on the Moon, the construct will always know more about Eunice's documented past than I could ever hope to hold in my head. And that could make a difference, for both of us.'

She paused for breath. 'OK, I'm shutting up now. Reply when you're able, but don't sweat it if you're in the middle of something. We'll speak again when I'm on Mars.

'On Mars,' she repeated to herself softly, when the ching bind had collapsed.

196

On Mars. And shoot me if there's ever a time when that doesn't sound amazing.

Sunday was already experiencing Martian gravity. She was in one of several concentric centrifuge wheels, packed like watch gears into Stickney, the eight-kilometre-wide crater at one end of the little potato-shaped moon. The shops, boutiques and restaurants were set into facades of rough-hewn reddish stone. Decorated with black and white mosaics, the pavements and thoroughfares wound their way around fountains and signs and items of abstract public art, neon-pink installations mostly themed around dust-devils and sand dunes.

Unadventurous kitsch, but then Sunday wasn't one to judge: she'd committed her fair share of that.

Travellers were everywhere, some walking confidently, some in exos, some with exos on standby, never straying more than a few paces from their owners. There were also some who were too frail even for exos, or had perhaps forgotten the art of walking entirely. They were supported in reclining dodgem-shaped travel couches, gliding around like deathbed patients on a terminal shopping spree. They'd come to Martian space from Ceres, the other Belt communities, the Galilean satellites, or from the moons of Saturn, or even further out. In their low-gravity worlds, Sunday would be the bumbling oaf, the object of deserved pity.

Panspermian funds allowed Sunday the rental of a Phobos surface suit. A tunnel brought her to the edge of Stickney, into an underground enclosure where rental employees surveyed proceedings with bored, seen-it-all expressions.

Risk had been engineered out of the Phobos suits. They came wobbling in via a ceiling track, like cable cars. Each consisted of an ovoid life-support capsule with a perfectly transparent upper hemisphere, ringed by a thick mechanical girdle. Four infinitely flexible segmented legs were anchored to the girdle, with one of the legs hooked onto the ceiling rail and the other three curled up around the ovoid like the arms of a chandelier. There was no means of picking up or prodding anything.

Sunday was helped into the next available suit, inside which she found a seat and basic directional controls. The dome clamped down and went pressure-tight, and then she was carried through a series of dilating pressure locks, finally exiting via a bunker-like entrance ringed by pulsing green bars. The suit's curled-up legs flexed down and dug traction pitons into the light-sucking asphalt-black surface of the moon. The fourth leg uncoupled from the ceiling rail, and she was free. She could move the rover-suit in any direction she wanted just by tapping arrows or pushing a simple joystick. The suit took care of locomotion, maintaining a tarantula death grip against the moon's feeble gravity.

Wherever Sunday looked there was another primary-coloured spider clambering with fluid agility over the soot-black undulating ground. No matter what contortions the legs had to perform as they navigated craters and grooves at all scales, the pressure capsules followed graceful trajectories. The more distant the spiders, the more acute the angle of view. She watched them tilt around the curvature of the world.

'Phobos feels like a long way from Earth,' Eunice said, her suited figure walking alongside Sunday's rover. 'But that's not how it works, when you factor in the orbital-transfer mechanics.'

'Right. I was wondering when you'd pop up.'

'Not like I was going to miss an opportunity to revisit the old place, given the time I spent here.' Eunice's purposeful, bouncing stride belied the feeble gravity.

'I don't see how this place can be anything other than a long way from home,' Sunday said.

'Energetics, dear girl. Delta-vee. If you start from Earth, it costs you more fuel to land on the Moon than it does to reach Phobos. Counter-intuitive, I suppose – although not if you have a thorough grasp of the principles.'

'That's me ruled out, then.'

'Nature gave us this stepping stone for free. It's just been sitting around Mars, waiting to be exploited. So we came and we saw and we conquered.' Eunice swivelled her helmet to track Sunday. 'Where are you going?'

'Your old base camp. Where else are you likely to have buried a clue?'

'Let's look at Mars first,' Eunice declared. 'Then we'll go to the base camp. You owe me that much.'

Sunday felt that she owed the construct nothing, but she caught her tongue before answering. Any utterance that was not the sort of thing she might have said to her living grandmother was at best noise, at worse a potentially damaging input.

'You'll get your wish.'

The rover-suit's whirling, whisking limbs made brisk work of the necessary kilometres, processing the terrain with furious scuttling pre-cision. Soon Mars began to rise over the horizon's sharp black ridge.

Sunday did not stop until the clock was reading two hours, halfway into her rental agreement. Then it was time to take in the glory of this new world.

Mars ruled the sky. It was half-illuminated, the shadowed hemisphere serving only to emphasise that this was a three-dimensional thing, a sphere bulging out towards her. With no air between her and the atmosphere of Mars – and very little air in the atmosphere to begin with – the ground features appeared preternaturally sharp, defined with a mapmaker's fastidiousness. The lit hemisphere was a warm salmon hue, tinged here and there with dusty swathes of ochre and burnt sienna. White snow frosted the visible pole. Cutting across the face, the clawmarks of some staggering canyon system gouged deep into the flesh of the world. *Valles Marineris*, Sunday thought: she knew that much, at least. And that fracture zone, where the canyons dissolved into a quilt of shattered intricacy, was the Noctis Labyrinthus, the Maze of Night. The three volcanoes beyond the maze: Ascreaus Mons, Pavonis Mons, Arsia Mons.

She was about to voke the aug to request a detailed topographic overlay when she realised that she was already travelling with the best possible guide.

'Fond memories?' Sunday asked.

'It wasn't like this when Jonathan and I landed on Phobos,' Eunice said. 'A planetwide dust storm had brewed up while we were on our way, so when we got here we couldn't see much at all. We had no choice but to sit it out before we could head down to Mars.'

'There were already people down there, though.'

Eunice used one gloved hand to screen glare from her helmet. 'They had enough provisions and supplies to see out the storm, provided it didn't last for months. But they couldn't move around much, and it was far too dangerous to send anything up or down. This was before the elevator, of course.'

'That much I figured.'

'It wasn't like Earth. Miss your landing point on Earth and you're never far from rescue. Didn't work that way on Mars, especially not in those days.'

Eunice had been thirty-one when she came with her husband to Phobos in 2062; not much younger than Sunday was now. She had been the ninety-eighth human being to set foot on that rusted soil, just before the influx became an inundation.

'Can we look at the camp now?' she said. 'Clock's ticking on my rental agreement.'

'Follow me,' Eunice said, sighing. 'It's not too far. Nothing's far on Phobos.'

The dust storm wasn't the worst thing that could have happened. Nevertheless, none of the early explorers had been pleased to have their journeys to Mars interrupted by surface weather. Phobos had benefited, though. Long a convenient staging point for Martian exploration, by 2062 an entire transnational shanty town had spontaneously self-organised on the little moon, consisting of a ramshackle, barely planned assortment of domes, surface shacks and dugout habitats, and home to a semi-permanent population already numbering dozens.

Even in those early days, some had already decided that they actually preferred life in orbit, rather than down in the Martian gravity well or back on the Moon or Earth. They got all the scenery they could take just by looking out of the window or venturing onto the moon's surface, and the steady succession of arriving and departing ships made for endless variety. Their technical services were also highly valued, in a variety of enterprises ranging from vehicle maintenance to the supply of narcotics and paid sex.

Most of that original shanty town was gone now, swallowed into the Stickney developments. But there had been a few outposts scattered elsewhere on Phobos, including the one where Eunice had spent most of her time.

When something began to push over the horizon, Sunday assumed they were coming up on the camp. But the object reared too high for that.

It was as dark, if not darker, than the rest of Phobos, and it rose a good ninety metres from the surface. They crept up to the shattered terrain around its base, where it had daggered into Phobos countless ages ago. A couple of other suits were wandering around the scene, shining spotlights onto the object's upper reaches. Where the lights fell, they picked out intricate carved detail: flanges, pipes, repetitive iterations of the same elements, like spinal vertebrae or ribs. Bony outgrowths fused with ancient fossilised machine parts. Rocket exhausts like eye sockets, docking ports like gaping jawbones or reproductive organs. Hull armour spidered with fontanelle cracks.

'They called it the Monolith,' Eunice said. 'Found it in photographs of Phobos, way back at the beginning of the twenty-first century. Couldn't resolve the thing itself, just its shadow, but the shadow told them it had to be big. Needless to say, it was a prime target for close-up examination by the first landers.'

Sunday's eyes tracked the mesmerising, morbid detail. The object was lumpy and asymmetrical, but it was clearly a vehicle of some kind, nose-down in the crust. 'Somehow, I think I'd have heard about a crashed alien spaceship by now.'

'Some of the early explorers got bored, cooped up here with a lot of time on their hands and not enough to do. One of them was a woman called Chakrabarty. Indian, I think. Or maybe Pakistani. One day, for kicks, she draws up a plan, very detailed and meticulous, and starts carving stuff into the Monolith. Her team had cutting gear, explosives, everything she needed. She started at the bottom and worked her way up. It was pretty easy. You can climb all the way up without any kind of safety line, and even if you fall off the top, it's no worse than jumping off a garden wall back on Earth.'

'This was all done by ... this one woman?'

'Chakrabarty started it. Then she went down to Mars and a while later word came back that she'd been killed – suit malfunction, I think. Her plans were still on file at the camp, though. After that, it became a sort of tradition. Anyone who was stuck here for more than a few days ... they'd suit-up and head out to the Monolith to add a contribution to Chakra's Folly. It was a way of honouring her memory – and of saying, *We were here, we did this*. Millions of years from now, the Monolith's still going to be here. Until Phobos falls into Mars.'

'Is it finished now?'

'They reached the top decades ago. They've even sprayed the whole thing with plastic, to stop vandals and micrometeorite damage.'

Sunday made out fist-sized craters where tiny particles had hit Chakra's Folly after it had been carved and decorated, chipping away at the details. She presumed the damage had been done before the protective layer was added.

'Did you add to it?' she asked.

'I suppose I must have.'

'You suppose?'

'I don't remember whether I did or not. Is that good enough for you?'

Sunday tempered her frustration. She couldn't blame the construct for not knowing things that it had never been told. 'There must be a record of who did what somewhere.'

'Don't count on it. And maybe I didn't add anything. At this point, there may be no way of ever telling.' Eunice stooped to pick something up from the ground, some chunk of material lying loose on the surface – blasted from the Monolith, perhaps – but her fingers slipped right through it. 'You didn't need to come all this way to examine the Folly,' she said, standing up with a grunt of irritation. 'You could have called up a figment of it and examined it in detail back on the Moon. Anyway, I don't think this can be the reason I wanted you here. Everything about the Folly is public. I couldn't have hidden a message in it if I'd tried.'

'Something worked into the pattern, perhaps?'

'Difficult. They didn't like it when you deviated from Chakrabarty's plan. It was supposed to bring bad luck.'

'Like you ever believed in that.'

'I wouldn't have gone out of my way to court trouble.' Eunice craned her head back, holding one hand above her visor. 'It's magnificent, though. No, really: isn't it?'

'It's a shame Chakra never got to see it finished.'

'We're seeing it for her,' Eunice said.

Sunday wanted to dispute that – there was no 'we' as far as she was concerned, just her own pair of eyes, her own mind and her own feelings. As absurd as it made her feel, though, she did not have the heart to contradict Eunice. Let her believe she was capable of honouring a dead woman's memories, if that was what she wished.

It did not take long to reach the Indian encampment, once they'd set off from the Monolith. It surmounted the horizon like an approaching galleon, masts and sails the towers and reflector arrays of a long-abandoned communications node. Smaller buildings surrounded the main huddle. It was a ghost town, long derelict.

'Bad blood between the Indians and the Chinese back in the mid-fifties,' Eunice explained, Sunday reminding herself that this was the mid-*twenty*-fifties she was talking about, not the twenty-one-fifties. 'Never blew up into anything involving tanks and bombs, but there was sufficient animosity for the Indians not to want to have anything to do with the Chinese encampment. So they came all the way to Phobos and built this place, practically walking distance from the original shanty town.'

'Couldn't they have done us all a favour and left the Old-World politics behind?'

'We were young, the world was young.'

Sunday couldn't tell if anyone had been near the outpost lately. There were no footprints on Phobos, and the indentations left by the surface suits were indistinguishable from the pitting and gouging already worked into the terrain over billions of years. Still, why would anyone bother giving the settlement more than a glance?

Maybe in a hundred years historians would look back on this neglected site and find its dereliction unforgivable. But here, now, it was just more human litter, roadside junk left behind when people had moved elsewhere.

Off to one side, Eunice walked by a curious, rack-like structure that had been planted into the Phobos topsoil. It had a makeshift, lopsided look, as if knocked together in a burst of misguided enthusiasm after a lengthy drinking session. Eunice brushed her hand against the wheels that had been fixed into the frame, mounted on vertical spindles so that their rims could be easily turned. 'Tibetans and Mongolians,' she explained. 'They were on the original Indian mission, or ended up here later – I can't remember which.'

'What the hell are those things?'

'Prayer wheels. What the Tibetans used to call 'khor. Ceramic gyro-scopes and reaction-control discs from spacecraft stabilisation systems. The things painted on the rim are Buddhist incantations, mainly – the eight auspicious symbols of the *Ashtamangala*. Supposed to notch up good karma by turning the wheels whenever you were coming and going from the camp.'

Eunice's ghost-hand brushed through the prayer wheels without turning them.

'Don't tell me you believed that stuff.'

'You don't have to believe something to keep on good terms with your neighbours. Their cooking was great, and it cost me nothing to turn their silly old wheels. I even suggested we should rig them up to dynamos, make some extra energy.' She made a tooth-sucking noise. 'Didn't go down well.'

'So why touch the wheels now?'

'Old habits.' Eunice hesitated. 'Respect for the people who once lived here. There was one ... there was this young Tibetan. I think space had already got to him by the time he reached Phobos. Cooped up here, the poor kid went completely off the rails. Just sat there rocking and chant-ing, mostly. Then he latched on to me. My fault, really. Had this helmet ... I'd painted a lion's face around the visor. We'd all customised our suits, so it was no big deal to me.'

'And?'

'This poor young man ... there's this figure, they call her the Dakini. *Khandroma* in Tibetan – "she who traverses the sky". One of her mani-festations is Senge Dongma, the lion-faced one. She's on some of those wheels. When I showed up with my helmet ... let's just say he had a few adjustment issues.'

Sunday had no recollection of ever having heard this story before. Yet it was out there, somewhere in Eunice's documented life – either in the public record, or captured in some private recording snared by the family's posterity engines. The construct could not have known it other-wise.

How marvellous a life was, how effortlessly complex, how full of astonishments.

'You pushed him over the edge,' Sunday said. 'Into madness.'

'Wasn't my fault that he was already primed to believe that claptrap,' Eunice said. 'This was before the Mandatory Enhancements, remember. But he was a sweet little boy. I tried to downplay my karmic stature as best as I could, but I didn't want to undermine his entire belief system.'

'How considerate of you.'

'I thought so.'

At the base of the comms tower was a low rock-clad dome – inflated and pressurised and then layered over with a scree of insulating rubble, fused to a lustrous ebony. Radiating out from this central dome were three semicircular-profiled tunnels connected to three hummocks, each of which had an igloo-like airlock and a thick-paned cartwheel-shaped window set into its apex.

The entire Indian complex was smaller than one wing of the household, but this was where Eunice had spent months of her existence, holed up with a dozen or so fellow travellers while they waited for the storm to blow over.

'How did you ... pass the time?' Sunday asked. 'You couldn't just ching out of it, could you?'

'We had a different form of chinging,' Eunice said. 'An earlier type of virtual-reality technology, much more robust and completely unaffected by time lag. You may have heard of it. We called it "reading".'

'I know about books,' Sunday said. 'It's one of your stupid books that's brought me here.'

'Well, we read a lot. And watched movies and listened to music and indulged in this strange behaviour called "making our own entertainment".' She paused. 'We weren't just sitting around watching the days go by. We had work to do, keeping the base operational, drilling into Phobos, even, very occasionally meeting the Chinese and other settlers in Stickney. Just because the governments made us build separate bases didn't mean we couldn't hang out.'

Sunday had walked the suit all the way around the main dome and its three satellites.

'I can't see a way in. There are airlocks on each of the smaller domes, but they're all sealed over. Even if they weren't sealed, I'm not sure this suit would fit through the doorway.'

'The camp was abandoned by the end of the century, which is when I'd have had to come back here. But that sprayed-on sealant must be newer than that.'

'Did it occur to you sixty years ago, while you were busy thinking of ingenious ways to waste my time, that I might not even be able to get in there now?'

Eunice bent to peer through the viewport in the nearest airlock, wiping the glass with her ghost-hands. 'You're making an unwarranted assumption. There may be no need for physical entry into the domes. There's aug here, self-evidently. If it reaches into the domes, then we can ching inside.'

'I already tried that. There's no way into the domes, active or passive.'

Eunice stalked around to the next airlock. 'Let me make absolutely sure of that.'

Sunday had equipped the construct with a suite of routines to maximise the effectiveness of the simulation, even when the aug was thin or local data traffic highly congested. Those same routines made Eunice's conversations all but secure, even with only modest levels of quanglement. Perhaps Eunice would be able to sniff a way into the dome using the same box of tricks.

Sunday wasn't optimistic about that. Unless there was something inside capable of surveilling – a security camera, a robot, a distributed sensor web – they were back to square one. And why would there be anything like that in an abandoned encampment?

'OK, I've found a way in. Impressed, granddaughter? Damn well should be. I've lost none of my edge.'

'Yes, I'm ...' But Sunday trailed off. Was it right to be impressed that software had done the job it was designed to do? Wasn't that exactly the point of it? 'Just tell me what we've got.'

'Active ching, my dear. There's a ... robot. Someone left it in there, and it's still motile.'

'Someone just *left* a robot in there?'

'Do you want the ching or not? You don't need to know the coords – I can put you through from my side.'

'Where will I end up?'

Eunice gestured vaguely. 'The dome to the left of us, I believe. It doesn't really matter, because I'll be right with you and I know the layout of the place. Once inside, we can make our way to my quarters.'

'Give me the bind,' Sunday said.

It was, by some distance, the crudest ching she had ever experienced – cruder even than the proxy she'd used on the Moon, during Chama's expedition through the Ghost Wall. She had a point of view, but no sense of being elsewhere – her body, as far as her mind was concerned, was still in the rover-suit. When she tried to look around, her viewpoint juddered like a camera with a sticky bearing.

'Are you here?' Eunice asked. She was standing next to Sunday, cradling her helmet under one arm. The helmet, Sunday was astonished to see, had gained a custom paint job in the seconds since she had last seen Eunice.

A lion's roaring face, coloured gold and ochre, with startling blue eyes and a toothsome, red-lined jaw gaping around the visor.

'Very nice,' Sunday said.

'There's no air, according to your sensors, but it feels odd to wear a suit in here.'

A circular window crowned the apex of the dome, but it didn't admit much light. Sunday's robot had a torch built into its head, which must have activated as soon as the ching bind went through. She steered its dim yellow beam around the airless room, picking out a miserable assortment of junk and detritus. The room looked as if it had suffered an earthquake, or been looted. There were bunks, equipment lockers, ancient and broken computer systems. Printouts, photographs of loved ones, children's drawings were still fixed to the in-curving walls.

Her robot was slumped, knees drawn up to its chest, back to the wall. She tried standing up. The robot hesitated, then jerked into shambling motion. It had a limp and its fine motor control was shot. It was obviously very damaged, which might have been the reason it had been left to moulder in the camp. There was something attached to its chest, a kind of mechanical spider with jointed white limbs and a flattened crablike body. Sunday presumed it was a repair bot that had broken down in the process of trying to fix the larger unit.

She dislodged it with a stiff flick from her forearm and gauntlet. The fingers were seized into uselessness, like a frostbitten hand.

'This way,' Eunice said, picking a path between piles of junk.

They navigated the connecting corridor between the domes, Eunice looking back impatiently as Sunday struggled to keep apace. Decompression, when it happened, must have been sudden. There were flash-frozen plants, their vines still curling around the corridor walls. When Sunday touched them, they snapped into green shards like brittle sugary confections.

'I don't like this place. Hope no one was here when the pressure went.'

'Do you see bodies?'

'No.'

'It was abandoned long before it fell into decay, I'm sure of that. No one's been inside these walls for a very long time.'

206

'Why would they? It's the dead past. Anyone sensible has got better things to do with their time.'

Eunice flashed her a cocky smile. 'Then what does that make you?'

'Find your room, then let's get out of here.'

The main dome had interior partitions with pressure-tight doors between them. The doors were all open now, the air long since fled. There was a lounge/commons area with a round table, its black top engraved with a zodiacal design, and brightly coloured chairs that were normal enough save for the fact that they had seat belts and foot stirrups. There was a mug still on the table, with a snap-on plastic lid and a drinking nipple. Sunday moved to examine it, but the robot's seized-up grip wasn't wide enough to grasp it and she knocked it off the table. The mug drifted to the floor without breaking. On its side were the words *Reykjavik 2088*, above the five rings of the Olympics symbol.

'This way,' Eunice said. She stepped through one of the partition doors, Sunday following into the room beyond.

Sunday waggled the torch beam around. 'Sure this is it?'

'Yes, quite definitely.' Eunice didn't need to explain herself. If she was certain, it meant that the records placed her in this part of the Indian base. There would be images, movies that had been gorged by the construct's ravenous curiosity. 'But I may not have been the last occupant, and there's no reason they'd have kept this place as a shrine to my greatness.'

'Then we're wasting our time, aren't we?'

'My older self obviously thought otherwise, or she wouldn't have buried those papers in Pythagoras.'

'Well, that worked well, didn't it? If your older self didn't anticipate that part of the Moon being swallowed by China, maybe she got her plans wrong here as well.'

'Do have a little faith, child.'

In one angle of the segment-shaped room was a combination bunk/hammock, optimised for sleep in microgravity conditions. Next to that was a fold-out desk, with a screen and mirror above it. Elsewhere there were equipment lockers and shelves, furnished with boxes, cartons, medical supplies and general spacefaring kipple.

Sunday scuffed her hand along one of the shelves, bulldozing dust. After depressurisation the dust had had decades to resettle, forming a cloying grey sediment on every surface.

Sunday saw something on the bunk. She limped over and tried to pick it up, but her hands were useless.

'It's your glove,' she said. 'The other half of the pair. It's just like the one Geoffrey found in Copetown. But I can't grab hold of it.' Then a thought occurred to her. 'Even if I *could* grab onto it, how the hell am I going to get it out of here?'

'Break the window in the ceiling and throw the glove out – just make sure you don't put it into orbit.'

'Then what? By the time it makes it back down to the surface, it could be anywhere on Phobos!'

Eunice had her helmet under her arm and was scratching the back of her head with her other hand. 'It's not the glove,' she said quietly. 'The glove's a gift, reassurance that you're close. But it's not the glove. That's not how I think.'

Sunday moved to another part of the room. She had noticed the mirror before, but it was only now that she happened to stand in front of it and glimpse herself. For an instant, the realisation of what she was looking at, what was being reflected back at her, did not quite click. She was chinging an androform robot, as she had expected: hard-armoured and articulated like a human being. The light in the crown of the robot's head dazzled her as it bounced back from the mirror.

But it wasn't an androform robot. It was a spacesuit, with a helmet on.

And there was something behind the visor.

Sunday looked at the face of death, looking back at her. There was a skull inside the helmet. A skull with skin pasted on, skin like rice paper.

'Eunice ... this isn't a robot.' Horror made her own voice sound unfamiliar.

'I'm sorry?'

'It's a spacesuit with a dead body and I'm walking around in it. Please tell me you didn't know this.'

Eunice looked at her. There was no change of expression on her face, no dawning comprehension. 'How could I possibly have known, Sunday?'

'You knew. You looked for something to ching, and you found ... this. You found a way in. You couldn't have done that without realising that the ching coordinates pointed to a suit, not a robot.'

'I ... improvised, dear. It's a suit with servo-assist and a camera built into the helmet. It moves, it sees. How, in practical terms, does that differ from a robot?'

'Because it's got a corpse in it.' She was too angry to swear, too angry even to sound angry.

'Fate presented us with this opening; I took it.'

'How can you be so callous? This is ... was a person, and you're using them like . . .' Sunday flustered, 'like some cheap tool, like some piece of disposable equipment. And I'm locked in with them, in a . . . a *coffin*.'

'Get over it. Do you think this person gives a shit, Sunday? Whoever they are, whoever they were, no one cared enough to come and look for them. They sealed this place up, not even realising there was a dead body inside. That's how missed this person was.'

'You're not making this any easier.'

'We've found them now, haven't we? When we get back to Stickney we'll alert the authorities, and they can come and open up the camp. They'll probably be able run a trace on the suit and find its owner. But in the meantime? Am I going to refuse to make use of this suit just because someone died in it once upon a time? This is serious, Sunday.'

She swallowed her revulsion. 'Let's get this over with. And if you ever do something like this to me again—'

'You'll do what? Erase me, because I had the temerity to make a decision? I thought you were smarter than that, granddaughter. By the way – while we've been talking, I happened to notice that that locker isn't where it ought to be.'

'What?' Sunday asked, wary of a diversion.

'Check the dust tracks on the floor. It's been moved. Those may even be my own footprints.'

Sunday could no more grip the locker than she could the mug or the glove, but in Phobos's gravity it wasn't hard to shove it sideways until it toppled in slow motion. Sunday directed the helmet torch at the portion of the wall that had been hidden by the locker until then.

Eunice's intuition had been correct. It was a painting, more properly a mural: brushed directly onto the dome's curving wall.

Sunday stared at it in wonderment. For a moment, she forgot all about the corpse suit.

'I know this.'

'Of course you know it. It's a copy of the one in my room, back in the household. I take no responsibility for the original, but I'm certain I made this copy.'

'You painted this?'

'Projected the original onto the wall, copied it. It doesn't make me an artist.'

She wished that the construct had permitted the tingle of recognition to endure for at least a few moments before shattering the spell. Eunice was quite right, of course. Sunday had visited her grandmother's abandoned bedroom on a handful of solemn occasions – it had always felt like the room of someone dead, not merely absent – and she recognised the mural from those visits.

'Who'd have thought it?'

The construct looked at her sharply. 'Who'd have thought what, child?'

'That you, the great and fierce Eunice Akinya, could ever have been homesick. Why else would you have brought this piece of your past with you?'

Executed with childlike boldness, the mural was a vivid, colour-drenched painting of Kilimanjaro. The mountain's steepness was exaggerated, its snow-cap diamond-faceted against deep-blue sky. Cutting across the middle of the painting was a horizontal swathe of trees, depicted with naive exactness and symmetry. Ornamenting the trees, perched on the branches like jewels and lanterns, were many colourful birds with long tails and horned beaks. In the foreground were ochre grasses and emerald shrubs. Woven into the grasses, striped and counter-striped like partial ciphers, were many different kinds of animal, from lions to zebra to giraffe and rhino, snakes and scorpions. There were even Maasai, their tall black and red spear-clutching forms the only recurrent vertical elements in the composition.

'I wasn't homesick,' Eunice said, after a great while. 'Home-proud. That's not the same thing.'

Sunday blinked the mural. 'I've captured an image. But I'm not sure this is the thing we were meant to find.'

'And I'm sure it is. When I came back here, I must have changed the picture. It was well done, wouldn't you say? Perhaps I redid the whole thing, to make sure the joins wouldn't show.'

'What are you on about?'

'It doesn't match. I have a memory of the original, and . . . something's different.'

'Tell me.'

'Let's be sure of ourselves, shall we? I can't be certain that my memory of the mural is accurate. But your brother's still in Africa. Have him visit my room and blink the image up to us. Then we can talk.'

Jitendra was on the drowsy cusp of consciousness, in the same kind of room where she had been revived earlier in the day. Sunday sat down in the chair next to the bed and was smiling when he surfaced, squinting against the light and licking sleep-parched lips. 'Welcome back, lover. We're on Mars. Almost.'

Jitendra had already been reassigned voluntary muscle function, so he was able to tilt his head and smile back. His face was slack, but the tone would return soon enough.

'We made it,' he said, slurring and pausing. 'Not that I ever had doubts ... but still.'

'It's still a miracle.' The technician had given her a box holding six little cuboid sponges, stuck on the end of sticks like lollipops. They were soaked with something sweet, chemically tailored to Jitendra's palate. She leaned over and dabbed his lips with one.

'Thank you,' Jitendra said.

'How do you feel?'

'Like I've been dead for a month.'

'You have, Mister Gupta. It's called space travel.'

He struggled into a sitting-up position, propping himself with an elbow. He was wearing silver pyjamas. They had even shaved him, so that when Sunday kissed his cheek his skin was peach soft and perfumed, smelling of violets. Jitendra took in his surroundings, studying the white room and the false window with its ever-breaking waves. 'Everything went OK, didn't it?'

Sunday dabbed at his lips again. 'Not a hitch. They brought me out sooner, but apparently that's what happens sometimes. Just time to take a little stroll outside, see the scenery.'

'Please don't tell me you've seen Mars ahead of me.'

'No,' she said, just a bit too quickly. 'Not yet. It was on the other side. We'll see it together.'

'I'd like that.' Jitendra rubbed his slightly stubbled scalp. 'I need a haircut.'

'We found something,' she blurted.

'We?'

'Eunice and I. I need to talk to my brother, but ... I think I already know where we're going next.'

Jitendra sat in silence, waiting for her to elaborate. 'Are you going to let me in on the big secret?' he asked eventually.

'It's Mars,' Sunday said. 'Which is where we were going anyway, of course. But there's a complication.'

Jitendra managed a smile. 'Why am I not surprised?'

When Mars lifted into view its aspect was different, but she made no mention of that. In a way it helped, because this was a different face of the world, not the one she had already seen, and she could study it afresh without having to pretend. Sunday regretted her lie, but it had been a small one.

They were standing next to each other, far enough away from the other tourists that they could imagine themselves alone on this airless ridge, the only living people on Phobos. Soon this would be the memory she chose to hold on to, letting the earlier one wither. And in time she might even come to believe that this was, indeed, the first time she had seen Mars rising, in all its ancient, time-scarred immensity.

'It's wonderful,' Jitendra said.

'It's a world. Worlds are wonderful.'

They stood in silence, transfixed, until a soft chime from the console told them it would soon be time to return their rented suits, and make ready for the rest of their journey.

'Before we go inside,' Sunday said, 'you should see Chakra's Folly. Reckon we've still got time. On the way, you can tell me all about the Evolvarium.'

'Why are you interested in that all of a sudden? I thought that was more my area.'

'Because that's where we're going.'

CHAPTER THIRTEEN

The ching was passive, but the resolution more than adequate for his purposes. He exited his standing body, rose into the air and drifted over the treetops, gaining speed and altitude. Sometimes it was good not to take the Cessna, or one of the other machines; just to become a disembodied witness, with a viewpoint assembled from distributed public eyes. The scene was rendered with exacting thoroughness down to the last leaf, the last hoofprint or elephant footprint in the dust. Any uncertainty in the image flow was seamlessly interpolated long before his brain had to fill in any gaps.

He found the herd soon enough. Whatever status Matilda might have lost among the other females when she was startled by Eunice's figment had been regained over the ensuing weeks. Her position and body posture were as authoritative as ever. She was leading her family along a narrow trail bordered by acacia and cabbage trees.

Revelling in the freedom – as much as he loved flying the Cessna, there was something delicious about lacking body and inertia, the ability to traverse the sky like a demon, at the merest whim – Geoffrey scouted the other herds, taking the opportunity to refresh his memories of their structures and hierarchies. He also pinpointed the roving bulls, solitary or in small, quarrelsome gangs. The minds of bull elephants, soaked with testosterone, preoccupied with status and mating, felt infinitely more alien to him than those of the matriarchs and their herds. And yet he'd known many of these bulls when they were juvenile males, as boisterous and carefree as the rest.

Minds were deeply strange things. When these elephants were young, it had required no great effort to see the sparks of human awareness in their curiosity and playfulness. It was even possible to think that their minds were in fact more human before adulthood clamped down and locked those attributes away, secure behind iron walls of dominance and aggression.

Elephant society was a product of necessity, shaped by environmental factors over countless millions of years. But what did that mean, here and now? Things were changing for the elephants; had been changing for centuries. Humans had come, and the humans had done things to the climate that had made the world convulse. Steamships to space elevators: all that in a Darwinian eye-blink, a strobe-flash of massively compressed change. Elephants were still dealing with the fact that monkeys had fire and spears; they hadn't even *begun* to process the industrial revolution, let alone the space age or the Anthropocene.

Bolder changes still were coming down the line, changes that even humans would struggle to accommodate. Panspermian Initiatives, the Green Efflorescence.

Observing elephants, monitoring them – even creeping into their skulls – that was acceptable to Geoffrey. But making them into something else, rewiring their society as if it was no more than a defective mechanism, transforming it into something better equipped to survive ... ? He wasn't sure how he felt about that. People had done enough harm, even with the best of intentions.

When he chinged back into his body, someone was waiting for permission to manifest. The tag was unfamiliar, so for a moment he presumed it was Sunday, coming in via an unorthodox, highly quangled routing.

He took the call in the research shack. He had made coffee before chinging and now, as the figment assumed reality, he drained the bitter dregs into his cup.

'I hope I haven't caught you at an inopportune moment, Mister Akinya. I did say I'd be back in touch, didn't I?'

Geoffrey studied the blank-eyed man, with his sea-green suit and toothless gash of a mouth, his skin so pale that it might have been grafted from a reptile's belly.

'Kind of hoping you might have forgotten, Truro.'

'Well, I can't fault your honesty. But no, we don't forget our debts. Especially when they've been extended. Remortgaged.'

'If Sunday cut a deal with you, that's between you and her.'

'Ah, but it doesn't work like that. If it ever did. We've done you two favours now, Mister Akinya. I'd very much like us at least to begin to discuss something by way of reciprocity.'

'You can start by telling me where you're chinging from.'

'Oh, not so very far from you. Your sister correctly deduced that I was based on or near Earth. As it happens, I'm practically within spitting distance. I'm calling from Tiamaat, not too far from your Somalian coast. You'll have heard of it, of course.'

214

'I'm not an idiot. Why have you waited until now to contact me?'

'You needed time to reflect, to assess your obligations to family. Sunday has arrived at her destination: we facilitated her visit, and the quangled bind from Phobos. She is awake. History has begun again. It felt like an appropriate time to resume negotiations.'

Geoffrey knew that Sunday was safe. He had received her message and made a point of blinking her a view of Kilimanjaro by way of reply.

'I'm not sure anything needs negotiating.'

'Chama Akbulut . . . found something, didn't he? On the Moon, in the Chinese sector?'

Geoffrey picked a fly out of the coffee's cold meniscus. 'If you say so.'

'I'll confess, there are two reasons why we ought to meet in person, and with some urgency. One is the business with Chama, Gleb and the phyletic dwarves. It's a marvellous little project and it has my absolute support. There's something else, though. You've come to the attention of . . . well, I shan't say for the moment. But a colleague of mine has requested an audience.'

'Thing is, my calendar's a little full.'

'And this is science, Mister Akinya. Whatever your plans, I doubt there's anything so pressing that it can't wait a few days.'

Geoffrey opened his mouth to argue, but beyond the usual vague notions of getting ahead on paperwork, he had no detailed intentions. 'You're not going away, are you?'

'As you'll find, I'm a remarkably persistent soul.'

'You're going to keep bothering me, I suppose I might as well get it over with.'

'Splendid,' Truro said, as if he had been expecting no other response. 'You shall come to Tiamaat, and the pleasure will be all mine! I have your ching coordinates. Shall we say . . . this location, tomorrow morning? Ten a.m.? Very good.'

The knob clicked, the door emitting a mouselike squeak of protestation as it opened. Eunice's room was cool, the windows permanently shuttered. A ceiling fan stirred the air to no detectable benefit. Geoffrey had peered into this room at various points during his childhood and adolescence, but not often since his late teens. Eunice's figment had sometimes manifested here, but as often as not it had appeared somewhere else in the household or its grounds. Whatever the case, Geoffrey had usually done his best to be elsewhere.

The room was a time capsule, a piece of the twenty-first century lodged in the present. The rose-printed wallpaper was paper, not active material:

it was pasted onto the walls and couldn't be altered at a moment's whim. Rectangular fade marks hinted at the locations of old pictures, join lines where the sheets didn't quite match, and little white lesions where the paper had been scuffed. The rug on the floor was a kind of textile rather than a self-cleansing frond-carpet. When he stood on it, it didn't ooze over his shoes and try to pick them clean of nourishment. The furniture was wooden: not the kind of wood that grew purposefully into furniture shapes, but the kind that started off as trees, before being hacked and rolled and sawed and steamed into shape. There were things in this room older than the Cessna.

One wall wasn't papered, or had been papered and then painted over. The mural didn't fill the entire area; it was bordered in white and smaller than Geoffrey remembered. The wall faced east, towards the real Kilimanjaro.

'I was right,' Eunice said. 'You can blink it for Sunday's sake, but I've seen it through your eyes now and that's much the same thing.'

'I haven't seen the other one. What's different?'

'Directly below the mountain, here.' She was pointing at a long-legged bird, maybe a crane or ibis. 'The etymology of Kilimanjaro isn't very clear, but it may mean "white mountain" or "white hill". This bird is white, do you see?'

'I do.'

'In the version on Phobos, it's a different bird. I saw it immediately, but I had to be sure. Sunday would never have realised, but—'

'Get to it, Eunice.' His nerves were addled after the visitation from Truro. 'Some of us have lives to be getting on with.'

'It's a peacock,' she said, 'painted in exactly the same position. That's the only point of difference between the two murals. We have stills of the Indian camp taken around 2062, and some of them show the mural. There was no difference between this one and that one at that point, so I must have made the change when I returned to Phobos in 2099.'

'Fine. And this is supposed to mean something to me?'

'From white mountain to peacock mountain, Geoffrey. Must I labour the point? The original mural refers to Kilimanjaro; the one on Phobos can only refer to Pavonis Mons.'

'Pavonis Mons,' he repeated.

'On Mars. It's the—'

'Highest mountain. Or volcano. Or something.'

'That's Olympus Mons, but you're on the right lines. Pavonis Mons is still pretty impressive. Main thing is, I was there. If there was no documented link to my past, then you'd be forgiven for dismissing the mural.

But *I was there*. I walked on that mountain. It was 2081; I was fifty-one years old, pregnant with Miriam. We know the exact coordinates.'

'Then all Sunday has to do is ...' Geoffrey trailed off. 'She mentioned complications, Eunice.'

The figment swallowed audibly. 'There are ... difficulties.'

'Such as?'

'That part of Mars ... the Tharsis Bulge ... it's changed a little since my time.'

Memphis motioned Geoffrey to take a seat until his call was done. Geoffrey poured himself some water from the jug set on a low table near Memphis's desk.

'What can I do for you, Geoffrey?' Memphis asked pleasantly, when he had come out of ching.

'I have to go away, just for a couple of days, leaving tomorrow morning. Could you check on things while I'm gone?'

'It is rather short notice.'

'I know, but I'd feel a lot happier if you could do that for me.'

Memphis shook his head, a gesture of good-natured exasperation that Geoffrey remembered well from his earliest days. *What are we going to do with you, young man?*

'Couple of days, you said?'

'That's all. And you don't need to spend hours out there.'

'Could you not ching, from wherever you'll be?'

'That may not be possible. Anyway, I'd rather someone went there in person. You know how it is.'

'Yes,' Memphis said, in long-suffering tones. 'One does. Well, you would not ask this lightly, I think. I will inspect Matilda's herd from an airpod. Will that suffice?'

'If you could also land and inspect the perimeter monitors, and then check on the camp, that would be even better.'

'Will one inspection per day suffice?'

Geoffrey shifted on his seat. 'If that's all you can give me—'

'Which is your way of saying you would rather I made at least two.'

Geoffrey smiled softly. 'Thank you, Memphis.'

'This mysterious trip of yours ... you'll be sure to tell me what it's all about, when you get back?'

'I will, I promise. I don't want there to be any secrets between us.'

'Nor I.'

There was a lull. Memphis looked ready to return to his work, so Geoffrey made to stand up. But his old mentor was not quite done.

'Now that Eunice is never coming back, we should give some thought to what happens to her room. She would not have wanted it kept as some miserable, dusty shrine.'

'There are plenty of rooms in the household going spare.'

'When we have many guests – as we did during the scattering – we are considerably stretched. If the subject upsets you, I won't raise it again. But I know your cousins will be anxious to move on.'

'Bury the past, you mean.'

'We must all do that, if we are to keep living,' Memphis said.

In the morning, Geoffrey saw a glint of moving silver, an aircraft with an upright tail fin, sharking low over the trees. Gradually he heard the drone of ... He shook his head, ready to laugh at the patent absurdity of it. The only thing in his experience that made a sound anything like that was the Cessna, and the Cessna was sitting in plain view.

'Eunice,' he said quietly, 'I could use some help here.'

She was with him in an instant, as if she had never been more than a few paces away. 'What is it, Geoffrey?'

'Need a reality check. Tell me I'm not looking at an aeroplane even older than my own.'

Geoffrey was shielding his eyes from the sun. Eunice echoed his gesture, but at the same time – from where, he hadn't noticed – produced a pair of slim grasshopper-green binoculars, which she held to her eyes single-handed, as daintily as if they were opera glasses. She tracked the moving form of the aircraft, now almost nose-on.

'If I'm not very much mistaken, that is a DC-3. Is there any particular reason why a DC-3 would be coming down to land, miles from anywhere, in the middle of equatorial East Africa?'

'It's my ride,' Geoffrey said.

Eunice lowered the binoculars. 'To where?'

'Somewhere interesting, I hope.'

The DC-3 dropped under the treeline, its engines throttling back. They walked over to meet it.

'They were extraordinarily numerous and long-lived,' Eunice said as they picked their way through dry brush. 'Sixteen thousand, and that's not including all the copies and knock-offs. Even when they were old, you could strip out the avionics, put in new engines and begin again with a zero fatigue rating. Dakotas were still flying when I was a child.'

'Did you like planes?'

'Adored them.' Eunice was stomping her merry way through thigh-high grass as if it wasn't there at all. 'Look at it this way. You've been born in a time when it's possible to *fly through the air in machines*. Who wouldn't fall in love with the idea of that?'

The DC-3 sat tail-down at the end of the airstrip. It was quite astonishingly beautiful: a gorgeous sleek thing, as curvaceous and purposeful as a dolphin.

But, incongruously, there was no sign of a welcoming committee. A door had been opened and a set of steps lowered, but no one was standing at the top of those steps, beckoning him aboard.

'Are you sure this is for you?'

'I thought so,' he said, but with ebbing confidence.

Yet what else could it be but the transport Truro had promised? Then he saw a neat little logo on the tail fin, a spiral galaxy painted green, the only marking anywhere on the highly reflective silver fuselage.

If that didn't clinch it, nothing would.

They climbed aboard. It was cool inside, with seats and settees laid out lounge-fashion and a bar situated at the rear of the fuselage. The compartment ran all the way to the nose: there was no cockpit, no flight controls or instrument panel, merely a couple of additional lounge seats for those who wanted to take advantage of the forward view.

Behind them, the steps folded back into the plane and the door sealed itself. The engines revved up again and Geoffrey felt the aircraft turning on the airstrip.

'And you've no idea what this is about?'

'You, ultimately,' Geoffrey said.

Soon they were bouncing along the airstrip, and then aloft, climbing shallowly, skimming the treetops by no more than hand-widths.

'Well, this is grand fun,' Eunice said, striding imperiously from window to window. 'I'm still here, too. Whoever's sent this thing is allowing you full access to the aug. That's reassuring, isn't it? You're not being kidnapped.'

'I never thought I was.'

Eunice soon tired of the view and sat herself down in one of the seats. 'So who sent this aircraft?'

'The Panspermian Initiative. You know about them – you used to hang out with Lin Wei.'

'I don't know anyone called Lin Wei.'

'You should do, but there's a part of your life missing. Sunday established the connection with Lin, but she doesn't have enough information to fill in the rest of the void.'

'Have to take your word for it, then. So we're going to see this Lin Wei?'

'I doubt it, seeing as she's dead. My point of contact is someone called Truro.'

'Whom you trust enough to get aboard this plane?'

'I'm in his debt. Actually, we're all in his debt, but I'm the one who seems to be expected to do the paying back.'

'The Panspermian Initiative,' Eunice said languidly, drawing out the words as if she was reading them, signwritten across the sky. She was tapping the aug, glugging gallons of data. 'You need to watch people like that. All that species-imperative stuff? Self-aggrandising horse-piss.'

'They think we might be in a critical period, a window of opportunity. If we don't seize the moment now, we might never get beyond the system, into the wider galaxy.'

'Which would automatically be a good thing, would it?'

'You weren't exactly short of grand visions in your day.'

She scoffed. 'I didn't have any noble intentions for the rest of humanity. I was in it for myself, and anyone else smart enough to go along with me.'

'No,' Geoffrey said, shaking his head. 'You were a pioneer and a risk-taker, sure, but you also had ambitions. You didn't go to Mars just to stamp your footprint into that soil and come home again. You wanted to live there, to prove it was something we could do.'

'Me and a thousand others.'

'Doesn't matter – you got there as soon as you could. But your problem was that you couldn't stand still. You had to keep moving, pushing outwards. You liked the idea of living on one planet more than the actuality. That's why you left your husband behind.'

'Jonathan and I grew apart. What has that got to do with anything?'

'If you were alive now, with enough influence to be part of this, you'd be one of the main drivers.'

'Spoken with the assurance of youth. Well, I'm sorry to prick your bubble, but did you ever wonder why I came back to the Winter Palace? Everything Eunice Akinya used to stand for started to bore me senseless.'

'So you decided to become a witchy old recluse, counting her money and tut-tutting at her offspring.'

'Since you put it so charmingly, yes.'

They had been travelling for two hours straight before they left Africa behind, crossing the buttressed white margin of the self-renewing sea wall and into the airspace above the Indian Ocean.

There were boats at sea, fishing and leisure craft, even some of the elegant multi-masted cyberclippers: benign *Marie Celestes*, holds abrim with bulky, non-perishable cargoes. To the south, the edge of one of the floating platelets, an artificial island capped by its own fevered little weather system. Another island, smaller this time, bore a dense thicket of skyscrapers, as if Singapore had become unmoored and drifted halfway around the world. As the DC-3 approached, the city revealed itself to be a congregation of stack farms, rising two kilometres from sea level. The stacks were mossy with vegetation, green-carpeted up their sheer flanks. Robot dirigibles harvested the tops of the stacks, crowding around them like fattened bumblebees as they waited their turn. Aside from a skeleton staff of technicians, no one would live on that island.

The DC-3 kept flying. Geoffrey checked his watch. It was two in the afternoon; they'd been in the air for four hours. He hadn't expected the journey to take this long.

Just when he was starting to worry that the plane was going to carry him all the way to India – however many hours that might entail – something loomed from the ocean haze. Whatever it was rose straight from the sea, a solid-looking mass with a rounded, symmetrical summit. It was a structure, a very large one, with the open maw of a snorkel facing him. The DC-3 was headed straight for it.

Geoffrey knew better than to be alarmed; if the Pans were going to kill him, there were simpler ways of going about it than a plane crash. The engine note changed, the floor tilting as the aircraft lost altitude.

'Do you know what that is?'

'An aqualogy transit duct,' Eunice said. 'They're built up from the seabed, raised on stilts of artificial coral, grown and replenished like the self-renewing sea walls.'

He'd moved to the forward seats for the best view. A pale, batlike craft emerged from the snorkel and sped south. One of the harvester dirigibles loitered near the entrance, awaiting clearance to proceed. Rafts of green biomass drooled from its collector baskets.

The DC-3 had approach priority. The descent steepened, and then they were inside the snorkel, flying down a completely enclosed air-corridor. Geoffrey tried to judge the angle of descent, but without a visible horizon it was hard to estimate. It felt much steeper than his usual landing pattern in the Cessna, but at the same time there was a sense of calm routine, the ride elevator-smooth. He hadn't even been told to sit down or buckle-up.

The corridor darkened as the sunlit mouth receded. Red lights slipped by on either side, marking their progress. Once, another batwing craft sped by in the opposite direction: silver-bodied with the Initiative's green whorl painted on its skin.

'We've descended a long way,' Geoffrey said. 'We must be underwater by now.'

'They're blocking me.'

'What?'

'Aug degradation. The duct must be interfering with the signal. I imagine that's not accidental.'

'Can't you do anything about it?'

'Dear me – that almost sounds like concern for my welfare.'

'It's not. I just value a second pair of eyes.' He paused. 'Eunice?'

His visual field clotted with error messages. She was gone.

His ears popped. The ride levelled out for a stretch. Then, softly enough that he almost thought it might be his imagination, the DC-3 was down. It rolled for a short while, as smoothly as if sliding on ice, and then came to a halt. The tunnel had widened out into a larger space, lit by banks of blue lights.

The door whirred open, the stairs lowering simultaneously. Geoffrey grabbed his overnight bag and climbed out of the now silent transport. He stepped onto hard black ground, sheened like wet asphalt. The chamber was large enough to hold half a dozen other aircraft, though none were as old as the DC-3. Nearby a harvester was having its collector baskets raked clean.

Without Eunice, and without the aug, Geoffrey felt more vulnerable than he'd been expecting. He didn't want to think about all the mega-tonnes of seawater somewhere over his head, especially as some of it appeared to be dripping through the ceiling.

'Well, thanks for the welcome,' he said quietly.

A merwoman strode out of the darkness. Her mobility prosthesis encased her body from the ribcage down, gripping corset-tight. Mechanical legs emerged from the exo's pelvic girdle, spaced wide on complex joints. They were articulated backwards, giving the merwoman the look of some giant strutting bird. The exo whirred and clanked, as if it wasn't in the best repair. The framework was bottle-green, traced with luminous kelp-like patterns.

In impeccable Swahili she said, 'Good afternoon, Mister Akinya. I hope your journey was a pleasant one.'

'Whose idea was the Dakota?'

'Truro thought you'd appreciate the antique touch. Rest assured, though, that you'll be going home by conventional means. I am Mira Gilbert – UAN Office of Scientific and Technological Liaison. It's a pleasure to welcome you to Tiamaat. I trust the absence of aug isn't too distressing?'

'I'm coping.'

'We have our own local aug here, and something very like the Mechanism. You'll be given access to the baseline functions, but before that, I'm afraid we'll need to neutralise any recording devices you might be carrying.'

'I'm not.'

'That also includes your eyes, Mister Akinya. Their capture-and-record function must be disabled.' Her tone was apologetic but insistent. 'I trust this isn't too great an inconvenience? Any information already on the eyes should be safe.'

Geoffrey bristled, but he'd come too far to throw a tantrum now. 'If that's what it takes.'

'Please follow me.'

She whirred around in the exo and clanked away, leading Geoffrey through a door in the side of the cavern and along a dank, wet-floored corridor.

'You speak Swahili very well,' he told her.

'Helps, in this region. I understand you've been in space recently?'

'The Moon and back, assuming that counts. Do you leave Tiamaat very often?'

'I don't leave *water* very often, let alone the city. Frankly, I can't wait to get out of this clanking contraption. It's not that I minded meeting you, though.' After a few paces she added, 'I have been to space, though. I was a pilot, before I was seconded to Tiamaat.'

'How long have you been . . . ?' He felt tongue-tied.

'Aquatic? Thirteen years now. Takes a little while to get used to the alterations – the brain has to learn a whole new way of moving, a whole new hydrodynamics. The first six months were difficult. After that, I never looked back.'

'And could you be . . . reversed? If you wanted to?'

'Perhaps,' Gilbert said, managing to sound as if the notion had never really occurred to her. 'Some have defected back to lubber. But they must have been 'formed for the wrong reasons.' She turned to look back over her shoulder. 'People think becoming like this is the magic spell that'll sort out their lives, put an end to all their worldly woes. Nowadays the psych screening's much more rigorous. There's also a huge waiting list for new surgery. You can't just wake up one morning and decide to become aquatic.'

'You're not worried about overcrowding, surely?'

'Not really. There's more surface area down here than on all the dry land masses combined. Earth coexists with a planet as large as Mars, and all you have to do to cross from one to the other is swim. But there are bottlenecks. Our clinics can only cope with so many transformations, and with the germline programmes making ever more headway, there'll soon be second-generation aquatics who never came through the clinics – merchildren born of merpeople. Then we'll have to impose much stricter quotas. Needless to say, our offspring will have priority. It's not too late to join us, though.'

'Become a citizen? Thanks, but I've got other plans for the rest of my life.'

They rode an elevator upshaft and emerged into a clean white-tiled room. With the tiled floor eventually giving way to a shimmering rectangle of turquoise water, accessed at various points by stairs and ramps, it resembled a large indoor swimming pool. Dim greenish light filtered through heavily strutted ceiling windows. That must be ocean above his head, he thought: enough of it that the full glare of sunlight was reduced to this soupy, olive-stained radiance.

'You can locomote the rest of the way if you want to,' Gilbert said, 'but it would really make a lot more sense if you travelled by water instead. Do you swim?'

Geoffrey couldn't recall the last time he'd set foot in water. 'A bit.'

The merwoman gestured to a white door in the tiled wall to Geoffrey's right. 'Wetsuit in there. Leave your clothes and belongings there – they'll be forwarded to your quarters later.'

With some diffidence, Geoffrey locked himself in the changing room and removed his clothes. He bundled them up in a wireframe basket, then examined the waiting wetsuit. It was fixed against the wall by some hidden means, legs and arms spread wide. It was a vivid yellow-green colour, with a texture like fine-grained sandpaper. He was just starting to work out the best way to get into it when the suit peeled open along hidden seams, exactly as if a kindly poltergeist were offering assistance.

Geoffrey turned and shuffled backwards, arms and legs mirroring the suit's posture, and waited for the fabric to seal itself around his body. At first it tightened alarmingly, sucking onto his skin as if vacuum-formed. Rather to his surprise, he found that he could still breathe without difficulty. He felt, in fact, completely unclothed, and when he brushed his bare fingertips across his fabric-clad chest, it felt as if he was touching his own skin. High-res tactile-transmission system, he supposed, the kind they had in spacesuits these days. He walked out of the room, feeling more self-conscious than he would have liked. The suit enclosed him from ankle to neck, but its tight-fitting contours were barely sufficient to preserve his modesty.

'Good,' Gilbert said, giving him no more than a momentary glance. 'Now for the aqua-mobility harness.'

She walked him over to the far wall, where a dozen or so sleek white devices were racked in a line. They resembled the partial skeletons of marine mammals, each with a segmented spine, a fluke, articulated side-flippers, a lacy suggestion of a skull. There was also a kind of cracked-open ribcage.

'I'm meant to get into that?'

'You want to keep up with me,' Gilbert said, 'you'd better. Back into the harness, it'll do the rest.'

Geoffrey did as he was told, selecting the first of the harnesses. The ribcage pincered slowly around him, clutching his chest firmly, the padded insides of the 'ribs' reshaping to provide maximum surface-area contact. The skull enclosed his head, forming an openwork cage equipped with a breathing apparatus and suction goggles. He felt the harness detach from the wall mounting, so that he was bearing what little weight it possessed. It felt as flimsy as a cheaply made carnival costume.

'What do I do with it?' Geoffrey asked, feeling awkward. He could speak and see freely: the breathing apparatus was still hinged away from his mouth and nose, and the goggles had yet to clamp down onto his eye sockets.

'Step into the water. The harness will sense your intentions and operate accordingly.' With this, Gilbert divested herself of the exo. She slipped out of it and slid into the water, sleek as an otter. Released from the exo she was effectively naked, but her form was so thoroughly alien that Geoffrey might as well have been watching a wildlife documentary.

He took one of the sloping ramps and walked into the blood-warm water. When he was up to his waist, the harness latched on to his legs and coaxed them gently together. Without any apparent conscious volition on his part, the harness then pushed him into a horizontal swimming posture. Before he had a chance to gag on the water the mask and goggles had covered his face. The view through the goggles was as bright and clear as day, lacking any optical distortion or cloudiness.

'Follow me,' Gilbert said, and he heard her clearly through the water. She flexed her body and torpedoed past him, executing an exuberant barrel-roll.

He kicked his legs and paddled his arms. Miraculously, he surged forwards, the harness flexing all the way along its spine, taking his legs with it. The feeble paddling of his arms was amplified a dozen- or hundredfold by the elegant wide-spread flippers, which extended a good two metres either side of him.

Gilbert was still ahead, swimming underwater at least as fast as someone might jog on dry land, but Geoffrey was only a body length or so behind her. For all the power she put into her swimming, it was evidently a very efficient process, judging by the lack of turbulence in her wake.

'Not claustrophobic, are you?' she asked.

'If I was, now would be a bit late to find out.'

'We'll take the express tube. You'll like this.'

Around the pool's submerged walls were several tunnel mouths, each ringed by a hoop of glowing primary colour. 'Red are the exit tubes, we don't take those,' Gilbert said. 'Wouldn't be able to swim against the up-current anyway, even with power-assist.'

She aimed for the tunnel mouth ringed in glowing purple, appearing to accelerate into the maw at the last moment. Geoffrey followed, muscularly signalling his intention to steer and feeling the harness respond almost instantly. Indeed, it appeared to be adapting to him as quickly as he was adapting to it. He was swimming underwater as effortlessly as a dolphin.

He grinned. It would be madness not to enjoy this.

He felt the surge as the tunnel's current seized him, and then he was racing along it, glassy walls speeding by, Gilbert not far ahead. As the tube twisted and turned, the water inside it flowing up and down, he wondered what drove that flow: he couldn't see any visible fans or pumps, unless they retracted out of the way as the swimmers passed. Perhaps it was peristalsis, a gentle but continuous impulsion, driven by the walls themselves.

He had no sooner formulated that idea than they were, startlingly, *outside* – crossing between one part of Tiamaat and another, with only the tube's glass between them and the crush of the surrounding water. They were crossing through a forest of night-lit towers, turreted and flanged and cupolaed, submarine skyscrapers pushing up from black depths, garlanded with myriad coloured lights. The buildings were cross-linked and buttressed by huge windowed arches, many stories high, and the whole city-district, as far as he could see, lay entwined in a bird's-nest tangle of water-filled tubes. He could, in fact, make out one or two tiny moving forms, far above and far below – swimmers carrying their own illumination, so that they became glowing corpuscles in some godlike arterial system. Elsewhere there were ocean-swimming aquatics, moving outside of the tubes, and all manner of submersible vehicles, ranging from person-sized miniature submarines to servicing craft at least as large as one of the cyberclippers he had seen from the air.

Geoffrey reeled. He knew about Tiamaat; he knew about the United Aquatic Nations and had some idea of what they were getting up to under the waves. But the scale of the thing was startling.

He realised that he'd been operating under a gross misapprehension. Living on dry land, it was easy to think that the aquatics constituted no more than a faltering experiment in undersea living, like an early moonbase.

But this was a kingdom. For a moment, dizzied, he began to wonder if it was *his* existence that was the failed experiment.

As quickly as it had been disclosed, the view of Tiamaat was snatched away and he was back inside, the tube hairpinning again, ducking and diving with joyous abandon through a series of vertical S-bends until it deposited the two of them in another swimming pool – or rather what he now appreciated to be a kind of interchange between the various tube systems, with its own colour-coded portals. It was a bigger junction, and they were not alone this time. Other aquatics loitered in the pool, not too close to the entrance/exit points with their strong currents. There were even some visitors or newcomers, wearing harnesses like his own. They were gathered into groups, talking and laughing.

Some were fully aqua-formed, like Gilbert, but there were others who still retained basic lubber anatomy, with a normal complement of limbs. Some of these borderline cases appeared happy with prolonged submersion, while others wore lightweight breathing devices of various kinds. From what Geoffrey had gathered, the process of full aqua-transformation wasn't an overnight thing; there were many way stations along the route, and not everyone opted to proceed with further surgery once they'd received the basic modifications.

Gilbert swam to an orange portal, and then they were rushing down another tube – not as far, this time – until they came out into another junction, this one not much larger than the first. This pool had its share of portals, but there were also colour-coded exits that were not yet open to the water. Gilbert swam to one of these exits and pressed a webbed hand into the panel to its right; the circular door rolled aside, revealing an illuminated, water-filled corridor.

After a short distance they emerged into a pool that was scarcely larger than a private jacuzzi. It occupied a curving, green-walled room with windows set into one side. Geoffrey made to stand up, pushing his head into open air, the mask and goggles unclasping automatically with a soft *pop* of released suction. Water stampeded off him in a thousand beetle-sized droplets.

Through the windows in one half of the room he saw another aspect of Tiamaat's abundant underwater sprawl: towers, a fungal growth of geodesic domes, glowing from within with floodlit greenery. Tiamaat went on for kilometres.

A kind of channel or ditch ran away from the jacuzzi, through an arch, into an adjoining room. Gilbert swam ahead, but with her face and upper body mostly out of the water. Geoffrey, now upright, shuffled behind. The harness retracted its flippers, tucking them away like folded angel's wings. He'd only been aquatic for a few minutes, and already walking felt like an absurd evolutionary dead end.

The water-filled ditch led them into Truro's presence.

'So very glad you accepted my invitation,' he said grandly. 'You were, of course, never under any binding obligation to deal with us again.'

'That's not how it felt,' Geoffrey said.

'Well, let's look on the positive side. You're here now, and we have every likelihood of finding common ground.'

Truro had changed. He wasn't the man in the sea-green suit any more.

Now he floated in a green-tiled, kidney-shaped pool, bubbling with scented froth. His head merged seamlessly with the smooth ovoid of his torso, all details of his underlying skeleton and musculature rendered cryptic beneath layers of insulating blubber. His grey skin, which was completely hairless, shone with waxy pearlescence. He had no external ears and scarcely any nose. His nostrils were two muscle-activated slits that opened and closed with each breath. He had large, almost round eyes, very dark and penetrating. They blinked a complicated double-membrane blink.

'Why didn't your figment look like this?'

'It would only have complicated the issue further, I think. Besides, when I manifest I tend to revert to my former anatomy. Call it a nostalgic attachment.' Truro touched a web-fingered hand against the area where, prior to his surgery, his nose must have been. 'Not that I have any regrets. But sometimes, you know, for old time's sake.'

Consoles and data displays with chunky waterproof keypads bobbed in the water like brightly coloured bath toys. Geoffrey couldn't remember the last time he'd seen actual, solid data-visualisation and interface systems outside of a museum. Books were more common than screens and keypads.

Truro barged the yoke of a keypad aside, clearing room in front of him. 'Come in. Join me,' he said, ushering them forward. 'We've much to talk about.'

'May I leave you now, sir?' asked Gilbert.

'Of course. Thank you, Mira.'

When they were alone, Geoffrey divested himself of the mobility harness, leaving it propped against a wall while he returned to the pool. He eased into the turbulent, fizzing waters, sitting cross-legged opposite the merman.

'So what do you think of the old place?' Truro asked, leaning back with his muscular arms resting along the pool's tiled edge, webbed fingers trailing in the water.

'The tiny part of it I've seen is impressive enough.'

'It's a wonderful life, down here. We're aquatic apes, at heart. Returning to the seas is only the expression of something deep within us. A calling, if you will. And each year, more people respond to that call.'

'I thought you Pans wanted a migration outwards, not back into the oceans.'

'Many paths to the one goal. We can return to the seas and take the seas with us to the stars.' Truro smiled quickly, as if his own words had betrayed him. 'Sometimes rhetoric gets the better of me. Please don't take anything I say *too* seriously. That wouldn't do at all.'

'I'm happy on dry land, thanks.' Geoffrey paused, sensing that the quickest way to get this over and done with was to go straight to the point. 'Can we talk about the phyletic dwarves, since that's obviously why I'm here?'

Truro's unusual countenance evinced pain at this abrupt curtailment of preliminaries. 'That's part of it, certainly. Matter of fact, I've Chama on hold right now. Said I'd let him know when you got in.'

'I didn't think Chama was meant to have any contact with the world beyond the Descrutinised Zone.'

'And what are private quangle paths for, if not for circumventing such tedious legal constraints?' Truro reached for the floating keypad and depressed one of the spongy controls. 'Chama, you can manifest now. Geoffrey Akinya is here.' Turning to Geoffrey he added: 'I'm giving you local aug access. Excuse me while I make my own arrangements.'

The merman fumbled in the water for a pair of lurid yellow goggles, which he slipped over his dark, seal-like eyes with elastic straps.

'You don't have retinal implants,' Geoffrey said, startled.

'Removed at the time of my aqua-forming. Does that appal you?' Truro looked to his left, towards an area of tiled flooring where Chama's figment was now standing. 'Ah,' he said, beaming magnanimously. 'Good to see you.'

Chama looked at Geoffrey. 'How are the elephants?'

'They're doing fine. They barely noticed I was gone.'

Time lag slowed Chama's response. 'Gleb and I've had a lot of time to talk things over, and we're even more convinced that this is the way forward.'

'Chama's already filled me in on the background,' said Truro. 'From our standpoint, there are no insurmountable technical challenges. We would need to extend neural intervention to all the elephants in your study group, with the exception of perhaps the very youngest calves, and limit the interaction with non-augmented herd members wherever possible. But from what I gather, as things stand we can proceed immediately, on a trial basis.'

'Quangle paths are allocated?' Chama asked, as if they were merely fussing over details.

'Already in place,' the merman said. 'The anticipated load isn't exorbitant, and we should be able to manage things without drawing undue attention.'

'There's a lot more to it than that,' Geoffrey said, alarmed by how readily his consent was being assumed. 'The ethical considerations, for a start.'

The merman scratched under one of his blubbery, hairless armpits. 'My dear fellow, there could hardly be anything *more* ethical than actively furthering the welfare of a species, surely.'

Geoffrey smiled, suddenly grasping his place in things. 'This is how you operate, isn't it? Always going a bit too far, always counting on people falling for your arguments that what's done is done, that the best thing they can do is cooperate.'

'Look at it this way,' Chama said. 'When it comes to long-term funding, who'd you rather do business with – us or your family? We're in it for the seriously long game. And we've every incentive to protect you and the Amboseli herds from outside interference.'

'You're good at this,' Geoffrey said.

'We have to be,' Truro said. 'It's how things get done.'

'We can begin almost immediately,' Chama said briskly, 'starting with some simple test figments: dropping ghost images of other elephants into their visual fields, distant enough that olfactory and auditory hallucinations won't be required. We'll run exactly the same assessment protocols on the Lunar dwarves.'

230

'You just have to give us the ching codes,' Truro said. 'Then we can really start to make things happen.'

'Collaborate with us,' Chama said pleadingly. 'Do something bigger than your family. Something that'll still have meaning centuries from now.'

'Join the Pans,' Geoffrey said, his own voice sounding hollow and drained of fight.

'Become a fellow traveller, that's all. No one's asking you to swallow the ideology in its entirety.' Truro was speaking now. 'Still, I won't insult you by reminding you that there's a debt to be paid, for what Chama did for you on the Moon. It was all to do with your grandmother, wasn't it?'

Geoffrey saw no purpose in lies or evasion. 'I'm sure Chama's told you enough.'

'The basics. Just when we thought we had Eunice Akinya pinned down . . . she surprises us all. She was close to us once, did you know?'

'I've heard about her Pan involvement.'

'That business on Mercury . . . such a *tragedy* it ended the way it did. There's so much we could have done together, but Eunice had to go and betray Lin.'

Geoffrey saw his moment. 'Did you know Lin Wei? My sister was hoping to find out what really went on there.'

'No, I never had the pleasure of meeting the first Prime Pan . . . Lin Wei drowned, of course. They told you that.'

'Yes,' Geoffrey said.

'Arethusa knew her very well indeed. When the current Prime Pan learned of your . . . interest, you became of . . . shall we say reciprocal interest to Arethusa.' Truro appeared to be having difficulty finding the appropriate words. 'No disrespect to Chama or the elephants, but that's really why you're here. Arethusa *demands* an audience.'

'Since I've already been dragged here,' Geoffrey said, 'I may as well speak to anyone who wants a conversation. Will the Prime Pan be coming here?'

Truro's minimalist features nonetheless evinced apology. 'The mountain must go to Mohammed, I'm afraid. Are you up for a bit more swimming?'

CHAPTER FOURTEEN

According to the aug they were somewhere over the equatorial highlands of Syrtis Major, on the other side of Mars from Pavonis Mons.

They had gone down in the cheapest kind of cut-price shuttle. Sunday had no regrets about taking the fast way: she was too excited for that. Jitendra shared her anticipation, his grin only intensifying as re-entry commenced. They'd gone from Stickney's centrifugal gravity to the free fall of the shuttle, and now weight was returning as the shuttle hit atmosphere and enveloped itself in a blistering cocoon of neon-pink plasma. As the deceleration peaked, the seats adjusted to provide full-body support. It was more gravity than Sunday had experienced in years. She loved watching the plasma snap and ripple around the hull, like a flag in a stiff breeze.

And then it eased, and they were flying as much as falling. The shuttle's hull was reshaping itself all the while, optimising to the changing conditions, resisting gravity to the last instant. Gullies and craters slid underneath, sharp-shadowed, Sunday certain that she could stretch out her hand and feel the leathery texture of the surface, scraping beneath her palm like the cover of an old book. So far, at least, there was nothing down there to suggest that they were anything other than the very first people to reach this world. No settlements, no roads, not even the glint of some long-abandoned mechanical envoy, dust-bound for centuries. It was staggering, all that emptiness.

Jitendra saw something, pointing excitedly at a dark worming trail, the furiously gyring knot at its head etching a meandering track across the surface. 'It's a vehicle, I think. A Mars rover, or maybe some kind of low-altitude aircraft.'

Sunday had already voked the mag to maximum. 'Kicking up a lot of dust. Moving pretty quickly, too.'

'It's a dust-devil,' Eunice said, cutting into Sunday's thoughts. 'Just a whirlwind.'

She turned to Jitendra, and repeated Eunice's words.

'Oh,' he said, on a falling note.

'Raised on the Moon,' Eunice said disapprovingly. 'Doesn't have the first foggiest notion of terrestrial planet weather systems.'

Sunday voked, 'Didn't think you'd show up until we were down, Eunice.'

'There's local aug, enough of a network for me to utilise. I'm synching with my Earthside self as we speak. That's going to take some time. Have you heard from your brother?'

'We talked just before I got on the shuttle. He knows I'm OK.' Sunday still had one eye on the scrolling view. 'Have you been in contact with him?'

'Not since he went off-grid.'

Sunday tensed. 'What do you mean, "off-grid"?'

'Your brother's currently a guest of the United Aquatic Nations, in Tiamaat. Truro sent a plane to pick him up.'

'I wasn't expecting him to forget the favours we owe him for. The only reason I'm here is because the Pans took care of my ticket.'

'They're more interested in us than I expected, though. This isn't just about reciprocity. I worry that it's me they're really after.'

'You don't exist. And at the risk of wounding your ego, not everyone in the known universe is obsessed with you and your secret history.'

'Let's be honest, though, a fair few are.'

'But only because you spent half your life turning yourself into a puzzle. Geoffrey blinked me a copy of the mural in your bedroom – seems you were right about the alterations in Phobos.'

'Good to have my suspicions confirmed. I'm not infallible, and I can't vouch for the absolute reliability of my memories.'

'Trust me, I never once thought you were infallible. What do you know about Truro?'

'He's not top dog, although he's not far off it either. He answers to the Prime Pan, whoever that is. Here's the catch, though. Sift through my logged conversations – as I myself have done – and you'll find ample evidence of occasional traffic between myself and Tiamaat. Highly quangled, so you can't get into deep content, but someone there was clearly of interest to me. For years, decades. Going all the way back to Mercury.'

'You have a theory.'

'My ... death has stirred up ghosts, Sunday. I can't be certain of anything. But there aren't many people I'd have been capable of sustaining a lifelong association with, without one or both of us going mad with boredom. What I'm getting at is this: did the Prime Pan know me? Did I know the Prime Pan?'

'Tell me what you're thinking.'

'Not yet. I'll wait for more data, until I'm not only fully synched but back in touch with Geoffrey.'

Sunday seethed. 'I'm ordering you to tell me.'

'And I'm refusing. This is a deep-level epistemological conflict, granddaughter. You can't force me to *be more like myself* and then throw a tantrum when I decide to act entirely in character. Live with your handiwork, my dear. You made me the high-minded bitch that I am.'

It wasn't long before human presence asserted itself in the form of what might have been a pipeline or power-conduction conduit lancing across the surface in bold tangents. A little later, as the line zagged to match their course, they passed over a frogspawn clump of silvery domes, an outpost or some kind of maintenance complex. Even at full magnification, Sunday couldn't see a living soul. Then, five or six minutes later, the line met another trunk branching in from the north, and there was something like a village or hamlet at the junction: multiple domes, square buildings, a geometric quilt of copper-green hexagons spreading to the south – solar collectors, or perhaps cropbeds – and a pale finger-scratch arrowing west that was too purposefully Euclidean to be a dust-devil track.

She followed it – they were moving west as well – until she picked out the bumbling, bouncing form of what was unmistakably a surface vehicle. It was a silver beetle with six huge wheels, plodding its way home.

After that, signs of civilisation only increased. More villages, and then a town, domes laid out in curling galactic spirals from a central core. She couldn't see anyone moving around, even at full magnification, and when she tried to ching down to street level her request was politely rebuffed.

The town had a railway line, also punching west, slicing through some craters, angling around others, occasionally diving underground for no particular reason. Then she saw a train, speeding along the track in the opposite direction from their motion – six silver cylinders with surprisingly blunt test-tube-shaped ends.

They followed the railway line until it passed through another big town, and then a city twinkled on the western horizon. Crommelin Edge, said the aug, and Sunday remembered that this was where they were going to be processed for final Martian immigration. The elevator's anchorpoint was halfway around Mars, so Crommelin Edge – located close to the equator, close to the zero meridian, in the cratered plateau of Arabia Terra – was one of the two main entry points for arriving travellers.

The shuttle made a pass over the city, sloughing altitude and speed. The settlement took the form of a crescent, partly tracing the outer wall of its namesake crater. Scant evidence of planning here, just a bubbling froth of variegated domes and other structures, cubes and rhomboids and cylinders, pylons and vanes, looking less like an organised settlement than a bag of marbles and toy building blocks spilt out onto the floor and gathered into rough formation. The artist in Sunday appreciated the ordered form of the spiral she had seen earlier, but there was something haphazardly human about this arrangement that also appealed to her. She liked her cities best when they contained gnarly, counter-intuitive geometries.

The shuttle came down on a landing strip surrounded by domes and soggy-looking amoeboid terminal buildings. The hull flicked to perfect transparency and their seatbelts slithered away. Service vehicles were already surrounding the shuttle, while a docking tube extended itself into position, flexing and probing like the trunk of an inquisitive elephant. The sky over the spaceport was a darkening mauve, fretted by wisps of high-altitude clouds.

'Welcome to Mars,' said a piped voice. 'The Mars Sol Date is one hundred and two thousand, four hundred and forty-seven sols. Local Mean Solar Time is eighteen hours and thirty-one minutes. For the benefit of passengers arriving from Earth, it is sixteen thirty-five Coordinated Universal Time on March thirteen.'

Cavernous and bright, the terminal could have been any shopping mall from Mombasa to the Moon. Exos loitered to assist those struggling with the gravity, but no one was having any obvious difficulties. Adverts jostled for attention, pushing services and products that were for the most part uniquely Martian.

Sunday wasn't at all surprised when she was taken aside for additional interviewing and background examination. They had reported the dead body on Phobos before boarding the shuttle and had been detained while bureaucratic procedure was observed. No crime had been committed: she'd been perfectly within her rights to trample all over the moon, and she'd broken no rules by chinging into the abandoned camp. Of necessity, they had to wait while the Stickney authorities sent their own investigators into the sealed-up dome, verifying Sunday's side of the story, but once that was done, they were allowed to be on their way.

Flags had been raised, though. It was difficult enough travelling incognito as an Akinya, but now there was the matter of the corpse and her Panspermian affiliation.

They were in the holding area when word came down from Phobos: the investigators had run a trace on the suit and crossmatched the DNA of the body inside with their records. The corpse belonged to Nicolas Escoffery, a Martian citizen who'd gone missing on Phobos nearly fifty years earlier. Escoffery was a broker in second-hand equipment, a wheeler and dealer who made frequent trips between the moon and the surface, and whose operations often skirted the edge of legality. At the time of his disappearance, Escoffery was under investigation for customs irregularities and appeared to have made efforts to conceal his true whereabouts. An area of Mars had been searched, but no one had guessed that he was actually on Phobos.

'Wouldn't happen now,' it was explained to Sunday. 'You just can't get away with that kind of crap these days.'

How Escoffery had died was a different matter. He hadn't been imprisoned in the camp, and the doors hadn't been sealed over until after his death. The best guess was that his suit had malfunctioned, its servo-systems jamming into immobility, turning itself into a man-shaped coffin. Sunday remembered the white spider she had dislodged from Escoffery's suit, though, and wasn't so sure ... but she thought it advisable to say no more on the subject.

They were eventually allowed on their way. As distasteful as the authorities found Sunday's Panspermian association, it wasn't a sufficient pretext for denying her entry. All the same, she could sense the resentment that they hadn't found something to pin on either her or Jitendra.

They collected their luggage, which was already waiting by the time they cleared immigration. Sunday made a conscious effort to put recent events behind her. She wasn't looking forward to what was ahead, and she could still see that paper-skinned skull, grinning through her own visor ... But that was over, and if she dwelt on it, it was going to ruin this delicious experience: her first few steps on another world. She could return to this place a thousand times and it would never be this new.

'We're here,' she said, hugging Jitendra. 'I can't believe it. Under my feet ... it's Mars.'

Literally so. In the arrivals plaza, a strip of flooring had been cut back to raw Martian soil, like a lumpy red carpet. It must have been sprayed over with some atom-thin polymer to eliminate dust, but she could not have told that from the feel of the ground under her feet or the palm of her hand. For a ridiculous moment she had to fight the urge to kneel down and kiss it.

Jitendra finished rearranging the contents of the suitcases, to make them easier to carry. 'We need to celebrate. Get a drink, now. Before the moment passes.'

'So there's this amazing, precious experience, this once-in-a-lifetime thing, and before it has a chance to form deep neural connections you want to batter it into submission with toxic chemicals?'

Jitendra gave the matter due consideration. 'Basically, if you must put it that way, that's exactly what I had in mind.'

'Fine,' Sunday said, deciding that it was much easier to go along with him than otherwise. 'I'm up for that as well.'

But first there was some business to attend to. The Pans had given Sunday a ching address to call upon her arrival. As tempting as it was to put the matter off, it would only be delaying the inevitable. She found a quiet corner of the arrivals lounge and voked the request.

The bind went through with a high level of quangle, and she found herself in a room which – judging by the high aspect of the sun – lay some distance west of Crommelin. Under her feet was glass, and under the glass was empty air, plunging all the way down to the scoured red ground, so far below that she might as well have still been in orbit. To either side, ancient weathered cliffs receded into mist-hazed obscurity. A handful of sleek discus-shaped buildings were cut into the cliffsides, or buttressed out from them.

'Welcome, Sunday,' she heard. 'How was your journey?'

'No complaints, apart from the friendly welcome at Crommelin.'

'You'll have to excuse our customs and immigration staff: they preach courtesy and respect while demonstrating exactly the opposite.'

Sunday took a nervous step sideways, distrusting the flooring. Even in ching it was hard to suppress vertigo, or the instinctive urge for self-preservation. This was especially the case when the proxy was a living, breathing human organism.

The warmblood belonged to a woman of about her age and build, although the skin was paler than her own. She wore a business outfit: colour-coordinated skirt and blouse, dark green offset with silver piping, black stockings and sensible low-heeled black shoes.

Sunday certainly wouldn't have trusted heels on that floor.

She flexed the warmblood's fingers. She'd only chinged this way a couple of times before but had already cultivated an intense loathing for the arrangement.

'Where am I?'

237

'The Pan outpost at Valles Marineris,' the voice said. 'We're on the very edge of the deepest canyon, the greatest rift valley anywhere in the solar system. I thought you would appreciate seeing the view through human eyes. My transform-surgeon, Magdalena, consented to be driven.'

'It's very thoughtful.'

'Entirely appropriate, too. You're both sculptresses. You work with stone and clay, Magdalena with the living flesh. Now you are as one.'

Sunday turned from the view of Valles Marineris. Her speaker faced her from a kind of bed, resting on an oblong of white self-sterilising frond-carpet. The bed was as heavy and complicated-looking as some ghastly iron lung or CAT scanner from the medical Dark Ages. It was plumbed into the wall behind it, and it hummed and gurgled like an espresso machine. It was actually more like a bath than a bed, for the occupant was mostly immersed in fluid, contained by high-walled, slosh-proof sides. The treacle-thick fluid had a bluish chemical tint.

'Come closer,' the patient said. 'I won't bite. Biting is one of the very many things not presently an option for me.'

Two green-uniformed female nurses stood by the bedside: one with a surgical trolley, the other with a kind of Pan-compliant clipboard and stylus computer. Without a word they took their leave, striding like catwalk models, one of them pushing the trolley before her. A door in the rear of the room snicked open and shut like an iris.

Sunday came closer. She couldn't smell anything through the ching bind, but wondered if the fluid – or indeed the patient – had a strong odour.

'I am Holroyd,' the voice said. 'You mustn't be alarmed. I'm actually in no great distress, and despite appearances I do not believe success to be completely ruled out, at least not yet.'

There was a man in the fluid, but only just. Her first thought had been: cactus. His form, what she could see of it, was covered with jagged dark growths, erupting from every inch of his skin. They were glossy and leaflike, sharp-edged, studded with barbs and thorns. His upper torso, his submerged limbs, his head and face ... there was no part of him where the growths were not rampant. His eyes peered through tunnels of pruned-back growth. She wondered how much of the world he could see.

'What happened to you, Mister Holroyd?'

He did not sound in the least bit upset by the directness of her question. 'Hubris, I suppose. Or impatience. Or some combination of the two.' She couldn't see a mouth making the words. 'I was a genetic volunteer. A Pan, of course – an old friend of Truro's, too, though I doubt we'll ever meet again. Our paths have taken us in very different directions. His to the oceans. Mine to . . . well, this.'

'Did Magdalena do this to you?'

'Magdalena was part of the team that, with my consent, proceeded with the genetic intervention . . . now she is part of the team attempting to undo the effects of that intervention.' A hand, spined and spiked to the point of uselessness, like a cross between a mace and a gauntlet, emerged from the cloying fluid. There were wounds in the armour, pale healed-over scars and white-seeping gashes. 'The intention was to change my body, to armour it to the point where, with only the minimum of additional life-support measures, I could survive outside without a surface suit. Thermal insulation, pressure and moisture containment . . . they were within our grasp. I'd still need an air supply, of course, and there'd always be parts of Mars that would be unendurable, even for me, but it was worth attempting. A gesture of intent, if nothing else. A sign that we are here for good. That we'll do whatever we can to make this work. Even change our basic humanity.'

'How did it go wrong?'

'There are no catastrophes in science, Sunday, only lessons. I'd far rather live in a universe capable of producing monsters like me than one where we understood all the rules, down to the last tedious footnote. I'm evidence that reality is still capable of tripping us up. As I said, I am not in pain. And recently we have made . . . I won't call it "progress", that's too big a word. But there have been intimations, hints of the possibility of a modest therapeutic breakthrough. The game is not yet lost!'

'I hope things work out for you, Mister Holroyd.'

'I try to look on the bright side. That's vital, don't you think?' The hand and arm sank beneath the surface of the fluid. The bed made a decisive clicking noise and the fluid began to bubble vigorously. 'Well, to business, I suppose – and you'll excuse the abrupt shift in tone, I hope. I'm delighted you've made it to Mars, and you have my assurance that the Initiative will do all in its power to facilitate your . . . enquiries. You will spend the next two nights in Crommelin Edge, and I hope you'll take the time to see something of the city and the crater, get your Mars legs. After that, we've arranged transportation to Pavonis Mons, or as close as we can reasonably take you. We will of course assist with any further logistical requirements that might arise, within the limits of funds and resources, of course. I hardly need add that there must be some reciprocity, however crass that sounds.'

'I understand, Mister Holroyd. I wouldn't have been able to get to Mars without Pan sponsorship. I agreed to take on some commissions, and I'm ready and willing to fulfil that commitment.'

'Very good, Sunday. I've been looking at some of your work, did you know?'

'I didn't, sir.'

'I'm no expert, but I like what I see. There are visible and public ways that you can help the Initiative, and we'll come to those in due course. But to begin with, I wonder if we might consider a more personal study, as a kind of warm-up exercise?'

'I'm open to ideas.'

'I never doubted it. But you may not . . .' Holroyd faltered. 'I appreciate that this may not be easy for you, but I wonder if you'd consider a piece that drew its inspiration . . . from me?'

'As you were, sir, or as you're meant to be?'

'No,' Holroyd corrected gently. 'As I am, here and now. In all my splendid ugliness. A monument to ignorance and possibility. Hubris and hope. There: I've already given you a title. How can you possibly say no?'

Sunday had never felt less enthusiastic about a commission, or less bothered about the title. 'I don't suppose I can, sir.'

The door opened and one of the green-uniformed nurses came back in with a trolley. Gleaming chrome instruments rested on it, including something that looked very much like a pair of pruning shears.

'I really need that drink now,' Sunday said, when she'd come out of ching.

'Difficult client?'

'A prickly customer.'

They found a bar called the Red Menace, on the edge of a glassed-over mall filled with high-end boutiques and expensive souvenir shops. The Red Menace's stock-in-trade was bad-taste Martian-invasion kitsch, from the slime-green cocktails to the skull-masked bartenders and clanking steam-actuated Wellsian tripods that brought the drinks, clutching glasses in their tentacles and carrying bar-snacks in baskets tucked under their bodies. Heat-rays pulsed through puffs of dry ice, while portentous military music throbbed from underfloor bass speakers.

Sunday should have been appalled, but in fact the bar suited her mood exactly. She was just wiping the salt off the rim of her second Silver Locust – Jitendra was on his third – when she became aware that someone was looking at them from the entrance, standing very still and peering through the scudding gouts of dry ice clouding the bar.

Studying the tall black-skinned man, a sense of profound wrongness washed over her in a clammy wave, as if her every waking assumption had just been annihilated. The shock stole her breath. The universe appeared to stall, stretching a moment into a lifetime.

The shape of his face, the light on the cheekbones, the wide imperial brow. It was one of the cousins.

She touched Jitendra's hand, and although the effort was almost unbearable, forced herself to breathe and then to speak. 'Look.'

Jitendra looked at the man and put down his drink. With a calm that felt far out of place, he said, 'It's not a person.'

She turned up her own aug threshold, letting the tag inform her that the figure was a golem.

'Hello,' it said, arriving at their table. 'I'm glad you made it here safely. Do you mind if I take a seat?' The golem tilted its face towards the third chair, the one nobody was sitting in.

'What do you want with us?' Sunday asked.

The golem lowered itself into the seat. 'I am Lucas Akinya's designated legal presence on Mars.'

'It's autonomous,' Jitendra whispered. 'Do you think it was here all along, or came with us on the same ship?'

'Who knows? Lucas and Hector probably have thousands of the fucking things, all over the system, ready to pop up like a slice of toast whenever they need a legal presence.' She glared at it. 'I'll ask you again: what do you want with us?'

'This visit of yours,' the golem said, 'has raised a number of flags. We've spoken to Geoffrey. Keeping secrets is not one of his core skills.'

She could see the trap she was being steered into, of disclosing more than she needed to. 'And what secrets would those be?'

The golem was keeping its voice very low, smiling all the while. 'You claim to be here on Panspermian business.'

'I don't "claim" anything.'

'How would you characterise your ongoing business relationship with these people?'

'I'm an artist. The Pans need art to get their ideas across. Doesn't mean I've bought the T-shirt'

The golem paused. Its cleverness was paper-thin. It could emit statements and responses that sounded plausible, but the swerves and hairpins of normal human conversation left it befuddled. 'This visit to Mars comes hard on the heels of your brother's visit to the Moon. Even the most casual observer might reasonably posit a causative link between the two developments.'

'Conclude what you like. Not my problem.'

'Geoffrey was tasked to investigate a matter on behalf of the family. Whatever he may have told you, visiting you was not the sole purpose of his trip.'

'In which case you've just made a big fucking mistake in mentioning it now, haven't you?'

The golem's face became a death mask pulled too tight. 'There is something else,' it continued, after a pause. 'An incident on the Chinese Lunar border, and a demonstrable Panspermian connection. Your associate Chama was arrested and then released, under terms of restraint.'

'It was nothing to do with me.'

'The incident took place near Eunice's crash site.' The golem leaned forwards and spoke with particular intensity. 'What did Geoffrey find in the Central African Bank? Apart from the glove, which we know about.'

'I've no idea.'

'It behoves you to show responsibility, Sunday. In these times of economic uncertainty, the continued good standing of the Akinya name must be paramount in our concerns.'

'Good standing?' She was thinking back to her treatment at immigration. 'They hate our name, even here. You think I give a damn about preserving that?'

Again the golem appeared unsure how to respond. 'Akinya Space is a building block,' it declared. 'Thousands depend on us directly for employment and welfare. Millions indirectly, through secondary contracts and business transactions. Billions more, by dint of our mere existence. Our machines bring valuable raw materials from across the system, from the main belt to the Trans-Neptunian iceteroids. Without that dependable flow, the entire infrastructure of human settlement and colonisation would falter.'

'I'm not trying to bring down human civilisation, Lucas. That would imply that I give a shit about it.'

'Our concern is that Eunice may have had self-destructive impulses. We worry that whatever was in that box was a metaphorical time bomb, planted under the family by a bitter, resentful old woman.'

'You don't believe that.'

'Please do not doubt the seriousness of my concerns, or the lengths Hector and I will go to to protect this family.'

Sunday sat in silence, as if she was giving the golem's words due consideration. Only when a suitable interval had passed did she allow herself to start speaking. 'Cousin, we're not in Africa any more. This is not the household. We're on Mars now, a long way from home. I owe you nothing. This is my life and I do what I want with it. I do not want to speak to you again while I'm here. I do not even want to see you again. So please leave us alone, before I make exactly the kind of scene you'd really like to avoid.'

'This may not be Africa,' the golem said, 'but nor is it the Descrutinised Zone. You're in the Surveilled World now, Sunday.' He moved to stand, rising from the stool with the oiled precision of a periscope. 'And it runs on our rules, not yours.'

CHAPTER FIFTEEN

She worked quickly, but not because she considered the commission beneath her. It was simply the way she always approached her art. Preparation, forethought, hours of meditation, then an explosion of swift and decisive action, like the quick and merciful descent of a sword. Execution, in every sense of the word.

The morning after her arrival in Crommelin, she had chinged back to the Pan lodge on the edge of Valles Marineris, into a proxy this time rather than the warmblood body of Holroyd's nurse. She had made her preferences known, and the Pans had abided by them. Now Magdalena was free to do her chores, and Sunday was wearing a wasp-waisted black mechanical mannequin. It was a recent model, ornamented with pastel-glowing vines and limb-entwining daisy chains.

'I meant to say that I've arranged a guide for you,' Holroyd announced. 'He has experience in the Evolvarium, which you'll definitely need. Not many people go anywhere near that place without good reason, usually involving a commercial interest. You're still certain you don't want to subcontract this operation to . . . specialists?'

'I came to Mars for a reason, Mister Holroyd.'

'That was before you found out where your grandmother had buried the next item.' Holroyd waited for Magdalena to snip away a thumb-sized growth from one of his chest-spines, leaving a weeping milky wound. If there was pain, he was careful not to show it. 'That development is . . . unfortunate,' he went on, 'but I suppose we can't blame her for not seeing this far ahead.'

'She could have saved us all a lot of bother and just put the first and last clue in the same place,' Sunday said.

'That obviously wasn't her intention.'

The sculpture was nearing, if not completion, than at least the point where the probability of success or failure could rightly be judged. Sunday had begun with an upright cylinder of lustrous silver-grey material, mounted on a plinth. The material, which stood nearly as tall as Sunday herself, was active clay: an inert medium saturated with nanomachines at a density of five per cent by both weight and volume. The machines were programmed to respond to gestural and proximal cues from Sunday's proxy-driven hands, moving not just their own bodies but the inert matrix in which they were embedded.

Sunday couldn't see the machines themselves, but their effect on the material was obvious enough. She only had to skim her fingers near the working surface and the clay would repel, flinching back in channels or grooves or wide, scalloped curves depending on the precise orientation of her hand and fingers. As it deformed, the clay turned reflective. It obeyed pseudo fluid dynamics, knotted with eddies and turbulence, forming rippling, surflike sheets or bubbling globular mirrored extrusions, like mercury slowed down a thousand times. Once her hand was withdrawn, the active clay froze into its last configuration. By bringing in the other hand, creating opposing vectors of repulsion, Sunday could coax the matter into solid geometries of surprising complexity.

'I don't know what she had in mind for us. All I know is it can't be personal. She didn't know it was going to be my brother who looked into that bank vault.'

'She knew it would be one of you, though. Definitely an Akinya. Whatever she's doing, she seems very determined to keep it in the family, doesn't she?'

Sunday flicked her wrist through part of the sculpture, cleaving matter the way prophets parted waters. The sculpture didn't really look like a man, she had to admit. More like a lung, or a tree dipped in molten lead. But the prickliness of it, the densely packed spines and thorns, was suggestive of her host.

'If she's testing us, I suppose there has to be a reason.'

'Gold at the end of the rainbow? Or just a dead woman playing malicious games with her descendants?'

'I don't know. Whatever Eunice planned, though, it was put in place before her last mission. She may have gone a little mad up in the Winter Palace – who wouldn't? – but she was sane when she took *Winter Queen* out for its last expedition.'

'Plenty of imagery and footage from then, in that case.'

Sunday nodded, cajoling an arc of clay out on its own lazy Martian parabola, freezing into the crooked curve of a gull's wing. She didn't get to work with active clay very often; it was too expensive for her usual commissions and there were strict conditions on the importing of nano-technology into the Zone. 'That's what unsettles me. Ever since she

came back, the whole time she's been up there, orbiting the Moon ...
she's known about this ... plot of hers.'

'You speak as if she's still alive.'

'I don't mean to, but when you dig into a person's past, and you
have—'

'I know about the construct, Sunday. A data entity like that, distributed
cloudware – we could hardly fail to detect its presence in the Martian
aug.'

She hid her shock. If the Pans were going to rip into her secrets, she
was damned if she'd give them the pleasure of looking surprised about
it.

'Of course. It's just that sometimes, if only for a moment, I forget that
it isn't my grandmother.'

'An understandable error. But not, I'd imagine, one that you make all
that often.'

'I try not to.'

After a moment, Holroyd said, 'Your grandmother was born in a
different world, Sunday. A different century. She lived through difficult
times; saw the best and the worst of what we are capable of. So did
billions of others ... But she was in a privileged, possibly even unique
position. She may not have experienced wars first hand, but she would
have met many people who were touched by them, and touched badly.
There were no Mandatory Enhancements in Eunice's day, either. She
would have understood that there are times, many times, when we can't
always be trusted to do the right and proper thing. Even with the
Mechanism guiding our actions, even when the neuropractors have
knifed villainy out our heads.'

'I'm not sure where this is leading, sir.'

'All I mean to say is ... no one would have been better placed than your
grandmother to see the truth about humanity. And given everything that
happened to her, no one would have been better placed to stumble on
dangerous knowledge.'

Sunday paused in her sculpting. 'Dangerous knowledge?'

'I speculate, that's all. But if your grandmother did learn something,
by whatever means ... something that she didn't think the rest of us
were ready for ... do you *really* think she'd be so selfish as to take that
knowledge to her grave, for all of time?'

246

CHAPTER SIXTEEN

Geoffrey went deep. At length the transit flume opened out into a submarine chamber the size of which he could only guess at. It was large, definitely: probably big enough to have swallowed both wings of the household and a fair part of the grounds as well. It was spherical and the walls were black, but the equator of this sphere was dotted with entry and exit flumes at regular intervals, and these luminous red and green circles offered some sense of scale and perspective.

Opposite him – the water was as clear as optical glass – hovered a glowing image, projected onto the curvature of the sphere's far side. For a moment he took it to be Earth, seen from space: it didn't look all that different from the view he'd had coming down the Libreville elevator. A moment's further scrutiny told him that this was not Earth, nor any world in the solar system. It had surface oceans and continents and weather systems, but they were fundamentally unrecognisable.

Like an eclipsing moon, a partner world to this alien planet, a dark form interposed itself between Geoffrey and the image.

Through the harness's headset he heard, 'You can leave him with me, thank you. I'll show him out when we're done.'

And at the same time as he heard those words, spoken in almost accentless Swahili by a woman's voice, he felt a subsonic component, deep as an elephant's musth rumble, conveyed through the water, into his belly, into his nervous system.

As if the Earth itself had made an utterance, shaping words through the tectonic grind of crustal plates.

He glanced around. His guides had departed.

'Welcome, Geoffrey Akinya,' the female voice said, with the same accompanying rumble. 'Thank you for agreeing to see me. Your meeting with Truro – it was suitably productive?'

Geoffrey was staring into the water, still trying to map the shape and extent of the dark form and hoping it was not as far away – and therefore as *large* – as his eyes were insisting.

'Arethusa?' he asked.

'My apologies. One tends to assume that my visitors need no introduction, but that's an inexcusable rudeness on my part. Yes, I am Arethusa.'

Geoffrey decided that it might be prudent to answer her question. 'Truro had some ... interesting proposals.'

'And your response?'

'I suspect I'm not really in a position to say no, after what happened on the Moon.'

'You feel indebted.'

'*Made* to feel indebted. Amounts to the same thing, I guess.'

'I was informed about Chama and Gleb's endeavours with the phyletic dwarves. It's a small aspect of our work, but an important one nonetheless. They deserve success. I'm sure you could play a vital role in making that happen.'

'And risk ruining my entire career.'

'Or creating a shiny new one. Why be a prisoner of your past?'

He took that as an invitation to steer the conversation in the vague direction of Eunice. 'I was told you knew Lin Wei.'

'We were close. She spoke often of your grandmother.'

'You never met Eunice yourself, though?'

'Lin painted a vivid picture. Warts and all, as the expression goes. Did you know your grandmother well?'

'Not particularly. She was already in the Winter Palace by the time I was born, and she didn't ching down to Africa very often. To be honest, I don't think she was interested in us any more.'

'But she's of interest to you, now.'

Obviously Arethusa knew about the glove, the burial in Pythagoras, the Martian angle. 'I've become tangled up in something I'd rather not have had anything to do with. But my sister's been digging into Eunice's past a lot longer than I have. There's this project of hers—'

'The construct, yes. I know of it. A valiant effort.'

'I'm surprised you approve. It's a thinking machine, for a start. And Sunday told me that my grandmother broke her side of the bargain with Lin Wei.'

'Water under the bridge. Lin Wei bore her no ill will, in later years. I see no reason why Sunday's project shouldn't be celebrated.'

'There are gaps in the construct's knowledge. It doesn't even remember Lin Wei.'

'No?'

His eyes had acclimatised to the darkness by small degrees. Arethusa was an elongated form, hovering in the water at an angle, her head closest to him, her tail further away and lower. He was fairly sure that she was a whale. The size and shape, the flippers on either side of her streamlined body, the subsonic communication. The only remaining question was whether she'd been born a whale, or had attained this form by post-natal genetic and surgical intervention.

He knew of nothing like her, anywhere in creation. A whale with a human-level intellect, or a person turned cetacean. He wasn't sure which would be the more miraculous.

'You know what really happened on Mercury?'

'I know that there was deceit,' Arethusa replied, with evident caution. 'More recently I've found myself wondering how far down that deceit extended.' She paused, and with a languid wave of her flippers began to gyre her massive form.

Across metres of water Geoffrey felt the awesome backwash. 'When was the last time you two spoke?'

'Just before she died. I chinged up to the Winter Palace, spoke to her in that mad jungle of hers. I may have been one of the last people to speak to her.'

'I'm surprised you had much to talk about.'

'I felt obliged. Your grandmother played a pivotal role in Ocular.'

He recalled what Sunday had told him. 'That was some kind of telescope, right?'

'A machine for mapping exoplanets,' Arethusa corrected in scholarly tones. 'The Oort Cloud Ultra-Large Array: a swarm of eyes, cast into the outer darkness, linked together laser-interferometrically so they could function as a single vast lens wider than the solar system. Even half-finished, it was an astounding technical feat. But it broke Lin Wei's heart, to see what became of her beautiful child.'

'I know a little about Eunice's connection.'

'Your family was brought in to help with the heavy lifting. In return, we gave them the Mercury leasehold. Akinya Space built their polar facility, saying it was for physics research.'

'Which was a lie.' Geoffrey presumed there was now no harm in recounting what he had been told. 'They were doing illegal work on artilects.'

'That was what we thought at the time. But Eunice was much too clever to allow herself to be nearly caught out that way. If she really, badly wanted to conduct illicit artilect studies, she'd have found somewhere else to do it, somewhere just as far away from the Cognition

Police as Mercury. There's a whole system out there, after all. No shortage of dark corners.'

'What are you saying – that there was something else going on, apart from the artilects?'

'The facility drew power from the Ocular launch grid. It was doing *something*.'

'Eunice put up a smokescreen to conceal a smokescreen?'

'You've heard of hiding in plain sight? Even Lin Wei didn't guess at the time. She was so fixated on the idea that illegal artilect research was going on, under the camouflage of physics research, that it never occurred to her to look closely at the camouflage itself, at the very thing that Eunice was making no effort to conceal.'

'Then ... it was physics all along?' But Geoffrey couldn't see where else to take that thought.

'Physics all along,' Arethusa said.

'This is just supposition,' Geoffrey said. 'Eunice is gone. Lin Wei is gone. If the Gearheads didn't find anything intact on Mercury back then, there won't be anything there now, all these years later.'

'So look somewhere else. Doubtless you've noticed the planet projected onto my sphere.'

'I was wondering when you'd get to that. Is it a real world, or a simulation?'

'Real enough. It's an Ocular composite image of Sixty-One Virginis f, a planet we call Crucible. It's just under twenty-eight light-years away – hardly any distance at all in cosmic terms. A hop and a skip. I showed Crucible to Eunice because there was something about it, something remarkable that Lin Wei would have wished her to see.'

'And you'd know all about Lin Wei's intentions, wouldn't you?'

'There's an odd undercurrent to that question,' the vast form retorted, with unmistakable menace.

'Suit yourself,' Geoffrey said. He was thinking of the girl at the scattering again, the figment that bore a striking resemblance to the younger Lin Wei. 'This discovery,' he went on. 'Shouldn't it be public knowledge?'

'Soon it will be. The discovery was made late last year, less than four months ago. We're still in the embargo phase, meaning that ... at this point in time ... there are probably fewer than a dozen people in the solar system currently privy to this data. All but one of them has an intimate connection with Ocular. You're the exception.'

Geoffrey wondered where all this was leading. 'So what did you find?'

'I can't take any credit for the discovery. It was made by Ocular itself, or rather by Arachne, the controlling intelligence at the heart of the instrument. Arachne is an artilect – a very smart one, forged from the fruits of Eunice's lab. The Cognition Police know about Arachne, and technically she – it – is within their threshold of concern. But they've given the project a special dispensation. Arachne is a harmless orphan, floating in deep space, blind to the world except for what she sees through Ocular's own eyes. What she found was stupendous and world-shattering. That was why she brought it to my attention.'

The image had changed while Geoffrey's attention was distracted. It was still the same blue planet, but now the cloud cover had been scoured away, the blue-green marble polished back to oceans and ice and land masses.

'I'm not—' Geoffrey began.

'Let's zoom in,' Arethusa said, 'down to an effective resolution of about three hundred metres. That's not enough to image fine-scale structure like roads or houses, but it's more than adequate to pick up geo-engineering, cities, deforestation, agricultural utilisation, even the wakes of large seagoing vessels. The area you're seeing now is about one thousand kilometres across, centred very precisely on the equator.'

Geoffrey stared at the thing Arethusa was showing him. It was obvious to his eyes that it had no business being there.

'Arachne called it Maximum Entropy Anomaly 563/912261. Obviously it needed a better name than that. That's why I decided to call it Mandala.'

'Man-da-la,' he repeated, stressing the syllables slowly. 'It's a good name.'

'Yes.'

And he marvelled. If the malleable skin of Crucible – the very planetary crust – had been warm wax, and into the wax had been embossed the hard imprint of an imperial seal, a seal of great intricacy, the result might have been something like this Maximum Entropy Anomaly, this Mandala.

At its heart was a system of concentric circles, ripples frozen in the act of spreading, but that basic organisation was obscured within layers of additional geometric complexity. There were squares, triangles, smaller circles – some positioned at the middle of the main formation, others at some distance from the centre. There were spirals and sinusoids. There were ellipses and horsetails and comma-like formations. It was, as near as Geoffrey could judge, marvellously, hypnotically symmetrical, in both the vertical and horizontal planes.

'And this ... thing – it couldn't be a mistake, something ... I don't know, imprinted on the data by ... what did you call her?'

'By Arachne? No. She's infallible. I've injected enough test patterns into the Ocular data stream to be certain that she's absolutely dependable. Of course, we ran even more exhaustive tests, and we'll have run many more by the time we go public with this. But there's no doubt – Mandala is real.'

'OK,' he said slowly, sensing that Arethusa's assessment of his intellectual worth might depend acutely on his next utterance. 'It's real. And I see that it isn't natural. Nothing natural produced that, not in ten billion years. But do you know what it is?'

'To the best of my knowledge ... a system of mirrored channels, cut into the planet's surface. Lined with something highly reflective, which is sometimes exposed and sometimes covered by water.'

'Sometimes?'

'Crucible has two large moons. Their tidal effects produce an ocean swell, or rather a pattern of ocean swells, which sometimes lead to the channels being inundated. Water isn't a good reflector, so the effect is very pronounced. Water races into the channels and fills them in a complicated fashion. In a similarly complicated fashion, the water drains or evaporates from the channels again, leaving the mirrors exposed once more. The pattern doesn't appear to be quite the same from cycle to cycle. Whether that is down to chance, or whether the system is running through iterations ... computational state-changes ... we can't know. Not until we have a much closer look.'

'Are there moving parts?'

'That's a good question, and the answer again is we don't know – our resolution isn't sufficient to discern that. But here's the thing: whether or not any part of Mandala moves, the entire thing must be self-renewing, or under constant repair. Whether it's ten thousand or ten million years old, it must repair itself. If we dug channels like that on our own Earth, even with the best materials currently at our disposal, do you imagine they'd last more than a few millennia without upkeep?'

'Maybe it's not even that old.'

'I very much doubt that it was built within the span of human history. Given the age of the galaxy, the ages of the other stars and planets ... that would be an almighty coincidence, wouldn't it? That someone made this thing, and we just happened to evolve a civilisation and the means to detect it a cosmic eye-blink later?'

'You think it's a lot older.'

'Yes, but not hundreds of millions of years, either. Crucible has plate tectonics, like our own Earth. Land masses move around on her surface. We trace their interlocking coastlines and deduce where they once fitted together, like Africa and the Americas. No structure that large could endure plate movement without being deformed or destroyed. Mandala's geometric symmetry is as perfect as we can measure with our current methods. It can't be much older than tens of millions of years. Which, I admit, is still a cosmic eye-blink.'

Geoffrey felt as if he'd stepped off a mental cliff and was still falling. Wisely or not, he rejected any notion that Arethusa might be lying. This was real – or at least she believed it to be so. Ocular had found something of epochal significance, one of the two or three most important discoveries in the history of the human species, and he was in on it from almost the outset. Stupendous and world-shattering, Arethusa had called it. That, he was forced to admit, was no exaggeration.

This knowledge changed everything. Sooner or later the world would know, and from that moment on ... every thought, every action, every desire and ambition would be indelibly coloured by this discovery. How could it be otherwise? There was another intelligence out there, close enough to touch. And even if they were now gone, then the mere existence of their handiwork was wonder enough to fundamentally change humanity's view of the universe.

Well, perhaps. The world had absorbed the dizzying lessons of modern science easily enough, hadn't it? Reality was a trick of cognition, an illusion woven by the brain. Beneath the apparently solid skin of the world lay a fizzing unreality of quantum mechanics, playing out on a warped and surreal Salvador Dali landscape. Ghost worlds peeled away from the present with every decision. The universe itself would one day simmer down to absolute entropic stasis, the absolute and literal end of time itself. No action, no memory of an action, no trace of a memory, could endure for ever. Every human deed, from the smallest kindness to the grandest artistic achievement, was ultimately pointless.

But it wasn't as if people went around thinking about that when they had lovers to meet, menus to choose from, birthdays to remember. The humdrum concerns of normal life trumped the miraculous every time. Eunice's death had been a seven-day wonder, and the same would be true of the Ocular discovery when it went public. Maybe a seven-month or seven-year wonder, Geoffrey thought charitably. But sooner or later it would be business as usual. Economies would rise and fall. Celebrities would come and go. There would be political scandals, even the occasional murder. And the knowledge that humanity was not alone in the universe would be as relevant to most as the knowledge that protons were built of quarks.

253

But still ... That didn't mean it *wasn't* momentous, that it wasn't an awesome privilege to be one of the first to know.

Quite why Arethusa felt he deserved that privilege, or what he was expected to do for her in return, were entirely separate mysteries.

'Forgive my scepticism, but ...' he ventured. 'Are you absolutely certain that it can't be a naturally occurring phenomenon? I mean, think of anthills ... beehives. They have structure, organisation, that might imply conscious intent. Even geological or chemical processes can create the illusion of design.'

'It's good that you have doubts, but I don't think you've considered all the options yet. This is an order of magnitude – no, make that two or three orders of magnitude more complex than anything nature is capable of. That's a planet like Earth, Geoffrey. Its weather and surface chemistry obey predictable rules. There's only one conclusion, which is that Mandala was made. It's artificial, and it was designed to be seen. The people ... the *beings* ... that did this – they'd have known exactly how visible they were. They'd have known that instruments like Ocular would be capable of viewing them from dozens of light-years away. And still they did this, knowing full well that another civilisation would be able to detect their handiwork. It was deliberate. It was made to be seen.'

'Like a calling card,' Geoffrey said.

'Or, perhaps, an invitation to keep away. A territorial marker. Maybe a helpful warning sign, like a radiation or biohazard symbol. I don't know. I've been thinking about this image for months and I still haven't got any further with it. Ocular will continue monitoring Crucible, and the signal-to-noise will improve ... but there's a limit to what we can find out from here. We'll have to get closer.'

'You mean go there?'

'If it takes a thousand years, that's within our scope. Don't look so surprised, Geoffrey – I credited you with more imagination than that.'

He shivered, for it was uncomfortably like being spoken to by his grandmother.

'It takes months just to get to Jupiter.'

'But the Green Efflorescence already demands of us that we achieve the means to cross interstellar space. We are already on that path. If Crucible is the spur that brings that goal closer, so be it.'

'You said this discovery was made late last year.'

'That's correct.'

'That's also around the time my grandmother died.'

'And you're wondering if the ... shock of it was what pushed her over the edge?'

Geoffrey doubted there was much in the universe capable of shocking his grandmother. 'Or something,' he allowed.

'She was surprised, as you'd expect. Brim-full of questions. Probing, insightful questions. Sharp until the end, your grandmother. But once she'd absorbed the news, once she'd asked me enough to satisfy her curiosity, it was almost as if she decided to put the whole business out of her mind, as if it really wasn't that important, just something we'd been talking about to pass the time. As if the discovery of intelligence elsewhere in the universe was no more consequential than, say, the news that a mutual acquaintance of ours was dying of some very rare illness. I'd told her the most astonishing news imaginable, given her this secret known only to myself at that point, and she was amazed, and then merely interested, and ultimately nonplussed.' Arethusa paused. 'That was when I started to wonder whether something had gone wrong in her head, after all those years of seclusion. Had she lost the capacity to be truly astounded, because nothing astounding had happened to her for so long? But how could anyone become that jaded?'

'Based on what I knew of her, everything you've just told me makes perfect sense. She was emotionally detached, cut off from the things that used to matter to her. I'm not sure she cared about anything by the end.'

'There's still the fact of her death happening so soon after my visit.'

'It could be a coincidence.'

'I'd agree if there'd been a single sign that she was in any way ailing, losing her grip on life.'

'You chinged up there. That means you were seeing whatever the proxy made you see. Maybe she was more unwell than she let on.'

'That's possible,' Arethusa allowed. 'But even if she was ill, the timing still troubles me. I show her the images of Crucible, and a few weeks later she dies? After one hundred and thirty years of *not* dying?' A pause. Then: 'You've been there, since she died? To the Winter Palace?'

'Not me. Just Memphis – I suppose you'd call him our retainer. Been with the family for years, and the only one of us who was still dealing with Eunice on a face-to-face basis, even though he's not an Akinya.'

'I should very much like to speak with Memphis. It sounds as if he knew her better than the rest of you.'

'Good luck getting much out of him. Memphis isn't exactly one to go blurting out secrets.'

'Because he has something to hide?'

Geoffrey laughed. 'I doubt it. But Memphis was loyal to her when she was alive, and he's not going to suddenly change now that she's dead.'

'And you've already spoken to him about Eunice?'

'I've asked him this and that, but he's not one to betray a confidence. Whatever passed between them, I'm afraid it'll go to the grave with Memphis.'

'Unless you make your own independent enquiries.'

'I do have a life I'd quite like to be getting on with. I'm a scientist, not an expert in digging into private family affairs.'

'Surely you grasp that this is about more than just your family now, Geoffrey. You are right to point out that I only chinged to the Winter Palace. Given my circumstances, that was unavoidable. But you could visit in person, couldn't you?'

'It's a bit late for that.'

'I'm thinking of the things she may have left behind. Records, testimonies. An explanation for her death. You should go, while there's still a chance of doing so.'

'The Winter Palace has been up there for decades. It's not going anywhere soon.'

'On that matter, your family may have other ideas.'

Text appeared to the right of Crucible. For a moment the words hung there in Chinese, before his eyes supplied the visual translation layer.

It was a request for 'disposal of abandoned asset'. The asset in question was an axially stabilised free-flying habitable structure, better known as the Winter Palace. The request came from Akinya Space, to the United Orbital Nations Circumlunar Space Traffic Administration.

It had been submitted on February 12.

The day he got back from the Moon. The day he handed the glove to the cousins.

'If I were you,' Arethusa said, 'I wouldn't wait too long before taking a look up there. Of course, if you need any help with that, you know who to call.'

CHAPTER SEVENTEEN

Even with her eyes cranked to maximum zoom, Sunday couldn't see the far end of the cable car's wire. It was braided spiderfibre, strung between pylons. A dust storm was curdling in from Crommelin's far rim and all she could presently see was the line, suspended like a conjuring trick before it vanished into a wall of billowing butterscotch.

The car, as big as eight container modules blocked together, had two floors, a lavish promenade deck and a small restaurant. At least a hundred people were milling around in it with room to spare. The golem wasn't on the car – unless it was wearing someone else's face, and the Pan intelligence suggested otherwise – but that didn't mean Sunday wasn't being watched, observed, scrutinised to the pore. Certainly there were golems and proxies aboard, and in all likelihood one or two warmbloods as well. Chinging struck Sunday as profoundly meaningless in contexts like this. The whole point of being in the cable car was physical proximity to the landscape. One could passive ching as close as one wished, but that wasn't the same as being here, suspended by a thread of spiderfibre. Or was she just being old-fashioned? She wondered what June Wing would have to say on the subject.

Jitendra came back from the other side of the observation deck carrying two coffees in a plastic tray. 'We're getting much lower now,' he said excitedly. 'The car's dropping down from the main cable – there must be winches in the trolley, so we can go up and down according to the terrain.'

Sunday accepted the coffee. 'You can draw me a sketch of it later. I'm sure I'll find it riveting.'

'Aren't you enjoying this?'

'Would be, if I'd come to gawp at the scenery. As it happens, there are a couple of other things on my mind.'

Jitendra's good mood wasn't going to be shattered that easily. Sipping his coffee, he studied his fellow tourists with avid interest. 'And you're sure this is the right car?'

'I just got on the first one that came in. That was what Holroyd told me to do. Said our guide would make their presence known eventually.'

'Fine. Nothing to do but wait and see, then, is there?'

The scenery, she had to admit, was something. No, she hadn't come to play tourist – but she had come to *play at* being tourist, and the two were only a whisker apart.

In Crommelin, billions of years of ancient and secret Martian history had been flensed open for inspection, naked to the sky. Over time, over unimaginable and dreary Noachian ages, wind and water had laid down layers of sedimentary rock, one on top of the other, deposition after deposition, until they formed immense and ancient strata, as dusty and forbidding as the pages of some long-unopened history book. Crommelin's interior – wide enough to swallow Nairobi or Lagos whole – was a mosaic of these sedimentary layers. Here, though, something remarkable and fortuitous had happened. Not so long ago – aeons in human terms, a mere Martian eye-blink – an asteroid or shard of comet had rammed into the ground, drilling down through Crommelin's layers.

The impactor, whatever it had been, had made stark and visible the sedimentary deposits, exposing them as a grand series of horizontal steps, dozens upon dozens in height. Awesome and patient weathering processes had toiled on this scene to produce a landscape of alien strangeness. Flat-topped mesas, pyramids and sphinxlike formations rose from a dark floor, tiered sides contoured in neat horizontal steps as if they'd been laser-cut from mile-thick plywood. Some of the formations were bony, making Sunday imagine the calcified vertebrae of colossal dead monsters, half-swallowed into the Martian crust.

Others had the random, swirling complexity of partly stirred coffee, or caramel syrup in vanilla or pecan ice cream. It was gorgeous, moving, seductive. But like everywhere else on Mars, it was also both deadly and dead.

The cable car dipped again – Sunday felt the descent this time as its suspending line spooled out a little more – and they sailed over the edge of a tawny cliff as high as any building in the Zone. Her stomach did a little butterfly flutter. Tiny bright-green and yellow multilimbed robots clung to the cliff's side, glued like geckos. She voked a scale-grid. Actually, they weren't tiny at all, but as large as bulldozers. Not rock climbers, or even ching proxies, she was given to understand, but scientific machines, still conducting sampling operations.

The cable car rose and dipped again, clearing a long stepped ridge. Another line came in from the north-east, intersecting theirs at an angle.

258

Sunday watched as a car on the other line lowered down to a railinged platform buttressed off the side of one of the rock formations. A handful of suited figures were waiting on the platform to board; others got off the cable car and began to follow a meandering metal path bolted to the cliffside. The cable car climbed away, reeling in its line to gain height, and soon it was lost in the butterscotch dust.

A sharp voice asked, 'Sunday Akinya?'

The voice belonged to a proxy, a brass-coloured robot chassis with many gears and ratchets ticking and whirring in the open cage of its skull. Its eyes were like museum-piece telescopes, goggling out of its dialled face.

'Of course,' she said. 'Since you're obviously not Holroyd, I'm guessing you're our guide?'

Sunday was alone. Jitendra had wandered off to use one of the swivel-mounted binoculars situated around the promenade deck.

'Gribelin will meet you in Vishniac. He knows the Evolvarium. He's already been very well paid, so don't let him talk you into any extra fees. Here are your train tickets.'

The proxy offered her its hand to shake and Sunday slipped her hand into its brass grip. The ruby-nailed fingers tightened. An icon appeared in her left visual field, signifying that she was now in possession of the relevant documents. Two seats, a private compartment on the overnight bullet from Crommelin to Vishniac, leaving tomorrow.

'This Gribelin doesn't sound very trustworthy.'

'Gribelin's mercenary, but he's also dependable. There's a coffee bar in the public concourse at Vishniac – he will be waiting for you.'

Sunday studied the bind tag. The proxy was being chinged from Shalbatana, but with the Pans' expertise in manipulating quangle paths that meant little.

'Did Holroyd mention the golem?'

'We know about that and we'll do what we can to slow it down, but beyond that there are no guarantees.'

'Can't you just . . . stop it? Have someone break its legs?'

'It wouldn't achieve anything, other than drawing the wrong sort of attention. Your cousin could easily obtain another body, even if it didn't look like him. We can stop him chinging ahead to Vishniac by renting all available proxies at that end, but we can't be seen to act in open opposition to Akinya interests.' The proxy looked around, its telescope-eyes clicking and rotating. 'We've block-booked half the train, so the golem won't be able to buy a ticket at the last minute. All the same, you mustn't give it the chance. The station isn't far from your hotel, so don't arrive any earlier than you need to.'

'We won't,' Sunday said.

'Holroyd will be in touch when you return. I was told to let you know that he's very satisfied with the work so far.'

'I'm ... glad to hear it,' Sunday said.

The brass proxy nodded and walked away, melting into the milling tourists.

'Give them credit,' Eunice said. 'They've covered all the bases, or as many as they're able to. Block-booking the train, renting the proxies in Vishniac ... that's only the half of it, too. I've been having difficulties synching with my Earthside counterpart ever since we arrived. It's not just that your brother's in Tiamaat, either. Someone's going to a lot of trouble to tie up Earth–Mars comms by all legal means available.'

'Then they're on our side, even if it inconveniences you.'

'My suspicion,' the construct said, 'is that they're on whichever side works best for them from one moment to the next.'

Sunday felt a touch on her arm. She turned, expecting it to be Jitendra, or just possibly the proxy, back to tell her something it had forgotten to mention before. But the young man looking at her in a crisp maroon and silver-trimmed uniform was one of the cable car's staff. 'The suit you reserved, Miss Akinya,' he said, smiling from beneath a pillbox hat. 'We were expecting you about ten minutes ago.'

Sunday narrowed her eyes. 'I didn't book any suit.'

'There's definitely one reserved, Miss Akinya. I can cancel it, of course, but if you'd care to take up the reservation, we'll be making our next stop in about ten minutes?' His smile was starting to crumble around the edges. 'You'll have about an hour on the ground before the last pickup of the day.'

'Did Jitendra book this?'

'I don't know, sorry.'

'No, he didn't,' Eunice said, answering her question. 'Not unless he managed to do so without me knowing about it, and as clever as Jitendra undoubtedly is, he's not *that* clever. So someone else has booked this suit for you, and if the Pans knew about it, the proxy would presumably have mentioned it.'

'If you'd care to come this way,' the young man said.

'I wouldn't,' Eunice said.

'It can't be Lucas. If Lucas wants to talk to me, he can just stroll straight on up, the way he did when we landed.'

260

'So you don't know who's behind this. All the more reason to be suspicious of it, you ask me.'

'Which I didn't.' Sunday looked through the windows, wondering what was the worst that could happen.

The suit would be the property of the cable-car company, so she could presume it would be in good repair, and it wasn't as if she'd be going off into the wilderness. The metal walkways down in the crater were fenced off, there were safety lines, the Mech would be as thick as anywhere else in Crommelin and there were sightseers coming and going all the time.

No possible harm could come to her: this was, if anything, an even safer place than the Descrutinised Zone.

'On your head be it,' Eunice said.

'Just do one thing for me. Tell Jitendra where I've gone. You can do that, can't you?'

'It won't overtax my capabilities, no.'

'Tell him to hang around at the cable-car terminal where we got on. I'll be back as soon as I'm able.'

'Why not tell him yourself?'

'Because he won't like it.'

'Indeed. That's because it's a mistake.'

'Then allow me the luxury of making it on my own, Grandmother.' She caught herself. 'I didn't mean to say that.'

'But you did,' Eunice answered, looking back at Sunday with a smile of quiet delight. 'You forgot, just for a moment. You forgot that I'm not really me.'

Sunday turned away, before the construct could see the shame on her face.

There were three other tourists on the landing platform: the last drop-off of the day. The suit was a little stiff, its locomotor functions lagging intent by just enough milliseconds for her brain to register the resistance. In all other respects it appeared to be in perfect working order, with a clean visor and all life-support indices in the green. The railing's cold came through her glove. She could feel the scabby roughness where the paint had flaked off the metal.

One of the cable-car employees latched a gate behind the surface party and the car pulled away, receding and rising into the air at the same time. She watched it fade into the dust, hoping Jitendra wouldn't be too alarmed by this sudden course of action.

Three metal-fenced paths led away from the landing platform, soon winding their way out of sight around rocks and cliffs. There was no guided tour, not even a suggested direction of progress, so Sunday waited until the other tourists had drifted off before choosing her own route, the one that struck her as the least popular.

The paths were bolted to the sheer sides of the rock formations, suspended dozens and sometimes hundreds of metres above solid ground. The floor was coated with some grippy anti-slip compound. A continuous rail along the cliffside allowed her to clip on a sliding safety line, with the other end tethered to her waist. There was no real possibility of falling, but she clipped on anyway.

Sunday walked as quickly as the suit allowed, conscious that she would need to be back at the platform for the final cable car of the day. The suit had more than enough reserves for an overnight stay, if it came to that, but it wasn't a prospect she viewed with any particular enthusiasm. For Jitendra's sake she vowed not to be late for the pickup.

But – and this was the thing – the scenery in Crommelin was literally awesome. There really was no other word for it. The Moon had its magnificent desolation, airless and silent as the space between thoughts, but it had taken rain and wind, insane aeons of it, to sculpt these astonishing and purposeful shapes.

Nature shouldn't be able to do this, Sunday thought. It shouldn't be able to produce something that resembled the work of directed intelligence, something artful, when the only factors involved were unthinking physics and obscene, spendthrift quantities of time. Time to lay down the sediments, in deluge after deluge, entire epochs in the impossibly distant past when Mars had been both warm and wet, a world deluded into thinking it had a future. Time for cosmic happenstance to hurl a fist from the sky, punching down through these carefully superimposed layers, drilling through geological chapters like a bullet through a book. And then yet more time – countless millions of years – for wind and dust to work their callous handiwork, scouring and abrading, wearing the exposed layers back at subtly different rates depending on hardness and chemistry, until these deliberate-looking right-angled steps and contours began to assume grand and imperial solidity, rising from the depths like the stairways of the gods.

Awe-inspiring, yes. Sometimes it was entirely right and proper to be awed. And recognising the physics in these formations, the hand of time and matter and the nuclear forces underpinning all things, did not lessen that feeling. What was she, ultimately, but the end product of physics and matter? And what was her art but the product of physics and matter working on itself?

She rounded a bend. There was a figure, another spacesuited sightseer, leaning over the outer railing, arms folded on the top of the fence. Sensing her approach – her footsteps reverberated along the path – the figure looked at her for a few seconds, then returned its gaze to the canyon below. She continued her progress, never doubting that this was the person who had arranged for her suit.

The figure's gold and chrome suit differed from hers. It was older-looking – not antique-old, but certainly not made in the last twenty or thirty years. The suit appeared well looked after, though, and she didn't doubt that it was still in perfectly serviceable condition.

Sunday joined the figure, hooking her own arms over the railing and looking down. As the day cooled, winds stirred dust eddies in the nooks and chicanes of the crater formations. Panther-black shadows stole up from the depths.

The figure touched a hand to Sunday's sleeve, establishing a suit-to-suit link. 'I know who you are,' she heard, the voice female, the words Swahili but with a distinct Martian lilt. No translation layer was in effect, at least not on her side.

'That's easy to say,' Sunday answered.

'Sunday Akinya.' The woman said her name slowly, so there could be no mistaking it. 'You've come to Mars to find out about your grand-mother.'

'Knowing my name's no great trick. Despite my best efforts, it's not like I'm travelling incognito, is it? You could easily have run an aug query on me before I left the cable car, or at any time since I landed.'

'And the other part?'

'Doesn't take a genius to draw that conclusion, does it? My grand-mother died recently. Within a few days of her scattering I'm on my way to Mars. How likely is it that the two events aren't related?'

'Maybe you had to get away from things for a while. But that's not really the case, is it? You're searching for something.'

'Aren't we all?' Sunday turned to look at the woman but her visor was mirrored, throwing back Sunday's own reflection and a fish-eye distortion of the landscape. 'You know my name. How about telling me yours?'

'Soya,' the woman answered, easily, as if the information cost her nothing.

'That's an African name, I think. And you appear to speak Swahili very well.'

'My ancestors were Nigerian, but I was born here.' Soya deliberated. 'Your intentions are to travel west, I think. We needn't go into specifics, but you have in mind somewhere quite dangerous.'

'Say it, if you're so damned sure.'

'I'd rather not. We're *quite* safe from eavesdroppers here, which is why I went to the trouble of renting that suit for you, and making sure aug reach was disabled – did you even notice that? But it's not wholly safe. Nowhere is.'

'Fine, talk in riddles, then.' Sunday admitted to herself that she hadn't noticed the absence of the aug. Unlike some people, and especially those who lived beyond the Zone, she didn't swim in it every waking moment of her existence. It was there, on tap when she needed it. And right now she would have been very glad of it. 'Are you working for the same people as Holroyd?' she ventured.

'I'm not "working" for anyone at all. I'm just here to warn you to be careful.'

'Is that a threat?'

'What could I threaten you with? Violence? Don't be silly. No: the people you need to be careful of are those who've bankrolled this expedition. Holroyd's people, in other words. They've been very helpful so far, haven't they?'

Sunday saw no point in denying it. 'We currently have a mutually beneficial relationship.'

Soya laughed at that. 'I don't doubt it. But let's not pretend that they're in this out of the goodness of their hearts.'

'Never said they were. They're helping me, and my brother's helping them. Everyone's a winner.'

'You may see it that way. I'm not sure they do.'

Sunday was wearying of this. 'Get to the point, whatever it is.'

'Let's be clear. I'm not saying the Pans are evil. They're zealous, certainly, and a little scary when they talk about their long-term goals, and how the rest of us are going to get sucked along for the ride whether we like it or not ... but that doesn't make them villains. But in it for themselves, when push comes to shove? Most definitely.'

'We're all in it for ourselves on some level.'

'Indeed. Why are you here, if not driven by intellectual curiosity? Isn't that a fundamentally selfish motivation, when you get down to it? You want those answers so you can feel better yourself, not because you think they'll necessarily do the rest of us any good.'

'Until I get the answers, I'm not going to know, am I?'

'*If* you get the answers,' Soya corrected. 'That's the point. The Pans have been watching you every step of your journey, haven't they? Always there, always willing to be helpful. Who were you meeting on the cable car if it wasn't the Pans?'

'I can't do this without them. I'm not the spoilt rich kid you might have heard about.'

'I don't doubt that. But be clear about one thing: whatever you find here, your powerful new allies are likely to be at least as interested in learning about it as you are – and they may well decide to cut you out of the loop at the last minute.'

'This is nothing to do with them. Or you, for that matter.' Sunday stepped back from the edge, but took care not to break contact with the other woman. 'OK, you've told me your name. But that means nothing. Who are you, Soya? What's your agenda?'

'Consider me a friend,' Soya said. 'That's all you need to know for the moment.' Using her other hand, the one that wasn't resting on Sunday's sleeve, she reached up and touched a stud in the side of her helmet. The visor de-mirrored instantaneously. Soya looked around, letting Sunday see her face behind the glass, and for a moment it was all she could do to keep her balance.

The face was her own.

CHAPTER EIGHTEEN

They flew Geoffrey back to Africa early the next day. The sickle-shaped craft was supersonic, a gauche indulgence when even the fastest airpods didn't break the sound barrier. Geoffrey was the flier's only occupant, and for most of the journey he stood at the extravagant curve of the forward window, hand on the railing, Caesar surveying his Rome.

Once they were over open water, back into aug reach and outpacing every other flying thing for kilometres around, Eunice returned.

'I've been worried about you. I hope no mischief occurred while I was absent.'

'I'm capable of taking care of myself, Grandmother.'

'Well, that's a development, you calling me "grandmother".'

'It just slipped out.'

'Evidently.' She fell silent, Geoffrey hoping that was the last she had to say, but after a suitable interval she continued, 'So what happened down there? Or are you not going to tell me?'

'We talked about Lin Wei, the friend you duped.'

'I don't even know of any . . . oh, wait – you mentioned her already, didn't you?'

'What did you actually *do* on Mercury, Eunice?'

'Whatever anyone does: collected a few souvenirs, soaked up the local colour.'

He abandoned that line of enquiry, guessing how far it would get him. 'Lin Wei came to you just before you died.'

'How would you know?'

'Because I think I might have met her. She didn't "drown" at all. Or if she did, it was only a metaphorical drowning. Becoming one with the sea. Changing name and form. She's a whale now, did you know? Calls herself Arethusa.'

'Try to make at least *some* sense.'

'Ocular found something. You remember Ocular, don't you? Or perhaps that's another part of your past you've conveniently buried.' He

266

gave an uninterested shrug. 'What does it matter? I'll tell you anyway. Lin found evidence of alien intelligence, the Mandala structure, and she thought you ought to know about it. Obviously still felt she owed you that, despite whatever it was you did to her.'

Eunice was standing next to him at the window, with the African coast racing towards them. The off-white wall of the coastal barrage was like a sheer chalk cliff rising from the sea. Fishing boats and pleasure craft slammed by underneath. They were flying at scarcely more than sail height, but even at supersonic speed the Pan aircraft would have been all but silent.

'My involvement with Ocular was no more than peripheral,' Eunice's figment said.

'Maybe that's what the public record says. But Lin must have known there was more to it than that. Reason she made a point of keeping her side of the bargain, by giving you this news. And then a little while later you go and die.'

'And that sequence of events troubles you?'

'Starting to feel like a bit too much of a coincidence. Lin must have felt the same way or she wouldn't have told me. She came to your funeral, you realise. That little girl in a red dress, the one none of us knew? It was a ching proxy of Lin Wei, manifesting as a child. The way she'd have been when the two of you were friends.' After a moment he added, 'I'm going up to the Winter Palace. If there's anything I need to know about it, now's the time to tell me.'

'What would I know?'

'You lived there, Eunice. You created it.'

'I wish I could help you, Geoffrey. I would if I could.' She turned to face him. 'I'll say one thing: be very careful up there.'

He knew something was not quite right as soon as the Pan flier dropped subsonic and began circling over the study station, selecting its landing site. The Cessna was where he'd left it, pinned like a crucifix to the tawny earth. Parked a little distance from it – not too far from the station's triad of stilt-mounted huts – stood a pair of clean, gleaming airpods. One was amber, the other a vivid, too-bright yellow. He could see figures on the ground, coming and going from the huts. People, robots and golems. Something on the ground like a foil-wrapped mummy, with a robot or golem bent over it.

'Put me down,' he snapped. 'Anywhere.'

The flier VTOL'd onto the nearest patch of open ground. Geoffrey dropped out of the belly hatch before the landing manoeuvre was complete, flinging his bag ahead of him. He thumped to the hard-packed earth, pushed himself to his feet, grabbed the bag and started sprinting the remaining distance to the huts. A shadow passed over him as the Pan flier returned to the sky. Geoffrey barely registered it.

'Geoffrey,' Hector said, noticing his approach. 'We tried calling you ... tried chinging. You weren't reachable. Where the hell have you been?'

'I told you to keep away from here,' Geoffrey said. He coughed as dust, stirred up by the flier, infiltrated his lungs.

'It's Memphis,' Lucas said. He was standing next to the mummy-like form lying on the ground.

'What?' Geoffrey asked, stupefied.

'Memphis was late back at the household,' Hector explained. 'This morning.' He was flustered, sweat prickling his forehead. 'He was expected at a particular time – we were supposed to be meeting him, to talk about the household accounts.'

'No ching bind could be established,' Lucas said, repeating himself a moment later. 'No ching bind could be established.' As if this very fact implied the opening up of an entire chasm of existential wrongness, a baleful perversion against the natural order of things.

'We came out here straight away,' Hector said. 'His airpod ... we could see where he'd landed.'

Geoffrey pushed Hector back until he was standing next to Lucas, who was staring blankly at the ground. He coughed some more dust from his windpipe. The ocean, the turquoise realm of Tiamaat, the night dance of the merpeople, felt like a lovely dream from which he'd just been abruptly woken. No medical diagnosis was needed to tell Geoffrey that Memphis was dead. His body was visible through the protective chrysalis that had been sprayed around him. Through its emerald tint, Memphis's bloodied and crushed form looked like a toy that had been given to a boisterous, vengeful child. He would have been unrecognisable were it not for his signature suit, caked with dirt and blood but insufficiently so to conceal the familiar pinstriping. One of Memphis's black leather shoes had come off his foot, exposing a dusty sock. The shoe was on the ground, outside the chrysalis.

'What happened?' Eunice whispered, appearing next to him.

'Not now. Of all times, not now.'

She kept looking at the body, saying nothing. The robotic form that had been stooped over the chrysalis rose to its full bipedal height. It was one of the household's usual proxies, Geoffrey saw – Giacometti-thin, with holes and gaps in its limbs, torso and head-assembly.

'There's nothing you could have done,' the proxy stated, with a smooth Senegalese accent. 'Judging by these injuries, he was killed very quickly. There will have to be a full medical examination, of course, given the *accidental* nature of his death, but I doubt there will be any surprises. You say his body was found near elephants?'

'He was working with them,' Lucas said, glancing at Geoffrey.

'Elephants didn't do this,' Geoffrey said.

Hector placed a hand on his shoulder. 'I know it will be hard for you to accept ...'

Geoffrey nearly wrenched his cousin's hand off. 'It wasn't the elephants.'

'These are crush injuries,' the proxy said hesitantly, as if it didn't want to get dragged into a family dispute. 'And this wound in his abdomen ... it *is* consistent with a tusk injury.'

'Seen a lot of those, have you?' Geoffrey asked. 'I thought accidents were supposed to be rare these days.'

'I've seen wounds like this in the textbooks,' the proxy replied.

'The doctor's only trying to assist us,' Hector said placatingly.

'He's right,' Eunice said, in little more than a murmur. 'It's not the proxy's fault, or the fault of the physician on the other end.'

But Geoffrey still couldn't accept the evidence of his senses, or the honest testimony of the medical expert.

'Elephants didn't do this,' he said again, only softer this time, as if it was himself he was trying to convince.

'He should not have come out here alone, at his age,' Hector said.

'He was only a hundred,' Lucas pointed out.

'He's not been looking strong to me lately. This was a risk he should never have taken. What was he doing out here, Geoffrey?' Hector had his hands on his hips. 'This was your work, not his.'

In a monotone, Geoffrey said, 'Memphis always helped me.'

'You should not have asked it of him,' Lucas said. 'He had enough to be doing at the household. You imposed on his good nature.'

Geoffrey took a swing at him, but missed. His own momentum sent him spinning off balance. He would have fallen had Hector not reached out to steady him.

'This isn't the time for recriminations,' Hector said, directing the comment at his brother. 'This is upsetting for all of us.'

'Get a grip on yourself,' Eunice admonished, her arms folded disapprovingly. 'If the Mech was any thicker, it would have dropped you like a stone just for thinking violence.'

Geoffrey gave a last cough. There was dust in his lungs, up his nose, in his watering eyes. 'He was just doing routine work for me,' he said in a wheeze as Hector relinquished his grip. 'While I was away.'

'You still haven't told us where you were,' Lucas said.

'Because it's none of your fucking business, cousin.'

The proxy swivelled its head, reminding them that it was still present, still being chinged.

'I've called for a scrambulance. The body will be taken to the hospital in Mombasa. They'll do what they can, but I should tell you now there's little prospect for revival.'

Hector nodded gravely. 'Thank you for your honesty, Doctor.'

'If I'd been able to get to him sooner ...' The proxy shook its head. 'I do not understand why he allowed this to happen.'

'Allowed?' Geoffrey asked.

'In a place this dangerous,' Lucas said, looking around, 'he should not have been on his own. The Mechanism can't be all places at all times – it's not god. A watchdog should have come out with him, in case he got into difficulties.' He pointed at the encased form. 'Look, he's not even wearing a bracelet. What was he supposed to do if a snake bit him, or he sprained his ankle and couldn't walk back to the airpod?'

'He knew what he was doing,' Geoffrey said.

'He must have been startled,' Hector said. 'That's the only explanation. The elephant was on him before he had a chance to do anything about it.'

'I doubt very much that he suffered,' the doctor said. 'As you say, if he'd had any inkling that he was in peril—'

'We would have found a dead elephant near his body,' Lucas said. 'Or dead elephants.'

Eunice looked Geoffrey in the eye, then absented herself.

CHAPTER NINETEEN

Sunday and Jitendra were on the overland bullet train, speeding west through the plains of Chryse in the middle of the Martian day, when Geoffrey chinged in.

Sunday knew at once that something was wrong.

'If you can,' his figment said, 'take this call somewhere private. I don't mean from Jitendra. It would be good if Jitendra could be with you. But you shouldn't be in public.' Geoffrey's face told her everything she needed to know, except the worst part of it. 'I don't have good news.'

The Pans had paid for a private compartment in the train so there was no need for Sunday to take the call anywhere else. She allowed the figment to continue speaking, cursing the distance that prevented her from responding to him in real-time. Cursing physics, the basic organising framework of reality.

'It's just after noon here. This morning I came back from Tiamaat. I was due to land at the study station, but as I came in I saw that something was happening on the ground. The cousins were there, and they'd found Memphis.' Geoffrey swallowed, moved his jaw. 'He was dead, Sunday. Something had happened out there and ... he was dead, on the ground, just lying there.' Geoffrey stopped and looked down at his feet. 'There was already a doctor on-scene when I arrived, but too much time had passed. They've taken Memphis to Mombasa, but it's not looking good ... I don't think there's going to be much they can do.'

Jitendra had already closed his hand around hers, though she barely felt his presence, the train compartment, the pressure-tight glass, the rushing red scenery beyond, everything receding into galactic distance.

'I don't know what happened,' Geoffrey went on. 'He'd agreed to help me with the elephants while I was away. The doctor says he was crushed ... as if he got into trouble with the elephants. But that can't have happened. Memphis knew the herd almost as well as I did – I wouldn't have asked for his help otherwise, and there's no one else I'd have trusted to do the job properly.' He closed his eyes. 'That's all I have right now. I'll call you as soon as there's more news, but I think you should be prepared for the worst.' He opened his eyes, started to say something before abandoning the attempt. 'I feel I ought to say that I wish I could be with you, but that's a lie. I wish you were here, back with me, in Africa. Right now Mars feels like a very long way away.' He nodded, his eyes meeting hers with uncanny directness. 'Take care, sister. I love you.'

Geoffrey was gone. The train sped on its way, oblivious to her news. It should be slowing, she reckoned, allowing her thoughts time to catch up. That would be the decent thing.

She did not know what to do or say, so when Jitendra tightened his hold on her and said that he was sorry, she was as glad as it was possible to be in that moment.

'I have to get back to Earth.'

'Wait for what the doctors have to say. Neuropractors can do wonders nowadays.'

'You heard what my brother said – it had been too long.'

Jitendra had no answer for that. He had meant to be kind, she knew, but there was reasonable hope and there was false hope, and she would not cling to the latter.

'I have to get back,' she repeated.

'It . . . won't make any difference.' Jitendra was speaking very carefully. 'It's taken you a month to travel here, and even if we got back into orbit and miraculously found a slot on the next swiftship out . . . it'd be five weeks, at least, before we'll be anywhere near Earth.'

'Every week I spend here, Earth is further away.'

'If there's going to be a funeral, then you'll have either already missed it, even if you leave now, or they'll have to wait until you get back. Who was closest to Memphis? You and your brother. And your brother's back in Africa. He's not going to let anything happen until you get home, is he?'

'Please don't talk about funerals,' Sunday said. 'Not yet. Not before we've heard from Mombasa.'

But he was right. She had already been thinking of funerals.

CHAPTER TWENTY

Chinging in from Mombasa, where Memphis's body had been examined in detail, the neuropractor delivered her verdict to the family members gathered in the household.

They *could* bring him back to life, the figment said, that was always an option, albeit an expensive one. But so much of his brain would need to be rebuilt from scratch that the end result wouldn't be the man they had known. The basic structural organisation of his personality had been blasted to shards. 'There is no gentle way of putting this, but what you would be getting back would be a baby in an old man's body,' the figment informed them, Geoffrey unable to shake the sense that this was all fractionally too rehearsed, a speech that the neuropractor kept up her sleeve to deliver on occasions such as this, while trying to make it sound suitably impromptu and sincere. He wanted to resent her for that, but couldn't. She was just being kind.

'A confused, frightened baby with just enough recollection to know what it was missing,' the specialist went on. 'Memory. Language. All traces of family and friendship. The hard-earned skills and knowledge of a lifetime. And with not enough life ahead of it ever to recover what was lost. We will of course abide by your wishes, but I urge you to give deep consideration before taking this course.'

No discussion was required. For once, the Akinyas were all in agreement. The decision was entirely in their hands, as Memphis had no family but the one that employed him.

'We wouldn't want that,' Hector said softly, Geoffrey nodding his assent, and knowing as he did so that he was answering for Sunday as well.

'I think you're doing the right thing,' the specialist said. 'And I am so sorry that this has happened.'

Geoffrey was still trying to come to terms with what the day had delivered. Everything felt unreal, off-kilter. Memphis had been part of his life in a way that Eunice never had. She was a reclusive figure who sometimes beamed herself down from the Winter Palace, but who never walked the household in person. Having her removed from his life was the same as having a part of his own past dismantled, boxed away for posterity. He was sad about it, but it didn't rip him apart.

It was different with Memphis. He'd always been there, a living, breathing, human presence. The smell of him, the prickly texture of his suit fabric, the squeak of his shoes on waxed flooring as he patrolled the household's corridors at night, more vigilant than any watchdog. Kind when he needed to be, stern when the moment called for it. Always willing to forgive, if not necessarily forget. The most decent human being Geoffrey had ever known.

He remembered Lucas's words: *You imposed on his good nature.*

The implication wounded, but he had done exactly that. Always had done.

'Thank you for letting me know,' Sunday said, when she chinged back in response to his earlier transmission. 'Right now, I don't really have a clue what to say. I'm still processing it. I'm so sorry that you had to see him ... the way he was. But whatever you might think, this wasn't your fault, OK? You asked Memphis to do something for you, but that doesn't mean you have to take responsibility for what happened to him. Memphis was old enough to make his own decisions: if he'd felt your request endangered him, he'd have told you so. So don't go making this any harder on yourself than it already is. Please, brother? For me?' Sunday collected herself; from the figment, it was hard to tell if she'd been crying or not. 'I'm on my way to Pavonis Mons right now. Keep me informed, and I'll be in touch as soon as I'm able.' She touched a finger to her lips. 'Love you, brother. Be strong, for both of us.'

He nodded. He would try, although he did not expect it to be easy.

Geoffrey had to get out of the house, so he went for a walk in the gardens, forcing his mind from its rut as best as he was able. Everywhere he went, though, he found evidence of Memphis's handiwork. Choices about the redevelopment of the grounds, the refurbishment of ornamental fountains, the arabesque detailwork in the enclosing wall, the selection of flowers and shrubs in the beds – all these things had ultimately fallen to Memphis. Even when the family had been presented with a series of options, Memphis would already have whittled down a much larger set of possibilities, to the point where any one of the final choices would have been acceptable to him. One of his greatest, subtlest gifts to the Akinyas had been granting them the illusion of free will.

*

Later that afternoon, when Geoffrey had returned indoors, Jumai chinged to say she was on the train from Lagos. Geoffrey was momentarily befuddled, until he remembered that he had in fact called and left a message with her, shortly after the body was taken away. Everything had been a blur. Jumai had been working, so couldn't take the call there and then. He was still startled that she was on her way.

'Get off the train in Kigali,' he told her. 'I'll meet you there.'

'All right,' she said, doubtfully, as if that wasn't the kind of reception she'd been expecting.

'It will be good to see Jumai again,' Eunice said, announcing her presence.

'You never knew her,' Geoffrey snapped. 'You never knew anyone at all.'

It was only later that he realised she'd had the good grace to keep out of his skull while he'd been wandering the grounds.

It was a two-hour flight, and mid-evening by the time he landed in Kigali. Rain was descending, soft and warm, honey-scented, dyed scarlet and cobalt and gold by the station's old-fashioned neon signage. He'd just missed Jumai's arrival: she was sheltering under the concourse's overhanging roof, while taxis and airpods fussed about and vendors packed up for the night. Two black bags, sagging on the damp concrete either side of her feet like exhausted lapdogs, were her only luggage.

'You didn't have to do this,' Geoffrey said when they were in the air, wheeling over night-time Kigali on their way back to the household.

'I knew Memphis pretty well,' Jumai said, as if he might not remember. They'd both got wet between the station and the airpod, but were drying off quickly with the cabin heater turned up. 'I was part of your life long enough, don't forget.'

'I'm not likely to.' But while he'd remembered to call Jumai – she'd have been hurt if he hadn't – it was only now that he was beginning to remember how closely braided their lives had really been. Weeks, months, in Amboseli. Memphis had often come out to the research station while Jumai was fashioning the architecture for the human–elephant neurolink. They'd often ended up eating together, late at night, under a single swaying lamp around which mosquitoes orbited like frantic little planets, caught in the death-grip of a supermassive star.

Long stories, silly laughter, too much wine. Yes, Jumai knew Memphis. *Had known*, he corrected himself. *All past tense from now on.*

He started crying. It was ridiculous – there'd been no particular spur to it, save the helter-skelter progression of his own thoughts, but once he started he could not stop himself. How foolish he had been to think he could keep it together, at least until he was out of anyone's sight.

'I'm sorry, Geoffrey.' Jumai squeezed his hand. 'This must be really hard on you. I know how much he meant to you.'

'It's hard on Sunday as well,' he said, when he was able to speak.

'Is she flying in?'

'Not really an option – Sunday's on Mars, on her way to Pavonis Mons.'

They were crossing the southern tip of Lake Victoria. The clouds had parted overhead, the waters as still and clear as if they were cut from black marble.

'What's going on, Geoffrey? Eunice dies. Memphis dies ... Your sister decides to go to Mars.'

'Something. I don't know what.' After a moment he added, 'I might need to go back into space myself. There's a job ...' He closed his eyes. 'It's related, but I can't say much more than that. I might have to break into family property.'

'Is that why I'm here? Because I can be *useful* to you?'

'You know me better than that.'

'Perhaps.' She was silent for a few seconds. 'Well, as it happens, I just quit in Lagos. Bad day at the office.'

'Really?'

'Yes, really. Nearly got spiked. Figured it was time to bail out, before we hit something really nasty. And for what? A dickhead of a boss? Bank accounts from a hundred years ago, the tawdry blackmail secrets of the rich and famous?' She looked cross-eyed and appalled, as if she'd just picked something repulsive out of her nose. 'Frankly, if I'm going to die on the job, I'd rather it was for something more interesting than century-old scandal fodder.'

Geoffrey considered the Winter Palace.

'I'm afraid century-old scandal fodder may be the best I can offer instead.'

There was a silence. The airpod made a tiny course adjustment. Once in a while another one zipped by in the other direction, but aside from that they had the night sky all to themselves.

'You want to talk about what happened,' Jumai said after a while, in not much more than a whisper, 'it's all right with me.' When Geoffrey was not immediately forthcoming, she added, 'You said they found him near the elephants, that there'd been an accident.'

'Something out there got him. But it wasn't elephants.'

'What, then?'

276

'I don't know. Something else. Memphis knew his way around the herd. Elephants didn't do this.'

After a while she said, 'It must have been quick.'

'That's what the doctor thought. He couldn't have had any warning, or he'd have . . . protected himself.'

'I've never seen anyone do that.'

'I have,' Geoffrey said, thinking back to the day they had found the death machine, and Sunday had nearly died. 'Once, when I was little.'

It was during breakfast with Jumai the following morning that the thought struck him, the one that, in retrospect – and given his ideas about the cousins – he might reasonably already have entertained. Perhaps, on some unspoken level, he had indeed done that. But he had not come close to voicing it to himself at the level of conscious assessment. And now that he had, now that the thought had pushed itself into his awareness like a rhino charging into daylight, it was all he could do to sit in stunned wonderment, awed at what his mind had dared to conjure.

'What are you thinking?' Eunice asked.

'I'm thinking it would be a good idea if you fucked off.'

'Geoffrey?' Jumai asked.

He was staring past her, through the window, out to the trees beyond the border wall. Eunice was gone.

'I'm sorry,' he said distractedly. 'It's just—'

'It was a bad idea me coming here, wasn't it?'

'That's not it,' he said.

But in truth it was disconcerting, having Jumai back at the household, but them not sleeping together. Doubly so in that Memphis was not around. Time and again his thoughts kept plummeting through the same mental trapdoors. *Memphis should hear this. Memphis will know. What will Memphis have to say?* And each time he caught himself and swore that that would be the last time, and each time he was mistaken.

They'd slept in separate rooms, and met in the east wing for breakfast. The household staff vacillated between subdued discretion and the putting on of brave faces, acting as if nothing had happened. This grated on Geoffrey until he realised he was doing exactly the same thing, smiling too emphatically, cracking nervous little half-jokes. They were all simply trying to do what Memphis would have wanted, which was to keep on with business as usual exactly as if nothing had happened. They were all overdoing it, though.

'You don't have to apologise,' Jumai said. 'You're bound to be upset by what's happened. But if this is making you feel awkward, me being here, I can leave at any time.' She dropped her voice to a stage whisper. 'It doesn't prevent me working on that, um, commission.'

'Honestly, it's not you,' Geoffrey assured her. 'I'm glad to have some company. It's just . . . there's a lot going on in my head.'

Like the ghost of his dead grandmother, bothering him from beyond the grave. Like the possibility that one or both of the cousins had killed Memphis.

There it was, stated as unambiguously as possible. No pussyfooting around that one.

The cousins killed Memphis.

He'd hoped, upon erecting this suspicion, to be able to knock it down immediately. Bulldoze the rubble away and forget about it. Until that point he hadn't hated the cousins, after all. Or at least if there were degrees of hate, his was on the mildly antipathetic end of the spectrum, repelled by their manipulative gamesmanship, sickened by their avarice, disgusted by their attachment to family above all else. But not actually despising them. Not actually wishing pain upon them. Most of the time.

But the idea that they might have killed Memphis, or made his death probable . . . well, when framed so plainly, why exactly not? The cousins bitterly regretted bringing Geoffrey in to help them, that was clear. Since his return from the Moon, they'd been well aware that he was keeping information from them, and that this deceit extended to Sunday. It was all to do with Eunice, so what better way to limit any further damage than by removing the one man who'd had more access to the old woman than any of them? Killing Memphis blocked Geoffrey's investigations in that particular direction. It also meant that anything damaging that Memphis might have had cause to disclose was not now likely to come to light.

And yes, *murder* . . . a difficult thing, that, in the Surveilled World. Easier to steal the Great Wall of China. The very word had the dark alchemical glamour of crimes now banished to history, like regicide or blasphemy.

But still. Murder wasn't impossible, even in 2162. Even beyond the Descrutinised Zone, in the loving panoptic gaze of the Mechanism. Because the Mechanism wasn't infallible, and even this tireless engineered god couldn't be all places at once. The Mandatory Enhancements were supposed to weed out the worst criminal tendencies from developing minds before people reached adolescence . . . but those very tendencies were imprecise, and it was inevitable that someone, now and then, would slip through the mesh. Someone with the mental wiring necessary to premeditate. Someone capable of malintent.

And if you wanted to commit a crime like that, the Amboseli Basin was far from the worst place you could think of.

When had Memphis died? When Geoffrey was away, not keeping his eye on the old man.

Where had he died? Out in the sticks, where the aug was stretched thin, the Mechanism ineffectual. Memphis wasn't even wearing his biomedical bracelet – although that could easily have been removed after his death.

Who'd found him? Hector and Lucas. The cousins.

Geoffrey closed his eyes, trying to derail his thoughts, to get them off this tramline. It didn't work.

The cousins killed Memphis.

'I'm sorry I dragged you into this,' he said.

'Dragged me into what? We've barely begun.'

'Family,' he said. 'Memphis. Everything.'

'You've given me an out from Lagos, Geoffrey. I'm hardly going to resent you for that.'

'Even if there's an element of self-interest?'

'Like we said, it's business. So long as we're clear about that, all's well.' She picked at her food like a bird rooting through roadside scraps. Geoffrey didn't have much of an appetite either. Even the coffee sat heavily inside him, sloshing around like some toxic by-product. 'Has there been any talk . . .' she began, then faltered.

'Of what?'

Jumai set her face in an expression he remembered well, drawing in breath and squaring her jaw. 'I'm assuming there are funeral arrangements. I couldn't make it back for your grandmother's scattering, but now that I'm here—'

'There's nothing in hand. Memphis never talked to me about what he wanted to happen in the event of his death, and I can't imagine he was any more frank with the rest of the family. Even Sunday wasn't as close to him as I am. Was.' He dragged up a smile. 'Still adjusting. But I'm glad you mentioned the funeral, because I hadn't given it a moment's thought.'

'Really?'

'I've been so fixated on what happened, and what it means . . . but you're right. There will be a funeral, of course, and I want my sister to be part of it.'

Jumai looked doubtful. 'Even though she's on Mars?'

'She'll be back sooner or later. Memphis doesn't have to be cremated and scattered in a hurry, the way my grandmother was. There wasn't time for everyone to get back home then, especially not when some of us were as far out as Titan. It won't be the same with Memphis.'

Jumai nodded coolly. 'And you'll make damned sure of that.'

'Yes,' Geoffrey said. 'Because I owe it to my sister. And it's what Memphis would have wanted.'

'That's one thing I never understood about your grandmother,' Jumai said. 'I can understand why no one wanted to move the scattering to suit my needs. But why did the rest of you have to get here so quickly?'

'Because that's what Eunice wanted,' Geoffrey said. 'A quick cremation, and a quick scattering. She didn't want to wait a year, or however long it would take for the whole family to get back to Africa.'

'She told you that?'

'No,' he answered carefully. 'But Memphis did.' And then he thought about that, and what exactly it meant.

After breakfast Jumai went to swim. Geoffrey returned to his room and sat on the made bed. He slid open the lower drawer of the bedside cabinet and took out the shoe he'd brought with him from the study station. He held it in his hands, chalky ochre dust soiling his fingers. The laces were still tied: the shoe had slipped off the old man's foot without them coming loose. Geoffrey touched the knot, wondering if Memphis had been the habit of tying his left shoe first or his right. He had a picture in his mind of Memphis resting one foot on the Cessna's undercarriage, doing up his laces, but he couldn't remember which shoe Memphis had started with. Details, ordinary quotidian details, beginning to slip out of focus. And no more than a day had passed.

He put the shoe back in the drawer, slid it shut. No idea why he had been moved to pick it up, as Memphis's chrysalis-bound body was being loaded into the medical transport. Hector and Lucas might even have seen him do it, he wasn't sure.

He moved to his desk, settled into the chair and voked a request to the United Orbital Nations for information relating to the status of asset GGFX13419/785G, aka the Winter Palace. The data was open and public, but even if it hadn't been, his request was coming through Akinya channels.

Text floated before him:

On: 20/2/62 07:14:03:11 CUT
Subject: Request for disposal of abandoned asset
Asset code: GGFX13419/785G

Asset type: Axially stabilised free-flying habitable structure
Status: Disposal authority granted
Disposal mode: Discretionary

'What's troubling you?' Eunice asked.

He thought about not answering her for a moment, before giving in. 'They're going to tear down the Winter Palace.'

'Let them,' she said, shrugging with blunt indifference. 'I don't live there any more, Geoffrey. Last thing anyone needs is more junk cluttering up Lunar orbit.'

'It's not junk. It's history, part of us. Part of what's made us the way we are. The cousins can't just trash it.'

'Evidently they can.' She was looking at the text, accessing the same data.

'Unless someone stops them,' Geoffrey said.

'You wouldn't be planning anything foolhardy, would you?'

'I'll get back to you on that one.'

Geoffrey voked the text away and went outside to find the cousins. He encountered Hector first. He was coming back from the tennis court, sweat-damp towel padded around his neck. A proxy strode alongside him, swinging a racquet. Geoffrey blocked the path of the two opponents.

'Whoever you are,' he told the proxy, 'you can ching right back home.'

'This is unfortunate, Geoffrey,' Hector said, staring him down. 'I'm used to your rudeness, but there's absolutely no need to inflict it on my guests.'

'I was going anyway,' the proxy said. 'Nice game, Hector. Let's do it again sometime.' The proxy became slump-shouldered and loll-headed as soon as the ching was broken, the racquet dangling from one limp hand.

Hector took the racquet, clacking it against his own, then told the proxy to store itself.

'There was no need for that, cousin.'

'You'll get over it.'

The proxy scooted away, walking like a person in a speeded-up movie. Hector dredged up a pained smile. 'And there was me, thinking we were all getting on so well yesterday.'

'That was then,' Geoffrey said.

'Anything in particular I can help you with?'

'You can start by telling me what really happened out there.'

'Out *where*, cousin?' Hector unwrapped the towel and began rubbing his hair with it.

'Memphis dying. That was so convenient, wasn't it? Solved all your problems in one stroke. No wonder you're in the mood for a game of tennis.'

'Go back inside, take a deep breath and start again. We'll both pretend this conversation didn't happen.'

'I'm not saying you killed him,' Geoffrey blurted. He'd gone too far, he realised immediately, let his temper get the better of him. Off in the distance, Eunice was shaking her head.

Hector gave him an appraising nod. 'Good. Because if you were—'

'But it works for you, doesn't it? You can't wait to bury Eunice and everything she did. You just want to get on with running things, and not have any nasty surprises jump out at you from the past.'

Hector flung his towel onto the path, knowing a household robot would be along to tidy it away. 'I think you and I need to have a little chat. You've been acting very strange since you came back from the Moon. Strang*er*, I should say. What were you doing in Tiamaat?'

Geoffrey stared at him blankly.

'What, you think an aircraft can't be tracked?' Hector pushed. 'We knew where you were. Cosying up to the Pans now, are you? Well, they've got money, I'll give you that. Comes at a price, though. I wouldn't trust them any further than I'd trust *us*, if I wasn't already an Akinya.'

'Man has a point,' Eunice commented.

'I'll choose my own loyalties, thanks,' Geoffrey said.

'No one's stopping you,' Hector said. 'Big mistake, though, thinking you can make the Pans work for you. What have you got that they want, exactly? Because it isn't money, and if it's charm and diplomacy they're after ...' Hector tapped the doubled racquets against his forehead. 'Oh, wait. It's one of two things, isn't it? Elephants or elephant dung.' He lowered the racquets. 'You think you're ahead of them, Geoffrey? Able to make them work for you, not the other way around? You're more naive than I thought, and that's saying something.' He paused, his voice turning earnest. 'Lucas and I didn't give a fuck about Memphis either way, I'll be honest with you. He was old and past his best. But whatever happened out there, you had better get it into your head that we had nothing to do with it. Whereas you sent an old man to do your dirty work, when you had better things to do. It's not me who needs to take a good hard look at his conscience.'

'I won't let you take down the Winter Palace.'

'Meaning what?'

'I don't need to spell it out. Eunice is gone, Memphis is gone. Now the only link to the past is ... that *thing* up there. And you can't let it stand.'

'Lucas was right – he did warn me it was a mistake to ask you to do anything useful. I should have listened.' He pinched sweat from the corners of his eyes. 'You enjoy certain benefits, cousin. You think yourself to be above the rest of us, but you're always willing to scuttle back to the household when the need suits you. A room you don't pay for? Free meals and transportation? Dropping the family name when it helps open doors?'

Geoffrey glared. 'I've never done that.'

'You need a dose of reality, I think. I won't throw you out of the household, not when you have a guest here, but consider all other privileges rescinded. Forthwith. I'll arrange a train ticket for Jumai and an airpod back to the railway station, but it'll be at my discretion, not yours. You've shamed yourself, Geoffrey. Stop before you do any more harm.'

He moved to punch Hector.

It was a stupid, unpremeditated impulse, not something he'd been planning. If he'd thought about it for more than the instant it took the fury to overcome him, he'd have known how utterly pointless the gesture was going to prove.

Hector didn't even flinch; barely raised the racquets in involuntary self-defence. He simply took a step backwards while the Mechanism assessed Geoffrey's intent and intervened to prevent the completion of a violent act. It had been different out at the study station, when Geoffrey had clashed with the cousins: there, the aug had been thin, the Mechanism's omniscience imperfect.

No so here, in the well-ordered environs of the household. A million viewpoints tracked him from instant to instant, an audience of unblinking sensors wired to the tireless peacekeeping web of the Surveilled World. In the dirt under his feet, in the granite glint of a wall, in the air itself, were more public eyes than he could imagine. His movements had been modelled and forward-projected. Algorithms had triggered, escalating in severity. From that nodal point in equatorial East Africa, a seismic ripple had troubled the Mechanism. At its epicentre, one calamitous truth: *A human being was attempting to perpetrate harm against another.*

The algorithms debated. Expert systems polled each other. Decision-branches cascaded. Prior case histories were sifted for best intervention practice. There was no time to consult human specialists; they'd only be alerted when the Mechanism had acted.

Geoffrey had barely begun to initiate the punch when something axed his head in two.

It was 'just' a headache, but so sudden, so agonising, that the effect was as instant and debilitating as if he'd been struck by lightning. He froze into paralysis, not even able to scream his pain. Eunice broke up like a jammed signal. Unbalanced by the momentum he'd already put into his swing, Geoffrey toppled past Hector and hit the ground hard, stiff as a statue.

The paralysis ebbed. He lay helpless, quivering in the aftershock of the intervention, dust and gravel in his mouth, his palms stinging, his trousers wet where he had lost bladder control.

The intervention was over as suddenly as it had arrived. The headache was gone, leaving only an endless migraine afterchime.

'That was ... silly,' Hector said, stepping over him, stooping to tap him on the thigh with the racquets. 'Very, *very* silly. Now there'll have to be an inquiry, and you know what that will mean. Psychologists will be involved. Neuropractors. Our name dragged through more dirt. All because you couldn't act like a responsible adult.'

Geoffrey pushed himself to his feet. Through the shock of what had happened, the fury remained. Absurd as it was, he still wanted to hit Hector. Still wanted to punch that smile away.

Eunice hadn't reappeared.

'This isn't over,' he said.

Hector averted his gaze from the sorry spectacle before him. 'Go and make yourself presentable.'

CHAPTER TWENTY-ONE

Geoffrey was still shaking, still doing his best not to think through the consequences of what had just transpired, as he tossed his soiled garments into the wash and changed into fresh clothes. His instinct was to blame Hector.

But even if Hector was responsible for him committing the violent act, he could not be held accountable for the intervention. That was the *point* of the Mechanism: it was oblivious to persuasion, supremely immune to influence. Nor was it done with him. It might take hours, it might take days, but he would be called to account, by shrinks and 'practors, subjected to exhaustive profiling: not just to make sure he was suitably repentant, but to satisfy the Mechanism's human consultants that the impulse had been an aberration, not the manifestation of some deeper psychological malaise that required further surgical intervention.

So he was in trouble, unquestionably. But he still had every reason to distrust the cousins, every reason to think that they would not waste a moment in erasing Eunice's legacy.

Still in his room, with the door ajar, he used Truro's secure quangle path to ching Tiamaat.

'There's been a development,' Geoffrey said, when the smooth-faced merman had assumed form.

'You're referring to the disposal plans?' Truro, who was half-submerged in pastel-blue lather, gave a vigorous blubbery nod. 'I assumed that would have come to your attention as well. There's no timescale for the operation, but we can safely assume it will be sooner rather than later, now that permission has been granted.'

'There's something else. I've just done something ... impetuous. Or stupid.' Geoffrey lowered his gaze, unable to look at the Pan directly. 'I confronted the cousins.'

'Perfectly understandable, given the circumstances.'

'And I tried hitting one of them.'

'Ah,' Truro said, after a moment's reflection. 'I see. And this ... *act* – was it—'

'The Mechanism intervened.'

'Oof.' He blinked his large dark seal eyes in sympathy. 'Painful, I'll warrant. And doubtless fairly humiliating as well.'

'I've had better mornings.'

'Any, um, history of this kind of thing?'

'I don't routinely go around trying to hit people, no.' But he had to think carefully. 'Got into a fight when I was a teenager, over a card game. Or a girl. Both, maybe. That was the last time. Before that, it was just the usual stuff we do in childhood, so that we understand how things work.'

'Then I doubt there'll be any lasting complications. We're animals, at the core, even after the Enhancements: the Mechanism doesn't expect sainthood. All the same ... it does complicate things *now*.'

'That's what I was thinking.'

'Usual protocol in this situation would be a period of ... probationary restraint, I think they call it – denial of aug and ching rights, restricted freedom of movement, and so forth – until a team of experts decides you aren't a permanent menace to society and can be allowed to get on with your life without further enhancement ... with a caution flag appended to your behavioural file, of course. The next time you're involved in anything similar, the Mechanism won't hesitate to assume you're the initiating party ... and it may dial up its response accordingly.'

No bones: the Mechanism would kill, if killing prevented the taking of an innocent life. Just because it didn't happen very often didn't mean that the threat was absent. Geoffrey's crime put him a long way down the spectrum from the sort of offender likely to merit that kind of intervention. But still ... just being on the same spectrum: he wasn't too thrilled about that.

'What do I do?'

'We need to get you to Tiamaat before probationary restraint kicks in. A human has to be involved in that process, probably someone with a dozen or so pending cases already in their workfile. That means we may have an hour or two.'

'Once I'm in Tiamaat, how does that help?'

'We have ... ways and means. But you need to get to us, Geoffrey. We can't come to you now.'

He looked around the little room, underfurnished and impersonal, like a hotel he'd just checked into. He realised he wouldn't miss it if he never saw it again. Other than a few knick-knacks, there was nothing of him here.

'I'll see what I can do.'

'Make haste,' Truro said. 'And speed. Haste and speed, very good things right now.'

Jumai was swimming lengths, cutting through the water like a swordfish, all glossy sleekness and speed. She made this basically inhuman activity appear not only workable but the one viable solution to the problem of moving.

'I thought we might take a flight, around the area,' he said vaguely when she paused for breath at one end of the pool, elbows on the side.

'Is there stuff you need to deal with, to do with Memphis?'

'Nothing that can't wait.'

'You all right, Geoffrey?' She was looking at his trousers and shirt. 'Why've you changed?'

He offered a shrug. 'Felt like it.'

She shrugged in return, appearing to accept his explanation. 'Mind if I do a few more lengths?'

He nodded at the clear blue horizon. It was untrammelled by even the wispiest promise of clouds, the merest hint of the weather system they'd flown through around Kigali. 'There's a front coming in. I thought we'd try and duck around it.'

'A front? Really?'

'Revised weather schedule,' he offered lamely.

'And this can't wait?'

'No,' he said, trusting that she'd understand him, read the message in his eyes that he couldn't say aloud. 'No, it can't.'

'OK. Then I guess it's time to get out of the water.'

She changed quickly, hair still frizzy from being towel-dried when she rejoined him. Geoffrey was anxious, wondering when the iron clamp of probationary restraint was going to slam down on him.

'What's up?' she asked him, sotto voce, as they headed towards the parked airpods.

'Something.'

'To do with me being here?'

'It's not you.' He was answering in the same undertone. 'But I need you with me.'

'Is this about the job?'

'Might be.'

He beckoned the closest airpod to open itself. Jumai climbed in confidently, Geoffrey right behind her. It was only as he entered the cool of the passenger compartment that he realised how much he'd been sweating. It was drying on him, cold-prickling his forehead.

'Manual,' he voked, and waited for the controls to slide out of their hidden ports, unfolding and assembling with cunning speed into his waiting grasp. A moment passed, then another. His hands were still clutching air.

'Manual,' Geoffrey repeated.

'I'm afraid that manual flight authority is not available,' the airpod said, with maddening pleasantness. 'Please give a destination or vector.'

Jumai glanced at Geoffrey. 'You're locked out?'

'Take me to Tiamaat Aqualogy,' he said.

'That destination is not recognised,' the airpod replied. 'Please restate.'

'Take me to the sea, over the Somali Basin.'

'Please be more specific.'

'Head due east.'

'I'm afraid that vector is not acceptable.'

'You're not allowed to take me *east*?'

'I am not permitted to accept any destinations or vectors that would involve flight over open water.'

Geoffrey shook his head, confounded. 'Who put this restriction on you?'

'I'm afraid I'm not permitted—'

'Never mind.' Geoffrey clenched his fists, giving up on the airpod. He cracked the canopy, letting out the bubble of cool, scented air, letting the African heat back in. 'Fucking Lucas and Hector.'

Jumai pushed herself out. 'They'll have locked them all down, won't they?'

'All the airpods,' Geoffrey said. 'Not the Cessna.'

It was parked at the end of the row of flying machines, already turned around ready for taxi. 'Engine start,' Geoffrey voked before they'd even got there. The prop began to turn, the hydrogen-electric engine almost silent save for a rising locust hum that quickly passed into ultrasound. That was good, at least: he didn't think that the cousins had the means to block his control of the Cessna, but there was little he'd put past them now.

'If you knew they couldn't stop the Cessna,' Jumai said, 'why didn't we—'

The hydrogen feed line was unplugged, lying on the ground next to the plane. Geoffrey had connected the line when he'd arrived, still focused enough to do that, but he had no idea when the cousins had come along to remove it.

'Watch the prop-wash.' Geoffrey opened the door and allowed Jumai to climb under the shade of the wing into the co-pilot's position. He removed the chocks and joined her in the cockpit. Skipping the flight-readiness checks, he released the brakes and revved the engine to taxi power. The Cessna began to roll, bumping over dirt and wheel ruts on its way to the take-off strip. Only now did Geoffrey check the fuel gauge. Lower than he'd have wished, but not empty. He thought there was enough to make it to Tiamaat.

'We're running away, aren't we?' Jumai said, fiddling with her seat buckle. 'That's basically the deal here, right?'

Geoffrey lined up the plane for take-off. 'I screwed up. I hit Hector.'

She said it back to him as if she might have misheard.

'You "hit" Hector.'

'Tried. Before the Mech intervened and dropped a boulder on my skull.'

'Ho boy.' She was grinning, caught somewhere between delight and horror. 'Way to go with the conflict resolution, Geoffrey.'

'I'm at war with my family. Escalation was the logical next step.'

'Yeah. You know, I think that's what they call pretaliation.' She was shaking her head. 'And now what?'

He pushed the throttle to take-off power. The Cessna surged forward, the ride bumpy at first until sheer speed smoothed out the undulations in the ground. 'We're on our way to Tiamaat.'

'Too cheap to send their own plane?'

'They can't now I've got myself into trouble with the Mechanism. They won't be rushing into a direct stand-off with the family, either.'

They were at take-off speed. He rotated and took them into the air.

'Something about you has changed,' Jumai said. 'I'm not sure it's good, but something's definitely changed. You used to be boring.'

'And now?' Geoffrey made a steep left turn, bringing them back over the white and blue 'A' of the household.

'Less so.' Jumai loosened her seat buckle. 'So – how far to the coast?'

'About five hundred kilometres.' He eyed the fuel gauge again, wondering if he was being optimistic. 'Call it two hours of flight time. And then we still have to get out to Tiamaat.' He patted the console. 'But we're good.'

'We'd be better off walking.'

'She's an old machine, but that's good – cousins can't touch old machines.'

'Maybe it isn't the cousins we should be worrying about,' Jumai said. 'Especially if you've just pissed off the Mechanism.'

Geoffrey smiled. The household wheeled below. Two figures were standing by one of the walls, looking up at him with hands visoring their eyes. He waggled the wings and aimed for the ocean.

Not that it was ever going to be that simple, of course. They had not been in the air for more than ten minutes when two airpods closed in, one on each side, pincering the Cessna with only a wing's width to spare. Geoffrey took his eyes off the horizon just long enough to confirm that it was the cousins. They were flying in the same two machines that had been parked on the ground near Memphis's body: Hector to starboard, Lucas to port.

'I think they want to talk,' Jumai said. 'Someone keeps trying to push a figment through.'

'They can fuck off. We're long past the point of reasoned discussion.' He had been rebuffing figment requests since he had taunted the cousins from the air. There was nothing he wanted to hear from them now.

'They're getting pretty close. I know airpods can't collide with each other, but ...' She left the sentence hanging.

'Don't worry,' Geoffrey said. 'If they do anything that even *looks* as if it's an attempt to force us down, suddenly I'm not going to be the main thing on the Mechanism's mind.'

'That'll be a great consolation as they're scooping me off the ground.'

'We're not going to crash. Anyway, this should be a walk in the park for you, the queen of high-risk data recovery. You laugh in the face of explosives and nerve gas.'

'Geoffrey,' a voice said, cutting through his thoughts like an icebreaker. 'I'm sorry to use this channel, but you've left me with no option.'

'Get out of my skull, Lucas.'

Jumai looked at him in dismay, not hearing the cousin.

'I would,' Lucas said, 'if I thought you'd accede to communication through a more orthodox channel.'

'What's happening?' Jumai asked.

'Lucas has found a way into my head,' Geoffrey said, having to shout to drown out the voice that was still droning on between his ears. 'Don't know how.'

He didn't. Even Memphis couldn't reach him when he didn't want to be reached, and there was no reason to suppose that the cousins had any secret voodoo that offered them a back door into Geoffrey's mind.

They'd have used it already if that was the case, when they were trying to contact him about Memphis being killed.

'It's simple enough,' Lucas was saying. 'You've fled the scene of a high-level intervention before a risk-assessment team had the chance to interview you. The Mechanism takes a fairly dim view of that. They'd shut you down again if there wasn't a risk of endangering both you and your hostage.'

'She's not my hostage,' Geoffrey said.

'Tell that to the authorities, cousin. The Mech's given me direct-access privilege because I'm kin and I might be able to talk you out of making this worse for yourself.'

'Well, you can tell them you tried. Now fuck off.'

'Geoffrey, listen to me. We understand that this has been a difficult and emotional time for you, but don't compound matters by behaving rashly.'

'Don't blame me, Lucas. You started this, by sending me to the Moon.'

'There are things best left in the past,' Lucas said. 'If you cared about this family, and its obligations, you'd understand that. There are millions of people who depend on us, who depend on stability.'

'Our stocks barely faltered, Lucas. Other than us, no one gives a shit about Eunice.'

'Which is exactly why none of this is worth what you're doing. She's history, Geoffrey. A ghost.'

'Leave it to the Mechanism. This isn't your problem any more.'

He hadn't expected Lucas to take him at his word, but after a few moments the cousins' airpods peeled away, leaving the Cessna alone in the sky. Geoffrey was surprised at how shaken that left him feeling. He twisted around in his seat to watch the two vehicles dwindling aft.

'Lucas is gone,' he said softly.

'There was nothing they could do,' Jumai said. 'You said it yourself – knocking us out of the sky was never an option.'

But eventually the Mechanism came, as he had always known it would. They were over the ocean by then, and the fuel warning had sounded three times. Two Civil Administration vehicles approached, official blue-and-whites garbed in aug-generated EAF and AU insignia, vectoring out to sea from Nairobi or maybe Mombasa, bigger and faster than the cousins' airpods, blunt-hulled, stub-winged, barnacled with duct-fans, rhino-ugly with angular chiselled hull plates and the hornlike black protuberances of weapons systems. Quite something, in this day and age, to be confronted with such an overt display of peacekeeping authority.

Geoffrey couldn't remember the last time he'd seen anything like it, on Earth at least. *All this, for little old me?* he felt like asking. *Really, you shouldn't have.*

'Maybe quitting the day job was a mistake,' Jumai said.

'They think you're my hostage,' Geoffrey said. 'At least, that's the stance they've decided to take, so I wouldn't worry if I were you – they're not going to say or do anything that might put you in danger.'

'Until they dig around in my background and decide, hey, maybe his Nigerian ex-girlfriend might be an accomplice after all.'

'They're still not going to do anything stupid. I haven't committed any crime. I just fled the scene of one I didn't succeed in committing.'

'Tell that to the judge.' She was looking through the windows, jerkily alternating between starboard and port like someone following a vigorous tennis match. 'I've seen some mean machinery in my time, Geoffrey, even driven some of it—'

'They're designed to intimidate. Which is why we won't be intimidated.'

The enforcement vehicles, insignia hovering around them like bright neon banners caught in their slipstreams, were much bigger than the Cessna. But that worked to Geoffrey's advantage, too. The pilots would look at his little white toy of an aeroplane and see something preposterously old and fragile, not realising that the ancient airframe was in fact much tougher than it looked.

'Geoffrey Akinya,' a voice said, cutting through everything just as Lucas's had done. 'This is the Civil Administration. Please return to your place of origin.'

'Sorry, no can do,' Geoffrey said.

'An intervention was necessary to prevent the completion of a violent act, Geoffrey.' He was being spoken to like a child, with great forbearance. 'Under such circumstances, a process of review must always take place. Submit yourself to probationary restraint and you have nothing to fear. I urge you now to turn around.' The voice was deep, male, unmistakably Tanzanian.

'You can't stop me, can you? There's nothing in the world you can do to make me alter my course.'

The vehicles came closer. They were as big as houses, armoured like bunkers. This kind of military-spec enforcement technology was like a coelacanth: it had no business still existing in the present. Yet, Geoffrey now realised, it had been there all along, a covert part of his world, tucked decently out of sight until he transgressed against the Mechanism.

'This is your last warning,' the voice said. 'Turn around now.'

That was when the fuel ran out. Geoffrey had never ditched an aircraft before, never even considered that he might one day face the possibility of ditching. Ditching was what happened when things went wrong, when things were miscalculated.

Yet here he was, ditching the Cessna. He came in at just above stall speed, full flaps, and flared steeply at the last moment. The wheels bit water. The aircraft slowed quickly, nose pitching into the sea, and then leaned slowly to starboard until the wingtip was submerged. The engine had stopped. The Cessna rocked in the green swell of the Indian Ocean, silent save for an occasional creak from the airframe, as if it had always been waiting for its time as a boat.

'Life jacket under your seat,' Geoffrey said. The sea air tickled his nose. 'We have to get out. She's not built for floating.'

Jumai extracted her life jacket. 'Meaning we swim for it?'

'Not much choice, I'm afraid.'

'There are sharks in these waters.'

He nodded. 'We should be all right. The Mechanism's probably already clearing any large predators from the area, or euthanising those that don't take the hint.'

'You hope.'

'Right now, being eaten is the least of our worries.'

The Administration vehicles loitered overhead. That was good, in one sense, because it meant they wouldn't have to wait long for rescue – Mechanism or not, Geoffrey didn't relish the prospect of spending hours in the ocean. Bad in another sense, though, because once Geoffrey and Jumai were floating, it wouldn't take the authorities long to work out a way of scooping them into custody.

But the Cessna was definitely sinking. Water had been lapping in from the moment they ditched, splashing through the door seals and engine openings. With their life jackets on, Geoffrey and Jumai climbed onto the sloping surface of one wing, but that would buy them minutes, no more. Jumai was sitting on the inclined wing, her feet dangling over the edge. Geoffrey stood, hands on hips, knees bent for balance, anxiously surveying the horizon. He'd been able to see land from the air, but not now they were down.

'Whatever happens,' Jumai said, 'I'm sorry about your plane.'

'Me too.'

There was a clunk from under the fuselage: softened by suspension, as if the submerged undercarriage had just touched dry land. With a lurch, the Cessna righted itself, the wing becoming horizontal once more. Geoffrey staggered, nearly losing his footing. Jumai reached out and grabbed his ankle, and nearly lost her own purchase in the process. Water sluiced away in rivulets.

With the smoothness of a rising elevator, the Cessna emerged from the sea.

'The fuck?' Jumai said.

Geoffrey offered her a shrug of incomprehension.

There was a black road under the wheels. The black road was rising, forcing itself into daylight: ocean was sluicing off the road as well, down its broad curving flanks. Geoffrey turned slowly around, half-knowing what he'd see. In the opposite direction, the road ran into a sheer-sided black tower, its rounded, tapering form rising to a hammerhead lookout deck.

'We're on a submarine,' Geoffrey said. He had to say it twice just to convince himself. 'We're on a submarine.'

Jumai dropped from the wing onto the slick rubber-treaded deck. 'And is this good, or bad?'

'I think it's good. For now.'

The submersible was from Tiamaat; he knew this even before a door opened in the base of the tower and an exo'd merperson came striding out. He squinted against a sudden salty lash of sea-spray.

It was Mira Gilbert. Behind her were three other exo-clad merpeople.

'Hello, lubbers!' she said, beckoning. 'Come inside. We'll secure the plane, then get under way.'

Geoffrey climbed off the wing, touched a hand to the side of the engine cowling, reassuring it that he would be back. In truth, he had little idea what was going to happen next. His ordered plans, such as they had been, were in tatters. He had done a shameful thing, then fled the scene of the crime. He had refused to submit to Mech authority, and now he was surrendering himself to people he barely knew, let alone trusted.

It wasn't too late. The Administration vehicles were still loitering. He could still take his chances with the ocean, let them swoop him into their custody. For a moment, caught between branching possibilities, two versions of his life peeling away from each other like aircraft contrails, he was paralysed.

'We're waiting, Mister Akinya,' Mira Gilbert said.

'You don't need to be a part of this,' he told Jumai. 'You could still—'

'Fuck that,' she said, shooting a dismissive glance at the hovering machines. 'Sooner take my chances with the aquatics, if that's all right with you. If you're smart, you'll do the same.'

She was right, of course. He'd committed to this path from the moment he tried flying the airpod. No point in second-guessing himself now.

So they went inside, and the Administration vehicles were still loitering when the submarine filled its tanks and slipped under the waves. The craft turned out to be the *Alexander Nevsky*, one of Tiamaat's small fleet of subsurface freighters. The *Nevsky*'s function was to carry or haul cargoes that were too heavy, bulky or hazardous for the elegant, hyper-efficient wind-driven cyberclippers that now moved nine-tenths of the world's global freight.

The *Nevsky* was a good hundred and fifty years old, rehabilitated from some dark former career as a nuclear-deterrent vessel. Now the only atomic technology aboard was its engine. Missile bays had been gutted of their terrible secrets and turned into storage holds. Behind it came a ponderous string of cargo drogues, hulled with sharkskin polymer to minimise drag, each as large as the submarine itself.

The *Nevsky* demanded little in the way of a crew, judging by the exceedingly sparse onboard provisions for cabin space. In fact, it probably ran most of its duties entirely unmanned, save for any passengers who might be along for the ride.

'How did you get here so quickly?' Geoffrey asked Mira Gilbert when they were under way again, and after he had asked for the twentieth reassurance that the Cessna was being taken care of.

'The *Nevsky* was already operating in the area,' the merwoman said. 'Routine cargo run. I podded aboard when it looked likely we'd be able to make a rendezvous.'

Geoffrey and Jumai had been given dry clothes, towels and brimful mugs of salty sea-green chai. They were underwater now, travelling at maximum subsurface cruise speed, but there was no way to tell that from inside the *Nevsky*. No aug reach, no means of opening a window through the iron dermis of its hull.

'I don't know how much Truro told you,' Geoffrey said, 'but I'm in a lot of trouble with the Mechanism. I don't think they're going to let me get away with it this easily.'

'We can hold them off for the time being,' Gilbert said. 'Technically, you trespassed on Initiative property, you see.'

'By ditching my plane?'

Gilbert nodded enthusiastically. 'Over our submarine.'

'I didn't know it was there,' Geoffrey said in benign exasperation. 'How can that *possibly* count as trespass?'

'It's all for the best. You're in our immediate jurisdiction now, which means we can activate various quasi-legal stalling measures.'

Geoffrey shivered. It was cold inside the *Nevsky*, even with the warm clothes they'd been given. 'Won't that get you into a stand-off with the Mechanism?'

'You came to us, not the other way around,' Gilbert said. 'That changes the landscape. There are now ... procedures which can be brought into play.'

'Such as?' Jumai asked.

'If Geoffrey applies for Tiamaat citizenship, the Mech has to wait until we've completed our own battery of psych assessments ... which, within reason, could take just about as long as we like.'

'And then what – you hand me back anyway?'

'We'll cross that bridge later. For now, let's get started on the citizenship application.' She smiled at his hesitation. 'It's just a formality. You're not signing over your immortal soul to Neptune and his watery minions.'

'What do I have to do?'

She voked text into the air. 'Just read these words, and we're good to go.'

CHAPTER TWENTY-TWO

During the night they had crossed and recrossed the complex fault-and-rift system of the Valles Marineris many times. As they swooped over impossibly high and narrow bridges – barely wide enough for the train's single gleaming monorail, which gave the disconcerting illusion that they were flying over these immense gaps – Sunday had looked out for evidence of the buildings she had seen from Holroyd's room, set into the canyon's walls. A window, a nurse, a green-thorned man in a surgical bath. But she'd seen no sign of human habitation at all, not a single light or pipeline or road in all the empty hours. Valles Marineris was wide enough to span Africa from the Pacific Ocean to the Indian: you could lose entire countries in that kind of area, let alone buildings and windows.

She reminded herself of that over and over, but her brain simply wasn't wired to grasp scenery on Martian scales.

She hadn't been able to sleep, not after the news from Earth. Geoffrey had called back and the update was no better than she'd been expecting, which was that Memphis had been dead for so long that there was no hope of recovery. She had no reason to doubt the truth of that. The one thing the family wouldn't skimp on was medical expertise, and the doctors in Mombasa were as good as anywhere.

So Memphis was gone: an entire thread ripped out of her life without warning, a golden strand unravelling right back to her childhood. She couldn't deal with that, not right now. She did not need consolation because she did not yet feel anything that she recognised as grief. Instead there was a peculiar vacuum-like absence of other emotions. It was as if her mind had begun to make mental houseroom, clearing itself of furniture it no longer needed. Something else was going to be moving in, for months or years. Sunday wondered how grief would feel, when it arrived.

Jitendra returned to the compartment looking brighter and better rested than she felt he had any right to. He'd gone to get himself some breakfast, Sunday apologising for not having an appetite, and hoping he didn't mind eating on his own. He was finishing off a paper-wrapped croissant.

'We're nearly in Vishniac,' he said, rubbing a hand over a freshly shaven chin to dislodge crumbs. He looked different, and it took her a moment to identify the change. Normally he kept his scalp shaved so that the transcranial stimulator could work effectively, but now his hair was beginning to grow back. 'I'm guessing our ride will be waiting for us,' he went on, between mouthfuls. 'Sure you want to go through with this? It's not too late to call it all off.'

'It'll take my mind off things,' she said.

'This happening, maybe it'll knock some sense into those cousins of yours.' He offered her the remaining half of the croissant. She shook her head. 'You sure? Got to eat.'

'I'm fine,' she said.

But she didn't feel fine. She felt sick and light-headed, not quite in her own body, as if she was elsewhere and a ching bind was collapsing. It was not simply the news of Memphis's death, though that was a significant part of it. She had been feeling disorientated ever since Soya had contacted her in Crommelin.

Soya of the mirrored visor and the face that echoed her own.

That's all it had been – an echo. Later Sunday had played back the retinal capture, and while Soya's face was very similar to Sunday's, it was not an exact likeness – although in the moment, with the distortion of the intervening layers of glass, she could forgive herself for thinking otherwise. But a family resemblance? Unquestionably.

Which threw up more questions than it answered.

She did not think she recognised the name, but in fact that had been her own memory at fault. Eunice's mother, of all people, had been named Soya. But that particular Soya had been dead more than a hundred years, and at least as crucially she had never left Earth. Born in the second half of the twentieth century, she had, by the standards of her age, lived a long and blessedly happy life. But she had not lived long enough to see more than the first flowering of her daughter's accomplishments. In any case, the images of Soya Akinya did not match the face Sunday had seen, even those few grainy still frames that existed of Soya as a young woman. The Akinya genes were present in both women, but they had expressed themselves quite differently.

How easy it would have been to run an aug trace, if she hadn't been stuck in that tourist suit. But that had evidently been the point: not just

298

to shield their conversation, but to disclose as little as possible about Soya's true identity.

All of that was suitably destabilising, but what had unsettled Sunday just as much as seeing her own face was the warning Soya had given. Not that Sunday had ever assumed the Pans could be trusted unquestioningly – she would be naive not to think otherwise – but given the fact that she had no alternative *but* to trust them, what precisely was she meant to do with that information?

And how did Soya know about the Pans, and Sunday, and Eunice's trail of breadcrumbs anyway?

It was not good to feel like a cog in a machine, even a willing and submissive cog. Who could she turn to now? Sunday wondered. Jitendra for love and affection, all she could wish for in a partner. But Jitendra couldn't help her make the decisions now being forced upon her. Her brother? In a heartbeat. But Geoffrey was on another planet and all her communications to him went through the Pans ...

That left Eunice, an art project she herself had assembled and breathed life into. A patchwork thing, a collage, a wind-up doll. Eunice might serve as a handy, easily queryable repository of all-world-knowledge relating to her late namesake, and she might have a few data-sniffing tricks up her sleeve, but the idea that Sunday might turn to the construct for counsel, for wisdom, for *succour* in a time of crisis ...

That was ridiculous.

I'm Sunday Akinya, she thought. *I'm thirty-five years old. I'm fit and well. I am not the ugliest woman ever born. Barring accidents I'll probably see out another hundred and twenty years, at the very minimum. I'm a talented if obscure artist, I live on the Moon and I'm currently walking around on Mars, with my boyfriend, with an expense account some people would kill for, if killing were still possible.*

So why am I not having fun?

The Vishniac railway station was much smaller than the one in Crommelin, and smaller than those at many of the intermediate stops they had made on the way. It was pressurised – the train had passed through an airtight collar as it dived underground – but the air was cool and it felt thinner in her lungs, somehow. That was undoubtedly an illusion, owing as much to her mental state as her knowledge that they had gained considerable altitude. A few dozen passengers had alighted, and it did not take long to verify that the golem was not among them. Sunday waited, apprehensively, until the train slid out of the station, picking up speed so quickly that she felt the air being sucked in its wake. Then it was gone, and there was still no golem.

There were no customs or immigration formalities for travel between Martian administrative sectors, so they were quickly through the station and into the shabby glitz of the Vishniac public concourse. It had the look of a place that had been fresh and modern about thirty years ago, but had since been allowed to fade. Sunday located the café where they had been told to meet Gribelin; it was tucked between a florist and a closed-for-business nail salon.

Their guide was already there, sitting by himself at an outlying table with one leg hooked over the other, sipping from a white coffee cup not much larger than a thimble. His bug-eyed goggles appeared to have been surgically grafted to his face. He was bald and cadaverous.

'Mister Gribelin?' Sunday ventured.

He set the coffee down on the glass-topped table with a precise and delicate *chink* and stood up, retrieving a knee-length leather overcoat from the back of his chair. He was tall even by Lunar standards, towering over both Sunday and Jitendra.

'Can't hang around,' he said, without a word of welcome. 'Your friend caught the next train out of Crom. He's been right behind you all the way.'

'How long does that give us?' Sunday asked.

'Two hours, maybe less. Means we've already pissed away most of our head start.' He shrugged on the murky brown coat. It had wide shoulder patches and a collar that went halfway up the sides of his skull. Now that she had a good look at him, Sunday saw fine tattoos covering every visible piece of skin, from his face to his scalp and the back of his head. The tattoos were of weird little dancing stick figures, executed in primitivist lines and squiggles.

She had nothing against weirdness – hell, she lived in the Descrutinised Zone – but she'd been hoping for a driver who exuded quiet authority and confidence, not someone who looked borderline psychotic.

'So much for your cousins seeing sense,' Jitendra said gloomily.

'Maybe the golem's on autopilot. Either way, I'm not in the mood to talk to it.'

'You all right?' Gribelin asked her, casually, as if he had only marginal interest in the answer.

Her face was reflected back at her from his bug-eyes. 'Had better weeks. Can we just get going?'

'Sure thing, sweet cheeks.'

They took an elevator. In the enclosed space, Gribelin gave off a hard-to-place mustiness, like the contents of an old cupboard. A garage lay three or four levels under the concourse. It was pressurised and floodlit, but even colder than the public spaces above. Sunday coveted Gribelin's coat and boots. The floor was covered with a tan-coloured tar of compacted oily dust that stuck to her shoes. They walked past rows of bulky machines, some of them as large as houses: cargo haulers, excavators, tourist buses, all mounted on multiple sets of springy openwork wheels.

'Here's your ride,' Gribelin said, stopping at one of the trucks. 'Don't scuff the paint job.'

He cranked down a ladder and made his limber way up into the cab airlock. Halfway up he paused, looked down and reached for Sunday's luggage. She passed him her bag, then Jitendra's, and then followed him up into the vehicle, trying to kick as much of the muck off her soles as she was able. The paint, what remained of it, could fuck itself.

It was a six-wheeled truck with a crudely airbrushed dragon on the side. Up front was a rounded accommodation and command bubble, with engine and cargo space at the rear, comms blisters and deployable solar vanes on the roof, now tucked back like retracted switchblades. Clamped to the front like a trophy, under the chin of the command bubble, was an androform maintenance robot.

There was more room inside than Sunday had been expecting. Two small sleeping cabins – one for Gribelin, another for his passengers – and a mini-galley with four fold-down seats. They took seats either side of their guide in the command bubble. The truck smelled as musty as its owner, dirt and mould in the corners, cigarette burns in some of the upholstery.

Gribelin had one hand on a steering yoke, the other on a bank of power-selector levers. They hit the steep upgrade of the garage's exit spiral; the truck laboured, then found its stride. Gribelin floored it, there was a lurch of wheelspin and then the curving walls were speeding by only a hand's width from the wheel rims. They climbed and climbed, barely slowing when the ramp flattened and the truck barged through a trio of self-sealing pressure curtains.

Then they were outside. For a few minutes they rumbled along surfaced roads, between low banks of bunkerlike buildings with narrow slitted windows and faded, weatherworn plastic logos on their roofs. The roads were perforated sheets, raised up on stilts. Signs on masts advertised the businesses along the route, with enormous neon-lit arrows pointing off to airlocks and parking ramps. Power lines ran overhead, sagging low above the road and its intersections. It was sprawl, the outskirts of a one-horse town on a planet where even the biggest city was small by Earth or Lunar standards. Sunday saw a repair crew working with welding torches on part of the road, but no pedestrians at all.

The buildings thinned out and soon they passed through a gate in a concrete dust-wall, flanked by flashing beacons, beyond which the road abandoned its lofty ambitions and settled for being a two-lane dirt track. Boulders and large stones, bulldozed out of the way and left along the sides, formed a crude demarcation. Every few hundred metres they passed a transponder or beacon on a flimsy pole, and that was the extent of the road markings.

Not that it appeared to matter to Gribelin, who was only pushing the truck harder. Sunday watched the speedometer climb up to one hundred and sixty kilometres per hour. Dust billowed out of the wheels, and wind-sculpted undulations in the road caused the truck to nose up and down like a small boat in high seas.

'How long until we reach the Evolvarium?' she asked.

Gribelin made a show of opening a hatch in the dashboard and rolling himself a cigarette before answering, stuffing it with some dark-red weed.

'Eight, nine hours,' he said eventually. 'Can't be more precise than that.'

'I wish we had more time on Lucas.'

He drew on the cigarette, examined it carefully before answering. 'That your buddy in the train, the golem?'

'He's not my friend,' Sunday said.

'Figure of speech, sweet cheeks. Kind of obvious you're not on kissing terms.' The truck reached the summit of a hill; Gribelin upshifted one of the power-selector levers. They passed the wreck of another vehicle, turned turtle in the dust. 'The golem'll need to hitch itself a ride out of town, unless it's planning on walking. Maybe you'll get lucky and there aren't any rides until morning. Who's on the other end of the proxy?'

'My cousin, back on Earth.'

He nodded slowly. 'Same place you're from, right?'

'The Moon,' Sunday said. 'There's a difference.'

'Earth, Moon, just tiny pissholes in the sky here. What is this, some kind of family feud?'

'Something like that.'

'Next time, maybe give some thought to settling your scores back home.' He scratched at the skin around the edge of his goggles. 'Had enough Earthside politics exported up here to last six fucking lifetimes.'

'Thanks for sharing. You're being paid handsomely for this little job, aren't you?'

He shrugged at Sunday's question. 'No complaints, sweet cheeks.'

'Then please shut the fuck up until I ask you a direct question. I've just lost someone very precious to me and the last thing I need is a dose of small-minded Martian nationalism.' She took a breath. 'And if you call me "sweet cheeks" one more time, I'll personally rip those goggles off and ram them down your windpipe.'

Gribelin grinned, took another draw on his cigarette and leaned over to say in Jitendra's ear: 'I'm liking her more by the minute. She always this way?'

CHAPTER TWENTY-THREE

Whatever the *Nevsky* had just docked with – there'd been a dull metallic *clunk* as it engaged with *something* – Geoffrey knew it could not be the aqualogy. They hadn't come far enough. Yet communicated in that *clunk* had been an impression of immense, dull solidity. A station, perhaps, rooted to the seabed, or a much larger ocean-going vessel.

Merpeople led them down damp black corridors of armoured metal with flume tubes stapled to the ceiling and water-filled channels sunk into the floor. Through doorways Geoffrey saw more merpeople, lubber technicians and robots toiling under bright lights, surrounded by pallets stacked with elaborately decaled cargo pods. A striding exo-clad merwoman was actually checking something off on a clipboard using a glowing-tipped stylus.

Shortly after he grasped that they'd arrived in the launching facility for one of Tiamaat's surface-to-orbit lifters, they showed him the rocket itself.

Blunt-nosed and pale green, it sat in its silo like a cartridge in a chamber. Loading belts poked through the walls, thrusting across open air to reach into the lifter's cargo bays. The lower part of the three-hundred-metre-tall rocket was already submerged. Even as Geoffrey watched, the tide rose perceptibly, lapping over the aerodynamic bulge of its engine fairings. They were flooding the chamber in readiness for launch.

'Basically just a big bottle of fizzy water,' Mira Gilbert said as they viewed the rocket from one of the silo's observation windows. 'Given a good shake, waiting for someone to pop the cork.'

The rocket's fuel was metallic hydrogen. Geoffrey knew just enough about MH to be suitably unnerved being this close to so much of the stuff. Nothing exotic or rare about MH: it was out there in bulk quantities, found naturally in the solar system, absolutely free for the taking. The snag was that it only existed at the bottom of the atmospheres of gas-giant planets like Jupiter and Saturn, where it had been formed by the brutal crush of all that overlaying gas. Under barely comprehensible pressures of many dozens of gigapascals, normal hydrogen underwent a phase transition to an ultradense electrically conductive state. The key to MH was its metastability: after the pressure was withdrawn, it didn't immediately revert to normal hydrogen. That didn't mean it was *safe*, by any definition, just that it was stable enough to be transported and utilised as an energy-dense rocket propellant with a potential specific impulse far beyond anything achievable through purely chemical reactions.

They weren't mining it yet. Akinya Space had a share in the programme established to develop MH extraction technology, literally lowering a piezoelectrically stabilised bucket into Jupiter's atmosphere on a spiderfibre cable and ladling out the stuff, and there'd been some promising feasibility demonstrations, but doing that on a cost-effective, repeatable scale made space-elevator technology look like the work of Neanderthals. It was decades, maybe even centuries down the line, and a dicey investment given that MH had no clear economic application for deep-space propulsion, only the short-haul business of escaping planetary gravity wells. So for now they manufactured it, at ludicrous expense, in mammoth orbital production platforms, tapping the kinetic energy of incoming spacecraft to drive diamond-anvil pistons that were themselves as large and complex as rocket engines.

'The tanks aren't completely full of MH,' Gilbert said. 'That would be *really* terrifying. The MH tank is tiny, just a little bubble right down at the base of the vehicle. Problem with MH is that it burns hotter than the surface of the sun, and we still can't make pumps or nozzles that can tolerate that kind of heat without melting. So we have to dilute it, to lower the burn temperature to the point where we can *just* handle the reaction, and for that we use liquid hydrogen.'

'In other words,' Jumai said, 'MH is so scary that it makes normal hydrogen, this horrible flammable substance, this stuff that explodes and kills people, seem like the safe, cuddly option.'

'It gets better,' Gilbert said, cheerfully indifferent to the dangers. 'You're going up in it, both of you. Lifters are normally cargo-only shots but they *are* fully human-rated. It's bumpy, but you don't need to worry about that: you'll be sedated for the ride.'

'All that, just to get us to the Winter Palace?' Geoffrey asked.

'The launch was scheduled anyway,' Gilbert said, deflating him slightly. 'Besides, you're not the only living, breathing passengers.' And she nodded down towards one of the conveyor belts, at the torpedo-shaped cargo pod that was being fed into the lifter's side. It was much larger than any of the other containers they had seen, and it was accompanied by six or seven technicians, mer and lubber, riding alongside like pall-bearers, giving every impression of attending to the pod with particular diligence.

'What's inside that?' Jumai asked.

'Not what,' Gilbert corrected gently. 'Who.'

CHAPTER TWENTY-FOUR

The ground refused to stop rising. Ever since leaving Vishniac they had been driving into the cold afternoon of an early spring day on Mars, ascending, always ascending. They were high up on the Tharsis plateau now, nine kilometres above the mean surface level of the rest of the planet, traversing a vast continent-sized lava bulge higher than Kilimanjaro, higher than Everest, higher than any spot on the surface of the Earth. Even now the terrain forged up towards the cone of Pavonis Mons.

Peacock Mountain. They couldn't see it yet – the summit was mist-shrouded, and the volcano wouldn't appear as much more than a gentle bump even in clear visibility.

And this wasn't even the tallest volcano on Mars.

They'd passed nothing in the way of functioning civilisation. A handful of abandoned vehicles, the descent-stage of a long-abandoned or forgotten rocket, the shrivelled, wind-ripped carcass of a transport dirigible that must have come down decades ago. Once they'd passed near a tiny hamlet, a cluster of pewter-coloured domes with fantails of dust on their leeward sides. Lights were on in the comms towers above the domes, but there was no other indication that anyone lived there. None of these dismal landmarks merited even the briefest of glances from Gribelin. Sunday supposed that he drove this way often enough that the scenery offered little in the way of interest. That had been two hours into the trip. They'd gone a long way since then.

'Here's your fence, kids,' Gribelin said eventually, slowing to guide the truck between a line of transponder masts, most of them leaning away from the prevailing wind direction. 'Don't mean a whole lot, truth to tell. Machines sense it, and they know they'll be punished if they cross over. But that doesn't mean they don't try it on for size now and then. Also doesn't mean we're going to run into machines as soon as we cross it.' He tapped a finger against a fold-down map, a physical display of the area east of Pavonis Mons. The display flickered and bled colour under his fingernail. Contour lines showed terrain elevation. Cryptic symbols, horse heads and castles and knights and pawns – like chess notation, except that there were also scorpions and snakes and skulls – were dotted in clumps and ones and twos throughout the roughly circular demarcation of the Evolvarium. There were hundreds of pawns, not so many scorpions, snakes and horse heads, only a few knights and skulls and castles. 'It's a big area, and there's a fuck of a lot of room to get lost in,' he said.

'Are those symbols telling you where the machines are?' Sunday asked.

'Telling me where the best guess for their location might be, based on the last hard sighting, which could be hours or days ago. Bit of a head-trip for you, the concept of not knowing where something is?'

'I'm from the Descrutinised Zone,' Sunday said. 'There's no aug, no Mech, in the Zone – at least, not as most people would understand those terms.'

'But that's intentional,' Jitendra said. 'In the Zone, they've chosen to go that way. I can't imagine why you wouldn't want to know where these machines are.'

'There are public eyes in orbit,' Gribelin said, 'but when the dust's up they can't see shit. Machines are sly – they'll exploit the dust whenever they can, and if there's no dust many of them are able to kick some up or tunnel underground or use camouflage. Your next question's going to be: why don't they just carpet-bomb the whole fucking landscape with eyes?'

Sunday bristled. That had indeed been her next question. 'And?'

'Machines ate 'em. You're basically throwing down foodstuff, nourishment, in a desert. Yum, yum.'

'Fix trackers to the machines, then,' Jitendra said.

'Same problem. Any kind of parasite like that, anything not directly beneficial to the host, gets picked off and eaten like a grub.' He tapped the map again. 'Lame as it is, this is the best we've got. Based on intel compiled and shared by the Overfloaters, when they're feeling in a compiling and sharing mood.'

'Overfloaters?' Sunday asked.

Jitendra cut in before Gribelin had a chance to reply: maybe he wanted to show that he wasn't completely ignorant of the situation here; that he had done at least some homework. 'The brokers who run the Evolvarium. Think of them like ... cockfighters, trying to create the ideal fighting animal. They're always dreaming up new ways to stress the population, to force the machines to keep evolving. And whenever the machines throw up something useful, some innovation or wrinkle on an existing idea, the brokers race each other to skim it off and make some money on the technologies exchange. That's why this place is on June Wing's radar.'

'June Wing?' Gribelin asked.

Jitendra smiled quickly. 'A . . . friend of mine. With an interest in fringe robotics. How much do you know about us?'

'Just that there's a job, that the fish-faces are behind it, and beyond that I'm not to ask questions.'

'You knew about the golem,' Sunday said.

'The Pans said not to hang around once you were off the train. I was also told to watch out for a claybot, in case your follower got the march on you. As to why the golem's on your tail, sweet cheeks, I didn't ask and they didn't tell.' He grinned a mouthful of weirdly carved and metal-capped teeth at her. 'Shit, I called you it again, didn't I?'

'We're not tourists,' Sunday said levelly, deciding to let her earlier threat slide. 'The Pans will have told you to take me as near as possible to a set of coordinates in the Evolvarium. There's a reason for that.'

'Which is?'

Sunday and Jitendra exchanged glances before she spoke. 'There's something buried in the area, something that belongs to me.'

'Belongs?'

'Family property,' she said. 'But not property that I'd want the golem to get hold of ahead of me.'

'And you know it's buried?' Gribelin asked.

'If it isn't, what are the odds of it still being here?'

'Pretty fucking slim.'

'I still have to be sure,' Sunday said.

Gribelin's skull bobbed up and down as he shrugged. 'Your call.'

After a moment she asked, 'What are those things on your skull?'

'Ears.'

'I mean the tattoos. Do they signify something? They look like rock art or something.'

'Rock art.' He grinned again. 'Yeah, that'd be about right.'

They passed their first carcass an hour into the Evolvarium.

Dust-scouring wind and the graft of enthusiastic scavengers, both human and mechanical, had stripped the war machine back to a rust-coloured skeleton, a hundred metres from tip to tail. Formed from dozens of articulated modular segments, the ruined robot resembled the vulture-picked spine of some much larger creature. The dust was thin on the Tharsis Bulge, a layer only a centimetre deep covering laval rock, so the war machine's metal bones were exposed almost entirely to the sky. Gribelin slowed to skirt around the corpse, eyeing it warily.

'Been here longer than most,' he said in a low murmur. 'Deadsville, completely harmless and pecked clean of pretty much anything usable. But sometimes active units use it as a place of concealment. Ambush predators. I think we're good today, but—'

'Would they attack us?' Sunday asked.

'Mostly, the machines are smart enough to leave us alone.' He shot her a glance, Sunday's face bulbous in his goggles. 'Basic self-preservation: fight each other, use whatever they can, evolve, but don't piss off the Overfloaters.'

'You said "mostly",' Jitendra said.

'Darwinism in action, my friend. Every now and then something comes along and tears up the rule book.'

'You're risking a lot, bringing us here,' Jitendra said.

'I know the terrain.' He eyed the map again. 'And I know who to keep away from. You think I'd be here if I didn't believe the odds were in my favour? Your friends are paying well, but nothing's worth suicide.'

At four in the afternoon, a quill of orange-red dust feathered up from the horizon. It scribed its way across the landscape, propelled by an invisible hand. Sunday's first thought was that they were watching a dust-devil, but Gribelin's map showed a pawn symbol close to their present location.

'Sifter,' he said. 'Your basic low-down grazing caste. Chew through the dust and the top layer of rock, looking for anything recyclable. What they can use to repair or fuel themselves, they use. What's left over, they barter between themselves or trade on up the food chain.'

'What's that?' Sunday asked, pointing dead ahead, up the gently rising lie of the land. A grey-black smudge floated in the sky, like a dead fly on the windshield, just above the horizon. It dangled entrails, as if it had been swatted. She had tried zooming, but the aug was all but absent.

Gribelin tugged down a pair of binoculars fixed to the ceiling on a scissoring mount and settled his goggled eyes into the rubber-shielded cups. '*Lady Disdain*,' he said quietly. 'Not usually this far east. Might be following the sifter, looking for anything thrown up behind it.'

'Can we avoid her?' Jitendra said.

'Only if Dorcas is feeling nice.' Gribelin steered left, the Overfloater craft veering slowly to the right in the window. He slid the binoculars towards Sunday. 'Be my guest.'

The rubber eye-cups were greasy with sweat and tiny skin flakes. It took a moment for the binoculars to sense her intended point of interest. The view leapt, stabilised, snapped to sharpness, overlaid with cross hairs and distance/alt-azimuth numerics.

The Overfloater machine was a fat-bellied airship, approximately arrowhead-shaped. Slung under it, blended into the deltoid profile of its gas envelope, was an angular gondola. The 'entrails' were sinuous, whiplike mechanical tentacles, a dozen of them, emerging from the base of the gondola. The airship skimmed the surface at a sufficiently low altitude that the arms were able to pluck things from the ground. That was what *Lady Disdain* was doing right now: loitering, examining.

It brought to Sunday's mind one of Geoffrey's elephants, nosing the dirt with its trunk. Or a family of them, bunched into a single foraging organism.

'Is Dorcas a friend of yours?' Sunday asked.

'Friend,' Gribelin said, chewing over the word as if it was a new one on him. 'That's a tricky concept out here. Pretty much dog eat dog all the way down. Machines fuck each other over, Overfloaters fuck the machines over, Overfloaters fuck each other for a profit margin. I fight for the scraps. Me and Dorcas? We go back some. Don't exactly hate each other. Doesn't mean we're kissing cousins either.'

'Wouldn't you rather be at the top of the rat heap?' Sunday asked. She had some idea of how it worked: how the machines, in their endless evolutionary struggle, occasionally splintered off some novelty or gadget or industrial process that the rest of the system could use. Like the technology behind the prototype claybot, the one she'd chinged to the scattering. That rapidly morphing material had been a spin-off from the Evolvarium, and now it stood to make trillions for Plexus. 'Floating up there like a god, being worshipped. Because that's what's going on here, isn't it? Gods hovering over mortals, taking amusement in their endless warfare and misery.'

'Wouldn't go that far,' Jitendra said. 'These machines might be super-adaptive, but there's no actual cognition going on down here. The machines don't understand that they're machines. All they know how to do is survive, and try not to fall behind in the arms race. They're no more capable of religion than lobsters.'

'Nice if it was that clear-cut,' Gribelin said. 'Me, I ain't so sure. Spend as much time out here as I have, you'll see some things that make you question your certainties.'

'Really?' Jitendra asked sceptically.

'You think these machines don't grasp what they are, that they don't get the difference between existence and non-existence?' He

311

paused to take a sip from his liquor bottle, flicking the cap off with his thumb while steering one-handed. 'Once, out by the western flanks, I saw a sifter begging for its life, begging not to be destroyed by a rogue collector.'

'An evolved response, like a whimpering dog,' Jitendra said dismissively. 'Doesn't prove there's anything going on inside its head.'

'You'd seen what I saw, you'd feel differently.'

'Show me the imagery, I'll make up my own mind.'

'Not enough public eyes to catch it,' Gribelin answered. 'My own eyes were surrendered to the Overfloaters. They wiped the evidence.'

'I can see why they might want to,' Sunday said.

Lady Disdain was powering downslope, three or four tentacles dragging the ground. Sunday had a better impression of the manta-like vehicle now. It was enormous – as it had to be, given the tenuousness of the Martian atmosphere. Ducted engines as large as ocean turbines were bracketed to the drab green gondola.

She felt that it ought to make a sound, a terrible droning approach, but there was nothing.

'Can you outrun it?' Jitendra asked.

Gribelin gave a brief shake of his head. 'Not a hope in hell, and even if we did, we'd only run into more Overfloaters further into the Evolvarium. But don't worry – I'm sure I'll find a way to sweet talk Dorcas.'

'Using your natural charm and diplomacy,' Sunday said.

'You'd be surprised how far it gets me.'

The airship circled the moving truck then headed slightly south, dropping its triangular shadow over them like a cloak. Gribelin was still driving, but he was making no effort to push the truck to its limits. Sunday looked up, watching as the underside of the airship, hundreds of metres across and speckled with patch repairs, began to eclipse the sky. The gondola was as large as the Crommelin cable car, aglow with tiny yellow windows.

Figures stole around up there, backlit and mysterious.

Something clanged against them. Sunday jumped. Jitendra grabbed for the nearest handhold. Gribelin swore, but appeared otherwise resigned. The truck pitched as if it had just run into a sand-trap. The ground pulled away, dust cataracting from the wheels. *Lady Disdain* was lifting them into the sky, hauling them up with one or more of her tentacles.

Fifty metres, then maybe a hundred. The horizon began to rotate, the deltoid canopy gyring slowly overhead. The tentacles held them level with the front of the gondola so that they were looking back at the deep, slanted windows of what was evidently the airship's bridge. The bridge was wide, and there were at least six visible crew, none of whom were obviously proxies.

One figure drew Sunday's attention. A woman garbed in a long black coat that went all the way to her boots strode from one side of the bridge to the other, pointing and jabbing at her underlings. She came to rest at a console or podium, then angled some cumbersome speaking device to her lips.

A head and shoulders appeared in the truck, hovering above the dashboard and rendered with slight translucence.

'Can't you see we're in the middle of something here, Gribelin?' She was ghost-pale, slender-faced, with a sharp chin and long ash-grey hair brushed in a side-parting so that a curtain of it covered half her features. Her nose was pierced and many rings hung from the lobe of her one visible ear.

'We're kind of in the middle of something, too, Dorcas,' Gribelin said. 'As you've probably worked out. You mind letting us go, while there's still some daylight?'

'You cross the 'varium on our terms, when we feel like letting you. Why do I have to keep reminding you of that?'

'Look, it would be nice to chat, but . . .'

The woman combed fingers through her hair, allowing it to fall back into place. 'You're not usually in this much of a hurry. Anything to do with the vehicle following you from Vishniac?'

Sunday glanced at her driver. 'Ask her how far behind it is.'

'No need, I heard you anyway,' Dorcas said. 'You weren't aware of it until now?'

'You know how tenuous things get out here,' Gribelin said.

'Especially after someone went to a lot of trouble to tie up all the proxies and swamp the public eyes with dumb queries. You usually operate alone, Grib. Why do I have the feeling someone's pulling strings behind your back this time?'

'Tell me about the vehicle,' Sunday said. 'Please.'

Something in Dorcas appeared to relent, albeit only for the moment. 'A rented surface rover, a little smaller than your truck. About two and a half hours behind you, maybe a little less.'

'Lucas,' Sunday said, as if there could be any doubt. 'Quick off the mark, too. He must have arranged the vehicle rental before the train got in.'

'Not a friend of yours?' Dorcas asked.

'I'm on an errand for a couple of clients,' Gribelin explained. 'A golem's been following them since they left Crommelin.'

'This errand . . . it wouldn't be anything that will get in the way of my business, would it?'

'You know what the Evolvarium is to me, Dorcas – just a place I like to get in and out of as quickly as possible.'

'And your clients?'

Sunday leaned forward. 'We'll be in and out of here as swiftly as we can, and nothing we do will have any impact on your line of work.'

'And I'm supposed to just take that on trust?'

Sunday closed her eyes while she organised her thoughts. 'I'm going to tell you the truth. Whether you believe me or not is entirely up to you. My name is Sunday Akinya.'

'As in—'

'Sixty-odd years ago, my grandmother buried something here, smack in the middle of the Evolvarium. Of course, it wasn't the Evolvarium then. It was just an area of Mars that meant something to her. Now I'm here to find out what she considered important enough to bury, and that means I have to locate the burial spot and dig.'

'I've already told her she's crazycakes if she thinks there'll be anything to dig up,' Gribelin said, 'but she's fixed on seeing this through.'

'You have coordinates?'

Sunday nodded. 'There's some uncertainty, but I think I can get close. My grandmother spent time at an abandoned Russian weather station near here, before she came back to bury whatever it was. The station's location is known, and there haven't been any geological changes since she last visited.'

'We're about two hundred kays out,' Gribelin said. 'We can be there in two hours, maybe three if we have to run around any big players.'

'By which time it'll be dark,' Dorcas said. 'Not much you'll be able to do then.'

'At least we'll be there first.'

Dorcas considered this at length before responding, taking whispered asides from her crew while she contemplated her answer. 'We've always had a good working arrangement, haven't we, Grib?'

'It's had its ups and downs,' Gribelin said.

'Neither of us is a philanthropist. But over the years we've mostly managed not to tread on each other's tails.'

'Fair assessment.'

'Even, some might say, helped each other when the situation demands it.'

'Which it does now.'

'Indeed. In that spirit, I'm going to make you an offer. I'll get you closer to the landing site in much less than three hours. We'll use the full resources of *Lady Disdain* to search for your object, and I'll hand it to you intact when – if – we locate it. In return, you'll give me twenty-five per cent of whatever you're being paid. Whether or not we find anything.'

'I'm not made of money,' Gribelin said.

'But someone else is. One way or the other, I'll find out who's involved and what they're paying you.'

'I wouldn't dream of fobbing you off, Dorcas.' For a moment, Gribelin looked paralysed with indecision, before deciding that honesty was the only viable option. 'It's the Pans,' he said, letting out a small audible sigh. 'You'd have figured that out sooner or later, based on the comms trickery.'

Dorcas sneered. 'Why are you letting the Pans yank your chain?'

'They pay well. Amazingly well. And my clients—'

'We're not Pans,' Sunday said emphatically. 'We've just got mixed up with them. What I want, and what they want ... they coincide, up to a point. That's why they've paid for me to be here, and why they're helping slow down the golem. But we're not Pans.'

'Yes.' Dorcas allowed herself the thinnest of smiles. 'Think I got that the first time.'

It was teatime on the *Lady Disdain*. They knelt around a table while one of Dorcas's underlings attended to their white porcelain Marsware cups. Tactical status maps, vastly more complicated than Gribelin's simple readout, jostled for attention on the table's slablike surface. These real-time summaries of the Evolvarium were accompanied by a constant low murmur of field analysis from the crew. Around the walls, systemwide stock exchange summaries tracked technologies commodities from Mercury to the Kuiper belt. Histograms danced to hidden music. Market analysis curves rose and fell in regular sinus rhythms like the Fourier components of some awesome alien heartbeat. Newsfeeds dribbled updates. Outside, the sun was beetling towards the horizon as if it had work to be getting on with.

The chai was watery but sweet – infused with jasmine, Sunday decided. She and Jitendra were kneeling on one side of the table, Gribelin and Dorcas on the other. Kneeling was very nearly as comfortable in Martian gravity as it was on the Moon, which was to say a lot easier on the knees than on Earth.

The conversation was flowing in at least two directions, maybe three. Jitendra relished the chance to learn as much as he could about the history and organisation of the Evolvarium, and his questions were divided equally between Dorcas and Gribelin. Dorcas, for her part, appeared willing to humour him ... but she had her own interrogative agenda, too, with her probing directed mostly at Sunday. She wanted to know more about this buried secret, and why it might be of interest to more than one party.

'I can't tell you what she buried there,' Sunday said. 'If I knew, I wouldn't have had to come all this way. I can't even be sure this is where she meant me to go.'

'And the Pans?' Dorcas asked. 'What's their angle?'

Remembering Soya's warning, Sunday wondered how much she was at liberty to discuss. 'They have an interest in my grandmother,' she said, circumspectly. 'She knew Lin Wei, who's as close to being the Pans' founder as anyone.'

'And that's all it is – mere historical interest?'

'I suppose they can't help being curious now,' Sunday said.

One of Dorcas's staff approached, leaned down and whispered something in her ear. She nodded, danced her fingers above the table. The positions of some of the Evolvarium players shifted around. 'Revised intel,' she explained. 'Increased sifter activity in sector eight, and two new hunter-killer subspecies out in three. Meanwhile, the Aggregate's been unusually active these last few days.'

'The Aggregate?' Jitendra asked, beaming like a kid who was getting all his presents at once. 'Have you encountered it?'

'Grib's had his share of run-ins with it, haven't you?' Dorcas said.

'I keep out of its way, best as I'm able.'

Dorcas gave a knowing nod. 'Sensible man.'

'What is it?' Sunday asked.

'What happens when a bunch of machines get together and decide to act in unison, rather than fighting for scraps,' Jitendra said. 'A kind of emergent proto-civilisation. A quasi-autonomous motile city-state made up of hundreds of cooperating machine elements.'

'A nuisance to some,' Dorcas said. 'An incipient Martian god to others. Isn't that right, Grib? Or is that something you don't like to talk about these days?'

'All in the past, as you well know.'

Dorcas smiled once. 'Did he tell you about the tattoos? I'm guessing not.'

'If I was bothered about the tattoos, I'd have had them removed.'

316

'Which would cost money, which you'd sooner spend on whores, narcotics or truck parts.' Dorcas gave a little throat-clearing cough, now that she had their attention. 'Thirty, forty years back, Gribelin ran into a little group of mental cases just outside the Evolvarium. Something about the scenery, the emptiness, the mind-wrenching desolation reaches in and presses the "god" button some of us still have inside us. What were these people called, Grib?'

'Aggregationists,' he said tersely. 'Can we move on now?'

'They're all gone now. Word is their leader, the crackpot behind the whole thing, woke up one morning and realised he was surrounded by lunatics. Not only that, but fawning lunatics he'd helped along with their craziness. The Apostate, they call him. He cleared out and left them to get on with it. You met him, didn't you, Grib?'

'Our paths crossed.'

Dorcas poured some more chai for her guests. 'Whatever became of the Apostate, the Aggregate's doing pretty well for itself. It's entirely self-sufficient, as far as we can tell, so it doesn't have to deal with sifters. It's also strong enough to be able to deter most mid-level threats, and agile enough to keep out of the way of anything large enough to intimidate it. If the original construct was a nation state, this is a walled city.'

'I guess the next question is . . . is there any way to make money from it?' Jitendra asked.

'If there is, no one's thought of it yet,' Dorcas said, not appearing to mind the directness of his question. 'The Aggregate doesn't shed bits of itself, and until it dies, we can't very well pick it apart and look inside. But someone will get there eventually. Our . . . rivals won't stop trying, and nor will we. So far, it's rebuffed our efforts at negotiated trade. But everything has a price, doesn't it?'

'Be careful you don't end up evolving anything too clever,' Sunday said. 'We all know where that leads.'

Dorcas smiled tightly. 'We have sufficient demolition charges on just this one ship to turn the entire Evolvarium into a radioactive pit, if we so wished. No one takes this lightly.' She directed a sharp look at Sunday. 'Of course, you'd rather we didn't do that any time soon, wouldn't you? Not while this secret of yours is still to be unearthed.'

'I don't even know if there is a secret,' Sunday said.

'You've come this far, you can't have too many doubts. Nor the Pans, given their level of interest. What do you imagine she might have left behind?'

'For all I know, it's just another cryptic clue leading to somewhere else.'

Dorcas raised a finely plucked eyebrow. 'On Mars?'

'Anywhere.'

'And if at the end of this there's nothing, no bucket of gold, what then?'

'We all go home and get back to our lives,' Sunday said.

Another aide came to whisper something to Dorcas. She listened, nodded once.

'The other vehicle has crossed the perimeter,' she said. 'Its point of entry was very close to your own, and it's following roughly the same course you were on before we picked you up. You say there's a golem in that thing?'

Sunday nodded. 'It's pretty likely.'

'Then it must be acting near-autonomously by now. Does it know exactly where the burial might have taken place?'

'The people behind the golem,' Sunday said circumspectly, not wanting to give away more information about her family than she needed to, 'they're smart enough to have joined the same dots I did.'

'Not much we can do about that,' Dorcas said. She put down her teacup and rose from a kneeling position, smoothing the wrinkles out of her long black coat as she did so. 'No matter: we have a good two hours on the rover, and we're very nearly at the location.'

'You don't expect to find anything, do you?' Sunday said.

'The machines are thorough, but if something was buried sufficiently far down ... well, there's a possibility it's still there, albeit a remote one.'

'Except Eunice wouldn't have seen any reason to bury something so deeply,' Jitendra said.

'Let's err on the side of optimism,' Dorcas said.

CHAPTER TWENTY-FIVE

Of the Russian weather station, of the evidence of Eunice's return decades later, nothing now remained. All traces had been erased by wind and time; all artefacts and trash long since absorbed and recycled by the Evolvarium's machines. But the location was known to within a handful of metres, and as *Lady Disdain* adjusted her engines to maintain a hovering posture, there could be no doubt that they were sitting over exactly the right patch of ground.

'If there was anything large and magnetic sitting right below the dust, we'd already know about it,' Dorcas said. 'I'm afraid that's not looking good right now. Same for gravitational anomalies. If there's something buried right under us, within a couple of metres of the surface, it must have the same density as the rock, to within the limits of our mass sensors.' She was standing at a pulpit-like console, arms spread either side of an angled display. 'There are a few more things to try, though, before we think about looking deeper.'

'Ground-penetrating radar?' Gribelin asked.

'Already down to a depth of three metres, over a surface area of fifty-by-fifty. We can expand the search grid, of course – but that'll take time.'

Gribelin had his arms folded across his chest. 'What about seismic?'

'On the case – again, the data will take a little while to build up.'

From the gondola's downward-looking windows, Sunday watched as the tentacles picked up loose-lying boulders, lofted them high into the air and then flung them back down at the ground. Other tentacles, spread out as far from the airship as was possible, brushed their tips against the surface to catch the vibrations transmitted through the underlying geography. The arrival times of the impulses would enable Dorcas to build up a seismographic profile of the local terrain, pene-trating much deeper than was possible with radar. It was slow and haphazard, though – the airship obviously didn't come equipped with specialised seismic probes or the routines to crunch the data swiftly – and Sunday wondered what effect all that crashing and banging was having on the Evolvarium's native inhabitants. If they wanted to approach this search in a discreet manner, without drawing attention to their activities, this struck her as exactly the wrong way to go about it.

'Eunice, Eunice, Eunice,' she said under her breath. 'Why couldn't you make this simple for us?'

Now that the construct was denied her, she missed having it around. Eunice might be an illusion, a parlour trick that only looked and spoke like a thinking human being. But her eyes were not Sunday's eyes. And she had seen things Sunday never would.

'This wasn't exactly how I was hoping things would pan out,' Gribelin said, his musty aroma announcing his arrival by her side a moment before he spoke, 'but I think we can trust Dorcas.'

Sunday was effectively alone now, the other Overfloaters busy with their instruments and technical systems, while Jitendra dug into first-hand summaries of the Evolvarium's history. 'You think or you know?' she asked.

'Nothing watertight where Dorcas is involved, kid.' His voice was a low confiding rasp. 'We'll just have to take things as they come and ... be flexible. She can be slippery, that's a fact. But then so can we.' He shifted something around in his throat, some loose phlegmy package that obviously felt at home. 'My manner back there ... when I first picked you up ...' He trailed off, as if he needed some invitation to continue.

'Go on,' Sunday obliged.

'This line of work, you get to meet all sorts. Rich kids, especially. Thrill-seekers. I knew there was money behind you, but ... you're not really here for the thrills, are you?'

'I had a good life on the Moon. I didn't want any of this. It came after me, not the other way round.' Sunday fell silent for a moment. 'You wouldn't be apologising, would you, Gribelin?'

'For giving you a hard time?' He shrugged, as if that was all that needed to be said on the subject. 'From here on, though ... whatever happens, when I take a job on, I don't let my clients down.'

'And if our host has other ideas?'

'We'll play things by ear. And if things get ... intense, you and the beanpole do exactly what I tell you, all right? No second-guessing old Gribelin. Because if the shit comes down, there won't be time for a nice chinwag about our options.'

'We'll listen,' Sunday said. 'Not as if we're spoilt for choice with guides out here.' Softly she added, 'Thank you, Gribelin.'

He made to turn away – she thought he was done with her – but

320

something compelled him to halt. After a silence he said, 'You asked about the marks on my skull, back when we were driving. Dorcas mentioned my run-in with the Apostate. I figured you'd be even more curious after that.'

'The way I see it, it's none of my business.'

'Way I see it, too. But not everyone would agree.' Gribelin looked down before continuing, 'I went a little mad out there. They put ideas in my head. Little dancing men, figures scratched in rock. The Apostate had gone mad himself, once, but I think he got better. It took me longer, and maybe some of it's still lodged inside me. But that's between me and the god I don't believe in.'

The shadows had lengthened and evening winds had begun to howl in from the northern lowlands when Dorcas lifted her gaze from a hooded viewer. 'I don't know quite what to make of this,' she said, fingering the fine-adjustment controls set into the viewer's side.

'Not sure how to break it to me that there's nothing here?' Sunday asked.

'No.' Dorcas pushed her hair back over one ear, to hook it out of her eyes. 'How to break it to you that we've found something. There's an object down there. It's metal, and it's not too far from the surface. Which, frankly, isn't possible.'

But the digging would have to wait until daybreak. It got cold at night, and cold made everything harder, but that was not the reason for their delay. At night, as the cold and darkness clamped down, the bottom-feeding castes became much less active, generally opting both to conserve energy and cool their external shells as close to the ambient surroundings as possible, so that they were harder to detect. The predators, conversely, became more active. Kills remained difficult, but the likelihood of success, once a pursuit or strike had been initiated, was now much higher. There was never a good time to be down on the surface, Dorcas explained, but night was worse than day, even for Overfloaters, and they would not risk drilling until sunrise.

'And the golem? We've gained this lead on it – what's the point of throwing it all away now?'

'Your golem is on land,' Dorcas said. 'That means it won't be going anywhere until sun-up, either. Not if it knows the first thing about the Evolvarium, and wants to make it through to dawn in one piece. So get some sleep. Be our guests.'

But Sunday couldn't sleep much, not while that thing was down in the rock, calling to her. So that night, while the Overfloater held station and a skeleton crew manned the graveyard shift, she stood in darkness aboard the gondola and watched. Radar and infrared sensors swept the parched, dust-tormented plateau. Very occasionally, halfway to the horizon or further, something would break cover. Fleeting and swift, it would slink across the land's contours. The ambush predators were experts at concealment, from jack-in-the-box variants that dug themselves into rock holes and natural fissures, compressed like springs, to shapeshifting forms that were able to pancake their bodies into the very top layer of the dust, to lurk unseen. There were things like flatfish and things like snakes. There were also stalking, prowling horrors that quartered the night on endless deterrent patrols, searching for the weak, the maimed or the dead. She saw one of these loping jackal-like things traverse the horizon line: it had so many jointed legs that it appeared to move in spite of itself, riding a bickering tumble of independent limbs. There was also something like a convoy of scorpions, one after another, that might (horrifyingly) have been a single entity, and a flat-topped creature like a house-sized hairbrush, supported on countless bristling centipede legs, that could have been a grazer or a killer.

It was wonderful in a way, she supposed. There was astonishing variation in the Evolvarium, a staggering panoply of evolutionary strategies, bodyplans, survival mechanisms. Life on Earth had taken three and a half billion years to achieve the radiative diversity that these swift, endlessly mutable machines had produced in a matter of decades. Artificially imposed selection pressures had turned life's clock into a screaming flywheel. The arms race of survival had been harnessed for the purposes of product development, feeding an endless supply of new technologies, new materials and concepts, into the systemwide marketplace. In that sense, it was almost miraculous: something for nothing, over and over again.

But it wasn't free, was it? The Evolvarium was death and fear, terror and hunger, on endless repeat. The machines might not have enough cognitive potential to trouble the Gearheads, but that didn't make them mindless, no matter what Jitendra might care to think. She thought of the sifter Gribelin had told them about, the machine that had begged. Maybe he'd been exaggerating. Maybe he'd been imposing human values on an exchange that was fundamentally alien, beyond a gulf of conceptualisation that could never be crossed.

She wondered. She wondered and knew that she would be very, very glad when they were out of this place.

Jitendra slipped his arm around her waist. 'I'm sorry about Memphis,' he said quietly. 'I'm sorry that we aren't back home, with your brother.

322

But I wouldn't have wanted to miss this for the world.'

'Really?'

'It's marvellous,' he said.

Beyond the horizon, red and green radiance underlit the night's dust clouds. Something was dying in fire and light. Sunday shivered.

CHAPTER TWENTY-SIX

By the time he came to groggy consciousness, Geoffrey was already halfway to the Moon, and a minor diplomatic squall was busy playing itself out back on Earth. Mechanism apparatchiks were not at all happy about Geoffrey having absconded before submitting to a pysch assessment, and they were taking an increasingly sceptical stance regarding Jumai's supposed innocence in the whole affair. The Nigerian had committed no direct wrongdoing, but the message – in no uncertain terms – was that it would be in her absolute best interests if she were to submit to Mech jurisdiction at her earliest convenience. In other words, she was a whim away from being declared a fugitive herself. Tiamaat, meanwhile – and by extension the Panspermian Initiative – was using every stalling measure in its arsenal, arguing that because Geoffrey had requested aqualogy citizenship, it had no option but to discharge its own procedural obligations in this regard, and that if it did not do so, it would be in grave dereliction of its charter.

Smoke and mirrors, bluff versus bluff, two geopolitical superpowers playing an old, old game. As long as it bought Geoffrey time, he didn't really care. Worse, as far as he was concerned, was the reaction of the cousins.

Lucas and Hector had been trying to ching from the moment he was picked up by the *Nevsky*. Their requests had been systematically rebuffed – and Geoffrey had been unconscious for much of the ensuing time – but the cousins hadn't been daunted. They'd had no trouble tracking the *Nevsky* – the movements of any seagoing vessel, let alone one as large and ponderous as a former Soviet nuclear submarine, were publically visible – and they'd had no trouble making the obvious connection between the *Nevsky*'s destination and the lifter's ascent into orbit. Geoffrey had dropped off the Mechanism's radar, so they couldn't be sure that he was in space. But he wasn't anywhere *else* under Mechanism jurisdiction either, which did rather argue for him being aboard the rocket. It would not have taken limitless resources to track the rocket's rendezvous with the deep-space vehicle *Quaynor*, and to presume that Geoffrey and Jumai were now aboard that ship.

When they had eventually given up on trying to speak to him directly, Hector had recorded a statement, one that Geoffrey had finally felt obliged to listen to.

'We know what you intend to do, cousin. We know what your new friends think they will help you to achieve. But you are wrong. *This will not work*. And you are making a very, very serious mistake. You have no business in the Winter Palace, and you have no right to trespass where you are not welcome.'

'I have as much right to it as you do,' Geoffrey mouthed.

'If you have ever thought of yourself as an Akinya,' Hector went on, 'do the right thing now. Turn around. Abandon this folly. Before you damage the family name beyond repair.'

'Fuck the family name,' Geoffrey said. Then, softly: 'Fuck the family while you're at it. I'm out.'

There was a dull propellant roar from somewhere in the ship, a ghost of gravity as the ship trimmed its course, and from that moment on the *Quaynor* was aimed like an arrow for the orbiting prison where his grandmother had ended her days.

'Not much to look at,' Jumai said, six hours later, when they had their first good view of the Winter Palace. 'I don't know what I was expecting. Bit more than this, though.' She paused to tap her medical cuff, instructing it to up her anti-vertigo dosage. Geoffrey had caught her vomiting into a sick bag a few hours into the flight, curled into a foetal ball in the module that had been assigned as her temporary quarters, making dry retching sounds. He'd asked her why she hadn't managed the nausea, and she'd said that the cuff's chemicals took the edge off her concentration, and for Jumai that was less acceptable than the occasional heave.

'We need you sharp at the station,' he'd argued. 'That means not being worn out from puking your guts up before we get there.' And he took her wrist, gently, and tapped up her discretionary dosage to match his own.

'Yes, Doctor,' she'd said, half-sullenly, but the message – he was relieved to see now – had got through.

'She had it built around her old ship, the *Winter Queen*,' he said, when the grey cylinder hung before them, massively magnified. They were still fifty thousand kilometres out, so the imagery was synthesised from distributed public eyes in cislunar space rather than the *Quaynor*'s own low-res cameras. 'I never went inside it, of course – never even chinged up there. But I know what it's like. Saw images often enough, whenever she deigned to address us from her throne. It's a jungle, humid and sticky as a hothouse. Ship's a rust-bucket; it was just about capable of keeping her alive, supplying power to the station, but no more than that. That's why the cousins can make a good case for decommissioning it – the reactor's almost as old as the one in that submarine.'

The cylinder had the proportions of two or three beer cans stuck together top to bottom, bristling with docking/service equipment at either end. It was rotating slowly, spinning on its long axis, bringing most of the surface into view. Between the endcaps, the station's outer skin was smooth, uninterrupted by machinery, sensory gear or anything that might indicate scale. Eunice had wrapped her own iron microcosm around herself, and she'd never felt the slightest inclination to see what was outside.

'She never left this?' Jumai asked, the horror seeping through her voice. 'I mean, not even to step outside, in a suit? In all that time?'

'We'd have known. There was never a point when someone, somewhere, wasn't watching the Winter Palace. Ships came and went occasionally – automated supply vehicles, Memphis on one of his errands – but no one else ever came *out*. Her star may have faded, but even in her last years she was still enough of a celebrity for that to have made the news, if it had happened.'

'But to live inside that thing – after all she'd done, all she'd seen. How could she do that to herself?'

'By going a little mad,' Geoffrey said.

'She could ching, I suppose. But that wouldn't have been enough consolation for me.'

'You're not my grandmother. Whatever she needed, it was in there.'

'That's not living.'

'Never said it was,' Geoffrey replied.

After a silence Jumai went on, 'Well, we dock first. That's clear. Then we see how easy it is to break inside. Figure you expect some complications, or you wouldn't have brought me along.'

'If you don't have to lift a finger, you'll still get paid,' he reassured her.

'You still think I'm a mercenary to the core.'

'I think you like risk. Not quite the same thing.'

'In your book.' Jumai gave an unconcerned shrug, her nausea blasted away for the time being. 'So: let's see what our docking options are.' And she reached out and tumbled the image of the Winter Palace like a toy suspended over a cot until she'd brought one of the endcaps into view.

She plucked her fingers to zoom in, frowning at the details. 'See anything out of the ordinary? You're the seasoned space traveller, not me.'

'Can't say I'm any kind of expert on docking systems.'

'You don't need to be,' said a voice behind them. It was Mira Gilbert, weightless now, fully divested of her mobility harness but equally at home in zero gravity as she was under water. She wore a skintight zip-up orange and grey outfit fitted with pockets and grab-patches. 'We've assessed the situation. Perfectly standard interfaces and capture clamps: the *Quaynor* will be able to hard-dock without difficulty.'

'You came just to tell us that?' Geoffrey asked. He'd barely seen Gilbert since his revival.

'Actually, I came to tell you that there's been a development back in the East African Federation. Public eyes detected the activation of the Kilimanjaro ballistic launcher.'

'Fuck,' Geoffrey said.

'Not sure what came up: could be a test package, a cargo pod, or something else. Right now we're leaning towards "something else". Whatever it was got pushed all the way to orbit, where it was met by another vehicle.'

'What kind?' Jumai asked.

'The *Kinyeti*, an asteroid miner registered to Akinya Space,' Gilbert answered slowly, so the words had time to hit home. 'Something with at least the range and capabilities of the *Quaynor*, if not greater.'

She pulled up an image: either a long-range real-time grab or an archival picture of the same ship. As far as Geoffrey was concerned, he could have been looking at another view of the ship he was travelling in. The *Kinyeti* had the same skeletal outline, built for operations in vacuum with no requirement to withstand atmosphere or hard acceleration/deceleration. It had engines and fuel tanks at one end, docking and mining equipment at the other, and a pair of contra-rotating centrifuge arms mounted at the midsection bulge of her main crew quarters, with habitat modules on the end of each arm.

He'd seen the *Quaynor*'s arms from inside the ship. They were static, welded into immobility, their only remaining function to serve as out-riggers for comms gear and precision manoeuvring systems.

'Been on high-burn ever since it met the blowpipe package,' Gilbert went on. 'Keeps that up, it'll reach the Winter Palace about ninety minutes ahead of us.'

'Has to be one or both of the cousins,' Geoffrey said.

'This caught us with our flippers off,' Gilbert said. 'We didn't think the blowpipe was working yet.'

'It wasn't,' Geoffrey told her. 'Not properly. They tested it when my grandmother was scattered, but it wasn't ready for *people* ... not by a long margin. Only Lucas or Hector would be fucking mad enough to risk their necks riding the blowpipe.'

'They want to catch up with us, they wouldn't have had much choice,' Gilbert said. 'Libreville would have taken too long to get to, and they didn't have access to their own rocket. Would've been blowpipe or nothing.'

'Someone means business,' Jumai said. 'But we knew that already. OK, what does this change?'

'Nothing,' Geoffrey replied. 'We're not turning around. Can we squeeze some more speed out of this thing, Mira? Now that we no longer need to hide our intentions?'

'Depends how fast you want to go,' the merwoman said. 'And how many space-traffic violations you want to stack up.'

'Enough to make sure the cousins don't get there ahead of us. All we need to do is shut them out – shouldn't be too hard, should it? We get in, find out what, if anything, Eunice left behind up there, and leave. And then, if at all possible, we can all get on with our lives.'

'*This* is your life now,' Gilbert reminded him gently. 'Citizen Akinya.'

Geoffrey touched the damp, warm glass of Arethusa's container, trying to make out the form it held. With the way the hold's lights were arranged, he could discern little more than a dark hovering shadow in the green-stained murkiness of the water tank.

'It's an extravagance, of course,' Arethusa confided. Her voice came straight into his head via the ship's onboard aug. 'Moving me around. I'm not just meat and bone, like you. I weigh fifty tonnes to begin with, and I also need thousands of litres of water to float in. But they can owe me this one. We have fuel to spare – or at least we did, before your family decided to race us to the prize – and in an emergency my suspension fluid can always be used for coolant or reaction mass or radiation shielding.'

'What would happen to you?' Geoffrey asked.

'I'd die, very probably. But I wouldn't object to the basic unfairness of it. Doesn't mean I'm tired of life, or ready to end it – not at all. But I've long since reached the point where I accept that I'm living on borrowed time. Every waking instant.'

'I still don't understand. Why now?'

'Why what now?' She sounded unreasonably prickled by the question. 'Don't tell me you just decided to leave the planet at the drop of a hat, Arethusa. Something's prompted this. Where are you going, anyway? You can't stay in the Winter Palace.'

'I don't plan to. But it's been time to move on for a while now. I bore easily, Geoffrey. Life in the aqualogy stopped offering me challenges decades ago, and for that reason alone I need new horizons. Ocular's finally given me the spur to make the transition.'

'To leave Earth.'

'I've been thinking about it for a very long time. But this news – the Crucible data, the Mandala and the death of my old friend Eunice – it really feels as if the time is right. *Carpe diem*, and all that. If I don't do this now, what else will it take? We Pans preach outward migration, exploration and colonisation as a species imperative. The least I can do is offer deeds instead of words.'

'You mean to stay in space, then?'

'I'm not going back,' she affirmed. 'And most certainly not after all the fuel expenditure it took to haul me up here. Do I want to look profligate?' She fell silent, ruminating in darkness. The tank chugged and whirred. 'There's a whole system to explore, Geoffrey,' she said eventually. 'Worlds and moons, cities and vistas. Wonder and terror. More than Lin Wei could ever have imagined, bless her. And that's just this little huddle of rock and dust around this one little yellow star.'

'You are Lin Wei,' he said quietly. 'You never drowned. You just became a whale.'

She sounded more disappointed than angered. 'Can we at least maintain the pretence, for the sake of civility?'

'Why did this happen to you?'

'I made it happen. Why else?' She sounded genuinely perplexed that the question needed answering. 'It was a phase.'

'Being a whale?'

'Being human.' Then, after a moment: 'We both became strange, Eunice and I, both turned our backs on what we'd once been. Me in here. Eunice in her prison. We both lived and loved, and after all that, it wasn't enough.'

The impulse to defend his grandmother was overwhelming, but he knew it would have been a mistake. 'At least you haven't turned into a recluse. You're still in the world, on some level. You still have plans.'

'Yes,' Arethusa acknowledged. 'I do. Even if, now and then, I scare myself with them.'

'Do you know why she hid herself away?'

'She was never the same after Mercury. But then again, who was?' Arethusa paused. She was still Arethusa to him: try as he might, he couldn't relate this floating apparition to his notion of Lin Wei, the little Chinese girl who had befriended his grandmother, back when the world was a simpler place. 'My doctors – the people who helped shape me – tell me I could live a very long time, Geoffrey. One way to cheat death is to just keep growing, you see. I'm still forming new neural connections. My brain astonishes itself.'

'How long?'

'Decades, maybe even a century: who knows? No different for you, really. You're a young man. A hundred years from now, do you honestly expect medicine not to have made even more progress?'

'I don't think that far ahead.'

'It's time we got into the habit. Every living, breathing human being. Because we're all in this together, aren't we? We endured the turmoil of climate change, the Resource and Relocation wars, the metaphorical and literal floods and storms, didn't we? Or if we didn't, we at least had the marvellous good fortune to have ancestors who did, to allow us to be born into this time of miracles and wonder, when possibilities are opening rather than closing. We're all Poseidon's children, Geoffrey: whether we like it or not.'

'Poseidon's children,' he repeated. 'Is that supposed to mean something?'

'We came through. That's all. We weathered the absolute worst that history could throw at us, and we thrived. Now it's time to start doing something useful with our lives.'

CHAPTER TWENTY-SEVEN

Sunday's boots crunched into Tharsis dust. This, she was startled to realise, was the first time that she had actually set foot on Martian soil. The strip of plasticised ground in the arrivals terminal hadn't counted, nor the spidering walkway in Crommelin. She was outside now, hundreds of kilometres from anything that might even loosely be termed civilisation. Between her body and the dust and rock of this vastly ancient planet lay only the thinnest membrane of air and alloy and plastic. She was a cosy little fiefdom of warmth and life, enclaved by dominions of cold and death.

She was accustomed to wearing a suit, accustomed to being outside in the Moon's vacuum and extremes of temperature. Mars was different, though. It lulled with its very familiarity. It didn't look airless, or even particularly antipathetic to life. She had spent enough time on Earth to recognise the handiwork of rain and weathering. The sky wasn't black, it was the pale pink of a summer's twilight. There were clouds and corkscrewing dust-devils. The ground, its temperature and texture transmitted through the soles of her boots, did not feel unwelcoming. She felt as if she could slip the boots off and pad barefoot through the dust, as if on a beach.

This was how Mars murdered, with an assassin's stealth and cunning. People came from Earth or elsewhere with the best of intentions. They knew that the environment was lethal, that only suits and walls would protect them. Yet time and again, men and women were found outside, dead, half-out of their suits. They weren't mad, exactly, and most of them had not been suicidal. But something in the landscape's familiarity had worked its fatal way into their brains, whispering reassurance, even friendliness. *Trust me. I look welcoming, because I am. Take off that silly armour. You don't need it here.*

This was not the Mars that Eunice had first set foot on a hundred years earlier, Sunday reminded herself. She might be a long way from Vishniac, and Vishniac might be a long way from the nearest city, but, crucially, there were cities. There'd been none in Eunice's time. No trains, no space elevator, no infrastructure.

If Sunday's suit failed now, which was about as mathematically probable as her being hit by a falling meteorite, Dorcas and her crew were close at hand. And if Dorcas and her crew ran into trouble, help would arrive from other Overfloaters soon enough. Vishniac could send an airship or plane, and by bullet train nowhere on Mars was more than a day from Vishniac. She was plugged into a planetary life-support system no less capable than the one clamped onto her back.

Sunday's courage wasn't lacking; she did not need anyone to tell her that. But it was a different order of courage that had brought Eunice to this world, one that had no currency on this prosperous and confident new Mars, with its casinos and hotels and rental firms. Even here, in the Evolvarium, the risk to which Sunday exposed herself was measured, quantifiable – and if she didn't like it, she could leave easily enough. And in the worst of scenarios, it would not be Mars that killed her. It would be the things people had brought to Mars, and set amok.

'We start here,' Gribelin said, nudging the drill into place. 'If we're off, it's not by more than a couple of centimetres, and we should be able to refine our bore once we get closer.'

'How long?' Sunday asked.

'To chew down?' He shrugged through the tight-fitting armour of his surface suit. 'Two, three hours, if it was solid Tharsis lava. But it's not. It's been shattered and poured back into the shaft, so progress'll be a lot easier. Shouldn't take us much more than an hour.'

The Overfloaters had lowered his truck back down from their ship, depositing it gently a few metres from the drill site. The truck had deployed bracing legs, and then Gribelin had swung a vertical drill out from the rear of the cargo bed, directing the heavy equipment into place with gestures, voked commands and the occasional shove from his shoulder. The drill was greasy with low-temperature lubricant and anti-dust caulk. He guided the bit into position, allowed it to rotate slowly as it chewed through the top layer of dust and reached rock. Then it began to spin faster, a tawny plume of digested rock arcing out from the top of it. Sunday could feel its grinding labours through the soles of her boots.

'See now why we held off until sun-up?' Dorcas said, angling her head back to track the plume's trajectory, making sure it went nowhere near her precious airship. 'Machines hunt with vibrations. Would've been a very bad idea to be sat here at night, practically inviting them to come and take a closer look.'

Sunday nodded: she could see the prudence in that, but she could also see the sense in being done with this as quickly as possible. The drill was already making tangible progress, its cutting head a hand's depth into the solidified lava.

There were five of them in suits: Gribelin, Jitendra and Sunday, Dorcas and one of her senior crew, another Martian woman who Sunday had gathered was called Sibyl. The Overfloaters had their own suits, very sleek and modern, with Neolithic and Australian aboriginal animal designs embossed on them in luminous holographic inks. Jitendra and Sunday made do with the units Gribelin carried on his truck for emergency use. They were clunkier, with stiffer articulation and no fancy ornamentation, but they worked well enough, and there was sufficient comms functionality to facilitate a sparse local aug. Tags identified the other suited figures, and a simplified version of the tactical map hovered in Sunday's upper visual field, ready to swell and assume centrality when she needed it. There had been no significant alterations to the map during the night, but in the morning the Overfloaters had acquired intelligence from their fellow brokers, and the positions of the Evolvarium's chief protagonists had been updated.

There were shifting networks of rivalry and cooperation, favour and obligation. It wasn't transparently clear that all this intelligence was reliable, but Dorcas was used to applying her own confidence filters. Her high-value allies had reported that the golem was on the move again, heading their way after spending the night immobile. 'But it's taking a big chance,' Dorcas had explained, while they were suiting up.

'Aren't we all?' Sunday asked.

Dorcas tapped a version of the map. 'Two C-class collectors moved into this sector since we passed through. A pair of hammerheads. Not the worst, but bad enough. If your golem carries on, it'll pass within two or three kays of their present positions.'

It's not my *golem*, Sunday thought sourly. 'Is that going to be a problem for him . . . I mean, it?'

Dorcas nodded sagely. 'He won't *automatically* be ambushed, not in daylight. But then again one or both of the hammerheads may decide to have a go at *him*, if it thinks the likelihood of reprisal is small. Which it would be – the golem's not even a warmblood – but the hammerheads probably don't know that.'

'Probably?'

'Don't put anything past these things. Sniffing comms traffic, distinguishing between a human pilot and a chinged proxy – that's within their cognitive bound, just as it's within ours.'

Sunday brushed a gauntleted finger against the largest icon on the map. 'The Aggregate?'

'Yes,' Dorcas said.

'Maybe it's me, but it looks closer than it did yesterday.'

'It's covered some ground overnight. It probably doesn't mean anything.'

'Probably,' Sunday echoed once more.

'It can't know what we're doing here,' Dorcas said. 'It can't know, and even if it did, it wouldn't be interested. I told you, it's like a city-state. We're nothing to it.'

Sunday watched the drill bite deeper, its progress plain to the naked eye – it had reached at least a metre into the ground, perhaps more. That there was something down there was now beyond doubt. The radar and seismic profiles had improved since Dorcas's first detection, and now revealed what appeared to be a purposefully buried box, not so very different in size and proportions from the container Chama had uncovered on the Moon. A rectangular shaft must have been excavated, the box lowered into it lengthwise and the waste material dropped back over it, before being tamped down. With better equipment, they might even have been able to peer inside the box without bringing it to the surface. Not that it mattered: they'd have the thing in their hands before very long. Gribelin was digging a circular shaft slightly wider than the original bore, and he would stop short of the item itself, for fear of damaging it or triggering some destruct mechanism or booby trap. To be sure, they would send in the proxy Gribelin carried attached to the front of his vehicle.

'When do we hit it?' she asked.

Gribelin stared at the drill for a long while before answering. 'Sixty, seventy minutes.'

'When I asked you before, you said it wouldn't take more than an hour.'

'I said it wouldn't take *much* more,' he snapped back at her.

'Golem's fifty kays out,' Dorcas said levelly. 'If the hammerheads are going to do anything, we'll know about it soon enough. Maybe luck's on your golem's side.'

'If we didn't have to drill here, maybe we could drive out and meet the golem halfway,' Jitendra said, stamping his feet nervously, as if the cold was starting to reach him through the insulation of his suit.

'And then what?' Dorcas asked. 'Use reasoned persuasion?'

'I was thinking more along the lines of a reasoned kick in the teeth.'

'There's no Mech to stop you, but you'd still be in a world of trouble

334

once news got back to the Surveilled World. And we don't know that the golem doesn't have a human or warmblood guide with it.' Dorcas nodded at the whirring drill. 'We'll see this through to the bitter end. It's not as if it's likely to be anything worth fighting over.'

'You still don't believe we'll find anything,' Sunday said.

'If that box has been down there for a hundred years,' Dorcas said, 'then everything I know about the Evolvarium is wrong. And I'm afraid that's just not the way my world works.'

'Much as it pains me to agree with the good captain,' Gribelin said, 'she does have a point.'

There had been days that seemed to pass more rapidly than that hour. Watching the drill was like watching a kettle. Eventually Sunday gave up and walked away from the site, as far as she dared. Even when she was two hundred metres from the truck, she could still feel the vibrations from Gribelin's equipment. Other than the rock plume, the sky was clear and cloudless, darkening almost to a subtle purple-black at the zenith. Pavonis Mons was a gentle bulge on the horizon – underwhelming, or would have been were she naive enough to have expected anything more spectacular. She was already on its footslopes. The mountains of Mars were simply too big to see in one go, unless one was in space.

Give her Kilimanjaro any day. At least that was a mountain you could point to.

The vibration stopped. She looked back just in time to see the plume attenuate, the last part of it bannering through the sky like a kite's tail. She watched Gribelin push the drill back out of the way, nothing in his unhurried movements suggesting that there'd been a fault with the machinery.

She walked back to the drill site. By the time she got there, Jitendra and Dorcas were leaning at the edge of the fresh hole, hands on knees as they peered into its depths.

'The good news,' Dorcas said, 'is that one of the hammerheads took the bait.'

'And?'

'It wasn't a clean kill. The vehicle is still approaching, although not as quickly as before. But it's damaged, and the other hammerhead may be taking an interest.'

'Will there be repercussions?'

'Reprisals? Probably not. Your golem resumed movement before sun-up, which is asking for trouble in anyone's book.'

'I hope no one else was hurt.'

'Their fault if they were,' Dorcas said.

Sunday took care as she neared the freshly dug hole. It was only about sixty centimetres across, but easily wide enough to become wedged in if she lost her footing.

'About this much to go,' Gribelin said, spreading his hands the width of a football. 'We'll back off and let the proxy dig out the rest.'

'Sifters,' Sibyl said, pointing to two pink plumes on the horizon, sailing slowly from left to right like the smoke from an Old-World ocean liner. 'We'd best not hang around.'

The truck and the airship backed off a couple of hundred metres. Gribelin's robot had detached itself from the prow of his vehicle and was now striding across the open terrain. Gribelin had gone into ching bind, otherwise immobile as he drove the proxy to the edge of the hole. It was the same kind of skeletal, minimalist unit that Sunday had chinged on the Moon, constructed from numerous tubes and pistons. It squeezed into the hole effortlessly, folding itself into a tight little knot like a dried-up spider, and vanished down the shaft. A few moments later, gobbets of rubble began to pop out of the opening. *If there's a booby trap*, Sunday thought, *we'd best all pray it isn't nuclear.*

But after a few minutes' further excavation, the proxy had unearthed the box. Deeming it to be safe, at least for the moment, Sunday returned to the shaft and looked down. The proxy had extricated itself, allowing her a clear view of the object. About two-thirds of the upright container had been exposed, revealing it to be of dull, anonymous-looking construction. The size of a picnic hamper, the grey alloy casing was scratched and slightly dented. Sunday made out the seam of a lid, and what appeared to be a pair of simple catches in the long side.

She nodded at Gribelin. 'Bring it all the way out.'

They retreated again and waited for the proxy to haul the box from the shaft and deposit it on the ground lengthwise, with the lid facing the sky. In all the red emptiness of Mars, it looked like something painted by Salvador Dali: a tombstone in a desert, maybe.

Sunday was the first to reach it. She sent the proxy away, not willing to let anyone else open the lid now that she had come this far. Different on the Moon, when Chama had been the one who had that privilege. Then, she'd barely known what she was getting involved with. Now it was as personal as anything in her universe.

Sunday knelt next to the box. Jitendra was behind her, but the others were still keeping their distance. *Let them*, she thought as she worked her gloved fingers under the catches and applied pressure. They flipped open obligingly, and Sunday had her first real inkling of disquiet. She'd never been entirely persuaded by Dorcas's argument that a box could not have been under the surface all this time and not be found by the machines. But catches that had been snapped shut sixty or more years ago and then exposed to six decades of Martian cold ought to feel tighter than these.

The lid swung open just as easily. It was only then that Sunday realised she should have considered the possibility that the box had been packed and sealed under normal pressure conditions rather than in the thin air on the face of Mars.

Too late . . . But no: it either hadn't been pressure-sealed, or the air had leaked away over the decades.

She looked inside. The box contained another box: a lacquered black receptacle with a flower pattern worked into its lid. There was just enough room around the outside of the smaller box to get her fingers in. She reached for it.

And felt something touch the back of her head.

'It's not a weapon,' Dorcas said. 'We need to be clear about that. I am not holding a weapon against your helmet. I would never do that. What I am doing is holding a non-weapon, a tool, a normal part of our equipment, in such a way that harm could conceivably come to you if I were careless. Which I won't be, provided you do nothing that might . . . distract me.'

Sunday was surprised by how calm her own voice sounded. 'What would you like me to do, Dorcas?'

'I'd like you to let go of that box, the smaller one, and step away from the big box. I'm right behind you, and I'm going to stay right behind you.'

Sunday removed her fingers from the gap between the boxes. She'd budged the small box just enough to feel that it was light, if not empty.

'I don't understand what's going on,' she said, standing and moving away from the box as she'd been told to. 'Other than the fact that it feels criminal.'

'Not at all,' Dorcas said. 'Quite the opposite, really. I'm intervening to prevent the execution of a criminal act. In the absence of an effective Mechanism, I'm obliged to do so. Now kneel again.'

'If there was a Mechanism,' Sunday answered, lowering down as she'd been ordered, 'I doubt very much whether you'd be holding something against the back of my helmet.'

'That's as may be. But as I said, what we're trying to do here is stop a crime, not create one.'

'The crime being . . . ?'

'The removal of artefacts from the Evolvarium without the necessary authorisation. I'm afraid everything here that isn't geology belongs to the Overfloater Consortium. You should have realised that before you came blundering in.'

From her kneeling position Sunday looked around slowly, careful not make any sudden movements. She had walked perhaps twenty paces from the big box when Dorcas ordered her to kneel again. The woman was still behind her. Sibyl, the other Overfloater, was holding a kind of pneumatic drill, double-gripped like a gangster-era machine gun. It was heavy and green and wrapped in a gristle of cabling. Gribelin and Jitendra were kneeling on the ground before her, their hands raised as high as their suit articulation allowed.

'Piton-drivers,' Dorcas said. 'We use them to fire anchors into the ground when we need to moor-up during a storm. They use compressed air to drive self-locking cleats fifty centimetres into solid rock. Just think what that would do to common-or-garden suit armour.'

'I didn't come to steal from the Overfloaters. You know why I'm here. Whatever's in that box is family property, that's all, and it was buried here before the Evolvarium was created. It's got nothing to do with you or your machines. If I take it, nothing changes. No one gets richer or poorer.'

'If that's the case,' Dorcas said, 'then you won't mind if I have it instead, will you?'

'I said it belongs to me, to my family.'

'Can you prove this?'

'Of course. I didn't end up here by accident. I followed clues, all the way from the Moon.'

'Then you can submit a claim for return of confiscated property through the usual channels.' Dorcas seemed to think for a moment. 'Of course, to prove that you followed those clues, you'll have to mention that incident with the Chinese, to which your name hasn't hitherto been linked.'

'Who's behind this?' Jitendra asked.

'There's no one "behind" anything,' Dorcas said. 'I'm merely asserting the rule of law.'

'It's just that you'd only know about what happened on the Moon if the Pans had told you,' Jitendra said.

'I'm not surprised,' Sunday said. 'If anything, I'm amazed it's taken them this long.'

'To do what?' Gribelin asked.

'To steal the box from under my nose. It's been too easy, hasn't it?

338

They've been falling over themselves to help us get this far. Now they've decided: enough is enough. We don't need Sunday to follow the rest of the clues. We can do that on our own, thanks very much, or just not bother.' She shook her head, disgusted at her own unwillingness to see things clearly until this lacerating moment. 'Soya warned me,' she said.

'Soya?' Dorcas asked. 'Who the hell is Soya?'

'Someone I should have listened to when I had the chance. Not that it would have made much difference. How far could I have got, without the Pans' assistance?'

'Maybe I'm missing something,' Gribelin said, 'but if the Pans are paying me, why is this shit happening?'

'Let's not allow this to come between us, Grib,' Dorcas said soothingly. 'We're both too old for that. You've done an honest job and you've been paid for it. You had no right to assist in the extraction of materials from the Evolvarium, so you could say that you're getting off very lightly by being interdicted before the crime could be fully actualised.'

'I told you what we had in mind. You said nothing about stealing the fucking box from me at the last minute.'

'Yes, well, that was before I was fully cognisant of the possibilities.'

'When did they contact you?' Sunday asked. 'Was it yesterday, after we'd been brought aboard? Was that why you delayed the dig, when we still had daylight to spare? So you could haggle terms with the Pans?'

'She's not going to admit to them being behind this,' Jitendra said.

'No,' Sunday said. 'You're right. But I thought they could be trusted – to a point, at least. I trusted Chama and Gleb. I even trusted Holroyd. And if they're screwing *me* over, what are they doing to my brother?'

'I very much doubt that Chama and Gleb had anything to do with this,' Jitendra said.

On an open channel, obviously not caring that her words would be heard by everyone present, Dorcas said, 'The box is secure. Send down two more crew to pick us up and start prepping for departure. I want to be out of here before the golem leads the hammerheads to us.'

'May be a bit late for that,' Gribelin said, angling his helmet to nod eastwards. Still kneeling, Sunday twisted to look as well, keeping her movements smooth and slow. She made out a plume of dust, a bumbling silver glint at the point where it met the ground.

Dorcas cursed, some Martian oath that the translation layer couldn't parse. 'I was meant to be alerted!'

'Nine kays and closing,' Sibyl said. 'There's still time, if we hurry.'

Dorcas prodded Sunday. 'Get up.'

'Make your mind up. You just told me to kneel down.'

This time the prod was harder, enough to rattle Sunday's head against the inside of her helmet. 'I won't ask again. Remember, bad things happen out here. No one's going to bat so much as an eyelid if you don't show up in Vishniac again. They went into the Evolvarium without an official escort – what were they expecting?'

Sunday rose. 'Whatever you think you're doing, understand this. You're not just stealing this box from me. You're stealing the corporate property of Akinya Space. Are you really sure you want to make an enemy of us?'

'Tell that to Lin Wei. I seem to remember Akinya Space stuck the knife in her business, all those years ago.' A prod, less violent this time. 'Now walk. All of you. Go as far as that ridge, and keep close to each other.'

Sunday pushed any thoughts of grand heroics out of her mind. She wasn't going to take a chance against the piton-driver, not when Dorcas was only a few paces behind her. The three of them did as they were instructed, leaving Sibyl free to retrieve the smaller box. Turning to look back while she walked, Sunday watched the other woman extract the lacquered box from the larger container without incident. She held it up to her visor and with one gloved hand eased up the patterned lid.

Sibyl examined the contents for a few seconds, poking a finger into whatever was inside, then closed the lid carefully. There was no way of telling what she'd seen.

'Keep walking,' Dorcas said.

Despite the order, Gribelin stopped and pointed. 'Hammerhead!' he bellowed, like a whaler sighting a spout.

'Move!' Dorcas snarled.

The hammerhead was some distance beyond the golem's rover, but it was rearing up now, assuming full and dreadful aspect. Sunday's visor graphed up a high-mag zoom, sensing her focus. A down-angled claw hammer, big as the rover itself, pivoted on the head-end of a mechanical spine as long as a train. The machine cut through the terrain in an S-wave, each of its house-sized spinal modules equipped with out-jutting legs, sinuous and in constant whipping motion. The golem was travelling quickly, kicking dust back at its pursuer, but the hammerhead looked to be gaining. They watched it scoop up boulders and fling them through the air, raining down on the golem with ballistic precision.

Sunday had been running from the golem from the moment it had announced itself in Crommelin, but now she welcomed its arrival. Given the alternative, she would far rather deal with Lucas than Dorcas and the Pans. Watching the hammerhead close the distance on the rover, she willed the golem forward.

It wasn't enough. A car-sized boulder spun through the air, barely missing the rover and landing slightly ahead of it. The rover bludgeoned into the obstacle, its nose digging down as its tail flipped up. Wheels spun in the air. The rover, its front end crumpled, fell onto its side. The hammerhead continued throwing rocks as it approached.

Sunday tore her gaze away from the spectacle long enough to see the airship reaching down its arms to scoop up Dorcas and Sibyl. It hauled them into the sky, along with their improvised weapons and the black box.

'Good luck!' Dorcas said over the suit-to-suit channel. 'We'll do what we can to push that hammerhead away, but I wouldn't stick around if I were you.' She let her piton-gun fall to the dust. 'I'll buy you a drink next time we're both in Vishniac, Grib.'

The gondola's airlock was open: another crewperson was waiting to receive Dorcas and Sibyl. The airship's engines swivelled on their mountings, the deltoid gasbag turning with the ponderousness of a cloud. Gribelin looked dumbstruck. He was hurrying back to the truck, kicking dust with his heels. He paused to scoop up the piton-gun, shaking the dirt from its workings. Sunday and Jitendra started after him.

But she couldn't not look at the golem. The hammerhead was on it now, rearing above the crashed rover. It swung back its head, angling it as far as the hinge allowed, then swung the hammer down, putting its entire body into the movement so that it looked, for an instant, as if the robot were no more than a whip being cracked. The hammer drove down onto the rover. The head angled back, swung again. The rover was being crushed and pulverised. Sunday thought of the golem inside, what must now be left of it. She hoped it had come alone.

They had reached the truck. The hammerhead had smashed the other vehicle six or seven times now. Bits of it had broken off, and now the Evolvarium machine was employing its cilia-like legs to pick through the debris. There was something obscene and avaricious about the haste with which it went about the task of recycling the broken machine, shovelling the prime cuts into a ring-shaped aperture just under its hinge-point. A horror of counterrotating teeth spun at high speed inside the maw, grinding and slicing.

Gribelin hauled himself onto the side of his truck. He looked back, still holding the piton-gun, and then switched his attention to the hammerhead. Sunday looked at it as well. It was still next to the wreck, but it had interrupted its feeding. The 'head' was swivelling slowly around, like a battleship turret moving onto its next target.

'It knows we're here,' Gribelin said.

'Then we'd better do what Dorcas just said,' Sunday answered. 'Get the fuck out of here.'

'Lucas couldn't outrun it, could he?' Jitendra asked, fear breaking his voice. 'What hope have we got?'

'Maybe Dorcas can scare it away,' Sunday said. Instead of heading towards the hammerhead, however, the airship was moving in the opposite direction.

'And maybe I trust Dorcas about as far as I can piss, right now,' Gribelin said. Through his visor, the set of his face was grim and calculating. He glanced at the hammerhead again, then his truck, then Sunday and Jitendra.

'Run,' he said.

Sunday frowned. 'What do you mean—'

'Run,' he repeated, lowering the muzzle of the piton-gun in her direction to dispel any remaining doubt. 'Run, sweet cheeks, and keep running. Hammerheads lock on to the biggest target they can find, and they're smart enough to go after a machine rather than a person in a suit. Until the machine escapes, or they catch it. Whichever happens first.'

Sunday wasn't processing. All she was seeing was a man pointing a non-weapon at her, blocking her access to the one thing that stood even a remote chance of outrunning the Evolvarium creature. 'Please,' she said. 'Let us in.'

From his position on the truck's side, Gribelin kicked hard. His boot caught her in the middle of her chest. She crashed back, falling against Jitendra, who stumbled and flailed before finding his balance. 'Gribelin!' he called. 'You can't do this!'

'Run,' Gribelin said again. He was in the truck now, venting its cabin air in a single explosive gasp so that he didn't have to go through the airlock cycle. Still on her back, Sunday watched him settle into the control position and work the levers. The stabilising legs spidered away. The wheels churned, found their grip.

'He's abandoning us,' Jitendra said.

'I'm not so sure,' Sunday replied as the truck backed away and turned. She rolled onto her side and forced herself up. She remembered what Gribelin had told her, that they should do exactly what he said if the shit came down. This predicament, she decided, adequately satisfied the requirements. 'But I do think we should run.'

So they ran, as fast as the suits allowed, which was nowhere near as fast as she would have liked, and maybe a fifth of the speed of Gribelin's rover, now scudding away from them with a huge peacock's tail of dust behind it.

'It's taking the bait,' Jitendra said, between ragged breaths. Sunday barely had breath herself. They were pushing the suits to their limit, their own lungs and muscles doing at least as much work as the suits' servos.

'Keep moving,' she said.

But she couldn't resist a look back. The hammerhead had abandoned its first kill. Now it was going after Gribelin, but not with any sense of urgency. Conserving its energy, knowing that it could catch him up in patient increments, over kilometres. She forced herself to keep running, or to maintain what was now little more than an exhausted shambling jog. She was starting to feel light-headed, with stars spangling the edges of her vision. The faceplate readouts were all in the red, warning her that she was pushing the suit beyond its recommended performance envelope.

Never mind the suit, she thought. *This is pretty far outside my own performance envelope.*

There'd been no stated intention, no agreement between them that they should run in a certain direction, other than away from the truck. But that had been sufficient shared volition, Sunday realised now, to send them towards the golem's wreck. It had looked awfully far away, but distances on Mars were deceptive. She crested a shallow ridge, and with a dreamlike lurch of contracting perspectives it was suddenly much closer.

It looked bad, too. She'd never had any real expectation that the attack had been survivable, but any hopes she might have entertained were now obliterated. The rover was in pieces. It had been ripped apart and pounded into mangled and flattened shapes, now barely recognisable as the vehicle parts they had once been. She thought of Dali again: of sagging watches draped over leafless branches. The Evolvarium creature had turned the rover into art.

The suit's warning alerts were now more than she could endure, and her own heart felt like a piece of machinery about to burst from her chest. Her lungs felt as if the sun had been poured into them. She could not keep running.

Lucas's proxy lay on the ground.

The golem had no need of a surface suit, and was dressed as it had been in the Red Menace. For an instant her eyes tricked her, telling her that half of it must be buried under dust, until she realised that half of it was missing. The golem consisted of a head, an upper torso, one left

343

arm. Lucas's proxy body had been severed in a diagonal line from the upper-right shoulder to the left hip. Sunday could not see the rest of it. Perhaps the other parts were in the remains of the rover, or scattered, or had already been digested by the Evolvarium creature.

It was the first time she'd seen the inner workings of a golem. There were glutinous layers, sheaths of active polymer, a skeletal structure of translucent white plastic, fibrous bundles of nerves and power-transmission circuits. A blue-grey blubber of artificial muscles, precisely veined with fluid ducting. Not much metal, and very little in the way of hard mechanisms. Purple ichor, some kind of lubrication or coolant medium, had spilt out of it and was already freezing on the Tharsis ground. The right side of its face was mashed in, the ear and scalp missing. An eyeball lolled out of its socket, trailing a rope of greasy fibre optics. The golem's intelligence, in so far as it had any, was distributed throughout its entire anatomy. But the eyes were still its primary visual acquisition system.

She stood next to it, hands on knees, waiting for the fog of exhaustion to clear from her vision.

The golem looked at her. The good eyeball tracked her in its socket, the other one twitching like a fish on land. The mouth moved, clicking open and shut in the manner of a ventriloquist's dummy, as if operated by a crude mechanism. For the moment, there was no animation in the face. It was like a limp rubber mask with no person wearing it, sagging in the wrong places. Then Lucas seemed to push through, his personality inhabiting the golem. The face tautened, filled out, and the mouth formed a smile.

'I'm in trouble,' Sunday said over the suit's general comm channel. 'I can't reach the aug, and aside from my brother and some people I don't trust any more, no one knows I'm here. That leaves you, Lucas. And I don't even know if you're hearing this, or if you still have a ching bind back to Earth.'

The golem spoke. She heard it in her head. 'I think we're both in trouble, Sunday.'

'When was the last time you received an update from Lucas?'

'I've been autonomous for hours now. I'm afraid it's highly unlikely that there'll be any re-establishment of contact, at least not before I become inoperable.'

'Is Lucas aware of my whereabouts?'

'Lucas knows that I followed you into the Evolvarium, and that your probable target was Eunice's landing site. However, he didn't know that for a fact.'

Sunday looked around. Gribelin and the hammerhead were a long way off now: from this distance, she couldn't see much more than the rover's dust plume. She hoped Gribelin was still maintaining his lead.

Jitendra staggered to a halt, bracing his hands on his hips. He saw the golem, shuddered instinctively. It was a natural reaction. It looked so plausible, so lifelike.

'It should never have come to this, cousin,' Sunday said, with genuine sorrow.

The golem's one good eye twinkled with bitter-sweet amusement. 'I was always prepared to put the family before my personal advancement. It's just a shame you didn't feel the same way. What have you gained, though? They took the item. You came all this way for nothing.' The face smiled. Purple ichor drooled from its lips. 'You wasted everything, Sunday.'

'I wouldn't say that.' She planted a foot on the golem's skull. 'There are always compensations.'

She felt the plastic crack wetly under her weight, like some large, brittle, yolk-filled egg. The pettiness of the gesture sickened her to the marrow. There was spite in her that she had never once suspected.

But at the same time she did not regret it at all.

Jitendra had been digging through the wreckage of the rover, the parts that hadn't been completely pancaked, for many hours now. He was looking for something, anything, that might enable them to send a distress signal. Sunday had helped, at first, but then the futility of the exercise had burst over her in a wave of bleak despair. He would not find anything of use, nor would they succeed in contacting anyone who could help. If they tried to walk, they'd still be inside the Evolvarium when night returned, and their suits would certainly not keep them alive for more than a couple of days. It was already long past noon and the sun was hurtling back down towards the horizon with indecent haste.

'I don't think we should stay here,' she said, for the third or fourth time. 'If the hammerhead comes back to take another look at the wreck . . .'

On the other hand, by remaining close to the wreckage of the rover they might be less conspicuous than two figures out in the landscape, far from any other manufactured thing. Did the machines hunt by heat or sound, primarily? And was there sense in staying close to the drill site, in the faint hope that the golem had managed to report home? She might have spurned the family, but they wouldn't let her die out here. Not knowingly, she hoped.

Gribelin was dead. She was certain of this now. Almost at the point when the dust plume faded into the pink haze of distance above the horizon, there had been a bright and soundless explosion. She had felt the report of it seconds later, rumbling through the ground like elephant talk. She imagined him allowing the hammerhead to come as close to the rover as he dared, before triggering something aboard the vehicle: a cache of explosives, some illegal weapon. Whether it had been enough to destroy the hammerhead, or merely to exclude the possibility of its catching Gribelin alive, there was no way of telling. A bonsai mushroom cloud had curled up, a brain rising swollen and cerebral from its own spinal cord, and there had been no sign of the hammerhead after that.

But the hammerhead was not even an apex predator.

'I want Eunice,' Sunday said. 'She'd know what to do. She always knew what to do.'

Jitendra kicked aside a buckled metal plate. 'There's nothing here we can use. And I'm not even sure it's a good idea to keep communicating like this. Maybe we should go into radio silence from now on.' He paused, his breath ragged from the exertion of searching the wreck. That was Jitendra's way of coping, Sunday thought: keep busy, until even he had no option but to admit the futility of it. 'So, which direction do we walk? The winds haven't been too bad since we came in. If our air recyclers hold out we can probably follow the vehicle tracks all the way back to Vishniac, even if we lose suit nav.'

If they lost suit nav, Sunday thought, getting lost would be the least of their worries. It would mean the suits were dying on them, and that life support would be among the failing systems. 'Maybe another Overfloater will take pity on us.'

'Yes. They do appear to be the kind and considerate sort, based on Dorcas's example.'

'I'm just saying. When you're out of options, you cling to the unrealistic.' But Sunday had been searching the sky for hours. There were no other airships up there. 'I could kill her. Better than that. I *will* kill her, if I ever get the chance.'

Which I won't, a quiet voice added.

'I don't think she meant us to die. On the other hand, I don't think she thought things through particularly well.'

'Do me a favour,' Sunday said. 'Can you – just for once – stop trying to look on the bright side *all the fucking time*? And stop trying to always see the good in everyone, because sometimes it just isn't there.

Sometimes people are just arseholes. Evil fucking arseholes.'

Jitendra dragged a piece of rover panelling next to Sunday and jammed it into the ground like a windbreak. 'We're going to be the hottest things for miles around. The more thermal screening we can arrange, the better our chances.'

'Our chances are zero, Jitendra. But if it makes you feel better . . .' She blinked hard. Her eyes stung with tears, but there was nothing she could do about that now.

'It would make me feel better if you helped a bit,' he said. 'Some of these pieces are too big for me to manage on my own.'

Anything to please Jitendra. And he was right. Better to be doing something. Better to be doing something, no matter how stupid and pointless, than nothing at all.

While the universe surveyed their ramshackle plans and laughed.

They made a crude shelter, open to the skies but offering some cover from anything approaching on or near the ground. Sunday doubted that it would make much difference – their heat was going to bleed out whatever they did – but if it made them slightly less visible then she supposed the effort was not entirely wasted. They had depleted some more of their suits' power and oxygen, but they had not surrendered. And when the work was done, the shelter fashioned to the best of their abilities and the sun lower still, they sat next to each other, shoulder to shoulder, hand in hand, maintaining tactile contact so they could talk.

'I'm sorry,' Sunday said finally.

'Sorry for being tricked and cheated?'

'Sorry for what I got you into. Sorry for what I got Gribelin into.'

'I'm sorry for him as well. But he was an old man, in a dangerous line of work. You didn't kill him; his job did.'

'Maybe we'd have been better staying together.'

'We're still alive,' Jitendra said. He tightened his hand around hers in emphasis. 'He isn't. That has to be the better outcome, doesn't it?'

'I don't know,' Sunday said, and the words surprised her because they seemed to come unbidden.

'I do,' Jitendra said. 'And while there's a second more of living to be had, I'll always choose life over death. Because anything at all could happen in that second.'

'Since when did you start believing in miracles?' Sunday asked.

'I don't,' he answered. 'But I do believe in . . .' Jitendra fell silent, long enough that she began to wonder if the tactile link had stopped working.

She followed his line of sight, out through the narrow vertical gap where two of the wreck's pieces didn't quite meet.

'Jitendra?'

'I haven't moved since we sat down,' he said. 'My line of sight's still the same. And I definitely couldn't see that hill an hour ago.'

Sunday adjusted her position and saw what he meant. She'd have seen it herself, had she been sitting a little to her left. It was no hill, she knew. The topography here was clear: other than the volcanoes and some ancient craters, there were no sharp protrusions in the terrain.

More than that, Jitendra was right. The hill hadn't been there while they made the shelter.

'The Aggregate,' Sunday said, and when Jitendra didn't answer, she knew it was because he had nothing better to offer.

And the Aggregate was coming closer.

CHAPTER TWENTY-EIGHT

Geoffrey checked his restraints. The *Quaynor* was burning fuel again, continuing with orbital insertion and approach/rendezvous with the Winter Palace. Up in the forward command blister – the nearest thing the ship had to a bridge – Jumai and Mira Gilbert were tethered either side of him, secured within a messy cat's cradle of bungee cords and buckle-on harnesses. The command blister was a metal-framed cupola set with impact-resistant glass and furnished with quaintly old-fashioned controls and readouts.

'Your family are still ahead of us,' Gilbert said, confirming the news that Geoffrey had been half-expecting. 'We had some delta-vee in reserve. Unfortunately, so did the *Kinyeti*.' She tapped at a fold-down instrument panel, muttering some dark aquatic oath. Reaction motors popped and stuttered, finessing the *Quaynor*'s course. 'Going to be a nail-biter, I'm afraid. We'll meet them on the same orbit. Unfortunately it looks like they'll make dock before we do.'

'How many docking slots?' Jumai asked.

'Close-ups show one at either pole. Anyone's guess as to whether both are serviceable.'

'Been a long while since there was any need for two ships to be docked at the same time,' Geoffrey said. 'If ever.'

The *Quaynor* wasn't new – Geoffrey could tell that much just from the rank mustiness of his living quarters – but he doubted that it dated from much before the turn of the century. Rather it had been tailored to Pan ideological specifications, which dictated a strict minimum of aug-generated contrivances. Glass windows, so that the universe might be apprehended photon by photon, on its own blazing terms, rather than through layers of distorting mediation. Control and navigation systems that required physical interaction, so that a person had to be present, in body as well as mind. Decision-making abdicated to fallible, slow-witted human pilots, rather than suites of swift and tireless expert systems.

'What are Hector and Lucas hoping to gain here?' Jumai asked.

Geoffrey scratched a nugget of crystal-hard dust from his eye. The period of unconsciousness in the rocket hadn't done anything to take the edge off his exhaustion.

'The cousins couldn't give two shits about what's inside the Winter Palace. Not for themselves, anyway. They just don't want *me* finding anything that might hurt Eunice's reputation or endanger the business.' He adjusted one of the restraints where it was starting to chafe. 'They'll be planning to scuttle it, one way or another. They already have the paperwork in place.'

Jumai asked, 'Reckon they brought bombs with them?'

'Plenty of stuff in a ship that can be used to make a bang,' Gilbert said. 'That's before we even get to the fact that there's a whole other ship stuck inside the Winter Palace.'

Geoffrey tensed at the arrival of a ching request. It was Hector, and the ching coordinates placed him near the Moon.

'I don't think we have much to say to each other,' he said, opting to keep the conversation strictly voice-only.

'You took the call,' Hector said, his reply bouncing back from the *Kinyeti* almost immediately, 'which suggests you think there's something worth discussing.'

'Is it just you, or did Lucas come along for the ride?'

'Only room for one of us, Geoffrey – I came up in a cargo shot, not the crewed capsule. Stress wouldn't have been good for Lucas, not after what he did to his leg.' He emitted a brief, humourless laugh. 'It was quite a trip. You should try it sometime.'

'I did it once,' Geoffrey said.

'Not this way, with no cushioning and the safety margins dialled to zero. The kick when I hit the bend at the base of the mountain ... that was something. The view, though ... once the pusher lasers had me and I was sailing into orbit. Glorious.'

'Glad it was worthwhile. You're brave or stupid, one of the two.'

Hector let slip another laugh. 'It's still not too late to make this good, Geoffrey. Whatever you think you're going to achieve in the Winter Palace, you don't have to go through with it.'

'So I should just leave you to destroy it?'

'We have a good life here, cousin, everything we need. Why are you so anxious to ruin things?'

'If Eunice wanted to screw the family, she had her whole life to do it.'

'You have a touching faith in human nature. I'd say she's perfectly capable of screwing us from the afterlife, if that's what she wanted.'

'Hector, trust my sister on this. Sunday knew Eunice inside out. Eunice didn't do pointless, spiteful gestures. And why the hell would she have something against us, anyway?'

'She lost her mind, cousin. Out there, on the edge of the system. From that point on, she wasn't thinking straight.'

'I don't think she lost her mind. I think she saw something out there, had some kind of experience . . . something that made her look back on everything she'd achieved up to that point and realise it wasn't necessarily worth all the blood and toil she'd put into it. But that's not going mad. It's called getting a sense of perspective.'

After an interval Hector said, 'Love to think you were right, but we can't take any chances here. Too much depends on us.'

'At least let me see what's inside the Winter Palace.'

'And if it's something that hurts us? Something we can't recover from?'

'I'm not going to destroy the business,' Geoffrey said, exhaustedly. 'I don't give enough of a damn about it.'

'And if we'd done something bad? Some crime only she knew about? If you found out that your own flesh and blood had done something unspeakable? Could your conscience allow you to keep the secret then, cousin?' He imagined Hector shaking his head, tutting beneath his breath. 'You wouldn't be able to live with that kind of secret.'

Softly Geoffrey asked, 'What kind of crime?'

'How the fuck should I know? Artilects, genetics, weapons: who knows what she got up to a hundred years ago? Who knows what anyone got up to back then?'

'This doesn't make any sense, Hector. We're almost talking like equals now. Why couldn't we have had this conversation weeks ago?'

Hector sighed, as if it bored him to have to explain something that should have been obvious. 'Weeks ago you were still family, Geoffrey. Now you're not. You've defected, turned traitor. Now you're a business adversary. Now you're an equal. That changes everything. I feel I can almost respect you.'

'Please turn around.'

'*Kinyeti*'s locked on, cousin. I'd maintain a safe distance, I were you.'

'What are you planning?'

'What I came here to do,' Hector said. 'Demolition.'

Rather than completing its approach, the *Kinyeti* came to a station-keeping halt fifty kilometres out, following almost the same orbit as the Winter Palace. Geoffrey wondered, optimistically, if Hector had had second thoughts. Perhaps, after all, he had begun to get through to his cousin, making him see sense.

But no. After ten minutes, a much smaller vehicle detached from the head of the mining ship and resumed the original approach vector. They studied the tiny ball-shaped craft at high-mag via the *Quaynor*'s own cameras. It was the kind of short-range ship-to-ship ferry that could also serve as an escape capsule or single-use re-entry vehicle.

'Should have seen this coming,' Geoffrey said. 'Hector doesn't want the *Kinyeti*'s crew getting any closer to the Winter Palace than necessary. Still playing family secrets close to his chest.'

'*Kinyeti* is withdrawing,' Arethusa said as the bigger ship fired a string of steering motors along its spine. 'Guess they'll be returning to collect Hector, but for the moment he's told them to keep the hell away.'

'They'll be paid well enough not to ask awkward questions,' Geoffrey said.

Once he was on his way, it only took Hector twenty minutes to complete the crossing to the Winter Palace. Using the capsule's micro-thrusters, he executed one inspection pass, spiralling around the station's cylinder from end to end before closing in for final docking. If the Winter Palace had queried the little ship's approach authorisation – and then given clearance to commence final docking manoeuvres – there was no practical way to intercept that tight-beamed comms traffic from the *Quaynor*. Geoffrey could only presume that they would be challenged on their own approach.

'Synching for dock,' Gilbert said as Hector's ship went into a slow roll, matching the station's centrifugal spin rate. 'Contact and capture in five ... four ... three ...'

The capsule docked. Clamp arms folded down to secure it. Two or three minutes passed and then there was an exhalation of silvery glitter from the airlock collar. A gasp of escaping pressure, held there since the last time the lock was activated, and then the seals locked tight. The tiny capsule was almost lost in the details of the station's endcap docking and service structures.

'Lining us up for the other pole,' Gilbert said, tapping commands into one of the fold-down keypads. 'Think we can pass through the entire structure?'

'It's just a big hollow tube, with *Winter Queen* running down the middle,' Geoffrey said. 'We shouldn't have any problems, especially as Arethusa already chinged aboard not so long ago.'

'I only saw what she let me see,' Arethusa warned.

Hector's transfer into the smaller ship had eaten into his lead over the *Quaynor*, but they were still thirty minutes from docking. Geoffrey drummed his fingertips, the seconds crawling by with agonising slowness. He couldn't see Hector taking his time inside, no matter the novelty value of being able to roam at will through Eunice's private kingdom.

They were fifty kilometres out when the first challenge came: shrill and automated, fully in keeping with Eunice's general policy of not extending a magnanimous welcome to visitors. 'Unidentified vehicle on approach heading one-one-nine, three-one-seven: you do not have docking or fly-by authorisation. Please adjust your vector to comply with our mandatory exclusion volume.' The voice, which was speaking Swahili, could easily have passed for his grandmother's. 'If you do not adjust your vector, we cannot be held responsible for any damage caused by our anti-collision systems.'

'Hold the course,' Geoffrey said. 'Let her – it – know we mean business. Eunice: are you listening to me?'

'I'm here,' the construct said, deigning not to project a figment into what was already a cramped space.

'Make yourself heard by everyone present, including Arethusa. No reason for them not to listen in on our conversation.'

'Sunday wouldn't like that.'

'Do it anyway. I'm ordering you.'

There was a barely measurable pause. 'It's done. They can hear me now.'

'Good.' Geoffrey looked around at his companions, trusting that they'd settle for asking questions later. 'I'm afraid there's no time to bring you up to speed right now, Eunice, but we need docking permission for the Winter Palace.'

'Tell it you're on Akinya business.'

There was little point seeking the construct's guidance if he was not willing to give her suggestions the benefit of the doubt. 'Mira – am I patched through?'

'Say your piece,' Gilbert said.

'This is Geoffrey Akinya, grandson of Eunice. I am aboard the deep-space vehicle *Quaynor*, requesting approach and docking authorisation.' He waited a moment, then, for all that it sounded pompous, added, 'I am on important family business.'

'Approach approval has already been assigned to Hector Akinya. No further docking slots are available.'

Geoffrey ground his teeth. 'Hector is docked at one pole; we can come in at the other.'

'No further docking slots are available,' the voice repeated, but this time with an edge of menace.

'I have the right to come in,' Geoffrey said. 'Disarm your anti-collision systems and give me clearance for the unoccupied dock. You have no choice but to comply with a family instruction.'

'Your identity is not verified. Desist approach and adjust your vector.'

'It doesn't believe you're you,' Eunice said.

Geoffrey bit off a sarcastic response before it left his mouth. 'Why did it accept Hector, and not me?'

'Hector came in on an Akinya vehicle, showing Akinya registration – the same way Memphis would have done. The Winter Palace had no reason not to let him through.'

He grimaced. 'Mira – can we fake a civil registration?'

'Not infallibly, not legally and most certainly not *now*, given that the habitat already has us pegged as being under different ownership.' Gilbert shot him an apologetic glance. 'You're just going to have to talk your way through this one, Geoffrey. Even Jumai can't help us until we're docked.'

'Need some ideas here, Eunice,' he said.

'If the habitat recognises the notion of family visiting rights, if it grasps that Hector is an Akinya and it therefore has an obligation to let him dock – then it *may* be running something a little bit like me. Much less sophisticated, of course – but a model of Eunice, all the same, and with an attempt at an embedded knowledge base.'

'All well and good, but I'm not sure that gets us anywhere,' Geoffrey said.

'Talk to it. Explain that you are Geoffrey Akinya, and that you're prepared to submit to questioning to prove it.'

'Think that's going to work?' Jumai asked him.

'Don't know. Any other bright ideas, short of fighting our way past anti-collision systems? Those are basically *guns*, in case you missed the briefing.'

'Thank you,' she replied. 'I do get the fact that there are real risks here.'

'I'm sorry,' Geoffrey said. And he meant it, too: of all the people he knew, it was hard to think of anyone less risk-averse than Jumai.

'Look,' she said, giving him a conciliatory look, 'if the construct says this is our best shot—'

'Are we still on air?' Geoffrey asked.

'Say your piece,' Gilbert confirmed.

He cleared his throat. 'This is Geoffrey Akinya speaking again. I have no formal means of establishing my identity, not at this range. But I'm willing to talk. Eunice knew me. Maybe not well, but as well as she knew anyone in our family. If there's something, anything, that I can say to prove myself . . . please ask. I will do my best to answer.'

There was silence. Jumai opened her mouth to speak, but she had not even begun to draw breath when the habitat answered again.

'Disengage all external comms except for this tight-beam link. Any attempt to query the aug will be detected.'

'It's done,' Arethusa said.

After a moment the Winter Palace said, 'Wooden elephants, a birthday present. How many were there, and how old would Geoffrey Akinya have been when he received them?'

He looked around at his fellow travellers. 'I would have been five, six,' he mouthed, keeping his words low enough not to be picked up on the ship-to-station channel. 'I don't remember!'

'I saw those elephants,' Jumai said, in the same hushed voice. 'You told me you didn't even think they'd come from Eunice.'

'There was a nanny from Djibouti looking after Sunday and at the time . . . I thought maybe she'd got them, or maybe Memphis.'

'Ask the construct,' Gilbert said.

'Can't. There's a copy of her assigned to me, like a cloud hovering around me in data-space, but she's not inside my skull. Without the aug she can't tell me anything.'

'I must have an answer,' the habitat said. 'How old was Geoffrey Akinya?'

'Six,' he said. 'Six elephants, and . . . I was six at the time. My sixth birthday.'

Silence again, and then, 'Approach authorisation granted. Proceed for docking at the trailing pole.'

Geoffrey let out a gasp of bottled-up tension. 'We're in. Or at least allowed a little closer.'

'How'd you figure it out, five or six?' Jumai asked.

'I didn't! It was a guess.'

'Lucky fucking guess.'

'She knew about the elephants,' Geoffrey said, as much to himself as anyone present. 'She may not have bought them . . . but I didn't even think she cared enough to know—'

'Enough to make it the billion-yuan question,' Jumai said.

'We're lined up,' Mira Gilbert said. 'Still off-aug, and we'll stay that way for the time being.' Then her tone changed. 'Wait. Something's happening with the *Kinyeti*. Thruster activity.'

'Where's she headed?' Geoffrey asked.

'Give me a few seconds to nail the vector.' Gilbert watched and waited, tapping commands into her fold-out keyboard and studying the complex multicoloured readouts as they squirmed through various scenarios. 'Resumed her approach for the Winter Palace,' she said, sounding doubtful of her own analysis. 'That can't be right, can it? He's only been in there, what, twenty minutes?'

'Maybe that's all he needs,' Jumai said.

'He still wouldn't want to call in the *Kinyeti*,' Geoffrey said. 'Not when he has his own means of getting back. So maybe there's a problem with the ferry, or he's told the *Kinyeti* to block our approach to the other dock.'

'We have approach authorisation,' Arethusa said. 'If he blocks us, this becomes an interjurisdictional incident.'

'I think it already became one the moment I signed up for citizenship,' Geoffrey said.

'I'm slowing our own approach,' Gilbert said. 'Want to see what the *Kinyeti*'s aiming for, before we get in any closer.'

Geoffrey reminded himself that he wasn't chinging here, his flesh and blood body safely back in Africa. He was physically present, aboard a huge, ponderous, fragile-as-gossamer machine, something that could no more tolerate a collision with another of its kind than it could execute dogfight course changes. And with two delicate ships being drawn to the candleflame of the Winter Palace, the chances of an accident, let alone a deliberate obstructional act, could only increase.

'*Kinyeti* is ten kays out,' Gilbert said, a few minutes later. 'Looks as if they're lining up for ... the docking node where Hector's already clamped on. That make sense to anyone?'

'Might be the only entry point they trust,' Jumai said.

Geoffrey nodded. 'Let's wait and see what their intentions are.'

A second or so later, Arethusa said, 'Pirates.'

She had seen it an instant before the rest of them: an eruption of pinprick light from either end of the habitat's cylinder, the bright spillage of magnetic and optical collision-avoidance devices as they directed mass and energy against whatever the Winter Palace's autonomous defence systems had identified as an incoming threat. Not an enemy, because the notion of 'enemy' required the supposition of intent, of directed sentience, but rather something dumb and non-negotiable, space debris or a marauding chunk of primeval rock and ice, sailing too close for comfort.

It took Geoffrey a moment to interpret Arethusa's statement. There were no pirates. But there were *proximal impact ranging and target eradication systems*, and in English the acronym was precisely the word

356

Arethusa had uttered. Guns, basically, but rigorously fail-safed, incapable of being directed at anything other than a real, imminent collision hazard.

Non-weapons.

They had stood down upon Hector's approach, but they had not shown the *Kinyeti* the same courtesy. A moment after he grasped what was happening, Geoffrey saw the flowering of multiple impact points along the *Kinyeti*'s hull, attended by puffs of sudden silver brightness as metal and ceramics underwent instantaneous vaporisation. The best the pirates could do was subject her to a continuous disruptive assault, aiming to break up her mass into smaller parts that could be individually bulldozed out of harm's way using further kinetic-energy volleys.

Most of the ship remained. One of her centrifuge arms had been ripped loose, cartwheeling away on its own new orbit, and all up and down her hull lay a peppering of craters and voids where she had been struck. One of her fuel tanks had been punctured and was now venting furiously, while there was evidence of systemic pressure loss from three or four rupture points in the forward module. The view was clouded by the debris and gases expanding away from the ship itself, cloaking her injuries.

But she wasn't dead. They knew this when a second stutter of heat and light signalled the *Kinyeti* deploying her own anti-collision systems, this time in a coordinated strike against the habitat. Quite what the legality of that action was, Geoffrey couldn't begin to guess: the number of instances of ships being attacked by other ships, or stations by ships, or vice versa, was surely so small that there could be little or no precedent for it in modern law. That the *Kinyeti* was protecting herself was beyond dispute, but equally, her crew must have realised that the habitat would not permit a closer approach, and that their actions were provocative.

From the *Quaynor*, all they could do was watch, transfixed, as the conflict ran its course. The *Kinyeti*'s assault had taken out the visible pirate emplacements ringed around either end of the Winter Palace. But the Winter Palace was rotating, and her slow spin brought undamaged emplacements into view. The Palace fired again, blasting another fuel tank, nearly severing the main axis and doing further harm to the command module at the ship's front. The gas cloud thickened to grey-white smog. The *Kinyeti* retaliated, less convincingly this time, as if portions of her own defence systems had been damaged or rendered inoperable. Blast sites pockmarked the Winter Palace – some landing far from the endcaps, cratering the unmarked skin of the cylinder, punching so far into insulation that they might have touched the bedrock of

Eunice's private hothouse. The Winter Palace kept spinning, as heavy and oblivious as a grindstone. More pirates revolved into view and rained hell on the Akinya craft. There was a sputter of retaliation, then nothing.

The Winter Palace, largely undamaged even now, maintained its spin as the debris/gas cloud slowly dispersed away from the wreck of the *Kinyeti*. The tattered, broken-backed mining ship was still moving, still on an approach vector for the habitat.

No further attacks were forthcoming.

'OK, would someone be so good as to clue me in on *what the fuck just happened*?' Jumai asked, doubtless rhetorically.

'Hector must have called for help, or he was late checking in,' Geoffrey said. 'Somewhere between his arrival and the point where it fired on the *Kinyeti*, the Winter Palace must have changed its mind about him being welcome.' He sounded awed and appalled even to himself, not quite able to process what he had just witnessed.

'There could still be survivors,' Gilbert said. 'I'm trying to establish direct comms. Resuming aug reach: we don't have much to lose now, and it may be our only way of establishing a path to the *Kinyeti*.' The merwoman paused, rapt with concentration. 'Oh, wait – here's something. General distress signal, point of origin *Kinyeti*. She's calling for assistance.'

'Can you patch me through?' Geoffrey asked.

'No idea if they can still hear, but you can try. Speak when ready.'

He coughed to clear his throat. 'This is Geoffrey Akinya, calling the *Kinyeti*. We saw what just happened to you. What is your status, and how may we assist?'

The reply came through on voice-only comms, sounding as if it had been broken up, scrambled and only partially reassembled. 'This is Captain Dos Santos ... Akinya Space mining vehicle *Kinyeti*. We have sustained damage to critical systems ... life support ... inoperable.' It was a man's voice, speaking Swahili at source. 'We can't steer and we have no delta-vee capability. Our emergency escape vehicle is detached.'

'They're screwed,' Eunice said.

'We saw the departure,' Geoffrey said, trying to tune out the construct but not wishing to de-voke her completely. 'I presume Hector took the vehicle?'

'I ...' Captain Dos Santos hesitated. Geoffrey could imagine him wondering how much he was at licence to disclose. 'Yes. Of course.'

'I'm Hector's cousin, if you didn't already know.' Geoffrey glanced at one of Gilbert's readouts, trusting that he was interpreting it correctly.

'It doesn't look as if you're going to smash into the Winter Palace now – your vector puts you passing close to the docking hub but avoiding an actual collision. That's lucky.'

'They must have vented enough gas to push them off course,' Eunice said. 'But they're still at risk from my guns.'

'They're your guns, you turn them off,' Jumai said.

'I can't, dear.'

'We don't know how many of the Winter Palace's guns are still operable,' Geoffrey said, cutting over the construct, 'and I doubt your information is any better than ours.'

'No, probably not.' The captain allowed himself a quiet, resigned laugh. 'What do you suggest, Mister Akinya?'

'We can't risk endangering this ship until you're out of immediate range of the Winter Palace,' Geoffrey said. 'Once we're satisfied that those guns won't be turned on us, we'll close in for docking. You'll have to ride things out until then. How many of you are there?'

'Eight,' Dos Santos answered. Comms had stabilised now: his voice was coming through much more clearly, and without dropouts. 'That's the regular crew, myself included.'

'We can easily take eight survivors,' Gilbert said. 'It won't overburden our life support, and at most we'll only need to hold them for a few hours before UON or Lunar authorities arrive.'

'There's also Hector,' the captain added.

'I was about to ask,' Geoffrey said.

'Hector was supposed to return on his own – we were never meant to get that close. Then he signalled for help.'

'He needed technical assistance?'

'Rescuing. Beyond that, I can't tell you anything. We think he may have been hurt, but that's just guesswork – we were on voice-only, no ching, and no biomed feed from his suit.' Dos Santos grunted: either effort or pain, it was impossible to tell which. 'But he wouldn't have called us unless there was a problem.'

'OK.' Geoffrey drew a breath, giving himself the space to collect his thoughts. 'Are you in suits, Captain?'

'Getting into them as we speak. Afterwards, we'll crawl into our storm cellar. That's the best armoured part of the *Kinyeti*. Should be able to ride out the worst of it in there, even full depressurisation.'

'Whatever happens, help is on its way. I'm sorry you were dragged into this.'

'We did what we were asked to do,' Dos Santos replied. 'That's all.'

'Good luck, Captain.'

'Same to you, Mister Akinya.'

Dos Santos signed off. Geoffrey remained silent for a few moments, wishing it did not fall on him to say what was surely on all their minds. 'We can't leave him there,' he said quietly. 'But at the same time, we can't endanger the *Quaynor*. We also have a duty of care to the *Kinyeti's* survivors.'

'If they make it through the close approach, they'll have nothing to fear,' Arethusa said. 'Mira said it herself: the authorities will already have been alerted to the attack, and they'll be on their way very shortly indeed. In a few hours, maybe less, this volume of space will be crawling with enforcement and rescue services.'

'I'm just as concerned for your safety,' Geoffrey said.

'If I'd wanted to be cocooned, I'd never have left Tiamaat,' the old aquatic answered. 'We have an advantage over the *Kinyeti*, anyway – we still have power and steering. Mira, I want you to take us all the way in, to the airlock we originally agreed to use, but in such a way that you minimise our exposure to those pirate emplacements which we suspect may still be operational. Can you do that?'

'I ...' Gilbert's hands danced on the keypads. 'I think so. Possibly. Whether the ship'll take it, I don't know. We'll be stress-loading her to the max, to match the habitat's spin.'

'They build safety margins into these things,' Arethusa answered.

'And I've allowed for the margins,' Gilbert said.

'Let me look at this,' Eunice said. 'I may be able to help.'

'Are you serious?' Geoffrey asked.

'Totally. Voke me active ching privilege. I need to drive your body.'

'No,' he said, even before he'd begun to consider the implications of her request.

'You think nothing of chinging into a golem when the mood suits you. Nor would you object if another person wished to drive your body as a warmblood proxy. Why does my request offend you so very deeply?'

He was about to say: *Because you're dead, and you were my grandmother*, but he stopped himself in time. The construct was a pattern of self-evolving data, nothing more. It embodied knowledge and certain useful skill-sets. That it just happened to manifest with the body and voice of his late relative was totally immaterial.

So he told himself.

'I don't know if Eunice can do a better job than any of us at flying this thing,' he told the others. 'What she thinks she can do and what she can really do are not the same things.'

'I flew ships like this before you were a glint in your mother's eye,' Eunice said. 'The avionics, the interfaces ... they're as ancient and old-fashioned as me.'

'If she can do this—' Jumai said.

'We should use all available assets,' Arethusa concurred. 'Mira, if you don't like what's happening, you can revoke Geoffrey's command privilege at any time, can't you?'

Gilbert gave the merwoman equivalent of a shrug. 'More or less.'

'I'll accept the consequences. Geoffrey – I can't force you to do this, but you have my consent to fly the *Quaynor*. If Eunice is able to help with that, so much the better.'

'You must do this,' Eunice said. Her tone turned needling. 'You let *elephants* into your head, grandson. Surely you can make an exception for me.'

'Give me the controls,' he said, popping his knuckles, spreading his fingers, loosening his shoulder muscles, just as if he was readying himself for an hour in the Cessna. 'Eunice – I'm letting you in. You know I can kick you out at any time, so don't overstay your welcome.'

'As if I'd ever do that.'

He voked the rarely given command, the one that assigned full voluntary control of his own body to another intelligence. There was nothing magical about it; it was merely an inversion of the usual ching protocols: nerve impulses running one way rather than the other, sensory flow leaving his head rather than entering it.

Still it was strange for him. People did this sort of thing all the time, hiring out their bodies as warmblood proxies. He'd never had cause to ching into a warmblood himself – but if the situation had demanded it, and there'd been no other choice, he supposed he'd have accepted the arrangement without complaint. But the other way round: to *be* the warmblood? Never in a million years.

And here he was being driven by his grandmother.

She stole his eyes first. Between one moment and the next, they weren't looking where he wanted, but where she needed to see – and her intake of visual information was so efficient that it felt as if he had gone into a kind of quivering optic seizure, his eyeballs jerking this way and that in the manner of REM sleep. Then she took his hands. They started moving on the fold-out keypads, rap-tapping commands into the *Quaynor*'s avionics. It felt, for an instant, as if his hands were stuffed into enchanted gloves that forced his fingers to dance.

Then she stole his voice. It still sounded like him: she could make him speak, but she couldn't alter the basic properties of his larynx.

'I have an approach solution. It's imperfect, and it will still expose us to the Winter Palace's countermeasures. If we were to attempt to match her spin precisely, we'd break up inside sixty seconds. This is a compromise that gets us to the dock and minimises our likelihood of suffering catastrophic damage. I will assume control all the way in, and make any necessary adjustments as we go. Do I have authorisation?'

'Do you need it?' Gilbert asked.

'I thought it best to ask first, child.'

'Do it,' Arethusa said.

The acceleration came without warning, without a cushioning transition from zero-gee. To his horror and wonderment, Geoffrey realised that he could hear the engines, even in vacuum. They had been cranked up so high that something of their output, some phantom of undamped vibration, was propagating through the chassis of the ship, despite all the intervening layers of insulation and shockproofing. It sounded like a landslide or a stampede and it made him very, very nervous. Red lights started flashing, master caution alarms sounding. The *Quaynor* was registering indignant objection to the punishment it was now enduring.

It had served its human masters well. Why were they putting it through this?

'She's holding,' Eunice announced, through Geoffrey's throat. 'But that was the easy bit.'

The *Quaynor* had to execute a curving trajectory to match, or even come close to matching, the Winter Palace's spin. In the Cessna, it would have needed nothing more than a modest application of stick and rudder. But curvature was acceleration, and in vacuum that could only be achieved by thrust, directed at an angle to the ship's momentary vector. The magnetoplasma engines could not be gimballed, and therefore the *Quaynor* was forced to use auxiliary steering and manoeuvring rockets, pushed to their limits. Under such a load, the possibility of buckling was a very real risk. Geoffrey needed no sensors or master-caution alarms to tell him that. He could feel it in the push of his bones against his restraints, the creaks and groans from his surroundings.

When something clanged against the hull he assumed it was the resumption of the Winter Palace's attack, but no: it was just a speck of debris from the wreckage of the *Kinyeti*. More came, in drumming volleys, and then they were through the thickest part of it. The acceleration and steering thrust intensified and abated in savage jerks as Eunice finessed her approach solution. They were very close now, fewer than a dozen kilometres from the station, and the extent of its damage – or lack of it – was becoming much clearer. A fraction, maybe one in five, of the pirate devices appeared unharmed. They wheeled slowly into view and then slowly out of view again, like cabins in a Ferris wheel.

'Maybe we still have approach authorisation,' Jumai said.

Something hit them. There'd been no warning, and they were so close to the Winter Palace that even a kinetic-energy slug arrived almost instantaneously. The *Quaynor* shook, and kept shaking, as the energy of the impact whiplashed up and down her chassis. Two or three seconds later, the habitat scored another strike. In the neurotic jitter of his vision, Geoffrey caught Mira Gilbert studying a schematic: an outline of the ship with the damaged areas pulsing an angry red. He wanted to speak, wanted to ask how serious the injuries were, but Eunice still had him in her thrall.

Then it quietened – there were no more impacts – and just as miraculously the acceleration eased, smoothed, reduced to zero. They had transited the volume of maximum hazard.

The *Quaynor* gave one more creak, and then all was silent. Even the master-caution alarm had stopped blaring.

'We're clear,' Eunice said. 'My guns can't touch us now – there's a zone of avoidance around either docking pole, and we're well inside it. Normal approach and docking will be completed in ...' She made a show of hesitation, although the answer was surely known to her in advance. 'Thirty seconds. Please fold away your tray-tables and place your seats in the upright position. Thank you for flying with Akinya Space.'

'Why did you shoot at us?' Gilbert asked.

'That wasn't shooting. That was a reminder not to take anything for granted.' She made him let out a small, prideful sigh. 'Well, grandson – now that my work here is done, would you like your body back?'

His eyes stopped their jerky dance. He could speak again, and move his hands normally.

'You did well,' he said.

'You feel the need to compliment me?'

'It's what Sunday would do,' he said, addressing the now disembodied voice. 'That's all.'

Soon came a gentle clunk, followed by a quick sequenced drumroll of capture clamps, primed like the petals of some carnivorous plant to lock on to any vehicle that made it this far.

Geoffrey began to undo his restraints. It had been difficult, but they had docked with the Winter Palace.

Now all they had to do was go inside and see what had become of Hector.

CHAPTER TWENTY-NINE

There was darkness, an absence of experience, then dawning amber light, the primal stirrings of consciousness. Then there was a room, warm and golden and as bedecked with finery as the inside of any wealthy merchant's tent, in any desert caravan from the *Arabian Nights*.

And Sunday was awake, looking at herself.

A memory stirred: an error she would not make twice. It was not her own face looking down at her, but there were sufficient similarities that a blood relationship could not be denied. A woman's face, close enough to her own that they might have been sisters or cousins. And she had seen this woman before, behind layers of glass, in a landscape older than Africa.

Her mouth was dry, her lips gummed together. Nonetheless she managed a word.

'Soya.'

'Glad you remember me. You were both pretty cold by the time we reached you. Your suits only had a few hours of effective life support left in them.' Soya was dressed in a white blouse, draped with about a dozen necklaces, some hung with jewelled pendants, some with wooden charms. She was all skin and bones, lean and angular where Sunday (as she would readily admit) was padded and ample. They had genes in common, but they'd been raised on very different worlds. Soya's legs, in leather trousers with calf-length boots, were stupidly long and slender. She was taller than Sunday, and towered over her even more so now that Sunday was lying on her back, on a couch or bed in one corner of the room. It had curtains rather than walls. Incense smoked in candleholders. The air smelled of honey, cinnamon, baking bread.

'Jitendra?' she asked, forming his name in three distinct syllables, each of which cost her effort.

'He's well, don't worry.' Soya was pouring something into a glass. Bangles clashed against each other on her wrist, making a constant metallic hiss whenever she moved. 'You don't remember much about being rescued?'

'No,' Sunday said.

'But you know my name.'

'We've met before.'

'Yes, we did.' There was a note of reproach in that. 'And still you got into trouble with those people. Well, you can't say you weren't warned.' Soya leaned down and offered the glass to Sunday's lips. 'Drink this.'

The liquid was sugary and welcome. It rinsed some of the dryness from her mouth and throat; notched her one step closer to the living.

'I don't know who you are, Soya.' Sunday dredged a hard-won memory from the recent past. 'You told me you were born here, on Mars. You said something about Nigeria. We're still *on* Mars, aren't we?'

'You've only been out about thirteen hours. It's tomorrow.' Soya smiled at that, and the smile cut through Sunday. She'd seen it a million times, in her own reflection. Just not as much lately as she might have wished.

'And that's all I get? We're related, Soya. I've known that from the moment I first saw your face. And why would you make contact with me if it wasn't connected with my family?'

Soya smiled, but with less assurance than before. 'I know you want answers, but you've had a difficult couple of days and you should probably rest first.'

'You just told me I've been asleep since yesterday.'

'After nearly dying.'

Sunday took a leap into the void. The question was absurd on a number of levels, but she had to ask it. 'Are you . . . related to Eunice? Are you some granddaughter or grand-niece I never knew about?'

'No, I'm not related to her. I'd offer you a cell scraping, if you had a means of testing it.' Soya looked down, fiddling absently with the necklaces. 'But you and me, that's a different story. We do have a common ancestor. But it's not Eunice.'

Sunday pushed herself up from the couch. Heavy blankets slid away from her. She was wearing lime-green football shorts and a cheap yellow tourist T-shirt with an animated space elevator printed on the front. The logo said *Pontaniak*.

'Who, Soya?' The other woman had half a head on her, but she still took a step away, as if she hadn't anticipated a show of determination quite this valiant.

'Jonathan,' Soya said. And as if that was not enough – there was only one Jonathan in Sunday's firmament – Soya added, 'Beza. Eunice's husband. The man she came to Mars with.'

Sunday shook her head reflexively. 'Jonathan Beza died more than sixty years ago. Eunice and he had divorced by then. There was an accident, here on Mars. Some kind of pressure blow-out.'

'And that precludes me from being related to him?'

'He remarried before his death. He had more children, and some of them had children themselves. Nathan even came to the funeral, and I know about all the others. There's no Soya anywhere in that family tree.'

'In which case you're looking at the wrong tree.'

It had not been Soya who said that. This voice was deep and sonorous, varnished and craquelured. It spoke Swahili, but with an old-fashioned diction that called to mind nothing in Sunday's experience but Memphis Chibesa.

She turned to follow the voice to its origin. There, standing in a gash of the curtain – like an actor hesitating to join the stage – was the oldest man she had ever seen.

'I am Jonathan Beza,' the man said. 'I am your grandfather, Sunday Akinya. I was married to Eunice. And yes, I am very much alive.'

Jitendra was looking to her for guidance. She signalled with the slightest nod that yes, she believed this man to be exactly who he said he was. As absurd as that was to take in, after everything she had accepted in her life.

'It was easier to die then,' Jonathan Beza said. 'You must remember that this was a different Mars, a different time. Even now, as you've experienced, there are places on this world where a person can disappear very effectively. Or be made to disappear.' He stopped to pour chai for his daughter and their two guests.

'You mean there was never an accident?' Sunday asked.

'There was. The same sort of accident that still happens very occasionally nowadays. It was real, and I didn't engineer it in any way. I should hope not: good people died in it, after all.'

'But you saw your chance to vanish,' Jitendra said.

'The thought had been at the back of my mind for some time. The Mech was so primitive back then we didn't even call it the Mech. The few implants I carried were easily disabled, or fooled into giving false reports. When the opportunity to fall off the edge of the world presented itself, I took it.' He fixed his gaze on Sunday. 'Your grandmother didn't know. She wasn't complicit in this. She even came to my funeral.'

'That was when she returned to Phobos,' Sunday said.

'Yes.'

They were sitting in a different curtained room. Sunday still had no idea where they were, beyond Jonathan's assurance that it was still Mars. There was no aug reach, no Eunice. In their place was a noise like distant engines and the occasional bump or sway that led her to think she was in a vehicle.

A possibility had presented itself, but she'd dismissed it instantly.

'You found us in the Evolvarium,' Jitendra said. 'Have you any idea what we were doing there?'

Jonathan said, 'Dying?'

'Other than that,' Sunday said.

'Yes, I have a shrewd idea what you were doing. Better than a shrewd idea, actually.' He paused, apparently to collect himself, marshalling energies before proceeding. Jonathan was small, wiry, obviously immensely old but nowhere near as frail as Sunday might have expected for one of his age. He was even older than Eunice: she'd have queried the construct for his date of birth, if the construct had been reachable. Born 2020 or thereabouts, if not earlier. A man now in his hundred-and-forties. That made him old, but not impossibly so. He wore the inner layer of a spacesuit, a tight black garment sewn with coolant lines and studded with the gold-plated discs of biomonitor sockets. His arms were scrawny but there was still muscle tone there, and no trace of arthritis or neurodegenerative tremor in his fingers. Sunday had watched as he poured the chai; he hadn't spilt a drop. His head was mostly hairless, save for a corona of fine white fuzz around his scalp, his face abundantly wrinkled, the already dark skin mottled by pure black lesions, yet remaining startlingly expressive. His eyes were clear and focused, his smile alarmingly youthful.

'Then you'll know it was a waste of time,' Jitendra said.

'I know Dorcas cheated you. That may not amount to quite the same thing.'

'How much do you know?' Sunday asked, directing her question at Soya. 'You were in Crommelin. You must be registered as a citizen or tourist to be anywhere on Mars, so you can't have dropped off the map the way your father has.'

Jonathan answered for her. 'Soya has been my lifeline, Sunday. She has been able to move in the Surveilled World, be my eyes and ears. She has arranged medicine for me, on the few occasions when I have needed it.'

'I have a false history,' Soya said, looking at Sunday and Jitendra in turn. 'My connection to my father ... and by extension your grand-mother ... isn't part of that history.'

'You could never do such a thing on Earth, or any place where the Surveilled World is fully developed. On Mars, now, it would be difficult. It was easier when Soya was born.'

'How old are you?' Sunday asked.

'Fifty,' Soya said. 'Does that surprise you?'

'I don't suppose it should.'

'Eunice wasn't her mother,' Jonathan said, confirming what Soya had already told Sunday. 'There was a woman, an investigator. Her name was Lizbet. She had her doubts about my death, and she followed them to me.'

'I never heard about any investigation,' Sunday said.

'Lizbet decided not to go public with her story once she'd heard my side of things. She became my companion, and we had a daughter. We were happy. Lizbet died twenty years ago.'

'I'm sorry,' Sunday and Jitendra said in unison. Then, on her own, Sunday continued, 'And what was your side of the story, Jonathan? Why this secrecy? What persuaded Lizbet to keep it to herself?'

'I know why your grandmother came back to Mars. My funeral was a useful pretext, but she'd have found a way to do it whatever happened. She spent time on Phobos, more than she needed to. I don't know what she got up to there, but I presume whatever it was led you here?'

Sunday eyed Jitendra before proceeding. 'We've been following some-thing ever since she died. It began with an anomaly in her private banking files. That led us from Africa to the Moon. On the Moon my brother found something in a safe-deposit box. That led us to Pythagoras. What we found in Pythagoras led me to Phobos. Phobos led me to the Evolvarium.'

'And now to me,' Jonathan said.

'Except I didn't find you,' Sunday said. 'You found me. Soya knew I was on the planet: that's why she contacted me in Crommelin.'

'It was easy to track your arrival,' Soya said. 'Given the timing, there couldn't be any other reason why you'd come to Mars, other than to find out what your grandmother had buried here.'

'I failed,' Sunday said.

Jonathan braced his hands on his knees and rose from his chair. 'Do you have any idea where you are?'

'Somewhere out in the sticks, I'm guessing. A camp or station everyone assumes to be unoccupied. Probably quite near the Evolvarium, since

I doubt we travelled very far overnight.' She was careful not to voice her suspicion that they were moving.

'Not near,' Jonathan corrected, with a smile. 'In. We've never left it.'

It came back to her in disconnected glimpses, as of a dream forgotten until some chance association called it to mind, much later in the day. Jitendra had seen it first: that hill, a feature in the terrain that ought not to have been there, glimpsed from within their makeshift shelter as they waited for night and whatever it might bring. A hill that was approaching.

The Aggregate.

Not a hill, but a machine as large as a skyscraper, crunching slowly across the Evolvarium. Sunday remembered what she had learned regarding the Aggregate, aboard the Overfloater airship. It was not one machine, but a society of them. From the level of sifters to apex predators, they had organised in the interests of mutual reliance and interdependence. It was a stinging affront to the basic function of the Evolvarium. Whereas the other machines toiled and clashed and evolved, sparking off industrial novelties as a by-product of their struggle for survival, the Aggregate gave nothing back. Whatever it innovated, it kept to itself.

It had sent out an envoy to meet them. With that memory came the aftertaste of the fear they had both felt as they crouched in their makeshift shelter. The Aggregate's envoy was a quick-scuttling thing like an iron ant, black-armoured and as large as the rover whose wreckage they had repurposed. Even if their suits had been working at full capacity, they could never have outrun it. It had ripped away the petals of their shelter, flinging them to the winds, and loomed over them in all its eyeless belligerence. Its head was a blank metal sphere, its torso a pinch-waisted cylinder. In addition to its pistoning black legs it had whipping cilia. It had plucked them from the ground, not without a certain carelessness, and a red-lit aperture had opened in its belly.

After that, Sunday didn't remember very much.

Yet here they were, in the Aggregate. There was no need to take Jonathan Beza's word for that. From a high vantage point, the queen of her own castle, Sunday was looking down on the very machine she had assumed meant to have her crushed and recycled for useful materials.

It was motley. Hundreds of basic organisms had fused or locked together to form the structural outline of the Aggregate, and that didn't begin to touch the implied complexity of its interior. Not a skyscraper, then, for that conveyed entirely too much symmetry and orderliness.

The Aggregate was more like a city block, a dense-packed huddle of buildings constructed at different times and according to varying objectives and governing aesthetics. It was approximately pyramidal in shape, wide and flat at the base, rising in steps and pinnacles and buttresses to a sort of summit, but there was nothing geometric or harmonious about it. Sunday saw where some of the machines had fused into the main mass, like gargoyles on a cathedral. Others must have changed beyond all recognition, so that it was not easy to tell where one began and another ended, or what their original forms and locomotive principles must have been like. From here, looking down, she couldn't see how the Aggregate moved its colossal bulk. She presumed countless legs and feet were deployed under the flat base of the city, working in concert so that the ride was mostly smooth. Dust welled up constantly from the Aggregate's margins, stirred by whatever mechanisms toiled underneath it.

'No one ever mentioned anything about this thing being inhabited,' Sunday said. They were in a many-windowed cupola, a hundred or more metres above the ground.

'They don't know,' Jonathan said. 'No one does, except Soya and me. Maybe some of the Overfloaters suspect, but that's not the same thing as knowing and it's certainly not something they'll talk about in polite company. They can't tell for sure, from the outside. The glass is one-way, and with all the waste heat and chemistry a machine like the Aggregate radiates, there's no way of picking out the signatures of a couple of human occupants. Especially when the Aggregate doesn't *want* anyone to know about us.'

'So you're its prisoners?' she asked. But that didn't work: Soya clearly had free roam of Mars, and must have come back here of her own volition.

'No,' Jonathan said. 'I'm its client. The Aggregate benefits from a human consultant. That's really all I am to it: just another modular component it can depend on when the need arrives. It makes me comfortable – more than comfortable, actually – and it tolerates my absence when I'm not here.'

'It lets you come and go as you please?'

'We agreed terms. It would rather put up with that than have me kill myself. Needless to say, I can't go very far – that's one of the drawbacks of being dead. But I'm not a prisoner.'

'I'm finding all this a little difficult to take in. I've spent my whole life thinking you were dead.'

'I'm afraid there was no other way. The best that Soya could do was warn you to be on your guard against the Pans. It was obvious to us that they couldn't be trusted simply to let you walk away with the prize.'

'You knew they were planning to steal it?' Jitendra asked.

'No, but there was a strong possibility of that happening. Had this all taken place in the Surveilled World, there wouldn't have been much scope for treachery. But the Evolvarium gave them the perfect opportunity to commit an unwitnessed crime.'

'I witnessed it,' Sunday said.

Jonathan allowed a thin smile to play across his lips. 'You don't count.'

'We'll see about that, when I get back to Earth. They're going to find out that I'm still an Akinya, and bad things happen when you cross us.'

'Yes ...' Jonathan stretched the word, managing to sound less than entirely convinced by Sunday's statement. 'Funny how you're so keen to slip back into the fold the moment you're wronged. You've been running away from your family all these years, but the moment life throws something at you that you don't like ... you're straight back into the arms of the household, a good little Akinya with the family behind her.'

Sunday bristled, but said nothing.

'I don't blame you for that,' Jonathan continued, conveying entirely the opposite impression, 'but it would be unwise in the extreme to underestimate the Pans. They're not just a movement with a few ships and people. Behind the Initiative is the entire geopolitical armoury of the United Aquatic Nations. Take them on, you're taking on half the planet.'

'You've kept up with Earthside politics, then,' Sunday said, her tone sour.

'I may be dead, but I'm not a hermit.'

'Well, it's all for nothing anyway,' Jitendra said. 'We don't have a clue what was in that box, and we can't even prove they stole it. Without corroboration, the evidence of our eyes won't be admissible in any court. Whatever's in the box may mean nothing to them without Sunday's background knowledge of Eunice. That's assuming they ever gave a shit. Maybe all they wanted was for us not to get our hands on it. Well, they succeeded. We're all losers now.'

'The Overfloaters must have been surprised,' Jonathan said.

'Surprised by what?' Sunday asked, irritated and fatigued.

'That the object was still underground after so many years. Did they not express scepticism that it would still be there?'

'Dorcas said it was strange that the machines hadn't found it,' Jitendra said. 'But there it was.'

'Or rather, there it wasn't,' Jonathan said. 'Come, let's go back downstairs. I have something you might be interested in.'

CHAPTER THIRTY

'And there was I,' Jumai said, 'thinking maybe I'd get paid for nothing. Silly me. As if anything's ever that easy.'

'I didn't mean to raise any unrealistic expectations,' Geoffrey said.

They were moving side by side down the docking tube, brushing themselves along with fingertip pressure against the rough-textured walling.

'Look at it this way, though,' he went on. 'You're hoping this is going to do wonders for your reputation. Wouldn't work if it turned out to be too easy, would it?'

'Fuck my reputation. Right now I'll settle for easy.'

They had matched the habitat's spin in the moments before docking, but as they traversed the connecting tube Geoffrey still felt weightless, albeit with the sensation that the world was tumbling slowly around him. The docking tube was aligned with the Winter Palace's axis of rotation, and he would therefore need to travel a lot further out before he felt anything resembling a normal gravitational pull. But even in the absence of visual cues that spin was impossible to ignore.

They were wearing spacesuits, of course: lightweight, hypermodern, form-fitting models from the *Quaynor*'s own equipment stores. Like the submarine harness in Tiamaat, Geoffrey's suit had put itself on around him, splitting open, encasing him from head to toe and reassembling along a dozen improbable seams that were now completely invisible and airtight. Technology had come a long way since Eunice's ancient gauntlet-like moonglove was state of the art.

Mira Gilbert's mobility harness was not optimised for weightlessness, and since the station was presently denying aug reach, there was no way for Arethusa to ching a proxy. Given that someone had to physically enter the Palace to locate Hector, Geoffrey was glad it was just the two of them. Arethusa would want to know what they found, and she would ching aboard as soon as that became feasible, but for now the Pans would have to be patient. Even Eunice couldn't stick her oar in.

They had passed without incident through the connected airlocks of the *Quaynor* and the Winter Palace, but now they came to the first obstruction: an internal door, armoured against pressure loss, blocked their progress. It was circular, cartwheeled with heavy bee-striped reinforcing struts. The manual control had no effect, and the door was certainly too large to force.

'I keep having to remind myself, Hector didn't come this way,' Geoffrey said. 'For all we know, this door hasn't been opened in years.'

'Give me a minute,' Jumai answered. 'I've cracked data vaults that haven't been opened in a century. This is just warm-up stuff.'

Jumai had spent her time on the *Quaynor* profitably, packing a holdall full of anything she deemed useful. Now she rummaged through the bag's weightless guts, pushing aside intestinal spools of data cables and stick-on sensor pads. She came out with a chunky rectangle of black plastic, geckoed it to the side of the door, over the operating panel, and connected a grey cable into her suit's forearm.

She tapped a panel on the forearm, which sprang open to form a surprisingly large keypad and screen. The suits might be modern, but they'd been customised according to Pan specifications, which meant physical readouts and data-entry options.

'What's the story?' Geoffrey ventured, when she'd been tapping keys and pursing her lips at scrolling numbers for several minutes.

'The story is . . . we're in.'

She tapped one last key, ripped the stick-on pad away from the panel. The door wheeled aside, recessing into a slot in the sidewall. The door's bare metal edges were toothed like a cogwheel.

'It was that easy?'

'Easier than it looked. Wanted to make absolutely sure there was nothing nasty beyond the door, like fire or vacuum or sarin nerve gas.'

'We're in suits.'

'I like additional guarantees.' Jumai packed her equipment away and sealed the holdall. 'No second chances in this line of work. Learned that in Lagos.'

They called back to the *Quaynor*, told them that they were passing through the door. There was still no aug reach, but for the moment simple comms were getting through.

'We've reached a right-angled bend,' Jumai reported. 'It's the only way forward. Looks like it runs all the way back out to the skin.'

'That makes sense,' Geoffrey said. 'The *Winter Queen* fills the middle of the habitat, and her engines and aerobrake would block our progress if we tried to pass along the axis of rotation. We have to go up to move

374

forward. Hector would have hit the same dead end coming in from his side.'

'Assuming he got this far,' Jumai said.

'He was inside this thing for a while before calling for help.'

They started moving along the radial shaft. It was wide and set with multiple hand- and footholds, and to begin with there was no sense that they were climbing either up or down. But every metre took them further from the axis, thereby increasing the tug of centrifugal gravity, tending to push them still further from the axis. For a while, it was easy and pleasant to drift, but there came a point when it took more effort than anticipated to arrest his motion. In that moment Geoffrey's inner ear decided, forcefully, that his local universe now contained a very definite up and down, and that he was suspended the wrong way up in what appeared to be an infinitely deep, plunging lift shaft.

Vertigo gripped him. He caught his breath and closed his eyes.

'Easy,' Jumai said.

He forced his eyes open. 'Has to be a better way.'

'Probably is, if we'd come in through the other lock. Can't see many people putting up with this shit. Then again, did your grandmother get many visitors?'

'No,' he answered, as with great care he inverted himself so that the force of gravity was acting in the direction of his feet, not his head. 'Just Memphis, and even then not very often.'

'Take it one rung at a time, and don't look down any more than you have to.'

'We'll never get Hector back up this shaft if he's hurt.'

'Comes to that, we'll call for help from the *Quaynor*. They can lower us a rope, or use the ship's thrusters to take some of the spin off the habitat.'

'Anyone would think you'd done this a million times.'

'It's all just breaking and entering.' He could imagine Jumai grinning. 'Used to delude myself that there was something in my brain, some developmental flaw which might mean I was predisposed to criminality. Wouldn't that be glamorous? But I was wrong. The scans came back and I'm ... almost tediously normal. Not a single brain module out of place or underdeveloped. I just happen to be more than averagely competent at breaking into things.'

Geoffrey forced a smile of his own. He might not have dragged Jumai out of Lagos – she'd quit of her own accord – but he couldn't deny that there had been a large measure of self-interest. However it had worked out, it was good to have her back in his life.

By turns, and his vertigo notwithstanding, he found a steady descending rhythm, always ensuring that he had three points of contact with the wall. The suit might well protect him in the event of a fall, but he had no desire to put that to the test.

When at last they reached the 'floor', they'd come – by the suit's estimation – a total of seventy-five vertical metres. Ambient gravity was now one gee, or as close as made no difference, and since the Winter Palace was only a little wider than one hundred and fifty metres across, they must be very close to the interior surface of its insulating skin. In the restricted space at the base of the shaft, Geoffrey could do little more than walk a few paces in either direction before he reached an obstructing wall or door. The gravity felt convincing enough in terms of the effort required and the load on his joints, but his inner ear insisted that something wasn't quite right.

Jumai was already tackling the door that was their only point of ingress into the rest of the habitat. It looked similar to the one they'd already come through, but when more than a few minutes had elapsed without her managing to open it, Geoffrey guessed that this door presented additional challenges.

'You think there's something bad on the other side?' he asked, hardly daring to break her concentration but not able to stop himself.

'There's pressure,' she said quietly. 'And unless these telltales are lying, it's not nerve gas or a wall of fire. That's not the problem, I'm afraid.'

'So what is?'

'Door's interlocked with the one back up the shaft. Give me a day, and more equipment than we came with, and I might be able to bypass that interlocking mechanism. But right now, and with this equipment, I won't be able to get us through this one without closing the other.'

'And thereby cutting off contact with the *Quaynor*.'

'Give the man a cigar.'

Geoffrey thought about this before answering. He didn't like it, and he doubted Jumai liked it either, but they had come a long way to turn back now. 'Have you ever been in a situation similar to this, in Lagos, or anywhere else you did contract work?'

'Crazy question if you were asking anyone else, but ... yes. Once or twice. Some of those server farms were designed by seriously paranoid arseholes.'

'And you still went through.'

'Had a job to do.'

'So your judgement was correct, in the moment. You made a decision ... and it paid off.'

'Wouldn't be having this conversation otherwise. I mean, I'm not saying I'd be dead, exactly, but sure as hell I wouldn't still be in this line of work.'

'In which case ... I think you should open that door.'

Jumai's hand was poised over the flip-out keypad on her sleeve forearm. 'Let's be clear about one thing, rich boy. No guarantees about what we'll find on the other side, or how the door mechanism will look to me then. Might not be as easy to retrace as it was to come this far.'

'Whatever it takes.'

After they had spoken to the *Quaynor*, Jumai said, 'You grown balls of steel all of a sudden?'

'Guess it's just dawning on me – I've burnt too many bridges to start having second thoughts now.' He knuckled his fist against the chest plate of the suit. 'Fuck it all. I'm Geoffrey Akinya. This is my grandmother's house. And I have every damned right to see what's inside it.'

'Hell, yeah,' Jumai said.

And tapped the keypad.

CHAPTER THIRTY-ONE

Jonathan Beza whipped the blanket free with a magicianly flourish, beaming at Sunday as if this was a moment he had been planning for years.

The blanket had concealed a box. It was, superficially, much like the box that Gribelin's proxy had unearthed the day before: the same dimensions, the same grey alloy casing. It looked older, though. Sunday couldn't put her finger on exactly why that should be so, but she knew she was looking at something that had been locked and buried a long time ago. The dents and scratches had provenance.

'I don't understand,' she said.

'Eunice came back for my funeral,' Jonathan said. 'This we know. But she didn't just come back for that. I ... followed her.' He hesitated, looking aside as if there was shame in what he had done. 'At a distance, obviously, and I don't think she ever suspected anything. It wasn't difficult to track her movements, and there was no Evolvarium then. I traced her return to her old landing site, near Pavonis Mons – the burial spot.'

'You saw her bury the box?' Sunday asked.

He shook his head firmly. 'No – I couldn't get that close, not without making my presence known. But when she'd gone, there was nothing to stop me returning to the landing site. I gave it a year or two, just to let the dust settle. Part of me worried that the whole thing was a trap to flush me out.'

'But it wasn't.'

'No,' he agreed. 'As much as it pains me, I think I was the last thing on her mind by then. Even my funeral ... it suited her to come back to attend it, but maybe she already had other plans ...' He trailed off. 'Perhaps you'd better open the box.'

'Do you know what's in it?' Jitendra asked.

'Yes, and it's perfectly safe. But it won't talk to me.'

As Sunday worked the catches at the side of the box, she said, 'I still don't get it. The box Dorcas stole – where did that one come from?'

'Oh, that,' Jonathan said, as if this was a detail he had nearly allowed to slip his mind. 'I put that there, obviously. I knew that the real box was meant for someone to find, someone connected to the family. For sixty years, no one came. Then Eunice's death was announced, and less than four months later her granddaughter shows up on Mars.' He touched his fingers to his chin, as if mulling a difficult problem. 'Hm. I wonder if those two things might possibly be connected?'

'I was keeping an eye on things for him,' Soya said. 'When it became clear that you intended to enter the Evolvarium, there was no doubt that you'd come for the box.'

'While Soya was meeting you in Crommelin,' Jonathan said, 'I was out there burying the decoy box. No one saw me do it. With the machines sniffing around, it wouldn't stand a chance of going undetected for more than a few weeks. But we didn't need that long, just the few days it would take you to cross Mars and reach the burial site.'

'It was good that I warned you that the Pans couldn't necessarily be trusted,' Soya said. 'It meant that you understood the situation the moment Dorcas turned on you. From what we can gather, you played your parts very well indeed. Dorcas never had the slightest idea that she'd been duped.'

'She got the wrong box,' Jitendra said, marvellingly.

'And left you to the mercy of the Evolvarium,' Soya added. 'She cut a lot of deals to make that snatch. Frankly, no one will be shedding any tears if the other Overfloaters rip the *Lady Disdain* to shreds.'

Sunday had finally succeeded in opening the catches. She eased back the lid, the hinges stiff but manageable. She wasn't sure what to expect this time. There had been a smaller box inside the decoy, but perhaps the point of that had just been to delay the Overfloaters. Inside this box she found a dense matrix of foam packing, and a rounded object poking through the top of the packing.

'Take it out,' Jonathan said. 'It won't bite.'

She understood the significance of his comment as she withdrew the ancient space helmet from the box. Even in Martian gravity it was heavy in her hands: like something forged from iron or cut from solid marble. She had never handled a helmet quite so antiquated.

But she had seen it before.

Vivid paintwork covered the helmet: slashes of yellow, gold and black, daubs of white and red around the visor's rim. The paintwork had chipped to reveal bare metal in places, was scuffed and dirty elsewhere, but the design was still clear. It was a fierce blue-eyed lioness, her mouth gaping wide around the faceplate.

'Senge Dongma,' Sunday said, in reverence and awe. 'The lion-faced one. This is Eunice's actual helmet.'

'Knew you'd recognise it,' Jonathan said.

Sunday bit back the admission that she would have recognised nothing were it not for the construct. 'I ... saw an image of it on Phobos,' she said. 'Very recently. Was this really hers?'

'This is what she buried. It's been in my care ever since.'

She turned the helmet around in her hands, wheeling it like a globe, cradling history between her fingertips. In forced exile from her own family, Sunday had handled remarkably few artefacts with a direct link to her grandmother. This helmet, had it been back in the household museum, would have been one of the most hallowed relics.

'This is all there was?' she asked. 'Nothing else with it?'

'Were you expecting more?' Jonathan responded.

'It *is* just a helmet. The other things we've found pointed to something – another burial. This doesn't.'

'You're sure of that?' he asked.

'It doesn't take me any further than Mars. I know she had this helmet when she was on Phobos, so she would have brought it down to Mars when the dust storm cleared. But we're on Mars already. It's a dead end.'

'Unless you're missing something,' Jonathan said.

'It's not just a helmet,' Jitendra said, 'is it? I mean, it *is* a helmet, but that doesn't mean it's just a lump of metal and plastic. There's computing power inside it. It will have seen and recorded things, while she was using it.'

She looked at Jonathan. 'Have you investigated that?'

'The helmet is old,' Jonathan said, 'but from a mechanical standpoint there's nothing wrong with it. It doesn't have an internal power supply of its own, though. It will only work when it's connected to a suit, via a compatible neck ring.'

'Tell her,' Soya said.

Jonathan shot his daughter a tolerant smile. 'The suit could be anywhere, if it still exists. Eunice only left the helmet here, at this particular burial site. But it doesn't have to be the same suit to make the helmet work. It just has to fit.'

'You'd still have to find an old suit,' Jitendra said.

'That's what antiques markets are for,' Soya said, with a glimmer of pride. 'It took me a long, long time, but I found one in the end, not far from Lowell. Not as old as the helmet, only about seventy years, but with the same coupling.' She whisked aside one of the room's curtains, revealing an old-fashioned composite shell spacesuit, olive drab and grey, with evidence of damage and repair all over it. The suit was complete from the neck ring down, hanging from a rack that had been bolted to the metal innards of the Aggregate. 'It's a piece of shit,' Soya explained. 'You'd trust your life to this thing only if it was the absolute last resort. But it can still juice the helmet.'

Sunday asked the obvious question. 'Have either of you tried it on?'

'Both of us,' Jonathan answered. 'Some kind of low-level sphinxware running inside it. Beyond a few gatekeeper questions, it won't talk to either of us. But it might work for you.'

There was no part of getting into that musty old suit that Sunday could be said to have enjoyed. The suit was a poor fit in all the critical places (it felt as if it had been tailored for a portly child, not a woman) and being seventy years old, it did nothing to assist in the process of being worn. Without the complicity of Jitendra, Jonathan and Soya, she doubted she would have been able to put the hideous old thing on at all. Conversely, without them there, she probably wouldn't have had the nerve to keep trying. Each component of the suit, as it clicked into place, added to her sense of imprisonment and paralysis.

The suit was not functioning, in any accepted sense of the word. Its motive power-assist was dead, so it required all of Sunday's strength and determination to move it even slightly. The best she could manage was a ghoulish, mummylike shuffle, and the effort of that would soon tax her to exhaustion. Not that she could go very far anyway. Its cooling and air-recirculation systems were only barely operative, so it was as hot and stuffy as the inside of a sleeping bag. It had no independent internal power supply, but needed to be connected to the Aggregate by an energy umbilical. Only then could the suit feed power to the helmet, which had to be locked into place before it would boot-up and function. Sunday felt ready to be buried. The air circulator huffed and wheezed like an asthmatic dog. Caution indicators, blocked in red, were already illuminating the faceplate head-up display. Even before it had fully booted, the helmet knew that it was plugged into a piece of barely safe garbage, and it wasn't too happy about it.

'The current user is not recognised,' the helmet said, its waspish buzzing into her ears in Swahili. 'Please identify yourself.'

With an assertiveness that rather surprised herself, she declared, 'I am Sunday Akinya.'

The helmet went quiet for a few seconds, as if it was thinking things over. 'Please state your relationship to Eunice Akinya.'

'I'm her granddaughter. I've come to Mars for this helmet. Please recognise my authority to wear it.'

'What brought you to Mars?'

She had to think about that, sensing that the suit might be looking for a very specific answer. 'Something I found in Phobos,' she said, cautiously.

'What did you find in Phobos?'

'A painting.' She took a breath, feeling sweat prickle her forehead. 'A mural. There was a mistake ... an alteration. The peacock should have been a different bird. A crane, maybe an ibis.'

'What brought you to Phobos?'

Had she passed the first test, or merely skipped to the next question having failed the first one? The suit gave no clue. 'Pages from a book,' Sunday said, swallowing hard. '*Gulliver's Travels*. It was a clear reference to the moons of Mars, and Eunice had only ever spent time on Phobos, so that had to be the right moon.' Through the helmet glass, which was beginning to mist up, Jitendra and the others were watching her with avid interest. They were ready to spring to her aid should something go wrong with the life-support system, but knowing that didn't alleviate Sunday's sense of confinement. 'I found the pages on the Moon – Earth's Moon,' she added. 'In the crater Pythagoras.'

'What led you to Pythagoras?'

'A glove, which we found in a safe-deposit box, also on the Moon. The glove used to belong to Eunice Akinya. There were ... gems in the glove. Plastic gems, three different colours. The numbers corresponded to a Pythagorean triple. Knowing Eunice's history, we were able to pinpoint a crash site in the crater.' She felt as if she was going to faint. 'That's all I've got. The existence of the safe-deposit box came from an audit of Eunice's affairs, after her death.'

'What was the significance of the coloured gems?'

'The colours had ... no significance.' But why would the helmet have asked her that if the answer was so simple? 'Except they had to be different colours so that we could count them.'

That was what Jitendra had said, at least – and she'd been more than ready to accept that explanation. But the gems had been stuffed into different fingers. Given the care they'd taken with the examination, they'd have been unlikely to muddle them up.

'You have failed to pass all security questions,' the helmet said. 'Nonetheless, you are recognised as having the necessary authority. Please wait.'

'Please wait for what?'

'Please wait.'

Even through the fogging glass, Jitendra must have seen the doubt in her eyes. He pushed his face close to the visor. 'What's happening?' he asked, voice muffled as if many rooms away.

'It asked me a bunch of questions!' she shouted back, making herself feel lighter-headed in the process. 'I failed at least one of them, but it's accepting me anyway. Can you crank up the cooling on this thing? It's like a Turkish bath in here.'

Jitendra and Jonathan exchanged words. Soya nodded and went to one side, out of Sunday's field of view. A moment later she felt knocking and tapping as Soya fiddled with the suit's backpack.

The faceplate continued to fog over, even as the air grew fractionally cooler than it had been before. Sunday wondered whether it was better to close her eyes than confront that misted-over glass only centimetres from her nose and mouth.

Then the mist began to clear. But just when the condensation had shrunk back almost completely around the faceplate's borders, it greyed over again. Sunday was about to call out to Jitendra when she realised the greyness wasn't more condensation; rather it had been caused by the head-up display obstructing her entire forward view. The head-up view was changing now, but the image that resolved wasn't the room inside the Aggregate.

What she could see was a broken aeroplane.

It lay upside down, snapped wings scissored across its fuselage. Dust had gathered in its lee. The plane slumped on the crest of a gently sloping ridge, bone-white against a horizon of darkening butterscotch. More dust spilt from the ruptured eye of its bubble canopy. Sunday thought of her brother, that this was some dire vision of the Cessna, crashed and upended. But this was not Geoffrey's aircraft.

To the right of the wreck, a hundred paces further up the shallow incline, sat a squat compound of pressure-tight huts. The huts' rib-sided shells had been scoured to a grey metal sheen by dust storms. Dust had also built up in their wind-shadows. Faded almost to illegibility was a hammer-and-sickle flag. A wind gauge, its cups as large as washbasins, whirred atop the roof of the largest hut.

Sunday found her point of view moving towards the aircraft. Acting independently of her volition, her line of sight dipped as if she was kneeling to peer into the inverted bulge of the shattered canopy. The seat was upside down, the buckled harness dangling open where it had been released. The cockpit was empty.

Her point of view turned from the aircraft, again without her direction, and approached the cluster of huts. The significance of the weather station and the smashed aeroplane was unavoidable. It was here, on the slopes of Pavonis Mons, that Eunice had landed and then sought shelter during a particularly ferocious storm. The plane had been intact when she brought it down, but had subsequently been plucked from its moorings by the winds, upended and crushed like a paper toy.

The station and the plane were gone now, but the documented fact of this episode had been the only thing pointing to a specific part of the terrain around the Martian volcano. Sunday already knew this. She could not have found the helmet without already making this connection.

So what did Eunice want with her now?

Metal steps, the lower treads buried in dust, led to the airlock in the largest of the Russian huts. The outer door and its interior counterpart were both open. Sunday's point of view ascended the steps.

Inside, it was brightly lit and wrong: physics and common sense were in dreamlike abeyance. It was not the interior of a Russian weather station on Mars but an annexe of the household. The light blazed in through square, thick-walled windows at a steep slant. It fell on recognisable furniture: chairs and tables, rugs and hangings, white-plastered walls. There were ornaments on the tables, dust-glints trembling in the air. In place of one wall, silk curtains billowed. Sunday would have been drawn to the curtains even if she'd had control of the suit's point of view.

A gloved hand reached out and parted the curtains. She pushed on through.

Outside it was Africa.

It was somewhere near dusk, some season when the skies held an abundance of clouds, gaudy with underlit colours: salmon-pink, vermilion, rare shades of rose and tangerine. Between the clouds, improbably, the slashes of clear sky were luminous cobalt. The trees, darkly silhouetted, reminded her of toy-theatre cut-outs.

The view tracked around. Kilimanjaro slid into sight, snowless. The household, blue-tiled and white-plastered, the walls reflecting sky in a hundred pastel combinations. A flight of cranes, like birds in a Chinese watercolour.

A stand of trees, more solid and real-looking than the silhouettes. Her point of view commenced towards that place of shelter. And the woman who had been leaning with her back against one of the trees, sitting down as she read in the last light of some long-gone day, made to stand up, neither hurriedly, as if she had been disturbed, nor languidly, as if she had all the time in the world. As if this was simply the ordained moment.

The figure rested one hand on her hip. The other grasped the book she had been reading, resting against her thigh. She wore riding pants and boots, and a white blouse with the sleeves rolled up to bony elbows. The blouse looked very much like the one Soya had been wearing.

'Good evening, Sunday,' the woman said.

'How do you know my name?' Sunday asked, wondering what she was dealing with.

'You told me, just now, when you answered the helmet's questions. Do you understand what I am?'

'Not really.'

'When I buried this helmet on Mars, it was already forty years old. I had its systems upgraded as best I could, but there were still limitations to what could be achieved. You are not interacting with Eunice Akinya, rather with a very simple model of her, with a limited range of responses and a very restricted internal knowledge base. Don't go mistaking it for me.'

'So . . . this is you speaking now?'

'This is . . . an interactive recording, a message to you, whoever you may be. The sphinxware wouldn't have admitted you unless you'd uncovered the trail that led to this point, so the chances are excellent that you're a member of the family, or at least someone with close ties to it.'

'As you just said, I've told you who I am.'

'You have, and we shall proceed on that basis.' Eunice – the recording of Eunice – glanced down at the book she'd been reading. 'Firstly, you've done well to come this far. That took resourcefulness. I trust there were no particular unpleasantnesses along the way?'

'You could have picked a better burial site on Mars.'

Eunice's eyes sharpened. 'There were local difficulties?'

'This is the middle of the fucking Evolvarium, Grandmother.'

'I have no idea what you're talking about. Evol-what? Succinctly, please.'

'Other than burying your helmet in a minefield, you couldn't have picked a worse spot on Mars. This whole area, for a thousand kilometres in any direction, is a no-go zone. It's a place where self-replicating machines are allowed to run riot. They evolve through generations, fighting for survival. Every now and then that evolutionary process throws up some gimmick, some idea or gadget that someone can make money from outside the 'varium. The machines are dangerous, and the people who run the place don't take kindly to outsiders poking around. Our guide was killed out there, and Jitendra and I came close to dying as well.'

'I'm ... sorry.' The contrition sounded genuine. 'I meant you to be challenged, but not put in real peril. Still, I can't be held accountable for what happened to Mars after the burial.' Again there was that sharpening of her gaze. 'It's an odd thing to happen, though. This is the only place like it on Mars?'

'I told you, you couldn't have picked a worse location.'

'Then that's strange. I'm not one for coincidences, Sunday. Not this kind, anyway. There must be an explanation.'

'You tell me.'

'I only know what I know. But how could my little adventure on Pavonis Mons have led to this?' She gave every impression of thinking about that, reopening the book and leafing through it, scratching her fingernail against the fine Bible-thin paper, even though her eyes were not on the close-printed text. 'After I lost the aeroplane ... but no.' A quick dismissive head-shake. 'That can't be it.'

'What can't be what?'

'I had to take shelter while the storm raged. The Russian station was still airtight, and it had power and the basic amenities. But I couldn't stay there for ever. The wind had damaged the aircraft, but I still needed a way out.'

Sunday issued a terse, 'Continue.'

As if Eunice needed permission.

'The Russians had left a lot of equipment in their station, some of it still semi-functional. Before landing, I'd scouted a number of abandoned facilities and assets in the area. If I could salvage some of that junk, I'd be able to keep myself alive longer. Batteries, air-scrubbers, that kind of thing. Maybe even rig up some kind of repair to the aircraft. But I couldn't go out there. My suit wasn't stormproof, and in any case it only had limited range. I couldn't have walked far enough to do any good.'

'So you were in deep shit.'

'Until I found the robots.' Eunice snapped the book shut again. 'The Russians had left them behind, in one of the storage sheds. I'm not surprised: they were old, slow, their programming screwed. Still, I didn't need them to do much for me.' She smiled quickly, as if abashed at her own resourcefulness. 'I ... patched them together, fixed their pro-gramming as best I could. Took me eight days, but it kept my mind off the worst. Then I sent them out in different directions, running on maximum autonomy. I'd told them to locate anything that looked potentially useful and drag it back to me.'

'I guess it worked.'

'No – rescue came sooner than I anticipated. The storm cleared, and my people were able to get me out. As for the robots ... I forgot about them. But they were still out there, running with my lashed-up programming. They were supposed to take care of themselves, and to act competitively if the need arose. Do you think ... ?'

'Do I think you inadvertently created the Evolvarium? I'd say yes, if I wasn't worried that your ego might already be on the point of stellar collapse.'

Eunice dislodged a fly from her brow. 'I've achieved enough by intent, without dwelling on the things I made happen by accident. Regardless, I'm truly sorry if circumstances were more complicated than I envisaged, but it appears you weathered the adversity. Congratulations, Sunday. You've come through very well.'

'My brother and I have been sharing the burden.'

'And does that mean you have the full authority of the family behind you?'

'I wouldn't go that far, no.'

'I never counted on it. The important thing is that you've demonstrated the necessary insight and determination to make it this far.' Eunice lifted her head to study the sun. 'My internal clock tells me that more than sixty years have passed since the burial. Is that really the case?'

'Yes,' Sunday said. 'And you've only just died. The reason I'm here is because of an audit the household ran just after your death.'

'A long time in anyone's book. How have things been, while I was gone?'

'With the family?'

'Everything. The world, the flesh and the devil. Us. Have we managed not to screw things up completely?'

'I'm here,' Sunday said. 'That should tell you something, shouldn't it?'

'I was born in 2030,' Eunice said. 'People told me it was the best and worst of times. To me it just seemed like the way of the world. Whether you're born with famine in your belly or a silver spoon in your mouth – it's always just the way things are, isn't it? You know no different. Later, I realised I was fortunate, extraordinarily so. Fortunate to have been born African, for one thing, in the right place at the right time. My mother and father always said we should make the best of things, so that's what we did. The world still had some catching up to do, mind. I grew up with the last wars ever fought on Earth. They never touched me directly, but no one could entirely escape their influence. Please tell me they were the last wars. I couldn't bear to think we'd slipped back to our bad old ways.'

'There haven't been any more wars, which is not to say things are perfect back on Earth. I tease my brother about it often enough. They still have police, armies and peacekeeping forces, the occasional border incident. But it's not like it used to be.'

'The Resource and Relocation crisis taught us to grow up,' Eunice said. 'We were like a house full of squabbling children for most of our history. And then the house started burning down. We had to grow up fast or burn with it.'

'We did.'

'What is it like out there now? Have you seen much of the system?'

'Not much. I was born on Earth, but I've spent most of my adult life on the Moon. This is the first time I've ever been anywhere else.'

'You never had the means?'

'It's . . . complicated.' Sunday nodded at the book her interlocutor was holding. 'Is that *Gulliver's Travels*?'

Eunice glanced absent-mindedly at the title. '*Finnegans Wake*,' she said. 'I liked Swift when I was little. Maybe Gulliver turned me into an explorer. But this is . . . denser. I still haven't got the bottom of it. So many questions. You could spend a lifetime on it and still not understand it.' She flicked open a random page, frowned at something written there. 'Who was Muster Mark? What do you suppose he wanted with three quarks?'

'I don't know.' Sunday was ready to leave the suit now. 'What's this all about, Eunice? Why did you bury the helmet? Why are you asking me these things?'

'You disappoint me, Sunday. To have so much of the world ready for the taking, and to have seen so little of it. I thought wanderlust ran in our blood. I thought it was the fire that made us Akinyas.'

'You saw it all, and then you came back, a sad old woman with no interest in anything except money and power and lording it over the rest of us. Doesn't that suggest all that exploring was really just a waste of time?'

'It would, if it hadn't changed me.' The book's leather binding offered a creak of complaint as she shut it. 'I've seen marvellous things, Sunday. I've looked back from the edge of the system and seen this planet, this Earth, reduced to a tiny dot of pale blue. I know what that feels like. To think that dot is where we came from, where we evolved out of the chaos and the dirt ... to think that Africa is only a part of that dot, that the dot contains not just Africa, but all the other continents, the oceans and ice caps ... under a kiss of atmosphere, like morning dew, soon to be boiled off in the day's heat. And I know what it feels like to imagine going further. To hold that incredible, dangerous thought in my mind, if only for an instant. To think: what if I don't go home? What if I just keep on travelling? Watching that pale-blue dot fall ever further away, until the darkness swallowed it and there was no turning back. Until Earth was just a blue memory.'

Sunday's scorn was overwhelming. 'You never had the nerve.'

'Maybe not. But at least,' Eunice answered mildly, 'I've stood on the edge of that cliff and thought about jumping.'

'I came to Mars. Isn't that adventurous enough for you?'

'You've only taken baby steps, child. But I can't fault your determination. After all, you found me.'

'Yes. And where has that got me?'

'To this point. And I'm not done with you yet. Not by a long mark. There's a choice that needs to be made, a difficult one, and in all conscience I just don't have the mental capacity to make it.'

'That's uncharacteristically modest of you.'

'Oh, I'm not talking about *me*. I'm talking about this thing I've become: this bundle of clanking routines stuffed into a hundred-year-old space helmet. That won't suffice, not when so much is at stake. That's why I'm going to leave matters in your hands. Return to Lunar space. Go to the Winter Palace, if it's still there.'

'It is.'

'If you've managed to find the helmet, then you'll get past the sphinxware guarding the Palace. And if you are, as you say, Akinya ... then the rest will follow.' She paused. 'At some point, you will be challenged by more sphinxware. The answer you give will be critical. But I can't tell you what that answer should be. I've been buried under Mars for sixty years.'

'And that's meant to be helpful ... how, exactly?'

Her eyes twinkled. 'Forewarned is forearmed.'

'Thank you,' Sunday said, drenching her answer with as much sarcasm as she could muster.

'I wish I could tell you more, but the simple fact is that I only know the things I need to know, here and now. Yet wisely or otherwise I have faith in you, Sunday Akinya.'

'You just told me you're a bunch of routines stuffed into a helmet.

How could you possibly know whether I'm up to the task?'

'Because you remind me of me,' Eunice said.

'You mean, up my arse with my own divine self-importance?'

'It's a step in the right direction.'

Sunday took deep and grateful gulps of air. Her clothes were soaked with sweat, sticking to her as she was extricated from the suit.

'I hope that wasn't too traumatic,' Jonathan said, pushing a glass into Sunday's clammy hand.

'You've had the helmet all this time, yet in sixty years you never figured out a way to break through the sphinxware?' She drank the glass down in one go. 'Even if you couldn't do it, surely someone else would have been able to?'

'There might have been a way,' Jonathan said, 'but would the risk have been worth it? If the helmet sensed it was being hacked, it might have erased its contents. Besides, it didn't really interest me.'

'I can't believe that.'

'You have to remember that I was the one who bored your grand-mother. When she'd grown restless of Mars, I was happy to put down roots. The helmet was from that other part of her life, the part I had nothing to do with.'

Soya dabbed Sunday's forehead with a cloth.

'Then why dig it up?' Sunday asked.

'I still wanted to make sure it reached the right hands. If that meant acting as a curator, so be it. If I hadn't, the machines would have recycled it decades ago.'

'You can't argue with that,' Soya said.

'No, but I'm not sure what either of us has achieved. Yes, there was a message from Eunice in the helmet, and it told me some stuff. But answers? All she gave me was some cryptic horsepiss about something being a blessing or a curse. She wouldn't say which. Other than that I need to get to the Winter Palace, which is back where I started.'

'She dragged you all the way to Mars ... to tell you the answer is on your doorstep?' Jitendra asked.

'I don't know what she was telling me.' Sunday accepted another glass of water from Jonathan. She was beginning to feel human again, save for the lingering aches and pains where the suit had been squeezing her. 'There was some stuff about looking back at Earth, seeing it from all the way out.' She paused and said doubtfully, 'Maybe there's more it can tell me.'

'You want to get back in that thing?' Jitendra asked, with what struck her as a particularly touching concern for her well-being.

'Maybe, when we're back in aug reach, the construct can find a way in without tripping the sphinxware to self-erase. But we have to leave the Evolvarium for that. She thinks she might have created this place, by the way. By accident!'

'She was here,' Jitendra admitted. 'No one can argue with that. And when all this is over, someone really needs to dig around and find out how the Evolvarium got started. Maybe I'll do it.'

'You'll ruffle a few feathers,' Soya said.

'Good. It's about time.'

'That'll have to wait, I'm afraid,' Sunday said. 'I need to get a message to Geoffrey, very urgently. Even if I left Mars right now, I'm still more than a month from home. That's too long. One of us needs to look inside the Winter Palace before Hector or Lucas gets the same idea.'

'We can reach Vishniac by tomorrow morning,' Soya said.

'Cross the Evolvarium at night?'

'It's safer when you have friends in the right places,' Jonathan said. There was a gleam in his eyes that didn't belong in a man that old. 'Trust Soya – she'll get you back in one piece. But promise me something – this won't be the last time we speak, will it?'

'We've barely begun,' Sunday said.

'Count on it,' Jitendra said. 'Even if she doesn't come back, I will. I'm serious about ruffling those feathers. And I have a feeling there's a lot you and I could talk about.'

'I think so too,' Jonathan said. Then he frowned slightly, turning back to Sunday. 'What you said just now, about it all being horsepiss?'

'What?' Sunday asked.

'Please don't take this the wrong way, but you sounded just like your grandmother.'

CHAPTER THIRTY-TWO

Geoffrey heard his own footsteps through the suit's auditory-acoustic pickup and the timbre was different now, each footfall accompanied by a distinct steel-edged echo. The open door had shown only darkness, and it was no lighter now that they were on the other side of it, cut off from the *Quaynor*. He felt as if he'd climbed into the hold of a ship: some huge metal-walled void with no windows.

'There's an image-intensifier mode on these things,' Jumai said, quietly, as if there were things astir that she did not wish to alert. 'Voke amplification, see what you make of it.'

Jumai was never more than arm's reach away, her form outlined on the helmet's display. Geoffrey did as she had suggested, voking the suit to apply a light-enhanced overlay. Grey-green perspectives raced away from him, curving in one direction, arrow-straight in the other. He pivoted around, Jumai manifesting as a blazing white smudge. The floor angled up behind her, commencing its great steepening arc, the arc that would eventually bring it soaring overhead and back down behind him. At right angles to the direction of curvature, the floor stretched all the way to the far endcap. He couldn't see anything of the endcap. There wasn't enough ambient light for that.

'This isn't right,' he said, shaking his head inside the helmet. 'It shouldn't be like this.'

'You want to let me in on what you were expecting?'

'I've never been here before,' Geoffrey said, 'but I'm very familiar with this space – from whenever she talked to us, whenever she delivered one of her sermons.' The words were a struggle. 'This wasn't just an empty shell. It was full of trees, full of greenery and light. Like a jungle. There were plants, borders, paths and stairs. It *rained*. There should be a whole closed-cycle ecology running in here.'

'Looks more like a big room full of nothing to me,' Jumai said.

'Arethusa was here. She chinged aboard, not long before Eunice died. She'd have noticed anything strange. She'd have said something to me.'

Jumai had her hands on her hips. She was looking up, towards the central axis of the empty chamber. 'Least there's a ship. That *is* a ship, isn't it?'

'I think so.' But he could hardly tell. It was nearly seventy-five metres away. All he could make out was a spine of organised darkness running from one end of the chamber to the other. 'We need more light,' Geoffrey said decisively. 'Is there a flashlight mode somewhere? I'm surprised it hasn't cut in automatically.'

'Maybe there are situations where you wouldn't want that to happen. Wait a second.' Jumai reached up and started fiddling with the crown of her helmet. 'Thought I saw something while we were suiting up. Got some flares in my toolkit, all else fails.'

Light blazed from her helmet. She doused the blue-white beam against the central axis, picking out details of the *Winter Queen*. Geoffrey felt his world lurch slightly back into sanity, if only for a few lucid moments. He was still reeling from the absence of the jungle. Even if the air in the chamber had been swapped for pure oxygen and allowed to consume itself, there'd still be ashes ... scorching. Yet there was nothing. The flooring under his feet had the improbable antiseptic gleam of an airpod showroom.

But the ship was real. He'd activated his own helmet lamp and was sweeping the beam along the nearest part of the *Winter Queen*. The deep-space explorer was a kilometre long, and even though part of that length was now absorbed into the endcaps, he still couldn't see more than a fifth of it. Yet the anatomy was unmistakable, from the cluster of fuel tanks above him to the delicate filigreed spine with its branching black complexity of fractally folded radiator vanes.

He'd seen this ship a thousand times, in countless family histories. Everything about it looked correct. But this wasn't the rotting, rusted, tree-encased carcass he'd been expecting. *Winter Queen* wasn't garlanded with humid green overgrowth and she wasn't laced with solar lights and an irrigation system. There were no spiral staircases rising from the floor to puncture her hull. She did not look as if she'd been stuck in here for decades.

She looked ravishingly, sparklingly new.

'Enough of this shit,' Jumai said. Her glowing form reached down and scooped something out of the holdall she'd dropped at her feet. She did something to the object in her hand and it quickened into impossible brilliance.

She tossed the little ball of light along the floor, where it bounced and rolled and then began to propel itself with a curious willingness, until it came to a rolling stop two or three hundred metres away.

Jumai did the same thing with a second flare.

They lit the entire chamber. Geoffrey squinted against the brightness until his eyes amped down their response. His suspicions were confirmed now: the ship looked as pristine as its surroundings. The two opposed centrifuge arms, one hundred and eighty metres from tip to tip, were still turning, whooshing around like the blades of a wind turbine. The capsule-shaped living pods at either end of the arms skimmed the ground with only a metre or so to spare.

'Why are they still turning?' Geoffrey asked. 'There's already gravity in this place.'

Jumai looked at the swinging arms. 'How fast are we spinning?'

Geoffrey recalled what he'd learned on the approach. 'About three times a minute, give or take.'

'Then they're not spinning fast enough to counteract the habitat's rotation, either. I thought maybe someone had gone to a lot of trouble to recreate weightlessness, for whatever reason. But that's not it. Those arms can't be swinging around faster than once every couple of minutes, relative to us.'

'Must be a systems glitch, then,' Geoffrey said. 'Something inside blew a fuse and the arms started up again. Or maybe it's just to keep the air circulating, like a god's own ceiling fan.'

Jumai scratched the back of her helmet, as if she had an itch. 'Air's breathable, you realise. Someone went to that much trouble. But I'm beginning to wonder if anyone ever actually put that to the test.'

'Memphis would have breathed it.'

'If he ever came this far. And if he did ... well, he lied to you, didn't he? Big time.'

Geoffrey wasn't keen to follow that thought to its conclusion. 'I see something,' he said. 'High above us, under the path of the centrifuge arms.' He pointed, and Jumai followed his gaze to the indistinct form he'd sighted, pinned to the ceiling like a squashed fly.

'Got to be Hector.'

'He's not moving.' Somewhere in the suit there had to be a mode for zooming in the faceplate view, but Geoffrey couldn't be bothered searching for it now. 'I wonder if he even knows we're here. There's no aug reach, but suit-to-suit comms are still good ...' He didn't want to voice the possibility that Hector might be dead, however plausible that now looked.

Jumai grabbed the holdall and broke into a surprisingly loose-limbed run, the suit easily accommodating her intentions. Geoffrey followed, keen to reach his cousin but anxious about what they might find. Whatever had hurt Hector might still be present. But where could anything or anyone hide, in this vast empty space? Unless Hector's attacker had retreated back into the far endcap wall, the only possible hiding place was the ship itself.

He didn't like that idea at all.

Even running against the spin of the habitat, Geoffrey didn't feel his own weight varying to any perceptible degree. They cut diagonally, Jumai tossing out another flare along the way, and slowed to a walk when they were about a hundred metres from the suited figure. The centrifuge booms were still turning, and now that they were closer there was a clear *whoosh* each time one of the capsules swept by them. The arms were not moving particularly quickly – scarcely more than running pace, compared to the floor – but Geoffrey nonetheless had an impression of enormous, dangerous momentum.

Hector – who else could it possibly be? – was on his back, spreadeagled and motionless, staring straight up towards the central axis and the *Winter Queen*. Next to him, resting on the ground, was a white rectangular box like a big first-aid kit. Traceries of luminous arterial red ran down the suit's matte-black limbs and defined the form of the chestplate and helmet. The Akinya Space logo glowed on the upper shoulder joint of the nearest arm.

Geoffrey approached the form, always keeping the centrifuge arms in view. As one of the capsules sped past him, he grasped what must have happened to his cousin. There was a door in the capsule: a dark circular aperture in the leading hemisphere.

'Hector was trying to get inside.'

'Figures,' Jumai said slowly. 'I mean, he would, wouldn't he? Comes this way, finds things aren't the way they're meant to be ... what else is he going to do but try to get aboard the ship?' She took a step back as the other capsule whooshed by. 'Think this was a surprise to him?'

Geoffrey had no adequate answer for that, only intuition. 'I don't like Hector,' he said. 'Don't trust him, either. But I don't think he was expecting to find this place empty.' He got up close to Hector's visor, trying to make out the face behind the glass.

There wasn't one.

'The suit's empty.'

Jumai knelt down and double-checked, as if he could possibly have been mistaken. 'I don't get it.'

'He must have removed the suit, then told it to wait here for him. That's what it's doing – just lying there, waiting.'

'I know there's air in here, but why would anyone be lunatic enough to get out of a perfectly good spacesuit?'

Geoffrey looked at the next centrifuge pod to swing past them, at the tiny door in its side. A suited figure could squeeze through that aperture – there'd have been little point in having it otherwise – but it would have been all but impossible to time the transition from floor to moving component. Unencumbered by a suit, though ... and for a man who was fit and agile enough to play both tennis and polo and excel at both ... Geoffrey wondered.

'I think he wanted to get aboard the ship. He couldn't do it with the suit on: too sluggish, too clumsy. So he got out of it. Told it to wait here, until he was ready to leave.'

'We haven't seen him,' Jumai said. 'There's another way out of the Winter Palace, of course.'

'But he wouldn't have left without putting the suit back on. I think he's still inside the ship.'

Cautiously, as if he might be working a jack-in-the-box, Geoffrey eased open the cover on the white container and saw four small cylindrical devices, packed like stubby beer bottles. There were four empty spaces next to them. He tugged one of the plump cylinders out of its cushioned support matrix.

It was heavy and cold, with a sturdy flip-up arming mechanism built into the cap. The label was in Swahili, with other languages printed underneath in smaller type. '"Caution: metastable metallic hydrogen,"' he read. '"This is a variable-yield explosive device. Do not tamper with, shock or expose to temperatures in excess of four hundred kelvin, magnetic fields in excess of one tesla, or ambient pressures in excess of one hundred atmospheres. If found, immediately notify Akinya Space, Deep-System Resources."'

'You don't think he came with just the four, do you?' Jumai said.

'Perhaps. On the other hand, maybe he took the other four into the ship.'

'And set the fuses. And then issued a distress call, because something happened to him in there.' Jumai was speaking very slowly, as if she did not much care for the direction her thoughts were taking her. 'Something that meant he couldn't get back out again on his own.'

'We might be in trouble,' Geoffrey said.

'You think those charges would be enough to blow up the whole habitat?'

'Don't need to be. There's a nuclear drive inside the ship.' He turned the demolition charge around, studying the fine settings around the flip-up arming device. There was a twist dial and a locking fail-safe. Tiny numerals were engraved into the twist dial. 'Must be a way to trigger these remotely. But there's also a timer mode. It goes ten, twenty, thirty, sixty, ninety.'

'Seconds or minutes?'

'Minutes, I hope.' Geoffrey slid the charge back into the box, treating it as gingerly as he would a Ming vase. 'We don't know that he set the timers, but it's a possibility we can't ignore.'

'He called in the *Kinyeti* more than an hour ago,' Jumai said. 'If he armed those fuses and *then* ran into trouble ... it can't be the sixty-minute fuse. But that still doesn't give us a lot of time to get out of here. We should start back now, and tell the *Quaynor* to pull away as soon as we're in the lock.'

'That's an excellent idea.' Geoffrey voked through visor menus until he found the option for suit removal. Typically, there were eight or nine hurdles to jump before the suit accepted that he really, honestly meant to get out of it. 'But one of us has to go up there and get Hector. I'll disarm the fuses if I'm able; otherwise I'll find him and get the two of us out of there as quickly as possible. And if I can't save Hector, I'll save myself.'

'No,' Jumai said. 'That's not how it's going to happen. And we don't have time to argue about it.'

Geoffrey's suit had begun to detach itself, opening like a crafty puzzle to reveal the human prize at its heart. The air in the chamber hit his lungs: he'd seen no point in holding his breath, so he gulped it down eagerly. Beyond a brief coughing fit triggered by the air's coldness, there were no ill-effects.

'Listen carefully,' he told Jumai. 'If Hector's hurt in any way, he won't be much use in that suit. I can carry him back the way he came in, if it comes to that, and he can get me through any doors we meet on the way – he passed through them on his way here, after all. But there's no way I'd be able to get him up that shaft we already came down.'

'So how the hell do you get out?'

'Hector's ferry. There'll be room aboard for both of us.'

He put a hand on the armoured swell of her shoulder joint, before she could voice an objection. 'I'm not suicidal, Jumai. But I can't just leave him to die aboard that ship. As soon as you're back in aug reach, tell Mira and Arethusa to decouple and get away as quickly as possible. The Pans'll wait for you, or leave one of the *Quaynor*'s own escape pods docked at the hub for you to use. If all else fails, vent the airlock and use the explosive decompression to push you away from the station. It'll only take you a few minutes to reach safe distance: I may not know much about spaceflight, but I know there are no shockwaves in vacuum, and the debris cloud will attenuate very quickly.'

'And you?'

'This is the only way.'

'It sucks.'

'Yes, it does. But the more time we spend discussing this, the less time we have for making it work.' Geoffrey raised his voice. 'Go. Now. We'll both be fine.'

Jumai hesitated, then started to retrace their steps. She turned back once or twice, but Geoffrey was waiting until she was gone before he chanced his luck with the centrifuge. If it went wrong, he didn't want Jumai risking her own neck to save his.

He waited for the next pod to come around, studying it more closely than he had before. The aperture was in the front, as the pod travelled, but if he simply stood his ground and waited for it to arrive he'd be swatted aside like a fly. Better to run alongside it, as fast as he could, and spring aboard. He couldn't match its speed, but he could reduce the relative motion to the point where he ought to be able to grab hold of the pod without being injured or flung aside. There were handholds around the pod's circumference: they'd been put there for weightless operations but they would serve his purpose equally well.

When he was certain that Jumai was either out of the chamber or far enough away that she couldn't see him, he stationed himself as close to the path of the pods as he dared. Divested of his suit, he felt the breeze as they passed. He gulped in deep cold breaths and began to jog. The next pod whisked past his right shoulder – it was moving faster than he'd anticipated. He increased his pace, transitioning from a jog to a run. He kept his eyes on the ground, tracking a fine seam in the floor, making sure he didn't deviate more than a few centimetres either side of it. The next pod arrived: it was still fast, but he'd cut down the relative motion to the point where jumping aboard no longer appeared insanely impossible. His feet hammered the metal plates. He was not yet running at his limit, but he might have to sustain this pace for several minutes. When the next pod passed, he upped his speed again. His lungs began to hurt. Now the relative speed couldn't be more than two metres a second, but this was not a pace he could sustain indefinitely. The pods had taken about two minutes to complete their revolutions before, but now they had to catch up with a moving reference point and the interval was closer to three minutes. He thought again of the timer fuses on the demolition charges. Was this madness, even attempting to get aboard the *Winter Queen*?

When the next pod came, he made his move. One chance only, he figured. If he was knocked to the ground, if his ankle twisted under him, he'd never have the strength to make a second attempt. Part of him hoped it would happen that way. Make a gesture, an effort to reach Hector . . . that would be sufficient, wouldn't it? He could go home with a clear conscience, knowing he'd tried.

He grasped for the handhold with his right hand, and an instant later had his left in place as well. For a second or so he was able to keep pace with the pod, but then his legs buckled under him and he was being dragged. Putting as much strength into his arms as he was able, he levered himself further from the ground. He was facing back the way he'd come now, like a rider about to mount a horse, his heels skimming the floor. With a grunt of supreme effort he managed to hook his right leg onto one of the handholds, like a foot into a stirrup, and then his left leg followed. He was aboard the pod.

But not inside it. He was facing the wrong way, gripping the outside, one slip away from tumbling off. He twisted around, keeping his hands and feet where they were. The only thing in his favour was that he was now slightly lighter than when he'd been standing: the centrifuge's own rotation was working against the overall spin of the Winter Palace.

Geoffrey adjusted his position. He moved his right hand onto the same handhold as the left, and then moved the left as far back over his shoulder as he was able without throwing himself dangerously off-balance. He caught his breath, knowing he could only hold the posture for a few seconds. He could not adjust the position of his legs unless he swung himself out into space again, holding on with just his hands. Taking another breath, calculating the movement he would have to make, rehearsing exactly where he would plant his feet when momentum brought him back into contact with the pod, he committed.

Something twisted in his wrist. The pain was intense, a dagger into a nerve, but it was also momentary. He forced himself not to let go, grunting away the discomfort. His left foot recontacted the pod, then his right. He scrambled for a more secure hold, his right heel sliding against the pod's curving side.

Then he was safe.

Geoffrey allowed himself a minute to gather his energies before continuing. It was not difficult to reach the entrance hole, although it required care. Under other circumstances, knowing that something had already happened to Hector, he would have entered it with immense caution. Scarcely an option now. He swung himself inside, and as he hit the padded floor all he felt was the relief of no longer having to clutch on to the handholds. His wrist ached, his shoulder muscles were protesting, his legs were burning from the exertion.

But he was aboard the *Winter Queen*.

The pod's interior was bathroom-sized. There were fold-down stools and a table, a couple of screens. Sufficient for a game of cards, but even without suits on, it would be very cramped in here with more than two people. The pods weren't meant for extended habitation, though. The idea would be to spend a few hours per day under normal or even slightly higher than normal gravitation, to offset the calcium depletion and muscle wasting of prolonged weightlessness. Given that Eunice had been alone on her final deep-space voyage, elbow room had hardly been an issue.

He looked up, along the spoke that connected the pod to the spacecraft's central axis. Ninety metres: more or less the same distance they'd already traversed after entering the habitat. There was a ladder, and just enough room for one person to climb it. Before cramp set in, he made a start on the ascent. His limbs protested, the ache in his wrist sharpening, but as he ascended, so his effective weight gradually decreased and the effort became endurable. Every ten metres or so the ladder reached a platform and swapped sides, so that there was no risk of falling all the way down. He wondered why they hadn't arranged an elevator, but a moment's consideration made it plain enough: the whole point of the centrifuge arm was to work bone and muscle. Climbing up and down was part of the exercise.

The air in the ship was free to mix with that in the chamber, but there was a metallic quality to it that he didn't remember from before. It smelled antiseptic, like a hospital corridor that had been vigorously scrubbed and polished. Nor was it as cold as the air outside. In addition to the warmth, ship sounds were now reaching his ears. He heard the electric hum of what he presumed to be the centrifuge mechanism, and beyond that the muted chug of onboard life support and air circulation, like a showroom full of refrigerators.

Three minutes after commencing his ascent, Geoffrey was weightless again. He had reached the transition collar where the rotary movement of the centrifuge met the fixed reference frame of the main hull. An oval hole slid slowly by, rimmed with cushioning. Hector had come at least this far.

Geoffrey pushed himself through the hole the next time it appeared. There was ample time to complete the manoeuvre, and he didn't doubt that there were safety mechanisms waiting to cut off the centrifuge's rotation should he somehow imperil himself.

He floated into the lit core of the *Winter Queen* and assessed his surroundings.

He was amidships: aft lay the engine assembly and the nuclear power plant; fore lay the command deck. He was hanging in a corridor, hexagonal in cross section, with panels and lockers arranged in longitudinal strips. Between the strips were recessed ladders, grip-pads and handholds. The main lights were on, and everything looked very clean and tidy.

Not at all like a ship that had been to the edge of the solar system and back – much less one that had been lived in for sixty-odd years. Geoffrey picked at the edge of a striped warning decal, bordering what the glass pane identified as an emergency bulkhead control. Not even a hint of dirt around the edge of the decal. His own fingernails were grubbier.

Nothing stayed that new, not with human beings in the loop.

'Hector!' Geoffrey called. 'Can you hear me?'

No answer. Not that that necessarily meant anything, since the ship was big and there were undoubtedly soundproof doors between its various internal sections. But which way had his cousin gone?

Tossing a mental coin, Geoffrey decided to check out the command deck first. Trusting his orientation, he set off down the corridor, using the handholds and straps for traction. He was glad he'd had time to adjust to weightlessness on the *Quaynor*.

The corridor jinked right, then left – squeezing past some fuel tank or external equipment module, he guessed – and then there was a door, blocking his path. A small window was set into the door, but all he could see through that was a short space and another door beyond it. Bracing himself, conscious that he wasn't wearing a suit and that he had no reason to assume the entire ship was pressurised, he reached out and palmed what was obviously the door's operating control. An amber light flicked to green and the door gapped apart in two interlocking halves.

He pushed through into the space beyond, the door closing almost before he'd cleared the gap. He arrested his drift and palmed open the second door. There was air beyond. He continued his exploration.

By his reckoning, Geoffrey thought he must be halfway to the front of the ship by now. The corridor he was moving along was wider than the others, and there were rooms – or more properly compartments – leading off from it. He spared them the briefest of glances as he passed. Most were large enough to serve as private chambers for individual crewmembers, and indeed one or two came equipped with bunks and other fold-out amenities. But again there was no sign that anything had ever been used. He passed a couple of larger chambers, a dining area, a commons room, a sickbay – all the chrome and pea-green equipment gleaming and shrink-wrapped, as if it had just been ordered out of the catalogue and installed yesterday. A zero-gee gym, a kind of cinema or lecture theatre. More storage lockers and equipment bays. Lots of equipment: spacesuits, vacuum repair gear, medical and food supplies, even a couple of stowed proxies, waiting to be called into service. The proxies were surprisingly modern-looking for a ship that hadn't gone anywhere since 2101.

Did they even have proxies back then? Geoffrey wondered.

He moved on. Around him the ship chugged and whirred and clicked. It was much warmer now, almost uncomfortably so, and Geoffrey was beginning to sweat under the spacesuit inner layer. He passed a pair of large eggshell-white rooms furnished with hibernation cabinets: stream-lined sarcophagi. They were Hitachi units, plastered with medical logos, instructions and graphic warning decals. There were six cabinets.

Which made no sense at all.

Winter Queen had made many journeys with a normal operating staff, but for her final mission Eunice had taken the ship out alone. There had been good reasons for that: automation and reliability had improved to the point where the vehicle could easily manage its own subsystems and damage repair, and beyond that Eunice had not wanted to involve anyone else in what was unarguably a risky enterprise, taking her much further out, and for longer, than any previous deep-space expedition.

That, of course, and her natural unwillingness to share the limelight.

But mass was fuel, and fuel was speed, and speed was time. Eunice would never have hauled the deadweight of five extra hibernation units and their associated mechanisms – many tonnes, Geoffrey guessed – if she only needed one for herself. *Winter Queen* had been outfitted and modified for each of its journeys. There was no reason for all that mass to have been left aboard.

Pushing questions from his mind for the moment, Geoffrey continued along the spine of the ship. He passed through another set of pressure doors, and before him lay the command deck. It was windowless: more like the tactical room of a warship than an aircraft's cockpit. Windows had little utility on a deep-space vehicle like this; it could steer and dock itself autonomously, and relay any external view to its crew via screens or aug-generated figments.

The ship was dreaming of itself. Screens and readouts wrapped the space like the facets of a wasp's eye, seen from inside. Lines of house-keeping data scrolled in green and blue text, updating too quickly to read. Schematic diagrams fluttered from screen to screen in a constant nervous dance, reactor cross sections, fuel-management flow cycles. Other displays showed zoom-ins of the solar system at different scales: planets and moons, their paths around the sun, various trajectories and intercepts available to the ship at that moment, depending on fuel and time/energy trade-offs. Simulations and projections, executing in neurotic loops, with only tiny, trifling variations from run to run, everything changing and shuffling at a feverish pace. Geoffrey could take in the totality of it, but no single display held still long enough for him to grasp more than the sketchiest of details. One thing was clear, though: the ship still thought it was a ship.

There were three chairs in the command deck – bulky acceleration couches, heavy and high-backed – and for all that the displays snared his attention, it could not have taken Geoffrey more than five or ten seconds to notice that he was not alone.

In the middle chair was Hector.

'What are you doing here?' he asked. 'Where's Dos Santos?'

'Dos Santos ran into trouble answering your distress call. I'm your next best hope.'

'Leave now,' Hector told him.

Geoffrey propelled himself through the space. Between the displays were margins of padded walling set with handles and elastic hoops. His foot brushed one of the displays. It flexed, absorbing the pressure before gently repelling him.

'What's happening?' he asked, facing Hector directly. 'Why are you still aboard?'

'Because I had to know,' Hector said. 'Because I had to fucking know. Why else? What happened to Dos Santos? Why are *you* here, cousin?'

Geoffrey's eyes amped up to compensate for the low ambient lighting on the command deck. Hector wasn't just sitting in the central command seat. He was strapped there, with a heavy X-shaped webbing across his chest and tough-looking restraints around his wrists and ankles. Like Geoffrey he was wearing only the inner layer of a spacesuit.

'I'm here because I thought you might be in trouble,' Geoffrey said, still trying to get his bearings. 'The station attacked the *Kinyeti* – the crew's still alive, but the ship's a wreck. Jumai and I came aboard afterwards, using the other docking hub. We found the four demolition charges you left behind and assumed you'd come aboard with the others. Is that the case? Did you arm them?'

'Not an issue now. There's still eleven minutes on the fuses, if my timing's right.'

Geoffrey shook his head. 'How can that not be an issue? Tell me where the charges are – I'll disarm them.'

'Just leave. You still have a few minutes.'

'You just said eleven minutes.'

'Different countdown.' Hector nodded, which was all he could do given the degree to which his movements were impaired. 'The screen ahead of me. It's the only one that hasn't changed.'

Geoffrey followed his gaze with a peculiar kind of dread. He saw what Hector meant. Three sets of double digits: hours, minutes, seconds. The hours had reached zero. There were four minutes left, and a handful of churning seconds.

'What the hell?'

'It initiated as soon as I hit a certain level of the ship's file system. Some kind of self-destruct, obviously.' Hector sounded insanely calm and resigned, as if he'd had years to accept his fate. 'I can't get out of this chair – it's locked me in. But you've still got time. You don't need a suit, and the elevator's still working to take you all the way back to the hub. Use my ferry – I assume it's still docked.'

Geoffrey was too stunned to answer immediately. 'The charges,' he said, when he could push a clear thought into his head. 'Tell me where they are.'

'You're not listening. It doesn't matter now. You need to leave.'

'Until we know what that countdown means, I'm not going to assume anything. Where are the charges?'

Hector groaned, as if all this was an insuperable nuisance. 'To the rear, next to the last bulkhead before the engine section. That's as close as I could get. I assumed it would be sufficient.'

'Maybe I should work on getting you out of that seat first.'

Hector rolled his eyes. 'With the heavy cutting equipment you happened to bring with you?'

'There's got to be something I can use somewhere on the ship.'

'Good luck finding it in . . . less than four minutes.'

Geoffrey pushed himself away. He left the command deck, working his way back down the ship as quickly as his limbs allowed. The doors opened for him, all the way back to the point where'd he'd come in. Through a small porthole he saw the centrifuge arms, still wheeling around. Hector was being optimistic, he thought. Even with four minutes, it would have been a stretch to reach space and safe distance before *Winter Queen*'s countdown touched zero. He doubted that he even had time to escape the demolition charges.

CHAPTER THIRTY-THREE

He pushed deeper into the ship, back towards the propulsion section, and at last found the devices. There were four of them, hooked into restraining straps on the wall just before the bulkhead. He slid one of the demolition charges out of its strap and studied the arming mechanism. It was set to the ninety-minute delay, but there was no means of determining how much time was left on the clock.

Geoffrey twisted the dial back to its safety setting, felt a click, and lowered the flip-up arming toggle. He repeated the procedure on the other three devices, then unzipped the top of his spacesuit inner-layer and stuffed the charges against his chest, metal to skin. Then he zipped up again, as well as he could. Hector must have had to do something similar to get the bombs aboard the ship in the first place.

Geoffrey made his way back to the command deck. He was still sweating, still struggling to catch his breath.

'How much time left?'

'I told you to leave!' Hector shouted. 'We're down to less than a minute!'

The clock confirmed forty seconds remaining, thirty-nine, thirty-eight . . .

'I disarmed the fuses.'

'What do you want, a gold star?'

'I thought you might like to know.'

'You should have left, cousin.' The fight had slumped out of Hector. 'It's too late now.'

Geoffrey tugged the charges out of his suit and stuffed them into a nylon tie-bag fixed to the wall near the entrance. He re-zipped his suit then eased into the command seat to Hector's left.

'What are you doing?' Hector asked.

'The ship wanted you in that seat for a reason. If Eunice meant to just kill you and blow up the ship, there are less melodramatic ways she could have made that happen.' Geoffrey buckled in, adjusted the chest webbing, then positioned his hands on the seat rests. Cuffs whirred out and locked him in place, as they'd done with Hector. He felt a momentary pinprick in both wrists. Something was sampling him, tasting his blood.

Fifteen seconds on the clock. Ten. He watched the last digit whirr down to zero.

'You didn't have to come back for me,' Hector said.

'What would you have done were the situation reversed?'

'I'm not really sure.'

Geoffrey heard a sound like distant drums beating a military tattoo. He glanced at his cousin. 'Those sound like explosions.'

'But we're still here. If the power plant was going to blow ... I think we'd already know it.' Hector looked to Geoffrey for confirmation. 'Wouldn't we?'

'I'm a biologist, not a ship designer.' He paused. 'But I think you're right.'

The detonations were continuing. He heard the sound, and through his seat he felt something of the shockwave of each explosion as it transmitted through the ship. But it didn't feel as if it was the ship itself that was breaking up.

Geoffrey looked around. The dance of readouts had calmed down. Before him floated a schematic of the entire ship, cut through like a blueprint, with flashing colour blocks and oozing flow lines showing fuel and coolant circulation. Most of the activity appeared to be going on around the propulsion assembly. On other screens, the trajectory simulations were stabilising around one possibility. He saw their future path arc away from Lunar orbit, away from the Earth–Moon system, slingshotting far across the ecliptic.

'We're getting ready to leave,' Geoffrey said, unsure whether to be awed or terrified by this prospect. '*Winter Queen* is powering up. Those explosions ... I think it's the station, dismantling itself around us. Freeing the ship.'

'I've got some news for you,' Hector said. 'This isn't *Winter Queen*.'

The explosions had doubled in intensity and frequency, now resembling cannon fire. Eight massive explosions shook the ship violently, followed a few moments later by eight more. One fusillade came from the front, the other from the rear. On one of the schematics, Geoffrey observed that the aerobrake and drive shield were decoupling from their anchorpoints in the habitat's leading and trailing ends. The ship was now floating free, cocooned in the remains of the Winter Palace.

He felt weight. His seat was pushing into his back. Half a gee at least, he guessed – maybe more. The ship clattered and banged. Moving forward, beginning to accelerate, the armoured piston of the aerobrake would be bearing the brunt of any impacts she suffered against the ruins of the habitat.

'If this isn't the *Winter Queen* ...' he said, leaving the statement unfinished.

'By the time I planted the charges,' Hector said, grimacing as the acceleration notched even higher, 'I'd already seen the state of this ship and the rest of the habitat. You think I didn't have questions by that point?' He clenched his fists, his wrists jutting from the restraining cuffs. 'I had to know, Geoffrey. There was still time to look into the system files. Maybe I'd stumble on a destruct option as well, save myself the worry of those charges not doing their job. So I came in here and sat in this seat, only expecting to be here a few minutes.'

'That's when the seat imprisoned you?'

'No ... I consented to this.' He smiled ruefully. 'I had immediate access to the top-layer files. It's an old system, but easy enough to navigate. At first, it was more than willing to let me have access.'

'And then?'

'I hit a point where it wouldn't let me go any further. Detailed construction history, navigation logs ... all that was blocked. No time to look for workarounds. But the ship said I could have access to everything I wished, provided I proved that I was Akinya. I didn't question it. Why wouldn't the ship want to know that I was family before giving me its deepest secrets?'

'So you let the cuffs close around you.'

'I had to buckle in first: the blood-sampling system wouldn't activate until I was secured. That was foolish ... but I didn't have time to sit and weigh the options. I wanted to know, very badly. And I assumed the ship would take a drop and release me again.'

The acceleration had been rising steadily ever since their departure, and it was a long time since Geoffrey had felt the ship crash into anything. Whatever remained of the Winter Palace, they must have left it far behind by now. He hoped that Jumai had got to safety, and that the Pans had managed to undock their ship in time.

'How did you call for help?'

'Still had a comm-link to my suit, and my suit could still get a signal to the *Kinyeti*.'

'You didn't tell Dos Santos much.'

'I told him I needed help. I knew he'd come as quickly as possible. There was still time to get me out.'

'After the ship had taken the blood sample ... did it keep its word?'

'Yes,' Hector said. 'That's how I found out that this isn't *Winter Queen*. It's ... something else. I found the construction history. This ship is sixty-two years old. It was built in 2100, when Eunice was off on her final mission. *Winter Queen* was a good twenty years older than that.'

Geoffrey nodded to himself, thinking that he understood Hector's error. 'Something happened out there, that's all. Her previous flight logs got wiped somehow, and everything was reset to zero.'

Hector sighed. 'All the files cross-matched. Nothing had been erased or lost. This ship only ever made one trip. It was built in deep space, and it came back to Lunar orbit, where it's been ever since. Box-fresh.'

'What do you mean, built in deep space?'

'Unless the files are lying ... this ship was manufactured on one of our Kuiper belt assets. A dormant comet, orbiting beyond Neptune.'

'You make igloos out of ice, Hector, not ships. I know that much.'

'I realise this is painful for you, Geoffrey, getting up to speed with what your own family has been doing for the last hundred years. *Of course* you can't make anything out of ice and dirt: that's not why we went to the Kuiper belt, nor why we spent a fortune planting flags all over anything bigger than a potato. We mine those iceteroids for what they can give us: water, volatiles, hydrocarbons. We send robots and raw materials out there and they build mining and on-site refining facilities, and then they package the processed material and catapult it back to us on energy-efficient trajectories. The robots and raw materials come from our facilities on the main belt M-class asteroids, where the metals are. It's a supply chain. Can you grasp that?'

'You still haven't told me how a ship could originate on a comet.'

'There are metals and assembly facilities in the Kuiper belt. We put them there, to mine the volatiles. Thousands of tonnes of complex self-repairing machinery, serviced by Plexus machines – even more tonnage. And that infrastructure was already in place by 2100, already earning back our investment.'

'You're saying it could have been reassigned to make a ship?'

'Saying it's possible, that's all. Maybe illegal – there'd have been any number of patent violations, unless our subcontractors were somehow in the know – but it could have been done. If Eunice wanted to build a copy of her ship, she had the means. All she would have needed were raw materials and time.'

Geoffrey closed his eyes. It wasn't just the steadily mounting gee-load, although that was a part of it. He needed to think. If they were on VASIMR propulsion now, the power plant was surely being pushed to its limit. He remembered how leisurely the departure of Sunday's swiftship had appeared.

'And secrecy,' he said.

'She had it. The Kuiper belt's a long way out, and it's not like anyone else was living anywhere near that asset.'

'Want to hazard a guess as to where we're headed?'

Hector looked at the trajectory display, but it was clear that he'd already digested the salient details. 'If that's to be believed, then we're going a long way out.'

'Maybe back to the ship's point of origin?'

'If I could get out of these restraints, maybe I could query the ship.'

Geoffrey struggled against his own cuffs, but they were still holding him tight. 'We're safe now, though,' he said, thinking aloud. 'The ship clearly wanted to make sure one or both of us was family, so it had to test our blood. It may also have wanted to cushion us during the escape phase. But that's over – so why would it insist on holding us here now?'

'Is that a rhetorical question, cousin?'

'Release me,' Geoffrey said.

The cuffs relinquished their hold, as did the ankle restraints. He was still buckled into the seat, and while the ship was under acceleration it might make sense to stay that way, but he was no longer a prisoner of the chair.

'You just had to ask nicely.'

Hector clenched his fists again, made one final attempt to break the restraints by force, then said, 'Release me.'

The ship let him go. Hector stretched his arms, holding them out from his body against the acceleration. Geoffrey remembered that his cousin had been confined to the chair for a lot longer than he had, and had spent much of that interval expecting to die. For the first time in a very long while he felt a dim flicker of empathy.

They were blood, after all.

'I guess the next thing is to tell it to stop and let us off.'

Hector strained forward. 'This is Hector Akinya. Acknowledge command authority.'

'Welcome, Hector Akinya,' the ship said, speaking in what Geoffrey recognised as the voice of Memphis, or one very close to it. 'Welcome, Geoffrey Akinya.'

'Stop engines,' Hector said, in the tones of one who was used to getting his way. 'Immediately. Return us to Lunar orbit.'

'Propulsion and navigation control are currently suspended, Hector.'

Geoffrey issued the same command, was met by the same polite but firm rebuttal. It was irksome to have Memphis speaking back, as if the ship failed to grasp that mimicking the voice of a recently dead man was an act of grave tactlessness.

'How long?' he asked. Then, sensing that the ship might need clarification: 'For how long are propulsion and navigation control suspended?'

'For the duration of the trip, Geoffrey.'

Hector looked at him, evidently sharing his profound unease at that answer. 'State our destination, and the duration of the trip,' he said.

'Our destination is KBO 2071 NK subscript 789,' the ship said. 'Akinya Space Trans-Neptunian asset 116 stroke 133, codename Lionheart. Trip time will be fifty-two days.'

Hector listened to that and shook his head.

'What?' Geoffrey asked, growing impatient. 'Is that the same place or not?'

'It's the same iceteroid where the ship was built. I remember the name, Lionheart. But that's *Trans-Neptunian*, for pity's sake. I've been as far out as Saturn, cousin. I know how long it takes, and fifty-two days won't begin to cut it.'

Geoffrey could only nod. He knew how long it had taken the swiftship to get Sunday to Mars, and Mars was a hop and a skip away compared to Neptune's orbit. 'Eunice's mission to the edge of the system took a lot longer than a hundred days, even allowing for the return time.'

'More than a year. So either the ship is bullshitting us, for no reason at all, or . . .' Hector didn't seem to know where to go with that.

'Or we're on a very fast ship.'

'Nothing's that fast.'

'Until now,' Geoffrey said.

Behind them, the command deck doors opened. Geoffrey twisted around in his harness, straining to see past the bulk of his seat. His heart skipped at the sight of a proxy, looming in the doorway. It was one of the shipboard units he'd seen earlier – a man-shaped chassis constructed from tubes and joints.

It was cradling a body, and he recognised it.

'This female has suffered minor concussion, but is otherwise uninjured.' The proxy spoke with the voice of the ship. 'Shall I convey her to the medical suite?'

Geoffrey unbuckled his harness. They were still accelerating, but the thrust appeared to have levelled out at around one gee. He could move around in that without difficulty, provided he took care. 'Do so,' he said.

410

'I thought you said you were alone.'

'I thought I was.'

Hector was in the process of undoing his own restraints when a ching request arrived. Geoffrey voked acknowledgement and placed Mira Gilbert's head and upper torso in the middle of the command deck. He voked Hector in on the conversation.

'Unless someone's spoofing the return signal, you're alive,' Gilbert's figment said. 'We've been trying to establish contact since ... well, whatever it was that happened. We'll get to that in a moment. Are you all right?'

Geoffrey took a moment to decide how to answer that question truthfully. 'I'm fine ... for the time being. Beyond that, things become a little murky. I'm with Hector – he's OK as well. Since you seem to be alive, I presume Jumai got word through?'

'Jumai reached the point where she was able to signal us. She told us to undock immediately and execute a safe-distancing manoeuvre. I told her I'd wait until she was in the lock, but she insisted on going back inside.'

'I know. We just found her.'

'How is she?'

'I'm guessing she made it onto the ship just before we departed. She must have been knocked around a bit, but the proxy tells me there isn't anything seriously wrong with her.'

Gilbert's figment nodded. 'OK – next question. The habitat's gone. Presumably you worked that much out for yourselves. How much control do you have over *Winter Queen*?'

'None whatsoever, and by the way, this isn't *Winter Queen*. It's some other ship Eunice sent back in its place. Similar, but not the same. And there's no sign that Eunice was ever here, either aboard this ship or anywhere in the Winter Palace.'

Hector shot him a warning look. 'Any other family business you want to reveal, cousin?'

'They already know more than you'd approve of – a little more won't hurt.'

'How can she not have been in the habitat?' Gilbert asked. 'Jumai said something similar, but we didn't have time to get the full story out of her before she went off-air again.'

'I don't know,' Geoffrey replied. 'Obviously none of us ever dealt with Eunice except via ching ... other than our housekeeper Memphis.'

'All right. As important as that is, there are actually more pressing matters right now. You say you can't control the ship – what have you tried?'

'Everything,' Hector said. 'Flight plan's locked in, and it won't let us change anything.'

'We're tracking you, but we don't have a handle on your trajectory yet. Where are you headed?'

'If the ship's to be believed,' Geoffrey said, 'an iceteroid in the Kuiper belt.'

Gilbert looked apologetic. 'You won't make it out of Earth–Moon space at this rate. You're running way outside the safe operating envelope for that type of propulsion system.'

Hector looked sceptical. 'You've figured that much out in just a few minutes?'

'You're lighting up near-Lunar space like a Roman candle. You need to find a way to throttle back, and urgently. At the very least, you're going to burn so much fuel you won't have a snowball's hope of slowing down this side of the Oort cloud.'

'The ship has its own ideas,' Geoffrey said.

'You'll have to do something. You've already reached the point where no local traffic has enough delta-vee to catch up with you – and that includes *Quaynor*, I'm afraid.'

Geoffrey nodded, although a fuller understanding of the situation did not make it any easier to accept. 'I need to check on Jumai. Maybe she can help us.'

'We'll keep reviewing the situation,' the merwoman said. 'In the meantime, good luck. I was about to wish you "godspeed", but under the circumstances ... maybe not.'

CHAPTER THIRTY-FOUR

Getting to the medical suite had been more difficult than Geoffrey had anticipated. The central corridor had become a plunging vertical shaft, one that could only be ascended or descended using the recessed ladders Geoffrey had noticed on his arrival. He'd wanted to go down alone – he'd tried to persuade Hector to stay on the bridge, monitoring the situation – but his cousin had been determined to accompany him. They had been able to secure themselves to handholds and grabs as they worked their way down, but the process had been time-consuming and fraught with hazard.

There was something troubling about the provision of the ladders, though. Whoever had decided they were necessary must have known that the ship would be accelerating hard. That, and the ship's confident assessment of their trip time to Lionheart, made it all the more difficult to accept that the engine was malfunctioning.

Geoffrey should have been encouraged by that, but he wasn't. He didn't like the idea of being trapped aboard a ship that was already travelling too fast to be intercepted.

'I don't remember what happened,' Jumai said, when the proxy had brought her round to consciousness and the ship had confirmed that her injuries were minor, the concussion having no long-term consequences. 'I was outside . . . and now I'm not.'

'You remember *Winter Queen*?' he asked.

She considered his question for a moment before answering. 'In the habitat, yes.'

'You're aboard it,' Geoffrey said, before adding, 'sort of.'

'We're prisoners,' Hector stated gravely. 'The ship has locked us out of its controls and we've been accelerating since we broke out of the Winter Palace. But it isn't Eunice's old ship, and we don't really know where it's taking us.'

'We found your suit,' Jumai said.

Hector nodded. 'Geoffrey told me you both came aboard to find me.

You were supposed to leave the station and get to safety before the charges blew. You remember the charges?'

She answered his question with one of her own: 'What happened to them?'

'I defused them,' Geoffrey said. 'But they were the least of our problems, as it turns out. The station was already counting down to its own demolition. It must have been designed this way, all those years ago – made to come apart, so that the ship could break out without damaging itself.'

'Did you say this isn't the *Winter Queen*?' There was a notch in her brow – a frown, or the crease of a headache, or both.

'It looks the same,' Geoffrey said, 'but it's younger, and it was built on the edge of the solar system. It's also ... doing things. Stuff that ships don't usually do, in my limited experience.'

'Your grandmother was a piece of work, do you know that?'

Geoffrey managed a graveyard smile. 'I'm coming round to that conclusion myself.'

'The ship is accelerating too strongly,' Hector said. 'That's what the people outside think, anyway. But clearly we're still alive, and the ship looks as if it's been designed to cope with this kind of thing.'

'You think Eunice gave it some tweaks?'

'If she did, it was a hell of a tune-up,' Geoffrey said. 'If the ship isn't lying, it's headed for an iceteroid in the Kuiper belt. It's an Akinya asset, a long way out. Ship says we'll be there in fifty-two days, which is nothing.'

'Doesn't sound like nothing to me. That's – what – nearly two months?'

'It should take a lot longer,' Hector told her. 'Our best swiftships – the best that anyone can buy, including me – have an upper limit of about two hundred kilometres per second, and most don't get anywhere near that. We'll need to be moving about five times faster.'

'That's impossible,' Geoffrey said.

'One thousand kilometres per second,' Hector said. 'Or one-third of one per cent of the speed of light. It may not sound very fast when you put in those terms, and frankly, in the grand scheme, it isn't. But if the ship keeps this up, the three of us will shortly be moving faster than anyone has ever travelled in the entire history of human civilisation.'

'Well,' Jumai said, 'this sure as fuck wasn't in my plans when I woke up this morning.'

'I suspect that goes for the three of us,' Hector said.

'You shouldn't have come after us,' Geoffrey said. 'You had a chance to get out.'

'So did you,' Hector said. 'Why criticise Jumai for doing exactly the same thing you did?'

'I wanted to save the station,' Geoffrey said. 'There was never much chance of me getting out in time.'

'Part of you must have still wanted to give it a try. That's basic human survival instinct kicking in, cousin. Yet you came back, and stayed with me until the ship's countdown reached zero.' Hector glanced away, then forced himself to meet Geoffrey's eyes. He held the stare, his chin working while he sought the right words. 'After everything that has happened between us, after what you thought Lucas and I had done to Memphis, I did not expect that.'

'I had to know what this ship is for,' Geoffrey said.

'Maybe you did,' Jumai said. 'But you couldn't leave him, either.'

Softly, Hector said, 'If Lucas and I have wronged you, it is only because we wanted the best for the family. Would we have involved you if that was not the case?'

'You opened something you weren't expecting,' Geoffrey said.

'That is true.'

'Maybe there was a point where we had the option of letting all this stay hidden. But after what we've seen now – the Winter Palace, this ship – I don't think we can go back. Not even if we wanted to.'

'The destruction of the habitat will have been visible to countless public eyes,' Hector said. 'The world will soon know what was inside it – if it doesn't already.'

'So you accept that the cat is out of the bag?'

Hector emitted a mirthless half-laugh. 'What choice do any of us have now?'

Geoffrey turned to Jumai. 'I can't say I'm happy that you chose to come back aboard the ship. But at the same time, I'm glad to have you here. Does that make any sense?'

'Maybe it will when my head clears,' she said.

When Jumai was strong enough to be moved, they had the proxy convey her back up to the command deck while Geoffrey and Hector took the ladders. They had been under way for more than three hours by this point, and the relentless acceleration had already taken them as far from the Moon as its own orbit around the Earth. In one of the viewing ports, it already looked smaller than it did from Africa. More than anything, it was this that touched Geoffrey on a visceral level.

It wasn't numbers any more; it was something he could look at with his own eyes and feel, deep in his guts. He didn't need to take anyone's word that they were going a long way out.

For most of the last hour Jumai had been sitting in the right-most command chair, attempting to find a way to unlock the ship's controls. She had been doing none of the command inputting herself since the seat would not recognise her as being of Akinya blood. But that didn't stop her directing Hector and Geoffrey.

It was to no avail. The control lockout was watertight, and all the usual circumventions proved futile.

'Not saying it can't be broken,' Jumai said, when her last attempt was rebuffed, 'but it's going to take someone a lot smarter than me to do it. Plus, they'd need to be on this ship already.'

'Maybe it can't be done,' Hector said. 'This has been orchestrated with exceptional thoroughness. Our grandmother was not one for leaving loose ends.'

'Except the ones she meant us to find,' Geoffrey said.

'This ship has been prepared for us,' Hector went on. 'It was waiting for an Akinya to enter it, and it has a destination in mind. I do not think it is any accident that those hibernation units were provided.'

'Why six?' Geoffrey asked.

'Eunice was taking no chances. The ship only needed one of us to trigger its countdown, but there was always the possibility that there might be other people aboard when that happened. As it transpired, it's just the three of us. But you've seen the provisions. Even if there were more than six, I think the ship could easily keep a few more people alive for fifty-two days.'

'And the return trip,' Geoffrey said. 'Let's not forget about that.'

'Let's hope sending us back was in her plans,' Hector said.

When Mira Gilbert next chinged in, it was with imagery of their own ship, captured by public eyes as it fled Lunar space. Geoffrey could appreciate her concern over the engine now. There'd been nothing that bright since the age of chemical rockets. The difference was that the ship was able to sustain its thrust for hours, not minutes. There was no sign of the drive flame guttering out, and even sceptical witnesses were beginning to speculate that the engine might not be as prone to imminent destruction as they'd first supposed. If anything, some of its initial instabilities were beginning to settle down.

The ship had emerged from the Winter Palace almost unscathed. The aerobrake had acted like a battering ram, shoving most of the debris out of harm's way. The centrifuge arms had decelerated and folded into their stowed positions, tucked along the sides of the hull like grasshopper legs.

'It may not be much consolation,' Gilbert said, 'but you're breaking news all over the inner system. You'll be systemwide when light's had time to bounce back from Saturn.'

'How does that help us?' Geoffrey asked.

'It doesn't. I warned you that you were already out of range of local traffic. Things are no better when we factor in faster ships. There are a couple of swiftships on Earth approach that might be able to match your instantaneous speed now, if they diverted immediately, but by the time they reached you they'd be out of fuel. That wouldn't help you at all.'

'No one is to risk anything on our behalf,' Geoffrey said.

'I agree,' Hector put in. 'And I speak for Akinya Space in this regard.'

'Once we have confirmation of your destination,' Gilbert said, 'we can talk about sending out a rescue party. But you're going to be looking at a long wait before anyone shows up.'

'The ship appears to have everything it needs to keep us alive,' Hector answered. 'We'll find out about the iceteroid when we get there. It's a mining facility, so there should be life-support equipment for visiting technicians.' Hector didn't sound sure of that, though. At this point Geoffrey didn't blame him for having doubts.

'We're just going to have to trust the ship,' Geoffrey said. 'We'll be entering hibernation soon – there's no point staying awake if our hands are tied. We all have friends and family elsewhere in the system. I think we'd all like time to make statements to them before we go under. We still don't have full aug reach, and we may never get it. We'll need your assistance to relay our messages.'

'I'll make sure they get where they're meant to,' Gilbert said. 'You have my word on that.'

There wasn't much to say, when it came down to it. They recorded their statements privately, committing them to the care of the Pans, and then returned to the command deck. Jumai made one last attempt to break the lockout, but she got no further than before.

'Whoever designed this,' she said, gesturing vaguely at the suite of readouts and controls, 'didn't throw it together in five minutes. This ship was designed from the ground up not to accept external inputs unless it wants to. Honestly, if it wasn't my life on the line here, I'd be impressed. As it is, I could cheerfully strangle whoever put this architecture together.'

'It's a little late for that,' Hector said.

Geoffrey was still thinking about what he had said to Sunday, and whether it needed amending. The last thing he wanted to do was add to her troubles, but he had still asked her to find someone who could take care of the elephants – at least watch over them – until he was back. He did not go so far as to voice his own fear, which was that he might never return. Geoffrey just hoped she was faring well on Mars. It would have been good to know that she was safe, before he went under.

'I suspect I know what you are thinking,' Hector said a little while later.

'What?' Geoffrey asked.

'You would have liked to have spoken to Memphis again before he died. You may find this difficult to accept, but I feel the same way. I did not kill him, Geoffrey. Nor did Lucas.'

Geoffrey looked away for a moment. 'I know. It was what you always said it was: just a stupid accident.'

Hector's face showed that he had been expecting any answer but that one. 'You were so certain we had done it. What made you change your mind? Did you play back our movements, examine data from the public eyes?'

'I didn't need to. I had a choice, when I came aboard the Winter Palace and found your suit. At that point, part of me was still willing to accept that you and Lucas might have been behind it.'

'No one could blame you for feeling angry. You were always close to him.'

'Another part of me knew it wasn't possible. We're family, after all. We may have different opinions about the way we live our lives, but that doesn't make us implacable enemies. Or it shouldn't. We've all had the enhancements, too. Why should you and Lucas be capable of premeditated murder if I'm not?'

'Some fish always slip through the net. It was not an outlandish possibility. When you tried to punch me . . . it's not as if you didn't want to draw blood, is it?'

The memory of that moment, the red rage, the numbing clampdown as the Mech retaliated, remained raw.

'I'm ashamed of what I did.'

'None of us has acted as well as we might have in this,' Hector said. 'Lucas and I . . . we should not have approached you the way we did. It would have been better if we'd just *asked* you for help, rather than offering money. Rather than bribing you. Then at least there would have been the implication that we trusted each other. But I am afraid business runs rather thick in our veins.'

'What's done is done.'

'I am still glad that you came back for me,' Hector said. 'Perhaps I would have done the same for you. The point is, the moment tested you, and you rose to the challenge. I have not yet been tested.' He paused, smiling slightly. 'I am not sure if we will ever be friends, in the accepted sense, but if we can somehow find a way not to despise each other, I think that will be an improvement. For the old man's sake, if nothing else. Memphis always did wish we could all get on like a happy family.'

'I still can't accept that he's gone,' Geoffrey said.

'It will take us all a long while to adjust. When this is over, we must find a way to honour his memory. All of us, as best we can.'

'I agree,' Geoffrey said.

Hector offered his hand. Geoffrey looked at it, allowing the moment to stretch. He did not want to give the impression that this was an easy or casual reconciliation, or that there was not still a vast gulf of trust to be bridged. But Hector was right. They had to start somewhere, and now was as good a time as ever. They might not, after all, get another chance.

He shook.

CHAPTER THIRTY-FIVE

It was the morning of the nineteenth of March, another spring day dawning in the northern hemisphere of Mars, the sky as clean and pink as bottled plasma. Soya had driven Sunday and Jitendra back to Vishniac, traversing the Evolvarium at night in a tiny four-wheeled buggy with a bubble-top pressure cabin. They had come out of the Aggregate's belly down a steel ramp which had folded back into the machine as soon as their wheels touched dirt. Jonathan had said that the journey was safe, that the other machines would keep their distance – none of them wished to provoke the Aggregate – but Sunday nonetheless sensed a constant low-level tension in Soya as they bounced and yawed across the endless high plains of the Tharsis Bulge. Now and then she'd bite her lower lip, clench her knuckles on the controls, glance nervously at the radar and sonar devices, or scan the horizon for the auroral flashes which signalled the death struggles of lesser machines. They had crossed the transponder boundary and put many kilometres between themselves and the technical limit of the Evolvarium before Soya allowed herself to relax. Even then, it was a twitching, high-strung sort of relaxation. She might be free of the machines, but Soya still wished to keep a low profile.

They had only been away from Vishniac for two full days, yet it felt like weeks to Sunday. And the little settlement, skewered by its railway line, so dismal and unprepossessing upon her arrival, now looked magnificent.

Soya parked the buggy in the same underground garage where Gribelin had kept his truck. 'I should be going,' she said, while Jitendra and Sunday grabbed their things. 'Got jobs to do for my father.'

'At least let us buy you a coffee,' Sunday said.

Soya resisted, but Sunday pushed, and at last they were riding the elevator back up to the public levels. In the elevator's unforgiving light, Soya looked older than before. Sunday began to appreciate the toll that her shadowy existence had enacted upon this woman. Then she caught her own reflection, and it was scarcely an improvement. Their genes were not so very different, she supposed. Both of them looked like they could use a few days off.

They found the same cafeteria where Gribelin had been waiting for them. While Jitendra was ordering drinks at the bar, Sunday held Soya's hand. 'I'm glad we got this chance to meet. Nothing's going to be the same now. I'll always know that you're out here.'

'I suppose we're cousins,' Soya said.

'Something like that. Whatever we are, I'm happy there's someone out here I didn't know about. Not just because you're a direct connection to my grandfather, although that's part of it, but just because . . .' Sunday faltered. 'I think we could both use more friends, couldn't we? And I meant what I said about coming back here. I will.' Although that might be easier said than done, she thought. It wasn't as if she could count on Pans for her expenses any more, was it?

'I would like to travel. There are problems with that, though. My past is a fiction. It's good enough to let me move around Mars, but I could never leave this planet.'

'What's the worst that could happen? They'd find out who you really are? I can't see that you've done anything wrong, Soya, other than maintain a falsehood to protect Jonathan. And who wouldn't do that? He seems like a good man.'

'If the world finds out who I am, then it will discover what happened to him,' Soya said.

'Maybe it's time. There's no rule that says he has to hide away for the rest of his days, is there?'

'I think he likes it better this way. Dropping out of history, like a deleted chapter.'

'Fair enough, that's his choice. But you don't have to sacrifice your whole life to serve him, do you? You've already done more than enough.'

'I'm not that old,' Soya said. 'There's still a lot of time ahead.' And she clearly meant a lot of time without her father, which was equally true, though Sunday had been careful not to voice that fact herself.

'Like I said, I'm glad we met.'

Soya appeared to come to some private decision. She reached around her neck, undid a hidden fastening and lifted away one of the wooden charms. 'This is yours now, Sunday. My father gave it to me. It used to belong to Eunice. It was a gift from her mother, Soya. Soya told her it was old, even then. I think it goes back a long way.'

'I can't.'

'You will.' Soya peeled apart Sunday's fingers and forced the charm into her palm. 'You have no say in this. No one ever does.'

Sunday stared down at the gift. Fastened onto a simple leather strand was a circular talisman, enclosing a more complex form that had been engraved and stained with fine geometric patterning. She allowed her fingers to curl around it, imagining her grandmother echoing the gesture, and Eunice's mother before her, a lineage of closing hands, bound in this moment as if time itself was membrane-thin, easily breached.

'Thank you,' she said softly.

Jitendra was coming back with a tray and three steaming mugs of coffee. Sunday was debating whether or not to show him the gift – wondering if it ought to remain a secret, between her and Soya – when without warning a proxy arrived and took his seat.

It was not a golem; this was a purely mechanical-looking thing, shaped like an improbably skinny suit of armour, all silvers and chromes and burnished blues. It had a minimalist face: a slit of a mouth, two round eyes like double craters.

'We need to talk,' the proxy said.

Sunday slipped the talisman into her pocket for safekeeping. She recognised the voice, but requested an aug tag to be on the safe side. 'Lucas,' she said, with icy politeness. 'Fancy seeing you here. The last thing I remember is my boot crushing your face. Didn't you get the message?'

'Shut up.'

Sunday had had enough of this crap. She braced herself and kicked out at the proxy, landing her heel in the middle of its abdomen. She pushed hard, toppling the proxy back. It went crashing, taking the table with it as its own foot flicked up. The spent drink containers left on the table by the previous customers went flying. From across the concourse faces swivelled towards the commotion like a bank of radar dishes.

Jitendra had frozen, the tray still in his hand.

'We're long past the point of reasoned debate, Lucas. Don't you get it yet? It's over, finished. The Pans screwed me. I came all this way for noth—'

'Shut up.' The proxy was getting back up, disentangling itself from the chair. 'Just shut up. Everything's changed now.'

There was something too calm about the way it was telling her to shut up. More in resignation than anger.

'How?' she asked.

The proxy placed the seat back upright, leaving the table tipped over. 'It's about your brother. I think you should listen.'

She wasn't talking to Lucas, she reminded herself. Lucas was another world away; this was just an emulation – cleverer and quicker than the simulation of Eunice running in the helmet, but no closer to true sentience. Yet for all that, the illusion was compelling. The urgency in its voice was all too real.

'Why do you care about Geoffrey?'

Jitendra had put the drinks down on the next clear table and was busy righting the tipped-over one, picking up the self-healing glassware and setting it down out of harm's way. The coffee dregs were being sucked into the floor before they had a chance to stick to anyone's shoes.

'As a rule, not much. But I do care about my brother. Hector got into trouble. Geoffrey ...' The proxy tilted its head downwards. 'Geoffrey tried to help him. Now they are both in difficulty.'

Sunday could have sworn she had exhausted her capacity to feel anxious after everything that had happened in the Evolvarium. But the proxy's words still managed to touch something raw. 'What do you mean?'

There was that not-quite-human pause while the proxy formulated its response. 'Hector tried to gain entry into the Winter Palace. Geoffrey went in after him, only a few minutes later. Something happened shortly afterwards. The Winter Palace is gone.'

Sunday wasn't sure if she'd understood correctly. 'Gone?'

'It destroyed itself. But Hector and Geoffrey are alive, for the moment. They're on a ship, together with Jumai Lule.'

'I don't believe it. My brother wouldn't work with Hector. This is some kind of trick to lull me into trusting you.'

'You don't have to take my word for it – consult the aug. The news has gone systemwide.'

Sunday doubted that the proxy would call her bluff that readily, so perhaps it was true after all. 'I need to talk to my brother.'

'You can't. They're asleep, and the ship is on its way to Trans-Neptunian space. It's moving very quickly, which in itself is noteworthy. We are concerned that the ship may damage itself, perhaps fatally. If it doesn't, it will reach its destination in a little over seven weeks. In truth, we don't really understand what's going on. But the landscape has certainly changed.'

'Not from where I'm sitting.'

'Sunday,' the proxy said, leaning forwards to emphasise its point, 'let us not pretend that you and I retain any great affection for each other. But *my* brother is on that ship, and your brother tried to help him. Shortly before he went under, Hector told me that we must reassess our position with regard to Eunice's legacy.'

'Are you saying you made a mistake?'

'We've both made mistakes.' The proxy folded its skinny mesh-muscled arms. She could see all the way through them, to metal bones and actuators, and out the other side. 'You said it yourself. The Pans screwed you.'

She'd been wondering if the proxy had the smarts to pick up on that. Evidently it did.

'How else was I supposed to get to Mars? Flap my wings?'

'The question should be: how are you going to get back to Earth, now that your friends have deserted you?' Quicker than she could blink, the proxy's hand whipped out and touched her wrist. Contact was made for only a fraction of a second – she felt the implication of a touch, not the touch itself – and then broken.

Then the icon popped into her visual field. 'I doubt the Pans will honour their obligation to return you home,' the proxy explained. 'In any case, the next swiftship with an available slot isn't due to break orbit for another week. But who needs commercial liners when you have Akinya Space at your disposal?'

She felt violated. Had the proxy asked her permission to establish a body-to-body link, she would have refused it.

Perhaps that was the point.

'What did you just give me?'

'Authorisation to sequester an Akinya deep-system vehicle currently in Martian orbit. It's a freighter, so don't expect the height of luxury, but it can get you home in five weeks, if you leave for the elevator today. You'll be back around Earth before Geoffrey and Hector reach their destination.'

'Maybe I don't want to go home. Maybe I want to follow my brother.'

'He's headed beyond the orbit of Neptune, Sunday. From that far out, the difference between being on Earth or Mars is nothing. Besides – even our fastest ship would take more than eight months to get there.' The proxy let that sink in before continuing. 'You can't do anything for Geoffrey here, and nor can I for Hector. That's why I'm still in Africa. And we all have to come home eventually.'

'I've only just got to Mars.'

'Mars isn't going anywhere,' the proxy said. 'It'll still be here waiting for you.'

So she went home. Vishniac to Herschel, Herschel to the elevator. As the thread-rider took her higher she watched Mars fall away under her feet, receding and paling like some memory of a dream that began to perish at the touch of daylight. Considered in those terms it had been a strange one, a restless fever stalked by scuttling iron monsters and grinning, bad-smelling madmen. She had nearly died in it, too, but now she was sad because there seemed to be something final in this ascent, some unaccountable certainty that there would be no return. *Goodbye, Mars*, she thought: *Goodbye, cold little world of broken promises*. The planet might not be going anywhere, but there was no reason to assume that the trajectory of her life was ever going to intersect with Mars again.

In orbit, she snatched only glimpses of the requisitioned freighter. Ugly as sin, all fuel tanks and radiators, with a random plaque of airtight shipping containers fixed around its skeletal chassis, thousands of them, like blocky 3-D pixels implying a fatter shape she couldn't quite visualise. The nameless vehicle had no permanent crew and only a tiny life-rated habitat module. They put Sunday and Jitendra asleep before loading them, and then there was nothing, five weeks of oblivion and then the grog and haze of revival. She'd felt like a god, like the centre of her own personal universe, when they brought her back to consciousness on Phobos. Now some switch had flipped in her skull and she felt like a piece of grit that the universe was trying very hard to expel.

But that passed, gradually. And from orbit Earth was marvellous, impossibly blue, lit up like an indigo lantern with its own interior glow. She longed to touch it, to stroke her fingers through that atmosphere, cleaving white billowing clouds and glittering salty seas, until she felt the hard scabbed crust beneath them. She wanted to walk on Earth, breathe its ancient airs, feel the tectonic murmur of its still-beating heart. To be somewhere where she didn't need to rely on machines and glass and pressure seals to keep her alive. Which was absurd, given the amount of her life that she'd happily spent in a roofed-over cave on the Moon. But Mars had done something to her.

'I can't go back to the Zone,' she told Jitendra. 'I mean, not right now. Not this moment.'

'One of us has to.'

He was right, too: their affairs couldn't just be left to moulder. So two days after revival, they separated: Jitendra returning to the Moon, and the Descrutinised Zone, where he would attempt to resolve any minor emergencies that had arisen since their departure; and Sunday to the elevator, and to Libreville, and to Africa. It was bad, saying goodbye to Jitendra. It might be many weeks, even months, before they were properly reunited – and Sunday doubted that ching was going to offer much in the way of consolation while they were apart. But she had to do this, and Jitendra understood.

She had not walked under terrestrial gravity for years, and the transition was far harder than she had anticipated. Medicine helped, and so did an exo – she did not feel in the least bit conspicuous wearing it, since her predicament was hardly a rare one – but what she had not counted on was the near-permanent ache in her bones and muscles, or the constant fear of tripping, of damaging herself. The ever-vigilant exo would not permit injury, and the ache was only a consequence of her body reconfiguring itself for locomotion on Earth. But neither of these realisations helped in the slightest. She still felt awkward, top-heavy, fragile as porcelain.

But that passed, too – or at least became no more than a tolerable background nuisance. She did not return to the household directly, for she was not yet ready to deal with Lucas. Instead she travelled, tapping funds that were effectively inexhaustible. Libreville to the Brazzaville – Kinshasa sprawl, where there were friends and fellow artists she'd once collaborated with. B – K to Luanda, where she spent long hours losing herself in the surge and retreat of the ocean, its mindless assault on the mighty Cho sea walls. She never had much trouble finding somewhere to stay, company to pass the evenings. Her friends wanted to know what had happened on Mars, why she had been all that way only to come home again. As politely as she could, she rebuffed their questions. Most of her friends were wise enough not to push.

But they wanted to know about Geoffrey, and she could hardly blame them for that. Unlike the death of her grandmother, this wasn't some seven-day wonder. *Winter Queen*, or whatever name that ship merited, had defied expectations by not destroying itself. It was still out there, further from the sun than it had any right to be given the mere weeks that it had been under way. It had long since stopped accelerating, but it would need to decelerate if it was to rendezvous with its presumed destination. The ship's exhaust would be directed away from Earth when that happened, much harder to detect from the inner system. But countless eyes would be straining for a glimpse of those improbable energies, trying to tease out a hint at the unexpected physics under-pinning them. Some of the minds behind those eyes, undoubtedly, would be half-hoping for the ship to wipe itself out in a single infor-mation-rich flash, all the better for unravelling.

In fact, she wasn't worried about that herself. By now she had some faith in Eunice. If the ship was capable of getting Geoffrey, Hector and Jumai most of the way to Lionheart, it wasn't going to screw up the last part of that journey. But she was much more concerned about what would happen to the three of them when they arrived. What awaited them out there? If the ship used up all its fuel getting to the iceteroid, could they get back home again – or survive long enough to await rescue? But again she fell back on that faith. This was engineered, part of a plan concocted by Eunice more than sixty years earlier. There had to be a point to it, beyond an elaborate form of punishment aimed at her descendants. So she hoped, anyway.

Meanwhile, Geoffrey was not in Africa. When he left Earth it had not been under ideal circumstances, and he could not have known how long it would take to break into the Winter Palace and ferret out its secrets. But he had surely not counted on being away for months. Since he had been involved with the Amboseli elephants, Sunday knew, Geoffrey had very rarely been away from them for more than a couple of weeks at a time. A month would have been exceptional. He'd often told her how much effort he had invested in establishing a rapport with the study group, and how easily that rapport could be undermined.

That, fundamentally, was what had brought her back to Africa, although she had not been quite ready to admit it to herself at first. The elephants had never meant much to her, even though she had shared very similar childhood experiences with Geoffrey. But if she had been pulled away from the Moon unexpectedly, and if something she had nurtured was in danger of suffering through neglect, she had no doubt that Geoffrey would have been there for her.

In Luanda her funds provided an airpod. Still awkward in the exo, she folded herself into its interior and told it to fly to the Amboseli basin. She would be within a stone's throw of the household, but the household could wait.

In the air, east of the Great Rift Valley, the airpod on autopilot, she chinged Gleb Ozerov. She hadn't bothered working out what time it was in the Descrutinised Zone. The zookeepers kept weird hours anyway, and after what she'd been through on Mars she was of the distinct opinion that they could damn well take her call.

Sunday had requested outbound ching, and after a moment of hiatus the bind inserted her bodyless presence into the menagerie. Gleb, who must have accepted the inbound call, stood next to a table-sized trolley, collecting leaf samples from the vivariums.

'It's good to hear from you,' he said, doubtfully, as if there had to be a catch somewhere. 'I was hoping you'd get in touch : . .' He put down his tools, dusted his fingers on his laboratory smock. 'I tried reaching you, but you were still on the ship. Are you all right?'

Sunday was already answering before Gleb had finished his piece. 'How much do you know about what happened on Mars?'

It wasn't just time lag that delayed his answer. 'I was hoping to hear your side of the story before making my mind up. Chama's been trying to find out what he can, but he's still under lockdown, which complicates things.'

'You screwed us. Your people, Gleb. The ones I thought I could trust.'

'*My* people.' He sounded stung by this, as if what she'd said was somehow beneath her. As if she had failed to live up to his hitherto unblemished image of her.

'Truro, Holroyd, whoever. I don't give a fuck. I was lied to. Told I'd be helped, when all they wanted was to get to the box before me. Jitendra and I nearly died out there, Gleb. The Evolvarium nearly ate us alive, and that wouldn't have happened if we'd got in and out without being betrayed. Gribelin died out there.'

Gleb selected another tool and nipped a leaf sample. He held the wispy green sliver up to his eyes for inspection, frowning slightly.

'Nobody comes out of this looking good, Sunday. But if it's any consolation, Chama and I had nothing to do with what happened on Mars. When Chama put his neck on the line in Pythagoras, he was doing you a favour.'

'To buy a favour back from my brother.'

'Perhaps. But beyond that, he had no ulterior motives.' Gleb placed the nipped-off leaf sample into one of his specimen boxes, clipping shut the airtight lid. 'Arethusa contacted us, it might interest you to hear – not long after that unpleasantness on Mars.'

'I've no reason to trust her either.'

'Trust who you like, Sunday – I'm not here to make your mind up for you. She spoke about Truro, though. Said things were possibly going to become difficult for Chama and me, since our sponsorship was so closely tied to Truro and his allies.' He paused to drag a stylus from behind his ear, using it to scribe a note on the specimen box. 'Arethusa said things were going to become difficult for her, too – it seems this whole sorry business has precipitated a bit of a rift.'

'I thought Arethusa was in charge.'

'So did she. So did *we*. But it appears there are elements who feel she's not been promoting the Panspermian ideology with sufficient vigour, at least in recent years.'

'My brother and I had our theories about Arethusa. If we're right, then there wouldn't be a Panspermian ideology without her.' Sunday hesitated on the threshold of what she hardly dared say, because it felt almost blasphemous to voice such speculation in Gleb's presence. But

428

the time for tact, she decided, was long past. 'I think I met Lin Wei, your founder. I think she's still alive. I think all of you owe Arethusa more than you realise.'

Gleb nodded slowly. 'I won't say the possibility had never occurred to us. Given your family's connection to Lin Wei—'

'She was at Eunice's scattering. Arethusa was behind the proxy, of course. And she could only have chosen the form she did because she half-wanted one of us to make the connection.'

Gleb wheeled the trolley to the next vivarium. 'She still has influence, still has allies. For the time being, I'm fairly hopeful that she can still protect Chama and me. Even ensure a continuation of basic funds and amenities. But that isn't guaranteed, and right now we need all the friends we can find. Actually, screw us. We don't matter at all. But the dwarves do. This collaboration is vital, Sunday. We can't let it fall apart just because of a squabble between Arethusa and her rivals.'

'Funnily enough, it's elephants I'm calling about.'

For the first time since she had chinged in Gleb smiled. 'Yours or mine? I should say, the dwarves, or the Amboseli herd?'

'Both, ultimately. Right now I need help with the big ones. You know about my brother's situation, I take it?'

'Difficult not to. I ... hope things work out, Sunday. Our thoughts are with Geoffrey.' Hastily he added, 'And the other two ... your cousin, and the woman.'

'Hector and Jumai. Yes, we're concerned about them all. But there's nothing we can do for them and there *is* something we can do for the elephants. Geoffrey wasn't expecting to be away this long, and I'm worried about the herd. That's why I'm back in Africa. I feel I should be doing something.'

'They are, fundamentally, elephants,' Gleb said thoughtfully. 'They've been managing on their own for millions of years. It would be presumptuous to assume they can't do without us for a little longer.'

'But they're elephants with machines in their heads, elephants my brother has been interacting with for most of his adult life. They're used to him coming and going, studying them. He *speaks* to them, for pity's sake. I don't know what his not being there is going to do to them. And that's before I start worrying about medical issues or pregnancies or anything else going on with the herd. My brother would have known what to do. I don't.'

'Did he leave specific instructions?'

She thought back to the message Geoffrey had recorded, before entering cryosleep. 'Nothing too detailed. I don't think he wanted to burden me, and anyway, he had enough on his mind back then.'

'If there was anything vital, he'd have told you.' She nodded, wanting to believe it, but Gleb sounded much surer than Sunday would have been. 'All the same, our hands aren't completely tied. Your ching tag places you . . . very near the herd.'

'On my way to it right now.'

'Chama and I know our way around the M-group – remember that we've been taking an interest in Geoffrey's work for years. We know the hierarchies, the bloodlines, and I can probably identify two dozen individuals by sight alone even though I've never been to Africa. You've never had much contact with them, have you?'

It felt like an admission of weakness, a duty she had shirked. 'Virtually none.'

'In which case we won't risk direct contact. Leave that to your brother, for when he gets home. But we can at least monitor the M-group, and any other parties that take our interest. And – not inconsequentially – maintain enough of a presence to deter any researchers who feel like claim-jumping. Although I hope no one would be that irresponsible, given the very public reasons for your brother's absence.'

'I hope not.'

'But human nature being what it is, we'd best take no chances. Will you be maintaining a physical presence in the area?'

'For the time being.' Which meant: until she had news from Geoffrey, good or bad. However long that took.

'Chama had best not risk involvement, at least until his hundred-day lockdown expires, and there's no reason for me to be there in person. But I can give you as much support as you need, for as long as you want it. That's my promise, Sunday. If you feel we've wronged you, then I aim to do my small part in rectifying that. I may not succeed, but I'm prepared to give it a damned good try.'

'Thank you,' she said. And it was a heartfelt thanks, although it was only in this moment that she realised how much she had been counting on his help.

The airpod's console chimed, pulling her back into its sensorium. She was nearing home.

PART THREE

CHAPTER THIRTY-SIX

When the hibernation casket brought him to consciousness, Geoffrey's first intelligible thought was that there'd been a mistake; that something had gone wrong with the process and it must only have been minutes since the casket's bioprobes had sunk their sterile fangs into his flesh and begun pumping his blood full of sedatives. It was a perfectly human response, after all. He had no memory of dreams, no sense of elapsed time. But it only took him a little longer to realise that matters were not as they had been when he entered the chamber. He was weightless, for one thing. They had been under thrust when he climbed in; now his body was at rest within the casket, cushioned against movement but otherwise floating, with the anxious feeling of falling in his belly.

A glass-mottled form drifted over him. His eyes tried to focus. They were bleary and the sudden intrusion of brightness and colour felt like a billion tiny needles pricking his retinas. He heard a clunk and felt cooler air touch his face. That was nice. The casket's lid was sliding off him. The blurred form pushed itself closer and assumed the approximate proportions of a human woman.

'Welcome back, sleepyhead.'

He grasped for her name. His memories weren't where he'd left them. It was as if they'd been temporarily boxed away in an attic: still in his head, but poorly organised and labelled. Dimly, he began to realise that he might have been in the casket longer than his initial impressions had suggested.

'Jumai?' he managed.

'Looks like we've got us a functioning central nervous system, at least.' She hauled in closer still, fiddling with his restraints. 'Hector was the first out. He's been through this kind of thing dozens of times, so it was no biggie to him. I've been up about ten minutes. I think we're all right, for the time being. The ship's in one piece, and we're ... somewhere, I guess.'

Her words were arriving too quickly, like tennis balls spat out by a service machine. Geoffrey tried to formulate a question. 'How long?'

'How long have we been under? Fifty-one days, as far as Hector and I can tell, which is exactly what we dialled in at the start. It's early May. Isn't that weird? I skipped a whole birthday while we were out.'

Geoffrey winced as the bioprobes withdrew from his skin. He tried using his arms. They barely felt like a part of him. He had spent some of the Earth–Moon journey unconscious, but nothing about that had prepared him for the fifty-one days he'd been under while the ship took them wherever it was headed. Nonetheless, his arms responded, albeit sluggishly.

'Muscle tone shot to shit,' Jumai said. 'What happens when you spend seven weeks weightless. The engine must have cut off within a few hours of us going under; we've been coasting most of the way, except for the slowdown at the end.'

Systems in the casket would have done their best to prevent muscle wastage and loss of bone density, but Geoffrey knew nothing was as effective as simply moving around under plain old gravity.

He fumbled his way free of one of the restraints and began to drift out of the casket. Jumai arrested his motion with a gentle application of the palm of her hand. 'Easy does it, soldier.'

'We've stopped?' he asked. 'We're still a day out, aren't we?'

'Ship must have shaved a little time off its estimate. As far as Hector and I can tell, we've reached our destination. He's trying to verify that it's the same place the ship said it was. I can tell you one thing already.'

'Which is?'

'Whatever shit we have to deal with out here, dying of sunstroke isn't going to be part of it.'

Half an hour later, Geoffrey had made his aching and uncoordinated way up front to join Jumai and Hector in the command deck. All three were buckled into their seats, even though the ship was now floating at rest. They had not needed to provide further blood samples, and what limited control they had possessed before going into hibernation was still theirs. The ship was even willing to let Jumai access some of its top-level systems. She had assigned external views to two of the displays: one showing the view back towards the inner system, the other of the object they were now holding station from at twenty kilometres.

It was the view back home that chilled Geoffrey the most. It was one thing to be aware that they were now beyond the orbit of Neptune, well into the long light-hours on the solar system's edge. Travel far enough, and that was what happened. It was another thing entirely actually to see how pitifully small and faint the sun now looked from this distance.

Geoffrey had never been further than the Moon in his life. The sun was now more than thirty times as distant as it appeared from his home, and the light it offered was over nine hundred times fainter. It was a bullet hole punched in the sky, admitting a pencil-shaft of watery yellow illumination, too feeble to be called sunshine. For the first time in his life he truly understood that his home orbited a star.

And he felt some sense of the true scale of things. That bullet hole was still the brightest thing in his sky, but he could imagine it shrinking, diminishing, sphinctering tight as he fell further into the outer darkness. Until even that pencil-shaft became just a wavering trickle of ice-cold photons.

He smiled at that, because he had not even come a thousandth of a light-year.

The sun might have been the brightest thing in the sky, but it was not the largest. The iceteroid, which sat in the opposite direction – its visible face illuminated – was fifty kilometres across at its widest point. It was a dark-red potato, its hidelike surface only lightly cratered. Like all Kuiper belt objects, it had been ticking around the sun largely unmolested for more than four billion years. Once in a stupendous while, the gravitational influence of one of the major planets might kick a Kuiper belt object onto a cometary orbit. For the majority of objects, no such glory awaited. They would spend their existences out here, going about their lonely business until the sun swelled up. If, that was, humanity's machines did not arrive first, to tap their riches.

'Is it ours?' Geoffrey asked.

'If we are where the ship claims to be, then this is Lionheart,' Hector said. 'We should be able to cross-check that in a little while, but for the moment I see no reason to doubt it. We've come a long way, and that's pretty obviously an iceteroid.' He dragged his gaze from the display for a second to meet Geoffrey's eyes. 'How are you feeling?'

'They say it gets easier.'

'It does. But fifty-one days is a long stretch even for the seasoned space traveller. The cabinets are modern, though. There should be no lasting effects.' He nodded at one of the schematic diagrams. 'The ship has even redeployed its centrifuge arms. It wants us to be as comfortable as possible. We should all think about spending some time under gravity, even if we have to do it in shifts while someone monitors things from up here.'

'You say the cabinets are modern,' Geoffrey said.

435

'Hitachi have been making them for a long while, but the ones we just used are not sixty-two years old.'

'You said that's how old the ship is,' Jumai said.

'Its basic systems are that old,' Hector replied, 'engine, hull, life-support, everything it needed to get back to Lunar orbit. Since then, though, it must have been outfitted with brand-new internal equipment. I suppose the cabinets may have been manufactured onboard, if the repair systems had the right materials and blueprints. But it's far more likely that they were simply bought and shipped up to the Winter Palace.'

'Without anyone in the family knowing?' Geoffrey asked.

'Only one person would have needed to know,' Hector said, 'and none of us would ever have had cause to question him.'

'Memphis.'

'Who better to supervise whatever provisions were needed? Materials and parts were being shipped up to the Winter Palace all the time, and not one of us batted an eyelid. How hard would it have been to slip six Hitachi hibernation caskets into one of those consignments? Hitachi would have had no reason to ask questions, and the units would have been installed by robots. Only Memphis would have had any real involvement.'

'Memphis knew,' Geoffrey said softly. 'All this time. He knew.'

'His loyalty to Eunice ran a lot deeper than we realised. He was ready to let the rest of us believe a lie because she asked him to. Even to the point of bringing back what we all thought were her ashes, and going through that whole scattering business.' Hector was doing his best, Geoffrey saw, but he couldn't quite keep the disgust out of his voice. He felt some of it himself. One thing to accept that Memphis had known things the rest of the family hadn't. Another that he had been willing to lie to their faces, and put them all through ... what, exactly?

He remembered Memphis meeting him, on the morning that the news of his grandmother's death had come in. The cool, indigo-shadowed gatehouse; Memphis putting his arm around Geoffrey's shoulders, offering strength and guidance when it was needed. All the while knowing that the Winter Palace not only did not contain a jungle, but had never been occupied. And if Eunice had not been living up there, and if the ashes Memphis had brought down were not hers, then what proof did they have that she had really died late last year?

'The only remaining question,' Hector went on, 'is a simple one. Why?'

'I can think of another,' Geoffrey said, 'although maybe they're connected. If Eunice didn't die in the Winter Palace, then where and when did she?'

'You don't even know for sure she's dead,' Jumai said quietly.

Geoffrey returned his attention to the iceteroid, shuttering out the thoughts he did not, for the moment, care to deal with. 'So we just sit here, is that the idea?'

'We can't leave,' Hector said. 'All we have is short-range manoeuvring capability – enough to make final approach to Lionheart. I can't believe that's accidental.'

'The ship's brought us this far,' Jumai said. 'Ball's in our court now.'

Hector voked an enlargement, zooming in on the central portion of the iceteroid. 'It's rotating very slowly,' he said, 'but I've corrected for that. This is what we'd see if we were hovering above a fixed point on the iceteroid's surface.'

The image switched through a series of colour enhancements, revealing surface detail. Spidering out from a central focus were the radial lines and scratches of concentric structures, like ancient crater walls. He voked another enlargement. The zoom jumped to reveal a sprawl of silver-grey grids and modules, pressed into the surface like a child's building blocks into wet clay. The concentric lines were pipes and tunnels connecting the blocks, the radial arms magnetic catapults. The focus was the main production shaft, bored deep into the iceteroid.

'What we're seeing here is more or less what I expected,' Hector said. 'There are production assets like this on thousands of Kuiper belt objects, running day and night, fully automated, for decades on end.'

'Is this one active?' Geoffrey asked.

'Wait a moment.' Hector held up a finger, his lips moving slightly as if counting in his head. Then he jabbed the finger precisely. Geoffrey caught a glint of brightness at the end of one of the launchers.

An instant later something razored a cold blue line across the display.

Then the blue line hazed, feathering like a vapour trail. He watched it darken to black.

'Package shot, on the nose,' Hector said. 'Once every ninety seconds. We've been tracking them since we got visual.'

'A package of what?'

'Processed ice, of course. Water, most likely, although it doesn't have to be. Boosted at high-gee in a magnetic cradle, followed by a shove from ablative pusher lasers once it's cleared the launcher. The lasers do most of the work. They can steer the package for quite some distance after launch by applying off-centred ablation. What you saw there was a vapour trail: the package's own steam-rocket exhaust.'

There was pride in Hector's voice; pride in a complex technical process working to plan. Geoffrey understood, or thought he did. Hector wasn't just thinking of this one launch event, or even this one iceteroid. He wasn't thinking of that single package, beginning its long fall home. He was thinking of the thousands of Akinya assets in the Kuiper belt, the tens of thousands more among the asteroids and iceteroids. Machines doing their work, tirelessly and efficiently, injecting ice and organics and metals into the vacuum, a corpuscular flow that most people barely knew existed. It didn't matter that this one package would take years or decades to reach its customers. What mattered were the thousands, millions, just like it already on their way ahead. That was the grander machine right there: a single industrial plant wider than the orbit of Neptune. A web of conveyor belts, centred on the sun and its little clutch of warm, inhabited worlds.

Not just any industrial machine, either. One that his family had brought into being, with blood and toil over a hundred hard years. They had built this machine and made it tick and whirr like a Breitling.

The launcher flashed again. The vapour trail gashed an electric-blue wound across his sight.

'Then we're wrong,' Geoffrey said. 'Or this isn't where the ship came from originally. If that iceteroid's still being mined—'

'That doesn't prove anything,' Hector said. 'A cubic metre of processed water ice, every ninety seconds? That's nothing compared to the mass of that 'roid. Even if we'd been tapping it for a hundred years, we'd only have extracted a few dozen megatonnes by now. Of course, the ice has to be refined, and some of it's used for the fusion generators powering the launchers and mining gear . . . but we're still talking about an insignificant fraction of the total mass.'

'He means there's still plenty of room for something else to be going on in there,' Jumai said. 'I think.'

'This is just camouflage,' Hector agreed, 'to keep prying eyes from looking too closely.'

'Until now,' Geoffrey said.

The iceteroid's slow rotation gave it many possible launcher trajectories. Depending on demand, there were few places in the system it couldn't lob a package towards. Most of them would be aimed squarely at Mars, which was by far the biggest consumer of water ice and organics. A smaller fraction would be shot Moonwards, silvered with a monolayer of reflective insulation, or aimed at Saturn or the Jovian settlements. The gas giants might be used to slingshot or laser-steer payloads elsewhere, if demand patterns shifted in the intervening time.

What could be aimed at a point in the sky, of course, could always be aimed at an approaching ship.

'We should be wary,' Hector said, apparently following the same thought train as Geoffrey and reaching a similar conclusion.

'Eunice arranged for us to come here,' Geoffrey said. 'We can be certain of that.' But he could understand Hector's trepidation. Hector had already run afoul of Eunice's secret arrangements, and his own ship had been ripped to shreds by her hair-trigger defences. He did not need to have witnessed the attack on the *Kinyeti* to remain mindful of the possibilities.

'Even if I trusted her not to screw up,' Jumai said, 'sixty years is a long time for stuff to keep working. She may have programmed this ship to return to Lionheart, and she may have programmed Lionheart to expect it. But what if some part of that plan didn't make it through the intervening years in one piece?'

'Do we have external comms?' Geoffrey asked.

'We can send and receive between us and Earth, if that's what you mean,' Jumai said. 'There's a message waiting for you, actually. Do you want to take it privately?'

He looked at Hector before answering. 'I don't think there are any secrets between us now, are there?'

'Perhaps not,' Hector said.

As he'd expected, the message was from Sunday.

'I'll keep this brief,' her figment said. 'If you're where we think you are, round-trip time for this message is going to be close to ten hours. Firstly, I hope you're all safe and well. We tracked your exhaust until the point when the engine shut off, by which time you were moving faster than any manned ship in history. We didn't see your slowdown, but that's to be expected: you'd have been firing away from us by then, and most of the radiation would have headed out of the system, not back towards us. We haven't been able to tap into telemetry from the ship, but aside from its speed, it looked to be functioning normally. Of course, if you're hearing this, we can presume that you've been brought out of hibernation. As to what you'll find in Lionheart, I'm afraid I can't give you much help. There's a lot to catch up on, brother. I'm with Lucas now: he told me what happened in the Winter Palace. I'm back on Earth, too – you'll know that from the quangle tags. I came back the fast way, on one of our own ships. What happened in the Evolvarium ... it's complicated, and I'm still not sure I understand it all.'

Sunday hesitated, before continuing: 'The Pans cheated us, Geoffrey. Truro, Holroyd ... the man I met on Mars. Whether that means we can't trust them at all, or that we can still trust some of them . . . I don't know yet. I think we can still trust Arethusa, and I don't have any doubts about Chama and Gleb . . . but whether they still count as Pans is harder to say.' She flashed a triumphant grin. 'They didn't win, that's the main thing. By now I'm fairly sure they'll have realised as much, which is why I don't really give a shit if they're listening in to this transmission. Are you hearing this, Holroyd, Truro?' Sunday raised a screw-you finger. 'We duped them – left them holding a decoy, while I got out with the real thing. I spoke to . . . a recording of Eunice. She told me that one of us needed to get to the Winter Palace.' Sunday smiled again. 'By which time you were already on your way. I wish I could have warned you what to expect, but there just wasn't a means to get through to you in time. But I still don't know what you're going to find in Lionheart. Eunice told me stuff . . . asked me questions. Decided I measured up, I think. But she still didn't give me any final answers. I'm hoping that's where you're going to come in. I wish I could be with you, all the way out there. But you've got Jumai and Hector, and that has to be better than nothing. There's something else, too. You're out of aug reach, so you can't access the construct in the usual way. But I had a better idea. I've uplinked a copy of her – you should find a memory file sitting in your shipboard inbox. Bandwidth was limited, so I had to strip her down a little – but the important stuff should still be there. You can do what you like with it, but if you think there's even a chance that Eunice's advice might come in useful, assign the memory file to a proxy. Bound to be one aboard somewhere.'

Sunday paused for breath. 'Reply, and I'll get it in five hours. In ten, you'll hear back from me again. The household is standing by, Geoffrey – all of us. I'm here, and the elephants are fine. And we want you all back in one piece, as quickly as possible. Take care, brother.'

'I will,' Geoffrey said.

'I'm glad she made it back,' Hector said. 'Although it doesn't sound as if she gained anything by going to Mars.'

That had been Geoffrey's thought as well, but he decided not to draw any conclusions for the moment. Sunday might have given the impression that she was speaking openly, but that didn't mean she'd told them everything.

'You haven't asked me about the construct.'

'I assumed that was between you and your sister,' Hector replied.

Geoffrey watched another ice package shoot away from the iceteroid, right on time, like clockwork.

'It's a long story,' he said. 'Do you trust Sunday?'

'We've had our differences.'

'I mean here, now. With everything that's happened to us, and what we now know.'

'I suppose,' Hector said.

'She created a simulation of Eunice, a construct. It doesn't know anything that isn't in our archives, anything that wasn't caught by the posterity engines – and if there's something the real Eunice didn't want the rest of the world to know, the construct won't know it either.'

'It doesn't sound very useful,' Hector said.

'On the face of it, no. But it's fast and it knows the public side of Eunice's life inside out, at a level of detail none of us could ever approach. It's already proven its worth. I think there's a chance we could still benefit from its input.'

'I have the file,' Jumai said, tapping a finger against one of the displays. 'It looks watertight, subject to the usual filters. I can assign it to the proxy that brought me to the medical suite, if you'd like?'

'We're confident it came from Sunday?' Geoffrey asked. 'That sounded like my sister, and the tags placed her back in Africa. But with the Pans involved, and knowing what they can do with quangle paths, I'm not sure I trust anything any more.'

'I see your point,' Hector said. 'If they faked the tags, there could be anything in that file – including an assassination programme, ready to be loaded into the proxy.'

'I said it looked watertight,' Jumai said, as if she hadn't been heard the first time. 'We can bounce it back to Sunday if you're in any doubt.'

'And wait ten hours for her to reply? And then be faced with the same qualms that the Pans might be hijacking the signal?' Geoffrey shook his head. 'That was Sunday. I'd put my life on it. Who else would bother telling me the elephants were fine?'

'You may be right,' Hector said. But he softened the remark with a smile. 'Do it, Jumai. Assign the construct to the proxy. If the Pans are that intent on killing us, that resourceful, they'll find a way to do it eventually. May as well save them the bother.'

Jumai tapped commands into the console. 'Assigning . . . done.' Almost immediately she added, 'The proxy's moving. It's on its way up to us.'

'Doesn't hang around,' Geoffrey said, pushing aside the ominous feeling in his belly.

'It's just a proxy. They can't inflict lethal injuries, no matter what's going on inside them,' Jumai said. 'Of course, I've never put that theory into practice—'

'I still don't know where Arethusa and the other Pans fit into all this,' Geoffrey said. 'Holroyd was the Pan Sunday met on Mars. I could imagine him betraying us. But I hope Sunday's right about Chama and Gleb. They're her friends. Hell, even I started liking them. I even liked Arethusa, although she scared the hell out of me.'

'There's a lot you need to tell me about,' Hector said quietly.

'We'll get around to it,' Geoffrey said.

Jumai muttered something under her breath. 'Drawing a blank here. I've been pinging Lionheart on every channel the ship lets me access. Either our signal isn't getting through, or they're not answering.'

'We can't just sit here for the rest of eternity,' Hector said. 'The ship is stopped, and it won't let us turn around and go home. It has power and supplies to keep us alive for a while, but it's not a closed cycle.' He nodded at the iceteroid. 'At some point we're going to have to deal with *that*. Like I said, we do have steering control. It would be enough to take us the rest of the way in.'

'And then what?' Geoffrey asked.

'I've already identified a docking structure, near the main bore. If it's anything like our other facilities, automated approach and capture should cut in once we're near. We wouldn't have to do anything – just sit tight.'

There was a knock at the door. The proxy had arrived. Geoffrey nodded at Hector to let it in. They had committed to a certain course of action the moment they assigned Sunday's file to the proxy; there was no point having second thoughts now.

'What name do you answer to?' Geoffrey asked the blank-faced machine.

'I'm Eunice. Who else were you expecting?' The effect was unsettling. The proxy might not have looked like anything other than a robot, but it was adept at mimicking voices.

'It's a shame it doesn't have her face,' Hector said.

'Be grateful,' Geoffrey replied. 'You might want to punch it.'

The proxy pushed itself into the room and came to a floating rest. It might have sounded like Eunice, but it still moved with the eerie precision of a machine. 'Would someone like to bring me up to speed, or am I meant to guess what's going on?'

'Do you recognise that?' Geoffrey asked, indicating the iceteroid. 'You damn well should. It's an Akinya asset, which you gave a name to. Lionheart.'

'After Senge Dongma, the lion-faced one,' the construct answered. 'It was one of our mining facilities. I also selected it as my refuelling point on my last voyage. *Winter Queen* was to set down here, refill its tanks and continue into deep Trans-Neptunian space.'

'We've been dragged here,' Hector said. 'This ship isn't *Winter Queen*: it looks similar enough but under the skin it's something much newer and faster. You must have known about it.'

'I know that there was a plan, and that Sunday followed some of the clues.'

'And the point of that plan was to lead us back to the Moon?' Geoffrey asked.

'Not solely,' Eunice said. 'There was more to it than that. Do you think it was accidental that I showed Chakra's Folly to Sunday, or asked her that question about the colours of the jewels?'

'I've no idea what you're talking about,' Geoffrey said.

'For the sake of transparency, you should know what I am. There is more to me than just the construct you've already met.'

'Delete it,' Jumai said. 'It's obviously got screwed up in the transmission.'

'Listen,' Eunice said sharply, making the word a command rather than an invitation. 'I am what I am. Sunday found my old helmet on Mars. I ... the living me ... had installed a low-level interactive persona inside the helmet. This persona, because it had been shaped by me, had the possibility of containing knowledge that the more sophisticated construct couldn't know. Sunday brought the helmet back to Earth. With care, she was able to bypass the sphinxware and integrate the two versions of me into a single construct – one with the personality of the original construct plus the additional information known only to the helmet version.'

'And that's what we're talking to now?' Jumai said.

'No,' Eunice answered patiently, 'because there simply wouldn't have been time to upload that version into the ship. Sunday whittled me down to the essentials as best she could.'

'There were two of you once,' Geoffrey said, 'one haunting me, the other haunting Sunday. Now there are ... what, three of you? Four?'

'It doesn't matter,' Eunice snapped dismissively. 'You only get to talk to this one, and if I ever make it back to the aug, all my existing facets can be reintegrated into a single working model. For the moment, the only thing that matters is my immediate usefulness. So tell me what you've been doing since you arrived around Lionheart.'

'Trying to work out our next move,' Hector said. 'According to the files, this ship originated here. Now it's returned home. But we're at stalemate. We're just sitting here, and Lionheart won't respond to our transmissions. What do you know about this place?'

The construct appeared to weigh up its options. 'All our facilities carry a degree of fortification against other commercial interests. In the case of Lionheart, I would have amplified those defences. But it should have recognised *Winter Queen* ... or whatever this ship is ... by now.'

'There's no sign that it has,' Geoffrey said.

'Have you considered a slow approach, trusting that the automated docking systems will cut in?'

'That was going to be our next move,' Geoffrey said. 'Provided no one talked us out of it first.'

The proxy swivelled its head to look at the display schematics showing the relative orientation of the vehicle and the iceteroid. 'The ship may have suffered directional comms damage during its escape from the Winter Palace, something that isn't showing up on the system overview. Or there may have been some unanticipated failure in the watchdog systems I installed in Lionheart, something that's preventing a correct reply protocol. Until contact is established, or the counter-intrusion defences are turned offline, there would be an element of risk in continuing with an approach.'

Hector looked incredulous. 'That's all you've got? An "element of risk"? That's like saying there's an "element of risk" in Russian roulette.'

Eunice hesitated before answering. 'There'll be a master security override in the airlock at the surface docking facility, but someone will need to disarm it first.'

'Before we dock?' Jumai asked.

'Preferably.'

'Send the proxy,' Hector said. 'It can cope with vacuum.'

'The airlock may block control signals,' Eunice cautioned. 'The system's designed to dissuade machine intruders. Anyway, the master override may require a human presence, maybe even an Akinya. It would depend on how I configured it.'

'And you don't remember?' Hector asked.

'If I did, I'd tell you.'

'We're ten kilometres from Lionheart,' Geoffrey said. 'It's insane to think of crossing that kind of distance. Even if we had the suits.'

'We do,' Hector replied. 'I saw them when I was scouting for bomb sites. There are also clip-on manoeuvring units for EVA operations. I've used them before – they're fairly intuitive.'

'It's still insane.'

Hector swallowed. 'And the alternative is ... what? Trusting that this ship will hold up all the way in?'

'You do have the aerobrake,' Eunice said. 'It's built for punching through atmospheres at Mach fifty. It can take some serious crap.'

'It's taken crap already, when we broke out of the habitat,' Geoffrey said.

'Line it up between Lionheart and the ship, it should still provide some protection,' Eunice replied.

'And there's no risk at all that it'll look like a battering ram?' Hector asked.

'One you'll have to accept. If you come in laterally, you're wide open to a broadside attack. I'll walk you through the turnaround. Do as I say, and then initiate a slow approach.'

'We're taking orders from a proxy now?' Hector asked.

'Looks that way,' Jumai said.

Geoffrey shook his head. 'We're not taking orders. We're just running a piece of tactical-analysis software and listening to what it tells us.'

'I'll remind you that I'm still in the room,' Eunice said.

'We know.' Geoffrey glanced at his cousin, seeing in his eyes that Hector was willing to accept the proxy's intervention, for now.

Hector's hands moved to the manual steering controls. 'Thruster authority is ours. We'll begin vehicle translation under Eunice's guidance. Jumai – this could get messy.'

'I can take messy.'

'I mean, it might be an idea for all of us to get into suits at this point. Go down to the locker, fix yourself up with one of the units, then slave the other two to yours and bring all three back here.'

'How do I slave suits?'

'You ask them nicely,' Hector said.

CHAPTER THIRTY-SEVEN

They really needed a name for the ship, Geoffrey thought. He was sick of calling it 'the ship', but didn't feel comfortable about reverting to the name *Winter Queen* when it was so demonstrably not the same vessel Eunice had taken to the edge of the system. Given the affection he felt for it, *Bitch* or *Murderess* were looming as distinct possibilities. Perhaps they'd have time to debate the matter when they had docked with Lionheart.

They were turning. It was slow, agonisingly so. Spacecraft were not like aeroplanes, made for hairpin turns and acrobatics. They were more like skyscrapers or transmission masts, with a very narrow range of permissible stress loads. Apply too much torque and a ship as big as this one would snap like a stick of candy.

'Two kilonewtons and hold,' Eunice said. 'Dorsal three, one kilonewton, five seconds.' She was doling out commands like a stern instructress at a dance class. 'Damn those centrifuge arms – they're throwing off my calculations, too much angular momentum along our long axis. Why didn't we stow them first?'

'You didn't suggest it,' Hector said.

'Dorsals four and six, one kilonewton each, three seconds. Aft: half a kilonewton, one second.' She paused, studying the results. As in an aircraft, there was a deceptive lag between input and response. 'That seems to be doing it.'

Eunice might have had the experience, but only Hector and Geoffrey were able to make the inputs. They were sitting next to each other, waiting on Eunice's commands. Geoffrey could sense Hector's tension, boiling off him like vapour. He'd spent half his life in space and had flown many different classes of commercial space vehicle. But nothing this big, this unfamiliar, or under such taxing circumstances.

By the time the ship had reorientated itself, Jumai was back from the suit locker. She was wearing everything but the helmet, her arm scooped through the open visor, and two other suits were shadowing her like zombies. She told them to stay put outside the command deck while she squeezed back into her seat.

'They're as modern as the hibernation units,' Hector observed. 'Give you credit, Eunice – you didn't skimp on the essentials. Geoffrey – get into your suit. We'd best be ready for the worst.'

'Anything from the iceteroid yet?' Jumai asked.

'Not a squeak,' Geoffrey said. He eased out of his seat, selected one of the two remaining suits and spread his arms and legs wide, like a man waiting to be measured by a tailor. 'Dress me,' he told it, and the suit obeyed, clamming itself around his body until only his head remained uncovered. Grimacing – the suit had pinched a fold of skin around his thigh – he scooped up the helmet and returned to his seat, leaving Hector to repeat the process with the other suit.

'Aerobrake is aligned,' Eunice declared, when everyone was secured. 'We'll initiate the approach now. Laterals one, three, six: two kilonewtons, ten-second burst.'

Geoffrey felt the push of acceleration. Almost as soon as he'd counted to ten in his head, it was over. They were weightless again, drifting towards Lionheart.

'Package launches continuing on schedule,' Jumai said. 'That's a good sign, isn't it?'

'As long as they keep away from us,' Hector said.

For all the countless billions of tonnes of ice still to be mined out of the iceteroid, its gravitational field was puny. They would not be landing on Lionheart, in any strict sense of the term; rather they would be docking with it. There was a part of Geoffrey's mind that couldn't really accept that, though. As the iceteroid swelled to dominate the displays, ominous as a bloodstained iceberg, blood that had coagulated to a dark, scabrous red, his brain began to insist that there was a definite up and down to the situation. It took a conscious effort to stop clutching his seat rests, as if he was in danger of falling ahead of the ship.

'Nine kilometres to dock,' Hector reported. 'We'll need slow-down thrust if approach control doesn't kick in. Jumai: keep signalling. We may break through at the last moment.'

'Do you have the faintest idea what we're going to find in that thing?' Geoffrey asked.

'I was hoping you'd have all the answers, cousin.'

'There are going to be a lot of people very interested in getting a closer look at this ship. Maybe Lionheart has something to do with that.'

'I'll remind you that this remains Akinya commercial property,' Hector said. 'People will get to look at it if and when we choose. I may have been wrong about wanting to keep Eunice's legacy locked away, I'll admit that much. But that doesn't mean I'm about to neglect my obligations to the family.'

Under other circumstances, Geoffrey might have taken that for a goad. But all he heard in Hector's words now were weariness and resignation, the drained convictions of a man surveying the grave he'd just excavated for himself.

'It really matters to you,' he said, marvellingly.

'Of course it does.' Hector sounded surprised that it needed stating. 'That doesn't make me a monster, any more than rejecting the family makes you one.'

'Seven kays,' Jumai said.

They had always known that Lionheart had the means to strike at them without warning, but it was quite another thing to have that truth demonstrated with such spectacular indifference to their sensibilities. The ice package emerged on schedule, ninety seconds after the last, but as it boosted from the launcher the steering lasers pushed it through nearly ninety degrees. All this happened too quickly to analyse: the first they knew of any strike was when the ship shuddered violently, and then kept shuddering, pitching and yawing as if on a rolling sea. Geoffrey braced for decompression, or something worse, but the air held. His heart racing, he searched the schematics for signs of damage. But Hector was quicker.

'We just lost a centrifuge arm – it wasn't shielded by the aerobrake. The other arm's still revolving – it's acting like a counterweight.'

'We should be able to stop it.' Geoffrey sounded calmer than he felt. 'Slow it, lock it down or something.'

The pitch and yaw were ebbing; they hadn't done anything, so the ship must have sensed the damage and acted accordingly. Geoffrey glanced at the console chronometer, counting back in his head. How many seconds had it been?

Hector's hands returned to the steering controls. 'Arresting forward motion.'

'You'll need to do more than that,' Eunice said sharply. 'You've been sucker-punched. Ship's still drifting off-axis. You'll lose aerobrake protection in about thirty seconds. Dorsal three, two kilonewtons, three seconds. Hit that mark. *Now.*'

'Overcorrecting,' Hector said, when the input had had time to feed through.

'You were slow. Laterals one and six, two kilonewtons, two seconds. Geoffrey: dorsal four, one kilonewton, one second: *hit it.*'

'We're still drifting,' Jumai said after a few moments.

'It's coming under control. Switch to vernier thrust. Laterals one and three, dorsals two and five: five-second micro-bursts.'

'Aerobrake is beginning to realign,' Geoffrey said.

'Good. Hold this drift for another ten seconds. Stand ready on laterals two and five, two-second bursts. That should kill it.'

When the ship was at rest, holding station relative to Lionheart, Hector said, 'The remaining centrifuge arm is static and locked down. I don't think we lost much air – the internal doors must have shut tight as soon as the centrifuge broke away.'

'Do you think we should pull back to ten kilometres?' Geoffrey asked. 'We were fine until we tried moving closer.'

Hector was already unbuckling from his seat. 'Maybe we were, but if we do that we're just back to square one – drifting with no fuel to get home. As far as I can see, there's only one course of action now.' He pushed himself from the seat, spinning around in the air. 'I'm going to reach that airlock, disarm the security system.'

'Across seven kilometres of open space?' Geoffrey asked.

'Better than ten.' Hector stabilised himself, brushing fingertips against the wall, and opened the door.

The ship shook again. The impact was much louder this time, and it triggered an avalanche of damage and warning indications. The after-vibrations rumbled like a passing express train, dying away over tens of seconds. 'Direct hit against the aerobrake,' Jumai said, when the diagnostic messages had localised the impact point.

'Even if we started pulling back now, it wouldn't make any difference,' Eunice said.

Geoffrey and Jumai abandoned their seats. 'There has to be an alternative,' Geoffrey said. 'If we give ourselves enough drift away from Lionheart, we're bound to fall out of range eventually.'

Hector was about to lower his helmet into place. 'Not how it works out here, cousin. Provided Lionheart can see us, it can hit us.'

'He's right,' Eunice said. 'Unless you can find another comet to hide behind, you have very little choice. The aerobrake won't hold indefinitely.'

Jumai and Hector were both now fully suited, with helmets on, although Jumai had not yet locked her visor down. Hector was on suit air: an image of his face, distorted and enlarged, had appeared on the external surface of his visor. He'd become a cartoon character of himself.

'Senseless the three of us crossing at the same time,' Hector said. 'Jumai knows more about security countermeasures than either of us, but if she runs into a gene-locked system she won't be able to disarm it. Besides, it's not her mess. That leaves you and me, cousin.'

'Fine,' Geoffrey said. 'We'll cross together.'

'Better if I cross alone, then you bring the ship in when I give the all-clear.'

There was another impact, just as brutal as the last.

'At this rate, there won't *be* a ship left to bring in,' Geoffrey said.

Hector opened his mouth as if to argue, then closed it and nodded once. 'Follow me and I'll show you how the manoeuvring units work. Eunice, stick by us. You might come in useful yet.'

Geoffrey should have anticipated a complication, but it wasn't until they had the thruster packs clipped on that he began to grasp what the difficulty might be. It wasn't with the packs themselves: as soon as he studied the controls, nestling under his arms like seat rests, Geoffrey understood what Hector had meant when he said that the operation was intuitive.

But they were bulky. At a push, two suited people could have squeezed into the ship's midsection airlock. With the thruster packs in place, the lock could only take one person at a time.

'We'll still go over together,' Geoffrey said. 'Cycle through and wait on the other side until I get there. We'll start our crossing after the next package arrives.'

Hector's cartoon face nodded. 'That's a good idea. At least we'll have ninety seconds of clear time. If we can get close enough to Lionheart, she may not be able to steer one of those packages onto us.' He reached out a gloved hand and tapped the airlock control. 'See you on the other side, cousin.'

The ship jolted. Hector propelled himself into the airlock and closed the inner door. The indicator next to the door flicked to red, signifying that decompression was in progress. 'Ninety seconds,' Geoffrey said on the pre-assigned suit-to-suit channel. 'That one felt pretty bad.'

The inner door twitched in its frame, jamming tight into its pressure seals.

'He just blew the outer door,' Jumai said, astonished. 'Didn't wait for the chamber to depressurise!'

'Hector, what are you doing? You've just dumped a roomful of air!'

'We won't miss it, and it was a damn sight quicker than waiting for the normal cycle,' Hector said, sounding pathologically calm under the circumstances. 'But don't worry. The outer door's closing normally, and it will still hold air. In a minute or so standard pressure should be restored.'

'He's leaving,' Jumai said. She had her open visor pressed up against the inspection porthole next to the airlock.

'Hector! We had an agreement!'

'Senseless both of us taking this risk, Geoffrey. You put your neck on the line when you came aboard this ship to find me. It's only fair that I reciprocate.'

Jumai worked the lock, forcing it to cycle back to readiness. 'Going to take a while. You can dump air a lot faster than you can pump it back in, and the inner door won't open until there's atmospheric pressure on the other side. Maybe if I had an hour I could find a workaround, but—'

'Never mind.'

Forcing himself to concentrate, Geoffrey stared at the thruster-pack controls again. They'd looked simple at first glance, but that had been with the understanding that Hector was going to show him the ropes once they were both outside.

'I have to follow him,' he said. 'If I don't, I'll never be able to look myself in the face again. But you stay here. We need one warm body back on this ship. The proxy doesn't count.'

The ship jolted again.

The airlock indicator flicked to green, signifying readiness. Other than the venting of some air to space, no damage had been done by Hector's sudden depressurisation. Geoffrey forced himself to breathe slower, though it did nothing to calm his racing heart. He was terrified. He didn't want to go out there, into open space. He'd never been outside a spacecraft in his life, much less in a situation where he might be swatted out of existence at any moment. But he'd told Jumai the truth. He had to be able to live with himself, and if he left Hector to his fate, that abandonment would corrode him from within.

The airlock opened. Geoffrey pushed himself inside, clunking against the outer wall with excess momentum. He nodded at Jumai's cartoon face, and then the inner door was closing.

The emergency vent control, the one that Hector must already have tripped, could not have been more obvious. It was a red handle the size of a shovel's grip, recessed into the wall so that it couldn't be activated unintentionally. Geoffrey took a good hold on it. There was another static handle next to it, providing a bracing point against the sudden decompression. He clenched that with his other fist.

'Venting,' he said.

He felt the tug as the air gasped from the lock but retained his grip. His head-up informed him that he was now exposed to hard vacuum.

Geoffrey eased out of the lock, taking care not to knock the thruster pack as he emerged. His instincts were to retain a point of contact with the ship, but that wouldn't get him anywhere. He had to submit himself to space, and trust in the harness.

He pushed away.

'I'm free,' he reported.

'Can you see Hector? He's out of my sightline.'

'Must be on the other side of the aerobrake.' Geoffrey positioned his hands over the matched thruster controls and applied a burp of thrust. 'Hector, can you hear me?'

'Still with you, Geoffrey. I gather you're outside the ship.'

'You knew I'd follow.'

Hector let out a sniff of amusement. 'I suppose I'd have done the same thing. Doesn't excuse either of us, though.'

The thrust had steered Geoffrey away from the hull. He looked back, seeing the ship in its entirety for the first time. The aerobrake was a braced circle blotting out a significant fraction of the sky, slightly dished on the surface he was looking at, aerodynamically convex on the other. Even with his eyes amped, there were details he couldn't make out. The shadows were black, the lit surfaces gloomy.

He would have to edge out from the cover of the aerobrake if he was to follow Hector.

White light rimmed the circular shield, turning it into an eclipsed sun with its own corona. The light faded. He'd felt nothing, heard nothing, but he knew that another package had just hit the aerobrake.

'Hector?'

'Still here. How's Jumai?'

'I'm fine,' she replied.

'Don't even think about coming after us,' Hector added.

Geoffrey arrested his lateral drift. He was beginning to emerge from the protective shadow of the aerobrake, with the iceteroid's launch systems looming into visibility again. Almost immediately, the visor dropped an icon over a tiny point of light. Next to the icon, distance and velocity numerics pointed to an object two kilometres ahead.

'I see you, Hector.'

'Good. You've made your point, now go back inside.'

Geoffrey stabbed at the arrow-shaped control studs, orientating himself in the same rough trajectory that Hector was already following. He applied a thrust burst, saw the hull of the ship begin to slide by. The aerobrake was looming closer. He studied its approach, hoping he'd given himself enough clearance not to ram against its underside or clip the edge as he passed. The icon put him eighteen hundred metres behind Hector now, but Hector was still pulling ahead. Strobeflashes of blue fire marked his thruster inputs. He was gunning it.

Geoffrey was sliding past the aerobrake now. He'd cut it close – as it neared, it looked as if he'd made a fatal misjudgement – but it whisked past him in absolute silence, and looking back he was at last able to inspect the damage to the ship. It was worse than he'd been expecting. The ice impacts had blasted away the aerobrake's ablative cladding in metre-thick chunks, exposing an underlying integument of geodesic support elements and shock dampeners. No matter that eighty per cent of the aerobrake was still intact, it was now useless for its intended function.

His suit veered sharply. A fist-sized boulder whipped by in the night. He guessed it was debris from the aerobrake: the suit had detected it and taken evasive action.

'Jumai,' he said, 'stay suited, and make sure you're clipped into a thruster pack. The ship can't take much more punishment.'

'Yeah. I figured that out for myself.'

The timbre of her voice was different, and it took him a moment to understand why. She was on suit air.

He looked back again: just in time to see a tiny figure emerge out of eclipse from behind the aerobrake.

Knowing there was nothing to be done – he could hardly argue with her, when he'd done exactly the same thing – he returned his attention to Hector's distant form. Twenty-one-hundred metres and receding. He gunned his own thruster pack again, feeling the pressure as it nudged his spine. He held the studs down as long as he dared, watching the relative velocity reach zero and then begin to climb into positive digits. Geoffrey guessed that he'd traversed a kilometre himself, about the length of the ship, since clearing the aerobrake. Hector must be nearing the halfway mark, and he was still out there, still alive.

Blue fire streaked past: superheated steam from an ice package, stabbing out from Lionheart like a chameleon's tongue. The entire cosmos pulsed white. He looked back, saw the aerobrake glowing against the dim grey nimbus of the inner solar system. The glow faded, darkening to red, then black. There was more damage.

'Jumai?'

'Still here. Am I the only one who's starting to worry about what we do without a ship to get us home?'

'We can manage without the aerobrake, provided we can top up the tanks with whatever fuel that engine uses,' Hector said. 'All I have to do is persuade Lionheart that we're its new best friends. Doesn't sound too difficult, does it?'

'When you put it like that ...' Geoffrey said.

'I'm about two kilometres out. I can see the lock from here. If the protocols are standard, I shouldn't have any difficulties working the outer door. I'm a little off-beam, so I need—'

Something white flashed ahead.

Geoffrey's first thought was that Hector had started correcting his angle of approach, or had even begun to reduce his speed in readiness for landing by the airlock.

That wasn't it.

'Hector?' he asked, dreading what his senses were telling him: that the flash had been much too bright to have been anything so innocent as a course correction.

Hector wasn't answering.

On the area of Geoffrey's visor reserved for comms status, a red warning symbol began to pulse.

'Hector!' he shouted.

But he knew the truth. He didn't need the helmet to tell him that. Hector wasn't responding because Hector wasn't there any more.

'He's gone,' Jumai said. 'Isn't he?'

The two of them were still falling towards Lionheart, towards the point or surface in space where Hector had been intercepted and neutralised.

There wasn't time for shock or grief, or even terror, over and above the fear that Geoffrey was already experiencing. Just the immediate and pressing calculus of survival. At his present rate of fall, Geoffrey would be passing Hector's place of execution in only a dozen or more seconds.

'Do nothing,' he told Jumai. 'No course adjustment, no speed adjustment, nothing. Not until we're almost there.'

'What happened?'

'Hector must have directed a burst of thrust towards Lionheart. I don't think it saw him until then. I don't think it *noticed* him. He was just too small a target compared to the ship, and with all the debris floating around from the aerobrake—'

'You hope.'

'If I'm wrong, we'll know it very shortly.'

He supposed that, of the myriad modes of death one might contemplate, being annihilated by a chunk of catapulted ice shot across space so quickly that it arrived without warning, was not the worst way to go. It would be painless. There would be no pain because once that ice touched him – once its kinetic energy began to convert into heat and mechanical forces – there would be no *him* to experience sensations of any kind whatsoever. He would no longer be an organism. He would be a pink nebula of rapidly expanding and cooling steam with some mixed-in impurities.

But he must have been right about Hector, because Lionheart refrained from killing him. He waited until the dull red world felt only a breath away, a hand's reach. He didn't dare begin to slow down until then. Although he knew that the suit had the ability to detect and avoid collisions autonomously, he wasn't trusting it to arrest his forward motion. Closing his eyes – he did not want to see the ground coming up if it was clear he wasn't going to stop – he jammed his thumbs onto the reverse-thrust studs. A few seconds passed before it occurred to him that if he didn't monitor his progress, he might push himself back out into space again.

More by luck than judgement, he found himself settling gently down – or was it sideways? There was still no appreciable gravity – onto Lionheart. There was red ground below him, grey bunkerlike surface installations all around, veined with pipes and gridded with radiators. The tallest structure was a buttressed tower with docking clamps arranged around its top, wide open like a grasping hand. That was where the ship would have berthed, if their approach had been orthodox. The airlock had to be nearby.

His feet touched down, crunching into the surface as if he was breaking through the crust of a cake, into the soggy interior. That was just momentum, not his own weight.

'I see you,' Jumai said.

She came down like a strobing angel, and at first he feared that she'd initiated slowdown too high up; that she might yet attract Lionheart's attention the way Hector had. But her judgement was no worse than his own. She landed a few metres away, and for a moment it was all they could do to stare at their own stupefied cartoon faces.

'I'm sorry about—' Jumai started saying.

'Later,' Geoffrey said, startled by his own callousness, but knowing that was how it had to be, until they were safe.

CHAPTER THIRTY-EIGHT

They found an airlock easily enough, set at ground level. Geoffrey didn't doubt that there was another one situated near the docking clamps, for the convenience of arriving ships. Jumai slapped her palm against the green-lit entry panel and the outer door opened without complaint. The iceteroid's defences, geared towards the interception of arriving ships, paid no heed to anything happening on the surface.

There was room enough for both of them inside the lock, even with their thruster packs. The outer door closed; air gushed in through slats.

'We've lost contact with the ship,' Jumai said. 'Eunice was right – the airlock's blocking signals.'

When pressure normalised, Geoffrey took off his helmet and allowed it to drift down to the floor.

'Eidetic scanner,' Jumai said, directing his attention to a hooplike device set just below the ceiling. 'And a gene reader, in that wall panel under the scanner. You'll need to make skin contact with it.'

Geoffrey ordered the suit to remove itself. He stepped out, wearing just his inner layer, shivering as the coldness of the air touched him for the first time. He positioned himself under the eidetic scanner, remembering the similar device in Chama and Gleb's menagerie. The scanner lowered down until it formed a halo around his head. The device would be primed to respond to visual memories of specific events or locations; it would easily be capable of distinguishing between memories laid down directly and those confabulated from second-hand experience. At the same time he pressed his bare palm against the grey rectangle of the gene reader. He felt the tingle as the reader drew a representative sample of skin cells.

'State your name,' a machine-generated voice said, in Swahili.

He swallowed before answering. 'Geoffrey Akinya.'

'State your relationship to Eunice Akinya.'

'I am her grandson. Please cease attack on the approaching ship. It is not hostile. Repeat, it is *not* hostile.'

If the scanner understood his words, or cared about them, it gave no sign. The hoop tracked up and down, ghost symbols fluttering across his vision – weird and senseless hieroglyphs, in colours that the naked eye could not quite perceive: yellow-blues, red-greens. The scanner was pushing deep and intrusive fingers into his skull. It was reading the architecture of his brain the way a blind person might trace the profile of a human face.

'Visualise the household, Geoffrey Akinya. You are walking through the west wing, away from the garden. It is late afternoon.'

Picking one memory out of the thousands he held felt dangerously arbitrary. He tried to focus on the details, the specific and telling texture of things. The gleam of polished flooring, the squeak of it under his shoes, the white-plastered walls, the way the light fell on the brown-framed cabinets and cases of the private museum. Dust in lazy suspension, pinned in bars of sunlight. The smell from the kitchen, which managed to infiltrate every corner of the household.

'Go to your room.'

He walked there, rather than simply imagining the transition. He pushed open the door, trying to recall the precise heft of it. He had been in the room recently, at least by his own sense of time, so it was not difficult to bring to mind its dimensions, the simple layout and sparse furnishings.

'Sit on the bed. Look around.'

He did as he was told, forcing the act of conscious and continuous recollection – not just bringing to mind disconnected objects and impressions, but replaying the visual scene as a smoothly flowing sequence, his point of view tracking fluidly.

'Focus your attention on the elephants.'

He had called them to mind, but only as one element of the room's interior. Then he remembered how the Winter Palace had also narrowed its focus onto the elephants, as if they were a key component in the establishing of his identity.

That had merely been a question about his age when he'd received the gift. This was an altogether more intense act of scrutiny. He sensed that to fail in this specific reconstruction would be to fail entirely. Lionheart was holding its breath, as he held his.

He visualised the elephants. He held them in his mind's eye as six distinct forms, recalling the weight of them, the smoothness of the carved wood in his hands, the sharpness of the tusks against his fingertips, the rough, dark feel of their bases. The elephants were all slightly different, even allowing for their diminishing sizes. He strove to visualise the distinguishing details, the subtle variations of head, ear and trunk postures, the leg positions. He concentrated until the act of sustained recollection was unbearable.

The image collapsed. The room evaporated from recall.

'Welcome, Geoffrey Akinya,' the voice said. 'You have authorisation to proceed.'

The eidetic scanner slid back towards the ceiling. He removed his palm from the gene reader.

'Cease the attack against the incoming ship,' he said again, hoping that the system was sophisticated enough to understand and comply. 'It is not hostile.'

'Approach defences have been stood down. Do you have further instructions regarding the ship?'

'Give me back comms.'

Jumai, who still had her helmet on, said, 'Link re-established. Eunice – do you hear us?' She waited a few moments, listening to the voice at the other end of the link. 'Good. The bombardment should have stopped. I think we've managed to persuade Lionheart that we're not a threat, but it's probably best if we keep the ship out of immediate harm's way for the moment. If we can work out how to bring you in under automatic guidance, we'll be in touch.'

'Much damage?' Geoffrey asked.

'Nothing that should prevent us from getting home, provided we can find fuel and make some basic repairs. You think it's safe to leave the packs and suits here?'

'Keep your suit on,' he advised. 'One of us should maintain a link back to the ship. Besides, it's cold.'

'You could put your own suit back on.'

'Or I could walk through that door *now*, and find out why we've been brought here.' He clapped his arms against his chest, deciding he could deal with the cold for the time being. 'Guess which one I'm going for?'

Geoffrey opened the inner lock and pushed through into the iceteroid. He was doing his best not think about Hector.

The door led into a reception bay and storage chamber as large as a warehouse, as deep as a cargo ship's hold. It plunged down many levels below the point where they'd emerged, all filled with racked machine parts and stacked cargo pods, gaudy with primary-colour paintwork, insignia and warning labels. There was Akinya property here, as well as products and supplies from companies that Geoffrey felt certain had not existed for decades. The ceiling, a level or so overhead, must have pushed above Lionheart's surface, forming one of the bunkerlike structures

Geoffrey had seen upon landing. It was windowless but covered with a matrix of lighting elements. A walkway, enclosed in a grilled tube with numerous hand- and footholds, pushed out from a small ledge at the airlock's entrance. The bay was brightly illuminated and smelled showroom clean. From somewhere below came the monklike chant of generators and heavy-duty life-support equipment. The throb worked its way through the grilled walkway, trembling it under the push of his fingers. Walking didn't really work in the iceteroid's practically nonexistent gravity. Geoffrey and Jumai were making long, slow arcing jumps, pushing back from the curve of the ceiling when they rose too high.

Geoffrey was glad to be moving. It was beginning to work the blood back into his limbs and fingers.

'Is this what you were expecting?' Jumai asked.

'Hector would have known better than me what to expect,' Geoffrey said, between breaths. 'But if you'd asked me to guess what the inside of one of our mining plants looked like, it wouldn't be far off this. There has to be pressure and warmth, for the technicians who come out here once in a blue moon. There have to be machine parts and supplies for the things the robots can't make on their own, or aren't allowed to make. And we know the facility's still working as an ice mine.'

'Eunice didn't drag us all this way just to inspect the troops.'

'No.'

At the far end of the covered walkway was another door, heavy enough to contain pressure, but not an airlock. It opened as they approached, revealing a cabin-like compartment set with restraints and four buckle-in chairs. It was an elevator, Geoffrey supposed, or what passed for an elevator on a world that was virtually weightless.

'We've come this far,' he said, in response to Jumai's unspoken question.

They chose seats and buckled in – Jumai having to adjust her restraint to fit around the extra bulk of her suit. Only when they were secure did the door close on them. Geoffrey felt an immediate surge of smooth acceleration. Insofar as he trusted his sense of orientation, it felt as if they were heading down, deeper into Lionheart.

'Eunice?' Jumai asked, more in hopefulness than expectation.

But there was no answer. The elevator sped on, still accelerating.

The ride lasted a minute or three, long enough – given their evident speed – to reach at least a couple of kilometres into the iceteroid's interior. It slowed quickly, but it was only when the door opened again that Geoffrey could be sure they had stopped.

They pushed out of the elevator into a white room about the size of a small hotel lobby. With its coved corners and bright handrails, it had the modular and utilitarian feel of a piece of spacecraft, transplanted deep underground. Circular doors led off from three of the walls into curving, red-lit corridors. The generator throb was much more prominent now, and the walls displayed a constant succession of scrolling status updates and complicated multicoloured diagrams. Nothing he wouldn't have expected in a remotely operated mining facility. That underlying throb might have been the vibration of monstrous drills, gnawing ever deeper into the cold husk of this stillborn comet . . .

Or something else.

The floor shook.

'You feel that?' Geoffrey asked.

'Package launch,' Jumai said. 'I felt one earlier, when we were in that tunnel. You must have been airborne when it happened. Seem to be going off on schedule, as before. Business as usual.'

They both tensed. What they heard were not footsteps, precisely, but the unmistakable approach of *something*, propelling itself limb over limb in the near-weightless conditions. It was coming along one of the red-lit shafts, its busy, bustling sound preceding it. Defenceless, Geoffrey's only response was to find a handhold and reach for it. Jumai made to seal her visor, then drew her hand slowly back before she'd completed the gesture.

The thing was a golem. He could tell that much as it came around the curve. It was humanoid, but it moved with the manic, limb-whirling energy of a gibbon, the quadruped gait too rhythmic and choreographed to look entirely natural. It was tumbling head over heels, yet maintaining impressive forward momentum. Only when the golem neared the door did its movements settle into something more plausibly organic.

Sunday's construct had emulated Eunice at the end of her public life, as she had been before going into exile. She'd lived seven decades by then, and taken no great pains to disguise that age. This was different. They were looking at a much younger incarnation now – perhaps half the age of the original construct.

The golem had arrived dressed in a simple one-piece black garment, marked on the sleeves with various flags and emblems. Eunice's hair was long and black, thick and without a trace of grey, though she had combed it back from her forehead and gathered it into an efficient bun, secured with a black mesh hairnet. The hairstyle was austere, suited for weightlessness rather than fashion, but the effect on the golem was one of understated and modest elegance. Geoffrey had seen countless images of his grandmother as a young woman, but he had never once thought of her as beautiful. She was, though. Small-boned, long-necked, with prominent cheekbones and wide eyes that cut right through him. And the thing he'd never really detected, in all those images – that quiet, knowing smile.

He still hated her for what she had done to Hector. Which was ridiculous, of course: this wasn't Eunice, even if it was convenient to think of the golem as such.

Yet he had to remind himself of that.

'I always hoped it might be you, Geoffrey,' she said, casting a long and appraising glance over him. She had come to rest standing up, her feet on the floor. 'I didn't count on it, and it wouldn't have mattered if someone else had come instead. They'd have been tested as well, and if they were blood Akinyas, with strong ties to the household, I don't doubt that they'd have passed the eidetic scan just as capably.'

He had too many questions to know where to start. 'The only reason I'm here is because Hector and Lucas decided to ask me to investigate the safe-deposit box. If they'd sent someone else to do that, you'd be talking to them now.'

'But would anyone else have had the fortitude to come this far?' She cocked her head. 'I extracted some of your memories, during the eidetic scan. Unethical, but it had to be done. I know something of what you've been through. And I'm sorry that it was necessary.'

'She's bullshitting,' Jumai said. 'Eidetic scans can't extract and process memories that easily. They look for correlations with known image patterns; they can't just rummage through your head indiscriminately, like someone searching a sock drawer. Machines just don't have the intelligence to make sense of the raw data. You'd need something with artilect-level cognition, at the very—'

'Then it's a good job there's an artilect running me,' Eunice said, cutting her off with savage discourtesy. 'Not one of those modern, declawed weaklings, either. Military grade, more than eighty years old, fully Turing compliant – the kind of thing that the Cognition Police were set up to pulverise.'

'Should you have told us that?' Geoffrey asked. 'Or are you not planning on us ever going home again?'

'No – you can go home. I'll put no constraints on that. I'd be a very ungracious host otherwise, wouldn't I? There's fuel here and the damage to your ship is nothing that can't be fixed, given Lionheart's resources.'

'For an artilect, you were pretty slow to realise we meant no harm,' Jumai said.

'I'm but one facet of the artilect,' Eunice said, 'and I was only activated after you had already established your credentials. Until then, Lionheart was guarding itself, as it has done for more than sixty years. If certain autonomic vigilance protocols acted with excessive zeal ... then you must forgive me.'

'If you've read my memory, you'll know that you killed one of us,' Geoffrey said.

'I didn't pick that up,' Eunice said, and for a moment there was something like contrition in her tone. 'It must have happened very shortly before the scan. The memories hadn't had time to cross the hippocampus, to be encoded into long-term storage. If there were casualties—'

'You killed Hector,' Jumai told her. 'He was your grandson as well.' She shook her head in self-disgust. 'What am I doing, trying to make an artilect feel guilty? She's only a mask. Behind her is just ... stuff.'

'Are you finished?' Eunice asked. 'I apologised. I did not mean it to happen. But the stakes have always been high. Impossibly so. Do you think any of this was done without good reason?'

'I have no idea what any of "this" is, other than a means of wasting time and killing innocent people,' Geoffrey said. 'We'll add Memphis to that tally as well. He'd be alive if I hadn't been dragged into your fun and games.'

'Memphis is dead?' The golem looked away, as if there was something on Eunice's face that she did not wish them to see. 'I didn't know,' she added, in a softer voice than she'd used so far. 'When did it happen?'

Geoffrey was about to say that it had only been a few days ago, but then he remembered the time he had spent travelling to Lionheart. 'Seven weeks ago. There was an accident, with the elephants.'

'If his death was a consequence of my actions ... I can't begin to tell you how that makes me feel.'

'You don't *feel* anything,' Jumai said.

'You're wrong about me,' the golem told her. 'This had to be done. Don't you understand?'

'We don't,' Geoffrey said.

'You came all this way. Surely you must have an inkling of what this is all about by now?' She searched their faces for a glimmer of comprehension. 'You don't know anything, do you?'

'My sister said you'd spoken of a gift, something that was both a blessing and a curse,' Geoffrey said.

'Yes.' Eunice nodded keenly. 'Yes, there was a gift. And you must know about the jewels to have made it this far. And the engine that brought you to Lionheart – surely that can't have escaped your attention? You made the connection, obviously?'

'The engine's better than anything else out there,' Geoffrey said. 'It got us to Trans-Neptunian space in weeks rather than months. Is that what this is all about?'

'No,' Eunice said, before adding, 'Well, yes, in one sense. But the engine is ... was ... only a means of bringing you here, and of demonstrating my, shall we say, sincerity?' She smiled encouragingly. 'So that whatever else I do or show you, you'll have good grounds to take my words at face value?'

'Every commercial interest in the system is going to want to pick that thing apart,' Geoffrey said, and suddenly Hector was speaking through him. 'The ship may be Akinya Space property, but we won't be able to sit on a secret like that for ever.'

'You won't have to – I've already made provisions for the engine. And keep in mind that while I live and breathe, I am still running this firm.'

Geoffrey sneered. 'I hate to break it to you, but the only reason we're here is because you upped and died at the end of last year.'

'You and I need a word,' Eunice said.

CHAPTER THIRTY-NINE

Jumai had given up trying to contact the version of Eunice back inside the ship. She had removed her helmet and now sat with it in her lap, eyeing Geoffrey as the elevator car sped deeper into Lionheart. The suit rendered her both monstrous and comical.

'You've come a long way,' the golem said, 'and I don't doubt that you both have lives and responsibilities of your own. Unfortunately, you are about to get a severe case of perspective readjustment. Even the most difficult decisions you've ever had to make in your lives simply don't register on this new scale.' She was sitting with her head low and fingers laced together, looking up at Geoffrey and Jumai as if pleading or begging. 'That was all inconsequential fluff, like choosing a brand of toothpaste.'

'We've both made life-and-death decisions lately,' Geoffrey said. 'So did Hector. So did my sister.'

'Decisions of strictly local consequence. If you died, your family would continue. If the family ended, that would be an economic catastrophe, but it would not be the end of all things. Do you see what I mean? Local responsibility. Contained consequences. That's not how it's going to be from now on.' Eunice looked down at her interlaced fingers – they were knitting and re-knitting nervously. 'A hundred years ago, more or less, I stumbled on something. It led, indirectly, to this moment. I've lived with the knowledge of that discovery ever since – although even I didn't grasp the full implications until decades later. Still, I knew it was some-thing worth keeping close to my chest. And I was right about that. If I hadn't, we wouldn't be here now. We'd be a lot of dead dust and rubble piles orbiting the sun, where once there were settled worlds and people.' She looked up sharply. 'Doubtless you think I'm exaggerating. I don't do exaggeration.'

The elevator had arrived. The door opened and Eunice made to stand. 'What do you know about Mercury, Geoffrey?' she asked, her tone turning brisk and businesslike again.

'Are you talking about the falling-out between Akinya Space and the Panspermian Initiative?'

'Very good. At least you're up to speed on that.'

'I'm not,' Jumai said.

'The Pans constructed a facility on Mercury,' Geoffrey said, recalling what he had already learned from Sunday and Arethusa, 'to build and launch Ocular. It was a telescope, a massive one – made of tens of thousands of individual parts, floating much further from the sun than we are now. To make that happen, they needed Akinya Space involvement. A deal was cut – we'd supply the components, shipping them from Earth and the Moon. In return, we'd get to piggyback our own research outpost on the Pans' facility.'

He looked at Eunice, waiting for her to contradict him. Instead she offered her palm, encouraging him to continue. 'The facility needed to be on Mercury because that was the easiest place in the system to tap into lots of free energy. The Pans had already put in place a solar collecting grid to power their assembly line and launcher; we used a fraction of that energy to run some experiments in propulsion physics.' Geoffrey took a moment to order his thoughts. 'That was a decoy, though. The real purpose of the Mercury facility was to conduct research into Turing-level artilects. By doing their dirty work on Mercury, my family hoped to keep away from the Cognition Police.'

'The Pans knew about this?' Jumai asked.

'No, and they weren't happy when they found out. They pulled the plug on the collaboration, booted us off Mercury. We managed to burn the evidence before the Gearheads got a close look: they couldn't pin anything on us, so they went home empty-handed. That was 2085 – fifteen years before Eunice went to the edge of the system.'

'At least we know what happened to one of the artilects,' Jumai said. 'What has Mercury got to do with this, here and now?'

'Ocular found something,' Geoffrey said, 'just before Eunice died. Arethusa – Lin Wei – felt enough of a debt to her old friend to believe that Eunice ought to be told about the discovery. That seems to have been the trigger for . . . something.' He offered an apologetic shrug. It was as much as he'd managed to piece together.

'There's a little more to it,' the golem said. Eunice was leading them down an ice-walled tunnel. It had been bored roughly, then fixed with spray-on sealant. A walkway had been fastened to the floor, handrails and grabs to the walls, lights to the ceiling. The air was turning cold again. 'Mercury was a double-blind. The artilect research was genuine, but that wasn't the sole point of our being there. The basic physics research wasn't just a screen. It was as equally valid – if not more important.' She was skimming the tunnel in long, loping strides – human locomotion, not the limb-over-limb tumble that the golem had demonstrated earlier. And looking back, smiling with uncontained pleasure. It was the delight of someone who hadn't had an audience in a very long while. She was enjoying the showmanship, her moment in the spotlight. 'On Mercury, we tested a hypothesis. We constructed a relatively small-scale experimental physics facility to probe certain obscure byways of high-energy quark-quark interactions. There were bigger physics labs elsewhere – in Earth orbit, on the Moon – but we needed discretion. Above all, we had energy in abundance.'

'What did you find?' Geoffrey asked.

'What appeared to be an unpromising little side-avenue . . . that turned out to lead to something astonishing. Utterly unsuspected, utterly unex-plored. We'd broken through into an entire garden of new physics. We were breaching unification energies almost without trying. Seeing exotic-matter by-products that shouldn't have been created since the universe was more than a couple of Planck-lengths wide.' Eunice shook her head in amazement. 'The wonder was that we didn't blow ourselves off Mercury. We came close, in the early days. Then we dialled it back a bit and became cautious. *Very* cautious. It was clear that the physics we were investigating needed a bigger experimental facility.'

'You say "we",' Geoffrey said. 'Who else was in on this? You can't keep that kind of thing secret if more than a handful of people are involved.'

'Only a handful were,' Eunice said. 'With artilects and robots handling the complex construction and analysis tasks, it was easy enough to run the physics facility with just a skeleton crew – and most of them thought they were working on minor refinements to propulsion design. As to who knew the full story, there were just two of us.'

'You were never a physicist,' Geoffrey said.

'I didn't say I was.'

They'd reached the end of the ice-walled tunnel. The door here was as heavy and sturdily armoured as a surface airlock, fixed inside a frame that was obviously well braced into the surrounding ice. It opened for the golem, and she led Geoffrey and Jumai through it.

Inside was a small control room – just a couple of consoles and buckle-in seats facing three large triangular-framed windows screened with heavy-duty slats. The wall behind them, flanking either side of the door, was lined with grey lockers and equipment racks. There was some kind of decorative sculpture on the wall to Geoffrey's right, while the one to his left was occupied by a single large display which appeared to show

Lionheart and its environs at a variety of logarithmic scales, culminating in one that was big enough to encompass the iceteroid's orbit around the sun. Geoffrey's eyes tracked to the smaller orbits of the outer gas giants; then inwards to the still smaller paths of Saturn and Jupiter. Mars, Earth, Venus and Mercury fell into an area he could easily have covered with the palm of his hand.

They were a long way out. Every now and again something would remind him of that, and the feeling was like vertigo. How could his grandmother ever willingly have sought this isolation, this sense of immense displacement from home?

'It's a shame your sister isn't here,' Eunice said. 'I'd have liked her to see this.'

'This' was the sculpture, on the wall to his right. It was a slightly irregular rectangle, about the size of a Persian rug, fixed vertically against the wall. The rectangle was in fact a mosaic of smaller pieces – black shapes, mostly about the size of his hand, which, to judge by their jagged outlines, must once have fitted together to form a single whole. Now there were gaps and fissures where they didn't quite join. There were also entire pieces missing from the edges and the middle – bites and absences where the grey backing of the wall showed through.

For all that their edges were irregular, the surfaces of the pieces – the visible faces – were as smooth as if they'd been chiselled along fracture lines. Aside from the occasional chipped or cratered piece, the dark mosaic was uniform in thickness. It gleamed with a magpie lustre, blues and greens shimmering back at Geoffrey, and within the shimmer the suggestion of faint intersecting scratches. Studying the scratches more intently, he made out what could almost have been totemic figures in cave art – a dance of headless, splayed-limb psychopomps made up of dashes and squiggles and spirals.

'Would Sunday have recognised this?' He wondered, momentarily, whether it might actually be his sister's work, but he didn't think so. With solid forms, her work tended towards the figurative. When she worked with abstract compositions, she employed every colour in the paintbox.

'That would depend,' Eunice said. She had positioned herself at one of the consoles and now opened the shutters covering the main windows. They whisked away with a series of loud clunks, leaving only glass between the control room and what was obviously a very large vacuum-filled cavity inside the iceteroid. 'That shielding was never going to make much difference if one of the reactions went critical,' Eunice remarked, 'but it made me feel marginally safer knowing it was in place.'

They might have been looking at the interior of the drilling operation, spotlit for visitors. The cavity was impressively large – an easy kilometre across, stretching away to the left and right around a great curve so that the far ends were not visible from their vantage point. If in fact there were ends at all, for, Geoffrey decided, it was just as likely that the cavity was toroidal, a doughnut-shaped hole dug out of the middle of Lionheart. Bolstering that suspicion was the fact that a metal tube came around the bend of the cavity, passed by the observation point and continued on its arcing trajectory around the other end. The tube was fixed to the inner walls of the cavity by cartwheel-shaped assemblies, each shock-absorbing spoke as thick as a railway carriage. The tube itself was as wide as a major thoroughfare. Like a sated python, it bulged here and there, and secondary pipes branched out from it at various angles, plunging into the cavity wall.

'A lot of metal,' Geoffrey said.

'Twenty million tonnes,' Eunice said, with a touch of pride. 'All of it shipped up from the main belt under the pretence that it was for normal mining operations. Would have been impossible if we didn't already have a massive system-wide manufacturing and transportation network in place. A few thousand tonnes diverted from this facility, a few more from that ... over time, it added up. But books still had to be cooked. One thing to keep a commercial secret from our competitors; another to run a secret project *within* the family. It took ten years, and there were many occasions when it nearly came undone. I couldn't have done it without help – someone to cover my tracks, make sure there were no loose ends in the administration.'

'So that's two people who knew, other than yourself,' Jumai said.

Eunice smiled tersely. 'I made the initial discovery. But – as Geoffrey so kindly pointed out – I'm no physicist. Never was. I could be guided into a kind of understanding, but it was never more than a shallow approximation of the real thing.'

Geoffrey asked, 'How could you make a discovery, without being a physicist?'

'By luck. Luck and the wit to know that what I'd found might be useful, and that I should speak to someone who might be better informed than me.' She touched a control and the shutters slammed back into place with the sound of a dozen rivet-guns firing simultaneously. 'The experiment's powered down now,' she said, 'but it still gives me the flutters, seeing that thing out there.'

'You needed the solar grid on Mercury to run the first experiment,'

Jumai said. 'Sun's colder than a witch's tit out here. How did you find the energy?'

Eunice laughed – not because it was a stupid question, Geoffrey decided, but rather one she liked. 'That's simple. I ran the second experiment off a small reactor derived from the first.'

She moved to the black tableau on the right-hand wall and detached one of the fist-sized fragments. It came off easily, leaving no trace of a hook or adhesive.

'A piece of Chakra's Folly,' she said, tossing the item to Geoffrey. In Lionheart's low gravity, he had ample time to catch it. 'The Phobos Monolith. Your sister would have seen it, I think – on her way to the Indian settlement where I spent some time before descending to Mars.'

Geoffrey caressed the black fragment, convinced that he'd already handled it. 'This is a piece of Phobos?'

'Something that ended up there. People have known about the Monolith for at least a hundred and fifty years – they saw the shadow it cast long before they got a good close-up look at the thing itself. For a while, there were cranks who thought it might be an alien artefact – a ship, a sentinel, something like that. But when we got there we found that it was exactly what all reasonable people had always expected: a very big boulder, jammed into Phobos like a splinter. Impressive, hard to miss – a viable tourist attraction. But not an alien machine.'

'Then why am I holding this?'

'I wasn't the first to see it up close. Not even the fiftieth. By the time I got there, nearly a hundred people had already come through Phobos on their way to Mars – I was the ninety-eighth. And countless robot eyes had already scanned and photographed the Monolith. They'd seen it for what it was: a clearly natural feature, the result of some ancient collisional process.' Eunice waited a breath, then added, 'But they'd all missed something.'

'Something you didn't,' Jumai said.

'I found debris,' Eunice said, 'near the base of the Monolith, loosely scattered over the Phobos surface material – bound there only weakly, due to the low gravity. That thing had been sticking up from the crust like a target in a shooting gallery for countless millions of years. Eventually something had hit it, some speck of cosmic dirt, and chipped off an entire face. I was looking at the debris, the shards of that high-velocity impact. Others must have realised what had happened, I suppose. But it had never occurred to any of them to pay attention to the debris.'

Geoffrey was still studying the piece in his hand. 'You realised there was more to it than just debris.'

'You can't have missed those fine surface markings. On the face of it, they could be anything: spallation tracks from cosmic rays, crystalline defects ... but something about them held my eye. I picked up another piece, lying close by. Then another. Eventually – and my suit air was running low by then – I found a matching pair. I fitted them together and saw that the scratches connected, and that they appeared to form part of some larger ... diagram.'

'I'd laugh if there was any possibility you might be joking,' Geoffrey said.

'I went back out there many times over the following weeks. I gathered as many of the fallen shards as I could find, bringing them back to the encampment. It was easy enough to keep the pieces hidden in my personal effects, and since we were going into a gravity well, not crawling out of one, there was no mass restriction for the trip down to Mars.'

'Did Jonathan know?' Geoffrey asked.

'I saw no reason to keep it from him. He was my husband, after all. And I didn't have any notion of what the scratches would actually turn out to symbolise. Obviously, their mere existence was astonishing. But beyond that ... even if I went public, I couldn't see it being more than a seven-day wonder. So what if the scratches appeared to point to an alien presence on Phobos? It couldn't be proved, not rigorously. Someone could always claim that the shards had been faked by one of the first hundred. And if aliens had been there, a million or a billion years ago, they'd done nothing beyond leave that one set of scratches. Like someone stopping to take a piss at the roadside before carrying on.'

'Graffiti. Scratched on the Monolith,' Jumai said. 'The kind of thing someone might do if they were stuck somewhere, bored, with nothing else to occupy them.'

'Jonathan had studied electrical engineering before making his fortune in telecomms,' Eunice said. 'As part of his studies, he'd taken modules in modern physics. When I showed him the pieces, arranged as well as I was able, he said that the scratched forms reminded him of something. They look like little men, don't they, or demons?'

'That's what I thought,' Geoffrey said.

'To Jonathan they were reminiscent of Feynman diagrams: little conceptual drawings encoding the interaction histories of subatomic particles. They weren't Feynman diagrams, clearly – that would be as unlikely as finding inscriptions in our own alphabets or number systems. But they were analogous. The lines are the trajectories of particles. The

470

squiggles are the forces mediating the reactions between them. The spirals are by-products of those reactions – other particles, packets of energy. That was just intuition, though. It would take a working physicist to say more than that. A good one, too. And someone I could trust.'

'And you just happened to know someone,' Jumai said.

'We established contact while I was on Mars,' Eunice answered. 'He was fascinated by the rock drawings. He said that they already encoded the entire edifice of existing physics, as well as implying the correctness of several models that were still at the preliminary stage. What was more important, though, was that the diagrams pointed to physics we hadn't begun to probe. Quark-quark interactions that seemed forbidden, on the basis of the known gauge symmetries. Do you know much about quarks? No, obviously not, or you'd have realised that they come in three colours: blue, red and green, like cheap plastic jewels. Or that when Sunday finds me reading a copy of *Finnegans Wake*, there's a *reason* for that.'

'I don't think we did too badly to get this far,' Geoffrey said.

'The point was, if the diagrams were right ...' Eunice shook her head, as if she was still experiencing the awe of that moment. 'We could do incredible things. We could build engines powerful enough to fling a ship to Neptune in weeks. But that was just the start of it – the *least* dramatic breakthrough.' She smiled again. 'My physicist was right, too. The engine that brought you to Lionheart was the fruit of that very early research. Really, it's just a standard VASIMR motor with a few wrinkles smoothed out. The kind of thing we'd probably have stumbled on eventually, given enough time. But this wasn't a stumble. We saw how to make it better, and it worked. You can't know how that made us feel. We'd proven that there was testable science in the rock diagrams. But if the least dramatic predictions gave us an engine five times faster than anything else out there, what would we be getting into when we started testing the *really* frightening predictions?'

'You tell us,' Geoffrey said.

'Even with the scope of the equipment in Lionheart, we could only probe the margins of the new physics. But that was enough, for now. These basic experiments have already pointed to a technology so potent that it would make the engine in that ship look like a toy.' Eunice gestured at the black mosaic. 'We can do much better than that. For a hundred and fifty years we've been locked into a few hours of space around one little star. Even being able to reach Neptune in a few weeks doesn't alter that. But now we have the means to break out of the solar system. A *stardrive*, if you will. If the physics is to be believed, then true interstellar travel is now within our grasp. Let's be clear what we're talking about here. It's still going to take a long time. A few per cent of the speed of light, that's what we're looking at. Pitiful and inadequate compared to the scale of things. Horsepiss against all that cosmic immensity. Even the nearest solar system will still be hundreds of years away. But that's hundreds, not tens of thousands!'

She was becoming increasingly animated, as if this whole speech was approaching a carefully scripted climax.

'We already think on that kind of timescale, as a species. We're starting to live long enough, and we've accepted the burden of century-long endeavours like the repairing of Earth's climate. So it's not completely abhorrent to think of interstellar travel in those terms. Of course, there's a catch.'

'There'd have to be,' Geoffrey said, 'or else why wouldn't you have gone public sixty years ago?'

She nodded, with what looked to Geoffrey to be inexpressible relief and gratitude, as if her most dire fear had been that he would not understand. 'I said it wasn't a toy. Sixty years ago, I did not think that as a species we had the wisdom to accept these gifts. Not at the end of that century, when there were still people who not only remembered wars, but had experienced them ... Would you have felt any more confident, in my shoes?'

Geoffrey discarded the flip answer he'd been about to give. 'No,' he admitted. 'Probably not.'

'The energy implicit in the rock diagrams would have been enough to wipe us out many times over,' Eunice said. 'We'd dodged that bullet once, in the era of nuclear weapons. Did we have the collective smarts to dodge it a second time? I thought not – or at least had such grave doubts that I could not leave matters to chance. So I didn't. I followed what struck me as the only rational course, under the circumstances. I decided to sleep on matters, and see what happened.'

'You didn't sleep,' Geoffrey said. 'You went into seclusion, for the next sixty-two years – or however long it was after you figured all this out. Then you died.'

'I didn't die,' Eunice said. 'I just put other arrangements in place. Lin Wei and I might have had our differences, but I'd always hoped that Ocular would find something remarkable. When Lin came to me, when she presented the evidence of the Mandala structure on Sixty-One Virginis f, a series of processes were set in irrevocable motion. For the first time, we had a clear objective: a target for interstellar exploration. It felt right that we should also have the means to reach that target, if we so chose.'

472

'But you can't decide if the time is right,' Jumai said. 'Maybe we're a fraction smarter than we were a hundred years ago, but is that smart enough? You're just an artilect. You can't possibly make that kind of choice.'

'I don't have to,' Eunice said. 'I've merely passed on my responsibility. Now it's yours.'

'You're not serious,' Geoffrey said.

Eunice's smile was not without sympathy. 'I did warn you that I was about to place a heavy burden on you.' She offered her hand, not for him to take, but to sweep majestically around the room. 'All this is yours now. The experiment, the rock carvings ... do with them as you will. If you think humanity deserves this gift, is ready for it ... then it's yours to disseminate. Not as a commercial property, but as freely distributed knowledge. We're rich enough as it is, wouldn't you say? We can afford to give this away. If we're wise enough to deal with this as a species, then we're wise enough to deal with it collectively.'

'And if we don't think we're ready?' Jumai asked.

'Forget about what you've seen in Lionheart, or better still destroy it. You have the resources of the family at your disposal; shouldn't be too difficult.'

'Everyone's seen what the engine can do,' Geoffrey said. 'Even if we wanted to keep this quiet, people will want to know how we did that.'

'Have the engine,' Eunice said dismissively. 'Without the conceptual framework of the new physics, it's an awfully long leap from that to the stardrive.'

'Even that small advance changes everything,' Jumai said. 'Just being able to get out here in a few weeks rather than months is going to shake things up. The outer solar system isn't going to look so far away any more.'

'So push the frontier back a little further,' Eunice said. 'It's what I always did.' She clasped her hands. 'Now, this may sound ungracious given that you've really only just arrived, but we should begin making preparations for your return journey. I was perfectly serious about not keeping you prisoner here. That wasn't the point of this exercise.'

'You'll let us take the ship back?' Jumai asked.

'After it's refuelled and repaired, which – with all of Lionheart turned to the task – shouldn't take more than a week. Then you can go back into hibernation. Perhaps when you arrive, you'll be closer to your decision.'

'I still don't know what happened to you,' Geoffrey said. 'I know you didn't die in the Winter Palace because there was nobody up there to die, and consequently no ashes to be brought home, either. Which means that the last time anyone saw you alive – anyone we can trust, that is – was before you left for your final mission.'

'Lin Wei was kind enough to think of me,' Eunice said. 'The least I can do is pay her back, in some small measure. Remember these numbers, and give them to Lin. I think they will answer at least one of your questions.' She reeled off a string of digits, then repeated them. 'Lin Wei will understand.'

'There's one more thing,' Jumai said. 'You talk as if you're the only person ... the only *thing* ... that knows any of this. Fine, you're an artilect – I'm ready to accept that there isn't another living soul in this iceteroid. But your husband knew, and you've told us about the physicist. You've also told us that it took insider help to pull all this off without the rest of your family finding out. So we're not the only ones, are we?'

'My husband died a long time ago,' Eunice said. 'Long before the true significance of the rock drawings became clear. And anyway, even if he'd lived, and known ... I'd still have trusted him to keep it all a secret. This information will be destabilising, whenever it's made public knowledge, and Jonathan liked stability more than anything else. That's why I left him on Mars.'

'And the physicist?' Geoffrey asked.

'He was a brilliant young Tanzanian,' Eunice said. 'A brave and courageous thinker. But the rock drawings destroyed him. Not as a human being, but as a scientist. He'd ... seen too much. Glimpsed too much of the inner workings of the universe, too soon and too quickly. He was a searcher after truth, and to have it revealed to him so readily, without effort ... the entire intellectual purpose of his life was undermined in one blow. Once the experiments were designed, he pulled back – left the detailed running and interpretation to the artilects.'

'And the insider?' Geoffrey probed.

'The same person,' Eunice told him. 'When he turned his back on physics ... he returned to Africa. He was a very good man, and none of this could have been achieved without him.' Then her voice softened. 'And now he has died, and you must go home to bury him.'

CHAPTER FORTY

They were in Lionheart for a week, as the golem had anticipated. The ship was allowed to approach and dock, and soon after that robots were swarming all over it, attending to the damage and preparing it for the return journey home.

'We never had a name for it,' Geoffrey said, 'since it obviously isn't the ship you left in.'

'Call it *Summer Queen*, if you like,' Eunice told them.

Since the repairs and refuelling were entirely automated processes, there was nothing Geoffrey and Jumai needed to do but wait until their ride was ready. They had been given the option of re-entering hibernation early, but both had decided against that. Neither wished to go to sleep until the ship was already on its way, putting distance between itself and the iceteroid.

Geoffrey couldn't speak for Jumai, but he had no difficulty analysing his own reluctance. He simply didn't have unquestioning confidence in Eunice, or in the artilect emulating her. It had already proven fallible, and for all that it articulated regret and sadness about Hector's death, and even Memphis's, he had no reason to suppose that those utterances carried the slightest emotional weight. It was making placating noises, but behind them, as Jumai had already pointed out, was just stuff. Machinery. And while machinery might ponder a set of actions that had led to a less than desirable outcome and adjust its future behaviour accordingly, it was a stretch to call that remorse.

Lionheart had been equipped to care for human visitors, and that was where they spent the week while *Summer Queen* – that name was as good as any – was overhauled. There was a suite of rooms and modules, a recreation complex, a gymnasium and a couple of centrifuges, one large enough to contain a commons and dining area – enough to keep a team of technical staff comfortable for months. They chose separate rooms and adjusted the furnishings accordingly to suit their preferences. There was entertainment, incoming transmissions – not full aug, but enough to keep them up to date on developments elsewhere in the system – and they had the means to send and receive private communications.

There was a limit to what Geoffrey was willing to discuss until he was face to face with his sister, but he told Sunday that they were both safe, and would be returning home as soon as the ship was cleared for departure. Allowing for the preparations, and the fifty-odd days of journey time it would take to reach near-Earth space, they would be back in two months.

'We'll be difficult to miss,' he said.

Then he called Lucas, and gave him the news about Hector.

Ten hours later, return transmissions arrived from Sunday and Lucas. Neither of them had a lot to say, simply expressing relief that Geoffrey and Jumai were alive, and would soon be on their way home. Lucas thanked Geoffrey for the news about his brother, but beyond that he was implacable, as if he wasn't entirely ready to take the news at face value. Even Sunday had appeared reticent to comment on it. She was in Africa, Geoffrey learned: after returning from Mars, she had travelled to the household to keep an eye on his elephants. Not just chinging, but physically there, in body and mind. He was grateful, and when he considered that by being in Africa she was necessarily neglecting her own life back on the Moon, her work and commissions, his gratitude became boundless. But Geoffrey and Jumai were coming back now, and Sunday didn't need to spend all that time waiting on Earth. He asked her to promise him that she would return to the Moon before his arrival.

Later, when Jumai and Geoffrey were dining in the centrifuge, being waited on by Plexus machines, she said, 'They're not sure we're us. That's why they're holding back, I think. That and the fact that we're obviously holding back something as well. Can you blame them? We've been duped and manipulated by artilects; Sunday's been cheated by the Pans. Right now no one knows who or what to trust. For all they know, we might be dead by now.'

Geoffrey agreed. The fact that they couldn't give a plausible account of what had happened in Lionheart wasn't helping their case, either. It would be better when they got home, and he could talk properly. Not just with Sunday and Jitendra, but with Lucas as well. There was no escaping that. Lucas would have to be told about Lionheart.

'That's not really true,' Jumai said delicately. 'Hector never got to find out why Eunice wanted us here.'

'So you're saying that because he was never let in on the secret, I don't have to share it with Lucas?'

'I'm saying you don't owe him anything. You didn't drag Hector into this – it was the other way around. Later, you saved his neck.'

'Didn't do him any good, did it? I just postponed it.'

'If Hector hadn't died ... it would probably have been one of us. So consider that score settled. Did you hate him at the end?'

Geoffrey had to search himself for the honest answer. The automatic reply was to say that no, he had forgiven Hector everything. But the reality was more complicated than that. 'We saw things differently,' he said, fingering the stem of his wine glass. 'I believe there are absolutes. Rights and wrongs, lines in the sand. Moral certainties. I think Hector was wrong to go about things the way he did. He and Lucas shouldn't have blackmailed me, they shouldn't have used the elephants as a bargaining chip, and they shouldn't have put the family name above all other considerations.' He smiled at himself. 'But I understand some of the cousins' fears now. More so than I ever have. I thought we might end up uncovering something, but I had no idea it was going to be this momentous. And Eunice was right: it is dangerous, and this knowledge shouldn't be shared until we're absolutely sure it won't rip humanity apart. Maybe we are ready for it, and maybe we're not – just yet. Either way, we know about it – you and me, and soon Sunday and Lucas. That means it's already out there, in a small way. And maybe Eunice was right about that but wrong about something else: that it'll take an enormous amount of luck for someone to go from *Summer Queen* to the physics behind the stardrive. If she's wrong about that, then the genie's already out of the bottle.'

He paused and gazed at the wine still in the glass. 'Which means Hector and Lucas were right to be cautious, right to be concerned about something from the past upsetting the present. They couldn't have known how potentially damaging it was all going to turn out to be, but their instincts were right. And if their instincts were right, then maybe their methods were as well. Maybe the means do sometimes justify the ends.' He emptied the glass and waited for Jumai to pour him another measure from the bottle, which was a satisfying Patagonian red – shipped up from the inner system in 2129, if the label was to believed.

The year of his birth, not that he attached any significance to that.

'So they were wrong,' Jumai said, 'but maybe they were right as well. And that line in the sand might not be as simple as it looks.'

'I didn't hate Hector,' Geoffrey replied. 'I used to, I won't pretend that I didn't. But not near the end. I can't say I ever got close to liking him, but when all's said and done ...'

'He was your cousin, and he did do one brave thing.' Jumai raised her own glass. 'To Hector, in that case.'

'To Hector.'

'Although Lucas will always be a prick.'

'One we have to work with, unfortunately,' Geoffrey said. He sipped the wine, placed the glass down and continued with his meal for a few mouthfuls. 'Although it's Sunday that worries me.'

'I don't see Sunday as the problem in this situation – especially as she already knows ninety per cent of the story.'

'It's the artilect,' Geoffrey said. 'Remember what Eunice told us, about how Memphis's entire mission in life was undermined by the rock diagrams? That's how it's going to be with Sunday. She's spent years creating the Eunice construct, and now I'm going to have to tell her it's all been wasted effort. That there's a simulation of Eunice in Lionheart that's at least as believable as the one she's created. How's she going to take that?'

'She won't have to.'

It was not Jumai that had spoken, but the golem. It had arrived unbidden and was standing in the doorway to the kitchen area.

'What do you want?' Geoffrey asked, considering its uninvited arrival a violation of their privacy.

'Sunday need never know about me. You haven't mentioned me in your transmissions home. I'd know if you had, and . . . well, you couldn't have, shall we say.'

'Because you'd have doctored our messages?' Jumai asked.

'Better that than have the authorities know the artilect law was breached,' Eunice said. 'Things may have relaxed in recent years, but you can never be too careful. No: the world doesn't need to know about me, and neither does Sunday.'

'I'm not going to lie to my sister, if she asks a direct question,' Geoffrey said.

'Tell her that Lionheart was being run by machines, and that the machines had a figurehead. There's no lie in any of that.'

He shook his head. 'You'll still exist.'

'No, I won't.' The golem moved to their table, drew out a chair for itself, sat down. 'I had a function, a very limited and specific one, which was to be here for you. I've done that now, and there's no further reason for my existence. You know what you need to know. If you return to Lionheart, the other machines will take care of your needs. They are fully capable of running the experiment should you wish to see it reactivated. And I, for my part, will cease to exist. The routines emulating me will be erased. There will still be an artilect, but it won't have a human face, or my memories. It won't even remember being me.'

478

'That's suicide,' Jumai said.

'It would only be suicide if I had ever lived.' Eunice hesitated. 'Might I ask one indulgence, though? *Summer Queen* will be made ready regardless of what happens to me, so it would make no practical difference to you if I ended myself now. I'd rather not, though. Not while there's still the possibility of conversation.'

'We can't mean anything to you,' Geoffrey said. 'You didn't even exist before we arrived. You said so yourself.'

'That's true.' Eunice looked at her hands, resting on the edge of the table. 'I was only actualised at the moment when you proved your identity, in the airlock. Before that ... I was a potential in the artilect, a set of dormant routines.'

'So you shouldn't have experienced anything before you were actualised,' Jumai said.

'I shouldn't have, and I can't say I did. But those years of waiting ...' She frowned, as if examining some puzzle or conundrum that refused to make sense. 'I felt them. Each and every second. And when you came, when human voices returned to this place ... I was glad. And I still am. And I do not welcome that which must be done.' Then her frown softened and she produced a sad and defiant smile. 'I'm not asking the world, am I? Just a little conversation and companionship, before you go.'

In that moment he thought he could forgive her everything.

'Of course,' Geoffrey said.

CHAPTER FORTY-ONE

Summer Queen took them home – back to the inner system, back to Lunar orbit. Jumai and Geoffrey spent a few days with Sunday and Jitendra in the Descrutinised Zone – Sunday had returned home for the last two weeks before his arrival – and then they all took the sleeper down to Libreville. As before, Geoffrey opted to be woken a few hours out from the surface terminal, when they were still high enough to see the blue-bowed curvature of the horizon, the immense, planet-girdling vastness of Africa. On the Moon, Sunday had told him about the pull Earth had exerted on her, when she came back from Mars. He felt something of that now: a deep biological calling, as if a ghostly umbilical linked him with this place where he had been born, where his ancestors had lived and died across numberless generations. That imperative would always be there, he sensed. The outward urge was just as powerful, just as heartfelt, but it wouldn't go unchallenged. No matter how far out people went, this longing would be present. They could try to ignore it, but this world had been their womb and cradle and that connection was too ancient and strong to be denied. He thought back to the day they had woken near Lionheart, when the sun had been reduced to a single white eye. To imagine going further out than that was to imagine a fundamental wrongness, an act of treason against his basic nature. He didn't think this made him weak, just human. But evidently his was not a universal reaction. His grandmother had stared into that void and shrugged. Is that the best you've got? Impress me. But by no reasonable measure had Eunice been ordinary.

Jumai, Geoffrey felt certain, felt much the same way he did. Giddy with the thrill of having gone as far as they had, but profoundly glad to be on her way home. When she joined him, looking down at Africa, she took a childlike delight in picking out places she knew, communities and landmarks along the coast from Lagos. He couldn't help but be caught up in her enthusiasm.

Yet it was strange to return. He'd had one set of burdens on his back when he came down the first time; now there was another. Even stranger not to feel entirely at odds with his family, although there would undoubtedly be complications and tensions to come, in the months and years that lay ahead.

'I've been talking to Lucas,' Sunday said, joining them on the viewing deck. 'The scattering's set for the day after tomorrow.'

'Did you tell him I was sorry we couldn't bring Hector home?'

'I did, but you can tell him to his face when you see him.' She rubbed a hand down her belly, in a gesture he didn't remember her ever making before. It must have been unconscious, because her eyes were still fixed on the ground, far beneath them. 'He's not going to blame you for what happened,' she went on. 'If anything, he's grateful that you tried to save Hector when you did. A lot's changed, brother. Which is good. We could hardly go on the way we were, especially not now.'

They'd said very little about Lionheart in the Zone, and even less on the elevator. None of them would feel entirely safe until they were back in the household, and even then they would need to be circumspect, guarding a secret that could not be allowed to permeate the Akinya business empire, let alone the outside world. Not until they'd all agreed on the best course of action.

'I'm just glad some of us made it back,' Geoffrey said. 'Including you and Jitendra.'

'Considering I smashed Lucas's proxy's face to a pulp with my foot, he was remarkably accommodating. I think we'll get on.' She set her jaw determinedly. 'We'd better. If the family can't organise a united front, what hope is there for the rest of humanity?' She leaned further over the rail, peering down at the wakes of huge ships off the Cameroonian coast: white vees, precise and economical as if they'd been inked in quick slashes by a master calligrapher. 'I'm still not sure where the Pans fit into all this harmony and niceness, though. They gained nothing, and I'm not even sure what they did counts as a crime. Still leaves a sour taste, though.'

'We needed them,' Geoffrey said. 'They needed us. It was a working relationship that served us all while it lasted.'

'Have you given any thought to—' Seeing his reaction, Sunday held up a hand before she'd finished her own sentence. 'Never mind. You didn't want to talk about them in the Zone; I shouldn't have expected you to change your mind this quickly. We owe Chama and Gleb some kind of answer, though.'

'We don't owe them anything. Any debt we had to the Pans was wiped clean the moment they decided to shaft you on Mars.'

'They're my friends,' Sunday said. 'Whatever happened, they weren't responsible for that. And they'll still be just as keen to continue work with the Amboseli herd.'

'Fine,' Geoffrey said dismissively. 'If they have a problem, they know where to find me. Now can we talk about something other than elephants?'

From Libreville, they rode a pair of airpods back to household – Geoffrey and Jumai in one, Sunday and Jitendra in the other. It was late when they arrived, the house magnificently gloomy and expansive, full of echoing halls and empty rooms. Lucas was waiting for them, evidently saddened yet bearing up – Geoffrey was surprised at first, until he remembered that he'd had many weeks to adjust to his brother's death. They hugged like politicians at a summit, holding an uneasy embrace before pulling away and meeting each other's gaze.

Later, when they were dining, Lucas declared, 'I am ready to turn over a new page. We had our ... differences, I won't pretend otherwise. But my brother would not have wished there to be any further animosity between us.' He blew out a breath through pursed lips, as if this utterance alone had already drained him to the marrow. 'I think it is fair to say that none of us knew what we were getting into.'

'I wouldn't quibble with that,' Geoffrey said.

'For what it's worth, you have my word that we will honour our pledges with regard to your funding.'

Geoffrey broke bread. 'That may not be necessary, Lucas. Although I do appreciate the sentiment.'

Sunday looked at him doubtfully. 'If you're still expecting research backing from the Pans, I think you might need to recalculate. I've been in touch with Chama and Gleb ...' She hesitated before continuing. 'They may not be able to count on the full support of the Panspermian Initiative any more.'

'They didn't do anything wrong,' Jitendra said.

'It's not them. It's the organisation. From what they can gather, the events on Mars have caused a rift. There's disunity at high levels – talk of splinter movements, even.'

'So much for finding out what those numbers mean,' Sunday said.

'Numbers?' Lucas asked.

Geoffrey was conscious that he'd yet to give Sunday a complete account of what had happened, let alone his cousin. But she knew about the numbers. He invited her to continue.

'My brother and Jumai encountered a construct in Lionheart,' she said, 'a low-level emulation of Eunice, a bit like the one guarding the Winter Palace. It mentioned a sequence of numbers, said they'd mean something to Lin Wei. We've no idea what they signify.'

'You could tell me now,' Lucas said. 'I could make enquiries.'

'They may not be the thing you need to know first,' Geoffrey said. He took a moment to refill the glasses, including Lucas's. 'We've been confronted with two difficult decisions, cousin. I'll come to the second in a moment – it's complicated, and you may need a little while to take it all on board.'

Lucas gave an easy-going shrug. 'And the first?'

'Whether or not to tell you about the second,' Sunday said. 'Hell, even I don't know more than the barest sketch of what happened out there. But my brother says you have a right to know, and I'm prepared to trust him on that.'

Geoffrey smiled and leaned in closer. 'Think of the most difficult business decision you've ever had to make, Lucas. The single hardest choice, in your entire life. Now multiply it by twenty.'

'You're not even close,' Jumai said.

Lucas looked like a man who suspected he might be the butt of a joke. 'Obviously there are commercial repercussions . . . we'll want to reverse-engineer *Summer Queen*'s engine, lock down all the necessary patents—'

'The engine's a detail,' Geoffrey said. 'All the construction schedules are aboard the ship. They're ours. But we don't get to make one yuan out of it.'

The skin at the side of Lucas's mouth twitched. 'If they're ours—'

'We get to build copies of that prototype,' Geoffrey continued, 'but we waive exclusivity on the design. The licence and all associated technical data are to be held and administered by the United Orbital Nations, or some equivalent body with reach beyond Earth – we'll figure out the details later. They'll assign construction rights to any commercial or transnational interest with the necessary background and experience in high-energy propulsion.'

'That's a world-changing technology. You're saying we just give it away?' Lucas squinted, as if his reality had suddenly loomed slightly out of focus.

'It's a sweetener,' Geoffrey said. 'There's no doubt that the new engine will change things – it'll shrink the solar system overnight, for a start. It could also do a lot of damage, if mishandled. Obviously we'll have to assess things very carefully. That's where you come in, Lucas. We want you to be a part of this.'

'After everything that has happened between us?'

'Hector would have been involved,' Sunday said. 'Whether he liked it or not, he'd have been in on this. Forced to accept his share of responsibility. Now you get to take his place.'

'I don't understand,' Lucas said. 'You say that this new engine is just a sweetener, as if it's not even the most important outcome of recent events.'

'It isn't,' Geoffrey said.

Lucas was looking down at his meal, as if somewhere in it there might be at least the hint of an answer. 'Then perhaps you had better start at the beginning,' he said.

When they had finished dining, and while Jumai was settling into her room, Geoffrey went wandering, listlessly at first and then with a growing determination. He patrolled the west wing, with its dark-framed cabinets and plinthed and labelled curiosities from his grandmother's life. That had always been the museum wing, but suddenly it felt as if the museum had swelled to encompass the entire building, for all that it was clearly much too large for the meagre collection it was required to house. He wondered what the point of all this was, now that he knew so much of Eunice's life had been a lie, or at least an incomplete and misdirecting version of events. Nothing that had really mattered to her was commemorated here. Not Phobos, not her friendship with Memphis, not the truth about Memphis himself, not Lionheart.

For one hot moment Geoffrey was struck by the mad impulse to grab a spade from the garden stores and start smashing wood and glass, reducing this lying past to shards and splinters. A few wheelbarrow loads, that was all it would be.

But the urge passed as quickly as it had arrived. Entirely too melodramatic, and in any case he only had to think of the patient hours Memphis had spent among these artefacts, tending them with devotion and loyalty. Even though he knew at least part of the truth.

He walked to Memphis's room and pushed open the door. Nearly four months had passed since he was last there, but hibernation had compressed that time into little more than a week and a half of lived experience. He'd been speaking to Memphis, leaning on him to visit the herds. Memphis had obliged, as he always obliged. The next time he'd seen him, Memphis had been lying dead on the ground.

'Why did you die?' he asked, to the back of the empty office chair, still parked at its desk. 'Why couldn't you have waited until all this was over? The one person I could have used, to give me some guidance—'

'He didn't mean to,' Eunice said.

He'd been wondering when the construct would reassert itself. There had been no sign of her in the Zone, and none on the descent to Libreville. He hadn't discussed the matter with Sunday – he was still skirting around the subject, hoping she wouldn't force him to speak about the artilect in Lionheart – and at the back of his mind was the faint and not unwelcome suspicion that his sister had used her privileges to remove the construct from his head.

Evidently not.

'How could you know?' he asked her, the wine fuelling his indignation. 'How could you possibly fucking know?'

She did not appear upset by his tone of address. 'I knew Memphis, Geoffrey, as well as anyone. He was an old man, but he still loved life. Whatever happened out there . . . it could only have been an accident.'

'After all the years he'd been helping me? Why then and there?'

'You don't still believe Lucas and Hector were behind it, do you? Not now.'

'No,' he said, and it was true; he didn't. Even though that realisation slammed one door and opened another, revealing an alternative no more pleasing to behold.

'Memphis had a lot on his mind after my death,' the construct said. 'Too much, for one man. When things started to get complicated, and when you started asking tricky questions . . . I think he found it difficult to focus on everything. That was all it was: the understandable carelessness of a man under pressure.'

'Then exactly whose fault was that?' Geoffrey asked.

'Mine, and mine alone,' Eunice said. 'I'm willing to accept that responsibility, if you accept yours.'

He kept having to remind himself that this version of Eunice was at least hazily cognisant of his grandmother's true history. Before his arrival at Lionheart, Sunday had already integrated the contents of the helmet with her own version of the construct. The file she had uploaded to *Summer Queen* had been stripped down, but there was no reason to assume that this version, the one haunting him right now, was not the most complex iteration to date. Provided that he dismissed all knowledge of the artilect.

'He never said a word about his past,' Geoffrey told her.

'There was no need. He'd shed it, moved on. Would it have changed anything, if you'd known Memphis was more than just a caretaker? Would you have respected him more?' She shook her head, answering for him. 'Don't say "yes" because then you'd disappoint me, and I'd rather you didn't. He was a good and loyal man, and he served this family well, and raised you and Sunday when your parents were halfway to Neptune, and neither of you turned into monsters, and that's *enough*. That's all anyone could ever ask.' She touched her ghost hand against the back of his chair. 'The scattering is tomorrow, isn't it? I'd like to see it. Would that offend you?'

'You don't have to ask my permission,' Geoffrey said. 'You can be there whether I like it or not, and I wouldn't even have to know about it.'

'That's exactly why I'm asking,' Eunice said.

CHAPTER FORTY-TWO

The next day he took an airpod out to the basin, grateful when no one else had made any overtures about accompanying him. Under other circumstances he might have put that down to their lack of interest, and been suitably offended by it. He doubted that was the case now. Sunday, Jitendra and Jumai knew he had matters of his own to attend to, and they were giving him the privacy he needed.

He flew low and fast, trying to empty his mind. It was easier said than done. Though the rains had come in force, greening land that had been parched in January, he knew the old landmarks too well for it to look truly new. He had put down too much of his life here, scratched too much of his history into the terrain. Every waterhole, every copse of trees, every trail had some personal significance, however slight. He had travelled far but he hadn't broken the ties to this tiny part of Africa. Or the ties hadn't let him escape.

He circled his usual study areas, relying on his own eyes to pick out the herds and lone males. It was trickier with the increased tree cover, but he'd had enough practice to be sure of not missing much. He knew the elephants' seasonal movements, their habits and customs and favoured meeting places, and his eyes and brain were attuned to picking out shapes and associations that might have eluded the less experienced.

It did not take him long to locate Matilda and her clan – they were less than half a kay from where he'd assumed they would be – and a quick series of looping inspections established that the M-group had suffered no losses since his last survey. Indeed, there were a couple of babies calved while he was away. There'd been several pregnancies in the group at the time of his departure, so that wasn't surprising. From the movements of the calves it was impossible to tell who the mothers had been – the babies ambled playfully from one adult to another, sharing in the overall protection and nurturing environment of the M-group.

He made one low pass, to let the elephants know he was arriving – or that someone was arriving, anyway, as they'd normally associate him with the Cessna, not an airpod – and then selected a landing site within easy range of the group. Thick lush grass buckled under the airpod's skis. He opened the canopy and climbed out, grunting as his shoulders protested with the effort. His muscles and bones were still aching after the prolonged period of weightlessness aboard *Summer Queen* and *Lionheart*, but not so much that he felt in need of an exo.

The day was hot, dry and windless. There were no clouds and that was a propitious omen for the scattering. He had learned of the plans and approved of them, although there was still a tiny twinge of doubt at the back of his mind. Memphis had never been one for the attention-seeking gesture, and perhaps he would not entirely approve of the arrangements. But then, if the Akinya family wished to honour him, wasn't that their prerogative?

That was for later, though. Geoffrey had other business now.

He sealed the airpod and strode through the undergrowth towards the herd. After a few paces he found a stick and grabbed it to beat the ground ahead of him. He carried nothing with him – no monitoring equipment, no sports bag stuffed with pencils and paper. Just the clothes he had on, which were already beginning to stick to his skin. He had made a mental note to allow himself time to change before they all went out from the household – Sunday wasn't going to get a chance to accuse him of smelling of dung this time. It wasn't the heat making him sweat, though. Geoffrey was nervous.

'It's me,' he called, as he always did. 'Geoffrey. I've come back.'

He pushed through the trees and bushes, whacking the ground with the stick and calling to announce his approach. From close ahead he heard the threat rumble of an adult female, and then he made out the humped forms of a couple of outlying herd members. He noted their shapes and ear profiles, recognising them as individuals. Still whacking the ground and announcing his arrival, he circled around the pair. He leapt a narrow brook and nearly twisted his ankle on landing. The stick had served its purpose, so he threw it away. He crossed behind another stand of trees and found a group of six elephants, with Matilda facing him. Behind the M-group matriarch stood Molly and Martha, two high-ranking females, both of whom had scarred foreheads, one tusk missing and heavily battle-damaged ears. Melissa, the young elephant that Memphis had helped Geoffrey inject with nanomachines, stood between Molly and Martha, her head lowered and her eyes brimming with alert watchfulness. Two yet-to-be-named calves moved among the larger elephants.

Geoffrey moved into sunlight. He walked slowly, but with all the authority and confidence he could muster. He didn't doubt that the elephants were aware of his fear, broadcast through the chemical medium of his sweat. But at least he could look the part.

Matilda broke away from the group, taking a handful of lumbering steps in his direction. She emitted a rumble and flicked dirt with her trunk. Not at him, exactly, but a kind of diagonal warning shot across his bows. There was something dismissive in the gesture, as if he scarcely warranted more effort than that. Geoffrey raised his open hands and stood his ground. Such behaviour wasn't out of character for Matilda. It didn't imply hostile intent so much as a ritualistic reminder of her status, the way a queen might demand that her courtiers approach the throne bent double and suppliant.

The other five elephants had begun to drift back, though their attention was divided equally between Matilda and the human who had interrupted their communal food-gathering.

Matilda stopped ten paces from Geoffrey. Her trunk was raised, her forehead wide and powerful as a battering ram. He could hardly see her eyes.

'I know what happened,' he said, pushing aside thoughts of how absurd it was, to be talking to an elephant. These words weren't for Matilda, though. 'I did what I'd been too fearful to do before. I correlated your movements, on the day Memphis died. And I know you were there. I know you were with him.'

He had meant to end it there, to turn around and return to the airpod. Now that the moment was upon him, though, he knew that he would always regret wasting this final opportunity.

He voked the command, opened the neurolink. Her brain appeared next to his, two weird squirming sea-sponges, pulsing with blood and heat and the endless chatter of electrochemical signalling. His own fear centre was already lit up like a football stadium, glowing across the night.

He wasted no time. Up through the tens, twenties, thirties. Forty per cent, then fifty. Her state of mind subsumed his own, crushing his fear, replacing it with something much closer to annoyance, only slightly tempered by wariness. Up through sixty, seventy per cent. Her body image had dismantled his own, distorting his perception of scale. He was huge but tiny; she was tiny but huge.

At ninety per cent, he allowed the neurolink to stabilise.

He knew what she had done. The mind dambursting into his was the mind of a premeditated and calculating killer. Memphis had been careless, it was true: too much on his mind, and when he went out to do Geoffrey's errands, he hadn't taken the precautions that would normally have been second nature. Above all, he had made the fatal error of trusting Matilda, simply because she had never once shown the slightest intent to harm him.

It must have been quick. One day, perhaps, Geoffrey would have the courage to review the record of events captured by her own eyes and those of any other elephants close enough to witness the murder – there'd been several. It didn't really matter, though. He had placed her at the scene of the crime and that was sufficient.

How was the easy part. Memphis had been distracted, and Matilda had closed in on him too quickly for him to react. The aug was thin here, the Mechanism toothless. Had the Mech detected the imminent nature of that violent and terminal act of aggression, it might have done something. But there'd been no time – either for the Mech to intervene, or for Memphis to save himself.

The why was more speculative. Geoffrey had a theory, though.

Matilda had committed the deed, but the fault was not really hers. She had developed a grudge against Memphis, and given his years of uneventful interaction with the herd, there could only be one explanation for that. Geoffrey had implanted the idea in her head that Memphis was an elephant-killer.

Because it was true. Because Geoffrey had known that his whole adult life, and longer. He had known it since the day Memphis came to rescue Sunday from the hole, the depression in the ground where the artilect had been washed out of the earth. When they had been making their way back to the airpod, following a trail through a grove of trees, a bull had blocked their path. Memphis had told Geoffrey to look away, and he had, for a few moments. But he had not been able to resist looking back, thinking that Memphis would never know. And he had seen the fallen bull.

It was only later that he had come to a full understanding of what had happened in that confrontation. Memphis had reached into the adult bull's mind and used his human privilege to submit a killing command to its implanted neuromachinery. A whispered death-order, one softly voked incantation, and that was all it had taken to bring the bull down. At any other time, Memphis might have risked sending a less lethal command, one that would simply put the elephant to sleep.

But he had taken no chances that day. Two children's lives were in his hands.

Geoffrey had carried the memory of that day ever since, so much a part of him that he barely noticed it. Memphis had taken no pleasure in the act; he'd done it not because he despised or feared the bull but because he had an absolute and binding duty of care to the children in his charge that took precedence over all other considerations. He had dispensed death only as a last resort, and to Geoffrey's knowledge that was the only time Memphis had ever been called upon to kill another creature. Kill rather than stun, so that the bull never troubled another human being. Geoffrey didn't doubt that the act had troubled Memphis in the days that followed.

But there had been no witnesses to that act, and the bull had not been part of a herd. Was it really possible that Matilda's decision to kill Memphis could be in any way linked to that incident from Geoffrey's childhood?

It wasn't quite the case that there'd been no witnesses, though. Geoffrey himself had seen what happened, or its aftermath, at least. And, years later, he had welcomed Matilda into his head.

He thought back to the time when he had allowed the neurolink to transmit his mental state into hers, letting her share in the pain of the scorpion sting. He had no conscious recollection of associating Memphis with the death of the bull. But had he inadvertently communicated that association to Matilda? Had he, in the opening of his mind, planted the symbolic notion in hers that Memphis killed elephants?

He wanted to dismiss the idea as absurd. But the more repellent he found it, the more it kept coming back. It wasn't Memphis's fault, for being inattentive. It wasn't even Matilda's, for taking defensive action against what she now understood to be a threat. She had her herd to think of, after all. She was only doing right by them.

Inescapably, he was forced back to one truth: the fault was his, and his alone.

Intentionally or otherwise, Geoffrey had killed Memphis.

All at once the resolve left him. He had intended to push the neurolink to one hundred per cent, just this once. But the moment had passed. If that meant he was too timid to follow his own investigations to their logical conclusion, then so be it.

'I'm sorry,' he said. 'I should have known better.'

He closed the connection and turned back for the airpod.

More visitors had arrived by the time he returned to the household, judging by the airpods gathered along the parking area. Jumai was waiting for him, already dressed for the scattering. She wore a tight-fitting black jacket and a slim black skirt, offset with flashes of red around the waistline. She brushed a hand against his arm as they met in one of the hallways, lowering her voice to a concerned hush. 'How did it go out there?'

'I had some unfinished business,' Geoffrey said.

She nodded slowly. 'And is it finished now?'

'I think so.'

'I'll be heading back to Lagos tomorrow. Not to my old job, but Lagos is still where my contacts are. I'm hoping I might be able to leverage my recent experiences into a new contract, maybe off-Earth. Still a lot of stuff out there that needs cleaning up.'

'Aren't you fed up with excitement?'

'If you mean do I want to dodge high-velocity ice packages for the rest of my life, then the answer's no. But I do need challenges. I certainly got them when I signed up to help you break into the Winter Palace.'

He smiled tightly. 'More than you were counting on, I'm sure.'

'Something's definitely changed. Maybe it's you, maybe it's me.' Jumai looked up and down the hall, holding her tongue as a proxy strode past – not one of the household units, Geoffrey decided. 'Look, I'll only say this once. Being here isn't normal for either of us, and I'm not one for funerals at the best of times. But when I get back to Lagos, will you come over and spend a few days? I mean, work permitting.'

'I'd like that.'

'I'll hold you to it, all right?' Only then did she drop her hand from his sleeve. 'You'd better go and scrub up, rich boy. I'll see you in the courtyard when you're done – Sunday and Jitendra are already there.'

'I won't be long.'

He went to his room, stripped and showered, and was halfway through dressing in clean clothes when his gaze chanced upon the six wooden elephants. He'd been too tired and preoccupied to pay any attention to them yesterday. Why should he? They were part of the furniture, that was all. The fact that the constructs guarding both the Winter Palace and Lionheart had questioned him about them was neither here nor there. It only meant that the elephants really had been a gift from Eunice, as he had believed at the time. Or rather from whatever intelligence had been masquerading as his grandmother, during all the long years of her imaginary exile.

But he realised now that there was rather more to them than that. He sat down on his bed, as momentarily dizzy as if he'd been knocked on the head. It couldn't be, could it? After all this time, so close at hand. So close to *his* hands.

He picked up the heaviest of the elephants, the bull at the head of the group. Not very plausible given elephant social dynamics, but he supposed that hadn't really been the point.

He stroked the elephant's body, reassuring himself that its composition was what he had always assumed, always been told: some dark, dense wood.

It was. He was sure of that.

But the base material, that was something else. Heavy and black and irregular, flat along the top and bottom, as if cleaved from some larger coal-like motherlode. He tipped the piece to look at its base, the elephant upside down, and made out the faint scratch bisecting it from one side to the other. He'd never noticed that scratch before, and even if he had, he'd have had no reason to attach any significance to it. But now he knew. It only took a few moments to confirm that there were similar scratches on the other five bases.

He knew exactly where they'd come from.

Thinking of what they had lost, what they had gained, what was yet at stake, Geoffrey sat sobbing, the bull elephant in his hand as heavy and cold as a stone.

Sunday and her brother walked out with the rest of the clan, the family and friends, into the evening air, Lucas with them, Jitendra and Jumai not far away. The sky was pellucid and still, as clear as that long-ago evening when they had come to scatter Eunice's ashes. She had not been embodied then, at least not in flesh and blood, but it was hard to dislodge the memory that she had been here, walking on African soil, breathing African air.

'I have been giving some thought to the matter we discussed over dinner,' Lucas said, his voice low enough not to carry more than a few paces. He walked with his back straight and his hands clasped behind his back.

'If you want evidence,' Sunday said, 'that's going to be a little difficult. At least for the moment. There's *Summer Queen*, obviously, but beyond that, you'll just have to take a trip to Lionheart and see the test machinery for yourself. The construct told my brother that it's fully operational.'

'*Summer Queen* itself points to new physics, or at least an area of current physics that we only thought we understood,' Lucas said. 'That in itself does lend a certain credibility to the rest of the story. You'll excuse any scepticism on my part, though, I hope. Even if it was Hector telling me these things, I'd still want more than mere words. It's difficult enough to accept that our grandmother knew about this new physics, everything it implies ... but to be asked to believe these things of Memphis? That he was not the man we imagined him to be?'

'He was old enough not to have a past fixed in place by the Mech, or posterity engines,' Geoffrey said.

'I admit that there are ... absences in his biography. But no more so than would be the case in a million people of his age.' Lucas touched a hand to his mouth, coughing under his breath. 'And there was once a physics student with a similar name, born in Tanzania at about the right time.'

'Then you accept that there's at least the possibility this is all true,' Sunday said.

'It would help if there was something ... more. I believe what Geoffrey and Jumai have told me, and I also believe what you have told me about your exploits on Mars. I saw some of that for myself, remember, even if it wasn't through my own eyes.'

Sunday flinched at the recollection of Lucas's ruined face, the dislodged eyeball, the milky eruption of the proxy's slick, wet innards.

'Might I interrupt?'

The girl asking the question was someone Sunday had seen before, under similar circumstances. She was even wearing the same red dress, the same stockings and black shoes, the same hairstyle.

Out of curiosity, Sunday requested an aug tag: The girl was a golem, although the point of origin of the ching bind couldn't be resolved.

'You're Lin.'

'Of course,' the girl said. 'I knew your grandmother.'

Geoffrey sneered. 'After what happened on Mars, I'm surprised you'd show your face.'

'Did I cross you personally?' she asked, shooting a sharp stare at him from under her straight black fringe.

'You never got the chance,' Geoffrey said.

'If I had something to be ashamed of, do you think I'd have bothered introducing myself? What happened on Mars was not my concern, and I wouldn't have approved it had I known. As it transpires, the gesture achieved nothing.'

'Chama and Gleb told me there was a rift,' Sunday said.

'The Mandala discovery has only stressed fault lines that were already present,' Lin Wei said. 'I think the world has a right to know that we've found evidence of alien intelligence on another world, and that it shouldn't have to wait until that data seeps into the public domain. Some of my colleagues have a different view. If I'm feeling charitable, it's because they don't think the rest of humanity is quite ready for such

494

a shattering revelation. In my less charitable moments, it's because they don't want to share their secret with anyone.'

'I can't help you,' Geoffrey said.

'The data will be made public sooner or later,' Lin Wei said unconcernedly, as if his help didn't matter one way or the other. 'I've put in measures to ensure that happens. Naturally, I have my critics, even enemies. Some of them are going to make life very interesting for me in the coming years. But that's not a bad thing: at least I won't be bored. I was ready to leave Tiamaat long before you gave me an excuse, Geoffrey. But I thank you for providing the spur.' She paused. 'I've a gift for you, but you'll have to come and get it. It would be far too bothersome to bring it back down to Earth again.'

Sunday searched her brother's face for clues. Geoffrey looked none the wiser.

'You don't owe me any gifts, Arethusa.'

'Oh, all right then.' She wrinkled her nose in irritation. 'Call it returned goods. Your little aeroplane, Geoffrey. It was retrieved from the sea, when the *Nevsky* rescued you.' What was that, Sunday wondered, but a sly reminder of the debt he owed her? 'In all the fuss, it ended up being loaded aboard the heavy-lift rocket. I've had it cleaned and repaired, and it's yours to take back whenever you like.'

'What's the catch?'

'None, other than that you'll have to visit one of our orbital leaseholds to retrieve it. But there'll be no diplomatic complications. You are, after all, still a citizen of the United Aquatic Nations.'

Sunday frowned, wondering exactly what she meant by that. There was still a lot she needed to talk about with her brother. She supposed there would be plenty of time in the days to come.

'Thank you for saving the Cessna,' he said.

'It was the least I could do. Well, almost the least. There is one other—'

But he cut her off. 'You can take a message to Chama and Gleb for me. Will you do that?'

'Naturally.'

'Thank them for helping Sunday, while I was away. And tell them that the elephant work can continue. I have no objection to the establishment of a linked community. The Amboseli herds and the Lunar dwarves – they can share the same sensorium, the way Chama and Gleb planned. I'll be glad to provide any technical assistance.'

'I think they'll be looking for more than just assistance,' Sunday said. 'Full collaboration, a shared enterprise.'

'Then they've come to the wrong man.' He walked on for a few more paces before elaborating. 'I don't work with elephants any more. That was something I used to do.'

Sunday could hardly believe what she was hearing. But she knew Geoffrey well enough to be certain that he wasn't just saying that for dramatic effect, expecting everyone to put an arm around him and tell him how wonderfully important his work was, how he was undervalued and underappreciated, how he owed it to the elephants to keep on with the studies. She'd had that conversation often enough in the past.

This wasn't it.

'You're serious.'

He nodded, but not with any sense of triumph. 'I think we both have enough to keep us busy, don't you?'

Lin Wei, to her credit, did not question Geoffrey's sincerity. Perhaps it was just an outburst, something he'd retract in the days to come, but everything in her brother's manner said otherwise.

'Chama and Gleb will be sorry. I know they were looking forward to your involvement.'

'They're smart enough to manage without me. It was always the elephants they wanted, not the researcher.'

Lin Wei said, 'I don't think it's very long to the scattering now.' She made a gesture in the air, shaping a square, and the aug filled the square with darkness. 'Can you all see this?'

They were still walking, but the square moved with them. One by one they confirmed that they were able to see it.

'Sunday told Chama and Gleb about the numbers, and they in turn told me,' Lin Wei went on. 'The numbers wouldn't have meant much to an outsider, but their meaning was immediately clear to me – as they would have been to Eunice.'

'So what do they mean?' Sunday asked.

The rectangle dappled itself with smudges of milky light. 'Ocular pointing coordinates,' Lin Wei said. 'That's what they are: a set of directions for the instrument. Before very long my adversaries will make it very difficult for me to access Ocular, but for the moment that is still my privilege – as well it *should* be, given that I conceived and birthed it. Needless to say, I did not hesitate to abuse that privilege by ordering Arachne to point Ocular in the direction corresponding to the coordinates.'

'Mandala?' Geoffrey asked.

'No. Crucible lies in the constellation Virgo, and this is in the direction of Lyra, a completely different part of the sky. Close to Altair, in fact –

one of the stars of the Summer Triangle. Arachne's search algorithms eliminated any starlike objects from the immediate centre of the field, but you'll note that there is still something there.'

'What is it?' Sunday asked.

'I thought perhaps you might be able to tell me, given what the two of you have learned of your grandmother. It's incredibly faint, and at first glance it appears quasarlike. But it's not a quasar. It's a . . . well, I don't know. Neither does Arachne. She's seen billions of astronomical objects, but nothing that looks remotely like this . . . energy source. That's what it is – an energy source, highly Dopplered, we can tell from the spectrum – moving away from us along what appears to be a radial line of sight. We'll have a better handle on that as time goes by, if we pick up lateral motion. But I don't think we will. I think we will find that this thing, this object, started off in the solar system, about sixty years ago. And ever since then it's been rushing away from us, falling into the summer stars.'

Geoffrey asked, 'How far out is it now?'

Lin Wei's smile was impish. 'I think I've given you enough to be going on with, don't you? Let's just say it's a long, long way – further than any human artefact has ever reached. And travelling at a quite ridiculous speed.'

'To nowhere in particular?' Sunday probed. 'There's no star along that exact line of sight?'

'There are stars, to be sure. But none that strike us – Arachne or myself – as an obvious candidate.' Lin Wei made a flicking gesture and the image disappeared.

'That's all you're going to give us?' Sunday asked.

'For now. You want more, come and talk to me. I think we all have rather a lot to discuss, don't you?'

'She's in that thing,' Geoffrey said. 'That's what you think. That Eunice is in a *ship*, a ship that's been heading away from Earth for sixty years.'

'She spoke to me once,' Sunday replied, 'about how it would feel to just keep going. To never go home again.' She paused, trying to call her grandmother's exact words to mind. 'Until Earth was just a blue memory. What I didn't realise was . . . she meant to do it.'

'She could still be—' Geoffrey began. But he caught himself before the sentence was out.

Sunday nodded. He didn't need to say what he was thinking. She was thinking the same thing herself.

She supposed the only way to know for sure would be to go out there.

To catch up with that impossibly distant thing and see what was inside it.

A sleeping lion, perhaps. *Senge Dongma.*

Jitendra said, 'I think it's time.'

He was right, too. Sunday could feel the ground rumbling under them as the blowpipe sent its tiny package racing under the plains. As one they turned to face east. As if of its own volition, her hand rose to her neck, fingering the charm she had been given on Mars, binding her to the past, binding her to the future.

They watched the spark rise from the mountain, a tiny bright star climbing against the turn of the heavens. It was travelling ballistically now, carried on the momentum it had gained in the long acceleration as it rode the magnetic catapult. Some of that momentum was already ebbing: the package was encountering atmospheric resistance, albeit from air that was half as thick as at ground level, and gravity was beginning to reassert its claim. Ordinarily the launch lasers would have cut in by now, projecting their ferocious energies onto the underside of the package to give it that extra push into orbit. Some of the onlookers, Sunday felt certain, must already have come to the conclusion that the blowpipe had mistimed. Others, she felt equally sure, were entirely ignorant of the usual mechanics.

The star kept rising – from the party's vantage point it appeared to be climbing vertically, but it was in fact following an arc, one that was already taking it east, out towards the Indian Ocean. Just when it looked on the point of falling, though, the lasers shone. Their beams scratched diamond-bright tracks in the sky, converging from Kilimanjaro's summit to meet at a fixed focus point in space, where the air became a little ball of ionised hell. The focus would ordinarily have been immediately underneath the rising object, but the arrangements were different today; the lasers were now directing their energies directly ahead of the package. It had no protection against that; it had been designed to be pushed, not to hit that plasma head-on. With no frontal shielding beyond that necessary to withstand the aerodynamic stresses, the effect on the package was rapid and glorious. The star's brightness flared by sudden magnitudes, until it looked as if a new day was dawning. Sunday raised her fingers against the dazzle, catching greens and pinks in the tiny blazing point. The light fluttered, and then – as quickly as it had begun – that little new sun began to break up, oozing molten droplets of itself. The colours subsided – gold turning to amber, amber to orange, orange to a slow dulling red. She tried to trace the falling sparks, but they were soon lost in the glow of the sky.

She knew the truth of it, that if any part of him was to rain down from that pyre, it would happen far out to sea. And perhaps no part had survived that incandescence. But from where Sunday was standing, from where everyone now stood, it was very hard not to believe that some part of their friend and mentor would end up touching the summit of that mountain, end up touching the snows of Kilimanjaro.

And that was enough.

We spoke of beginnings, at the start of this. It is well now to speak of endings. That was the last that Geoffrey had to do with Matilda, or the M-clan, or the Amboseli herds, or elephants in general. Or at least the last that any of us ever knew about. There was sadness at first, then anger and remorse, mingled with lingering self-disgust at what he believed he had caused to happen. Then just sadness again, long and slow-dying, like the endless collapsing roll of thunder across the plains. He could not have known, of course. And it took years before he was even ready to speak of what had happened, on that day when Matilda saw too deeply into his head, and understood Memphis for what he was.

Enemy of her kind. Murderer of elephants.

Even though Memphis had done it for no other reason than to protect us. But she could not see that. She was just an animal, after all, no matter how brightly her mind shone.

They're still out there, the phyletic dwarves. There's no harm in disclosing this information now. We don't know where they are, and in all likelihood neither do the orthodox Pans. After the sundering, after the great parting of the ways between Truro and Arethusa, Chama and Gleb took their work deeper underground than it had been before. But somewhere out there, in a solar system still big enough to contain hiding places and dark corners, still big enough for secrets, the elephants thrive. Once in a while, conveyed to us through a labyrinth of quangle paths, all but untraceable, we hear from the zookeepers. They are still happily married, and the great work continues. The elephants are doing well. One day we may yet be a part of it.

Data packets still bind the dwarves to the M-clan, providing that essential socializing framework, but please do not go trying to follow that thread; it'll get you nowhere. Besides, the bonds between the herds are much weaker now than they were when all this started. Twenty years on, the dwarves have grandchildren of their own, sons and daughters, matriarchs and bulls, family ties, the foundation of a complex, self-sustaining elephant society. One day, when resources allow, they may even be allowed to grow, to stop being dwarves. But perhaps that is for another century.

500

If Geoffrey misses his role in that enterprise, he is careful not to show it. No more, perhaps, than Sunday misses her former career as an artist, or Lucas misses his as a willing component in the family machine. We have all had other business to keep hands, hearts and minds occupied.

Sunday returned to the Descrutinised Zone, and for a little while she tried to submerge herself in the routines of her old life. She went back to the commissions she had abandoned, before her journey to Mars. Jitendra, too, tried to pick up the pieces of his former existence. But it was hard. They both carried too much knowledge, burning in their heads like a lit fuse. We all did.

For years Sunday had worked to bring the Eunice construct to fruition. That private project had been the mainspring of her life, the thing she cared about beyond any of her tiring, rent-paying commissions. She had abandoned physical sculpture in preference for the sculpting of a single human life, in all its dizzying fractal glory.

And she had not failed. But the construct had grown too clever, too complex. It had torn itself free of Sunday's plans, become something she could influence but not control. And although Geoffrey and Jumai had tried to shield her from the truth, she had made the necessary deductions for herself. The artilect running Lionheart was everything she had ever hoped her construct might become. The work she strove to complete had already been achieved.

The construct abides. Like the dwarves, it is out there somewhere. Being a bodyless spirit, haunting the aug, there would be even less point in trying to pin it down. We long ago assigned it all the autonomy it craved. Once in a while, we hear from it. Perhaps it thinks of the woman in whose shadow it walks, the figure it can emulate but never become. Perhaps it is content to become something else entirely. Sometimes, when it offers us wise counsel, when it advises us on the intentions of those who would act against us, we are grateful that it is on our side. At other times we slightly fear it. And sometimes we forget that Eunice is an it, not a she.

Of the real Eunice, the living woman, our dead grandmother, things are simpler. At least we know where she is now.

There will, of course, be those who criticise us for waiting as long as we did, before making this decision. What choice did we have, though? When this burden was placed upon us we were, to be frank, little better than children. We needed time to think, time to judge the readiness of the world. Eunice could not make this decision sixty years earlier; we could not make it rashly either. We wished to see how the world would adapt to the new engines, and the knowledge of Mandala.

It's been twenty years. But now we are ready.

This testimony, written in our shared hand as honestly as we are able, is our attempt at explaining ourselves. We did not go looking for this respons-

501

ibility, but we have done our best to measure up to it. Looking back across these years, at the way we were then, all our enmities are matters of vanishing consequence, the squabbling of infants. We have moved beyond such things. If nothing else, we owed it to Hector and Memphis to rise above our former selves. Because if we couldn't do it, if we couldn't put aside the past, what hope could there be for anyone else?

Twenty years ago the world saw a glimpse of what lay ahead. The improved engines have shrunk the inner solar system, brought Jupiter and Saturn closer, and accelerated the development and colonisation of Trans-Neptunian space. There have been accidents and stupidities, but for the most part the technology has been absorbed without catastrophe. As well it should have been, for what we gave you then was really nothing at all. The real test of our collective wisdom begins here and now.

We call it the Chibesa Principle. The improved engines were merely a glimpse of what this new physics can give us. Properly tamed, the Chibesa Principle will not only shrink the solar system even further. It will put human starflight within our reach.

But understand the risk, as well as the promise. Like the discovery of fire, this is not something that can be uninvented. And in the wrong hands, used maliciously or foolishly, the Chibesa Principle is fully capable of murdering worlds.

That is why our grandmother deemed us unready. But that was more than eighty years ago, and much has changed since then. We think things are different now, and that the species is ready to demonstrate its collective wisdom. If we are wrong, if our wisdom is lacking, the Chibesa Principle will burn us. And if that is the case, and if there is anyone left to cast judgement on our actions, we shall gladly accept history's verdict. But if we are right, it will give us everything that Soya Akinya showed her daughter, when she held her up in the velvet warmth of a Serengeti night: all these stars, all these tiny diamond lights.

We have been clever, and on occasion we have been foolish. For smart monkeys, we can, when the mood takes us, be exceedingly stupid. But it was cleverness that brought us to this point, and it is only cleverness that will serve us from now on.

We have no time for anything else.

502

ACKNOWLEDGEMENTS

Huge thanks are due to Tim Kauffman, Louise Kleba, Kotska Wallace and Joan Wamae – and not least my wife – for agreeing to read an early draft of this novel and offering their comments and suggestions. Up-and-coming writer Jonathan Dotse was also kind enough to make time during a visit to London to talk about Africa and science fiction, from a uniquely Ghanaian perspective. For specific discussions on exoplanets and break-through physics, I thank my brilliant and talented scientist friends Lisa Kaltenegger and Dave Clements. I am indebted to all of you for your time and insights. The faults of the book, of course, remain my responsibility alone.

I spent the first decade of my professional writing career under the able editorship of Jo Fletcher, not only a trusted colleague but also a good friend. By the time Jo left to run her own imprint we had already been discussing this book for several years. There's no doubting her influence on BLUE REMEMBERED EARTH, and some of that influence, I'm sure, will continue to be felt in later instalments of the Akinya saga. In particular, it was Jo's immediate fondness for the elephants that made me determined to make them much more than background dressing. Thank you, Jo!

By the same token, it has been a delight to work with my new editor, Simon Spanton – all round good bloke and a man with a deep passion for the core virtues of science fiction. It is no easy thing to take on an established writer halfway through their career; Simon has given me nothing but support and friendship. Respect!

Once again, it has been a pleasure to work with the brilliant and meticulous Lisa Rogers, who has been my line editor for most of my career – there is, I suspect, no sharper pair of eyes in the business, nor anyone better equipped to impose sense on my often muddled approach to internal chronology. Thanks, Lisa!

I am also hugely indebted to my agent, Robert Kirby, for years of support and enthusiasm. Like Jo, Robert has been in on this book since the beginning. Deep into a big project, it's easy to forget why one ever thought it was a great idea in the first place. Robert has always managed to give me that motivational impulse, whenever I felt my energy flagging. Again, it's been a pleasure.

The genesis of this book – one strand of it, anyway – goes back to the first in a series of visits to the Kennedy Space Center. My wife and I have been fortunate enough to witness two launches of the Space Shuttle Atlantis – literally unrepeatable experiences. For allowing me to get closer to a launch than I ever dreamed I would, I thank Tim Kauffman, Louise Kleba and Piers Sellers – all fine people, still committed to the idea of human space exploration. It has also been a pleasure and privilege to spend time with Steve Agid, who knows more about the past, present and future of manned and unmanned spaceflight than almost anyone on the planet.

Much of the technology in this book is speculative, but quite a lot of it is based on real ideas and proposals, none of which involve breaking the laws of physics. Space elevators, ballistic launchers, VASIMR drives, even metallic-hydrogen-fuelled rockets and the direct imaging of exoplanet surfaces, are all technologies that have been discussed in the 'serious literature' – indeed, some of these concepts are well on the way to being realised.

At the moment we lack a 'Theory of Everything', a single, all-enveloping physical theory that would tie together both the behaviour of matter at the grandest of scales – the dynamics of black holes and galactic superclusters – and the smallest, the fizzing, fuzzy realm of subatomic processes. Despite this, we have some promising candidate ideas. We also live in an era of truly exciting experimentation, with projects like the ongoing Large Hadron Collider pushing into energies which may enable competing theories to be tested against each other. It's too soon to say what the outcome of these studies will be. Perhaps conservatively, I have assumed that the theoretical physics of Eunice's time is not radically different from our own. However, the breakthrough on Mercury, with its supposed connection to quark-quark interactions and subsequent application as a new form of spacecraft engine, is entirely fanciful – very much 'made-up' science.

There is no such world as Crucible, although the star 61 Virginis is believed to have a planetary system, and the presence of an Earthlike world is not yet ruled out. The field of exoplanet research is moving so rapidly that I fully expect to be caught out by observations within the lifetime of this book. But that's the joy of speculating in a rapidly evolving discipline.

504

There is a monolith on Phobos, but no one seriously believes that it's anything other than a slightly unusual (but not all that odd) geological feature. Obtaining close-up images of this long-shadow-casting object will doubtless be a goal for future exploration of the Martian moons. I look forward to seeing what they find.

Two things motivated me to write a science fiction novel in which Africa was the dominant economic and technological power. The first was a simple: why not? I have never been to Africa, but I have no reason to suppose that there is anything that would prevent Africa, or a part of that continent, from assuming global dominance in one or more advanced industries. The second reason, which is rather more personal and heartfelt – and therefore rather more difficult to articulate – is to do with music. In the last five years I have come to love African music and it has formed a great part of my listening during the conception of this book. In particular I would like to mention the amazing Ugandan musician Geoffrey Oryema, who was very much my gateway into a realm of wonderful and surprising discovery. His beautiful song 'Land of Anaka', written from an exile's point of view, conveyed exactly the sense of overwhelming loss that I felt might be shared by space travellers, centuries from now, remembering an Earth to which they could never return.

Which is why I named my central character Geoffrey.